THE JOURNAL:

cracked earth
ash fall
crimson skies

DEBORAH D. MOORE

A PERMUTED PRESS BOOK

ISBN (trade paperback): 978-1-61868-632-9

THE JOURNAL
Cracked Earth, Ash Fall, Crimson Skies
© 2016 by Deborah D. Moore
All Rights Reserved

Cover art by Matt Mosley

PERMUTED
PRESS

Permuted Press, LLC
275 Madison Avenue, 6th Floor
New York, NY 10016
http://permutedpress.com

This is for my Mom and Dad.
I miss you both.
John — I don't know where you are now,
but maybe someday, you will…find me.

Go far from me

But stay close

For I want to be alone

With someone near.

D.D. Moore

THE JOURNAL:

Cracked Earth

Book One

INTRODUCTION

I first met Deborah in an online survival/prepper forum several years ago. I'll be honest in that, at first, she drove me nuts. It seemed like she *always* had an opinion on just about any topic that was posted, particularly those that centered on homesteading or living off the grid. After a while, though, I understood why she felt it necessary to address these topics again and again.

She knew what the hell she was talking about.

Deborah lived off the grid for several years. She learned, through trial and error as well as otherwise, what really worked and what didn't. Experiential learning often makes for the longest lasting lessons, the ones that you never forget.

Over the years, I came to value Deborah's opinion on many subjects, simply because I knew those opinions were based on hard realities, not simply book learning. Eventually, she, a couple of other friends, and myself decided to work together on a website. This was to be a place where we could share our various experiences, our knowledge, and our skills with the world.

That site, SurvivalWeekly.com, was also where the book you're holding was born. Well, truth be told, it may not have been born there but that was the nursery where everyone came to see the new arrival, so to speak. From the very beginning, it gained a loyal following, a following that grew with each installment. It quickly got to the point where people were quick to notice if an installment was late for some reason. As the story went on, fans were riveted. They clamored to hear more about how Allexa and the others in Moose Creek were faring under a range of different emergencies.

One thing I really appreciate about *The Journal* is that it is very much based in reality. We don't have characters who are some sort of super-soldier, capable of surviving eleventy million gunfights with nary a scratch. No, Allexa and her friends are all too human. They quibble and quarrel. They make mistakes. They aren't perfect. They fall in love and they lose loved ones.

In other words, they are just like you and I.

As you read The Journal and get to know Allexa, you're also getting to know Deborah, at least a bit. See, there's an awful lot of Deborah in that character. As the saying goes, "Write what you know." Well, that's what Deborah has done here. Deborah knows prepping. She's been there, done that. She's lived a prepping lifestyle since before the word "prepping" came into common parlance and for most of that time, she's done it all on her own. She knows what has to be done each and every year in order to make it through. Putting up the food, preparing the cords of firewood, laying in the necessary supplies in sufficient quantities, the list goes on and on. All of it while fully realizing there is a strong likelihood that there may be weeks at a time when just getting to the barn and back might be an ordeal due to the winter weather, let alone any sort of traveling.

That's not just admirable, it is downright humbling.

I'm not going to spoil anything for you by going into any detail about the events that transpire in *The Journal*. Suffice to say, disasters like those described herein are very possible in the real world. And, just like in *The Journal*, crises have a tendency to come in bunches. One leads to another and so on, sort of like dominoes. As you'll see, though, with some forethought and careful planning, life after a major disaster can be made at least a bit easier.

And that's the other thing I love about *The Journal*. Throughout the story, Deborah has included quite a bit of practical information about being prepared for disasters. Watch yourself, if you aren't careful, you just might learn a thing or two.

Jim Cobb
Author of *The Prepper's Complete Book of Disaster Readiness*
and *Prepper's Long-Term Survival Guide*

CHAPTER ONE

My phone rang with the forlorn tune, Hall of the Mountain King. "Allexa Smeth," I answered, already knowing who it was by the ring tone.

"Allexa, thank goodness I've finally reached you! Where are you right now? Are you still in lower Michigan at your sister's?" Liz Anderson, the county manager, who happened to be my sometime boss, had that impatient tone to her voice that I've come to recognize as her trying to do too many things at one time.

"Yes and no," I replied. "I'm still downstate, but I'm not at my sister's anymore. I'm in Indian River having lunch with a friend, about half an hour from the bridge." It had been too long since I'd seen my friend Soozie and I was enjoying our time together, even though I had left my sister Pam's a day early because of an unsettled feeling in my gut. "What's going on, Liz?" I asked nervously.

"I think it would be a good idea for you to get on *this* side of the bridge. We might have to shut down our borders and that starts with the Mackinaw Bridge."

"*What*? Why?" I asked, feeling my heart miss a beat. This could only mean bad news.

"I can't say too much on the phone, Allexa, but something strange is happening and I want all of my township emergency managers where they belong. You're one of the few EMs that actually take their position seriously and let me know when you'll be out of town." Liz sighed and took a breath before continuing. "Look, please get back into the U.P. as soon as you can, okay?" With that she hung up, leaving me staring at my cellphone.

Eight years ago I accepted the appointment of emergency manager for my small town of Moose Creek in the Upper Peninsula as a means of giving back to the community for the peace I finally found. The appointment was for the entire township of eight hundred people, not only for the two hundred souls that lived in the town itself. Very rarely have I been called on to exercise the knowledge I've gained from the ongoing education that's required, however, I made a commitment and I always honor my word. I lived deep in the woods with a bipolar narcissist for seven uneasy years, barely making it out alive. The town and the people healed me. I owe them.

"Well, Soozie, looks like I have to go," I said sadly, pushing my unfinished burger aside and easing up from the red and white vinyl seats of the booth we sat in. I looked around at the quaint restaurant, with the red stained-glass lampshades that hung over each table by heavy copper chains and snifter candle holders that sat, waiting for dusk to be lit.

"Before you leave, Allexa, I have something for you." Soozie slid a small package toward me across the scarred and heavily varnished wood table. I removed the pink tissue paper to reveal a beautiful brown leather book, laced up the back binder with strips of rawhide. "It's a replica of a Civil War diary," Soozie explained.

The smooth and rough textures of the leather held me. I decided right then to start using it tomorrow.

* * *

I came around the final curve of the road, and the bridge came into view. It never ceases to thrill me to get the first glimpse of those towering pylons strung with heavy cables. After being away, even if it's only been for a few days, the sight is still humbling. The Mackinaw Bridge is the longest suspension bridge in the United States at a little over five miles, and the only physical connection Lower Michigan has with its sister, the Upper Peninsula. The U.P. has been my home for the past eighteen years and I can't imagine living anywhere else.

The thrum of my tires against the rain/expansion grates rang in my ears when I got to the center of the bridge. The tug on my tires reminded me I was almost back in the U.P. I happily paid my toll and continued on I-75 until the Highway 123 exit. The two lanes of 123 meandered through pine forests and open fields, small settlements, and then finally into the town of Trout Lake where I stopped for a short break. I purchased a hand-dipped cone of Moose Tracks, a rich vanilla ice cream with swirls of caramel and fudge and chunks of peanut butter cups. It had been an arduous few days and I felt entitled to the decadent treat. Back in the car, it was another twenty minutes to the next turnoff onto M-28. From there it was a straight shot to Marquette, and still three more hours of driving.

It would be about 4:30 P.M. when I arrived, and with any luck, Liz would still be in her office at the State Police post.

* * *

"So can you tell me what's going on?" I asked Liz when I sat down in a soft black leather chair.

"Since talking to you, I've made a *lot* of phone calls, only to find out the rumored terrorist threats have been only a *drill*. One that no one bothered to tell me about." Liz leaned back and closed her big pale brown eyes. "I'm sorry to have yanked you away from your visit. This job gets to me sometimes," she confessed. "It's getting harder and harder to decide when to act on a rumor or lead, or when to wait until confirmation."

"Why a terrorist drill up here? That doesn't seem likely. What would be the point?"

"Not a drill with us directly involved. Though it is going on in several nearby major cities. It's to show how a takedown of infrastructure would disrupt commerce everywhere," she explained. "The main commerce being discussed would be food distribution. If the food stops, things will get nasty very quickly."

"It was only a drill then? That's a relief! My training doesn't include food riots," I joked, yet I was also serious.

* * *

Maybe the journal from Soozie will help me get more organized. This weekend I think I will do an inventory of food and supplies in preparation for winter.

I'm extra pleased with the garden. It has done great and I've canned more this year than ever before. Being a prepper has its advantages in the long run; at the same time it's a lot of work. I've been stocking over the summer the best I could, even with my hectic work schedule. With the threat of food shortages from a terrorist attack, drill or not, I'm extra glad I've done all I have.

* * *

Last week was the final day of work at the resort for the season. I'm *so* glad it's over. I look forward to it every spring, and then by September 1st, can't wait until it's done. I'm past tired, I'm exhausted. Doing five and six massages a day, three, four, even five days a week is getting too hard on my aging body. Twenty-eight years of it has taken its toll. Maybe I should consider retiring, at least then I would have more time for the garden.

On the last day I performed six massages and injured my shoulder. A brutal day. It didn't help that it was rainy, windy and cold. At least now I can rest.

What I would miss most about work is the people and the location. The resort is over twenty thousand acres of privately held nature reserve. Each day that I drove the five miles from the guarded gate to the compound where all the cabins are was a delight. The lush forests of deciduous trees give way to giant pines and then back again on the two-lane dirt road. I was always offered something new. It might be some new flower or mushroom growing alongside the road, or it might be the deer that stared at me before they sauntered off into the underbrush, knowing they were completely safe.

One of the most memorable sights I had was watching a young coyote jumping playfully in a field, catching grasshoppers to eat. I watched for five minutes before it realized I was there, then like a wisp of smoke it was gone. *The* most incredible experience was when I rounded a curve and came face to face with a moose calf once, one of the adolescents that occasionally hung around the entrance gate. I knew the moose were here but had never seen them. I stopped the car less than twenty feet from her, and watched the huge animal in the middle of the road. When I first saw her I thought she was a horse, however, when she looked at me with that unmistakable large head, the long, wide snout, and those long, gangly, powerful legs, there was no denying what she was. My first moose sighting was up close and personal. It only lasted a few minutes, then she turned, giving me a full, breathtaking side view, and deftly leaped the berm and walked off into the dappled shadows of the woods. My cellphone was dead so I don't have any pictures except for the ones in my memory.

Then there were the owner/members of the Resort. Being their massage therapist for the past sixteen years had given me an insight into a world of the elite and wealth that I never would have seen on my own. The members are wealthy—some very, some extremely. I often heard about their month long vacations to Italy in the spring, the weeks in the Bahamas during the winter, plus the trips to Europe with jaunts to Paris and London then on to Rome. What I admired most though, was that they were all really very down to earth people. I'd seen them shopping at the local big box stores or pumping their own gas.

One time I asked an older client for some advice on the British hierarchy, prepping for a costume party that I was hosting. After she explained the pecking order of a Duke to an Earl, a Duchess to a Lady, she laughed and said, "I must tell you the most amusing story about when Prince Philip came to visit!" I was amazed, though not surprised that she actually knew the British royal family. I have mourned the ones who have passed right along with their peers, not embarrassed to sob at the Resort held memorials. Yes, I would miss the people the most. Many of them had become dear friends, and I would see them next spring.

* * *

I did a cursory inventory of the freezer room pantry, the first of three separate storage areas. There wasn't as much beef or chicken broth as I would like, but it was something I could make. I also had some fruits, canned beans for quick use, one hundred pounds of flour, light bulbs, all kinds of miscellaneous stuff, plus all my herbs and seasonings. The wine rack my son Jason built isn't really full, yet I'd say there were four cases of wine, though some was my cooking stock: Marsala, Sherry, and Port. I wasn't worried about how much wine was (or wasn't) there. The freezer itself, even though it's only twelve cubic feet, was packed. I had lots of beef and chicken, some pork, some fish, ten pounds of butter, and a few bags of wild mushrooms. I could probably live off the freezer alone for many months. I have difficulty passing up a good sale.

The entry pantry was stocked with "stuff": paper goods mostly, and water filters. I have a year's worth of toilet paper, six months of paper towels, and if I run out, I could use towels and wash them, like Granny did. Installing shelves in there has helped organize that area. I also put in small tubs and labeled them (dental, deodorant, band aids, wipes, misc.), which helped keep track of what was where. There's also plenty of toothpaste, deodorant, and OTC pain meds.

My medical bag is good. A friend helped me with that last year — sutures, scalpels, iodine, tissues, blood pressure cuff and stethoscope, plus a dental kit. I certainly didn't need to worry about shampoo and conditioner now that my hair was so much shorter. A few weeks ago there was a 10 for $10 sale on popcorn so I loaded up and stored it in the front pantry. That's where Tufts' litter box is, so checking the stock reminded me to check in the barn for how much spare litter I have for the winter. I need to stock up on dish soap, since there are only four bottles under the sink. I have a couple of tubs of powdered washing soap out in the barn that should last a while, but not indefinitely. Then there was the back room pantry. I've outdone myself with the canning this year and am really pleased. I sure won't go hungry. All in all, I'm happy with my supplies and food stores. I've worked hard at it and it shows.

I do need to make a run to the artesian well soon; I'm almost out of drinking water.

* * *

I dug up some horseradish roots a few days ago. The plants did great this summer and the leaves were four feet tall. Earlier in the summer I dried some of the leaves for seasoning; on the other hand actually making horseradish from real roots is a new thing for me, so I asked the online prepper groups how to do it. Someone gave me a warning to wear my gasmask. I thought that was silly, but at least that warning got me to get out the N95 mask and the face-sealed goggles and surgical gloves. I set up a table on the deck with the food processor outside and set about making the horseradish.

I scrubbed the roots with no problem. I peeled the roots with no problem. It was a pleasant scent. I love horseradish. I took all outside and shredded the roots. When I took the lid off of the processor, my eyes burned through the goggles and my nose immediately started to run. OMG... the fumes! YIKES! I dumped the pulp into a glass bowl without going blind and reset it with a chopping blade instead of the shredder and pulsed it several times. Finally it got to the consistency that I wanted. I held the bowl away when I lifted the lid and even still, my eyes watered again. I dumped the chopped root back into the bowl and put a cover on it, then I lifted the goggles and wiped my eyes after I rinsed my gloved hands. I added half a cup of my own Apple Cider Vinegar, and stirred it all in. I covered the bowl with a plastic cap and then washed everything. I wasn't about to bring that stuff inside, so I took the prepared jars out to the deck and filled them with my fresh horseradish.

Next time I just might use the gas mask. It was quite an experience, and the end product is incredible. It was a good thing the weather was nice. It made me want an outdoor summer kitchen. Maybe next year.

* * *

Now that the resort had closed, it was past time I attacked my fall prep list. There was *so* much to do, and I still lament I must do it on my own. Looking over the list, I was pleased that I had tackled many of the really important items early.

The winter wood was delivered in May. I was thankful that Keith let me pay for it when work picked up. This is the first year I managed to stock a full eighteen months' worth of wood. Every now and then I get the feeling that we'll have a bad winter and I'm going to need all of that wood. It hasn't happened yet, still, one of these years it will.

I use propane for cooking, even though the cook stove lets me do everything I need. Even though I haven't used much of it, I still called for a winter top off for November 1st. One more thing off the winter prep list.

I hadn't rototilled the garden yet, but I had shut it down and let the chickens run free. This was a really great garden season. I was able to can more tomatoes than ever before, plus greens and squash and beans.

Back in late August sometime I ran into Mike T., a local farmer, and arranged to barter my tomatoes for some of his corn. Unfortunately, before I could collect, his corn was gone and I had to buy some. Oh well, at least I have two cases, and that's better than nothing.

I still need to shut the outside water off. An onerous task since I don't like going down in that eight foot deep pit where the valve is located.

* * *

I love productive days. The weather is holding, sixty-eight degrees today and mostly sunny, a good day to be outside. I dug up a pound of Jerusalem artichokes. Too bad they don't keep well; I'll keep adding them to meals before they spoil. I relocated some of them to another part of the garden. I hope that they take.

I cleaned out the onion beds, planted some garlic, and dug up as many of those darn creeping weeds with the geranium-like leaves as I could. The wheelbarrow was completely full. I knew they'd be back; at least these wouldn't be tilled in.

I took down the fence charger and pulled up the cord, storing it all in the barn for next year. One more task to add to the winter prep-fall chores list since it was a new addition this summer. I left the wire at the top on the fence in place. I will have to see how it fares this winter.

I washed sheets and hung them out on the line, then did all my laundry.

The day was still young, so I decided I'd go for a walk.

* * *

I ended up on the public side of Eagle Beach. It was wonderfully quiet this time of year since all of the tourists were gone and the kids were in school. I had the whole beach to myself. I walked for a bit and then found a large piece of battered driftwood to sit on. Where this piece of wood came from is anybody's guess. Lake Superior is a huge lake and it might have come from Canada or the other side of the bay. In spite of it being cool, I took off my shoes and dug my toes into the damp, rocky sand. I sat there for a while watching the waves gently lap at the shore, trying to think of what I wanted for this coming winter. Try as I might, my mind kept drifting.

I remembered a night so long ago, when my ex Sam and I were new to the area and still working on our house in the woods, long before we split up. It was a warm August night, the moon was new, and there wasn't a cloud in the sky. Sitting on the beach at midnight and looking at all the stars was mesmerizing. There is no light pollution up here and the sky was brilliant. From the bay, the view out to Lake Superior is more than 180 degrees. That night there were so many stars I could actually see a subtle curvature of the universe. I know it was an optical illusion, but the sky seemed to bend around us. I will never forget that night.

I dug my toes a bit deeper and felt something sharp. Digging with my fingers, I found a nice piece of hematite to add to my rock collection and stuck it in my pocket. After disturbing the sand, I was visited by a couple of squawky white and gray seagulls, curious if I dug up anything for them. They can be annoying little creatures and it's part of life on the lake. Almost immediately, there was another shriek, then another. They have some kind of code in that caw, I swear. Soon there were a dozen of those pesky birds swooping down, their raucous cry piercing the quiet, parading up and down the shore or fighting with the next one for a piece of twig. It was a good thing I didn't have any food or else they'd never leave.

My attention kept coming back to the first house on the other side of the break wall, which separates the public beach from the residential section with the marina. That first house is where John Tiggs and his co-workers live. I'd been seeing John as a massage client for a year now and I've grown dangerously fond of him. During our many hour-long sessions together, he has told me much about himself, past relationships and how he never wants to be emotionally tied to anyone ever again. I wish I could say the same.

I pulled my focus away from that house to watch an ore freighter chug its way across my view a few miles out. Last year during a particularly violent storm, a thousand-foot freighter took refuge in the much calmer waters of our bay. It was startling for me to see this huge ship anchored calmly. I had forgotten how vast our cove is, at least five miles across making the ship look like a small toy boat in a big bathtub. It stayed for two days and then left quietly during the night when the storm had passed.

* * *

The television news tonight covered a riot in Miami. It seems that an entire district didn't get their food stamps due to a computer glitch, so they stormed the local social services office. When they couldn't get in (some smart worker quickly locked the doors) the crowd went on a rampage, breaking into stores, looting and setting fires. Due to being short on manpower because of budget cutbacks, there was little that the police could do, so they barricaded the area off to keep more people from entering and let the crowd burn itself out. Apparently one of the caseworkers took charge of the rest of the employees and got them upstairs where they jammed the elevator doors open so it couldn't be called down.

The guy put an "out of order" sign on the elevator doors on the main floor and duct taped over the buttons so it wouldn't show where the elevator was. He used the janitor's keys and locked the stairwell doors behind him. The final count was seven dead, and 126 injured. One of the dead was a caseworker who wouldn't retreat. When he tried to get to his car, the crowd beat him to death.

If people will do this because their food stamps were late, what will they do if something really bad happens?

* * *

JOURNAL ENTRY: October 23

Today was my son Eric's birthday. It's hard to believe that he's older now than I was when he was born. I called him even though it was hard to wish him a happy birthday when he and Beth are splitting up. Damn, I really like my daughter-in-law. Eric is coping. That's the best thing the military did for him, gave him coping skills. He's a good man and a good father. Perhaps that's what I did for him: teach him how to be a good parent. I'm so proud of him and it makes me weep sometimes.

I'm proud of Jason too, in different ways. Jason has turned into an amazing father. Having an autistic child is difficult, however, he's done well.

* * *

I got my rototiller back from Jason and then hired his helper, Abe, to till the garden. My grip has been bad from all the massage work, but with a winter to recover, it would be better by spring. With the ground broken, I'll be able to run the tiller myself. Jason took the gutters down from the barn that feed the cistern, and then turned the cistern over while Abe tilled the garden. That's two more things off of my list.

A few days ago, I came across one of those hard-to-pass-up deals—a clearance sale on chicken legs, what I call a "use or lose" sale. The legs, all twenty-five of them, went into a big pot for soup, which I canned today. Eleven pints, heavy on the chicken, along with the two packages of boneless thighs, making eight more pints. I couldn't help it. When I see prices like that, I feel the need to buy it.

The weather is now cool, low fifties, cloudy and dreary. Saturday the temps are supposed to drop into the thirties for the high, so it looks like winter is closing in on us. I think I might run into town and get two more bags of chicken feed and see if rock salt is in stock yet. It should be—I've seen Christmas displays already! Geesh, what happened to the day *after* Thanksgiving?

* * *

JOURNAL ENTRY: October 24

I keep looking at my list, and looking at it again. Why am I hesitating to finish it? The water is a big issue. So many times after I've turned it off, I find something that I need to hose down, or wash outside, which means turning it back on. I'm also reluctant to empty and winterize the hot tub. This is the perfect time to use it, as the nights are getting chilly. I do love a good long soak. I give therapy all summer long and the hot tub is *my* therapy.

* * *

When I arrived for my morning massage with John, all the guys there seemed antsy and irritable, which is unlike them. They're usually pleasant and jovial. I wonder if they're having more problems from the locals.

These guys might be miners at a very controversial local mine, but they are also a bunch of the nicest guys I've met, and they're trying very hard to fit in with the community. Doing a massage off to the side in the large dining area lets me be the proverbial fly-on-the-wall. These guys are from all over, literally. Lance is from Ireland and I can listen to him talk for hours. Sven is from Sweden, John from North Carolina, and none of them are from Michigan. I think that was intentional.

Most of them have degrees in something related, like management or geology, or specialize in explosives, and they are all intelligent and polite. Their language is rather rough; it comes with the territory. Actually, that they talked like that in front of me made me feel more accepted.

I don't know why the guys are acting peculiar. John said some of them get "feelings" about earth movement, that there had been some, and that it was making them all extra cautious.

* * *

JOURNAL ENTRY: October 25

The weather report isn't good. We are expecting cold rain and thunderstorms for the rest of the week, so I drained the hot tub and dumped the two gallons of anti-freeze in, wrapped up the screen netting, and took down the umbrella. Another major project done, and I'm sure going to miss it. With it sitting outside on the deck, I can't afford the extra money every month to heat it during the winter.

* * *

I was on a roll. I'd been waiting for gas prices to drop so I could refill the drum. This morning it dropped, not much, down to $3.75. Outrageous, but I'm way too nervous about not having full drums. I've always had it refilled by now, however, it has been too expensive. I needed eighty gallons to refill everything. That came to a lot of money; on the other hand, I did feel better having the drums topped off even at that price. It took several hours of running back and forth this morning, twenty gallons at a time, trying to time the shift change at Fram's so it wasn't so obvious what I was doing, and now I felt so much more confident with full drums.

If a snowstorm takes down the power I need gas for the generator. Depending on how long it stays down, I could need a *lot* of gas. The two drums and four cans gave me 130 gallons to get through an emergency.

While I was doing that, I dropped off all the heavy comforters, blankets and pillows at the Laundromat. That storm front must have missed us. The weather was still reasonably okay to dry it all on the clothesline, even with the nighttime temperatures getting into the forties. That the rain had held off so far was a bonus. The temperature actually hit sixty-seven yesterday, not what was predicted at all.

* * *

JOURNAL ENTRY: October 26

Well, that was short lived. We're now under a severe thunderstorm warning with possible hail. The blankets are draped over chairs in the kitchen, drying very, very slowly. At least they won't get any wetter. I bet Jacob would love it here with all these "blanket tents" to play under. It is fifty-seven degrees and too warm to start the stove to help with the drying. Other than the pillows, it's also all too large to fit into the dryer.

I'm pleased that at least I got the gas in. I pushed some boxes out of the way, and parked the car in the barn. Quarter-sized hail can do some damage!

Everything has shifted fast. It's dark out now and a thick fog has settled in. I can hear the thunder in the distance. Tufts is not happy about staying in. He might be a big kitty but he's a coward at heart. The first crack of thunder and he'll be hiding under the bed.

* * *

Tufts the cat is my friend and companion. I remember when I first brought him home. I was his fourth home in four months, and he was scared to death. I had lost my longhaired white cat CeeCee six months before to cancer. That was a long and lonely six months for me. Then I saw an ad in the paper: "Free to good home, longhaired black cat, neutered, all shots, declawed, owner allergic."

I called and picked him up the next day. The first owner was moving into an apartment and couldn't take him, so he went to the pet shelter to await adoption. The next owner wanted another black cat for a friend to their current black cat, only that cat wasn't adapting. The third owner was more loyal to her other cat, which I understood. After a week with me, I saw the cat sitting at the glass door staring out, the sun shining in, illuminating the grayish tufts in his ears and on his tummy, and he became Tufts. He's been a wonderful, affectionate cat that needed one owner (not a family) and to be an only child. Now, his golden eyes greet me every morning and I spoil him rotten.

* * *

The storms have completely moved out and it's cool and sunny. I took all the curtains down, washed them, and put them out on the line. I can't believe how much I'm getting done. It's difficult to do all this by myself. I have to first remember what to do, then do it and do it right. Not doing a chore right is as bad as not doing it at all, especially when it might be one of those vital things like turning off the outside water, or filling the hot tub lines with anti-freeze. It could be disastrous if not done, or not done properly.

* * *

After I washed down the hearth of the wood cook stove, I brought in a full load of wood. I had to fire the stove up this morning. It was chilly, only forty-two degrees out, and I didn't expect the temperature to go much higher.

The fall colors are wonderful as usual, yet also go away quickly. With a predominance of maple trees up here, there is a vivid display of red, orange and yellow that draws people from all over for the Color-Tour, our last hurrah for tourism. It's hard to believe that the peak color was two weeks ago and now we have bare trees. What an amazing transformation.

At least there's been no snow yet. I remember one year when there was a foot of wet, heavy snow even before the leaves dropped. It brought down countless trees and took the power out. Mine was out for four days; others for over a week. The power company did massive trimming the next spring to keep it from happening again.

The forecast is for flurries on Sunday so I put the chickens' winter walls up on the inner yard, yet another thing off of my list. Putting those sheets of thin plywood over the secure fencing keeps the blowing snow out of their small yard and the roof keeps everything else out. The chickens are happy when they are able to get out to scratch around in the dirt, and happy chickens lay more eggs.

My best friend Kathy called last night to see if I was going into town today so she could hitch a ride. Her husband Bob was already in town for a daylong workshop and there was a hockey game they wanted to watch later. Since I had planned a quick run, I told her I could drop her off and save Bob from coming back those thirty miles to pick her up.

Jason is planning to come for dinner tonight with Jacob and requested "meat," so I need to shop. I suppose I could pull something out of the freezer...

I found a couple of steaks that should satisfy Jason's appetite. Those, along with some steamed carrots with Swiss chard and a salad will make a nice dinner.

* * *

JOURNAL ENTRY: October 27

A major hurricane is making its way up the East Coast. New York City provides over 350,000 free meals each day, on a *normal* day. I wonder what will happen if there is no food to give out during or after this storm?? People can get real ugly when they're hungry.

The weather here is strange, though I doubt it's an effect from the storm. The skies are clear at night so it got cold, only thirty-three degrees when I got up. When the sun came up, the clouds rolled in so there was no solar heating.

I left one cherry tomato plant in the garden, covered at night with a frost bag. The few tomatoes on it won't ripen without warmth, so I needed to pick those and bring them inside, then pull the plant up. There's also most of the short row of Swiss chard that seems totally unaffected by the cold. I picked some last night for dinner, so that I will leave alone to enjoy while I can. It's time to dump the flowers on the deck and put the planters underneath. One more thing to cross off of that nagging prep list.

Eric called to tell me that he is going to come up for Thanksgiving. Wow, two visits in two months. I wonder what's up?

* * *

Jason brought Jacob over around noon. He had a job to do that would take him a few hours, and since Amanda, my daughter in law, is still out of town, I agreed to watch my nine-year-old grandson. Jacob is autistic and takes a bit more attention at times, but he plays so well by himself that it was easy to continue with my chores. I dumped the flowers, hauled in wood, changed the litter box, and did some laundry. Then Jacob and I went for a short walk along my road.

Jason showed up around 5:30 P.M., just in time for dinner. I made two Cornish hens, stuffed with fresh herbs and cooked in the woodstove oven, served on a bed of basmati rice with a side of Swiss chard. It was nice to cook for someone beside myself. Jacob is a fussy eater, so I always keep chicken nuggets or noodles on hand for him. He loves noodles.

* * *

JOURNAL ENTRY: October 28

No snow, although it sure is chilly! It got down to thirty degrees last night. I built a nice fire in the cook stove, started a new book, and spent the day relaxing. The fire felt good, and I'm planning to cook a pot roast for dinner, a nice long, slow cook. Yum.

It looks like that hurricane is going to wreak some havoc on the East Coast. The media is calling it a "perfect storm," a nor'easter colliding with a cold front from the west. They are predicting that some areas might see fifty inches of snow! Even up here we don't get that in one fall. The most that I've ever seen is forty inches when I still lived deep in the woods. That was a blizzard to remember, long before the Weather Service was naming winter storms.

Over on one of my Internet groups, Survival Retreat, the speculations have already started on whether or not the hardest hit areas of the storm are going to be able to hold elections next week, or if they'll be suspended. That's never happened before.

* * *

Today is the last Monday of the month. I paid my bills for November online. Gosh, I love doing that! They are all done and will go out when they should, automatically. I still needed to plug in an amount for the propane bill, since the fuel will be delivered on Thursday. It felt really good to have enough in the checking for the rest of the year, with the balance in the savings, ready to transfer over, providing no expensive emergencies come up.

It was twenty-five degrees this morning, and the furnace failed to come on when it was supposed to. However, when I bumped up the temperature manually, it kicked right in. Hopefully it was only a glitch. The woodstove is going now and it's quite comfortable. The temperature outside has risen to forty-five degrees and the skies are a deep blue with near blinding sunshine.

I got another winter prep done. I recharged the generator battery for easy starting. It isn't hard to start it with the cord, but my shoulder still isn't one hundred percent and I don't want to re-injure it. The generator has the capability to start by either pull cord or key, and the key method requires a battery to furnish the necessary power. Jason got it all rigged for me after I got the right sized battery. When the gennie runs, it charges the battery, although if I don't use it for months on end, the battery gets drained. I finally got the trickle charger Jason suggested and can now keep the battery level where it needs to be. I didn't have these issues in the woods: Sam ran the generator daily to do his stained glass art and he did all the maintenance on the gennie. I sure had a lot to learn after we split up.

I had to do one last sweep of the deck. I don't know where all these leaves are coming from, there sure aren't any more on the trees!

It might be a good day to clean off my computer desk and the shelf overhead. Maybe my art table too. That might give me the incentive to start painting Christmas cards again. I used to hand paint all of our cards when I lived deep in the woods. Watercolor art came easy to me and I really enjoy it. I would work with two or three designs and then duplicate them individually. That last year in the woods I made seventy-five cards. After we broke up, one of Sam's friends asked if he could stay on my Christmas card list. That was flattering, but not so touching as when I found all of my cards in Mom's drawer after she died. She didn't keep any other cards, only mine.

CHAPTER TWO

The storm was ferocious. The perfect storm, called "Frankenstorm" because it's so close to Halloween. This was on a nationally known television commentary website: "Not even a back injury could keep him from coming onto the radio and telling the New York branch that if the storm didn't get them, the inevitable breakdown in the food supply and the subsequent rioting would surely result in their untimely demise."

That was even scarier than the storm. A breakdown in the food supply is almost a sure thing, considering the Just-In-Time system most major cities utilize, and for those cities, yeah, there *will* be rioting. It makes me shiver. The JIT system seems to be way too prevalent. What bothers me the most about this is that people *could* have prepared! They could have stocked up on food, water, supplies. They could have done a lot of things but they didn't, counting on the government to take care of them and then blaming others when that failed. I do hope that those affected by the storm *wake up* and realize that their safety, their future and their very lives are in their own hands, not the government's.

We're under a high wind advisory and Lake Superior is under gale warnings. It's cold, windy and snow is in the air, likely tonight. I'm sure glad that I don't have to go anywhere, though I did bring in extra wood.

The furnace kicked on as scheduled this morning, so it looks like yesterday was only a fluke.

Elections are a week away. I want all of my winter preps done before then. I'm slightly behind, nevertheless, if I push it, I might finish by my November 1st goal. I've used that date for my personal marker for seventeen years now.

Wow! I've been up here that long already? Yet there's no place else I'd rather be. The air is clean, the water is clean and there's no light pollution. There is little crime and it's so peaceful and *safe*. The little town of Moose Creek is literally at the end of the road. There's no drive through traffic because the road stops. The joke is that you either come here on purpose or you're lost.

* * *

JOURNAL ENTRY: October 30

I read a report today that said one-third of all Americans are not paying their bills on time now, and that more than forty-one percent of all working-age Americans are not working—the economy is that bad. That's the true unemployment rate! I'm thankful that I bought this house outright when I did. I have no car payment or mortgage, only utilities, insurance and taxes. I'm in much better shape than most people, even with a seasonal job. Plus, a large garden and canning helps keep food on the table.

I braved the well pit and shut off the water today. My prep list is almost done. Dawn mentioned Halloween cocktails tomorrow night. Any excuse for a party!

* * *

On Halloween I went into town early and got four more fifty pound bags of cracked corn for the chickens. While there, I picked up some more of Tufts' favorite crunchy treats. He's *so* spoiled. Since it's the official end of my season, I picked up my celebratory rib eye steak and a single slice of cheesecake for tomorrow. Dawn always puts out a lavish spread for her parties, so that will be my dinner for tonight.

I asked John to go with me but he had to work like usual. This is the second time that he's turned me down. Guess he doesn't like me as much as I thought. I can always hope though. Well, maybe not. Perhaps it is not good to mix business with pleasure.

* * *

There's been a lot of Internet traffic about looting and crime in the cities that have been hit hard by the hurricane. Eighty million households are without power. Without electricity, no surveillance cameras, and with the police busy elsewhere, it is a looter's dream come true. I'm sure whatever we are hearing is just the tip of the iceberg.

* * *

JOURNAL ENTRY: October 31

I was right. Dawn put on a spectacular party. Costumes were optional and only Guy and Dawn wore them. I love dressing up, but I just didn't feel like it this year. Dawn made an artichoke dip that she put into the body of a bread *spider*. It looked great and tasted even better. There were lots of appetizers from ham roll ups, raw veggies with plastic spiders nestled in between, chicken wings, a fruit tray, and the usual cheese and crackers, to the smoked oysters and our local whitefish caviar. It was good food and there was lots of it.

We all played cards after satisfying our appetites.

* * *

On November 1st, the gals restarted our weekly Ladies Lunch, one of those events to help stave off the boredom when winter sets in, our own Cabin Fever Reliever. It has always been on a Thursday because Mary's husband Alan plays poker on that day, which is the only day that he lets Mary do something by herself. Geesh, they've been married for forty-five years, you'd think they'd want some space. On the other hand, he is a control freak. Now Bob and Kathy, they have such respect for each other that it's a joy to be around them. Dawn and Guy I don't know well, not yet anyway. Dawn seems to do what she wants and Guy goes along with it. I'm the only single person in the group and the longer I'm alone, the more I like it. Usually. I do get lonely but I try not to let it show.

About two months ago, Dawn approached me about prepping. Their daughter turned them on to it. I've given Dawn and Guy what advice or suggestions that I can, and they've run with it. Then again, they've got the money to do it.

Sitting on their deck having cocktails, I asked them if they had any weapons and Dawn quickly said yes. I asked Guy how much ammo he had. Before he could answer, I said it wasn't enough. Dawn admitted that she didn't like guns; I told her to get over it. How else was she going to protect those four grandchildren if she was the only one there during a break-in? That really made her pause.

She also has extensive medical knowledge. I think her mother was a surgical nurse, so she could be a real asset, and lives within two miles of my place, an easy walk. I wish that she didn't smoke.

Beginning with the bird-flu scare some years ago, I've added to my own medical stores. Though masks and gloves can be used for many different situations, I really went heavy on them. At first I wasn't sure about what kind of masks, so I got a variety: regular surgical masks, respirators, N-95, N-99 and a gas mask. The gloves range from surgical, some latex free, some not, to several packs of food handler gloves. Those are *really* handy for cleaning the wood stove, enough to keep hands clean and free of the gunk. They also work for peeling beets. Once I went a whole day with pink palms.

Two years ago I added two stethoscopes (plus repair parts), a blood pressure machine, sealed goggles, scalpels and a variety of sutures to my kit. I even split an order of cast compound with Rick from the Michigan prepper group. I don't have everything that might be needed in an emergency, however, it's way more than most people have. I set much of this up in a grab-n-go bag. A doctor with nothing would be impressed with my medical kit.

Some preppers stock up only on food, some only on guns and ammo—*not* a prepper to me. I prefer to be the kind of prepper that covers all the basics: food, medical supplies and yes, ammo. No one ever really knows what we may be faced with, yet I'm trying to cover all the bases I can.

* * *

JOURNAL ENTRY: November 2

I doubt that it's even worth mentioning here, but I do like to keep records. Late yesterday evening, Yellowstone National Park had a serious tremor of a 4.5 on the Richter scale. Then the New Madrid Fault had a couple too, a 4.0 and a 4.4. There's no damage in Yellowstone, nor was there any in the New Madrid, since they were pretty deep. Still, it's something to pay attention to. With the hurricane damage on the East Coast, and now this, it feels like some higher force is shaking us up good.

* * *

It snowed this morning! It started out as sleet, switched over to snow and there is a light dusting on the ground. Sure glad I got everything done in time. Tufts doesn't like the snow pelting him in the face, and I can't blame him. I don't like it either, though I still need to face it to bring in wood. The temperature started out at thirty-three degrees and only got up to thirty-five.

There is looting and mayhem going on in the big city and all the other large cities that are still without power from the Frankenstorm. Society seems to have broken down completely. There were pictures on the news last night of the long lines just to get gas, and they had to start limiting it to ten gallons per person. Fights were breaking out; it's crazy in the cities. And to think that it will all be fixed in another week.

One news article said, "*If people will behave like this during a temporary emergency that lasts only a few days, what would they do during a total economic collapse? That is a frightening thing to think about.*"

Very frightening indeed.

I've been a bit dizzy the past few days. I think it's my eyes. I have to remember to stop and pick up my new glasses. Maybe I should run into town tomorrow and do that.

* * *

I picked up my new glasses and feel silly that I had forgotten about them. While in town, I picked up four more cases of quart canning jars. Funny though, it's the end of canning season, and the jars were not even on sale, much-less on clearance.

Jason said his dad was coming up to hunt. He promised me that we would get venison for the freezer. Since I keep little of the freezer meat, and only some of the sausage, I usually make my share into soup and stew meat, all canned. After they get the deer, then I'll get a couple of pork roasts to grind and add to the sausage. I don't have the freezer room. I have to remember to check the spices out in the small barn to see if the supply might be getting low, and I'm pretty sure I have enough casings for making the sausage.

* * *

JOURNAL ENTRY: November 4

Amanda is back from her visit to see her mom and stopped over last night with Jacob. She wanted to discuss Thanksgiving plans. This year it's at their house, so they get to do the turkey and most of the trimmings. My brother lives right across the road from me and his wife, Nancy, is making a couple of pies and I'm bringing my seven-layer salad, fresh bread and the wine. Amanda asked if I would make the gravy since she doesn't know how, plus the thought of handling/cooking the neck and gizzards makes her queasy. How did she ever make it into her thirties without learning to make gravy?

It is cold here, only thirty-three degrees this morning. I wonder how the people in the big city are managing the cold nights without power. I doubt this storm will wake any of them up.

There is another storm brewing out in the Atlantic. This one is a winter storm, a Nor'easter, which means even more snow for the coast. What little snow that fell here yesterday is now gone.

I'm not sleeping well again. It seems that every other night I don't sleep at all, and the other nights, it's a toss-up between really well and fitful. It's wearing me down. I'm not getting enough rest.

Spring Forward—Fall Back. We are now in Daylight Savings Time, gained an hour of daylight, I think. I can never keep that straight.

I think this is going to be a very boring journal; there is nothing happening in my life. I get up, check email, straighten up the house, do some laundry, plan the day's menu, let Tufts out, then in, then out. Nothing exciting.

I went for a walk today on my road. I like walking in the fall better because my little ten acres here are a blaze of color. I love the sharp, pungent scent of the pine trees and the smell of damp, decaying leaves when I kick the carpet up. The woods behind me are so grown that the breezes rarely filter down yet I can hear the upper branches swaying and creaking when the wind passes through, even with all the leaves down. These sensory things are just not there when walking on a blacktop road. It still may be exercise, though it is not nearly as enjoyable.

* * *

The news is too depressing to watch with more riots, more crime, and now some areas out east are turning away power crews from other states for the only reason that they're not part of their union! How stupid can they be?

I called Dawn to see how her prepping was coming along and if she needed any more suggestions, but they weren't home. So I called Kathy. I sure wish that I could talk her into stocking even a week's worth of food. She's got lots of tomato sauce from her Earthboxes and beans from her garden that now are in the freezer. Cheese, crackers and smoked oysters are staples there, to go with their rather extensive wine cellar. I worry about them if they couldn't get out due to a blizzard or if something worse happened.

I can only suggest.

Watching the news coverage of the storm, my anxiety level has gone up in some ways, and lowered in others. Things went south very quickly. Criminals are opportunists and they sure had the opportunity for looting and other crimes. Those who evacuated the cities late and are now waiting in lines are of the mentality that they cannot blame themselves for not having what it is they need or desire. They, like everyone else, had both the chance and the choice to prepare, and they chose not to.

When the scenario turns into reality, and they see they should have prepared, they must blame someone else. To blame themselves is tantamount to admitting that they are failures, and our current society has programmed us by telling us that there are no failures because everyone is a winner. That failure only gets reinforced when you've failed those you are supposed to protect or those who depend on you, like children, the elderly, or the disabled.

I looked over my food preps and know I'm in good shape for the winter, much longer if I stretch out my canning. I could fill out some spots in my supplies, but toilet paper won't keep me alive, so I'm not overly concerned with it since that's a convenience thing. For what I have and what I need to survive until next summer, I'm good.

When I see on the news and in real life what "civilized" people are capable of, even *knowing* that help is on the way, that the power will be back on eventually, and that this will all become a bad dream, what will they be like when they find out that the power *won't* be back on, or that help *isn't* coming? That's when my anxiety spikes and I check my ammo supplies.

CHAPTER THREE

It was a wonderfully casual morning with gray skies and a threat of snow showers that never materialized. Though it was only thirty-six degrees out, it felt strangely pleasant. I checked my Internet groups, sent some emails and had a late breakfast. Then around 11:00 A.M., I went to the Moose Creek township hall to vote. There was no line. There are seven hundred people in the township, though only four hundred fifty-seven registered voters, so I think that if we all showed up at the same time it would still only take an hour. I made my choices and went home after checking the post office for mail.

I'm feeling good about the day, but guilty about not meeting my November 1st deadline, and decided to go into the city, thirty miles away.

First stop was at a big-box store for laundry soap, toilet paper, paper towels, and cat food. Tufts is an important member of the household. He's the *only* other member of the household, so his food supply is a high priority to me. While there, I decided on a couple six packs of seltzer water (to go with my spiced rum), and grabbed a couple of bottles of wine. It was a lucrative work season, so I opted for the good stuff.

Then I headed over to Mack's, my favorite grocery store. I picked up romaine lettuce and celery, a head of cauliflower and some oatmeal, then checked the bargain bin for anything good. There was nothing this time. I was getting some sliced cheese at the deli when my phone rang.

I recognized the number, so I answered immediately.

"Hey, Rick, what's up?"

"Allex, I have to make this fast, so just listen." I sighed, thinking that this must be serious since he knows how much I hate being called *Allex*. "A 7.8 earthquake hit the New Madrid Fault a few minutes ago. That will likely mean loss of trucking, loss of power, loss of phones. The shit has hit, Allex! Whatever you're doing, get back home and hunker down."

He abruptly hung up. I stood there for a moment, stunned. Rick wouldn't kid around about something like this. If shipping shut down, food supplies will disappear in a hurry since they keep little inventory, only what's on the shelves. That won't last once word gets out and then there will be panic buying.

I collected my cheese and headed toward the checkout, trying to stay calm, before I realized that *nobody knew yet*. I had a rare opportunity to beat the rush. I went back to the meat department and loaded up four turkeys, two hams, six roasts, and a dozen good steaks, putting my few other purchases in the seat area to make room. I went back to the wine aisle for more wine, beer and rum. I saw a bottle of wine called "Earthquake," — how appropriate. I grabbed six. Then I nabbed two twenty-five pound bags of flour. It was getting hard to push the cart, so I headed toward the checkout, snagging two big bags of cat food. When I was passing the paper goods aisle, I left my cart, since it was too heavy to maneuver easily, and took two cases of canning seals off the shelf, one regular and one wide mouth, setting them on the bottom of the cart. Nobody buys canning supplies this late in the season.

I couldn't believe how calm everyone was. Either they hadn't heard yet, or the "someone else's problem" mentality kicked in. Here was a major disaster, though in another state. It wouldn't affect us, right? They really didn't understand our grid, or our transport system.

I picked Marie's lane. I like Marie and we've gotten to be friends. She never questions what I buy because she knows I live so far out of town.

"Hey, girlfriend! Getting Thanksgiving dinner early, huh?" she smiled and started ringing all of the meat up.

"You could say that. Can I get a couple of the tote boxes? This is going to be heavier than I thought," I chuckled, trying hard to act natural. I got four and put two turkeys each in two of the boxes and the rest of the meat in the third, the bottles in the last, and used plastic bags for the rest. I was surprised to see the total a bit under five hundred dollars, more than I'm used to spending, yet I thought it would be higher. I swiped my debit card, anticipating they wouldn't be good in the all-too-near future. Once boxed and bagged, I needed a second cart and one of the baggers to help me.

I turned to leave, and made a decision.

"Marie," I said quietly, "before you go home tonight, stock up on pet food for your two dogs and the cats, and get your other shopping done, too." When she asked why, I said, "Something has happened. You will find out tonight on the news. Just do your shopping tonight, okay?"

The parking lot looked like it should, but it sure didn't feel right. Maybe it was just me.

The young man helping me looked at the totes. "That's a lot of turkeys," he said.

"Yeah, I have a big family reunion coming up," I said politely. Rude would be remembered, friendly would not, and I don't want to be remembered for these purchases when others start getting hungry.

I loaded the rest of the groceries and headed for the exit. Another split decision. I made a left instead of a right. I had three more stops to make, and if all went well,

I'd be on the road home in less than an hour. The first stop was the bank, where I withdrew a thousand dollars from my savings account. I'd done that before, so no one even blinked. Next stop was the bulk food place that has some things which no one else does, and in large quantities. I went right to the back and got a half wheel each of parmesan, asiago, cheddar and American cheeses, then two twenty-five pound bags of Basmati rice, Jason's favorite. I didn't need anything else from there so it was a quick check out.

The final stop was to top off the gas tank. I was only a quarter-tank down, so that didn't take any time at all and I was back on the road. It only took forty minutes to get through those three extra stops.

When I got onto County Road 695, the straight stretch to home, I pulled over. My hands were shaking and I dropped the phone twice. I sent out a group text to Soozie, Suzy, Clark, Jane and Pam. Those close friends and my sister would understand the agreed upon code: "Alas, Babylon!" and I added: "New Madrid, 7.8."

Then I called Jason. I asked him if he'd heard what happened, then remembered that he doesn't have a television, and rarely listens to the radio. I said that I was on my way home, and asked him to meet me at my house in forty minutes.

When I arrived, we watched the news in stunned silence and viewed the aerial pictures of the area. Such devastation! There is actually a crack in the Earth. All this within a week of the damage on the East Coast. How will our country deal with this?

I'm still stunned that I was able to do that last minute shopping without being caught up in a mob. All of the meat is in coolers and the rest of the stuff can wait until tomorrow before I put it away. Right now, I'm exhausted.

* * *

JOURNAL ENTRY: November 7

I slept surprisingly well last night with no dreams that I can remember. I love the lazy mornings now, when I can casually stay in bed and ease myself awake. Then I looked at the clock—7:30 A.M., and realized it was Wednesday! I need to be over on Eagle Beach to give John his weekly massage in 30 minutes. Since it's only a seven mile drive it doesn't take long, but I haven't loaded up my table yet, and I needed to hustle!

* * *

John met me at the door of the house that he shares with a dozen other miners. I could smell the aroma of the breakfast that Steve had cooked and my stomach gurgled. I set up my massage table and got ready to work. The sounds of anxious, almost frantic, newscasters coming from the TV in the other room caught my attention and I peeked around the corner. All the guys were staring at the big-screen TV. None of them had gone to bed yet. Usually the night shift at the mine is brutal and once home they eat and go to bed. Not this time. The horrors of yesterday's quake took on a surreal feeling as the images were played over and over. There were still no death count totals, however, it's reported being very high

An hour later I slipped John's payment into my pocket and packed up my table. I really like this moment, because John hugs me like he enjoys holding me. Neither of us gets hugs and they feel so very good. He gave me an extra-long one today so I asked him if he was okay.

"Quakes always make us really nervous," he said in his charming North Carolina drawl. "None of the guys want to go down into the mine right now, yet the bosses are pushing us pretty hard to finish the portal by December." He paused. "We had a rock slide last night. Sammy had his hand on a railing and got two of his fingers crushed. It's the first accident this mine has had and the project heads are not happy about it. I just wanted to punch someone. Fingers are nothing. Nothing!! I've brought guys back out in body bags! Crushed fingers are nothing! Sean is talking about quitting, so is Adam. Liam already did."

I didn't know what to say, although I could tell that he was done venting. I told him he could call me anytime to talk, gave him another long hug and said that I'd see him next week. My mind was reeling over what he had said, over the earthquake and over the election results. I felt numb.

* * *

I left Eagle Beach and went to Jason's over on the Dam Road. Last night I had made a list of supplies that I thought they could use, and needed to check with them first. Amanda was still sleeping, but Jason was up, having gotten Jacob off to school. I almost offered to do the shopping for them, but Amanda loves to shop, and would have been royally pissed if I'd left her out of it. I went over the list with Jason.

"I understand, Mom, but I can't afford all of this. We recently bought Jacob all new clothes for school. He's growing so fast." This I understood; he's already nine, and because he's growing, the extra clothes in larger sizes would be needed regardless. Not to mention all the food supplies I had listed.

I handed him $500 in cash, then reached in my pocket and gave him what I'd just earned. "I doubt they'll be taking checks or debit cards before long." He looked at me with concern. "I think this is that important, Jason. You and Amanda have to go together. It might be bad in the stores, or soon will be, and you have to be there to protect her. Two of you will be less of a target. Call the school and have them drop Jacob off at my house if you start to run late. Shop fast and shop smart. Don't forget to fill your gas tank. In fact, do that first!"

Back at home, I plugged in the extra refrigerator in the barn and repacked the meat. The turkeys were still well frozen, so they went into the lower part, leaving me plenty of room to freeze the rest of the meats. The steaks I bagged individually and vacuumed sealed. The roasts I cut in half and then vacuum sealed. The hams were my quandary, so I stuck them in the fridge with the frozen turkeys. They would hold for quite a while and may become a Christmas treat. With it bouncing between thirty and thirty-five degrees, nothing was going to thaw anytime soon.

The cheeses were good in the cold pantry with the low temperatures. I've had hard cheese last a very long time that way, so I'm not concerned. The American cheese would have to be used within a few months. Thankfully, Jacob loves grilled cheese. Once opened, or cut into, I would wrap the cheese in vinegar-soaked cheesecloth and that should hold it even longer.

I found room for the paper goods in the cat pantry, and then put the flour in the metal trashcan in the cold pantry. The wine went on the wonderful oak rack that Jason built for me years ago.

It was 5:15 P.M. Central time, right in the heart of rush hour, when the second quake hit. It measured 8.2 on the Richter scale.

* * *

JOURNAL ENTRY: November 8

The first quake was downgraded to a 7.6 with the epicenter slightly north of Memphis. It lasted four minutes. All along the Mississippi River bridges have collapsed or are severely damaged. Aerial views show a crack in the Earth.

It's mind boggling, but at least the levees are holding. The second quake remains at an 8.2 and centered in what was Hannibal, Missouri. Hannibal is gone, leveled. The tectonic plate was shoved out of place during the seven minutes of shaking, and now the Mississippi at this juncture is spilling back into itself, forming a new lake. The death toll is staggering—thousands, maybe hundreds of thousands, with thousands more missing and even more thousands injured.

There is no way to get an actual count right now because the devastation is too great. There are fires and gas explosions everywhere, hampering any rescue efforts, which are minimal. Roads are filled with debris from buildings and crushed cars. Asphalt and concrete have buckled. Emergency vehicles can't get anywhere. Gas stations are burning out of control from ruptured fuel tanks and natural gas lines have ignited everywhere. FEMA is overwhelmed. They were completely tied up on the East Coast with the hurricane victims, and now this. They can't even do anything since there has been no call from either governor requesting help.

Missing Missouri Governor Sarah Astor was home with her family in Hannibal. Tennessee Governor Johnny Perkins is also missing. Both governments are in chaos. All shipping traffic on the Mississippi has been halted. Some of the barges were shoved into the riverbanks, while others that were not so lucky were sunk. With virtually all the bridges compromised in one way or another, the vehicle traffic is non-existent. It's the same way for any east-west trains. The only route is through northern Minnesota and it's blocked by the first blizzard of the season.

Reports just came in that there were two 4.5 tremors in Utah within the last twelve hours, and a 6.7 in Yellowstone. They had to evacuate and close the park because the ground is so hot that it was melting the soles on shoes. Another 6.3 Richter scale earthquake occurred off the coast of British Columbia.

What is happening?

* * *

That's it, no more runs to town.

I dressed in my usual slacks, long sleeved shirt and vest. The vest is important to hide my shoulder holster. Ever since the first quake, I've been wearing it even around the house.

County Road 695 into town was absent of any traffic, though that's not unusual. I wanted to make this a fast trip so light traffic was a bonus. I pulled into the mall parking lot. My goal was to get to the hardware store in the strip-mall section next to the grocery store. I grabbed one of the cloth shopping bags from the back seat and headed in. The selection of batteries was poor; others had obviously thought about them too. Damn! I could kick myself for forgetting I needed batteries! I managed to obtain three packs of D cell and two of C. They were not enough since they were only double packs.

When I neared the checkout, I saw the shotgun leaning behind the counter. The young man, maybe thirty years old, saw me glance at it.

"Getting that bad already?" I asked, putting the batteries on the counter.

"Yes," he replied tensely. "It's cash only and I don't make change." That surprised me. I handed him enough bills and left.

Next door at Mack's, I got a bonus. Who looks for batteries in the shampoo aisle? I found four more packs of D, C, AA and AAA. Since there were lots of nine volt, I took two in spite of the fact that, offhand, I can't think of anything I have that uses nine volt. Apparently nobody else does either.

Out of curiosity, I wandered through the store a bit. It's only been three days, but the beer, wine and liquor section was stripped clean. The rest of the shelves were near bare. In the cereal aisle two women were arguing over a canister of oatmeal. I watched in silence as they struggled over the box. The box inevitably broke, spilling its confetti-like contents, joining the Fruit Loops and Cocoa Puffs already littering the floor. One woman glared at the other and stomped off, cereal audibly crunching underfoot while the other stood there staring at the floor and cried. I slipped away before either knew that I had seen their petty quarrel. In the produce section, it was worse. Things were mixed in together, rotten or dumped on the floor that was already sticky with crushed tomatoes and mashed bananas. The sickly sweet stench of unidentifiable fermenting fruit was overwhelming. I did not want to be there.

I found Marie's lane and set the batteries from the basket on the conveyor, leaving my cloth bag in the seat of the cart. Her eyes pooled with tears and she grabbed my hand.

"Thank you. Thank you for the warning. I did what you said," she choked up while ringing up my purchase. I smiled because I didn't know how to answer. She looked for a bag and I said I'd put the batteries in my bag with my stuff from next door. I pushed the cart out beyond her station to get the batteries off the end, and she came from behind the register and gave me a hug. It felt somewhat awkward because Marie is six feet tall and I'm only five-foot-five.

"You take care of yourself, Marie, and if your gut says don't come in to work, then *don't*. It's going to get even worse. You know that don't you?" I whispered. She nodded and I grabbed my now heavy sack and left.

* * *

I got to my car and hit the release button on the key fob to open the hatch. My eyes were darting around the lot, trying to stay aware of my surroundings. I noticed two young men walking down the parking lane. They both appeared to be in their early twenties and were sloppy looking with long greasy hair and torn jeans. One carried a baseball bat while the other had what looked to be a metal plumbing pipe and they were looking at me.

Oh, crap.

I set my bag in the car and turned my body slightly, slamming the hatch shut with my right hand while the left hand hit the lock on the fob, before dropping the keys into my left pocket. My right hand then slid inside my vest and released the strap on the Kel-Tec that was snug in its shoulder holster. They were now seven cars away.

"That's far enough!" I yelled, trying to sound cold and confident, not sure if I had succeeded. The sight of the gun pointed in their direction stopped them. I held the standard two-handed position until they backed away. My concentration was on the two punks in front of me and I didn't hear the cart approach from behind.

"Ma'am," a nervous voice said and I turned quickly. Two cars over, with an empty slot between us, was a young man. I pointed the gun up when I saw the child in the cart. "Please, will you stay until I get my son in the car seat? I didn't think it would be this bad," he pleaded. The young father looked miserable.

"Be quick!" I commanded and turned back to the punks who had stopped retreating. They apparently realized this new person was not a threat to me but to them, and they turned to leave. The father put the child in the car, strapped him in, and loaded the few groceries that he had found. He was about to enter his vehicle when I yelled, "Hey, put your cart in the corral! If we want civilization to continue, *we* must remain civilized."

He hurriedly pushed his now empty cart into the metal corral. "Thank you, lady. You're absolutely right about staying civilized."

I unlocked my car, slid in, re-locked the doors and set the 9mm down on the seat next to me. Looking at the handgun, I realized that I had better put it back into its holster. Right after I strapped the Kel-Tec back into the holster, my hands shook nervously from the adrenaline rushing through my veins. Although I've had my Concealed Pistol License for eight years, I have never pulled my gun before.

I just wanted to go home.

CHAPTER FOUR

From what I saw yesterday, I am even more concerned with my friends on Eagle Beach. They're not from here and have no family close by. I am familiar with the schedule the "house parents" keep. I knew Steve cooked breakfast and left for home around 8:30 A.M. By 8:20 A.M. I was parked at the end of the road, waiting to flag him down. He was the one in charge and I needed to talk with him.

When I saw his red pickup, I got out of my car. He stopped, looking perplexed. "What's up, Allex? Car trouble?" he asked.

"No, Steve, it's fine. Can we talk for a couple of minutes?" Not waiting for his answer, I opened the truck door and climbed in. "I didn't want to do this in front of the guys. No sense in worrying them," I said. "Supply lines are already shutting down, I'm sure you've noticed. It's not my business what you're stocked up on at the house, though I'm going to suggest a few things. First, if you can, get to the bulk food store and get as many non-perishables that you can: pasta, rice and canned goods—anything that doesn't need refrigeration."

"I've been working on a list, and I see I've got too much that won't keep," Steve said, looking down the road, already lost in thought.

"That place has a whole house generator, right?"

"Automatic turn on when the power goes out for more than five minutes, propane fueled. You're going to tell me to get the tank topped off, right?"

"Yep." I smiled. "I have a feeling that the power might not last much longer, Steve. That gennie will keep the freezers going. You should use that food first, *and* you need power to run the blower for that outside woodstove. Without it, it's going to get mighty cold in that house, especially facing Lake Superior like it does."

"I hadn't thought of that," he confessed. "How do you know all this, Allexa? And what's your interest?"

"Well, Steve, I don't know if you've ever heard the term 'prepper' but that's what I am. I have spent years trying to be prepared to survive just about anything. I've had numerous conversations with others who are a lot smarter than me about what we depend on and what could go wrong with it. We've discussed what we need and what would happen if we don't have it. I suppose that's why the township has appointed me the emergency manager and kept me through three administrations. I'm really good at thinking about the worst possible things that can happen and then trying to see our way past them." I laughed. "What's my interest? None, except that you've got a dozen guys back there that are depending on you, and it's part of my job to help you do that. Besides, I really like those guys. Oh, and Steve? Don't forget to stock up on some things for your own family!"

* * *

JOURNAL ENTRY: November 10

It's been four days since the first earthquake hit down south. So much has happened it feels like much longer. Yesterday I had left a message for the new township supervisor, Anna, but she hasn't called me back yet. I'll have to track her down. We need to talk about the safety of the town. Though I rarely have the occasion to use all my knowledge and training as the town's emergency manager, I do take the position seriously. I feel a strong urge, though, to get my own house in order before I can help others.

* * *

My cold weather lunch has normally been a pint of homemade soup mixed with a pint of a canned vegetable. When I was grabbing the two jars off the back pantry, it occurred to me that I'm going to have to do some rationing myself! The majority of my pantry food is supposed to get me through the winter. Now it might have to last a lot longer, unless I want to go vegetarian. Yuck. I put one jar back.

I still wasn't over my encounter from yesterday, and needed to stay busy and do normal stuff, so I baked. First I baked a loaf of whole wheat bread, then a focaccia. I don't know why I did the focaccia since I don't normally eat sweets. Still, it smells heavenly in here. I used apples, raisins, lots of cinnamon and walnuts.

Knowing that power could go off at any time, I'm trying to stay ahead doing chores, even to the point of doing small loads of laundry. Today I washed only the clothes that I wore yesterday.

Then I gathered the empty water jugs for a trip to the spring. Only two were completely empty, and the third was half full. I poured the water into a couple of buckets, trying to collect as much water from the spring as possible. It's only a thirty minute jaunt round trip, though it might be a long time before I can go back. I was nervous the whole time. Once I got there and remembered how isolated it was, I knew that it was a stupid thing to do.

The roads were eerily free of traffic, but now I have twenty gallons of fresh spring water to drink. I'll set up my water filtration system if need be, however, not until I can't get the artesian water. I know I shouldn't be making those kinds of trips alone anymore. Still, it sure is hard. I've been alone and independent for so long that it's a tough habit to break! I'll have to work on that.

The news tonight said a total of eleven states had been affected by the quake: Minnesota, Wisconsin, Iowa, Illinois, Indiana, Missouri, Kentucky, Tennessee, Arkansas, Louisiana and Mississippi. Damage was concentrated along the Mississippi River and the New Madrid fault line and branched out from there. There is still no word on a total number of dead. They may never know.

There was a power outage here tonight that lasted a half hour. Is this just the beginning?

* * *

JOURNAL ENTRY: November 11

Last night I actually slept with the window open! It was something normal in a not-so normal world. When I went to bed, it was forty-five degrees, an acceptable temperature to me for having the window open. This morning it's fifty-eight degrees and windy, with the forecast of thunderstorms. Tomorrow the temperature is supposed to plummet to thirty degrees and we're expecting snow. I guess when the power and the Internet go, we will all know the weather the old fashioned way: step outside and look. Right now I can see sunshine, a welcome sight, yet over the Big Lake, there are blue-black clouds forming.

It's Sunday and I'm not a churchgoer. At the same time, it has occurred to me that the church might be the place to take the pulse of the community. What a wakeup call.

* * *

I parked myself in the back pew of the Methodist Church. Carolyn, the minister, is a friend of mine. The buzz, of course, was the earthquakes, and discussion of them being a punishment from God. The rest of the talk was the concern for limited supplies that was already being felt. To give her credit, Carolyn emphasized the need for the community to band together to take care of each other whenever possible. Some of the people were *handwringers* and some were downright hostile. It was surprising to me to see which side some were on.

It *didn't* surprise me that Lenny Bagget was hostile; it did surprise me to even see him in church. Adam Grant has always been a gruff, take-charge kind of guy, but he and his wife Carla were on the side of the handwringers. Many were concerned about how they were going to eat, which gave me an idea. I left a note in the collection plate for Carolyn to contact me, and I slipped out the back unnoticed.

Back home for lunch, I found I really missed the combination of a meat soup with veggies, so I came up with an acceptable compromise. For lunch, I poured one jar of turkey soup and one jar of canned green beans into the pan, mixed them up, and then ladled half of it back into one of the empty pints for soup tomorrow. Now I don't feel so denied. I've got all this food that I grew and canned for myself that I'm finding it very difficult to *not* eat what I want to. It's frustrating but I know it's necessary. Tonight is linguini with clam sauce and mussels from the freezer, all from storage. I have to keep eating from the freezer while the power is still on. That's my goal—at least one meal a day from the freezer. It would be disastrous to lose all that frozen food when the power grid goes down.

The temperature got up to sixty-four degrees and then the rain started, lowering the temps. By tomorrow it's supposed to drop thirty degrees! I brought in more wood.

* * *

JOURNAL ENTRY: November 12

It's been a week since the first quake. Now that reality has hit, I think I had better make a stronger effort to check in with the township supervisor. After all, I *am* the township emergency manager. I'm wondering if that's such a good position to have right now. During a disaster it's a lot of responsibility and pressure. I hope I'm up to it. The times I've had to put that hat on are few and far between and my training didn't cover national disasters, only localized events.

The very first thing I need to do is call Liz since she's the one I ultimately report to. I'm hoping she will give me some clue what I need to be doing. I haven't been trained for anything on this scale.

It was a short conversation. She is overwhelmed herself and had little time to spare for me.

* * *

"I've known you for eight years, Allexa, and you're one of the few local EMs that take their position seriously. Follow protocol and do what you think best for your town, you know it better than I do. I've got my hands full here," Liz said matter-of-factly during our brief conversation. I could hear her shuffling papers in the background.

"Can we get any food supplies? And what about law enforcement?"

"I know that you have several retired officers up there. Do you think they will be willing to pitch in? I can send the sheriff up in a few days to deputize them and anyone else that you think would be good to have," she replied, deftly skirting the first half of my question.

"That would be helpful. I'm sure Ken and Karen Gifford would come back on, and perhaps Bill Harris," I said, knowing that she would be familiar these three state troopers. "And I have a list of all the CPL holders."

"How did you get that list? CPL holders are not a matter of public record."

"Don't ask. But since I have mine, we kind of know each other. Besides, you know what a small town this is," I reminded her. "Let me know when the sheriff can be here and I'll have everybody ready."

"Good luck, Allexa. You may well be on your own, you know," were her last words.

"Wait! What about food?" I asked. She had already hung up.

* * *

I'm assuming that Anna is now the supervisor, since she ran for election unopposed. I had THE disaster talk with Dennis when he got elected, and Lenny before him — now it's time for the conversation with Anna. She isn't the type to want to hear what I have to say and I'm not looking forward to it. Hopefully with all that's gone on in the past week, she'll be more receptive to some hard truths.

At the top of the list of things to do was to check with Joe at Fram's Store. I stopped there before going to the township office and left word that I needed to see him in Anna's office.

Joe arrived shortly after I did and we discussed what was in the small grocery store. I reassured him that we had no intention of confiscating his inventory, which seems to be holding, mainly because he maintains a back room stock, not a JIT system. He also had the gas tanks filled a week before all this happened. He didn't like it that I said that we might need to ration the gas, however he saw the wisdom in it. There really is no place to go, so we decided to limit gas to ten gallons per person per week, and that will mostly be used for generators if the power goes out. I also suggested he that limit store hours, so there won't be panic buying like in the city. I then suggested that he might also want to consider hiring a night watchman. That was a shock to him, because this is a fairly crime-free community and there hasn't ever been the need for guards before. Half the people in town don't even lock their doors.

Along with the store is the only Laundromat in town and a café that serves breakfast and lunch. The biggest draw is that both areas are Internet hot spots. One of the downsides of being so rural is the dependency on only a few relay towers, and those towers need power. When the power goes out, so does the connection. Joe has a huge backup generator for the store complex, and since he provides the electricity for the tower on top of his building, the Internet should still work. I say "should" because it's never been fully tested.

I like Joe. We've been friends a long time, and I suggested that he take some of the food stock home with him; a couple cases of veggies at the very least. He glumly nodded and left.

Anna is a very petite gray-blond, with never a hair out of place and always nicely dressed. She looked shocked and ruffled while she slumped in the oversized brown leather chair and drummed her manicured fingertips on the glass desktop.

"On our own? No help from anyone? What are we going to do?" she asked after I relayed the information from Liz to her. She was *so* not ready for this.

"The first thing we're going to do, Anna, is stay calm. The town will look to you for guidance. You are the elected official here. In a disaster situation I'm to take point, however, I think you should be there too. Together we can do this. Okay?" She had that deer in the headlights look, and merely nodded. What is it with the nodding lately? Everyone seems to have lost their voices. "For now, I think we should start with some lists. Who do we think will be leaders? Who do we think could cause trouble? Who are the seniors that might need help or checking on? Is there anyone else like Gregg, who is severely disabled? Oh, and who has wood heat?"

"I don't know, Allexa. Are these really important issues?" she asked me dismissively.

"They might be, Anna. I think we should have the answers before we need to ask the question, especially concerning the elderly and the disabled," I stated firmly.

"It's only been a few days, and we really haven't been affected by the earthquake. No one seems to be all that worried."

"They may not be worried right now but what about tomorrow or the next day when everyone starts to realize just how short our local food supply is? We are going to want to know who is out there that needs our help," I insisted.

Stubborn as she was being, she finally saw my point after a discussion. The sun was going down by the time I left her office.

* * *

JOURNAL ENTRY: November 13

The power went out for a couple of hours this evening, but it's back on now. We get our power feed from Wisconsin and they are closer to ground zero than we are. I'm wondering how long the power stations will continue to be operational. It would only make sense for all the nuclear reactor plants to go into a systematic shutdown to prevent a major incident, like the Fukushima, Chernobyl, or Three Mile Island situations.

Hundreds more minor aftershocks continue to hamper any rescue efforts along the New Madrid fault. It's a mess down there.

CHAPTER FIVE

The power went out again early this morning and hasn't come back on.

I had another meeting scheduled with Anna today. It's a good thing the township hall is only four miles down the road from me. I might be using up my allotted gas just going to town, although that will last only while the roads are open. The weather was mild until yesterday, when the temperatures dropped into the twenties and we got a dusting of snow. This is only the beginning. Average snowfall here is almost *200* inches in a season, and I've seen 360 inches in some areas. If that happens *no*body will be getting around.

Anna's office has only one small window, and with the gloomy gray skies, it was dark in there. I brought one of my battery-operated lanterns and set that on her desk while we went over our lists. She looked longingly at it, so I gave it to her. I didn't tell her I had a few more. I reminded her that it took batteries and she needed to get some from Joe.

We decided to post important notices at the township hall and at the post office. There hasn't been any new mail in a few days, yet D.J., the postmaster, is there anyway. The office area where our postal boxes are is open twenty-four hours, and it is a good place to leave important information. Fram's might be another good place for notices. We decided that the first notice will be a special town meeting scheduled for Friday at noon.

Considering the fuel delivery disruption, we discussed the rationing issue and Anna decided to simply shut down Joe's gas supply to save it for the EMS, fire trucks and the road crews, eliminating the need for rationing. People might be more accepting of that. If someone needed gas it would be allotted on a case-by-case determination. A few of us would need a few gallons each week to get to the offices: Anna, myself, Pete the township handyman, Mike the fire chief, and Maye, the newly elected clerk. Everyone else lives within walking distance. It might be a long time before fuel comes available, so I think it was a wise move, and I was secretly glad that I didn't have to make that decision.

Anna's come around quickly; I think partly because her brother Dennis, the former supervisor, is a nurse in the city and has relayed some horror stories about these past few days. Thankfully, she's willing to work with me in a joint effort to ensure the safety of the town.

We now have a more accurate view of our resources and a better picture of our growing needs. We had lists of who was where that might need help and I'll combine them into one list later tonight when I get back home. Our biggest dilemma is going to be food. I said I was working on something and needed to talk to Pastor Carolyn before I discussed it. Anna seemed satisfied with that but I think that she just doesn't want to dwell on it. I was not about to shatter her snow-globe world with the fact that food is really our *major* concern, or would be shortly.

We also have lists of everyone over sixty-five years of age. I was surprised that there are seventy-eight seniors, and many of those were living alone, plus everyone who was disabled or has medical issues. We have a list of known hunters, a guesstimate of those with wood burning stoves, and who had a CPL. I had to educate Anna that it meant a Concealed Pistol License. I still needed to call Karen, Ken, and Bill about being deputized. Thankfully, the cell phones are still working. The tower I see from my computer room has a massive battery system that is constantly being charged by the grid. When the power is out the batteries take over and can last about a week. After that, no more cell service and no more Internet until power to the grid is restored.

* * *

JOURNAL ENTRY: November 13

The house was really cold when I got home. I was away so long that the fire in the stove had gone out. I need to ask Don if he could come over during the day and put in a couple of logs when I'm gone for an extended period. A big advantage to my brother being right across the road is that he's close and I trust him with the keys. With the stove cold, I used up some propane and lit the gas stove with a match. Mac and cheese for dinner may not be very nourishing, but it was hot and quieted my grumbling stomach.

More news from the disaster zones today...tent cities are going up all around the East Coast, trying to shelter the victims from the hurricane. With the nor'easter that hit right after the earthquakes, it seems to be a losing battle for FEMA and the Red Cross. People are really angry with the government for not doing more. What is the government supposed to do? Those that are screaming the loudest are the ones who refused to get out before the hurricane made landfall, despite being strongly encouraged to do so. I still don't understand that mentality. I just don't.

The news helicopter photos of Missouri are surreal, like clips from a bad movie. One report said the National Guard was called in; another said it was the Army. One interesting and sad item was the destruction of a zoo. Buildings were toppled and fences were ripped down by the falling debris, which means animals are now on the loose. I must be getting punchy because all I can think is "Lions, and tigers and bears. Oh, my!"

It's late and bad jokes are not my style. I need sleep.

* * *

The morning was bitterly cold when I went to Eagle Beach to see John for his weekly massage. It was pleasantly warm inside and lights were blazing in every room. It was obvious that the generator was working well. Steve was still cooking breakfasts, which seemed odd. Usually by the time I arrive, everyone has eaten and he's in cleanup mode. It seems that not all of the guys are doing their shifts at the mine, and are just hanging around the house. From what I've heard of Green-Way Mining Company, that won't be tolerated for very long.

John was unusually quiet and preoccupied. When I asked him what was wrong, he said he couldn't reach his family in southern Indiana.

"I know they're all grown adults with families and lives of their own, but they're still my family and I'm worried. I can't reach my mom either," he mumbled into the face cradle of the massage table. I stilled my hands on his back, trying to give him some of my positive energy.

"Well, it's likely that they're fine and that it's because the cell towers are down. I'm expecting my cell to go out soon. The tower near me has only a few more days of backup power," I said trying to be reassuring. It got me thinking about lost communications. What would we all do? It's been so easy to pick up the phone and call whomever we wanted. Even though it's only been a few days, I needed to talk to Eric. What if I never heard from him again? My sons mean the world to me. I understood how John was feeling.

* * *

Back home the chores still needed to be done. I hauled in extra wood and more kindling since the nights are getting very cold. I fed the chickens and let them out into their sheltered yard. Then I started up the generator so I could have water to wash dishes. After the dishes I washed the globes on all the oil lamps and topped the kerosene off. While the gennie was going, I took a quick shower and washed my hair, glad again for having my hair cut, donating eighteen inches to Locks for Love. I filled a bucket of water for flushing and then shut the gennie down. An hour in the morning and an hour at night should keep the deep freezer going for a while. One of my goals is still to use something from the freezer every day for dinner. In time I'll be able to keep some of it in coolers on the deck, but not until the temps stay below freezing. This food *cannot* go to waste!

Tonight dinner will be chicken legs and the last of the romaine lettuce for a salad. I'm really going to miss salads. I still have half a head of garden cabbage in the fridge. Cabbage keeps so well, especially when it's that fresh. I need to grow more of it next year. There had been a half row of Swiss chard, however the chickens made short work of that. Next year I'll protect it better. I will keep this head of cabbage for fresh coleslaw. When it runs out, I will use the coleslaw I canned last summer. I wish I could thank David, the group's canning guru, for that recipe, but he hasn't been online lately. In fact, all the Internet groups are strangely quiet. I think we're all quite busy just surviving.

* * *

JOURNAL ENTRY: November 14

While I had the generator running this evening, I watched the news for a bit. The Mississippi river is slowly draining because of the new "dam" near Hannibal. There's talk of blasting it open, except they were afraid of triggering another quake. The Army Corp of Engineers is there now, scratching their heads like the rest of us. It's possible that they can blast in increments to relieve the pressure. What they don't want to do is send a twenty-foot wall of water cascading downriver. What bridges along the river that didn't collapse during the actual quakes are being examined, and most of them have structural problems, which make them unsafe for heavy traffic. The good news is that some of the bridges can be used for foot traffic. The death toll keeps climbing, and now there is a plea for body bags. At this point, one of the new concerns is disease, however they haven't said *what* disease they are concerned about.

* * *

Carolyn finally got back to me. I put a couple of logs in the stove and headed over to her house across from the church. In her seventies with a crop of curly gray hair and lively blue eyes, she's fit and spry, and has a delightful sense of humor, though there's not much that's been funny lately.

"I did see you hiding in the back pew on Sunday, Allexa," she smirked. "Do I have a new convert? Or is something else on your mind?"

"Definitely something else, Carolyn," I said. "I was listening to some of the concerns of the congregation, mainly about our food supply. It's a valid concern, and I have an idea for feeding the masses, and I think you are the perfect choice. Before you say anything, hear me out. I'd like to see a soup kitchen started. The Catholic Church isn't suitable, since people have to go down that flight of stairs to get to the kitchens. Your church has that short ramp, making it much more accessible, and your area is bigger."

"Go on," she said, looking interested.

"Do you know the story of *Stone Soup*?"

"You mean the one where a stranger comes into the poor town looking for food and no one has any? He claims that he has a magical stone that will make soup; all he needs is a large pot of water over a fire. After putting the stone from his pocket into the pot, he says 'it will be good, but it will be better if there were a couple of carrots to put in,' and someone brought out some carrots. And so on with potatoes and onions until there was a pot of real vegetable soup and everyone was fed," she said.

"Yes! That's the story. What if you had a soup kitchen where people could bring a can of something to donate to the pot and then have a meal in the warmth of the church basement? We could call it The Stone Soup Kitchen." I let it sink in for a moment.

"Hunting season started today," Carolyn said thoughtfully. "I'm sure a couple of the guys would be willing to donate some venison to add protein to the pot. And I love the name: The Stone Soup Kitchen," she said, letting the name roll around in her mouth. "Yes, that would be the perfect name. I like it a lot. Why are you doing this?"

"First of all, Carolyn, I care about this town and the people here. Second, as the emergency manager for the township, I know people are easier to take care of if they're not hungry. I am *not* going to confiscate anyone's food. If someone was smart enough to stock up for the winter, then good for them, it's their food. If we make it easy for people to voluntarily share or donate, I think we will have a much better response. You could even ask for plate donations to be a can of something, since money is useless right now. What do you think?"

"I think God was wise in putting you in our community," she said and gave me a warm hug.

"And all this time I thought it was my ex," I said under my breath. She ignored me.

We went over some details about what would be needed — cooks, someone to set up chairs and clean up, all volunteers from the congregation, and we discussed the different possibilities for meals. I suspect soup might get boring after a while, nevertheless, at least it would be food. I plan on announcing this at the town meeting tomorrow and she will make it part of her sermon on Sunday. It's hard to estimate how many people are left in town, and I think after the meeting we might have a better idea. I know many are leaving to stay with relatives in other towns, since our town is so isolated. A soup kitchen feeding a hundred people might work, but for how long?

I made another last minute decision, which seems to be frequent for me lately, like people only nodding at me. "You could start it on Thanksgiving. There's an extra turkey in my freezer that you can have." I thought she was going to start crying, so it seemed like a good time to make my exit. I was back at home before noon.

Has it really been only nine days since the first earthquake? It feels like so much longer.

Same chores needed to be done: chickens were let out, fed and watered; wood was brought in to replace what was burned yesterday, floors swept and dishes washed. I took some fish out of the freezer for dinner and will fix some rice to go with it. I also took out a pound of hamburger meat for tomorrow.

I went across the road to talk to Don about coming over to add wood to the stove when I have to be gone and told him about the town meeting. Nancy, his wife, was adamant about not getting involved. Their two freezers are stocked full, and they won't need anything or anyone for a long time, at least not until they run out of gas for their generator. I tried to talk to them about their dependency on power, but since they're older, they feel they know better than me, and they are sure that the power will be back up soon. I hope they're right yet I fear they're not.

It was another cold day and a colder night. Power came back on around 9 P.M., and was off again forty-five minutes later. At least I was able to save generator gas, fill a couple of buckets with water and recharge the cell phone. I wonder how much of a charge that short time on the grid will give to the cell tower batteries.

* * *

The town meeting was really short. Only a dozen people showed up and they immediately complained that we weren't doing enough, which soon turned into complaints that we weren't doing anything. They were upset over the gas situation. They were mad that Fram's couldn't get any more food or beer, and they were just plain angry about everything. They refused to shut up and it got very frustrating. It ended in a shouting match from the audience, so the board members packed up their notes and went back to their offices, closing the doors behind them. I went home very discouraged. I hope Carolyn has better luck on Sunday.

* * *

JOURNAL ENTRY: November 16

The weather is surprisingly beautiful: blue skies and sunny, and the temperature got up to fifty-eight degrees, so I walked for an hour trying to burn off my frustration.

I need to do something more. I'm tired of simple dinners and I wanted to *make* something! The nice thing about pasties is they don't take much to make and they're simple. I made a large batch of pastry dough and set it aside to rest, then peeled and diced one large potato, two small carrots and a couple of onions, all still raw from the garden. I browned the hamburger meat that I thawed yesterday and mixed everything together. I divided up the dough into eighteen balls and rolled them out. The veggie mix went in the center and then I rolled and pinched the sides. No, they weren't pretty but they held.

Eighteen golden brown pasties were lined up on cooling racks on my work island. I set four of them aside for me and then wrapped the rest up in a towel, rack and all, and set it in a cardboard tote. I added a case of ramen noodles for Jacob, one of the roasts from the outside freezer, a bottle of wine, and a box of .308 shells and then drove over to Jason's. He and Amanda were delighted with my surprise visit. I could tell they were trying hard to ration what they had, so the extra food was well received. We had a nice, short visit. The sun was getting low, and even though it was only 4:40 P.M. I needed to get back before dark.

* * *

It's another cold morning, only thirty degrees with a heavy frost on the windshield, not that I'm going anywhere. I think I should make it a habit of parking in the barn now.

I'm still feeling mixed emotions about yesterday's failed meeting. I had such high hopes. Maybe that's the problem. I expected too much. I know this town of Moose Creek. We have so many independent souls, yet the remaining ones all have their hands out and get angry when they aren't given everything that they feel they should have. I think those are the ones who showed up to the meeting. They are so used to getting a response from stomping their feet and throwing temper tantrums. It's not going to work this time though, and they will learn that soon enough.

I hope Carolyn has better luck. Her congregation is used to being polite and listening, something that didn't happen at the meeting. She'll get the Stone Soup Kitchen running, and that's the important thing. I talked to her this morning and told her what happened last night. I think she's going to be doing some scolding tomorrow. Maybe I'll show up to watch. Meanwhile, I'm taking the day to recoup from the stress. I don't like all of this responsibility and I like it even less when nobody listens!

* * *

I just came back from a long cathartic walk in the woods. It reminded me of all the walks I took at my previous house in the woods. Oh, how I miss that place. That life taught me so much about myself and about prepping. Ever since I was a too-young bride of nineteen and got caught in the mob of the grocery store a few hours before a snowstorm in Detroit, I knew that I had to keep more than one or two days of food in the house. Little-by-little, I learned. With the arrival of the boys, I learned even more, since they depended on me. It really wasn't until I moved to the woods, however, that I understood having adequate supplies can be a life or death thing. Right from the start, my ex-husband Sam and I decided to winter in. The snow was too deep to drive through and the house was over a mile from the plowed road. I found out that pulling a heavy sled on snowshoes is tough work!

The second winter was different. I stocked up heavy *before* the snow flew when I was still able to drive the supplies in. With the winter lasting almost five months, I had to store at least that much in food and supplies, everything from tomatoes to toothpaste, flour to TP. Every year it was a little easier, since I had the previous year's inventories to reference for how much I needed of what. I made it my mission to have whatever I *might* need for whatever I *might* want to cook. I selected menus sometimes that would keep me entertained during those long cold months. When Y2K was approaching, I doubled what I stocked, just in case. That "just in case" cost us our relationship. Sam was furious that I believed Y2K could happen, and I was just as angry that he didn't.

I know that my approach has changed drastically from that time, and much of my supplies are now long term: buckets of wheat berries waiting to be ground into flour instead of pre-made flour, berries that will last years instead of months; sugar and salt that will never go bad since they *are* preservatives and need no preserving, along with rice and pasta that, if kept dry, will last indefinitely. It isn't just food anymore. Now it's nails, screws and fencing. It's tools and water filters and a bicycle I don't ride yet might need to. It's also school supplies and larger-sized clothes for Jacob. It's twenty years of lamp wicks because they were on clearance for only fifty cents. This approach evolved on its own when I became more aware of the world and the mess I saw it in. Look at us now; the country is quite literally ripped in half. The East Coast is drowning in seawater and sludge, and the supply lines are almost shut down from the earthquakes in the Midwest and West. Some things don't change though...there are still nitwits who refuse to listen.

CHAPTER SIX

Last night it was really windy but it only dropped to forty-eight degrees. I was able to sleep with the window open again. There won't be too many of those nights left this year. With the sun shining and blue skies, people are bound to be in a good mood. I hope.

I was curious how Carolyn was going to handle the sermon today, so I took my place in the back pew to listen. She's an excellent speaker, and she's had lots of practice. She began with the tale of the seven years of plenty and the seven years of famine, and morphed into the five maidens who ran out of lamp oil when their five sisters were prepared and had enough to see them through the night. She then launched right into preparedness in modern times, and how we've had more than seven years of plenty, and shame on us for not setting aside enough to see us through the darkness of the days to come. If we all came together we just might make it, she insisted.

She leaned on the podium and said, "Let me tell you a little story." When she relayed the story of "Stone Soup" and explained how the congregation was going to start The Stone Soup Kitchen, the audience nodded in agreement and whispered among themselves.

I stayed until the end so I could talk with her, and because everyone was excited, I couldn't get her alone.

I saw her shake her finger at Lenny and say, "If you would have given the board the courtesy of your ear instead of your mouth on Friday, you would have known about this already!"

I smiled. He was totally chastised and positively contrite!

I tried to sneak out, but Carolyn saw me and asked me to wait. She excused herself from her flock and pulled me aside.

"I have to thank you. This is exactly what the town needs to pull it together again," she said with a wide grin and her eyes glowed with an inner happiness.

I told her that I would be by on Tuesday with the turkey that I promised, and I wanted to leave it with *her*. I didn't want anyone to know that it was me providing the bird. Carolyn thought that I was merely being humble. I let her think that, but truthfully, I simply don't want anyone knowing that I have food.

"If you bring it by around nine in the morning, only I will be there," she told me. I think she wants to talk more.

* * *

JOURNAL ENTRY: November 16

The power came back on at noon, and then it was off again an hour later. On at two, off at five. During the on times I actually had Internet! The news is not good — reports from the group and across the country on TV about the Middle East crisis. (When was there ever not a Middle East crisis?) There is massive bombing going on between Hamas and Israel and it's escalating hourly. I sure hope no one hits the nuke button.

A few on the groups have checked in, although Internet is spotty, exactly like the power is right now. In a reverse situation, the bigger the city, the more likely it is to have power and Internet. The needs of the many.

I spoke briefly with my sister Pam. I have missed our chats! We use to talk almost daily, and it's hard to realize it has been two weeks. She said the small town she lives in (in Lower Michigan, which is ten times bigger than my town) has undergone big changes. Most of the stores on the main street have been looted and are now boarded up. The police and fire departments remain functional, yet the firemen now just keep the fires from spreading. The grocery store that she loved walking to every day is now closed.

* * *

Pam was one of those I texted on The Event Day with the code of *Alas, Babylon*. Since she doesn't have a car, she called her daughter, telling her that it was an emergency, and they drove to the store where she bought extra flour, sugar, canned goods, kitty litter, cat food, laundry soap and a couple of cases of water. She's not the prepper that I am; still, I'm confident that if she can stay safe, she'll be okay.

No word from any of my group members: Dot in Tennessee, or Kris in Minnesota. Carol in Tennessee is okay! She is much further away from the fault line. Carol wrote that she felt the quake but had warning from the animals and was able to get the gas shut off and power switches thrown just in case. She's a wise woman to listen with her eyes and understand what the dogs and horses were saying with their actions. The quakes were felt as far east as Washington, DC, and as far west as Yellowstone, which is still a concern.

The power was back on, for several hours. This corner of the township is on three separate "legs" with the power company. Don, right across the road, is strangely on a different leg than I am and he didn't have power. I think this surge might have replenished the batteries at the cell tower, so my phone and Internet might be good for another week. I hope so. Being out of communication is the pits!

While the power was on, I filled the buckets and washed clothes again, did dishes, and took a shower. It's funny how a hot shower makes all the difference in the world for your attitude. Being clean, I feel civilized, which makes me think back to that guy in the parking lot with his young child. I wonder how they are doing.

I called Liz to check in and let her know that we're holding on, and to see if there could be any relief for us, food wise, and to inform her that we're all set for deputizing. I talked to Ken and Karen about it after church. They were reluctant; nevertheless, they understood the necessity. I wasn't surprised that Harris would jump at the chance, though only if he could be compensated somehow. The county is in bad shape for food like everyone else, especially since so many are gravitating to the city to be taken care of. That meant that I couldn't get any food or medical supplies sent in. At least our EMS has the basics and there hasn't been any real emergency, at least not yet. Someone is bound to get stupid though, it's only a matter of time. We really *are* on our own.

I met Sheriff Lacey at the township office and we went over to Ken and Karen's house. Since Harris wants to be paid, I declined to invite him. This is all gratis work that we're doing and if he can't help out in time of need for his own community, I don't want him. We now have two official deputies. I hope we don't need them. At the same time, it's a matter of having them and not needing or needing and not having.

* * *

JOURNAL ENTRY: November 19

There's rioting in Springfield, Missouri, and I-72 going east-west and I-55 going north-south have been completely shut down with gridlock traffic trying to escape. There's more upheaval in Quincy, where the new Mississippi Lake is forming and getting bigger every day. Those not affected by the quakes are now being flooded out. Militias are forming everywhere. I wonder if that will happen here, too. It could be done in a controlled manner with Ken and Karen in the lead. The two of them might need help.

With no good news to write down I'm feeling numb. Even before the power quit again, I turned the TV off. I can't listen to it anymore.

Tufts is mad at me. He went out this morning and hasn't come home. It's been eight hours and I'm worried.

Dinner was going to be some fish, but now I'm not hungry.

* * *

Tufts finally came in early this morning. I almost wept with relief and I would have if I weren't mad at him for making me worry. I know that he's only a cat, however he's *my* cat, and my companion. I don't even want to think about alternatives.

I got dressed while the coffee was perking. The auto timer on the coffee pot is one of those things that I really miss. I still have a bit of flavored creamer and after that's gone, it's either black or back to tea. I think I'd rather have the tea. Meanwhile, I'll savor the coffee. I used to make perk coffee all the time in the woods. There is nothing like the aroma wafting through the kitchen while the coffee bubbles through the filter, yet it does take time. Maybe I'll try the French press tomorrow. It's much quicker and makes a great brew.

I went out to the shed where I keep my long-term storage and removed a bucket of rice. While I was locking back up, it occurred to me that I had better make this more secure, but shoved the problem to the back of my brain for now. A five-gallon bucket holds thirty pounds of rice. Carolyn and the Stone Soup Kitchen should be happy with that. I put the bucket in the hatch of my car and backed up to the barn. In the refrigerator were those four turkeys, barely beginning to thaw. I pulled out two of them and set them in the open hatch. A few weeks ago I had gotten twenty pounds of red potatoes in a box of scraps for the chickens. The chickens won't eat potatoes unless they're cooked because they are too hard to peck. I hefted the box into the back next to the turkeys. I might regret not keeping those potatoes but I have a bushel full of my own, and more canned.

As promised, there was nobody at the church, not even Carolyn. I left to take care of my second stop first—the guys on Eagle Beach. Steve was still there cleaning up. The rest of the house seemed empty. It was too quiet.

"They've all gone to bed already," Steve told me when I asked. "Green-Way was pretty upset that they weren't going to the mine and threatened to fire them. John's already asleep. I thought you weren't due until tomorrow."

Steve looked beyond tired. When I explained what I brought for the guys in the house, he perked right up.

"You're an angel! I didn't know how to break it to them that there wouldn't be turkey for Thanksgiving."

I left him one of the birds and five pounds of potatoes with a plea that he not tell anyone where it came from.

When I got back to the church, Carolyn had finally made her way there and had opened the basement doors for me. I handed her the frozen turkey and then grabbed the box of the remaining potatoes.

"What's this?" she asked me, eying the box.

"Something extra for the soup." I grinned, putting the box on the back counter before heading back to the car.

"And this?" she asked, her eyebrows raising when she saw the bucket marked "Rice 30 Lbs."

"More extra," I laughed. Helping like this was lifting my spirits and I sure needed it. I felt almost giddy. I felt like Santa! When she saw how much rice there was, her eyes brimmed with tears.

"This is wonderful," she sniffled, "and I don't even like rice."

"Carolyn, I won't be able to do much more, if anything, but I wanted to give the Stone Soup Kitchen a good start. You'll have to make it last."

* * *

JOURNAL ENTRY: November 20

I can't believe the weather! Upper forties for the lows, upper fifties for the highs and it is sunny. I took a peaceful walk around the perimeter of my ten acres, re-marking the trees with plastic ribbon tape, hot pink this time. Not that it matters at all anymore. Still, it was something to do, and it was a productive reason to be outside. Last night was the third night in a row that I've slept with the window open. I get the sinking feeling that we will pay for this good weather at some point.

I got an email from Liz, which was sent to all township EMs. The respite of electricity yesterday may well have been our last for a very long time. It seems that the federal government has required all power generating plants to divert their resources to major cities, government offices and law enforcement only. Small towns, suburbs outside the city limits and all rural areas fall under "non-essential" power usage. Failure to comply will result in severe penalties. We just became a casualty in the needs of the many outweighing the needs of the few. This isn't going to go over very well with the few left in Moose Creek. Without power, hope is gone for any sort of normalcy.

* * *

I went to see John for his morning massage. When I was getting out of the car he came outside and stopped me quite abruptly.

"I can't pay you. The ATMs aren't working," he said, embarrassed and sad.

"That's okay, John. Pay me next time." I pulled the table out of the back of the car, knowing the ATMs wouldn't be working for a very long time.

"I don't like owing anyone," he said, "so this will be the last one until the ATMs are working again."

That made my heart lurch. "Tell you what. You've paid me well for the past year, so this one is on me."

He smiled gratefully. "But only for a half hour."

"Deal," I said smiling back. "Then maybe we should talk."

* * *

After the massage I put the table in the car and we sat on the steps of the porch, out of earshot of the few guys remaining inside. The waves from Lake Superior pounded the rock-strewn shore seventy-five feet away. The Big Lake was getting very rough.

"How are things going here, John? I don't see many around."

"Yeah, I know. Half the guys have left for the Green-Way house in Marquette. At the mine, they heard that they still have grid power and food there. Steve's obviously done some recent shopping, because we still have some food, and he's cut down on our portions. That's okay, since we're not burning as much. Did I mention that most of us haven't been down in the mine since that second quake, even though we still go there?" He took a long, deep breath and let it out while running his hands over his bald head, pushing off his ever present knit cap. "Hey, at least we're still eating, right?"

"Yes, and enjoy your turkey dinner tomorrow," I said. I had to slide that in, but it went right over his head.

When we lost power last week, I wondered what would happen here, and now that I know the power won't be back, I'm worried. This house Green-Way rents has a propane generator, and it won't last forever. I've seen the deep freezers — they won't last forever either. I'm pleased that Steve took to heart what I had suggested and did some shopping.

"Hey, maybe there's some use for my hobby now," John said, grinning. "Years ago, I went to a trade school and learned to be a gunsmith. I putter with that every time I go home on vacation."

He's a gunsmith? Wow. Could *that* ever be useful!

The wind off the lake was picking up and I shivered. I knew that it was time for me to go. I took his hand as I stood, pulling him up and hugging him. He held on tight, and his body heat felt good against me. Oh, how I wanted more than a hug. I knew it would never happen; he had already told me that he didn't want any emotional ties ever again. I finally stepped back.

"John, things are going to get much worse, and when they do, *find me*," I said and finally let go.

* * *

JOURNAL ENTRY: November 21

Tomorrow is Thanksgiving. Jason, Amanda, Jacob, Don and Nancy will all be coming over here since I have the wood cook stove and can cook the turkey. I also invited Bob, Kathy, Guy and Dawn. Kathy quickly said yes, and I told her to bring the wine. They don't have much food but they have a lot of good wine! Dawn is better prepared food wise and is in need of the social interaction. I want my family and friends with me again. I need to do something normal.

Though the weather is still mild, I can smell moisture in the air and there's a chill now too. No more Weather Channel on TV. No more instant access to the Internet; it's back to old-fashioned senses and observations to rely on now. I've lived here long enough to know that snow is coming.

How quickly we've stepped backward.

* * *

Thanksgiving Day! I've decided that I'm going to splurge. I will use up five gallons of stored gas to run the generator and have power all day long. When my guests arrive, there will be lights and water plus Jacob can watch all of the DVDs he wants. I'm stuffing one of the turkeys and will heat up one of the hams. Everybody will get to take leftovers home with them. I've got a green bean casserole from my garden beans, homemade rolls, butter from the freezer, and I even made a real pumpkin cheesecake. I'm hoping that Bob and Kathy will remember to bring wine. If not, I have enough. I want to make this Thanksgiving feast a memorable one.

Jason and Amanda were the first ones to arrive. Jacob was excited to come to Nahna's house. It seems like ages since he's been here. I have a collection pack of Muppet Movies and he's one happy camper right now, with microwave popcorn and clear Kool-Aid. Bob, Kathy, Guy and Dawn came together to save gas, and both couples each brought a few bottles of wine. Don and Nancy walked over, bringing another pie.

Our conversation centered on the earthquakes, the lack of food and the loss of power. They all wanted to know what I knew about all of it, which wasn't much. I told them that the power was gone indefinitely now, and why. It was received with stunned silence. Everyone has lost weight, trying to ration what they have left.

Guy and Dawn started prepping a couple of months ago, so they're in halfway decent shape. They've got a generator but limited gas and a hand pump for the well that isn't installed yet. They live on one of the local inland lakes, so at least they will have plenty of water for flushing and washing. They've got a woodstove for heat and Guy has cut and stacked an impressive amount of wood. Dawn's been working hard at stocking up, and she's expecting their daughter to show up any minute with four kids and a husband in tow. What food they have might not go very far once the kids arrive.

Bob and Kathy have a natural fireplace, although with the open floor plan and pitched high ceilings; the fireplace won't be able to keep up when it gets really cold. There is a gas fireplace in the basement, and it's a much smaller area to heat. They will eventually move down there. I know Bob recently had their one thousand gallon propane tank refilled. The basement is also a walk-out, with an enclosed area where the gas grill is, making it a perfect shelter for cooking and it's hidden from view. Their food supply is very limited, and what they have left is in the freezer. Rarely have they ever had more than a week or two of food in the house. Bob's been running their small generator enough every day to keep the freezers going. He was the one most shocked one when I said that the power was gone, period. He was sure that everything would be okay by next week. I don't know what to do about them, if anything.

Don and Nancy I don't worry about, they'll be fine. On the other hand, with them both in their seventies, hard work is getting harder to do.

That leaves Jason and Mandy. I'm his mother, I will always worry about him, but he's smart and young and healthy. So I will *try* not to worry.

I can't think about Eric right now. He's still in Florida as far as I know, and safe. We talked briefly a few days ago and they are all doing fine. He went out hunting and got another hog to refill the freezer. Fortunately, their power is still on. They weren't affected as much by the quakes like some of us. I know he wanted to come up, and I'm disappointed. Considering the circumstances, him staying home is understandable.

We ate very well: turkey with stuffing and gravy, thick slices of ham, the green and wax bean salad with fresh hot rolls and lots of butter. Everyone loved the salad and it was surprisingly easy; two jars of beans, drained and tossed with some bottled Italian dressing, plus a finely sliced onion that Kathy carefully picked out. Maybe it was the freshness of the garden beans that was a hit. Then someone suggested we play some cards, like we did when everything was normal. I sent extra food home with everyone except Don and Nancy, who don't need it, and I kept two slices of ham for my lunch tomorrow.

I checked the Internet after everyone left to find there is a cold front moving in tonight, and snow predicted for tomorrow, a LOT of snow. I knew I smelled it in the air!

This was the first night in a long time that I slept well. I had a full stomach, some fun with my family and friends, and forgot, if only briefly, about the trouble we're in.

CHAPTER SEVEN

The winds are howling outside, and there's already five inches of snow, at least that's how much that hasn't blown away yet. The morning started out at twenty-nine degrees, then dropped to twenty-seven degrees and stayed there.

I'm trying hard to stay on top of email while I can. Only a few more days left on the batteries for the cell tower. I'm guessing on that because I really don't know and there's no way to find out. After that I'll have to go into town with the tablet, which will *not* be convenient.

I finally heard from Suzy in Oregon. With her hubby driving trucks to Texas and Louisiana, she's often alone at home with their four kids. They're doing okay. The goats, cats and horse sensed the quake and aftershocks in Yellowstone, but the chickens were oblivious for the most part. Typical, I suppose. She's trying to keep the kids busy with tending the animals so they don't worry about their dad. He had just left on a trip to Louisiana when the quakes hit. With so much disruption everywhere, Suzy has decided to home school rather than risk the young ones being away from home if anything else happens. I certainly can't blame her. I worry about my boys all the time and they're grown.

* * *

JOURNAL ENTRY: November 24

It's a day for good news. I got an unexpected phone call from Eric! They are doing fine, and with Beth busy in her higher level of emergency management, she's asked him to move back in, temporarily of course, to take care of Emi and the livestock. He said no. I've got to hand it to him to stick to the rules that she laid out. He set up a bedroom for Emi at his new place and told me that he would pick Emi up from school and then go to Beth's. While Emilee picks up a few things and feeds the cat, Eric will feed and tend the horse and chickens, collect eggs, and then they will go to *his* house, where Beth can pick up their daughter when she gets off work. If she works too late, Eric will take Emi to school from his house. He works from home ninety percent of the time anyway, so it makes sense. Why should he sleep on an air mattress on the floor, when he could/should be sleeping in his own bed? Beth is learning that she can't always get her way.

I finally turned on the TV for some news. It's been seventeen days since the first quake and rescue efforts have turned into body recovery. The toll now stands at 78,523 confirmed dead, some not identified or even identifiable, with at least that many more missing. They've lost count of the injured. Unbelievable. It was said that the only way to deal with the sheer number of bodies is with mass graves.

One thing everyone will have to be cautious of now is all the inmates on the loose. It seems that they offered some maximum-security prisoners a reduced sentence if they helped with recovery and clean up. The prisoners just walked away. Now the population will have to contend with some real nasties wandering around. I suppose the officials felt that it was worth the risk, but then *they* likely won't have to deal with it. I'm forever thankful to be way up here in this small corner of the world. Even so, I wear my shoulder holster constantly now.

Oddly, there wasn't even a mention of the continuing relief efforts on the East Coast for the victims of the hurricane.

* * *

It is past the time to do something about the storage shed and I could kick myself for not taking care of this earlier when the weather was nice. Wallowing in self-pity distracted me from those details. Now I have to shovel the deck of the seven inches of snow before I can start bringing in some of those buckets of long-term storage. The only good part is that instead of carrying one or two at a time, I can put four on the sled to get them from the shed to the deck. I would have to bring them in one at a time anyway, and it's going to be slippery, thankfully there won't be too many to move right now.

I moved the futon away from the wall and made sure that the carpet was rolled back too. I'm really not sure how much is going to fit back there, yet I don't have any alternatives, I have to have this food easily available.

I overestimated the battery backup for the cell tower. I lost Internet and cell phone service at 4:15 P.M. Before it went out, I got an email from Kris in Minnesota. I hope she realizes how lucky she is that her town has a power plant! Those towns continue to use their own power, though any excess must be routed to someone else's emergency services, likely the Twin Cities for her town. Her hospital, schools, library, water treatment plant and local TV and radio stations will continue to function. Even though they have a bank, it won't open because most of the offices are shut down to transactions. The gas stations aren't getting any deliveries, so once the gas is gone, those close down too. Even the stores and bars will close once the supplies run out. I'm thinking that the library and movie theater are going to be very busy. I wonder if she has a bike to get around town on?

My bike is in the barn; I can't use it in the snow. Maybe I had better lock that up anyway. That one is easy, it's a metal barn and I can padlock the doors. Anyone with bolt-cutters could get in, but why make it easy? I suppose I could put some of the buckets in the barn, and rig an alarm to let me know if anyone opens the doors. More to think about.

I'm intentionally staying out of town. The township offices are closed today, and I will also avoid the church tomorrow too. I'm in a weird mood and not really fit company, even for Tufts, who hates this snow. I need some physical activity and I've got to shovel the deck because that's where the grill and gennie are.

I can still smell snow in the air and the clouds are getting darker and lower. I might be in for a real blast. I better bring in a bit more wood. My first burn pile is almost gone and that's good. I'd hate digging a path to it.

* * *

JOURNAL ENTRY: November 25

It was snowing *hard* when I got up this morning. There must be a fresh six inches already with no signs of stopping. I wonder if I should use the snow blower later. I wonder if they are going to plow the roads. I wonder if anyone cares.

With no phone, I feel totally cut off.

I had set the turkey carcass to cook for soup right after everyone left on Thursday. It was cool enough this morning to strip off the remaining meat, so now I will can it. That means going out to the other shed in this blizzard for the pressure canner and jars.

* * *

I got twenty pints of turkey soup out of the carcass. That's twenty more days of lunch, of surviving. It's funny how the perspective changes when the food supply is limited.

Dinner tonight will be a pork chop from the freezer, a half can of black-eyed peas and maybe some cornbread. I can have the rest of the cornbread for breakfast tomorrow and then add the other half of peas to my lunch soup.

* * *

The snow finally stopped around noon. I will measure it when I dig my way to a flat space. It looks like around fifteen inches fell. I bundled up and got the snow blower going when the wind stopped, around 3 P.M. At least I got paths cut, then it began to get dark and the wind started up again. I heard the plows out on the main road though they haven't come down the side roads yet. Even if I had someplace to go, I doubt that I could get past my driveway. If this side road isn't plowed, I won't be able to get into town for those on-going meetings, which might not be a bad thing. No, I can't say that. Though Anna may have the best interest of the town in mind, she really doesn't know how to go about it, since she really doesn't know how dark the human mind can get during times of desperation. I've seen that dark side with Sam and it isn't pretty.

* * *

Twenty inches of snow fell in the past twenty-four hours. This really is early in the season for this much snow. I wonder if the quakes shook up anything else, like the weather patterns.

I spent most of the day sitting by the stove, reading. It was nice but it got boring after a while. If the wind is down tomorrow I will clear the driveway and cut a path behind the house to the bucket shed.

I keep thinking about my women's group. Now that I don't have Internet anymore, I wonder how they are doing. I wonder if I failed them by not giving them enough survival information. I wonder if I failed them by not insisting they stay more on topic. I wonder if I failed them by not making them *think* more. I wonder if I should have closed the group when I had a chance. I really do feel like I have let them down.

CHAPTER EIGHT

I heard the plow truck this morning! Then they stopped and cleared out the snow they piled in my driveway. They never did that before. Since they did, and I had already cleared the drive myself with the snow blower, I went to the township offices to see what was going on.

Apparently Anna ordered the plow truck to clear the road just for me, so I could get into town. I'm glad she did. She sure needed the help and obviously couldn't call me since the cellphones aren't working. There was another town meeting scheduled for noon and I made it there by 11:00, with plenty of time to get brought up to speed on the weekend events.

It seems that a lot of people are upset over the limited gas situation, and the lack of food at Fram's store. I was not happy to see Lenny pacing at the back of the seating area but I was relieved to see Carolyn in the front. Lenny is the type that paces, working up his steam to lash out. He was effectively dodging the chairs in his way better than he was dodging the people that were milling about.

After the Pledge of Allegiance, Anna opened the meeting to public comment. All hell broke loose when Lenny started shouting at us. Anna stood up and told Lenny to shut up or Karen would escort him out. I hadn't noticed Karen and Ken standing on either side of the room serving as our new police force. I grinned. Lenny would be shamed by Karen ejecting him, but he would have been okay with Ken doing it. It's that macho thing. Anna reminded the audience that all who wished to speak would have their turn and were limited to three minutes each. I pulled a timer out of my pocket and set it on the table in front of me. All eyes went to that small device. There's no arguing with a machine.

"Now, Lenny, what is it you want to say?" Anna said, giving Lenny the first spot.

"First, what's *she* doing here?" he said while glaring at me.

"Allexa? Well, Lenny, you should remember that Allexa is the emergency manager," Anna replied. Her voice was saccharine sweet and I knew what was coming. "You were the one who appointed her eight years ago and authorized her to take all the classes that she needed to know her job well. Since we are deep in an *emergency*," her voice suddenly got very steely, "she's been activated and is my second in command. Do you object?"

"I guess not," he mumbled. "Anyway, why can't we get any gas? When will the power be back on? Where has all the food gone? If it weren't for Carolyn and the church, we'd all be hungry!"

Anna hit her gavel on the table for order after the crowd yelled in agreement.

I rose slowly, trying to keep my composure. Were they really that stupid? I said nothing for a few minutes and the room gradually came to a quiet stillness.

"I have a question for you, Lenny," I said, looking him in the eye. "What do you need the gas for? Your car? The four-wheeler in the driveway? A generator? The township needs that gas for the fire truck to put out the fire next door to your house so *your* house doesn't burn down. The township needs that gas for the EMS to get *your* sorry ass to the hospital when you have a heart attack! The township needs that gas for the generator to run the pumps that keep water coming to *your* faucet!" I took a short breath. "We just don't know when or even *if* we will get another gas delivery! Don't you understand that? And power? I'm assuming you're referring to the electricity that comes from Wisconsin," I continued. "You remember Wisconsin? One of the states affected by the *two massive earthquakes* that have taken this entire country to her knees?" I knew my voice was rising in pitch; I couldn't stop myself. "I talked with Emergency Management in the county seat a few days ago, before we *all* lost cellphone service, and was told we were SOL! We are too small to be of a concern to the government. Our power stays in a bigger city. So we are on our own. Do you hear me? *ON OUR OWN!*" I let that sink in a minute. "I tell you what, Lenny, and everyone here," I said sweeping my arm across the audience, "I will allot anyone who wants it five gallons of gas to get into town, but you can't come back."

Anna's head snapped around at me. I knew she wasn't expecting that. Frankly, neither was I.

"What do you mean, we can't come back?" Lenny's wife, Anne, asked. The room was silent.

"If you're going to take precious resources from the town, then you can't return to take even more. It's that simple. There are shelters in the city where you will be kept warm and fed. We can't do that on such a scale here. The County EM said they can't send us any food either. No power, no food, no gas, no help. So you are welcome to leave. Next spring, when we no longer need heating and we can all get a garden going, you can return. It's your choice.

"Rick, you have the floor, three minutes," I said when I saw his hand shoot up for a question.

"What about those of us who want to stay, but don't have a woodstove for heat? It's really cold out now."

"Good question, and one of the reasons this meeting was called. We would have addressed this already if the *last* meeting hadn't dissolved into a shouting match," I said, making it a point to look at Lenny, who looked down at his toes. "Anna?"

"We know it's cold out," Anna said, "and we know it's going to get colder since the winter is only starting. I have a list here of those who have wood heat and those who don't. This is completely voluntary. Nobody has to share their home with anyone else unless they want to. Nobody will be assigned, and it must be mutually agreeable. For those who may be going to another's home, understand and remember you are a guest there and can be asked to leave at any time. You should be willing to help with chores and not expect to be waited on in any fashion. You should also share any food that you might have." She pushed the clipboards to the front of the desk. "You can add your name to the lists on your way out. We will compare them and notify you later."

"If you were smart enough to stock up on supplies for the winter," I added, "good for you! I want this *very* clear—there will be *no* confiscation of food. I know this has been a concern for some of you." I noticed a few nods in the audience. "What you have is yours. Period. Fram's is running low, yes, and that's because he can't get restocked, just like he can't get more gas. There's nothing he can do about it and it certainly isn't intentional. Joe Fram has lived here in Moose Creek all his life, just like you, and you know he'd rather earn a buck, so he's not keeping anything from you on purpose." They chuckled over this. "Now, that being said, *if* you have anything to share take it to the Stone Soup Kitchen. That's where it will do the most good. Also, I'm using my authority to extend hunting season, but only on the condition that if you take anything out of the normal season, you take *half* of it to the Soup Kitchen. Half a deer should last you two weeks, and then you go and get another. It's simple. Do not abuse this, people," I pleaded. "If we work together, we *can* survive!"

The room erupted in applause, which was unexpected and embarrassing. At least the town's people were in agreement to do something proactive.

Another topic of discussion was what we were going to do about our trash. I hadn't thought much about it, the chickens get anything organic, I burn anything that's paper, and I have very little of anything else. That wasn't the case with most others. Usually, everyone takes their trash to the transfer station on Tuesday afternoon, but the compactor needs electricity to work. We used to have an actual dump many years ago that we might have to reopen. That's something that will have to be remedied before it gets to be a problem.

* * *

JOURNAL ENTRY: November 27

Yesterday, after everyone left the township offices, Anna and I went over the two lists. The one of the folks who had wood heat and were willing to take someone in was a lot shorter than the list of those who needed heat. We made notes beside each name for what we knew of the people: age, sex, health, where their house was, and anything that we thought was useful. Then we went over the list with Carolyn. We were able to make recommendations for less than a dozen people. It was a start.

I was surprised at how many people are so dependent on their propane gas or electricity for heat. We are in "wood country" and it's virtually free for the taking in the right areas, but it is still a chore to cut it, haul it, split it, stack it, let it cure and then haul it into the house daily to burn. The upside is that when the power goes, you still have heat and a means to cook. Those with a propane furnace rely on the power to run that furnace and are soon without heat.

Bob and Kathy are still holding on because although their furnace won't run, their gas fireplace in the basement will work being lit with a match and doesn't require a blower. Their extra bonus is they are one of the few that have a one thousand gallon tank and recently had it filled. Most of us only have a five hundred gallon tank. I talked with Kathy about this when they were over for Thanksgiving dinner. They have shut off all of the rooms in the basement except for the bathroom and the main area, which they now use as a bedroom and living room. They are getting a real taste of living in a one-room cabin. Bob is native to the area and has experienced many harsh winters. He knows how quickly water pipes can freeze without heat and then burst when heat is restored. He had the foresight to shut off all the water to the upstairs and then drained those pipes. Kathy hung blankets on the glass door to the lower deck to keep the chill out. Fortunately, the gas grill they've been using has a direct line to the tank, and doesn't use the smaller twenty-pound tanks like mine does. Now, if they only had stocked up on food.

On the rare occasion that I need something quick, I light the burner of the stove with a match, however the oven won't run without power. I'm completely dependent on the wood cook stove for baking. Because of the nature of how it heats I have to do any regular baking early in the day. Consequently, with all these meetings in the morning, I'm now out of bread. I'll have to remedy that tomorrow. I'm finding that I really have to pre-plan so many things now.

I pulled some chicken out of the freezer for dinner tonight. The freezer is finally starting to look less packed. Back in October I filled it with good sales. I can't complain about my *paranoid* prepper buying habits now. It's keeping me fed and alive.

* * *

It's hard to believe that tomorrow is the first day of December. Twenty-five days left until Christmas. What kind of Christmas will there be this year? We can barely drive anywhere, can't call anyone. I can't easily visit anyone except Don and Nancy, there's no mail and most people barely have enough to eat. I wonder if at some point I should make some cookies and visit David and Jane next door, twenty acres over. I know they use wood heat and have a generator, yet I have no idea how prepared they were for something like this. I have gifts for everyone already. I'm glad that I shop early and practical. I have a new Carhartt jumper and jacket for Jacob, in the next size up. His old jacket is getting tight on him but he loves wearing it since it matches his daddy's. I got Jason a set of four new LED flashlights and a knick-knack table for Amanda that looks like a sunflower. I bought that last June. I don't know when I will be able to give them their gifts and this saddens me. I think that the next time I'm in town at the offices, I will see if their road is clear enough for me to get down it, at least to see them. I almost feel silly. I just saw them last week. As the days get shorter and the snow gets deeper, I feel isolated from my family.

* * *

I had a visitor this afternoon. I heard a car pull into the driveway, and Tufts growled, sounding the alarm and headed for under the bed. He doesn't like strangers. It was a familiar jeep. I knew it was local, and I couldn't place it, until Lenny got out. What the hell?

I opened the sliding door and looked at him coming up the walk, carrying a heavy garbage bag.

"Can I talk to you for a minute, Allexa?" he asked meekly.

I was not afraid of Lenny, even if he is a jerk, arrogant, and even obnoxious at times. I opened the door for him to step in.

"Thank you. Nice and warm in here," he said making conversation, which made me a touch uneasy.

"What is it that you want, Lenny?" I said getting right to the point. He was making me nervous.

"Pastor Carolyn told me what you've done. *Are* doing," he said, his blue eyes magnified behind the thick lenses of his glasses welling up. "That the soup kitchen was your idea, and that it was you who gave the church the turkey so we all could have a Thanksgiving dinner."

Uh-oh. Where was this going? Was he going to hit me up for some food? This was exactly why I didn't want her to tell anyone!

"I wanted to thank you and apologize to you for being such a jerk," he said. "And I want to give you this to thank you." He handed me the garbage bag.

"What is it?"

"It's a hind-quarter. I got a deer yesterday, a six pointer," he grinned. "I gave half to the church like you asked us to do. I kept the other quarter for Anne and me. I figured if you could share with all of us, I could share with you."

"That's very generous, Lenny. Thank you." I meant it. I shifted the bag to my left hand, and held out my right. He looked down at my extended hand, pulled off his glove, and shook my hand.

Maybe the town will make it after all.

* * *

With the gift from Lenny, I've spent most of the day processing the meat. I cut all of the meat away from the bones and set the bones cooking for soup, along with my usual herbs and seasonings. I've cut most of the meat into chunks for either canning as stew meat or grinding into sausage. Glad I checked the premixed spice supply back in September. I pulled some of the pork chops out of the freezer to grind too. I've got enough to do some breakfast sausage. I need to check some of my older recipe books for how to make my own sausage spice someday.

I have been thinking about this turn of events. Lenny really surprised me. Carolyn surprised me too. Although she agreed not to tell anyone, she picked the right one *to* tell. I just might have an ally now. I wonder what he said to her that prompted the disregard for confidentiality?

The temperatures are rising a bit, yet the sky is still heavy. It's hard to tell if it's going to rain or snow. It would be better if it snowed. Even though there's still some on the ground, we need more. I recall one year when we didn't get the blanket of snow early enough in the season, but it was bitter cold. Without that snow to insulate the ground, the frost line went six feet deep and all of the water and sewer lines in town broke. It was a mess. I need to run the generator in the morning and pump some water to keep my water lines moving. It might be a good time to do a load of laundry too.

* * *

JOURNAL ENTRY: December 1

This morning when I got up, I noticed that I'm sleeping better. I still wake easily, as I always have been ultra-sensitive to sounds, but now all the sounds are from nature. There's no traffic on the main road, there's no refrigerator cycling and there's no hum to the clock. I'm wondering if it is the absence of electricity, that constant hum and discharge of power. Either way, I'm sleeping through the night now.

* * *

I took my usual seat in the back of the church. It was time to take the pulse of the community again. Most of the service was devoted to two memorials, residents who had both died yesterday. Since there is no funeral home and we have no access to a coroner now, the attending EMS issued death the certificates.

Beatrice was ninety-two, so her death was not a surprise. She ran out of her heart meds and refused to be taken into the city, saying that she had lived a long life and didn't want to take food away from a younger person. She also wanted to die in the home she had lived in for over seventy years, shared with her now-deceased husband, and raised her children in. This she did, surrounded by friends and family.

Gregg was our local quadriplegic. He dove into the lake when he was seventeen and broke his neck on a submerged boulder. He would often be seen tooling around our small town in his motorized wheelchair, almost every day, even during the winter. The chair also kept some of his body functioning. Without power, his batteries couldn't be recharged. He was fifty-two when he passed. He lived longer than the doctors expected him to. His mother had been his caregiver; she'd passed five years ago. Many of the neighbors looked in on him regularly, and one of them discovered that he was laboring for breath. Fortunately a landline was available there and they called the EMS, but he was already gone by the time they arrived.

Following the service we had lunch in the church basement: venison soup on rice. I smiled, knowing that Lenny and I had jointly provided today's meal. I saw that of the fifty people there, most had brought their own bowl and spoon. That *would* save on the soup kitchen having to clean up. Those of us who did not bring a bowl were offered one while in line.

I looked at those around me. Hazel, in her eighties now, was pitching in. She could always be counted on to volunteer at the Catholic Church across the street. It was good to see her crossing the ecumenical lines when it came to the needs of the town. I suppose that's not a big surprise, since the two churches have coordinated events for years. Because of the limited parking, they stagger services, and because of limited population draw, they set their rummage sale fundraisers for the same day and time. It has me thinking I should put in some volunteer time too.

Though the soup was tasty, it was lacking something. I pulled my ever-present notebook out of my vest pocket and jotted down a note to bring salt for the soup. I could spare a pound or two. I was listening to the conversations around me, which seemed upbeat for the most part, when three people approached me for gas vouchers. Once I had made that offer at the town meeting, I carried a half dozen with me at all times. At home, I had used the computer word processor while the gennie was running and made up some simple vouchers. They all said the same, five gallons, so no one could change the amount. On neon green paper, I imprinted each one with my raised notary seal, and left it unsigned. I signed one and handed it over, making a note of who it was, and wished them well.

When I saw the township handyman at another table, I excused myself to talk to him.

"Pete, this may seem insensitive at the moment, but can you still dig graves?" I asked. The town has their own cemetery and that's one of Pete's many jobs.

"I've already done that, early this morning," he replied. "Burial will be this afternoon."

I knew that Beatrice had been like a second mother to him and Gregg lived across the street, so it must have been painful.

"Thank you for attending to that so quickly. You do realize there will be more deaths this winter, don't you?" He nodded, looking sad. "Stick with early in the morning so no one sees you, dig a few more graves, maybe six, and cover them with tarps. It won't be long when the ground will be too frozen to dig."

"You really think we're going to lose six more?"

"I hope not. I think we should be prepared in case we do, don't you?" Pete nodded again and walked away. It was time for me to go, so I snuck out the back door to my car.

* * *

JOURNAL ENTRY: December 2

This evening I went across the road to my brother's house. Today is Nancy's seventy-second birthday. I took her a bottle of her favorite white wine that I bought months ago just for this occasion.

I canned a total of fourteen quarts of venison soup, which means two more weeks of survival. This soup has extra protein, an essential survival tool.

* * *

After the canner cooled down, I went into town again to see Jason. I'm not sure why I had the urgency, but I do miss the regular contact with him. I brought him some venison stew, a few boxes of pasta and a case of noodles. He's lost a noticeable amount of weight. I think he is giving up his food for Jacob, which I can understand. Amanda wasn't around and Jason wouldn't say why, and he was grateful for the extra food.

I stopped at the post office to check for messages and I was surprised to see that I actually had mail. It was my winter tax bill. I laughed out loud, and then headed to the township hall to bring this up with Anna. She agreed that we should suspend the property taxes until the banks reopen.

I visited the Stone Soup Kitchen to see if there was anything that I could help with. I was pleased to see the twins there, Jean and Joan Heckla. Now in their mid-sixties, they have never been apart. I stayed for an hour and chopped vegetables and listened to the chatter. The speculation was Pastor Carolyn had gotten someone in the congregation to donate a large bucket of rice. They talked about how blessed they were and thankfully nobody knew who the donor was.

The weather was strangely mild today. It got up to fifty-two degrees, and very windy. All of the snow from earlier is now gone, and the roads are muddy.

* * *

JOURNAL ENTRY: December 4

What a difference in the weather from yesterday. I had to get up during the night to close my window. This morning it started out at thirty-eight degrees and has been dropping steadily. The skies are dark and heavy and the wind is biting cold. I think we're in for more snow. Since I can't get weather from the Internet anymore, I put a flag on a long stick and fastened it to one corner post in the garden so at least I can see which direction the wind is coming from. Right now it's coming out of the north, which will bring snow off the Big Lake. A slight shift to the east will keep it here longer and produce lake effect snow, which is very common this time of year.

Lake effect occurs when the water is still relatively warm and the winds are cold. When the two clash, it creates massive amounts of snow.

Some days are plain boring. Today is one of them. I brought in a couple of days of wood and refilled the kindling bin. My drinking water is getting low, but I won't be making the trek down to the well by myself anymore. I set up my Berkey water filtration system and started up the generator. I filled only one of the five-gallon jugs. Five gallons will last me a couple of days and will give me time to take the other containers into town to fill at the township hall. With fewer people in town now, the water tower supplies nearly a week of the town's needs. Pete has been running the township generator four hours every other day, so at least adequate water is not an issue.

Cold this morning! It's only twenty-five degrees with a light dusting of snow. I was happy to see so little snow, as I had plans for the day. We aren't directly affected by the earthquakes down south, yet we are still feeling the backlash. The town has come together to support each other, though there are still problems, *lots* of problems, and many of those are beyond my scope and training to do anything about.

I'm very worried about the guys on Eagle Beach. I haven't heard from John since the cellphones went down and I promised not to come for his massages until he can pay me. Though I don't give a tinker's-damn about the money, a promise is a promise. Maybe I can casually stop in for a visit with Steve.

* * *

Before I headed to town today, I took the two buckets I set aside and emptied the mixed beans. Since I left them in their individual bags, I lined them up on the floor so I could see the variety: kidney, pinto, Lima, northern and split peas. Then I poured half the rice into that bucket. I got four half pint canning jars from the other shed, and filled two with soy sauce and two with Worcestershire sauce from my gallon jugs. I nestled one of each jar down into the rice, and divided the beans up equally, filling the rice buckets. I put them both in the back of the car and tossed a towel over them. I got two dozen eggs from the cold pantry and set them on the car floor next to my purse, along with a dozen cans of tuna fish for Jason. Then I loaded up my water containers and went to the township hall.

I had to stop at Fram's first to get some gas; I was getting pretty low. I signed for my weekly five gallons, and then parked across the street at the township hall. I shoved the covered buckets over to one side to make room for the water containers. After I filled them, Pete helped me load them into the car. He never even looked at the buckets. I used the town's landline phone to call Kathy on *her* landline so she knew I'd be stopping by. Living in the basement like they're doing, they'd never hear me knock and I really had to get some food to them. Our cell phones might not be working because of the lack of power, but these regular phones have been a godsend.

Bob was waiting for me with the garage open so I could use the interior back door, right next to the stairs going down. I handed him a bucket and followed him down.

"What's this?" he asked when I handed Kathy a dozen eggs.

"A gift for my best friends," I said, taking the bucket opener out of my pocket to pop the lid and expose the food. Bob didn't say anything but he reached out and gave me a long hug. It made me think of how I miss John's hugs.

"I know you've got plenty of water, and you can heat it on the grill. I don't know how often you've cooked dried beans…" I did know, and that was never, "… so I'd suggest putting some beans in a pot, cover them with boiling water and let them soak overnight, then cook them. Meanwhile, you can at least have rice with some eggs. Don't worry about the fresh eggs; the girls will keep laying them so I have spares. I'll bring more when I can."

Kathy came from under the blanket that she had wrapped around herself. She was wearing a turtleneck shirt, sweatshirt and sweat pants, with big pink fuzzy slippers that looked really warm.

"You were so right about stocking up. I should have listened to you." I could see how thin her face was getting. "Thank you for not saying 'I told you so.'"

I thought that her biggest thank you would be staying alive. "Say thank you by not telling *a soul* where you got the food. I don't need anyone breaking my door down. I'd hate to have to shoot somebody," I laughed.

"I know Christmas is still twenty days away, but can we come over?" Her lip quivered.

Bob put his arm around her and said to me, "James and Olivia both passed away a couple of days ago. They had no heat or food in the house."

Kathy's parents!

"Oh, Kath, I'm so sorry. Of course, please come over for Christmas. I have one ham left so we'll have a nice dinner. Come early, stay late," I offered, using one of Kathy's favorite phrases. I was getting good at keeping up my cheery front. Inside I was sobbing, I really liked Kathy's parents. I would mourn them later.

* * *

I drove over to Jason's next. The roads were good for the most part. When I pulled into their driveway, I saw that Amanda's car was still gone.

Jason met me at the door. "Oh, hi, Mom. When I heard the car I thought it might be Amanda." I didn't have to see his face to know he was disappointed that it was only me.

"Are you going to tell me what's going on?" I asked. He handed me an envelope. I set it aside. "She went into the city, didn't she?" I asked. He nodded and cried.

At that point, I picked up the envelope and opened it. In Amanda's neat scrawl, it read:

Jason, please keep one thing in mind as your read this: I love you with all my heart. I love Jacob with all my heart. But I also love my friends, and they need me more than you do right now. I'm taking the extra gas and going into Marquette to see them. I know that if I had waited until you were awake, you would have stopped me, and I have to do this. I have to be my own person and make my own decisions.

I know that you and Jacob will be fine without me. If I'm not back soon, you know your mom will take you and Jacob in. I wish I had a mother who loved me as much as your mom loves you.

I'll be home soon.

Mandy

I was stunned that she would actually leave. It's been a very long time since I've seen my son cry.

"When did she leave?"

"Last week."

A week and he hadn't told me.

"Do you want me to pull a few strings and see if we can find her?"

"No, she'll come home when she's ready," he said heaving a big sigh.

I reached across the table and took his hand in mine. "Whenever you need to, Jason, bring Jacob and stay with me. Just don't bring Downey," I said, looking around for their little Shih Tzu dog. "Where is he?"

"Mandy took him with her."

"Do you want to come with me now?" I asked while still holding his hand, wondering why she chose her *dog* over her husband and child.

"No, we're okay for a while, now. Thanks for the extra food. Jacob loves rice and his scrambled eggs."

* * *

Before going home I really needed to stop at Eagle Beach. I haven't seen the guys or John at any of the township haunts, not the meetings, not the soup kitchen, not the church services. I knew Steve would take care of them the best he could, and I wondered how long could he do that.

When I stepped into the kitchen, Steve looked up from the bread he was kneading on the counter, and smiled sadly. "Allexa! It's been too long since you've been by." He dropped his voice into a whisper, eyes darting around. "The guys loved the turkey dinner. Thank you again."

"Where is everyone?" I asked. The white trucks with the green leaf logo on the doors were very easy to spot, and there was only one in the parking area, along with Steve's red pickup.

His hands stilled. "Most of them have left for Marquette. There's only five here now. John's down by the marina shore trying to catch some fish. I'm really worried about them. There isn't enough food and they're too stubborn to leave. After I bake this bread, it's gone." Just then the door opened, letting in a gust of frigid Lake Superior wind—and John. My heart thudded against my ribs at the sight of him.

"Hi," I greeted him, smiling softly.

He looked up at the sound of my voice and smiled, those blue eyes sparkling. John absentmindedly handed Steve a stringer of three small fish and held out his arms while he walked toward me for a hug. Oh, that meant the world to me, and I soaked in the warmth of his embrace, despite knowing that for him it was platonic.

* * *

"Thought I would check in and let you know we're hanging in there, and that we could use some supplies," I said when I called Liz.

"Everyone needs supplies," she sighed. "Let me know what you need most and if something comes up I'll keep you in mind."

"We need everything," I laughed, "but I'd say gas would be the priority. With the Stone Soup Kitchen, the food is going further."

"The what?" she asked. I explained about the kitchen, its meaning, and how everyone was working together. I neglected to mention that I lifted hunting restrictions because I was unsure if that was overstepping my limited authority. "That is a great concept. Anything else?" Liz questioned.

"Yeah, I need a favor," I said and told her about how Amanda was missing. She asked for the make of the car and the addresses of where she was supposed to have gone.

"We have strict curfews in place. If she was caught, she might be in the detention center. I'll see if I can find anything out. We'd rather you feed her than us," she laughed sarcastically.

* * *

JOURNAL ENTRY: December 6

When I got home I tried to concentrate on the mundane, normal things. I fed and watered the chickens, brought in lots of wood and kindling, and cuddled Tufts for the longest time. It didn't help. I still feel sad and helpless.

CHAPTER NINE

With power off now for quite a while, it was time to fall back on some of the things I learned while living deep in the woods during the seven years I lived without grid power. We always had refrigeration and ice for our drinks. Water frozen in dish pans will keep the refrigerator cool, exactly like it did that antique icebox I used in the woods, only better. A refrigerator is nothing but a big cooler, and the insulation is more efficient. I filled my ice cube trays and set them on top of the hot tub. Like before, I'll keep breaking them into a zipper baggie and use when needed. Like riding a bike, there are some things we don't forget how to do.

I moved what was left in the small twelve cubic foot upright freezer into coolers and set them on the back deck and shut the freezer off. It isn't practical to continue running the generator just to keep the freezer going. There is little now to keep chilled: catsup, mustard, mayo, eggs, cheese and all the butter from the freezer. I still have a half head of garden cabbage, and I'm saving that for a special salad. The potatoes, onions, beets, turnips and two pumpkins I harvested from the garden are in the cold pantry. I even have a bag of apples! Maybe I'll have baked apples for dessert on Christmas, or an apple pie.

* * *

JOURNAL ENTRY: December 7

It occurred to me while thinking about using the refrigerator like an icebox that since the freezer is in the cold, unheated pantry, I could use that as the refrigerator. It sure will get cold enough in there even without ice. It also reminds me to ask Jason about building a spring house for the summer. We could do one down by the creek and have cold water constantly flowing through it. Or one could be built around the second well, once we get the hand pump hooked up and working. I wonder if it would be feasible to do both. Definitely need to bring that up to Jason, he's got a great problem-solving mind.

* * *

I was sitting in my rocker by the woodstove reading a romance novel when I heard a vehicle pull into the driveway. Tufts leaped from my lap, digging his back claws into my thigh before hitting the floor, did his usual growl and then hissed, slinked a few feet, hissed again and bolted for the bedroom. It was not like him.

Bill Harris got out of the deep blue extended cab four-wheel drive truck. Considering Tufts' reaction I went on alert. I don't like Bill either. I reached down and made sure the steel bar was in place in the track of the sliding door. The door would now only open three inches. I waited until he knocked, let him wait a bit more, then I slid the door open enough to talk.

"What do you want, Bill?"

Without even the pretense of niceties, he said, "Hey, Allex. Listen, I know you've got food. I remember one of your solstice parties and you've got lots of supplies. We're getting really hungry, how about sharing?"

A couple of years ago I held parties on the Solstice, partly to show my friends how comfortable we could be without power, *if* we were prepared for it. At that time Bill and his wife Marilyn were part of our card-playing group.

"That was years ago, Bill. I don't have any of that stuff left," I lied. "I have nothing to share with you. Please, just go away and leave me alone."

I started to close the door but he quickly reached for the edge and tried to shove it open. It stopped on the steel bar and he pulled his hand back. I closed the door and locked it. He glared at me through the triple-paned window with hatred and turned away. When he got to his truck, he opened the back door, instead of the driver's door. My alert kicked into high gear.

I grabbed the loaded twelve-gauge shotgun that was leaning against the wall and headed to the deck door. I only had a minute or two. I knew Bill, a former law enforcement officer, would never carry a loaded gun in his car, and now he needed to load whatever it was he had brought with him. From the deck, I quickly slipped behind the house and up the snow ladder onto the roof. I was glad I at least had shoes on though I didn't have time to grab a jacket. My hands were already getting cold and I stifled a shiver. I crouched down and hurried across the roof, the snow muffling the sound of my movement. I peered down at Bill as he aimed his shotgun at my glass door.

I braced the shotgun against my shoulder and pulled the slide to chamber the round. Bill looked up at the unmistakable sound. I pulled the trigger and the first round hit him in the leg, barely wounding him. He staggered backward, giving me a better target. I quickly chambered another round, took a steadying breath, and fired again. It was a direct head-shot. He never knew what hit him.

He'd told me several years ago that if things ever got as bad as I thought they could, he would just shoot me and take *my* stuff. Did he really think that I would forget that? I had thanked him for the warning. Apparently *he* forgot about *that*.

I ran over to Don's and told him that I needed help. He had heard the shots and had already gotten his boots and coat on to investigate. On our way back I told him what had happened. We loaded Harris in the back of the blue truck that Don drove, following me in my car. What's that old saying? Friends help you move, but good friends help you move the body. Don is a good friend. Oddly enough, it was Harris who told me that little ditty.

Once I got to Ken and Karen's house, our newly deputized officers, I asked Don to wait in my car while I talked to the couple. I explained what had happened, emphasizing that Bill had threatened me, pulled a gun, and was trying to rob me. I asked them what they wanted to do. My voice and my hands were shaking.

"Looks like a clear case of self-defense, to me. What do you think, Ken?" Karen said, turning to her husband.

"I've never liked Bill," Ken said. "He was a loose cannon and it doesn't surprise me that he got killed committing an armed robbery. We'll take it from here, Allexa. You go on back home. You need a lift?" I told him Don was with me and that I'd make it home okay.

I've had a hard time shooting raccoons. Shooting a person? Well, I can't begin to describe what's going through my mind right now. I had no appetite for dinner so I killed a bottle of wine instead, all the while praying for heavy snow to cover up the bloody mess that was now smeared across my yard.

* * *

JOURNAL ENTRY: December 9

I keep reminding myself that if I had given Bill some food, he'd have come back for more, again and again. I'm still feeling bad. Could I have done something different before? During? After? Well, of course I could have. I know that the sliding glass door is my vulnerable point. I could have boarded it up. I may do that now. I could have given Harris some food…that would only have delayed the inevitable, and would have put me at further risk from whomever else he might have told. I will have to live with his death on my hands. A death I can't share with anyone beyond the three that already know.

I have no source of comfort, other than Tufts. His silky head, his loud purr… He loves to rest his head on my arm like it's a pillow. It's nice but it's not enough. I'm still very much alone and feeling lonely.

* * *

I was too shaken up from yesterday's events to go into town, so I used the time for personal things. I started up the generator and took a long, hot shower, washing my hair with a bar of fragrant Shea butter soap. It cleaned my hair and my body, but not my soul. Then I did a load of laundry to hang on the wooden clothes rack to dry by the stove. While the washer was going, I turned on the TV to see if the satellite networks were still functioning.

It appears that in the early morning hours another quake hit the New Madrid Fault. Another big one, an 8.1 on the Richter scale, at the same location as the last. The portion of the tectonic plate that was lifted and created the new lake in Missouri was ripped in half, sending an avalanche of water down the now dry Mississippi River. A wall of water nearly fifty-feet high traveled at an incredible speed and washed away everything in its path. This time there were very few deaths, considering, although the exposed and vulnerable bridges were completely swept away. I'm totally numb.

* * *

Anna was already at the township hall when I arrived, and reminded me to check the bulletin board for the weekend news. Last Friday night there was a break-in at Fram's store. There are no suspects and witnesses are encouraged to talk to Ken or Karen. No money was taken and there isn't any food left to steal. Joe is keeping the store open only for gas and the hardware department he has in the back. The café is open, only serving coffee and tea for the Internet users. Wisely, he took all the coffee off of the store shelves and now keeps it locked in his safe.

The notice about the break-in was right next to a slightly larger notice about Harris being shot during an attempted home invasion and armed robbery, with a side note reminding that this was what could happen to those who step outside the law. It was signed by Ken and Karen. Thankfully, it did not mention whose home he was trying to rob, yet the timing is suspicious to me. Did Harris come to me only after he couldn't steal any food at Fram's? All those years ago, I tried, I really tried, to get my friends to stock up, but most of them ignored me. Some even scoffed at me like Bill did, which is when he stopped being a friend. That threat he made is why and when I stopped talking to my friends about prepping.

* * *

JOURNAL ENTRY: December 10

It's getting really cold outside. It's now down to twenty-eight degrees and will get lower overnight. How cold it is right now reminds me about those in town without wood heat.

* * *

"Anna, whatever came of those lists of folks who have wood heat and are willing to take in others?" I asked, sitting down across from her. "Weren't you and Pastor Carolyn working on that?"

"Funny that you should ask. We were going over the lists just yesterday," she replied. "For the most part, it's working out rather well. There have been a few issues though."

I raised my eyebrows, asking for more details.

"Rather than those seeking shelter, it was one or two offering that were the problem. Stanley was one. He took in two older women and then expected them to do all of the work: the cleaning, the laundry and cooking. He wanted to be waited on for his 'generosity.' They gave him an earful and walked out." Anna shook her head. "Then there are the successful arrangements like Rosemarie and her ten-year-old twins. Carolyn teamed them up with old Alice. Alice has a woodstove and plenty of wood, but has a hard time getting around. Those two kids can't do enough for her and she adores them. Rosemarie is happy and content to do any chores that need doing in return for keeping her children warm. It's a bonus that Alice's house is right across from the school."

"It's good to hear that things are working out for some. Are there any that haven't found a match?" It could be a problem if somebody still didn't have heat.

"Well, the problems are being matched to each other, so someone has to learn give in," Anna chuckled.

CHAPTER TEN

I felt weary when I woke this morning. My sleep was filled with nightmares of Bill Harris barging his way into the house. Every dream had a different ending, none of them good.

It's been snowing since I woke and it's really starting to pile up. This looks to be an all-day snow. I dressed early and filled up the spot for wood behind the stove. The usual chores include feeding the chickens and taking them fresh, warm water. With the cold as it is, I will keep them confined to the coop and not let them out into their inner yard, conserving the heat they generate. I've got lights and heat lamps for them, however with no power and no lights, they will have to survive on their own. The most that I can do for them is to add the extra bale of straw that I stored, which will insulate the floor some. The fresh eggs are an important part of my diet. I'm sure glad that I kept the one rooster so I can hatch eggs in the spring. The meat will be welcomed, and I really need to propagate the layers. I do have a roll of metallic insulation that I could cover their window with for extra protection. I'll have to pull it out and see if there's enough. Only problem with that is it would block all the light from their only light source, and chickens need the cycle for laying eggs.

I shoveled the deck off around 1:00 P.M. I have to keep that open for the grill and so I can get to the generator and the coolers. The way the snow is falling, I bet I will shovel again at least twice before calling it a night.

I pulled a small chuck roast out of a cooler to thaw for dinner. I'm hoping to grill it like a steak—my favorite way to have a roast, seasoned with olive oil, Worcestershire, and my own blend of peppercorns, rosemary, and powdered ginger, a touch of dried basil and sea salt, ground together. I haven't had much red meat in the past ten days, so I bet that the doctor would be happy with my lower cholesterol level. I'm trying to spread out the use of the few fresh root crops that I've got left. In another month or two something fresh is going to be non-existent. I still took two beets and slow roasted them in the oven because they are so much easier to peel that way. Once they are done, I'll keep them in a small glass dish to reheat at dinnertime.

I've started re-reading *Alas, Babylon,* my all-time favorite disaster book. I thought about re-reading *One Second After,* but that might be a bit too close to home right now. Then again, it might help me prepare for what could be in store for us.

* * *

JOURNAL ENTRY: December 12

With the temperatures this cold, Lake Meade, our local inland lake, now has a few inches of ice. Some of the braver, or more desperate, have moved their ice shanties in place to start fishing. I wish them a lot of luck. Personally, I'm terrified of being on lake ice. I've seen too many break through when they hit a thin spot. Still, it's nice to see the townspeople doing something normal. There were even a few ice-skaters out there too. It's interesting to see the transformation going on. There are no lights for decorations, and still I am seeing garlands of all colors going up, wreaths on doors, cedar boughs on railings and people walking around instead of driving. It's beginning to look like a Currier and Ives Christmas card!

Thinking of breaking through the ice reminds me of a story that I read years ago called *At Home In The Woods,* where the young wife ice-skated to town down the frozen river. She would carry a long, cut tree sapling with her just in case she fell through the ice. The pole would catch on the edges and she wouldn't sink. That gives me shivers up my spine thinking about it.

* * *

Fishing must have been good yesterday, enough that there is supposed to be a fish fry at the church tomorrow. It will be a nice change from venison soup. I think I'll make up a big batch of sugar cookies to take. It doesn't take much sugar and flour to make them, and I think it will be a nice touch. I even have some sugar sprinkles from last year to decorate. A couple dozen will give every person a cookie or two, and I doubt that anyone will mind the orange Halloween sprinkles. I must remember to take that canister of salt and a bottle of ketchup with me.

I also found out that the ladies have formed a knit and crochet club to do something positive and to keep busy. They are making hats and mittens to give away as gifts at Christmas. What's even better is that they are giving lessons by teaching the non-needle people how to knit or crochet by making squares that will be stitched together to make lap blankets or shawls. I wonder if someone can teach me how to knit socks? I will have to bring my craft box into the house and see what I've got, if I can find it out in the barn. It's been so long since I've done any of the handcrafts. This could even be fun, and it feels like forever since I've had any fun.

There was a brief burial for Bill Harris. Nobody asked who he attacked, nobody wanted to know. His wife Marilyn was given to the keys to his truck and his shotgun. Everyone understood. Whatever happened was his doing, not hers.

While in town, I went to see Jason and Jacob. Jason hasn't heard anything from Amanda and I didn't tell him I asked for it to be looked into on a more official level. There may be good news, yet it might be bad at this point; the good news may be no news. I brought him another case of noodles for Jacob, a dozen eggs, and a loaf of homemade bread. I also brought him a five-gallon container of gas for his car from my own storage, not from the township. He needs to know that he has enough gas make it to my house if he really needs to. I took his empty container back with me. Despite the fact that the school is still open, Jason has been home-schooling Jacob and enjoying it. He said that now with the extra gas, he can take Jacob in once a week to interact with the other kids.

Other than seeing my son and grandson, which always brightens my day, it's been dreary. The sky is a solid slate gray, not even lighter where the winter sun is supposed to be. The temps are hovering around a chilly thirty degrees, which could mean snow or rain.

* * *

JOURNAL ENTRY: December 14

What a great time everyone had at the Friday Fish Dinner! The guys all went fishing and then worked hard to clean their catch in time for an early dinner. Ken brought his wood-fired pig roaster to the church parking lot so the fish could be cooked in large batches. There is no cooking oil for frying but no one seemed to mind. It was delightful to see how polite everyone was, even the children, about taking only one cookie and a small squirt of ketchup to make sure everybody got some. There were six cookies left, which were all broken in half, so the dozen kids there could have an extra piece. I was amazed at how well the cookies were received! Someone brought a huge can of beans, enough for all to have a spoonful, and another brought two jars of olives. Still another made a big bowl of macaroni, tossed with Italian salad dressing. Rob and Cyndy brought their banjo and violin for some music. Nick, another member of their small band, showed up with his guitar. Music and some dancing, what a way to end the evening! Seeing everyone pitch in and work together made me forget my own worries, for a while anyway.

A few more inches of snow fell. If it weren't so hard to get around it would be very pretty.

* * *

This morning's chores included cleaning the woodstove. I took the top plates off and wire brushed the underside and then swept all the accumulated soot off the oven box into the firebox so it could fall into the ash pan below. I scraped the side and bottom of the oven box and pulled out that ash through the access door.

I worked quickly. It was getting cold in here! In the past when I did this I let the furnace run to keep the room warm while the fire was out.

The furnace is one of the things that I miss in the morning. I had the thermostat set to come on at 6:45 A.M. to raise the house temperature to sixty degrees. Even if it was only sixty degrees in here when I got up at 7:30 A.M. to start the woodstove, it was better than the fifty-five that it usually dropped to. The other thing the furnace did for me was warm up my sweatpants. I would lay them across the closed register in the bedroom at night. When I got up, they would be warm instead of freezing on my bare skin. Lately, I've been tucking the sweats under the blankets with me when I go to bed. There are many adjustments to make when the power goes out.

I sure wish I could get some news. Not knowing what is going on in the country or even in the state is very frustrating.

* * *

JOURNAL ENTRY: December 15

There was a break in the snow and wind this morning. I took the opportunity to snow blow the driveway and my paths. It seems that I do less and less of the driveway as the years go by—just enough to get the car into the barn or out onto the road. The second half of the horseshoe drive drifts horribly and isn't worth the effort to keep open. The wind was really fierce yesterday and the drifts got pretty deep in some spots. It's a good machine and I had it tuned up in the fall. All of it, including the paths to the woodshed and the small barn, took me only an hour. After I shoveled the steps to the sliding door, I salted them down out of habit. Then I shoveled the steps to the pantry entry and cleaned up the edges of the walkways the snow blower can't get.

The sky over the Big Lake seems perpetually black lately, heavy with lake-effect snow. Time to bring in more wood. It's a daily thing now, just to stay ahead of it. Going through the pantry with the double door system helps keep the cold air out and the warm air in, which is needed when it's only fifteen degrees out!

* * *

I was almost done bringing in the wood when I slipped. I hadn't salted down the back steps. There are only three steps but I slipped on the second one going out, and landed hard. I'm going to have one hell of a bruise on my hip tomorrow! I don't think that's going to be the problem, because I ultimately landed on my left ankle, which is my weak one. I have overextended the ligaments and tendons in that foot twice before, and each time it was worse. Ligaments don't heal quite like tendons do.

After I caught my breath, I scooted so I was sitting with my legs stretched out in front and ran my hands down, checking for breaks. I was already certain that wasn't the case, though wanted to be sure. I pulled myself upright and tested the foot. It was sore, though not too bad. In hindsight, I should have stopped right then, but I really had to finish. Stupid me. Two more loads of wood and I was set for several days. After removing my outer gear and hanging it to dry, I sat down in the kitchen to take off my boots. I couldn't get the left one off because the ankle had swollen. I hobbled over to the junk drawer and got the shears. They were old boots and I had to cut it off. When I set my foot across my right knee to do so, I saw that the zipper wasn't completely down. Once fully unzipped, I managed to barely get my foot out. At least I saved the boot!

The pantry where I keep Tufts' litter box is also my dry goods storage, plus bins filled with medical stuff. I hobbled over and got the one marked "bandages." After retrieving an Ace bandage, I sat back down, took off my sock, surveyed the bruising and wrapped the elastic bandage around semi-tightly. The two gel packs I usually use for my wrists in the summer were still in the freezer, and are now warm. I took them and two large baggies and once again hobbled to the door. On the deck, I set the ice packs on the hot tub cover, and then scooped snow into the baggies. Back in the kitchen, I put one baggie into the fridge, and sat down once more. Propping my foot up on a kitchen chair I draped the snow filled baggie over the bandages. Tears of anger and frustration were building while the ankle started to throb badly. This was a stupid and preventable accident. Now what am I going to do?

* * *

Don stopped over around 4:00 to invite me over for dinner and his birthday. I had taken the second snow pack off and was feeling a bit numb. I really wanted to go. I doubted I could walk that far, so I had to decline. At 5:30 I saw flashlights bobbing in the dark and the two of them brought the party to me! Nancy had even thoughtfully brought me a slice of the rib roast she had saved for Don's dinner, knowing that I might not get up to fix something for myself. She was right. I had contemplated warming up some soup later, now I didn't have to. They brought over two beers for Don, a bottle of white wine for her, and Don opened a bottle of my favorite red wine from the pantry. I had already lit one of the brighter lamps to read by, and Don got two more off the shelf and lit those, setting one on the island and the other on the second table. The lamps gave a nice glow to the room and chased the shadows out of the corners.

* * *

JOURNAL ENTRY: December 16

When I woke up this morning, I felt great. Then I stretched, and the pain in my foot shot up to my knee and made my eyes water. Tufts jumped off the bed and hid under the table in the kitchen when he heard me cry out. I lay still for a few moments, remembering what had happened.

The other two times I had injured this ankle, I don't remember it hurting this bad, and I am wondering if maybe it is broken.

* * *

My foot really, really hurts. I used the wall to support myself until I got to the kitchen where I could lean on the counters. This was so *not* good. I paused at the gas stove and saw that I had set a kettle of water out last night. The stove burners will light with a match so I pulled the grill lighter out of the drawer and lit the burner to heat the water for my tea. I really needed that tea—it was cold in here! Leaning against anything in my way, I hobbled toward the woodstove, when I noticed Mom's walking staff leaning in the corner. It sure helped to take the pressure off my foot. I opened the ash door and the grate, the first steps to starting a new fire. Then I noticed Jacob's favorite chair.

One of my clients at the resort had given me a "bungee" office chair, which was super comfortable to sit in, and had the awesome high-tech rolling casters. Jacob loves "getting a ride" on the chair, where I would spin him around and around. My heart clenched and I wondered how they were doing. I pulled that chair up the single step from the computer room and sat down. Relief! I scooted myself over to check the water for tea, and pushed off for a glide across the room to reset the stove fire. If my foot didn't hurt so much, I might have fun with this. It certainly will make it easier for me to stay off my feet.

After starting the stove, which is hard to do from a sitting position, I hobbled over to the computer room. Two things were on my agenda, retrieving a cane and my computer chair. Mom's walking staff feels awkward and I want to try using one of her canes instead. There were two in the crock stand next to the TV; a thin one with a standard curved handle and a ball headed one that was sturdy. After testing them out, I settled on the ball headed one because it's shorter and was a better height for me, despite it being harder on my wrist. Hopefully I won't have to use it for long.

My computer chair is on casters like the bungee chair that I can use to move around in that room, and then move to the other chair for the rest of the house. I'll have to move the rug-runners out of the hall and out of the bathroom. The dining room and kitchen are both tile and unobstructed.

I took a couple of Ibuprofen and washed them down with my tea. I moved the pot over to the stove to stay warm, and quietly sipped while I went over in my head what I needed to do today. First was to get dressed, then pull something out of the cooler for dinner tonight and tomorrow, maybe the next day, too. Next was to start up the generator so I could take a shower, draw off some water for the next few days and wash dishes—the usual things that don't wait just because I was clumsy. There was no guarantee that I wouldn't feel worse tomorrow.

CHAPTER ELEVEN

Monday is my usual day for going to town to check on things in the office, see what's happening with the town folk. Not today. My ankle is still swollen and it hurts. I think it would best to stay off my feet and keep that foot packed in snow. Twenty minutes on, twenty minutes off. During the twenty minutes off, I try to get something done like fill the woodstove to stay warm. Wood supply is good for another day or two, before I need to do something about it. My biggest problem at this point is clearing the driveway to get out. A foot of snow is a bit much to drive through. If I rest and ice today, maybe I'll be able to run the snow blower tomorrow. I have to get the car out since five miles is a bit much to walk into town, and impossible with an injured foot. So far the plow trucks haven't been by to clear the road though, so it might be a moot point. I might be stuck here.

I noticed a few days ago that the smoke diverter on my stove was hard to move and then it wouldn't move at all. There are two ways the smoke goes up the chimney. The first is directly out and the second forces the smoke around the oven box before going out the chimney. Since it was stuck in the "out the chimney" position, I wasn't too concerned, but in the "around the oven box" position, it was easier to maintain the temperature for baking. You can't set the oven for 350 degrees and walk away with a wood fired stove. Before I built the morning fire I pulled the wheeled-table closer to the stove and spread it with newspapers. The stove had cooled off enough during the night so I could handle the top plates to get at the diverter in the back section near the chimney. It was really chilly in here so I wanted to assess what needed to be done quickly. Fortunately it's a simple mechanism, and the grooves it slides in had built up soot, ash and general debris. After eighteen years I suppose that's to be expected. I wire brushed and swept, wire brushed and swept again, manually moving the diverter plate back and forth to loosen up even more. Finally it moved smoothly, and I put the stove back together. I used the papers to start up a fire. It took less than fifteen minutes to fix it. There is really not much that can go wrong that a good cleaning won't fix. Had this situation been different, I would have called Jason over to check it out, but in many ways I'm on my own, just like the town is. Maybe I should insist he and Jacob move in. On the other hand, I *did* fix it myself.

* * *

JOURNAL ENTRY: December 18

The wind died down to a light breeze today so I decided to chance clearing the driveway. There are a lot of advantages to living alone but being injured isn't one of them. Sure, I'd rather sit in the house next to the stove with my foot up, book in hand, sipping on tea, yet there aren't any cobbler's elves in Moose Creek to shovel my driveway. I re-wrapped the elastic bandage around my foot a bit tighter than I was doing before, put on thick socks and my high-top insulated boots. I decided against my coveralls since it was a real chore getting into them. Then again I've lost weight so it might be easier now. With my jacket, knit hat and heavy mittens on I was ready to tackle the driveway. I'm glad I waited... the plow trucks came by earlier and left extra in my drive entrance.

* * *

Snow blowing is slow work, and easier than shoveling. I limped slowly behind the machine, redirecting the chute when needed. When I got to the spot where Bill had fallen, I seemed to freeze up. All the memories of shooting him came flooding back, and so did the memories of him trying to force his way into my house. I feel worse than bad that the situation ended like it did, yet I can't let it run my life. I pushed the thoughts away.

When I turned back to finish the back portion and start on the leg that goes to the street, there was Don, with his monster of a machine, clearing the rest in half the time. When he was done, I thanked him. He mumbled something about being clumsy and I dutifully ignored him. I love my brother. I parked my machine back in its spot in the barn, feeling confident I could get out now if I had to. Right now, there was a cup of tea and a chair calling to me.

I'm really glad I took extra food out of the cooler two days ago. I was exhausted from all the work. I put a turkey leg in a roasting pan, sprinkled it with some seasonings and tucked it in the oven.

* * *

I finally had a chance to ask Anna what was going to be done about trash now that the dump compactors didn't work.

"Pete came up with a really good idea," she said. "He set up bins inside the school for separating the recyclables. With everyone burning anything paper or cardboard, that's not something that we have to worry about. People are feeding their pets what little table scraps there are, and he thinks that will leave very little actual garbage. He will take the remaining trash out to the old dump once a week."

"Excellent! What about those bins filled with glass, metal and plastic?" I asked.

"Well, there's an idea that came from the Lady's Knitting group. They are going to recycle what they can into useable crafts by making pincushions from tuna cans and such. Pete has already circled the word that anything put into the bins must be fully washed first. I'm really proud of all of them," Anna said.

"You should be, Anna. This is great, really great. Maybe I should put a bid in for some of the plastic bottles for next year's garden."

"What will you do with those?" she asked, obviously unfamiliar with drought gardening.

"When I lived in the deep woods, the only water that I had for the garden, other than rain, was from a cistern. All I had was three hundred gallons for a 100' x 150' garden. I couldn't afford to waste a single drop of water." I had her attention. "I took the caps off and cut the bottoms off of plastic bottles and then buried them, neck down, one-third of the way deep next to a plant. Then I'd fill the bottle, which took the water right to the roots where it was needed and did the most good. None of it was wasted on surface evaporation."

"That's amazing!" she exclaimed.

"It worked very well," I said. "I still use that method, but considering that next year I think it wise to expand my garden, I'll need more bottles. I need to talk to Pete about that. He should save all of the bottles. Others might want to do the same."

* * *

JOURNAL ENTRY: December 19

In the past, the school Christmas pageant always started at 7:00 P.M. Now, without lights, that's no longer an option. At 3:00 P.M. when school let out, the children stayed to give their performance before heading home for the Christmas break. Many in the audience brought flashlights or lanterns to light up the dim gymnasium, and several were placed on the stage for the children. Carolyn took her place at the aging piano, and began by playing Christmas tunes. The children came out in groups by grades and sang songs. It was charming, and I even teared up a little.

At first I didn't see Jason, and then when I saw Jacob on stage with his fourth grade class, I knew his daddy was close by. I scanned the front rows, knowing that Jason always sat where Jacob could see him. He was there — with Amanda!

* * *

I am so relieved that Amanda is back. I'm also very angry with her for putting her family through such torment. I know that I can't say anything to her, at least not until I find out the details when they come over for Christmas. Not saying anything is an additional source of torment for *me*.

It's only been six weeks since the event, and during that time I've seen my community suffer and there's nothing that I can do. I've watched my son suffer and I can't help him. I've seen friends die and cannot grieve for them. I've shot and *killed* a man, and I cannot grieve for *myself*. I'm suppressing everything that I feel so I can function at my best, and keep the promise that I made when I was sworn in. It's tearing me apart. I don't know how much longer I can keep this up. I don't know what to do anymore. I don't know *how* to help all those desperate people. I want to stop clearing the driveway, no more shoveling and no more going to the office. No more! No more anything except taking care of myself instead of everyone else. However, I did take that oath, and I did make that promise, so I went to the office even though I feel so helpless.

* * *

The sky was exceptionally dark this morning, even at 9:00 A.M. There was an ominous gloom hanging over the office as I settled into my seat. I laid the cane across the counter next to me since it was constantly falling over if I stood it upright. My "office" is only a corner of Anna's bigger office, and my desk actually looks out the only window at a perfect angle to watch Fram's store, which is why I was one of the first to see the gas tanker pull into his lot. Liz came through for us. This would go a long way to alleviate the tensions of the town folk wanting gas for their cars and their generators.

"Anna! We are getting an early Christmas present. Come look," I called to her over my shoulder.

"Gas? How did that happen?" she asked.

I told her of my conversation with Liz, well, most of the conversation. I haven't told anyone about Amanda and now that she's back, I won't have to. Gray, our head EMS, walked into the office and saw my foot up on the wastebasket.

"What did you do?!" he asked, not sounding happy. He's had to be the doctor in town, all minor stuff of course, and didn't need one more patient.

"Hey, I didn't fall on purpose and it's only a strain," I reassured him.

"Let me check." He removed the Ace bandage and then poked at my foot and moved it around.

"Ouch! Careful there," I said, not appreciating him making it feel worse.

"Strain, huh? This is a sprain, Allexa, and a bad one at that. You need to stay completely off this foot," he ordered.

"I promise to stay off it as much as I can, Gray, but completely is impossible. You know that," I said glaring at him over my glasses, wanting him to go away. He noticed the tanker across the street.

"Gas? I sure hope its diesel." His comment took me by surprise.

"Diesel? Why?"

"Well, all the county trucks run on diesel. You know, the *plow* trucks, my EMS truck, *and* the new fire engine. They all run on diesel. Only the older pumper runs on regular gas," he said with a hint of sarcasm in his voice.

Why didn't I know this? I had wrongly assumed that all of the trucks took regular gas. "Well, we'll take anything they've brought us."

Gray rewrapped my ankle, patted my knee and went back to his own office.

I picked up a stack of gas requests that were still sitting on my desk that I was getting ready to approve, though I needed to ask Joe how much regular gas was left. If all the essential vehicles took diesel, we might not have to ration so strongly. While I contemplated this, someone came walking across the street from Fram's, carrying a small box. He looked vaguely familiar, but he wasn't a local. I turned my attention back to my paperwork.

"I was told to ask for Anna," I heard an unfamiliar voice say to Joe, the zoning guy whose desk is in the lobby.

"In there," Joe said pointing with his thumb toward this office.

"Are you Anna? My name is James, I've got a package to deliver to someone named Allexa," the strange voice said. I turned in my seat at the mention of my name. Anna looked at me, and James followed her eyes.

"It's you!" he said.

That's when I recognized him. The young father in the parking lot at Mack's grocery store!

"Oh, my God! I never thought I would see you again to thank you!" he said, taking several long strides in my direction. I smiled and we shook hands.

"How's your little boy?" I asked.

"Oh, he's doing fine. So you do remember me?"

"Of course! Situations like that don't happen every day!" I said with a shrug and looked at the box in his hands.

"You know Marie at Mack's? She's my cousin. I told her that I had been assigned to make a delivery to Moose Creek. That's what I do: deliver gas around the U.P. Anyway, she said she knew someone in Moose Creek that she owed a big favor, but all she knew was your first name. To make sure I gave this to the right person, she said that you would know what you told her."

I reflected for a moment. "I told her to buy a bunch of pet food before she left work, the day of the first quake." He smiled and handed me the heavy box. I opened it and laughed. Marie had sent me a box of batteries! A, AA, C, D and one 9V—all of the types that I had picked up on the day of the parking lot incident. "Tell Marie I said thank you. And I hope she's staying at home! I hear town is very dangerous right now," I said.

"Oh, she's still working. The few grocery stores that are still open have guards. Marie is safe," he replied. "I really don't know how to thank you for what you did that day. I still can't believe those guys would have attacked in broad daylight! You might have saved our lives, you know."

"I only did what anyone else would have done," I said and shrugged again to ease my discomfort.

"Here's a copy of your receipt for five thousand gallons of diesel fuel," he said, handing some papers to Anna.

Diesel. How did Liz know?

After James left, and just before leaving for the day, I gave Anna a pack of D cells for the battery lamp that now sits proudly on her desk. In the short time I was at the office, there was a fresh four inches of snow on my car. I went back into the building and into Anna's office.

"Say, if this snow keeps up you might not see me for a few days," I warned her.

"Don't worry, I'll send the plow trucks after you," she threatened jokingly.

* * *

Back home, I re-stoked the fire, leaving the damper wide open. There would be no grilling tonight because I couldn't even *see* the grill from the back door. It's been years since we've had a blizzard like this. Don had apparently been over after I left since the wood supply behind the stove was full again. I really despise depending on others like this, yet I'm grateful I had those I *could* depend on when necessary.

A half hour later the kitchen was nicely warmed and I could finally take my coat off. I hadn't eaten all day, so I limped to the back pantry and selected a quart jar of chicken soup, and a pint of mixed veggies. I added a handful of rice and pushed the soup pot to the back of the stove to heat and cook the rice, and made myself a cup of tea. What a day!

I sat in the rocker with my tea in hand and briefly closed my eyes. I wasn't asleep long when I was woken by a knock on the door. I bolted out of the chair, my sprained ankle causing me to stumble, spilling my tea. Had I locked that door? Was the bar in place? A vision of Bill Harris flared in my mind and I reached for the shotgun, fear creeping up my throat. I looked out at a snow-covered figure.

He looked up, his clear, sad blue eyes peering through a veil of snowflakes. "You said to find you," said a voice with a soft North Carolina accent that kept whipping away with the wind.

My heart lurched in my chest! John! He had made his way to me. I tried and failed to open the sliding door. I had left the bar in place. I yanked it free and opened the door for him to come in. He smiled. His beard was snow packed and frozen. I began brushing the snow off of him while he stood there.

"It's so nice and warm in here," he mumbled, or sighed, I don't know which. Still, he was here and that's all that mattered right now.

"Let's get you out of those wet clothes," I said tugging his coat off, draping it over one of the other chairs. He was shivering. I dropped his hat and gloves on the floor and guided him to sit in the chair that I had just vacated. I limped into the other room and grabbed the comforter off of the couch and draped it around him. He shivered again as I knelt down to pull his soggy boots off and grabbed a towel for him to wipe the snow and wet off of his face.

"Did you *walk* all this way, John?" I asked. It was slightly over seven miles to that house on Eagle Beach, not really far, but too far to walk in a snowstorm.

"Yeah, I left this morning before it snowed so heavily. It was hard walking in all that wind. I wasn't sure I could make it. I stopped a couple of times to rest out of the wind, so that's what took me so long," he said, looking over at the stove.

"Are you hungry? There's some soup, would you like some?"

With the jacket off and knit cap on the floor, I could see how thin his face had gotten. It had only been two weeks since I had last seen him. Why didn't he come here sooner?

I ladled some chicken soup into a mug and gave it to him. He held the bowl in his hands and shivered again, almost spilling it. I placed my hands over his to steady him. His skin was so cold! He finished that bowl quickly. I refilled it but knew he had to slow down. His eyes began to droop as the exhaustion set in.

I left him there by the warm stove and began making up the futon couch for him to sleep on.

I pulled up one of the other chairs beside him, added more wood to the fire, and made tea for both of us. I wanted to know what had happened at the house on Eagle Beach.

"John, where are the others?" I questioned softly. There was anywhere from twelve to eighteen men staying at that house on alternating shifts. Though some had left, there were still a few remaining the last time I had visited.

"A lot of them got out early and went home," he explained while staring down into his tea. "You got anything stronger than this?"

I smiled. "I might. What do you want?"

"A beer would be good."

"You're in luck. I've got two left." I got one from the cold pantry, popped the cap and handed it to him.

He looked at me, then the beer, and drank half of it in one tip. He smiled. "Thank you. I've really missed beer. For the last few weeks I thought I'd never have another one."

"Do you want the other one?" I asked after he finished it in a second long gulp.

"No, but thanks," he replied while briefly closing his eyes and tipping his head back against the chair.

"You look really tired. I've made up the couch for you. Would you like to rest?"

"If you don't mind," his soft voice was apologetic.

I had some toiletry kits already made up, and set one in the bathroom for him and put a towel on the sink. The kit included a toothbrush, toothpaste, floss, a comb, razor, soap, deodorant, shampoo.

"I'll get you a pitcher of warm water if you want to wash up. There's a zip-lock bag on the sink with a few things you might need."

* * *

Ten minutes later he came out of the bathroom, smiling. "Just brushing my teeth makes me feel human again. Thank you!"

I walked up to him and put my arms around him for a hug. He sighed and hugged me back. Another time of not letting go. I stepped away.

"I'm really glad you're here, John, but you need some sleep. In the morning, I'll fix you a big breakfast. What would you like?"

He laughed. "Anything?"

I nodded.

"Biscuits with sausage gravy, eggs, bacon— and coffee, real coffee!" he said wistfully.

"I'll see what I can do." I led him into the other room where I had set up the futon. I turned on the battery lamp for him and left him to sleep.

CHAPTER TWELVE

I made sure that I was up at 6:12 A.M. to light my bayberry candle and welcome in the Winter Solstice. I was very quiet. Knowing that John was sleeping in the computer room on the futon made me smile. I have this content feeling that everything will be all right now.

I opened the stove to drop the ash, and stumbled back to the warmth of my blankets.

I surfaced from my cozy cocoon of dreams an hour later, dreams of radiating heat, only to find Tufts on my chest pawing at the covers. I shooed him away after the requisite scratch behind the ears and pulled my robe on again. I had left my sweatpants on, so all I had to do was slide into my slippers and hobble to the kitchen. I quietly set the water to boil and pulled out the French press, put two scoops of coffee into the bottom of the pot and filled it with boiling water to brew. I peeked around the corner to see that John was still sleeping with the thick blanket covering his bald head. I smiled. Snapping out of my reverie, I brushed the last of the ashes into the lower pan, shut the grate, and began to rebuild the fire.

John was up shortly afterward and heading for the bathroom. I added more wood to the fire as he came back into the kitchen. He smiled shyly.

The boiling water had effectively brewed the coffee in the bottom of the French press, and when he appeared, I pressed it, plunging the filter down to trap the coffee grounds. "Are you ready for some coffee?"

"You really have coffee?" he asked in disbelief.

"I don't drink it much, so there was some left over." I know I lied. I'm so used to *not* talking about what I have stocked up before the Event that it came naturally. There was enough coffee in storage to last John a long time. He smiled when he took the cup from me, and sipped. Was that a tear I saw?

"Have a seat, John." I pulled another chair next to the stove. "I'm betting you would really like a hot shower." He peered at me over his coffee cup like I was teasing him with a pot of gold and would snatch it away when he reached for it.

"Yeah, me too," I said, "however, the generator is buried in snow. We need to do some shoveling. I don't expect you to exert yourself without some food, so I made you some toast and jam," I said knowing the carbohydrates and sugar would help him a lot. His eyes widened when I lifted the cover off the griddle to expose three slices of nicely toasted bread.

"You're limping," he said, smothering a slice of homemade bread with my wild blueberry jam.

"I twisted my ankle a few days ago. It's fine, only a little sore," I lied.

Soon after, we both had shovels in hand and dug a path to free the generator of its snow-dome. I started it up and plugged in. Right after I moved in here, I had Jason wire the circuit panel to divert to a single plug if need be, for our frequent power outages. That plug fits the 5000-watt generator and it runs the entire house if used conservatively. My biggest concern then and always has been water. It's a good well, although the pump needs electricity.

* * *

I retrieved another package from the back storeroom and set it on the dryer in the bathroom.

"It's kind of generic, but you might want some clean clothes after you shower. There are sweat pants, t-shirts and socks. I'll get you a sweatshirt. Just put your clothes in the washer, I'll start it later," I said before I left him alone. Soon I heard the shower running and over the sound of the rushing water, I caught a definite groan of contentment. I don't think he meant for me to hear.

While John was showering, I got a jar of sausage patties from the back storage to break up for his sausage gravy, plus one of the few cans of milk. The chickens had slowed down laying, nonetheless, I was still getting four eggs a day and there was bacon already thawed. I added more wood to the stove to bring up the oven temp for the biscuits.

"John, what's the matter?" I asked when he returned. He looked so sad.

He took a deep, shuddering breath. "That felt so good. I can't understand why I waited so long to come here," he said.

I can't understand that either, still, it was his choice. The clothes fit him fine, though a little loosely.

"I don't want to run the generator too long. While I take a quick shower, would you please fill these three buckets from the kitchen sink? You can leave them on the floor. Then I'll shut the gennie off and finish fixing our breakfast."

I've found that having something to do is often the best tonic and John needed something to do.

I showered in record time and while toweling off, I started the washer filling so the clothes John put in there could soak. The room was chilly and prompted me to dress quickly. I combed my wet hair then fluffed it so it would dry quicker.

John was sitting in front of the stove when I came out.

"If you show me what you do with the generator, I can do that for you," he offered.

Oh, my, if he wants to help like this, maybe he plans on staying. I smiled gratefully and put a knit hat over my wet hair to go back on the deck to show him what to do.

* * *

"Is that...?" John asked wide-eyed, looking at the biscuits in a basket, sausage gravy with eggs and bacon on his plate.

"That's what you said you wanted," I said, knowing that he was impressed. Shame on me, I was *trying* to impress him. "Don't get used to it though. I did this for a special reason. It's your first day here and you need food. If you decide to stay, it won't always be like this, it can't be. As a rule, I only have two meals a day. No real breakfast, just toast, with soup for lunch and a more hearty dinner. I hope you can adapt."

"One meal a day will be more than I've had in the last two weeks," he admitted as he dug into his food. I chuckled over the ecstatic expression on his face while he ate, his comment haunting me.

After he'd finished eating, I poured him the last of the coffee.

"Oh, that was wonderful. Thank you. I really should have come here sooner."

"Why didn't you?" That question had been plaguing me.

"I dunno, Allex, pride maybe, and I didn't want to be a burden to you." He looked away. "We all kept waiting for things to go back to normal. Then the generator quit and with it went our heat. We were burning logs in the fireplace but it wasn't enough. When Steve and Sandy stopped coming, I knew it was bad, and I didn't want to abandon the others. We ate what was left in the refrigerator and when that was gone, several of them piled into the big van and went to Marquette. There were only three of us left," he explained, a sad cloud passing across the back of his eyes. He took a sip of coffee. "There wasn't much left this past week, except cheese puffs. When I woke up two days ago, the guys were gone and so was the last truck. I waited a while thinking that they went in search of food, but they never came back. That's when I remembered what you had said to me the last time you were there, to find you. It's okay, isn't it?"

I took his hands in mine. "Of course it is, John, absolutely! I meant it. In a way, waiting like this has made it easier, I couldn't feed all of those men. I *can* feed *you*."

* * *

We talked for another hour or two about the different things that were going on in the country. The guys on Eagle Beach never knew about the Stone Soup Kitchen. Perhaps it might have made a difference.

Awhile later, we went out to the barn with a pail of water for the chickens and the basket to collect eggs. Once in the barn, I remembered to grab the mattress pads, and since my ankle was still sore I had John climb the ladder to get one off the top shelf. I also grabbed the blow-up mattress and foot pump. We struggled to get those bulky things back to the house in the high winds.

My inner doubts were fading. John and I seemed to work well together, at least so far. It was only changing his bedding around, yet it was a start. He didn't question what I was doing or why, like so many men do; he mimicked what I did and we were done in no time. When he offered to bring in wood, I assured him that there was plenty for now. He could do that tomorrow. He seems anxious to earn his keep.

While he was re-shoveling the deck and all the steps, I started on dinner. Remembering a comment from what seems like so very long ago, I know that he likes pasta. A jar of homemade sauce from homegrown tomatoes, plus a jar of meatballs from when I emptied the freezer back in October. We would have spaghetti and meatballs with garlic bread. Everything was from storage except the bread. I had made two loaves of Italian bread last time and froze one in the cooler outside. All I had to do was heat everything through and cook the pasta. I hope he likes spaghetti pasta. Pasta stores so well that I have lots of every shape that's made.

* * *

Dinner was a big hit. I even opened a bottle of wine. I felt I deserved it and John would appreciate it. There's tension building between us, in just this short time. I know I have felt this attraction for many months, though I'm not sure I'm ready to change our relationship. My emotions are too much in flux, too much pressure; everyone wants something from me. I don't know what's real and what isn't. I know I can't shut down; I also can't open up. Not just yet.

* * *

JOURNAL ENTRY: December 22

After such a heavy snowstorm we've been graced with incredible blue skies and blinding sunshine this morning. I can't see any clouds except for the ever-present blackness over Lake Superior. The trees are bent in a cloak of icy white. Some have already cracked and are broken from the weight of so much snow. Those trees will make for good firewood for next winter.

* * *

John and I finished our morning coffee and toast. He emptied the last of the blueberry jam on a single piece of toast. I retrieved a jar of strawberry jam from the back pantry and set it in front of him.

"I don't see you eating much of this, yet you seem to have a lot of it," he said, spreading the second slice with a scoop from the fresh jar.

"I know it might seem odd, John. I love to can, to cook, to make things, even if I don't always like to eat it," I laughed. "I've got pickles from three years ago. I had an abundance of cucumbers that summer and I just can't let good food go to waste. I made seven quarts of pickles, though I rarely eat more than one jar a year. And the jam? My friend Kathy and I love to pick wild blueberries. It's a wonderful way for us to spend some time together during the hectic summer when I'm always working and she's entertaining houseguests. It's peaceful, quiet and productive." I smiled at the memories. "Our favorite place to pick is up on the Plains, near the mine. Usually I freeze the blueberries so I can put a handful on my oatmeal in the winter, and a few years back I had so much that I made a lot of jam too. It's a good thing that I did. The next two years were a bust for any wild fruit."

"What's the matter?" he asked, when he noticed that sad thoughts were on my mind.

"Thinking of picking blueberries reminded me of when Kathy's dad came with us. Oh, how he loved to pick berries! In June, the three of us would travel over an hour to the strawberry farm. Kath and I would pick, and James would playfully flirt with the ladies. At eighty-six he wasn't able to stoop to pick berries, so we picked for him. He so enjoyed the outings," I said with melancholy and took a sip of coffee. "He and Kathy's mom died a couple of weeks ago."

The tears prickled behind my eyes. I took a deep breath, and another sip of coffee. John got up, took my hand and pulled me into his arms.

He looked down at me, reached out and tucked a wayward strand of hair behind my ear, grazing my cheek with his fingers. "Any time you need a hug, just say so," he said softly, and dropped his hand to his side.

"Talking about Kathy reminds me that she and Bob will be coming over for Christmas dinner. I'm hoping that my son Jason will come too, with his family. I haven't talked to them lately. He knows that they are always welcome." My knees were shaky with John standing so near and I could still feel the trail his fingers left on my face. I turned to clear the dishes to avoid his eyes. I didn't want him to see my hunger when he didn't feel the same.

* * *

Chores still loomed before us. I needed the driveway cleared so I could get to town and we needed wood for the stove. I showed John the woodpile and handed him the carry sling.

"This is the last of the first burn wood. It's wood that was left over from last year and since it's now two years old it needs to be burned first."

The clear skies also meant lower temperatures, and thankfully the wind had died down. The snow crunched underfoot as I limped my way through the deep drifts to the barn.

We both worked quickly. This was the shortest day of the year and dusk was already threatening. By the time I finished removing the snow from the entire drive, the plows still hadn't come by. Now I could get out of the driveway, although I might not be able to get to the main road. Come to think of it, I haven't heard the plows out on CR 695 either. I might be the emergency manager, but I can't do anything if I'm snowed in.

Back in the house, I was pleased with the pile of wood John had stacked behind the stove. He had also fed wood into the stove, so it was pleasantly warm inside. I opened the warming door over the stove and set my gloves there to dry. John picked his up off the floor and set them there too, giving me a sheepish grin.

Dinner was simple. I warmed a jar of hamburger meat, some onions, and a few crushed herbs then added a jar of green peas. I thickened the broth to make gravy and served it on top of penne pasta. John finished off the bread sopping up the gravy. I guess it's oatmeal in the morning instead of toast. It also means making bread sometime tomorrow.

* * *

The next day, I lit the stove slightly after daybreak, which is now around 8:15 A.M. I've found from experience it's easier for the woodstove to maintain a baking temperature early in the day, so I make bread right after I get up. I mixed a double batch in a big bowl, adding a couple of eggs to make it a bit richer and more flavorful. I kneaded it while thinking about the day to come, then set it to rise in the oiled bowl next to the warmth of the stove and covered it with a towel.

Christmas is in two days, and I still haven't planned out an actual menu for Christmas dinner. I sat down to do that at the same time John made his way into the kitchen.

"Good morning," he mumbled, still half asleep.

"Good morning. There's coffee on the stove." Tufts finally wandered out from under the bed. I know he's been out and about during the night because his food is gone and the litter box is used. He's avoided John, not sure what to make of him. Tufts doesn't like strangers. Maybe he's decided that John isn't a stranger anymore. It's good to see him getting underfoot again.

With two of us doing the few chores, it all gets done quickly. John likes keeping the wood full, and I do understand that. If we get hit with a surprise blizzard—and without a weather report, it's *all* a surprise—having a few days' worth of wood already inside can be a lifesaver. Early this afternoon, while he was getting wood, I heard voices. Don had come over to give me a hand, and met John loading up the sling.

I had put the two loaves of bread in the oven a half hour earlier, and the baking aroma permeated the kitchen. When the two walked in, John stopped, closed his eyes, breathed deep and sighed.

"I see you've got some help," Don said *looking* uninterested, though he arched his brow at me to ask a silent question.

"And I see that you've met John," I said meet his gaze and just smiled. "John's my friend from Eagle Beach." *That* took him by surprise, and it showed.

Don stayed for a cup of coffee and a chat with John. They discussed numerous things, then when it came around to guns, Don was impressed by the fact that John is a gunsmith. Don was getting ready to leave when I was taking the bread out of the oven. "Before you go, Don, how are your supplies holding out? Do you need anything?" I asked.

"Only gas for the generator to keep the freezers going. Since now we can pack things outside we don't run it as much. Nancy has been canning up a storm. Say, do you have any extra jars that we can use? And what about rice? She stocked up on pasta, but we've gone through the ten pounds of rice that she had stored." Don had a lot of food in freezer storage, where I had a lot in dry storage.

"Tell you what," I said, "I'll trade you a five gallon bucket of rice and a dozen quart jars for a half dozen nice steaks, rib-eyes if you have them."

"Deal!"

John and I loaded up the sled with the rice and an unopened case of quart jars, then we snow-shoed across the road. I had to show John how the shoes were strapped on. He's a quick study and got the hang of it real fast. Knee-deep snow is hard to walk through regardless how far one has to go.

* * *

When we returned home I opened the bag from Don and discovered a dozen large rib-eye steaks. I set two of them on a plate to thaw for dinner and put the other ten in one of the coolers on the deck. I sat by the stove. My ankle was really starting to hurt. I had definitely overdone it today. John saw me wince when I got up for an ice pack.

"Sit!" he commanded. "What do you need?" I told him where the ice packs were. He gently pulled my boot off, set my foot on a pillow that he placed on a chair, and pressed an ice pack around my throbbing ankle. I sighed.

"Don't move for at least a half hour. You need anything, tell me. Okay?"

"Okay. Pull up a chair and talk to me. Tell me about your family, your home, anything." All he needed was a little prompting.

"My daughter Christine is now thirty and finished school as a dental hygienist about five years ago. She had a nice job in Fort Wayne, Indiana at a clinic, until it cut back the staff and she got laid off. It's a good thing she's single, since the only other job she could find after six months was in Greenwood, near Indianapolis, and she had to move." He paused to adjust the icepack on my ankle that had slipped to the side. "My mom lives in Louisville, Kentucky, so at least Christine is closer to her grandma now. My mom loves to travel," John smiled. "She's been all over the states, seeing everything the travel brochures talk about. The Grand Canyon, Mount Rushmore, the Badlands. I think her favorite is Bourbon Street during Mardi Gras. She's quite adventuresome for an old lady." The sound of his laughter filled the room and made me smile.

I've never heard him say this much in the year I've known him. Of course, he was usually face-down on the massage table.

Forty-five minutes later, the ice pack was warm and my butt was numb. I needed to move. I stood, took a step, my ankle gave out and I stumbled. John caught me by the shoulders and prevented me from falling. We stood there for a moment, then he pulled me closer, his face hovering mere inches from me. He lowered his head and kissed me, barely brushing my lips. Then he deepened the kiss. Shock waves of pleasure assaulted my senses and I leaned into him, returning his kiss. His lips seared mine with a passionate heat I had not expected. Desire flooded my body and I moaned as he brought me tighter against him.

"I've wanted to do that for a very long time," John whispered.

CHAPTER THIRTEEN

JOURNAL ENTRY: December 24

I had planned on going into the office despite the fact that it's Christmas Eve, however, the roads still haven't been plowed. John walked out to CR 695, which was finally cleared a few minutes after noon. My road is knee deep in snow, so I still can't get out. I almost don't care anymore.

John and I seem to be avoiding each other, embarrassed by our brief intimacy last night. It was a wonderful, tender kiss that was filled with unspoken promises. Unfortunately, it has left a tension in the air.

I asked him to gas up and start the generator so I could do some laundry. His clothes have been soaking long enough. I found a camouflage one-piece coverall that Eric left behind his last trip here for John to wear while I washed everything he's been wearing the past few days. He has so few clothes. I need to find a way to get to the Eagle Beach house so John can get some of his own things.

As I was hanging the heavier wet clothes on the drying rack by the stove the plow went by! At least everyone should be able to get here tomorrow.

* * *

"John, let's go over some of the things that I've found necessary to adapt to without power," I said while he sat attentively. "The generator can run the whole house provided we use only one 220 line, and that's the well pump for water. The clothes dryer takes a great deal of power and puts too much of a strain on the generator and could possibly damage it, which we can't risk."

"That makes sense."

"I'm keeping a pot for hot water on the stove at all times for dishes, washing, and whatever else we might need it for. If you use the pot, refill it and remember to wipe off the bottom so it doesn't leave rings on the stove surface. If I think of anything else, I'll mention it."

"Fair enough," he said, giving me one of his shy smiles.

* * *

It was close to 4:00 P.M. when I heard the engine rumble of a car in the driveway. A surge of panic rose in my throat and I had a flashback to when Bill Harris showed up. It wasn't him, of course. It was Jason. Out of the car came Amanda and Jacob. When I opened the door, Jacob ran up and flung himself into my arms. It was so good to see him!

"Jason, Mandy, this is John Tiggs, a friend I've known for a long time. He's staying with me now," I added, making the introductions.

"I'm glad you're not alone here anymore, Mom. I've worried about you being on your own." Jason shook John's hand. "And I wonder if we could stay tonight too," he asked.

"Of course you can!" I said, before realizing the sleeping arrangements would have to be adjusted. "Just put your stuff in the computer room and make yourself a drink. John, can we talk for a minute?" When he came over, I said quietly, "I should have talked to you about this first, but I didn't know that Jason would be here today and wanting to spend the night. Ummm…" I hesitated, "will you sleep in here tonight so they can have that room?" I gazed into his blue eyes, hoping he'd say yes, afraid he'd say no.

"Allex," he said softly, tucking a strand of hair behind my ear, "once you let me share your bed, I won't go back to the couch. Are you okay with that?"

I swallowed, hard, my voice gone and nodded. He obviously had thought about this for some time. Ready or not, our relationship instantly changed. When we walked back into the kitchen, John slid his hand into mine, and we officially became a couple.

* * *

"I was just getting ready to organize dinner. Are you hungry?" I looked from Jason to a much thinner Amanda. Jason had fixed himself what looked like rum and cola, Mandy had a glass of water and things seemed tense.

"Oh, yeah," Jason answered sullenly. "Yesterday, I ran out of that food you brought last week. I still had some ramen noodles for Jacob for this morning, but that's why we came early. I hope you don't mind."

"Of course I don't mind! Don't be silly. You're always welcome here. I was thinking of some chicken on pasta for dinner, there will be plenty for everyone." I gave John's hand a squeeze and let go, so I could collect items from the back pantry.

Jason grilled Jacob a cheese sandwich and cut it up small. Jacob's eyes lit up when he saw it and ate every last bite. Oh, my, the little guy was really hungry. My heart hurt for my grandson.

"How would Jacob like some popcorn?" I looked at Jason. "And I know there are juice packs still in the pantry."

"Oh, I'm sure he would love some," Jason was holding his emotions in check, but this bit of normalcy was taxing him.

"John, would you start the generator again? It won't be for long." He grabbed his jacket and a flashlight.

Once the power came up, Jason put a pack of popcorn in the microwave. When it was done, he put a second one in. "For later." He grinned.

The water I had put on for the pasta was boiling and I stirred the fettuccini in. "Mandy, would you stir this, please?" When she was close enough, I asked, "Where have you been? We've been so worried!"

"I don't want to talk about it," she said, and turned her back on me, unwilling to share what had happened.

The table was aglow with lamp light when we sat down to eat. By the time we were done, Jacob was already curled up on the futon, fast asleep. Jason pumped up the air mattress, and everyone settled in for the night, exhausted from the busy day.

As I snuggled up next to John, I could hear Jason and Amanda in the other room, arguing. I fell asleep troubled.

* * *

I stretched under the covers and bumped into something. Startled, I froze and then remembered that John was with me now. I turned slowly to see his blue eyes opened and amused.

"Merry Christmas," he said and kissed me lightly. I smiled, and kissed him back, deeper. "Easy, Allex," he pulled away, "this is too tempting and I want our first time together when we're completely alone."

Last night we slept. Just slept. I sighed, but agreed, and slipped out of bed.

We woke to a fresh blanket of snow on the ground. The house was quiet but not cold like I thought it would be. Jason had gotten up during the night and put more wood in the stove.

It was Christmas morning, and I was disappointed that I didn't have a tree. There were no colored lights, but I could give my family love. Right now I think that mattered more than presents. Then I remembered I did have presents!

I started a fresh pot of coffee, for which Amanda was very grateful. It might not have been up to her Starbucks standard, but it was more than she had had for a couple of weeks, and she sipped it with pleasure.

Jason noticed I was limping and using a cane and wanted to know what happened.

"It really was nothing. I forgot to salt down the steps and slipped when I was hauling in wood."

"And why were *you* hauling in wood?" Jason demanded, glancing over at John. John's mouth tightened in defense and his chin rose just enough for me to notice.

"Jason, I know you're being protective, but this happened days before John got here. And since then, I haven't lifted a stick of wood and he helps with all the chores."

John looked Jason in the eye and said, "Your mother can be a stubborn woman, can't she?"

I pouted, which made Jason laugh, since he knows I have a hard time sitting still for long. With the tension eased, I reinforced my support for John by slipping my arm through his. I could *feel* him relax. I sure don't need Jason and John being at odds with each other. They are both so important in my life now.

I passed out what few presents that I had from my early shopping in the fall. I apologized to John for having no gift for him, but he silenced me with his finger on my lips.

"You've already given me the best gift possible," he smiled. "I'm sorry that I don't have one for you."

He moved away to help set the leaf into the table before I could protest.

* * *

Jason retrieved the ham from the barn while John relit the stove. I convinced John to let Jason bring in wood because I needed him to help me in the back. John reluctantly gave up that one duty, "just for today."

My thoughts kept slipping into town. I haven't been to the office since John arrived a few days ago. I'm sure things are going fine. If not, there is nothing that I could do anyway.

It was 2:00 P.M. and the rolls were going into the oven when Bob and Kathy arrived.

After introductions all around, I brought out a tray of deviled eggs that I had kept secret from everyone. Deviled eggs, cheese and crackers, plus some of the venison summer sausage that Jason and I made last fall were the appetizers I had selected.

Bob was so happy with the little appetizer spread that he insisted on opening one of the six bottles of wine that they had brought.

"How did you keep these crackers so fresh?" Kathy questioned while she munched a second piece, obviously enjoying the food.

"As an experiment, I dry canned a few boxes of different kinds of crackers last summer. I wasn't sure how they would turn out, but I'm happy with them. I only have a few jars, but this is a good occasion to use them," I told her.

"This is great! Will you marry me?" Bob asked jokingly after eating several appetizers, his favorite part of the meal.

John immediately tightened his arm around my shoulders possessively and retorted, "She's taken. She's mine and you can't have her!" He grinned.

Bob laughed. "You've made a wise choice, my friend."

A few minutes later Jacob came into the kitchen.

"Nahna, can I watch a movie?" he asked, tugging on my arm and my heart. Jason started to explain that he couldn't, but I stopped him.

"This is a special day for all of us. John will you start the generator? We'll run it for a few hours. Jacob can watch anything he wants. We can have lights and running water and I can use the other stove to help re-heat things for dinner." It was Christmas Day, I had my friends and my family here, plus I had John. We had plenty of food for everyone and I was determined that we would all have a good time.

I had already decided on using the remaining ham for dinner; along with it, a green and wax bean casserole with cream of mushroom soup and a baked garden pumpkin filled with rice pilaf. I've done the pumpkin-rice before and it's not only good but fun to scoop out some rice and squash at the same time. Fresh bread rolls, too. For dessert we had baked apples.

With everything heated at the same time, dinner went smoothly, the wine flowed freely and the conversation was lively. Kathy told of how quiet Moose Creek was at night, except for last night.

"We've been getting used to it being very quiet at night," she said, "so when the music and ruckus started last night it really surprised me, especially the music!"

Living right in the heart of town, they heard everything.

"I think Buddy was holding a private party at The Jack," Bob chimed in. "He must have found a case of booze hidden somewhere."

I explained to John that "Buddy" is the nickname for Carl McCoy. He and his wife Patty own the local bar, The One-Eyed Jack. Not many people in Moose Creek like Buddy, but The Jack is the only bar, so he is at best tolerated, but still a creep, nonetheless.

After dinner, Kathy helped me divide up the leftover ham three ways, but I insisted she and Jason split the rice pilaf and the rolls. I could always make more. It was one of the things I had planned for. By having a wood burning cook stove, I had a capability to bake whenever I needed, provided the flour held out.

"Bob," I interjected into a conversation he was having with Jason about plumbing. "Would you like an after-dinner scotch? Kathy, how about you?" Bob's eyes lit up and so did John's. I didn't know John was a scotch drinker. I would have offered him some sooner. These touches of normal habits are what I've prepped for.

"Well, I see I said the right thing," I laughed. "John, would you get some glasses down from that shelf, please?" I pointed to the rack where the wine glasses hung. On the shelf above it was a variety of drink glasses. I hobbled into the back pantry and retrieved a bottle of scotch, rum and schnapps.

Jason got the bag of ice cubes off the deck for us, and Kathy, Bob and John bonded over Famous Grouse on the rocks. Jason opted for the Captain Morgan's Private Stock spiced rum, while Mandy and I sipped a shot of peppermint schnapps.

It was a good time to ask Bob and Kathy about Al and Mary, our other friends.

"Oh, I thought you knew," Kathy said. "They went downstate to stay with their boys in Traverse City when this all began." Good, that was one less couple I had to worry about.

With the generator still running I did the dishes instead of waiting for morning. Then I found out why Jason wanted to stay one more night

"Mom, do you mind if we all take showers?" Jason asked while he helped me dry the dishes. My gas water heater stays hot on a minimal amount of propane, which still flows without power, where his electric water heater didn't work at all.

While Amanda was taking her shower, Jason came to me for a favor.

"May I have five gallons of gas before we leave in the morning? Amanda barely got back home and I had to siphon some from my truck to get us here." He knew I had a drum of gas in storage.

"Absolutely. Do you want a couple more cases of noodles for Jacob, too?"

"Thank you," he hugged me tight. "One will be fine for now."

CHAPTER FOURTEEN

The next morning I fixed a big breakfast, hoping it would last until supper. While Amanda collected their belongings and Jacob's toys, Jason put some gas in their car, and then filled the five-gallon container he'd brought while I watched from the back door.

At about noon, they were ready to leave. Jason mentioned that he took a little extra gas, and I knew he would. He's always been very with honest with me. Well, mostly. I still wonder why he didn't tell me about Amanda leaving.

After they left, I told John that I needed to go to the office for an hour or two. He looked confused. He didn't know that I was the township emergency manager.

"Do you want me to come with you?"

"No, that's not necessary, but we need to cover something before I leave," I replied. He got a big grin.

"Not *that*," I blushed. "You need to be armed. What would you prefer to have an automatic or revolver?"

"Automatic."

"Nine millimeter or twenty-two?"

"A nine."

I got up, reached into the clock and pulled out a gun. His eyes widened. I thumbed the safety on, ejected the clip, ejected the chambered round and handed it to him, handgrip first.

"Beretta 92FS, nice gun!" he exclaimed while he pointed it at the floor, sited it down, weighed it.

"Will that do?"

"Nicely! Do you happen to have a holster for it?"

"I'll get one."

"What are you carrying?" he asked when I returned from the back room after locating the appropriate holster. I showed him my Kel-Tec 9mm and he grinned. I slid it back into my shoulder holster.

"I know you don't need to be told to not let anyone in you don't know, but I have to say it anyway," I shrugged. "You've seen the supplies. Those are for *us*, John—you, me, my family. That's what I've prepped for. Your job today is to protect all that," I said with a grin, then kissed him. "I won't be gone long. I hope."

* * *

"Where have you been?" Anna asked when I arrived at the office. I reminded her where I lived, that nobody plowed my road. I couldn't get out.

"That won't happen again. Sorry." Anna looked like she hadn't slept in days. She sank into her oversized chair. "It's been a busy weekend. Have you driven through town yet?"

"No."

"Someone has been trying to burn down the town!"

"*What?!*"

"Shoreline Treasures was the first casualty, and then the real estate office burned."

I was more distressed that the real estate office suffered. It was a great building! Originally a bank, it was built to fit the area, a log cabin. It was beautiful with its hand-hewn beams and rustic stain. When the bank pulled out, it made its way into several, unsuccessful businesses before settling into a real estate office, which had maintained now for over ten years. Shoreline Treasures was a gift shop that was closed during the winter.

"Any suspects?" I asked, dazed.

"Since it started right after Buddy's bash, Ken and Karen are going over the guest list, figuring that someone got really drunk and then got pissed off over something. Now everyone left in the town is pissed off."

"When did this happen?"

"Christmas Eve," she said shaking her head. "Of all the nights! It's disgraceful, considering how well the town has pulled together so far."

"Do they have any suspects?" I asked again.

She looked sullen and didn't answer right away. "Yeah. Lenny." She took a deep breath, "It's only a suspicion right now. You know Lenny is a hothead."

"I'm confident Ken and Karen will figure it out," I said, not entirely sure if I was convinced myself. "I need to contact Liz. Is there someplace I can have some privacy?"

Anna left me alone in the office knowing the importance of my call. I quickly dialed the County Emergency Manager. The phone rang and rang, unanswered. I hung up and dialed 911. "This is Moose Creek emergency management," I said when the call was answered. "I'm trying to reach Liz Anderson and no one is answering her phone." After a pause and some clicks a male voice answered.

"Tom White."

"Tom, Allexa Smeth in Moose Creek. I'm trying to reach Liz Anderson, but she's not answering." The line seemed to go dead. "Tom?"

"We found Liz yesterday. County ME said it was a heart attack." His voice broke.

No words came to my mind.

"I'm acting CEM. Is there anything critical that you need?" he asked, sounding overwhelmed.

"Food."

"You and everyone else," Tom sighed. "I'll see what I can do, but I can't promise you anything."

"Thanks. Please, send my condolences to Liz's family." I hung up, stunned at the news.

* * *

"What's wrong?" John asked when I let myself into the house.

I struggled to get the words out. "I lost someone today." I broke down in sobs. John wrapped his arms around me. I shivered despite his added body heat.

"Who?" he asked gently, wiping the tears from my face.

"Liz Anderson, the county emergency manager. Liz wasn't just my boss, she was my friend." I pulled away from John to get a hanky from my pocket.

"What happened?" John asked. He was pressing something into my other hand. I looked down at the golden liquid in the glass and took a sip. Brandy.

"They believe it was a heart attack, too much stress I imagine." John took the glass from my hand and hugged me again tightly. It felt so good to have someone understand my distress. When he kissed my temple I looked up at him, wanting more. The kisses that followed stirred something deep within me and I forgot the stress I was under. I forgot about Liz for the moment. And we both forgot about dinner.

* * *

"Anna, is there any way I can borrow a snow mobile from someone?" I asked.

"For how long?"

"An hour or two, that's all."

"I'll have George bring ours up," she offered. I wanted to get John back to Eagle Beach to collect some more of his own things.

"Thanks, we won't be long."

"We?" I heard her ask while I walked out the door.

* * *

John and I arrived back at the township hall at the same time George was parking their new snowmobile. He went over the controls with John, assuming that he would be driving. I knew John had never ridden one before, though he had a motorcycle back home in North Carolina, and could adapt quickly. John made a slow circle, and drove around the parking lot a few times to get the feel of the machine. I took the towing sled out of the car and tied it to the back of the snowmobile like I'd done a hundred times before in the woods, then I got on the back of the sled behind John and tightly held on to his waist.

He was definitely having fun.

The roads were fairly clear, but snow packed, which was good, since a snowmobile needs snow for the treads to grip. When we got to the entrance to the Eagle Beach subdivision the road changed. It hadn't been plowed since the first snow and was deeply drifted. I whispered to John the advice I was given many, many years ago: if you get into deep powder, *don't stop!* From that point, it was close to a mile to the house that John had shared with his co-workers. The snowmobile took the drifts easily.

When we pulled up to the house, we sat there for a few minutes, taking in the beauty of the Big Lake. The wind had whipped up the shoreline, spraying the trees and the deck with the glory of Lake Superior. Icicles dripped from the handrails looking like shimmering Christmas ornaments. Small ice floats appearing like a frozen wasteland crowded each other in the bay, held motionless by the small pools of thin ice that might have been open water yesterday. Chunks of ice, farther than the eye could see, jagged and gem-like, edged the horizon where the open water of the deep lake undulated with massive waves that were made small by the distance.

We let ourselves in through the garage, where John used a hidden key to open the interior door.

He asked me to wait upstairs while he took a big duffle bag and a flashlight and descended alone into the gloom of his old basement room. I wandered through the kitchen. Ice crystals had formed on the metal faucets, but all looked neat and clean, though it was obvious that anything consumable had been stripped from the place. The glass door commercial coolers that once were filled with all manner of drinks for the guys was empty. The nearby storage shelves now only held empty boxes.

After a few minutes, I called down the stairs to John, asking if he was okay. Moments later, I could see the bright white beam from the flashlight getting larger as he made his way back up the stairs.

"It took a little longer than I thought it would. Sorry if I alarmed you," he said with a hint of sadness in his eyes, making me wonder what else was down there. "Let's get out of here," he said.

* * *

At home, he dumped the bag out in the middle of the kitchen floor. He had packed his pillow, cellphone and charger, a couple of books and clothes: t-shirts, jeans, a sweater, socks, underwear and two pair of shoes.

"I think all the clothes will need washing. I'll start the generator," he said, appearing distracted.

I sorted his clothes and started the washer. Then I got the last beer out and handed it to John.

"Are you going to tell me what's wrong?" I prodded gently. He stared at the beer a long time before taking a large swallow.

"Those last few days that I was at the house I slept on the couch, near the fireplace," he said between gulps. "I didn't know that Henry was downstairs. He still is."

* * *

JOURNAL ENTRY: December 28

I'm really feeling down.

After everything else, Liz is dead, someone is trying to burn the town down, and there's a dead body on Eagle Beach. Not to mention I'm still waking in the middle of the night with cold sweats from bad dreams.

With all my preps, I felt I had so much, enough to last me forever, at least well past the next growing season. I did have extra, but I didn't count on so many depending on me. Will I have enough, or will I let everyone down? The responsibility is overwhelming.

I wonder if that's how Liz felt?

* * *

On the morning of the 29th, I ventured into town to find Gray so I could tell him about the body on Eagle Beach. While at the EMS office, I ran into Marilyn Harris. I felt guilty because only four of us knew I had shot her husband, and it still haunted me, likely always would. She seemed happy to see me,

"Oh, Allexa, I'm so glad to run into you!" She hugged me and handed me a set of keys. "I didn't know who to give these to. I'll need a ride back home."

"What's this, Marilyn?" I asked really confused, examining the keys in my hand.

"I know that Bill had a dark side and I'm not going to justify it. But maybe I can apologize in a small way," she explained. "Bill had a Passat Wagon TDI, a diesel. I want the township to have it. Actually, I think I'd like Karen and Ken to have it like some sort of patrol car." Then it dawned on me: a diesel vehicle. With the new shipment of diesel gas, this would help a *lot*. I hoped I thanked her enough.

"Do *you* know who my husband was trying to rob? Who shot him?" Marilyn asked me directly.

"Marilyn, I think it's best that none of us know," I said. "Besides, what would you do if you knew?"

"Probably thank them," she snorted. "I said Bill had a dark side, and he did, sometimes he...got physical. Didn't you ever wonder why I dropped out of the ladies groups in the summer? Bruises show." She smiled. "Now I don't have to worry."

I was stunned.

"You will make sure that Ken and Karen get the car, won't you? It's the least that I can do." I thanked her again and had Pete take her home.

CHAPTER FIFTEEN

I needed some fresh air and alone time today, so I took a quiet walk, along the road. The undisturbed snow was beautiful. It all looked smooth, like ice cream with glitter, and helped to lift my mood.

When I returned home, John had all the guns laid out on the table and was systematically disassembling, cleaning and oiling them. It was a joy to watch. He grinned when I walked in. I think he really needed something to do, something productive and worthwhile, something he was good at. No matter how much we might like each other, being cooped up together in a small house can be very taxing on the nerves. After I watched John work on the guns, I took Jim Cobb's *Preppers Home Defense* book off of the shelf, and set it on the table.

"This author is a friend of mine," I explained, "He's written a couple of books on home defense and also on disaster preparedness. Although I found many of his ideas useable for here, I want your opinion." I wasn't pandering to John's male ego, though guys *do* need to be needed, but John's thoughts and ideas were just as important and valid as mine.

He watched me closely while I talked, then asked what was bothering me.

"You seem upset, Allex. What's the matter?" John has gotten to know me well in a very short time.

Has he really been here for only ten days?

I couldn't help it. The tears welled up behind my eyelids and were soon flowing down my cheeks. He held my hands and let me cry. I told him I was worried about our food lasting. Those blue eyes crinkled with a mirth *I* certainly didn't feel.

He stood, still holding my hand, and led me to the back room where the main food pantry is.

"Look around, Allex, really look around! There is enough pasta here alone to last us months. I was trying to do a quick calculation, hope that's okay, and I came up with almost a hundred pounds of various types of pasta. If we had to eat nothing except macaroni, and ate a pound a day, it would still last us three months. We don't need to do that because there are the cases of tuna fish and salmon and mackerel that you were smart enough to buy and store. Look at all the soups and tomatoes and vegetables you canned, from the garden that *you* grew."

The jars glistened in the dim light. "How can you possibly let this worry you?" he asked drawing me close and whispering into my hair. "*You* have provided us with enough to eat for at least a year, maybe two, since I don't know what else you have."

John gave me one of his sweet smiles, and then got serious.

"I owe you my life, you know. So please don't cry or I'll think you regret taking me in."

"Oh, no, no! I don't regret having you here, not at all! Don't even think that. If I saved you, then you saved *me*, John. And you're right—we will be fine. I tried hard to plan having enough to share with my family, and that now includes you."

I hugged him tight, and decided he needed to know what else we had.

* * *

John was bringing in wood the next morning, while I made a list of what I had and where I stored it. He really needed to know what our supplies were. The first list was the easy one for me since it was the long term storage.

"One hundred and fifty buckets?" he asked, quite shocked.

"Well, I know there could have been more, except the last two rows I put in I didn't stack as high, so I had room for the ten cans of coffee."

He was right, I shouldn't have been worried about our food supplies, not with a half-ton of wheat berries, and the same in rice, five hundred pounds of beans, two hundred pounds of sugar and a hundred pounds of salt.

I handed him the second list, and then the third. He looked up at me and smiled. "Any other surprises?"

When I handed him the ammo inventory, he started laughing. "What were you planning for, the end of the world?"

"Isn't that pretty much what we're facing, John?" I asked in all sincerity.

He looked back at the ammo list. "Do you have weapons for all of this?"

"Except for the 308, that's Jason's." I smirked. "What? You want to clean and oil the rifles now?"

* * *

JOURNAL ENTRY: December 31

For New Year's Eve, John and I grilled a steak and six shrimp each. I know that was excessive, but the fresh meat won't last forever, even frozen, and the shellfish even less time. We split a potato, and then shared my only bottle of bubbly. We were in bed and asleep by 11 P.M.

I was awakened by the roar of a snowmobile. I got up to use the bathroom and saw flames!

* * *

"John! Get up! There's a fire!" I shook John while I pulled on my clothes. He woke instantly and grabbed his clothes.

It looked like my barn was on fire! I grabbed the fire extinguisher and handed it to John. It took a few seconds to put on jackets, boots, hats, and gloves as it was near zero out, and then we ran outside.

Flames were licking up the side of the building. Someone had tried to set my *metal* pole barn on fire! John made short work of the flames with the extinguisher before I even got a shovel out to start tossing snow on the building. I could smell the gasoline on the ground in the fire-heated slush. If that gas had reached the 4x4 wooden studs, it could have been disastrous. My car was in the barn, along with the drums of gas and the chickens. I sank to my knees in the snow, shaking.

"Who would do this to me? To us?"

"Let's get back inside," John said when he pulled me off the ground and led me back to the house. "Stay here," John commanded, "I'll be right back."

A few minutes later, he returned with a bucket filled with snow and glass, the remnants of what had caused the fire. It was a Molotov cocktail.

* * *

The New Year started with blue skies, glorious sunshine and the memories of last night's fire. I reached over to find John's side of the bed empty, the sheets already cool. I quickly slipped into sweatpants, my warm robe and slippers, and went in search of him.

He looked up from the table and smiled. "Let me get you some coffee," he said. We both drank it black because milk and coffee creamer was a luxury that I hadn't factored into my preps. The few cans of evaporated milk that I had needed to be rationed.

"You're up early," I said, sitting down across from him and sipping the hot brew, thankful that the stove was already going and the room warmed.

"I didn't sleep well, either," he said.

"Sorry I disturbed you." I frowned.

"It wasn't you; it was the fire that disturbed me. We need to think about who would do this," he said to me with a touch of anger.

"Trying to burn down a metal building seems stupid, unless it was only a warning. But a warning about what? And from who?" he thought aloud.

"I've been thinking all night and all I can come up with is that somebody is mad that I pushed for gas rationing. Though it doesn't make sense to use up gas making bombs to get more gas. If anything, I should tighten the rationing!" I exclaimed out of frustration. "I think I'm going to talk with Ken and Karen this morning."

"I'll come with you. I don't want you out there alone," he said resolutely. Reaching for my hand, he added, "*You* were the target, you know. Not me, not us, *you*. No one knows that I'm here except for your family and they wouldn't hurt you."

"We can't both leave. Someone has to stay here, John. What if they come back and toss a gas bomb at the house? If no one is here, the place will burn down! Even if we were both here, there could still be extensive damage because the siding is all wood."

Then it dawned on me. "John, we don't have another extinguisher. I had only the one!"

I slumped back in my chair. Damn! I should have had a spare! It was a minor item, and was now a major hole in my preps.

Reluctantly, he agreed to allow me to go alone, provided I promised to come right home when done with the meeting. I did tell him about the new patrol car and that if it was ready I intended to deliver it today. That didn't sit well with him, but I still had a job to do and he reluctantly accepted that. When I left the driveway, I followed the snowmobile tracks out our road while I could, then they disappeared once I hit the main road.

* * *

Both Karen and Ken were surprised by the attempted arson. I handed the small ice cream bucket of "evidence" to Ken. They were no closer to a suspect than they had been before. Lenny was under constant surveillance so they knew that it wasn't him. However, this was the first time that anyone had heard the vehicle. There were plenty of snowmobiles in town, so it only narrowed the list down slightly.

"This is the first attack on a personal residence. The other fires have been on unoccupied businesses," Ken said, thinking aloud and trying to process the information. "On the other hand, he might be getting bolder. Anyone you've ticked off lately, Allexa?"

"Only half the town," I said. "Everyone blames me for the gas rationing, not that there is anywhere for anyone to go. I've offered gas to anyone who wants to leave and not come back. Otherwise, I've really tried to help Moose Creek, not hurt it. So, what should I be doing? Anything special? Different?"

"Well, we know that you're armed, so that's a good start. Too bad you live alone," said Karen.

I told them about John, and that he was staying with me. Karen was pleased, though Ken wondered if the attack came from a past spurned boyfriend. I laughed.

"Ken, I haven't even dated anyone in over two years, and I've never dated anyone from town anyway. Besides, no one knows that John is staying with me except my family, and now you two. It wouldn't explain the attacks on the businesses."

"Well, just be extra cautious, be aware of your surroundings. Watch if anyone is following you," Karen reminded me. I rolled my eyes at her and she laughed.

* * *

The paint job was not quite finished on the new patrol car, so I went back home to find John happily cleaning my shotgun.

I pulled a couple of cookbooks into my lap and worked on menus for the week. What we were eating was getting boring, and it was time to fix that.

I can't dwell on the fire. Cooking is a good diversion for me, so I picked something for dinner I haven't fixed in a while, stuffed manicotti. I cooked three manicotti tubes in some boiling water until they were softened. I didn't want them too cooked or they wouldn't absorb the tomato sauce. I drained a jar of chicken, reserving the liquid for soup tomorrow, and then shredded a half-cup of the meat into a bowl. I added one slice of bread, torn into pieces, a minced onion and a quarter cup of shredded Parmesan cheese. I tossed that all together, mixing in some herbs for extra flavor. Handling the pre-cooked tubes gently, I stuffed in the meat mixture and set them aside. The tomato sauce had already been made and canned last summer. I poured enough of the contents of the jar into a baking dish to cover the bottom, and then placed the pasta tubes on top. The rest of the sauce went over the top and then the pan went into the oven to bake.

* * *

We spent a leisurely morning on the 2nd just enjoying the quiet and each other. It was close to eleven o'clock that we finally lit the fire and had our first coffee of the morning. A truck pulled up in the driveway after we enjoyed our first sips of the black brew. Naturally we went on alert, but it was only Karen. When I introduced her to John, she—and he—relaxed.

"There was another fire overnight, up on the dam road," she began. "No, it wasn't Jason's house. It was Marjorie Brewer's and she at was home." Karen took a deep breath and eyed my coffee cup. I poured her a cup and she continued. "Now we've got him for arson *and* murder. There were snowmobile tracks circling the house. We're closing in, Allexa, but you can't let your guard down."

"I won't, Karen. Promise. John won't let me," I laughed to break this tension.

* * *

I went to the office long enough to pick up and deliver the new patrol car. What made it easy was that Ken and Karen were both at the township going over maps, marking where the fires had occurred. I left my car in the parking lot and walked over to the auto shop. I gave Harry a voucher for payment and drove the car over to Fram's, filled it with diesel, signed the receipt, and went back to the office. Our two police officers were just coming out and had huge, astonished grins on their faces when they saw the sign on the side of the car that read "Moose Creek Township Law Enforcement."

"This is a gift from Marilyn Harris. It's her way of apologizing for Bill's actions," I said as I handed them the keys. "It's all gassed up and takes diesel fuel. You have an unlimited account for it, but remember we don't have unlimited supplies."

"If it's from Marilyn apologizing for Bill, maybe *you* should have it," said Karen.

"Oh, no! Besides, she was specific that it should be for you two. How is the investigation coming?"

"We think we know who it is. I don't want to say anything at this time, not until we're positive," said Ken.

"Are you going to need back-up? I'd suggest Lenny," I said, much to their surprise. "He's got a CPL and is a very good shot. It would also go a long way to pulling him back into the respectability in our town."

* * *

Late in the afternoon on January 3rd, Karen stopped by. She gratefully accepted a cup of coffee and one of the scones I had made this morning, not questioning baked goods. I wonder if she would get the joke if I made donuts for her.

"There was another fire last night," she said. "One of the camp cabins on the Sullivan Trail. Fortunately it was not occupied. I just don't know what to make of this. The fires seem to be random, yet they are not. Any ideas?"

"Have you been over any of the lists Anna and I made in November?" I asked. "We compiled lists of all those who needed medical continuance, the elderly, those who live alone, and are rural, of the CPL holders." I caught her quick glance at the CPL remark and smiled. "Don't ask! Yes, I know who they are."

"Can you make this any stronger?" she asked, extending the coffee cup towards me.

John pulled a bottle of whiskey from a cupboard and showed it to her with raised eyebrows.

"Oh, yeah," she said excitedly. "It's always five o'clock somewhere. No, I haven't seen those lists; I suppose I need to. I think we can eliminate some of the elderly. Most can't handle a snowmobile like that."

She sipped her fortified coffee and sighed. "What about the medical list? Anything peak your interest?"

I retrieved a folder of things that were ongoing in the township since the event. I flipped a few pages and turned it to her. When her eyes scanned the list, something caught her attention.

"Can I take this?" she requested.

"John, will you start the generator?" I asked. "I'll make you a copy. The medical list was viewed by Gray and then enhanced," I said to Karen. "Someone catch your attention?"

"Yeah. Someone that is already on our radar is on that list," she said. "If it's any consolation, if it *is* who I think it is you're not a target. It really may have been all random."

* * *

JOURNAL ENTRY: January 3

This arson business has me confused and concerned. Everyone left here in Moose Creek *wants* to be here. They love the town and the people in it. It doesn't make sense for one of our own to do this kind of damage.

* * *

When I put my coat on this morning to feed the chickens, I found a couple of slips of paper that I had put in my pocket the last time I was in the office. These were phone messages that I had forgotten about. One was from Pastor Carolyn and the other was from Tom White at the County EM office. I was curious what he wanted. I had inkling what Carolyn wanted.

John was not happy that I wanted to go to the office again without him as my bodyguard. I reminded him that all the attacks had taken place at night, and I would stay at the office once I got there.

I drove to Jason's first. It had been over a week since they were over for Christmas and I needed to know that they were okay. When I neared his place, I saw the burnt out shell of the Brewer house, ringed with police tape.

With Amanda at home to watch Jacob, Jason was out cutting wood for the stove. The house was on the chilly side, so I kept my coat on.

"Did you bring any food with you?" Amanda asked when I walked in.

"No I didn't. If you make a list of what you need I'll do what I can."

She snorted. "Mom, we need *everything*. I should have listened to you about stocking up."

I knew better than to say I told you so.

Jason came in right then with an armload of snowy wood. After setting it down near the stove to dry, he gave me a hug.

"Did either of you hear or see anything around the time of the fire next door?" I asked them while Jason warmed his hands over the woodstove.

"No, we slept right through it," Jason said. "Amanda and I put some blankets on the windows to help hold the heat it, and they also muffle the noise. Ken and Karen were already here asking us questions. I'm sorry we couldn't help."

"I'm just glad you all are okay. Don't forget to get that list together, Amanda," I said, and gave each of them a hug before I left.

My next stop was Carolyn. Luckily, I tried the church first and she was there, helping out in the Stone Soup Kitchen.

"I'm so glad to see you!" she said, giving me a brief hug. "Let's go upstairs to talk. I was hoping to see you at church last Sunday." We went up a short flight of stairs to her office.

"Food donations have really fallen off, Allexa. Is there any chance you can help us out again?" she asked sheepishly. "We've had some fish, but it's been so cold that the fish aren't biting like they usually do."

"My own supplies are limited and dwindling, Carolyn." I noted how her face drooped with disappointment. "Would another bucket of rice help? I think I've got some bouillon too. That will be the last though, I'm sorry." I knew I had more, but I can't be *everyone's* supply line, and the people have to learn to stand on their own. I prepped for *my* family, not the whole damn town!

* * *

The township offices were in an uproar. It seems that there was yet another fire last night: the Catholic Church, and this time there was also a witness!

"I was walking home after having a beer at The Jack," Lenny said excitedly, "when I heard a snowmobile coming up behind me. I stepped closer to The Out-Riggers to get out of the way and must have been out of sight. This sled raced by, then slowed in front of the Catholic Church and I saw the driver throw something," he continued to his captive audience. "A few seconds after the sled took off again there was a burst of flames up the front door!"

"What happened then, Lenny?" I prompted him.

"I ran across the street and scooped up snow and threw it at the flames, over and over." He took a breath and went on. "My hands were numb but the fire was contained. Then I called Mike to make sure the fire was completely out." He smiled proudly.

"You did good, Lenny. You saved the church." He grinned even wider.

* * *

Ken and Karen have made an arrest!

When I went to the office on the 4th, I found our team of deputies in a back office, with Junior Simms handcuffed to a chair. Karen spotted me and came out, closing the door behind her.

"Junior? Are you sure?" I asked. Junior was in his late twenties and had never caused any real problems, even when he drank too much at the Jack. I heard he had been a troubled teen, getting into fights and vandalizing public property, though he seemed stable in the past years and lived alone in one of the older homes on the edge of town, working odd jobs to pay the rent.

"He's already confessed, now he's babbling," Karen said. "Once we picked him up, Gray went through the house looking for meds or drugs. What he found were empty prescription bottles, and confirmed that Junior was being treated for schizophrenia and paranoia. He was on a literal cocktail of mood stabilizers. Every fire target was totally random. He thought that someone was after him, but didn't know who. He just drove around until a voice in his head told him to stop. Weird, huh?"

Then she smiled. "We got him now, in part to your lists. He showed up several times. I just don't know what we're going to *do* with him!"

"What do you mean?"

"We don't have a jail. We don't have *anything* up here. I'm afraid that if we try keeping him here, even overnight, the town folk may lynch him! Ken thinks we should take him into Marquette, and let them deal with him."

"That might be for the best. Congratulations on the arrest, Karen. You and Ken deserve our gratitude. Oh, and you might want to call Sherriff Lacey *before* you make the trip to town with your prisoner."

* * *

While I was there, it was time to make the phone call that I had forgotten about.

"Tom, Allexa Smeth in Moose Creek, returning your call. I hope you've got good news for us up here, like some food?" I said after he picked up on the fifth ring.

"Uh, no, sorry. How would you like a job though?" he asked, getting right to the point.

"A job? What do you mean?"

"I need help. An assistant. You've already had the training, and I think you would be perfect."

"Thanks for the confidence, Tom, but I'm needed here. I must decline," I said politely.

"Just think about it, okay?" he said and hung up abruptly, like Liz used to do. Apparently he got *that* part of the job down quickly.

John was delighted about the news of the arrest. It was a night to celebrate: steaks on the grill, a baked potato, and some canned coleslaw, topped with one of the few bottles of wine left.

CHAPTER SIXTEEN

"A job in Marquette?" John asked, clearly not happy with the news when I told him.

"Don't worry, I'm not going to take it. I thought you would like to at least know about it." I was a little affronted that he was angry with me about the job offer.

"I'm sorry for snapping at you like that, I'm just tense that's all. These past two weeks have been…"

"Been *what*? I thought you were happy here," I said with concern.

"Oh, I am, *I am*. That's part of it. It's all been overwhelming. You. Here. I really thought I was going to die, Allex, and now… Marquette is so far away and it's still dangerous. I don't want anything to happen to you, that's all."

"Well, I'm not taking the job, I already told Tom that. I'm not going anywhere." We were both on edge, and we needed a diversion.

"I know that I said that one of us needs to stay here, but with the arrest of the arsonist, I think we can bend those rules a bit." I smiled up at him. "How would you like to go to Bob and Kathy's for dinner? We'll take the food over. Besides, I think that we need some company other than each other."

"I think that's a great idea," he said with his soft North Carolina accent that melts my insides.

* * *

Karen took my suggestion and called the Sheriff's office before transporting Junior Simms. The dispatcher turned down their request because the jail was at double capacity already. Then they were told to deal with it themselves.

Downtown Moose Creek once had a courthouse, town offices and a jail. After the new modern offices were built, the building was sold and has been the Down Riggers Bait and Gift shop for two decades. Part of the gift shop includes the old jail cell on the lower level. Ken contacted the owners this morning and asked to use the old jail cell for a few days. The owners reluctantly complied. Ken went to Fram's and got a chain and a padlock to replace the dismantled old locks. It should help to keep Junior secure while they decided what to do with him. Despite the fact that they tried to keep Junior's whereabouts quiet, word still got out.

* * *

"Kathy? Bob?" I called out several times while I pounded on their front door. After a few minutes, Bob opened the door, the chain still engaged. When he saw it was only us, he removed the chain and opened the door.

"We can't be too cautious right now, you know," Bob explained when he saw me looking at the rifle in his hand.

"No problem, Bob, I think that's wise. Can we come in and visit?"

He led us downstairs to the basement, which was decidedly warmer than the living room, though still cool. Kathy greeted us both with hugs and John set the picnic basket down on the covered pool table.

"What's this?" she asked.

"Well, we needed to get out and I thought it would be nice to visit," I replied while I unpacked pasta, sauce, corn, canned salmon, eggs and bread. "And bring dinner with us. Hope you don't mind the intrusion," I said, which got a laugh out of both of my friends.

We cooked the pasta on the grill then poured the sauce into the same pan to heat. After slicing up the bread, we took our full plates and sat near the fireplace to eat.

"In spite of what a simple meal this was, Allexa, it sure tasted wonderful," Kathy remarked as she sopped up the last of the sauce with a piece of bread and Bob poured more white wine for all of us.

The guys had just stepped out to the enclosed porch for a cigar when we heard the gunfire.

John rushed back in, his calm buzz gone. "That sounded like a .22! And it was close." Another shot rang out, then another. "A .223 and a .38." John could distinguish the sounds, which surprised Bob.

"Three different calibers. Someone might need help," I said.

Bob looked at Kathy and said, "You stay here, please! And lock the door behind us!" He looked at us. "What do you have?"

When I told him that we both had nine-mils, Bob grabbed another rifle and handed it to John. The three of us left the basement, went upstairs and out into the street. When we cleared the tree line, the frozen grass crunching beneath our feet, we saw a group of guys with rifles or clubs in hand, running in all directions from the gift shop. One stopped and looked at the three of us. Bob and John instantly leveled their rifles at him. The guy turned away and ran down the street away from us.

* * *

Ken decided to take the first shift of guard duty so Karen could go home and catch a nap. He was caught unaware when a dozen men stormed the building.

"Get out of the way, Ken. We want Junior. We don't want to hurt you," Buddy sneered, leading the group of locals.

"Carl," Ken said, using Buddy's given name, "you don't want to do this. Just go on back home now, all of you." The crowd was forming in the store. When nobody moved, Ken racked the twelve-gauge shotgun, chambering a load, making it ready to fire. The liquid courage Buddy had fed his friends faded fast with the resistance to their demands. A second shotgun was heard racking from behind and Karen appeared in the doorway with her shotgun ready. Then Lenny stepped around her and leveled *his* gun at the mob.

"This isn't over, Ken," Buddy threatened, encouraging his followers to leave. At the last minute, Buddy turned back and fired at Junior, who was curled up in a corner. Ken used the butt of his shotgun on the back of Buddy's head, knocking him out. The shot, which echoed through the building, ricocheted off the old walls, sending out a shower of plaster and dust, missed its target.

Once the first shot rang out, the crowd started to stampede, and someone tripped or was shoved and his gun discharged, sending the round wild, hitting Karen. No one really knows yet who fired the third round that hit Ken.

* * *

Karen staggered out of the gift shop and leaned against the doorjamb. Once she recognized us, she slumped over. Lenny, a former member of the EMS team, was tending to Ken, who had taken one in the shoulder. Karen had a graze on her calf. Junior was still curled up in the corner, and Buddy was now handcuffed to the bars.

Inside the Down Riggers, I used the still working landline to call our fire chief, who used his 800 radio to call Gray. Since Gray was taking a rotational turn sleeping in the Fire/EMS building, he arrived in minutes. He took over working on Ken, while Lenny cleaned and dressed Karen's calf.

"Karen, what the hell happened here?" I yelled frantically, no longer containing myself.

* * *

I borrowed Gray's radio to get to dispatch and demanded to talk to Tom White, and I was pissed enough that I was put right through to him.

"We now have both of our officers down and *two* prisoners instead of one, because *your* dispatcher wouldn't take an *arsonist and murderer* off our hands! And you want me to *leave* here?" I yelled, trying to explain what happened here.

119

I was mad, really mad.

"Have Gray transport Ken to the hospital. I'm sending two scout cars. I'll find out about dispatch on this end," he said after I explained the situation. Then he hung up.

Karen was shaken, but doing okay otherwise. When the backup arrived, she went home. One police cruiser took the two prisoners to Marquette, while the other parked himself at the EMS building.

CHAPTER SEVENTEEN

"I'm correcting an oversight," I said as I placed a long Styrofoam box on the kitchen table.

John unfastened the tape to reveal an AR15 in its original Cosmoline packing grease, and still wrapped in plastic. He looked like a kid being handed the keys to the candy store.

"You'll have to clean it up of course," I said. "Considering yesterday, I think we should have the heavier firepower, don't you?"

While John cleaned the rifle, I worked at putting a casserole together for Karen. John leaned over my shoulder. "Looks good, when's dinner?"

"This one is for Karen. Want to take a quick trip with me?"

* * *

Not only was Karen home, so was Ken, which surprised me. He sported a sling and she had a limp. They were both in good spirits, and also pissed off, so this was a good sign.

"Ken, can you shed any light on who shot you?" John asked.

"Not at all," Ken frowned. "Once I saw Karen there, I knew that I was good. Lenny was a bonus. You were right about him, Allexa. Anyway, my attention was drawn to Buddy and Junior. I didn't see anything. They definitely pulled a .38 out of me. It's not something that *we* use anymore, only .357s, and the shotguns."

"I've got a question that has been puzzling me, Ken, please don't be offended," I said carefully. "I'm wondering, considering the scope of the offenses, why didn't you just execute Junior right away? Obviously, that's what the townspeople expected, or they wouldn't have confronted you yesterday. Way out here, we're in a 'wild west' situation, and on our own. No one questioned the Harris situation, have they? It was justified. Wouldn't it also have been justified to terminate Junior?"

There was a long pause before Ken answered. "I've been thinking about that all night. Perhaps it would have been the thing to do, but I spent twenty-eight years on the police force, arresting those who took the law into their own hands. It's a hard thing, a *very* hard thing to be on the other side now. It crossed my mind when we first arrested Junior, I'll be honest about that. I couldn't do it though," Ken replied while nervously shifting his weight in his recliner. "What if I had shot him? And what if the world comes back to normal next week? I would have that boy's death hanging on me for the rest of my life. Yes, he's crazy, *right now*, without his meds, but with them he was a ghost in this town, quiet and unseen, and not bothering anyone. I went to school with his mother. I've watched him grow up," his voice hitched. "I just couldn't do it, Allexa. Can you understand that?"

"Yes, I can, Ken. You might want to think more about it, though, because it's bound to come up again, maybe soon. People are getting hungry, real hungry, and with the deeper snow now, hunting is sporadic at best. There's bound to be more violence, more theft, and then what are you going to do? What are *we* going to do? Stealing food could become a hanging offense." Our two new officers had nothing to say. "We should go so you both can get some rest. Tom will want his officer and cruiser back soon."

I left the casserole on the table, leaving them to figure out how to heat it.

* * *

On the morning of the 7th, I made some quick calculations regarding a five-gallon bucket of rice. It holds thirty pounds, which equals seventy-five cups of raw rice, which is one hundred and fifty cups cooked. At one-quarter cup of cooked rice per serving, that's six hundred servings in a bucket. With fifty people left in town that doesn't cover two weeks' worth of food. They will just have to make it stretch even further. I took one more bucket of rice and a one pound carton of salt to Pastor Carolyn and told her it was the last, and I had shared all I could. She said she understood and thanked me for all I had done. I decided against adding the pasta or bouillon and I'm confident Carolyn will keep my donations a secret. I know I could give her more, however, that would only encourage dependency on the part of the town. They now needed to stand up on their own, leave, or die. Many of them would indeed leave when this bucket ran out. Would it be too late to go to the city? Would they even be allowed in? I should ask Tom White about that next time we talk.

* * *

I walked into the house after my visit to Pastor Carolyn. Jason and Jacob were there visiting with John and I swept Jacob up into a hug, which made him giggle.

"Where's Amanda?" I asked Jason when I saw the sadness in his eyes. "She went back to Marquette, didn't she?" I asked flatly.

"This morning. I begged her to stay but it didn't do any good. She hates it here. Sometimes I think she always has. She's gone to stay with Lori," he said with a tear in his eyes. "I'm out of wood to burn and the snow is too deep now for me to cut more, plus I can't leave Jacob alone. The house is really cold, and Amanda took the bucket with the last of the rice. I didn't know where else to go, Mom. Can we stay with you for a while?"

"Of course you can. We can use the extra security, too, right John?"

"Actually, we can. Did you bring your .308 with you?" John asked. He was really getting into the guns, ensuring that all of our weapons were cleaned and ready for possible use. It was a huge relief to me.

"It's out in the truck. I brought some clothes, more of Jacob's things and his school books. I wasn't really sure…"

"Jason, you know me better than that. I would never turn you away." I gave him a hug before retrieving the linens and bedding for the futon that he and Jacob would share.

"If Jason is going to be here, we need to redistribute the chores," I said to John, and then turned to Jason. "Right now, John shovels, brings in the wood, gases and starts the gennie and maintains the guns." I looked back at John. "Which chores do you want to give to Jason?"

He smiled. I knew giving him the choice would make things go much easier. "He can have the generator duty and the shoveling. If it's a heavy snow, we can share the shoveling."

John's choice didn't surprise me. I know that he really likes hauling in the wood for me. Maybe that's it; it's a chore that's a direct benefit to *me*. That's sweet. In all this violence, this mayhem, this *change*, my heart swelled with pride at the generosity of my new mate.

"I will give him the chickens to tend too," I piped in. "I've still got plenty to do with the cooking, baking, laundry and housework, though I do expect you to take care of your and Jacob's room," I said to Jason. "We all pitch in during the day to keep the stove fed."

"I think this is more than fair for what you're giving me in return. Mom, John, thank you," he said, giving me a big hug.

Jacob came into the kitchen and asked for Sponge Bob. Jason got up to take care of that. "Mom, the TV isn't working, no cable signal," he called out from the other room. That's one more thing for me to look into at the office when I have access to a real phone.

By the time I had washed two loads of laundry and hung the wet clothes on the wooden racks to dry, it was getting dark. I refilled the water buckets that I had emptied then put their t-shirts and underwear in the dryer while Jacob watched the end of a movie. I began to fold clothes and asked Jason to shut down the gennie.

John's remark about all of that pasta keeps creeping into my head. I took out a box of multi-shapes from the back and made macaroni and cheese for dinner. Even Jacob ate some!

* * *

DEBORAH D. MOORE

JOURNAL ENTRY: January 7

The past couple of days have been full, even traumatic, for most of us, and we were all exhausted. John put wood in the stove for the night. When we snuggled into bed, he told me the snow is still falling, and is already at a good six or eight inches in only a few hours.

I'm beginning to wonder if the earthquakes have had some kind of impact on the weather.

CHAPTER EIGHTEEN

Over coffee and toast, the three of us discussed the snowstorm that was still swirling around us with an intensity I haven't seen in years.

"I think we should start melting some of this snow for our water needs," I suggested. I've been through this before, years ago, and there is nothing like experience to show that a full pail of snow renders only two inches of water when melted. It's a harsh reality for those who think it's easy, and a dependable method of having water.

"I suppose when I shovel the back deck I could shovel into buckets and bring them inside," Jason offered. "Since I have to clear the deck anyway to access the generator, I might as well make it useful."

The first pail of snow took hours to melt down and produced very little water. I did this intentionally so John and Jason could see firsthand how little was gleaned from the melting.

"If we start with hot water," I said, pouring warm water from the pot on the stove into the kettle with the snow, "it speeds things up a bit. Once it comes to a boil, we will add snow." It melted almost immediately. I added more and more again, until the snow stopped melting on contact. Then I let it heat and come back to a boil. Heating warm water takes a lot less time than trying to heat the frozen water we call snow, but it's still time consuming.

"Say, Mom, what if we now start using two pots? We can double the production."

Melting snow gave my guys a new project and kept them busy while the wind howled outside. It made me smile to see them work so well together. It then occurred to me that they weren't too far apart in age.

The storm raged on. It's been thirty hours now.

* * *

The plows came by around 4 P.M. on the afternoon of January 9th. There looks to be close to twenty-four inches of snow. It's hard to tell truly how much because of all the drifting, and the winds are still blowing.

The guys are continuing to melt snow, but are losing interest. It's a lot of work for a small return. They've realized the benefit of having the generator for our water needs.

Shortly after the plows came by, so did Karen. She waded through the drifts and got within twenty feet of the house. It startled me that she was wearing a facemask.

"Karen, what's up? Why the mask?" I asked while staying on the porch.

"I needed to warn you," she said. "Ken is sick. We think that he picked up a virus when he was being treated in the hospital."

"Are you okay?" I asked with worry when she put her hands on her knees and struggled to breathe.

"So far I'm okay. I'm just out of shape," she laughed. "Besides, twenty-eight inches of snow is no picnic to walk through! Are you going to clear your driveway soon?"

"We'll get right on it. So, what does Ken have? When did it start?" I asked, knowing John and I had been there not so long ago, in close quarters with someone who is now sick, maybe very sick.

"So far it *seems* like any other flu, but I called Gray in and he called the ER. Anyway, there's an epidemic of a nasty flu going on. I thought you should know, since, well, you were in the same room with us." She paused. "Allex, it's a really nasty bug. People are dying. Dying! We've gone into isolation. You should too," Karen cautioned.

Yes, John and I were exposed to Ken, before he was contagious, I hope. At least before he had any symptoms. Maybe we were okay.

"We'll do that, Karen. We'll be okay. You need to let Anna know what's going on," I reminded her.

"Already done that."

"Thanks. Did Gray give you any indication of an incubation period?"

"It's fast, forty-eight hours."

Forty-eight hours? That *is* really fast, but if that's the case, we'll know soon enough if we were contaminated.

After Karen left I called Jason and John together. I pulled out a bin containing medical masks and gloves from the front pantry.

"We really don't need these, at least not yet," I said. "If John or I are contagious, which I doubt, then you and Jacob have already been exposed. We will have to wait and see. It won't be long if we are. This is for if we have to leave here, be in contact with others, or if somebody comes here. I feel fine, if only a bit rundown and tired, but I've felt that way since the start," I mused. I reached over and cupped John's face with my hand. "How are you feeling?"

"I'm fine, really."

We no sooner cleared one major problem and another is on us immediately. The stress alone could do me in. I left the med box there in the kitchen, just in case. Facemasks will keep us from breathing *in* germs, and also from breathing *out* those same germs. Physiological, I know… Suddenly I was very tired.

I got the garlic and D3 vitamins from the cupboard, asked the two of them to take extra doses. I did the same. I knew that Jacob wouldn't take them, but if *we* stayed healthy, so would he.

CHAPTER NINETEEN

JOURNAL ENTRY: January 11

None of us has had any signs of illness. No headaches, no fevers, no coughing. I think we've avoided the flu that Ken brought back from the hospital. I'm wondering who else might have it now? Ken was there, so was Gray, and Gray's ambulance driver, Patty. Patty is Buddy's wife, and she is also the secretary at the school.

Uh-oh.

* * *

The wind had finally died down enough for the guys to get out and start clearing the snow. Jason did the handwork around the steps and porch, plus clearing off the deck so we could get to the generator. I think they are both tired of melting snow and are more than ready to appreciate running the gennie to pump the well. While Jason shoveled, John ran the snow blower up and down the drive. Although I'm anxious to talk to Anna about Patty, I know I won't get to town until tomorrow. I just hope someone else has made the connection.

Jacob is happy with the gooey cookies that I made today. He needs the calories. I think the guys will enjoy a few too, after they finish their snowball fight they think I don't see.

Tufts came out again and moped around, and then curled up behind the woodstove. He really doesn't like all the people in the house. In spite of that, I think he's adapting.

* * *

Anna looked like hell when I arrived at the office. She had the flu. Joe let me pass only when he saw that I had on a better mask than he did. I insisted that John wait in the car. Even with a mask and gloves I wanted him away from any exposure.

I leaned against the doorjamb of Anna's office, not wanting to get too close. "How are you feeling?" I asked. It was a stupid question, but knowing the symptoms might be good.

"Like a truck hit me and then backed up." She took a breath and coughed behind her mask. I stood there waiting for the spasms to subside. That cough was deep in her lungs.

"How are *you* feeling?" she managed to wheeze out.

"I'm fine," I said, not moving so much as an inch. "I'm worried about you. The town needs you. John and I were both exposed to Ken, but it was less than twenty-four hours after his exposure. We aren't sick, neither is Jason or Jacob. I'm keeping them all isolated, though John is out in the car. He wouldn't let me come here alone, and I wouldn't let him come in," I chuckled. "Anyway, I'm guessing there is a window before the new host is contagious, and we were lucky."

"Your mask is different from the ones Gray gave us," she said weakly.

"Mine is an N99. Yours looks to be surgical. Why no gloves, Anna?" Even knowing what I had on under my mittens, I was still careful not to touch anything.

"Gray gave us all some, however, I don't see the point," she said as another coughing spell hit her.

"You need to be at home and in bed."

"I know, I know," she replied putting her head down on her desk. "But there's something that I need to do first." Although it was hard for her to stand, she insisted. She gave me the oath of office to be her official and legal deputy. I told her that I didn't want the job. It was only when she promised that it was temporary that I agreed.

"Now," she went on, "I'll go home when I bring you up to speed on the school situation. When Karen noticed Ken was sick, she called Gray and he immediately made the connection that Patty had been exposed, too; however, she had already infected two teachers and from there it went from bad to worse." She paused to take a sip of water from a bottle of water. "Don't worry. Patty isn't any worse, and she's in isolation at home. We've closed the school for classes indefinitely but it's open as a triage area for the sickest."

"How many are sick?"

"Close to half the town," she answered. "Some seem to have a natural immunity, like Gray. I don't know what we would do without him."

This flu spread really, really fast, and so far, no deaths. I hope it stays that way.

I took off my mittens, surgical gloves and mask when I stepped outside. They all went into a plastic garbage bag that I had in my pocket. After I tied it shut and set it in the back seat, John drove us home in silence.

* * *

Most autistic children have an obsession-like focus on something, often letters or numbers. Despite having high functioning Asperger's, Jacob is no different. His plastic letters are like a security blanket to him.

"If he doesn't want to do his homework, then we take away his numbers and letters until he does, and today it's his math," Jason said. He knew his son well. Jacob is really smart, but like any nine-year-old, was always looking for a way out of schoolwork. Like any autistic boy, he can be very stubborn.

"Maybe we can try a different approach," I offered. I got my sprouter out of the cold pantry and washed it. Then I got a jar of mixed salad seeds, mung beans and the bucket of wheat berries. Once everything was set up, I called a pouting Jacob into the kitchen.

"We're going to grow something today, Jacob, and I need your help." He wasn't interested until I told him he could have one letter for every twenty-five seeds he helped me with. That boy really loves to count. He counted out fifty, then one hundred, then two hundred mung beans and put them in the sprouter. When it came to the wheat berries, he protested.

"Nahna, these are too small to count!" he exclaimed out of frustration.

"Then we need to count them in a different way," I explained, and retrieved my measuring spoons. I instructed Jacob to take the two hundred mung beans out of the sprouter and measure them with one of the spoons and then put them back. Next he used the same measuring spoon to measure the small seeds.

"Nahna, we have one big T of the big seeds, and one big T of the small seeds!" he happily proclaimed.

"That's right, Jacob. Sometimes we don't have to count, we can measure," I said. He seemed pleased with himself. "You will still have to count small seeds so I know how many letters to give you." He frowned, and then I explained the other spoons. He caught on to what I was getting at real quick. Jacob was doing double-digit multiplication in his head long before his classmates were introduced to the concept on paper. He took the one-eighth teaspoon and carefully counted the small amount of seeds that he scooped out then did the math in his head and gave me a number. I have no idea if it was right, but the figure wasn't the point. I gave Jacob his baggie of letters back.

"We're not done, Jacob." I brought out a packet of very tiny seeds. He took one look and picked up the tablespoon measure and put a spoonful in the last sprouter unit. I gave him his baggie of numbers.

Jason beamed; John looked astounded.

"We're still not done yet! Now comes the fun part. We need to water the seeds so they can grow." With the seeds in the different layers of the sprouter, Jacob added some water. "In a few days they will sprout and we can eat them, but you need to help me water them every day, okay?"

"It takes daddy's seeds in the ground a lot longer to grow, Nahna. Why are these different?" Jacob questioned.

"It's because they *are* different, plus we will eat them sooner so they don't have to get as big." He seemed satisfied with the answer and then carefully walked the unit over to the table where it was close to some sunlight, and took his letters to the other room to play.

CHAPTER TWENTY

I really don't feel the need to go into the town every day. Right now, every two days or so might be necessary to stay in the loop with this flu epidemic, especially now that I'm the Deputy Supervisor and Anna is sick. Maybe Monday, Wednesday and Friday; or maybe Monday and Thursday; it will depend on how Anna is doing. Once she's better, I won't come in so often.

We stopped at the offices first. John is still my shadow, which is okay with me. I really do feel safer with him nearby. The main door was unlocked, and I couldn't find anyone inside. Since it was warmer in there than outside, I had John come in to keep me company, while I sanitized Anna's desk. With gloves and mask, I cleared all of the papers off, glancing through them to see if she'd left me any notes. They all went into a cardboard box that I had sprayed down with disinfectant. I emptied the penholder, sticky notes and everything that she might have touched into the box, until the desk was empty except for the phone, which I sprayed liberally. The place stank of cleaner, and now I was confident the room was clean. I sat down to use the phone now that I was comfortable touching it. I still left my gloves on though.

The first call was to the cable company. Yes, service was suspended because of non-payment. Geesh, it's been only nine weeks. I had paid all my bills in early November before anything had happened. It's only January 14th. I explained where I was and that without power I couldn't pay online. She took my debit card number and said that it would be turned back on by the end of the day. The rep then told me that not all channels were available anymore. Most of the news stations were shut down by the government.

Swell, now the news is censored even more than it was before.

Before making any other calls, I set up my laptop and managed to get online with the township server. I wasn't sure I'd be able to with my personal computer; I had only used the township's equipment. Only 2,759 emails behind. I skipped over to my online banking to check account balances. Everything looked to be intact and since I haven't spent anything in weeks, I had no idea what the dollar was worth. I got into bill payment and set up automatic transfers to keep things paid. If we had any power at all, some normalcy would be very welcomed, and that made me think. I switched sites and looked up my account with our power company. They aren't delivering any power, however, I'm still being charged the $25 per month surcharge. If we ever get power back, everyone is going to have a huge bill that has nothing to do with electricity. I went back into my banking and set up an automatic payment for that $25.

Next call was to my cell phone company. When I explained where I was and that it was their tower that was down, they agreed to suspend but not cancel my Internet service. They also saw it reasonable to credit my account for the prior five weeks of cell service, as they could see it hadn't been used. The rep was nice and helpful and said the first time there was activity on the phone, charges would resume.

I had one more personal call to make, but would do it after I called Tom White. He must have been sitting right there, because he picked it up on the second ring, and had apparently programmed the phone with caller ID. Makes me wonder if there are those he doesn't want to talk to. I also wonder how long it will be before I'm on that list too.

"Allexa, how are things up in Moose Creek?"

"Cold, snowy, and overall, crap. Half of the town is down sick with this flu. I'm okay so far. Anna is sick and I haven't seen her in a few days, so I don't really know what her status is. What is going on, Tom? Is there any relief in sight? And what about food? That would help us out a *lot*. And can we get any kind of meds? That would really help Gray out."

"Do you have any idea how many you have left in town?" he asked.

"Not a firm number, maybe fifty. Does it matter?"

"Not really, because I have only so much in the way of resources," he said, sounding more tired that I felt. "I will try to get you a load of food, but I can't make any promises. If, and I do mean *if*, I can get something together, where do you want it?"

"I understand, Tom, really, and we appreciate all you can do. I think the best place for any delivery would be the Fire/EMS hall. Somebody is always there. When was the last time you had any sleep, Tom?"

"I was taking a nap when you called," he said with a faint chuckle. "I've been sleeping on the couch and haven't been home in a week."

* * *

The next day, John and I went over to the school to check in with Gray. I wish I hadn't. At least John didn't see what I did.

Fully gloved and armed with my N99 respirator, I made my way to the gym area. It was horrible. The six blue cots from the emergency storage locker at the fire hall were set up along with countless numbers of mattresses lining the floor. I counted twenty beds. People were coughing, wheezing and moaning. One person was having a seizure. I didn't know what to do, so I stood there quietly, taking it all in. That's when I noticed the one mattress on the floor off to the side: several lay on it, none were moving. Gray lifted his head off of the table where he'd been napping.

He saw me and motioned for me to come closer. "Don't touch anything," he commanded. I nodded, and held up my double-gloved hands knowing he could see the two different colors of gloves. I stepped closer.

"Are you sick?" I asked him. His eyes were bloodshot, but he shook his head. "Have you slept? Eaten? You can't help anyone, Gray, if you don't take care of yourself first."

"There's no food to eat and every time I close my eyes, someone else dies."

"How many so far?"

"Pete's mom was the first. He hasn't come back since he buried her yesterday," he said, taking a struggled breath through his mask. "Five more have passed since then. The worst are the kids. We lost two of them." Gray's voice broke on that.

"I'll be back within an hour," I said and I left.

* * *

When I returned with two cases of oriental noodles Gray asked where I had gotten the food. I said I picked up some supplies from Marquette. He didn't really care as long as he had something hot to fill the emptiness.

* * *

JOURNAL ENTRY: January 15

What I saw yesterday, I still can't get out of my head. Half of the town is sick and dying. Dying! I see that mattress with unmoving bodies in my sleep, only in my sleep the mattress gets bigger and the pile gets taller.

John had to wake me a couple of times during the night to pull me out of the nightmares.

* * *

I technically did not have the authority, but I ordered two firefighters, geared up with hazmat-suits, to load all of the sick into the two EMS vehicles and drive them, and an exhausted Gray, to Marquette General Hospital.

I found Pete at his house, drunk and weeping. At fifty-five years old, he was the baby in his family. He was the one who had never married and the one who stayed at home to take care of his aging mom. I left him alone with his grief.

Moose Creek is like a ghost town now. No one is on the street anymore and no one is in any of the offices. The Stone Soup Kitchen is also empty; not even Carolyn was at the church anymore. The only way to reach anyone is to go to their house and hope that they have the strength to answer the door.

I was surprised when Anna answered the door, and relieved when she said she was doing much better and should be back in the office in a few days. Anna had lived in Moose Creek her entire life and knew how brutal the winters were. Like many of us, she had stocked up on some of the necessary supplies in November. They were eating. It may not have been well, but they weren't starving.

Patty was next. I was shocked when Carl answered the door. John was beside me instantly with his Beretta aimed. Buddy took a step back with his hands opened wide. I can't help wondering why he was released from jail. Attempted murder is still a crime.

"I've no quarrel with you, either of you," he said, casting a worried glance at John. "I was wrong and I admit it. Okay? So what do you want?"

"I'm just checking on Patty, Carl. She was one of the first exposed with this flu and I want to know how she is." I refused to back down to this nasty, angry piece of work.

"I'm doing better than I thought I would be," Patty replied from behind her husband. She laid a hand on his shoulder to move him aside slightly. She must be one with a natural immunity that could still pass the virus. "Maybe you should go, Allexa, and leave us alone."

* * *

"Karen, can I be honest? You look like crap," I said when we arrived at her house.

"Thanks," she coughed.

"Flu?"

"I'm not sure. It might be only a cold. It started a couple of days ago, but it hasn't gotten any worse. I'm just really tired, drained, ya know? Either way, you need to keep your distance. You don't want even a simple cold." She shivered. "On a good note, Ken is improving every day. He was really bad off for a while. Provided he stayed upright, he could breathe. He's been sleeping in his recliner and would have been in hog heaven if he weren't so sick. We're both really weak." She pulled the hood of her jacket up and shivered again.

"Is there anything that you need? That I might be able to get, that is," I asked, not knowing the level of their supplies or how well prepared they were.

"We could use some food, but since everyone needs some, that might be asking for the moon." She coughed again.

"Well, funny you should ask. I happened to have gotten my hands on some supplies. I took what I could."

John opened the back door of the car and took out two cases of oriental noodles. When Karen saw the soup, I thought she was going to cry. I reached in my pocket and tossed her a bottle of aspirin.

"If you step inside and close the door, we'll leave this on the porch so you don't have to come out this far," I said before we left.

* * *

"Nahna! Nahna! It's growing!" Jacob exclaimed while pulling me over to the seed sprouter when we arrived back home. Sure enough, some of the seeds were showing signs of sprouting. The mung beans were splitting apart and the wheat berries were well on the way with a hint of green showing. I couldn't help but feel good over his joyous discovery.

Jason volunteered to make a tuna noodle casserole for dinner and I gladly accepted. I'm not sick, though after all that has happened I'm exhausted to my core. I'm beginning to question how much more I can take. I'm so tired, all the time.

* * *

JOURNAL ENTRY: January 17

I'm having nightmares of bodies, piles and piles of bodies. Last night Bill Harris emerged from the growing number of lifeless arms and legs stacked on the one sagging mattress. As he pushed his way to the top, he pulled his shotgun out and aimed at me. I froze when he pulled the trigger, coughing silently through half of a face.

* * *

John shook me awake.

"What's the matter, Allex? You were thrashing about like you were being chased!" He wrapped his strong arms around me and held me close while the trembling subsided.

"It was just a nightmare. I'm okay now," I said, knowing I couldn't tell him about what I saw. I couldn't tell him about Harris either, at least not yet.

* * *

I didn't go to the office today because it didn't appear that there would be much to do. Everything was shut down. I pulled the rocker up near the woodstove, took a spicy romance novel off of the shelf and read for about an hour.

* * *

I guess I was testy last night, I don't remember. John and Jason are now avoiding me. I've always been one to withdraw when upset or under stress. I don't rant and rave. I don't yell or lash out. Maybe Jason warned John that's what he was seeing: my withdrawal. I don't know. Reading is good therapy, being busy is better. I pulled out my favorite cookbook, *A Prepper's Cookbook: 20 Years of Cooking in the Woods.*

I thought of dessert first. A fruit focaccia would be good. I checked the pantry and decided on peaches I canned last summer. Last summer seems like a lifetime ago. I assembled the sweet and rich dessert, mixing, chopping, and then set it aside to rise. I will do a glaze when the focaccia goes into the oven.

For dinner I decided on chicken patties with mushrooms in wine sauce and basmati rice. Everything except the rice was canned over the summer. Having the chickens for fresh eggs made certain dishes so much easier. I assembled all the ingredients, and then I saw Jason whispering something to John, and John smiling.

The chicken patties, made with dried herbs and homemade breadcrumbs mixed with fresh eggs, onions and garlic, then pan fried, were really tasty, especially nestled into the rice and topped with the mushroom sauce. Jacob had plain rice and scrambled eggs. Between the four of us, there was not one piece of peach focaccia left. We all need the calories.

Taking care of my family is what I do best, and is definitely therapeutic for me. I slept well for the first time in many days.

* * *

JOURNAL ENTRY: January 18

Even sleeping well, I'm having strange dreams. Last night I was back at my home in the woods, an off-grid house set in the middle of 240 acres of woods, private and serene. Sam was there, charming as ever, but was also sad and distant. Out of the back window, I saw that an area had been cleared and there was a power pole. I asked him about it. He said that was the only way. I didn't know what he meant. I told him that we never should have left there. I went back to that window and saw a subdivision containing sixteen houses, in various stages of construction, all close to each other near my wonderful, once remote home. It made my heart hurt.

When I woke up, I was sad and puzzled by what the dream might mean.

* * *

I asked John if he would like to make a social call with me. I hadn't seen my friend Dawn since this whole mess started. I realized I worried about my friends who were ill-prepared for any disaster, long or short term. Dawn didn't fit that. During the heat of the summer past, she, Guy and I would sit on their deck overlooking the lake and sipping cocktails while I answered their questions about prepping. They were the *last* ones I was concerned about.

The mile long road leading to their house was snow covered with occasional deep drifts. My all-wheel-drive car barely made it through a few spots. We pulled into their long driveway and I parked in full view of the house. I stepped out and away from the car, my hands out from my sides, empty, and called to her. I saw a slight movement at a window. A moment later, the front door opened and Dawn came running out, throwing her arms around me, while Guy stayed at the door with his rifle in hand. John got out of the car, pulled his gun and everyone froze.

"John, Guy's rifle is not a threat to us. Please holster that," I said gently. Once the Beretta was back on his hip, I felt the tension drain from Dawn. I moved to John, slipped my arm through his and pulled him over to meet my friends.

* * *

Dawn's daughter and son-in-law and the four grandchildren had made it to the remote location from a neighboring town. Shortly after the earthquakes, Kara and Matt dropped the kids off with Guy and Dawn, and went back to their house to refill the van with whatever would fit.

"Oh, Allexa, it's so good to see you!" Dawn exclaimed with excitement. "I've been wondering how you were doing. We decided to just hunker down for a couple of months. Then when the neighbors all left, we knew it had been a good choice. Now we've got this whole end of the lake to ourselves. Matt and Guy have a regular routine going for hauling water up from the lake and for ice fishing. It's been a real bitch keeping the hole open with these temperatures, but it's working. And thank you for recommending the water filtration system! We would be lost without it. Can I get you a glass of wine?"

"I knew I didn't have to worry about you. Thank you, I'd love a glass," I smiled at her. "Without you going anywhere, you haven't been exposed to the flu, then?"

"Flu? What flu?" She looked alarmed as she handed me a crystal glass filled with a ruby liquid.

I explained what was going on in town, and in Marquette. "Don't worry, we aren't sick, and whenever I've been near anyone, I've used full precautions."

I knew that with her medical background, Dawn had prepped heavy on medical supplies. I asked if she might be willing to help out.

"At this point, I'm thinking only about key people. You know Ken and Karen Gifford. They've been pulled out of retirement," I explained. "Ken is recovering from the flu and a gunshot wound. Karen was grazed in the same shootout and now has a bad cold. If nothing else, they need their bandages redressed."

Dawn looked down. I could tell that she didn't want to get involved.

"Just think about it, okay? I know you considered your talent and knowledge to be a bartering tool. This might be a good time to test it."

I left it at that.

John and Guy had slipped away, giving Dawn the opportunity to ask me some questions.

"Where and when did you meet John? You've been single and unattached all the years I've known you. Tell me all about him!" Dawn probed, pouring more wine in my glass, and then she grinned at my embarrassment.

"There's really not much to tell, Dawn. He's one of the miners, and I've been giving him a massage every week for over a year. We've been developing feelings for each other for quite a while, but it would have been improper to have a relationship. Of course, all that propriety became moot with the disaster shutting us off from everything. About a month ago he showed up at my door and he's been with me ever since." I shrugged my shoulders, not knowing how to hide my discomfort in discussing my private life, even with a close friend.

"Well, I think it's wonderful that you finally have someone!" Dawn gushed. "Tell me what's going on in town."

We chatted for another hour, with me doing most of the talking, filling her in on various events and mutual friends.

It really was getting late. That's when I noticed that Guy and John were still nowhere around. We found them in the basement workshop. When Guy found out that John knew so much about guns, he asked for help. There they were, a rifle disassembled between them. John had just finished adjusting the trigger tension and was reassembling it when I mentioned that it was time to go.

CHAPTER TWENTY-ONE

I can't avoid the office completely, though I'd like to these days. After our morning breakfast of toast and coffee, John and I left around ten o'clock for town. I'm still thankful I switched over to almost all battery clocks years ago, so I can still keep track of the time.

I was delighted to find Anna in her office. She was still tired, yet managed to give me a weak smile.

"Allexa, I don't know how to thank you for all you've done this past week," she said. Then she coughed. I backed up and pulled up the mask that was already hanging around my neck.

"It was only a tickle, don't freak." She took a sip of bottled water.

"I'm not freaking, just being cautious," I said through the mask. "So what's the story with Pete? Is he back? I can understand how upset he was about Agnes' death, but we need him."

"He's back, with a mega-hang over!" she chuckled. "The school is now empty of—"

"Okay, that's good," I interrupted, having a flashback of that mattress piled with bodies. "Are there any messages for me?"

"Nope. Were you expecting something?" She raised her eyebrows in question.

"I asked Tom about getting us some food out here. I was hoping for a note that said when it would arrive. Though, like with the diesel, it might just show up. By the way, if that happens, it will go to the EMS building next door. Someone is always still there, aren't they?"

"Yes, Gray and Patty are taking alternate shifts. I sure hope something arrives soon," she said pushing herself away from the desk. I backed up again. "Okay, I'll stay here until you leave."

I laughed. "Gray's back then?" Last I'd heard he went to town with the twenty flu victims.

"Oh, yeah, he didn't stay at the hospital. He came back with the drivers. I understand he had a couple packs of noodle soup and then slept for a day, and is doing better now that he gets regular rest." She paused. "That was the right call, you know, sending everyone to the hospital. They would have all died here."

* * *

I climbed in the car, reached across the seats, and gave John a kiss. "How about a road trip?" I asked.

"Okay," he said after he pushed his knit cap back, rubbing his hands over his balding scalp—a movement that is *so* John—and tells me he's pausing to think. "Where to?"

"Marquette." I grinned. "I think it's time that we see what's going on, firsthand."

* * *

A hundred yards before the railroad tracks that take coal from the docks, there was a roadblock, manned by the Michigan National Guard.

"Ma'am, your business in Marquette?" asked the young girl in uniform.

I pulled my emergency management identification from the visor and handed it to her. "I'm on my way to see Tom White at the Post," I said, hoping she would take my bluff. She nodded, scribbled something down on her clipboard and handed back my ID. Then she looked into the car at John. Before she could ask I said, "He's my bodyguard. Is Washington open, or should I stick to Wright?"

"Washington is open, ma'am, but Wright Street is safer," she said, stepping away from the car to let us pass.

Washington was open but not safe? My curiosity was peaked. I followed CR 695 to the end and turned onto Lakeshore away from the power plant. It was always a pleasant drive; now it was eerily void of traffic. I turned right onto Washington Street, Marquette's main drag.

The movie theater was boarded up and the marquis still showed a movie from months ago. The bank on the corner had an armed guard stationed at the door, which meant the bank was still open. An entire block of stores was now blackened rubble. I had seen enough. Across from the park, a bookstore was open and seemed to be a thriving business. It also had a guard stationed at the door, holding an M-16. The guard watched us as we drove by.

I drove us past more burned out buildings, more armed guards, and more empty faces.

"I know you still have to see Tom, otherwise I'd insist that we get out of here," John said. He was getting twitchy beside me, and he kept watching the roadside, eyes darting, looking for any wrong movement.

We pulled into the Post parking lot; it too was nearly empty. I was familiar with the procedure, having been there to see Liz several times. I hit the call button located inside the solid glass vestibule of bulletproof glass. I introduced myself and asked to see Tom. A few minutes later I was buzzed in, given a clip-on badge, and directed to his upstairs office.

"You took quite a chance coming here without an appointment," he said while leaning back in his chair and eyed me. There was a time, years ago, that we had entertained the idea of dating, but his marriage ended that abruptly. "You're looking well."

"You look like you could use twenty-four hours of sleep and a week-long cruise to the Bahamas. Besides, I'm finding that just showing up gets better results."

He laughed. "Gosh, it's good to see you, Allex," he said leaning forward on his elbows. "What can I do for you?"

"Food, Tom. Moose Creek is starving. You know that no one can get past the checkpoints without a good reason, and I doubt that there's anything in the grocery stores anyway. Anything at all, a couple cases of soup, Spam — anything!"

He pulled a notepad out, wrote something at the top, and signed the bottom. He stood up and handed it to me. It was a request form for the bulk food store! "I still wish you would consider being my assistant, Allex."

* * *

After I left Tom's office with that requisition in my hand, I felt exhilarated, giddy with excitement. We went directly to the warehouse.

At the counter, I presented the paperwork and asked what I could have. The older woman handling the bulk orders asked how many I was feeding. When I told her seventy-five, she looked up. I smiled and shrugged, and said, "A whole town. Moose Creek."

While John wandered the aisles, I sat with a checklist: flour, sugar, salt and yeast, cases of soup, veggies, pasta and bags of rice. I checked off powdered milk, cheese, dried potatoes, canned meats and fish, along with fruit, cooking oil, shortening, dry mixes for seasoning and soup base, boxes of cereal for the kids, cakes mixes and chocolate chips, #10 cans of spaghetti sauce, chili and taco sauce, oatmeal, eggs, and even bacon was available.

The lady looked over my list. "You haven't put down any amounts."

"I don't know how much I can have. We'll take anything you can give us." She nodded. "What about non-food items?" I asked, then explained about the Stone Soup Kitchen, and our recent bout with the flu, hoping to get a couple boxes of food-handlers' plastic gloves. As I was finishing, John came back to the counter.

"Can I buy something?" he asked.

"Yes."

He hurried away with a wide grin on his face.

I was surprised that we could arrange delivery for the next day at noon. I felt short of breath and felt like weeping with relief.

* * *

JOURNAL ENTRY: January 20

Tonight I laid awake and thought about that dream of my house in the woods. Sometimes dreams are just dreams. Sometimes dreams are our subconscious trying to tell us something. Maybe it's time for me to completely forget about that life and move on. That house will never be mine again and I will never again have a say in what happens to it. I've known this in my head, but it's been hard for my heart to accept it.

I read over what I had written about that dream, and Sam. Sam is tall, handsome, and a charming bipolar narcissist with a truly evil streak. He no longer lives anywhere around here. He was a part of my life for nine years and those years shaped much who I am now and why I feel the way I do.

It's time to let go of my anger and fear of him now.

* * *

I wanted to be at the EMS building when the delivery arrived, so John and I left the house at 11:30 A.M. to begin setting up. After looking things over, I was really glad we got there early because the EMS building would not work. All of the EMS and fire trucks needed to be parked inside, which left little room for the space that was needed. Back at the township offices, Pete helped us pull long tables out of the storage closet and line them up so we could organize the supplies and disperse them. First we had to move out all the crafts the Ladies Knitting group was making out of the recycled trash. We moved plant stands that were made from two oil bottles with the bottoms glued together, and then flat dishes glued to the top and bottom that created a base and a place to put a plant. There were pincushions made from tuna cans, and rugs made from scrap material.

While the stuff was being moved, I headed to the EMS building to intercept the delivery truck. The driver wasn't happy about the change in location, however when I explained that it was right next door, he was okay with that.

At first it didn't look like much, but when we took the cases out of the van, they really began to add up. Several volunteers unloaded the supplies, while I gave directions where to put things. I signed the receipt and walked through the aisles to see what we had. When I stopped at the miscellaneous table, included were six boxes of food handler gloves and a case each of toilet paper, paper towels and tissues! I wasn't quite sure what to make of the gross of gallon and quart zipper baggies; still, I wasn't going to complain.

It seemed easier to put one or two cases of something on the table, and the rest on floor underneath, where it would still be easy to reach. It was starting to take shape, and now I needed a way to hand it out. I thought about giving it all to the soup kitchen, but that defeated the purpose of everyone having a choice of either sharing it, or fixing their meals at home. First we needed a count of how many people were still here that needed to be fed.

Neither Anna nor Carolyn could agree on a number of residents remaining. It could be as few as fifty, or as many as a hundred. Those out in the woods were more self-sufficient and were hunkering down. We probably wouldn't see them until spring. Between the three of us, we decided that the bulk items, like the three hundred pounds of flour and yeast, cooking oil and shortening, soup bases, and the #10 cans should go to the Stone Soup Kitchen for community meals. It would be too difficult to divide that up. With the remainder, we selected what it would take to feed one person one decent meal per day, then gathered a week's worth so we could hand out one bag per person. They could always get a second meal at the soup kitchen, which would be more than most were getting now. We will have to keep track of who came in and when. Unfortunately, this inventory room will have to be kept closed and locked except during selected grocery days. Since I procured the food, I left it up to Anna and Carolyn on how best to distribute. I was tired, emotionally drained and ready to go home.

Before leaving, I did a quick calculation. With the food here, it looked like we could keep fifty people fed for a month. It was a good start.

* * *

It was a night for comfort food. I mixed up a large chicken noodle casserole using a jar of chicken thighs I canned in the fall with egg noodles, one of the few remaining cans of mushroom soup, a jar of my garden peas and a mixture of cheeses on top.

As I put the dish in the oven to heat, John came into the kitchen with a devious look on his face.

"What are you up to?" I asked with a grin.

"I brought you a gift," he replied. From behind his back, he brought out a bag of lettuce that he had purchased at the warehouse. He chuckled at my astonished look. Tonight we could have a fresh salad. It made my day!

* * *

I'm sure John doesn't know that I remember today is his birthday, but I do. Alone in our bedroom last night, I asked him what he missed the most.

"My family," he answered. I could feel the sorrow in his voice, and I thought of my Eric in Florida. I wondered when I would hear from him again and my heart stuttered. We were silent for a while. I thought he had fallen asleep, and then he chuckled, "And smokes."

I had forgotten that he was a smoker. Apparently he had detoxed before he came here, since it's never come up. This wasn't what I expected, so there was no covert way to ask him about his favorite foods.

* * *

We try to have meals at the table and together, so after admitting I was getting bored with toast, I asked what everyone else missed eating.

"Oh, that's easy," Jason said. "Deep fried perch."

"I want French fries," Jacob quickly added.

John looked thoughtful and then said, "Pizza, with lots of sauce and gooey cheese."

We all laughed at that, and I knew that in the back of the freezer were several eight-ounce blocks of various cheese and I was fairly certain there was some mozzarella. I knew I had stored cans of mushrooms and tomato sauce and that a stick of pepperoni was in the cooler outside. All these years that I've been prepping, I've tried hard to always have on hand enough of whatever I needed to make whatever I wanted. Now I could make a pizza!

While John was outside getting wood, I pulled Jason aside and told him of the plans.

"How does Jacob like his pizza? I can arrange the toppings for what he'll eat."

"I'd say a good size single piece would be enough for him. He always ate those mini-pizzas. Only no mushrooms, and the pepperoni needs to be cut up small. I'll do it if you want."

* * *

After he was done loading wood behind the stove, John engaged Jacob in a game of Scrabble. I know how surprised he was at young Jacob's adeptness. That boy could spell anything and he added the scores in his head quicker than John could write them down. It was delightful to me to see those two bonding.

During the afternoon class lessons, Jason had Jacob make John a birthday card. It was impossible to hide making the pizza from John, but when we sat down for dinner, Jacob gave John a hug and the hand drawn card. I could see him getting choked up.

* * *

"How did you know?" John asked me later.

"You told me months ago, maybe even a year ago," I said, remembering the time when I asked, and why. I've had feelings for John for a long time; he just never knew it. "I'm really sorry I have no gift to give you."

He tightened his grip around me as we lay there in bed. "That you even remembered is my gift. I can't remember ever being so content, Allex, so needed, so wanted or so appreciated. Thank you." He kissed me softly.

CHAPTER TWENTY-TWO

Today was the first day of the food giveaway and I wanted to be there. Surprisingly, John let me go by myself.

Before we opened the doors, I called Pam again. She answered!

"When you called before I was out shoveling snow off the steps," she said. "When I tried calling back the line was dead. Our power was out for a while, and now it's back on and steady. Our power lines are tied to another town, and that town has a hospital so it stays on."

"Oh, that's good for you, since you're all electric," I said. "I've been worried about you."

"For the few days it was down, I stayed with Peggy and Keith," Pam continued. "I know I don't always get along with my son-in-law, but I love my daughter and they have a fireplace so we burned lots of wood. It helped, though not very much."

She had learned really fast it's not an efficient way to stay warm. Pam was stocked up from summer canning, and now her supplies were starting to run low.

"I saw the National Guard a few days ago," she said. "Several trucks cruised down Main Street. They never stopped though. It was like they were just watching, observing and wanting to be seen." She was also surprised at how the locals had come together during this crisis to take care of each other. Certainly nothing like the big city she had left only two years ago. I told her I would try to call again in a week.

I returned to the main room, buoyed by talking to my sister, when the doors were opened. At first there were only a few who came in, unsure if we were really giving out food. Once the word spread more and more arrived.

Anna manned the front desk, wrote down the names, and gave each person a card for how many household members they had. Carolyn, Kathy and I filled predetermined items and predetermined amounts into a bag or a box, much like they do at the Food Pantry at the thrift store in town. Yesterday, while I was at home, they had used those boxes of baggies and filled them with bulk items. Quarter pounds of sugar, half-pound of pasta, rice and salt, all of which came from the larger bags that didn't go to the Stone Soup Kitchen. Everyone got a roll of toilet paper, a bar of soap and paper towels. There were a few complaints but the distribution went smoothly.

I was happy to see Ken come in for their two bags. Karen was still coughing and didn't want to spread her cold. Ken was trying to handle the bags one handed since his arm was still in a sling.

"Let me put those in the car for you, Ken," I offered. When I did so, he thanked me for sending Dawn over. I had seen her earlier, getting their share for the grandkids, and she hadn't said anything about going there.

"She changed our bandages like a pro, then she gave Karen a bottle of liquid cold medicine and I finally got some sleep." He laughed then got serious. "This is all a good thing," he nodded toward the building and the food giveaway. "How long do you think you can keep it up? How long before people get a bit of strength back and get mean again?"

"I don't know, Ken. We'll keep it going as long as we can." With an afterthought, I told him Pete was sleeping here partly to protect the food but mostly so he wouldn't be in his empty house. "He will want to go home eventually, of course. While we have food to give away, this building will need protection."

* * *

After three hours, we closed and locked the doors, putting a notice on the door that anyone who did not receive their share could come back at noon on Friday.

When everyone went for their coats, I had to remind them to take a bag or box for themselves. Kathy needed two bags for she and Bob, and Anna was entitled to two for herself and her husband. Carolyn wasn't going to take hers until I insisted. If she didn't want it, she could give it to the kitchen. She took her share.

"You have four people at home, you need to take yours," Kathy said with her hands on now bony hips. I picked up an empty box and held it out to her. She filled it with the predetermined amount of items while Anna made notes that we each had taken our share this week. Satisfied, we shut the lights off and locked up. I offered Kathy a ride home and drove her the three blocks. Carrying the two bags of groceries wasn't so bad, but she was still weak.

* * *

I backed the car into the barn and slogged through the fresh snow to the side door. The heat of the house, warmed by the woodstove, felt welcoming as I shed my coat and boots. I asked Jason to get the box of food out of the car for me.

John had a scowl etched on his bearded face, wrinkles furrowed in his bald scalp. "Why did you take food? We don't need any."

"I know we don't need it. If I didn't take it, then others would question that. They might suspect that we have a lot of our own supplies, which could put us in danger." I still hadn't told either of them about Harris. "Don't worry," I said, tugging playfully at his short beard. "I will either sneak it back into the supply room, or find someone to give it to."

* * *

JOURNAL ENTRY: January 25

Tomorrow when I go to the office, I've got to get some news. I haven't a clue what's going on in our country!

* * *

This morning I found out why John allowed me go to the office alone. Jason was behind it. They were both aware that the coffee was running low. That's why I had switched to tea. Jason was more familiar with my storage than John was, and knew where he might find more. The morning of John's birthday when I said I was tired of toast, Jason wanted to do something about it. He knew that I would never allow him to share precious eggs, which were sometimes Jacob's only source of protein. He remembered items that I had forgotten about, like oatmeal.

Last summer, he helped me inventory my long-term food shed, where I stored food that tolerated not only the heat of the summer, but also the freezing days of the winter. Food like the wheat berries, sugar, rice, beans and cereals like grits and oatmeal in sealed five gallon buckets. Also items like coffee. There were ten cans! I had forgotten what was in there, and my inventory list was on my silent computer. The shed was half buried in snow right now and it took both of them to dig it out enough to open the doors.

For breakfast Jason fixed steaming bowls of oatmeal, sprinkled with dark brown sugar, also from a forgotten bucket. We each had a small glass of Tang *and* a full pot of coffee. I was very touched by their thoughtfulness.

After breakfast, I went back to the office to see if I could find any news on the computer. Not knowing what filters or restrictions might be on the township owned computers, I took my laptop and was glad I did, as the place was busy. I pulled out my wad of paper towels and disinfectant, sprayed my desk and chair, and wiped it all down. Others were forgetting we were still in an epidemic. I wonder how many of them would get re-infected from carelessness.

I set up the laptop on my desk in my corner of Anna's office. I still had the view of Fram's store, and remembered watching the tanker of diesel. For a moment I wondered how that young man, Marie's cousin, was doing and if his son was well.

I brushed them from my mind. I can help only so many. Right now, I needed to know what was going on in the world. I logged on using the local server.

I was able to surf the Internet for about twenty minutes, finding only local bits and pieces that had obviously been sanitized. A little spritz of cleaner and the news was all happy again. One article caught my attention—North Korea is preparing another long-range missile test with the intent of hitting the U.S. This time they are threatening to arm it with a nuclear device. They could be trying for an EMP. That's exactly what we don't need, complete power loss!

Another news clip was on the widespread nature of the flu epidemic. Officials were urging everyone to get their flu shot—isn't that a bit late?—and to cover their mouths when coughing. Oh, good grief. People are dying and they don't want to talk about it.

Rick in Wisconsin emailed me about the new trucking routes that were being established around the fault, up through Canada! The most used route is now across the west to I-29 up to Winnipeg, across Ontario, with routes cutting off down through Duluth, Sault Ste. Marie, and Toledo, the main crossing point to get supplies of food to the East Coast and Washington, D.C.

The next email was from Ken in Texas. Our government has pulled all troops from the Mexican border in order to keep peace in the major cities. Now the Texas Patriots are manning the crossing and patrolling the border, and are doing a better job of it. Something troubled me. I did a quick search on "peace in major cities." Virtually every major city east of the fault line is under martial law and is in twenty-four hour lockdown. Every city with a population over 100,000 is under martial law, but not locked down. The Upper Peninsula has escaped this, since it falls under the category *as needed*. The largest city is Marquette, and has a population of slightly over 21,000. From what Tom told me, there are curfews and travel restrictions, yet so far, no martial law.

I closed the laptop after saving a few things to read later. Yesterday, before he "let" me venture out on my own, John asked me to wear a watch and to promise to never be gone past 4:00 P.M., unless prearranged. How can I argue with someone who cares so much about me? It was 3:35 P.M. and I *wanted* to go home. My head was spinning from all of the news.

* * *

At home I put together a batch of pita bread. It was be a great way to have Jacob's sprouts, which were now ready to eat. Fresh greens, live food, and the most nutritious thing we can eat. The warm bread stuffed with the sprouts and a drizzle of salad dressing was wonderful. Jacob wouldn't eat them, of course, and had a grilled cheese instead.

* * *

JOURNAL ENTRY: January 25

This morning I woke to more howling winds and a ferocious snowstorm outside. It was just sunny yesterday! What a cruel reminder that our weather can change literally overnight.

One of the things that I downloaded but didn't read yesterday was a listing for local ham radio operators. Perhaps there is someone local that can shed some light on the news. That will have to wait until I get back to town or we can run the generator to power the laptop.

There was something that was in the back of my mind all night about the news that I read. It occurred to me this morning that there was no mention of the New Madrid Fault quakes. None. The news has shifted back to the hurricane victims, and the upcoming Super Bowl. What a strange country we live in, where a sporting event takes precedence over a major, multi-state disaster.

* * *

Jacob had his usual scrambled eggs for breakfast plus a glass of Tang. The three of us have agreed that since Jacob has taken to the new taste, it will be his. We can take vitamins instead. Vitamins are something I hadn't given a great deal of thought, so while the storm raged outside, the three of us did an inventory.

I'm disappointed. The tub that I marked as "vitamins/medical" was half-filled with the overflow of Band-Aids & bandages. This is all we have:

3 - Nasal spray
7 - Bottles of allergy pills
2 - Bottles of Ibuprofen P.M.
1000 tablets of aspirin
1000 tablets of Ibuprofen
1 - child liquid cold medicine
1 - adult liquid cold medicine
1 bottle of eye drops
4 bottles of multi-vitamins, 890 tablets
2 - D3, 200 tablets
½ bottle of garlic tablets

* * *

We also have single bottles of lysine, calcium, magnesium, zinc, fish oil, B complex, plus various odd stuff. I really fell short on this. Calculating it out, the three of us have less than a year of vitamins if taken once a day. I should have done more. I'm saddened by my failure in this area.

CHAPTER TWENTY-THREE

I don't remember a snowier winter. The weather is relentless. Another foot of snow fell yesterday, and it's still coming down.

Jason trudged his way to the barn to feed and water the chickens, and collect the few eggs. While in the barn, he found the tub I had marked *office supplies*, which are really school supplies: blank notebooks, ruled paper, pencils, crayons, rulers, protractors and odd stuff I found. Most were on sale from the beginning of the school year. He was interested in the notebooks so Jacob could practice his writing and spelling with a few lines to do math. I forgot about the flash cards that I had put in there. Jacob is a bit beyond them, but it's still good practice.

* * *

JOURNAL ENTRY: January 26

We may have to run the generator even though it's still snowing hard. The water supply is getting low and we all need showers. I'm going to do a load or two of laundry too, and get it drying on the wooden racks. I've been doing dishes by heating water on the stove like I used to, tedious and functional. I suppose we could take showers the same way with the bucket system I've got stashed in the barn, though we still need water to do that.

There's been so much going on in our lives with day-to-day living and surviving, we've forgotten to have some fun occasionally, so John and I spent an hour playing cribbage this afternoon. I've always enjoyed playing cards and board games, but it's been so long since I've had a partner. When looking for the cribbage board, I also found the dominoes, and the Obilqo block game. Now *that* game is going to be interesting, with Jason so meticulous and John an engineer. There are a few jigsaw puzzles in the back room, and somewhere in the barn is a box full!

* * *

Jason sat down at the table with me while I was sorting jigsaw pieces.

"Mom, before Amanda left again, she said something that I've been meaning to ask you about."

"What's that?"

"She said 'tell your mother not to come after me again.' What did she mean?"

I looked away for a moment. How do I tell my son I interfered? With the truth, I guess.

"I know you had told me not to, but I made some inquiries the last time she left." I briefly closed my eyes, sighed and dropped the puzzle piece. "I only wanted to know she was okay, Jason. I have no idea what happened, then suddenly she was back. When all of you were here for Christmas, I asked her what happened, but she wouldn't tell me. Do you know?"

He leaned back in his chair and ran his hands over his face. "Yeah, I know." He was quiet a long time. "She was staying with Lori, obeying the curfews. One day when she went to see her other friend, she was pulled over. They put her in the detention center for three days. They gave her car back and told her to go *home*. The detention center is not a nice place, Mom." He looked down and frowned at the thought.

"Oh, Jason, I'm so sorry. I didn't ask for her to be sent back. I just wanted to know that she was okay. The request obviously got misunderstood. I won't ask again, I promise."

* * *

JOURNAL ENTRY: January 26

It's 10:00 P.M. as I write, and it looks like the snow is finally easing up.

* * *

I was surprised when John said that he wanted to go to church today. I agreed to go only if we sat in back. Considering this was the first Sunday after the food bank opened, it didn't surprise me that the sermon was the feeding of the masses on a few fish and a loaf of bread. We even stayed for the long social hour afterward.

In the last couple of days, the ladies of the now non-denominational church have been baking rolls or bread daily to go with the meal. A few loaves were baked and sliced to give to those who asked for some to take home. The meals have expanded too. Now there are canned beef or chicken stews over rice or noodles, chili and meatless spaghetti instead of the thin soups they had before. I asked Carolyn about the meat shortage. With all the snow we've had, the deer have disappeared back into the swamps, and hunting has come to a halt.

The congregation is down by about half. Some people are still sick with the flu, other members are afraid to come into contact with others, while a few more have died. We probably won't have a true count until spring.

I was surprised to hear the generator running when we got home.

"I promised Jacob that if he did all of his math problems, he could watch his cartoons for an hour," Jason explained when I asked him why it was on.

"*Cartoons*? Are you doing anything else? Laundry or dishes or showers?"

"I did the dishes, nothing else. Why?"

"Shut the damn thing off!" I lost it. "Look, I stored two drums of gas, that's *only* 110 gallons. The generator uses one gallon every two hours. *Two hours*! If we run the generator only two hours every day, that's not even four months of use. Every other day, it's six months. The gas also goes for the snow blower, and come spring the chainsaw and log splitter! We do not have enough gas to just be watching *cartoons*." I turned back into the kitchen, angry. I was mostly angry at myself for being angry, but also angry at the world for putting us in this situation. I sat down at the table, my head in my hands. I could hear Jacob crying, and I felt even worse.

"Mom, we'll get more gas," Jason said.

"You don't know that. You don't know if we'll *ever* get more gas! What is out in the barn may be all we *ever* have! And that will have to be rationed for our very survival!"

John placed his hand on my back and made a small, soft circle, rubbing between my shoulder blades. Then I heard him set something down. He'd gotten some ice from outside, and poured me two fingers of spiced rum. It didn't seem to matter that it was only 3:00 P.M. I took a sip and felt it burn all the way down. The second sip was better. I looked up to see him smiling while the tears rolled silently down my face.

"I should apologize," I mumbled.

"No, Allex, you are right. Jason was wrong. Do not apologize for being right."

He sat down next to me and took a sip from my glass. "Eeew! You really like that stuff?" He made a face, which made me laugh.

"I could have handled it better," I sniffed. He handed me a tissue.

"Maybe, but there's no question in Jason's mind now how you feel about this. I think you made a big impact, one that he's not likely to forget."

Jacob came into the room then and ran into my arms.

"I'm sorry, Nahna. I love you," he whimpered, hugging me tightly.

CHAPTER TWENTY-FOUR

Jason was up early to clear the driveway from the latest snowfall, which seems to be a nightly occurrence. While he was doing that, he also made a trail for Jacob to run for exercise. It's like a maze, with lots of turns and twists, all built into the massive snow banks in the side yard. In two spots, he created short tunnels for his son to crawl through. Jacob loved it and was running through the maze, having lots of fun while Jason was doing handwork with the shovel.

John was watching them from the window while I was making bread when suddenly he tore open the door and ran outside screaming for Jason. Jacob had just gone into the longer of the two tunnels near the center of the maze when it collapsed! The guys jumped the walls where they could and busted through where they couldn't, digging with their bare hands. When they finally got close enough, John grabbed Jacob's feet and pulled him out from under the snow. He wasn't breathing. I knew that John had been in several underground mine cave-ins, and that his crews were all trained in CPR. John immediately gave Jacob a couple of breaths, and Jacob started coughing.

* * *

I was so scared and so helpless. Jason sat for the longest time in the rocker with Jacob on his lap, just rocking him, holding him and crying. He almost lost his only child. Jacob was unsure why his daddy was so upset, but understood that he was, so quietly held on. It looked like he was the one trying to do the comforting.

John went back outside and broke down both tunnels, then cleaned up the paths. Later he said that there was no reason why Jacob couldn't still run the maze, but the tunnels were a bad idea.

* * *

"John! Wake up! What's wrong?" I gently shook John, then more forcefully when he didn't respond. Suddenly he sat up and gasped for breath. His clear blue eyes were clouded with a distant memory and he was trembling.

"John?" I prodded, kneeling on the bed beside him, afraid to touch him. Nightmares can have violent consequences. He took a deep breath and closed his eyes.

"I was back in the mine," he said with his eyes still closed. "The rocks overhead started crumbling down on us. Some of the men were running for the portal. Others were already buried under white rock. All of them were screaming, and I was stuck in the whiteness up to my knees, unable to move and unable to help." He took another deep breath, shuddered again, and the trembling stopped. I tentatively put my hands on his shoulders and started to massage the tension out.

"I haven't had a dream like that in a long time," John confessed. "It must have been the incident with Jacob yesterday that triggered it." He turned to me and gave me a sad smile. "I'm sorry if I scared you."

The pre-dawn air chilled our skin and we slid back under the covers. We held each other for a long time. When John finally fell back asleep, I slipped out of the bed to light a fire in the woodstove.

* * *

"Allexa, do you have any baking soda?" Dawn asked when she stopped over this morning. "I need some for a rehydration and electrolyte formula for the flu victims."

"I thought you might be making biscuits," I teased, knowing Dawn's lack of baking skills. I got a thirty-six ounce container and gave it to her.

"I understand now why Kathleen always came here first if she needed something and couldn't get to town," she mused.

I couldn't help but laugh. That was different. Kathy always wanted herbs or something gourmet like a vanilla bean or saffron.

"What formula are you using, Dawn?" I asked. I had one from a nurse friend and wanted to see if they were the same.

"Well, for electrolytes: three-fourths teaspoon salt, one teaspoon baking soda, four tablespoons sugar, three-fourths quarts of water, and one cup of juice, or all water. And for rehydration: one pint water, one teaspoon salt, and one quarter teaspoon baking soda," she replied. "So, is there something you want to barter for this?" Dawn asked, holding the container of baking soda.

"Just use it wisely," I said, slightly offended by her question.

* * *

"Jacob is fine, Jason. The cave-in was an accident and it was caught immediately. You're making everybody nervous with your hovering so please back off."

"Mom, he almost *died* because of me," Jason said with distress.

"But he didn't! Take this as a learning experience," I said taking his hands in mine, "*for you.* You're such a good father, but you need to see the different shades of the picture: All of the what-ifs that seem to go more with a mother's view. I know I use to drive myself crazy removing all the potential what-if dangers from yours and Eric's life. I learned to temper that, by focusing on the most potentially disastrous and removing that. Instead of being fearful, be grateful, Jason."

"Grateful? That he almost died?" he asked, like he hadn't heard a word I said.

"No, grateful that he *lived.* You have the opportunity to learn firsthand the consequences of certain actions. Learn it! Don't let this accident go to waste! Be watchful but don't smother him."

* * *

Anna managed to collate a census from the food pantry activity. Going by these numbers, we have fifty-two people still in Moose Creek, and maybe that many more out in the woods. So there are barely over one hundred people left in the township, out of nearly eight hundred. We've had almost twenty-five deaths, so that leaves over six hundred residents that have left. At least I will now have a more accurate number when I have to go back and beg for more food, knowing I will have to do that soon. I looked at the tables of the dwindling food supplies and wondered how long this will last those fifty-two people. Two weeks? Maybe three? Then it will be back to Marquette, and back to pleading for my town.

What are we going to do when those six hundred people start returning? At least they won't want to come back until spring. Maybe, just maybe, things will be back to normal by then, or semi-normal, or partially normal, or some sort of normal.

Who said normal is just a setting on the dryer?

* * *

"I meant to tell you yesterday that I emptied that first row of wood in the woodshed," John said over coffee.

"That's good to know. We are right on schedule." I explained how I had calculated my usage, and that each row inside the shed should last one month. Our wood was in great shape. Kindling was holding up too. This made me think we need to do a mid-winter inventory. I had Jason check the gas level, the chainsaw supplies in the barn, and the chickens' feed. I had John help me in the pantries. Mid-afternoon we had a conference to share data.

"Jason, what are your totals?" I asked. I had a pretty good idea, but this would also drive home a point about conservation and about what we had.

"The two metal cans with chick feed are near empty, and there are three bags each of feed and scratch."

"Excellent! They're using only one fifty pound sack per month of each. Three more months will take us to spring when they can start to forage again. What else?"

"It looks like there's six gallons of Bars-oil, and six large bottles of gas mix for the chainsaws. But," he hesitated, looking a bit sheepish, "one drum of gas is really low, maybe fifteen gallons left. The other drum is still full."

"We're not too far off. I think we all realize we will have to be real stingy on the gas, unless some miracle happens that we can replenish the supply. Let's not count on it though. John, please share with Jason what we added up."

"I still don't know how or why you stocked like you did, but I'm certainly not going to complain," he said. "Other than having at least four more months of wood for the stove, we have thirty rolls of paper towels, nine filters for the water filter on the washing machine, and seventy-four rolls of toilet paper." He chuckled, and then read the rest of the list.

I added, "Please remember, everything we're inventorying here might never be replaced. Ever. These are all disposable stocks." I looked at these two men in my life appreciatively. "It's been almost three months. I think we're doing really well. Especially since I had no idea how many of us there would be." I smiled at both of them, lingering on John. I think he actually blushed.

"Next is the food," I went on. "We're in really good shape there. So I think we should celebrate. What would you like for dinner tonight?"

Without hesitation, they both said, "Lasagna!" and we all had a good laugh.

* * *

JOURNAL ENTRY: January 31

Jason spent some time over at Don's today. My brother and his wife really prefer to be left alone, so I'm not surprised that we haven't seen much of them. I'm still glad Jason went for a visit. I took Jacob for a sled ride, and gave John some needed alone time.

The short road I live on is a half mile loop, with both ends connecting to County Road 695. With very little traffic, I've found it a very safe place to walk. With Jacob sitting happily in the sled, I walked near the main road, though not up to it. I wanted to stay out of sight from any possible traffic.

Towing a nine-year-old up slopes was hard work. Still, our walk lasted almost an hour as we stopped to listen to the birds, or for me to catch my breath. We had a pleasant time together, but I was glad to get back to the warmth of the stove.

* * *

"Nancy was really excited about what she's going to plant this spring in their spot over here," Jason said when we got back home from his visit across the road.

"Here, as in *my* garden? They haven't even asked me if they can use that space again. I need that area this year!" I exclaimed.

"Mom, you can't hurt their feelings. They're not only neighbors, they're family," Jason admonished me.

"Aren't I *their* family and neighbor? What about *my* feelings?" I was stunned at my son's attitude. "They've never even said thank you for the three years I've allowed them that 12x12 patch. For three years I've sacrificed what and how much *I* want to plant so they could have something, and all this time the only thing she plants at their place are flowers. Considering the events of the past couple of months, they need to adjust their priorities, and I need to plant more food!" I declared.

I'm tired of being used.

CHAPTER TWENTY-FIVE

Friday was the third of the food bank days. Only twelve days since we started, and already things are bare and running low. I try to remind myself that a healthy portion went to the Stone Soup Kitchen and they are feeding most of the people. Nobody is starving. The first box of food that was forced on me I took to the Soup Kitchen. The second box I left with a grateful Bob and Kathy. This next box I decided to divide between my two neighbors, neither of which I'd seen come in to the food bank. It was a good excuse to check on them.

John and I donned our snowshoes and loaded the sled with a box filled with half of the supplies, then set out for Doreen's house to the north. There were no tracks— vehicle, human, or animal—on the long, sloped driveway. No smoke rose from the chimney. No sounds or movement could be heard or seen whatsoever. When we got near the raised wooden porch I called out. Somehow knowing there would be no answer, I remembered the only other time I'd been here. A few years back Tufts had gone missing for three days, and I was frantically combing the neighborhood for him. I admired and envied the large wraparound redwood deck that had a view of both the woods and the wooded drive that crossed our mutual creek, but my arrival had been less than welcomed. I called out a second time. We waited a little longer and there was still no answer, no movement, no sounds.

"What now?" John asked, catching his breath from the strenuous hike up the hill.

"I think we should try David and Jane on the other side," I suggested. "From the looks of it, Doreen must have left here early on, but I know David has a generator and wood heat. Chances are good they're still here."

My house sits on ten acres, Doreen's is on twenty acres to the north, and David's is on twenty acres to the south. The distance between my two bordering neighbors isn't that great, and it was slow going on snowshoes. The plow has been by regularly, clearing only the road, not the driveways, and snowshoes are a necessity. When we walked past our house it struck me how... *lived in* it looked. The drive was cleared of snow, there was smoke curling out of the stove pipe chimney, and there was evidence of Jacob's snow angels everywhere.

Yes, it looked lived in... and happy.

David's drive wasn't steep like Doreen's, but it was just as long. I could see a heat signature waving around the smoke stack, and then heard a dog barking inside.

"David! It's me, Allexa, from next door," I called out knowing he had his shotgun already pointed at us.

"What do you want?" he asked with a muffled voice from behind the closed door.

"We've only come to check on you and Jane. I brought some supplies from town. Do you need any food?"

"Leave it there and go," he demanded.

"No, David, I won't do that. We've been neighbors for eight years. You should know by now that I would do you no harm. I just want to talk to both of you for a few minutes, that's all." When I heard a chain scraping against the door, I asked, "May we come closer?"

"Are you armed?" he asked.

"Of course we are, David, you know better than that," I replied. "You still have nothing to worry about from us."

He didn't move and didn't answer. "Do you want this food or not? I can take it back to the food bank if you don't, and we won't bother you and Jane again."

We kept our hands visible, and soon he lowered the shotgun. We walked closer and stopped fifteen feet from the house. The smell kept me from going any further. Unwashed bodies, cigarette smoke, wet dog, dog crap and dog piss.

"Stay here," I whispered to John as I reached for the box. It was light, but full. I took a deep breath and ventured a few more steps to set the box down. When I stood, I noticed the antenna tower behind the house.

"David, do you have a ham radio?"

"Yeah, but it don't work. No gas for the generator. It needs electricity to power up."

"I could get you some gas, if you would let us listen to some real news."

Jane stepped up behind her husband. She looked awful. I could see how thin she was even through all of the layers of clothes that she wore to stay warm. Her hair was matted and dirty and her movement sent a fresh waft of eye-watering smells my way.

"Gas just to listen?" David asked warily.

"How long have you been without the generator? What else does it run?"

"It runs everything, especially the well," Jane said. "We ran out of gas around Christmas. Siphoned some from the car, but there wasn't much there."

"You've had no water for the past six weeks?" I asked, astounded. "Why didn't you ask for help, David? We're right next door!"

"Why would you help us? Besides, we got along. We melted snow," he answered. "Though it does take a long time and it's a lot of work."

"Don't I know it," John muttered.

"Because we're neighbors, that's why! You got an empty gas can? I'll get you some gas and another box of food from the pantry. We'll talk about the radio when we come back." I tossed the empty can he handed me into the sled and we left.

When we were up on the road and out of earshot, John said, "I don't know if I can go in that house. The smell…"

"I know, but I've got a plan."

* * *

Back home, I took the other box of supplies that we had split and added hand soap, shampoo and deodorant from my own supplies.

"If we give it to them this way, they won't know that it didn't come from the pantry," I said in answer to John's questioning look. "Will you run into town and fill that gas can?" I found my wallet with the extra gas ration tickets, pulled out two that were printed with "two gallons" and signed it. "Four gallons for now and more if this works out."

John smiled. He says so much when he says nothing. It tells me he trusts what I'm doing. I don't know if he realizes how much that means to me.

* * *

Two hours later we reloaded the sled with the gas and the other box. Although we didn't really need our snowshoes for walking the road, we wore them anyway. David's drive was covered with several feet of snow. He won't be driving out until after meltdown.

When we approached the house, I called out again. David opened the door immediately, and again we were assaulted by the rank odor.

"I wasn't sure you'd be back," he said.

"Well, we had to get the gas from Fram's. There's only four gallons here because gas is rationed." I set the can in the snow, and then picked up the box. "Here's more food and supplies. Since it looks like you won't be driving out for a while, I can get your share when I pick up mine, if you want me to do that for you."

"That would be great," he said hesitantly. "You want me to fire up the ham now?"

"No," I told him. "Why don't you use the gennie to pump water? I'm sure that you and Jane would love to have a hot shower, get cleaned up, have something to eat and run the vacuum. We'll come back tomorrow." We turned to leave and I glanced back. "Oh, and David? You're welcome. Neighbors *do* help each other."

* * *

JOURNAL ENTRY: February 7

I waited until the afternoon to go next door to give David and Jane more time to clean things up. Armed with surgical masks sprayed with a touch of perfume, John and I made the trek through the snow to go next door.

When I called out our arrival, it was a different person that answered the door, so it seemed. David was shaved, showered and had on clean clothes. He smiled when he opened the door, though it faded quickly.

* * *

"Come on in, you won't believe what I've been hearing on the ham," David said, opening the door wide. We put on our masks and went inside. I had never been in their home before. A small mudroom blocked the main entrance from the weather, and led into the living room, which held the woodstove, a now silent flat screen TV, a couch with a floral sheet pulled over it, various end tables, and the ham radio set up in a corner. Off to the left was the small kitchen, made smaller by the battered table and two mismatched chairs. A hallway was along the outside wall that led to the bedrooms and bathroom. A pile of dishes was still soaking in the crowded sink; otherwise the countertops were clear and clean.

Jane emerged from one of the back rooms and saw our masks on. There in front of me stood the woman I remembered. Her shoulder length chestnut brown hair was clean and brushed, and barely sweeping the dark pink sweater she wore. Her weight loss was more obvious with how the clean jeans hung on her hips. She no longer had the matted hair and vacant eyed look.

"What's with the masks?" she asked.

"I wasn't sure what we would find in here. When I got close yesterday, it smelled pretty bad. It's not my intention to offend you, but we all do what we gotta do, ya know? Besides, you probably don't know about the flu epidemic in Moose Creek. We just don't want to take any chances."

"I know it was a mess in here. I've been cleaning all day. It was impossible to wash anything without water, and what little we melted we had to use for drinking."

"I was listening to the radio some last night and again this morning," David said in a serious voice. "There's a gang on ATVs working their way up 695, heading this way."

"Was there any word on where they are now?" I asked in alarm. It's a long road between here and Marquette, over thirty miles.

"They were last seen at Ravens Perch."

Ravens Perch was a long bypass off of 695, several miles away. There were some nice homes and some older homes, and there were at least fifty and that would keep a gang occupied for a few days. There was very little between Ravens

Perch and Moose Creek, only a small settlement of a dozen houses called Midway. The gang was close.

"David, this is valuable news. I need to get this information to Ken and Karen. Maybe we can set up roadblocks or something." My mind was reeling. If the gang was heading to Moose Creek, we here were first and on their way.

"Ken and Karen?" he questioned. "I thought they were retired."

"Once all this started, they were pulled out of retirement by Sheriff Lacey. Law enforcement just doesn't exist up here, you know that. They've been doing a good job and we're lucky to have them." I turned to John. "You can stay and see what else you can find out. I have to get to town and warn them."

"I'll go with you, and we can come back later," he said, not wanting to stay. David and Jane were strangers to him.

"That okay with you, David?"

"Sure."

"Keep listening and write down anything that you think we should know," I reminded him.

Our first stop was Ken and Karen's house; they weren't there. I wasn't hopeful about the township offices since it was so late in the day, so we tried Anna's place. George said that she was at the office.

When we arrived at the township building, Anna, Ken and Karen were all there. I wasn't the least shy about interrupting their huddled conversation.

"Have you heard yet about the gang coming this way?"

"We found out a few minutes ago," Anna answered. "We really need to get you a radio or some way that we can reach you."

"How did *you* find out?" Karen asked.

"David Myers' ham radio. The latest word was the gang is at Ravens Perch," I said. "Have you thought of anything yet to stop them?"

"We were looking at the maps to see where the best place for a blockade would be," Ken said.

"I would suggest Big Guppy Creek. It's swampy on both sides. A load of timber would seal it off," I said. When he raised his eyebrows at me, I said, "Hey, it's my job to think of the worst case scenario. The Little Guppy is too close to where they are now and we need as much time as possible. Next we need to seal off 150 at the Hairpin, though that will depend on if it's been kept open. The snow is our best barricade if not, but that's secondary. The Big Guppy is our best hope of stopping them." I tapped my finger on the map. "We need a logging truck, already full would be ideal. Who's left in town?"

"I'll go talk to Danny Greenwald. Danny always has a few hundred logs stacked nearby," Ken replied.

"You look troubled, Allexa," Anna said when she sat down across from me.

"If we can't stop them, they'll be heading for Moose Creek, pillaging everything in their way. My plowed road is like a neon sign," I stated. "Is there any chance of getting reinforcements from Marquette?"

Anna scowled. "We tried that first, with no luck. In fact, it was Lacey who called to warn us. That was less than an hour ago."

"It's time that we organize our own militia."

It troubled me that the county sheriff waited to tell us about this threat.

"I agree. I think we certainly have enough guns in this town," Anna chuckled. "But do we have enough ammo?"

"Our shooters will just have to make every round count."

I mentally calculated what I had for our weapons, thankful that I had stocked up before the government controls went into effect. I hoped others had done the same. The government knew that they couldn't take our guns, so they took the ammo instead.

"Why would Sheriff Lacey warn us then not help us? That's confusing to me," Anna said, resting her chin in one hand.

"Anna, they want everyone *in* Marquette. They don't want us rogue communities functioning, that's why our power was shut off. It's a matter of control. Control the power, the food, the gas, everything, and you can control the people."

She stared at me in disbelief.

"Have you had any communication with other officials?" asked. She nodded.

"I'm going to bet that in spite of the surface helpfulness, they really haven't done anything."

She nodded again.

"I'll venture that they suggested that everyone should come to Marquette, where they will be taken care of. Of course, don't forget to bring any food that you have and all of your guns."

"How did you know that?" she asked, sitting up straight now.

"It was only a guess, Anna, but I would also imagine that when somebody did that, their guns would be taken away 'for the good of the community.' Any food they brought would be confiscated, again 'for the good of the community.' If they really wanted us to function, they would have found a way to leave our power on. In fact, how did this ATV gang get past the National Guard roadblocks? And why didn't Lacey stop them long before they got organized? I don't like the way this is shaping up. Not at all. That's not the issue at the moment. Right now we need shooters, and organization."

I looked at the enlarged map of the township.

"If they get past the roadblock here," I said, pointing to the area where the Big Guppy crossed 695, "the next spot to hit is only a few miles north in Midway. We know, and maybe they know, there's little there, so they might keep going.

"If we position shooters here, and here," I said, stabbing my finger at the map, "and here, all staggered so there's no crossfire, using the houses in Midway for concealment, good shooters can take quite a few and the wheelers won't know which way to shoot first. What do you think, Karen?"

"I think you have a devious mind, Allexa," Karen grinned. "If we can get everyone in place quickly enough, the surprise factor is to our advantage. It could work."

"So now we need to round up our militia. That will be your job, Karen. The next step is, what if they get through that trap? There are a lot of homes still occupied between there and here," I scowled, "including mine."

* * *

JOURNAL ENTRY: February 8

I pulled the FRS radios out of the faraday cage and put all fresh batteries in. The Family Radio System is limited in range, but should work well for this purpose. One radio each for me, John, and Jason. I gave Don one, too, with the instructions to keep it on and keep it close. I also delivered one to David.

* * *

"With your ham you might get enough of a warning to give us some warning. Will you do that?" I asked, holding the small unit out to David.

"Of course. Is there going to be shooting?"

"Likely. Does that bother you?"

"No, but I'm nearly out of ammo and it would be a shame to just get started and run out."

"What are you shooting?"

"308. Been good for deer," he grinned. "We've been living on venison. I have to tell you that mac and cheese you gave us tasted mighty good."

"Walk back with me and I'll give you a box. We could use an extra shooter."

* * *

"Mom, I should take the roof position," Jason insisted. "I've spent more time in a tree stand than you, and I know I'm better at the long shot."

"I agree. Why don't you take a look and see where your best vantage point is," I replied. I turned to John when Jason left. "He really is the best shot of the three of us."

"I know he is. I have no problem admitting that, Allex." He gave me a crooked smile and a quick hug.

* * *

"You were up there a long time," I said to Jason when he came in a half hour later.

"Once I got up there I realized that I might be seen from a distance, so I mounded up a line of snow to conceal me. Kind of like a snow fort," he grinned. "Plus, if the Wheelers do come down this road, we don't know which direction they'll come from, so I had to make the fort on three sides."

"That's a great idea," John complimented. "Will you show me what you have in case we have to switch positions?"

After they came down, we lined up rifles and ammo, both for window positions and for quick grabbing for the roof spot. We are as ready as possible. Now we wait.

* * *

JOURNAL ENTRY: February 9

The response from the community was stunning! Several women and every male from fifteen years old to seventy volunteered. They showed up at the township hall with rifles in hand and ammo filling their pockets once they understood the potential danger. The rest of the women prepared in town. Many of them were ready to shoot or make a stand, while the others offered whatever support would be needed.

Danny was sent to drop a load of logs at the Big Guppy, and Ken and Karen organized the volunteers. A total of twenty-five men and women, armed to protect their town and their lives, headed for the small settlement of Midway Village, less than a quarter mile stretch of a dozen homes. Lenny was sent ahead to be a lookout. His electric four-wheeler was incredibly quiet and he took up a position a mile south of the village slightly past a bend in the road. Having him there to give the alarm will make a world of difference to those waiting.

* * *

While the blockade of logs kept the gang from using the road, what I hadn't counted on was the creek freezing. A couple of the snowmobiles charged around the logs through the snow, only to discover a frozen marshland that was not even remotely capable of stopping the determined four-wheelers. Onward they came. When Lenny saw the first sled go around the bridge, he headed back the short distance to Midway to spread the warning. Fortunately, everyone was in place. Unfortunately they'd been there for hours, and many were getting tired. The roar of sleds and wheelers could be heard a mile off, and the adrenaline started pumping, wiping out any signs of fatigue.

As anticipated, when the Wheelers came upon the first of the houses, they slowed down for a better look, likely scoping out which would be worth ransacking first. Once most of them were within the fire-zone, the concealed shooters opened up. With fire coming at them from both sides, those that could roared past and kept going north. Out of two dozen men on eighteen ATVs, only ten were killed. Two of our men went down. George, a sweet old man, managed to drop two of the Wheelers before he was shot, and a youth I was not familiar with was fatally wounded. There should have been higher totals. It should have been like shooting fish in a barrel. In hindsight there was fear of hitting each other. The Wheelers' numbers were down, but not enough, and now they were prepared for resistance.

* * *

The FRS squawked. "I just spotted five machines pulling into our road. They're coming in slow and cautious," David whispered into the hand radio.

Jason zipped up his waiting snow coveralls, pockets already packed with full magazines, pulled on his hat and gloves, grabbed his rifle and was out the deck door within thirty seconds to take up his position on the roof.

"Don! Did you get that?" John called on into his hand-held unit.

"I'm on it. Out," my brother answered.

John opened two front windows just enough to stick a barrel out. He manned the bedroom window and I would take the dining room because it was closest to Jacob.

"Jacob, I need a really big favor. You need to keep Tufts from getting scared. Can you do that for me?" Tufts had finally come to accept Jacob, and spent most nights sleeping with him.

Jacob nodded.

"It's going to get noisy, so I want you to wear these, okay?" I gave him shooter earmuffs. He grinned. "You know what makes Tufts feel really safe?" I asked. "Being under the covers! So maybe you could keep Tufts under the blankets. Okay?" Jacob grinned again and put the muffs on. I covered him and the cat with two layers of blankets. With the windows open it would chill off fast in here.

David called on the FRS, "One of Wheelers is hanging back. He's mine. You've got four."

John had the AR-15, and the twelve-gauge, both with extra magazines. I had the M-14, extra mags and the twenty gauge. I gazed into his clear blue eyes. He gave me a deep kiss and turned to take up his position. I was hoping for a certain declaration from him that never came.

My window had a low sill, so I tossed a seat cushion on the floor to kneel on, set the barrel of the M-14 out the window and glanced down at the three full magazines on the floor by my side when the first Wheeler slowed in front of the house.

My insides turned liquid with fear, and I shivered. A shot then rang out from across the road. Don! The Wheelers turned as one unit towards Don's house. The furthest one to the south raised his rifle. Everything dropped into slow motion. He fired. My brother jerked from the impact and fell backwards, the wooden deck rails offering no protection at all. Instantly, Nancy burst out the front door from the relative safety of the house, screaming for Don. The third shot hit in the center of Nancy's bright yellow "Welcome to Florida" t-shirt and a large red blossom appeared. She crumpled to the deck.

"*Nooooooo!*" I yelled, the guttural sound escaping from my throat without me realizing it or recognizing it. Within seconds, another shot was fired, and that shooter's head exploded like a ripe watermelon. Jason got him! The other three now turned toward us, raising their weapons. There was a barrage of gunfire. John got the next one, then Jason nailed his second and John took out the final one. Somewhere in the back of my mind I heard Jacob crying for us to stop the noise but I had to ignore him. There was now silence and no movement. A distant double tap shot followed more silence. David had taken out the fifth gang member. Other than the fire at my brother and his wife, the gang members never got off a shot.

I could hear Jason trampling across the roof. He scrambled down the ladder and was back in the house within moments. I stood, my knees shaking with fear and anger. I'm sure I set my rifle down because it was no longer in my hands. When I tried opening the door, John grabbed me from behind and held on, stopping me from doing something perhaps very foolish.

"Wait for us! First, your coat and gloves. Make sure your safety is off!" John yelled and reluctantly let me go. I had to get across the road to my brother!

Jason was talking to Jacob quietly and he stopped crying. Everything remained fuzzy and surreal. The three of us went out of the door and cautiously moved toward the downed gang members, our handguns drawn. None of them appeared to be moving, but my anger was now boiling over. Purely in a vindictive action, I put a bullet in the head of the closest one.

We picked up our pace. John and Jason finished making sure this scum wouldn't move again. We came to the last one; there was little of his head left.

"Nice shot," John said, clapping Jason on the shoulder. Then he viciously kicked the body. We are all capable of extreme anger under the right circumstances.

"It wasn't soon enough, though," Jason choked. He was close to his uncle.

When I reached the porch, I almost lost it. There was the lifeless body of my only brother, lying half across the picnic table. His wife's body was by his side, a pool of crimson blood forming beneath her where it didn't drip through the slats of the cedar decking. I reached out and brushed a lock of gray hair away from Don's empty eyes, a gesture he never would have tolerated had he been alive. I sobbed while sinking to my knees, checking for a non-existent pulse.

"We have to move them inside," Jason said. "Mom... Mom!"

I turned to him, but didn't really see him.

"Mom. Focus! Go in the house and get us two blankets or sheets."

My world wasn't functioning. We put Don and Nancy each on a sheet, moving them one at a time, and laid them side-by-side in the kitchen. Burial would have to wait.

We were back across the road and nearly to the house when the FRS squawked again. "Here come more!"

We ran.

Jason, still in his insulated one-piece, grabbed his rifle and headed once more for the roof. I opened my window and took a deep breath. John came up behind me and said, "Don't hesitate, just shoot. There's no one left to hurt except those that deserve it."

Five more Wheelers came roaring down our quiet road. They slowed and drove their RV's around the other machines and the bodies on the ground then stopped. When the first one dismounted his machine, Jason fired from the roof. A clean neck shot nearly took his head off and the Wheeler crumpled where he stood.

I felt an angry chill surge through me and I fired, again and again. Although they shot back, they couldn't see us, but we sure could see them. I emptied my first clip and slammed another one in place as glass shattered in front of me. One of the Wheelers raised his hands in surrender. We weren't taking prisoners.

I lost a few windows, and it was over in a matter of minutes. There were now nineteen dead Wheelers, two men from town, and my brother and his wife.

* * *

Ken and Karen followed the four-wheel tracks down my road, and climbed out of their new scout car with weapons drawn. The road was a mess with bodies and four-wheelers. Some of the machines were overturned, a few still running. Several of the machines were riddled with bullet holes. One of those lying on the ground moved, twitched. Ken walked over and silenced him permanently.

* * *

"Allexa? Are you guys okay?" Karen called out nervously while Ken continued walking among the dead.

I grabbed my jacket and stepped out the door, glass crunching underfoot. "We're all right, but my brother...he... they're both dead." I choked on that word: *dead*. It didn't seem real.

"Karen!" Ken yelled. "We've got a problem." He made his way back to where we were standing. "I count nine here, plus the ten in Midway. We're missing five of these scumbags. We need to get into Moose Creek, pronto."

"I'm leaving two pickups here, plus Donnie and Josh to help get these pieces of crap off the road," he said to me. "They'll push the machines off to the side and we'll deal with them later."

"Go take care of the town, Ken, we'll finish up here," I said, gazing out at the road.

* * *

The Moose Creek Militia caught up to the Wheelers at Fram's, where they were attempting to steal gas. Fram's wasn't open. Joe had already shut it down. The pumps didn't work without the generator running the power. The Wheelers were frustrated and there was no one to bully or force to do their will. Not until Marilyn Harris made the mistake of pulling into the parking lot. The five outlaws, now grubby from days of travel and wreaking havoc on unsuspecting locals, turned to the big blue pick-up truck.

Marilyn got out of the driver's door, much to the dismay of Pastor Carolyn, who was riding in the shotgun position. She took with her Bill's twelve-gauge shotgun. Marilyn didn't have the same reservations that Bill did about a loaded gun in the car, and she didn't see any reason to keep it in the backseat either.

One of the prisoners smiled and walked toward her, hands open.

"Lovely lady, perhaps you can help us. My friends and I here are just trying to purchase some gas so we can get back home, but the pumps don't seem to be working," he said, walking with a slow and steady gait, maintaining eye contact with Marilyn.

Marilyn raised her twelve-gauge to firing position.

"You won't need that, we mean you no harm," he said, continuing to advance. When he was ten feet away, Marilyn fired, not only knocking him off his feet, but blasting him fifteen feet backward. The Militia arrived in time to see Marilyn's shot.

The remaining four gang members surrendered. Rising from behind their stalled machines, they raised their hands in defeat. Karen raised her freshly loaded shotgun, while Ken stepped closer. The various vehicles belonging to the other members of the newly formed militia came to a stop. The men and women emptied into the parking lot, creating a seemingly impenetrable line of rifles, shotguns, and handguns. One at a time, the prisoners dropped to their knees and assumed a well-rehearsed position: face down, arms outspread, ankles crossed.

Ken stepped even closer. "We don't have a judge here in this little town, so you four are stuck with me. I find you guilty."

He shot each of them in the back of the head.

The men and women of the Moose Creek Militia were stunned. From their midst, Buddy clapped. Soon, everyone was applauding and cheering.

Karen pulled Marilyn aside and asked, "Why did you wait so long to shoot, Marilyn? You let that guy get awfully close to you!"

Marilyn cast her eyes down sheepishly and replied, "I'm a terrible shot, and I didn't want to miss!"

* * *

Ken sat in the passenger's seat in the cab of the flatbed truck, with Bob Lakeland behind the wheel. Their gruesome cargo was covered with a tarp.

"Sheriff, I'm not asking *if* you will take these criminals back, I'm asking you where you want them," Ken explained over the radio to Sheriff Lacey.

"No, *you* don't understand! We will not keep these bodies."

There was a short pause.

"Yes, *bodies*. Every last one of those scum are dead. We lost four good people in Moose Creek, plus whoever these guys killed along the way. It was unanimous that you get them back. If you don't tell me where to take them, Bill, I'm going to dump them right here and right now."

* * *

What we didn't know when all this started, was *who* the gang was comprised of. Marquette has a maximum security prison where the worst of the offenders are kept. With limited resources in the county, some of the prisoners were out on a work crew, clearing snow, freeing up fire hydrants and shoveling roofs for seniors. They killed the single guard who was assigned to watch them, buried him in a snow bank and took off. Approximately two dozen of them raided an RV store, leaving with winter gear, helmets and eighteen four-wheelers and snowmobiles after killing the entire staff. From there, they overwhelmed the two armed guards at the sporting goods store and cleaned out the stock of high powered rifles, filling knapsacks with all the ammo that would fit. Two of the younger prisoners took turns raping the young girl behind the counter before beating her and leaving her for dead. She survived, barely, and will need reconstructive surgery that just isn't available anymore.

The prisoners had cut across to the loop that bypasses downtown, avoiding the local police. When they came to the National Guard roadblock, they must have figured something up that road was worth protecting and started their unopposed rampage. There was no way for them to know the roadblock wasn't to protect anything, it was meant to keep people on the other side *out* not in. Because these prisoners were from lower Michigan, they didn't know that once they started their northward trek of destruction, there was no place to go once they got here — no place except to go back to the waiting law enforcement. Clearly they hadn't counted on the resistance they were to encounter. Had they turned south instead of north, they might have been unstoppable.

CHAPTER TWENTY-SIX

JOURNAL ENTRY: February 7

It's been eight days since The Wheelers attacked us and we defeated them. The defeat was good and necessary, but it came at a great cost. Not only the four lives, two of them very close to me, but part of the cost was our innocence as a town, as a community.

I'm still sweeping up glass. Thankfully the glass door-wall was not one of the casualties, though the dining room window was and now we are lacking in natural light. The other window was in the hall and it was dark there anyway. Someday I hope that we can replace the glass. Jason and John scavenged some plywood from the barn to cover the outside and there was enough of the roll of metallic insulation to piece together a covering for the inside to keep out the drafts and cold. It's still only February, and March is and always has been our heaviest snowfall month.

Over the past several days, we've had another six inches of purifying snow. It's cleaned up the mess on the road. The ATVs that were left by the wayside are now mounds and formless humps and have taken on shapes that Jacob thinks look like giant turtles. At some point I'm sure the dealership will be out to reclaim them. Meanwhile they are a reminder to me of some horrible times.

* * *

We buried Don and Nancy in a single grave in the Moose Creek Cemetery last Monday. I would rather have buried them in one of her flowerbeds, but because of the deep frost line there is no digging in February here and Pete already had several graves pre-dug. Immediately after the burial, Jason went into Don's house to secure it. I knew why he waited. He loved his uncle and it would have been impossible for him to be there with them still in the middle of the kitchen. He got the woodstove fired up and then drained all the pipes of water. Don always kept a couple gallons of RV antifreeze, which Jason found in the basement after a great deal of searching. Don wasn't always the most organized person. With the pipes drained and the traps full of antifreeze, Jason stoked up the fire, and then dampened it down for a slow burn.

Jason is now considering moving into Don's house. There is a two-year supply of wood for the woodstove so they would have heat. One of the freezers is still full of food, partly with jugs of ice that have been frozen outside. My brother did an excellent job keeping the freezer intact. What canned goods were left he had brought out of the basement and lined the bookshelves to keep them from freezing. Pork and beans, soups and pasta sauces now took the place of the encyclopedia, novels and cookbooks. When I asked Jason why he wanted to move, he said it might be better if John and I had more privacy. They would still come over for dinner though, and I would bake for them. John grumbled about taking on Jason's chores, but Jason just laughed.

I'm still not sure the move is a good idea.

On the bright side, we were delightfully surprised yesterday by the arrival of another food warehouse truck at the township hall. When I questioned the driver about it, he looked at the paperwork and pointed out that our shipment was classified to be recurring. Recurring, meaning every month we would be getting food now! The relief flooded through me and we quickly refilled our near empty tables with fresh supplies.

"Allexa! Good to hear from you. I have to tell you, your little town has caused quite a stir here," Tom laughed when I called to thank him for the provisions.

"Oh? Why? For defending ourselves?" I know I sounded a little snarky, but I was still hurt that Bill Lacey had hung us out to dry.

"Well, honestly? Yes. The Sheriff's office is taking a lot of flak for not stopping that crew before they headed your way. You did what needed to be done and without hesitation. The word on the street is that the locals here have new respect for the people of Moose Creek. You might even get a float in this year's Fourth of July parade."

"We'll see when July rolls around, Tom. I can't even think that far ahead. The reason I called, though, was to thank you for the recurring food delivery. That means a great deal to me, and it means survival for Moose Creek."

"Are you sure you won't—"

"No, my place is here, Tom. You of all people should understand that now." I hung up on him this time, before he offered me a job again.

* * *

John surprised me this morning by wishing me a Happy Valentine's Day and presented me with a handmade card. He made me potato pancakes for breakfast, one of the few things he says he does well. They were indeed excellent. I know that I've not been very good company for him this past week. With all that's happened — the shootings, the deaths, the funeral and burial — I've been in a daze. He's been so very sweet and patient with me. Perhaps I can make it up to him later. Tonight.

* * *

JOURNAL ENTRY: February 15

John and I strolled over to David's with a box of food from the recently resupplied food pantry and a can of gas from the grateful town of Moose Creek for his warning about the Wheelers. There's no telling what would have happened if we hadn't known and been ready for them. The thought sent shivers up my spine. We listened to the ham radio, picking up bits and pieces of news, and I took in the changes in the house. Gone were the dirty floral sheets covering the furniture, no dishes were stacked in the sink, and I'm thinking they removed some of the carpeting, but I'm not really sure about that, all I know is the smell is gone. It's amazing what having water will do, that and knowing someone cares. We live surrounded by lakes, yet the water isn't that easy to come by.

More news confirms that most large cities are cesspools to live in. Martial Law is the norm and most law enforcement agencies have had to be augmented from the local population. The corruption that has infiltrated the ranks runs rampant. The politicians are so far removed from the man on the street that they don't have any idea about what is really going on. They likely don't *want* to know. It appears that the political corruption hasn't changed much.

One item of good news is that power is slowly being restored to the smaller towns and cities. I felt my pulse jump a few beats when I heard that. I wonder if there really is a chance we will have the electricity turned back on in the near future. We will have to survive until then.

* * *

With a slightly better attitude than I've had in days, I ventured into Moose Creek to see how the town was handling all that has happened. I was surprised, and yet not, to see it was business as usual. People were walking around, Fram's was still open for a few hours each day for hardware or the weekly gas allotments, notices were posted, and the township hall was back to being the hub of activity.

"Good morning, Allexa!" Karen greeted me cheerily.

"Well, you're in a good mood," I said. Her upbeat mood was contagious.

"I am! My work just got a lot easier," she said. "With all the weapons confiscated from the Wheelers, and especially the thousands of rounds of ammo, we no longer have to depend on our own reserves. They were beginning to get severely strained. Plus, our new deputy is down at the Big Guppy supervising the replacing of the logs. I might be able to take a real lunch break!"

"Whoa! What new deputy? And what about the logs? I thought Danny had already moved them out of the way."

In fact, I knew he had moved them. It was the only clear route, and was how Ken had taken the bodies to town and the food truck had gotten up here.

"What have I missed?"

Karen grinned. "We deputized Lenny Bagget yesterday. He's going to work out great. I can't believe we actually suspected him of those fires." She shook her head in disbelief. "He's eager to do even the crappy jobs, like organizing the mess Danny left."

The dozen logs Danny had put in the path of the Wheelers were dragged out of the way when they were no longer needed, and then haphazardly piled to the side. After further discussing the situation, it was realized that if those logs were needed again it would take twice the time to move them with the way they were now since they looked like a bunch of giant pickup sticks with bark. By making two piles, one on either side of the road, and arranging them in a 3-2-1 stack, replacing the barricade would take only half the time. We were well aware of how valuable a few minutes could be and what a difference it could make to our safety.

"I will be sure to congratulate Lenny the next time I see him," I commented. Things were taking on an interesting slant in our little town.

I wandered over to the Stone Soup Kitchen to put in an hour of volunteer work. Several ladies were working on a new batch of stew since someone had brought in fresh meat. A few men were there too, moving tables, sweeping and staying busy. Since I felt that I wasn't needed there, I went home.

CHAPTER TWENTY-SEVEN

The days seem to just slide on by. We have all lapsed into our own routines that see little change and even less variation. John hauls wood, I bake and cook, Jason shovels snow, and we all pitch in giving lessons to Jacob.

Jason is about to make the move across the road. I still don't like it. Jacob has been over there several times with Jason while he checks everything over and keeps it heated. The little guy is excited about having his own room again and I'm letting him take most of the toys that I've had here for him. I will keep a few here. The school supplies go with them too. After all, I stocked them for Jacob.

* * *

Several guys from town showed up this afternoon with the flatbed truck and the township backhoe to dig out the eight silent four-wheelers. I will be glad to see them gone. They are too much of a reminder of sadder days.

"Hey, Pete, come to take away my road junk?" I laughed as I walked up to the busy crew. Some days I have to laugh to keep from crying.

"Well, yes and no," he said.

It was good to see him smile. I know that he must still be feeling the pain from his mother's death, though hers was more natural and expected, and Don's was neither.

"I'm guessing you will tell me what that means, Pete."

"Once we have all of the machines freed, cleaned off and started, you get to take your pick of one to keep." I was startled into silence. "And Jason gets one, and so does David. The rest we'll load up and take back to Moose Creek."

"Why?"

"A gift from a grateful township." He looked almost hurt that I wasn't overjoyed.

"These machines aren't the township's to give away, they belong to the dealership they were stolen from," I insisted.

"Not anymore, Allexa. Anna will explain it better when you go into the office, but the dealership has given the township the machines, *all* of them, as a thank you for ridding the county of those renegades," Pete said with delight. My guess is he gets one of these too.

Well, they will certainly be better on gas! Now to pick one. I think I'd better confer with John and Jason; I'm likely to pick one because of the color.

*   *   *

Once that decision was handed off to my two guys with my preference voiced, I made I quick trip to talk with Anna.

"Pick out your new ride yet?" Anna asked when I arrived at the office.

"Yeah, the one with the camouflage paint job provided they can get it started."

"Why does that not surprise me," Anna chuckled.

"Why didn't you warn me? You know I don't like surprises like this," I scowled.

"Why haven't you been in to the office in," she glanced at the calendar, "five days?"

I dropped into the seat across from her instead of the chair at my desk. "Permission to speak freely, ma'am?"

"Why ask permission now? You've always spoken your mind."

I looked down at my trembling hands. "I don't know how much more I can take, Anna. I really don't. I feel like I'm being torn apart inside. I'm exhausted all the time and I'm not thinking clearly. See? I didn't realize that it had been five days since I left the house." I took a deep breath. "I feel like I'm on the edge of tears half the time and that's certainly not a good professional image to project!"

"I see you've lost more weight. Do we need to increase your rations?" she asked.

"No! No more food! I just don't have much of an appetite anymore," I confessed.

"What else is going on, besides the obvious?" she asked, genuinely concerned.

I leaned back in my chair, not knowing how personal to get. "Jason is moving out. He's going over to Don's house. I don't know if John loves me or is staying with me for the... benefits. I haven't heard from my other son in Florida since this all started, and the worry is tearing me apart." My voice cracked; I couldn't help it.

"I know what you need! A vacation!" she exclaimed and I started to laugh. I laughed until I sobbed. "First you need to read this," her voice gentled. "A communiqué from Sawyer Air Force Base routed through Tom White."

On Jan. 24, 1955, the United States government signed a 99-year lease with Marquette County. Almost immediately, construction of military support facilities began and K.I. Sawyer AFB was a reality and became an important part of Marquette County infrastructure. K.I. Sawyer Air Force Base was decommissioned in 1995 as a military facility, but had operated for nearly forty years, and was a major employer in the county.

Its closure meant the loss of hundreds of jobs, both at the base and the filter down jobs. It was re-purchased by the county and the new county airport, Sawyer International, took over and now occupies a portion of the base and has, or did have, scheduled airline flights and some general aviation activity. During this crisis, most domestic flights were curtailed, and limited military flights were resumed. The joke around the county for years was we had commuter planes landing on airstrips that could land the space shuttle, overkill to say the least.

To have a direct communiqué from there was curious, disturbing, alarming and hopeful. The message that was faxed over was already two days old, having had to wait until someone was at the office to turn the generator power on. The message was also maddeningly brief: just to contact them about a package that had arrived.

I called Tom White immediately. No answer. I called Dispatch and asked where I could find him, only to be told he had gone home for the day. I was happy for Tom that he went home, but it also meant that I would have to wait a day to find out what Sawyer wanted with me and what this package was. The last package I received was batteries. I doubt that's what this package was.

* * *

When I arrived home, there were three cleaned off four-wheelers sitting in the driveway. The camouflage painted one that I had tagged for myself, a hunter green one, and a deep blue one, all of them with the bells and whistles that would delight those that could afford such toys. At the time, I didn't know that David had already been given one, and these three were ours. Even John got his own set of wheels for his part in our town's violent history.

The snow on the shoulders of the road had been greatly disturbed, but the rest of the machines were gone. I'm still not sure how I'm going to feel riding a machine that had been used to wreak such havoc on our quiet community. There was still no word on what had happened during the rampage to the south of here. What damage and death the Wheelers had left behind may be never fully known.

John came out when he saw me pull in, I think so it wouldn't be a surprise to walk into an empty house. For the brief time I'd been gone, they'd been busy moving Jason and Jacob across the road. The house was indeed quiet and empty.

* * *

"What is this about Sawyer, Tom?" I asked when I finally got him on the phone. I'd been calling him since nine o'clock, dialing non-stop until he picked up twenty minutes later.

"Good morning to you, too," he replied. "Someone has landed with a military clearance, looking for you."

"Me?"

"Yes, *you*, by name. He also gave what he calls a password," and Tom told me what this 'someone' said. My heart almost stopped. Very few people knew what I used as a secret verification word, only close friends and family: Tufts.

"Where is this person now?" I managed to squeak out.

"They're being held at Sawyer. Does this mean anything to you?" Tom questioned.

"They?" my heart did a double trip. Could it possibly be? "Yes, it means something."

"Then I think you should make a trip down to Sawyer, Allexa. Conditions there aren't what they used to be, though it *is* very secure." I could hear Tom shuffling papers again.

"Who should I ask for when I get there? I could be there in less than two hours." I wrote down Captain James Andrews on a slip of paper.

* * *

I know that Anna was startled when I rushed out of the office. I couldn't take the time to explain what was going on and the possibility I was faced with.

I backed into the barn partway and started to pump gas into the car from the nearly depleted drum. John had seen me pull in, and came out to see what I was doing. When I told him what was going on, and what I thought was waiting, he took over pumping the gas and told me to do whatever I felt needed doing. I scurried across the road to tell Jason we'd be leaving shortly, and to keep an eye on the house. We'd be gone for several hours and he needed to tend the fire for me. I didn't want to say anything more since I didn't want to get his hopes up. It was enough that mine might crash; his didn't need that if I was wrong.

My hands were shaking so badly that I asked John to drive. I didn't trust my reflexes. He was well acquainted with the route, having flown in and out of Sawyer Airport every six weeks for the past two years. When we arrived, the place had a whole new look of military presence. Barbed wire was back, topping the chain link fence that the county put up, gray-green jeeps were everywhere, soldiers hustled between buildings and a new guard shack was added where there hadn't been one before.

I gave the guard my name and who I was to see while he looked over my Emergency Management ID. He glanced at John, who maintained a stony face when I told the guard John was my driver and my bodyguard. People seem to accept that for some reason. The not-so-young soldier told me where I could park and which building would have my contact.

"Why are you so nervous, Allex?" John asked. He placed his hand on my arm to slow down my pacing.

"I don't think this is so much nerves as anticipation," I said to him. My heart felt like it was going to pound out of my chest. The Captain I had spoken with had been gone for fifteen minutes now. I laid my forehead to John's chest, for comfort.

"Nahna!" I heard moments later and my granddaughter Emilee launched herself at me from a full run. I swept her up and hugged her as Eric reached us. I set her down and turned to my oldest son.

"Hey, Mom," he said with a very tired smile, and folded me in his arms. The tears just poured. They were safe and they were here! Eric looked over at John, eyebrows raised in question. I reluctantly let go of him.

"Eric, this is John Tiggs, my—"

"Please don't call me your driver and bodyguard, not to this man," John interrupted. He extended his hand, which Eric grasped firmly, both of them grinning.

"John is my... everything," I smiled at him, sniffled, and dug in my pocket for a hanky. Cloth of course, paper tissues were long a thing of the past. I slipped my arm possessively into his.

That's when Captain Andrews rejoined us. "I think I can safely ascertain that you recognize Sargent First Class Rush and his daughter."

I grinned and nodded, unable to say much.

"Since Sgt. Rush was unexpected, coming in on military stand-by, and unauthorized by the way, he's been held in custody until someone signs for the two of them. New statutes prohibit crossing state lines unless there is someone on the receiving end willing to vouch for, house, and feed a person. Will you take full responsibility for these two people, ma'am?" he asked, holding out a clipboard to me.

"Yes, absolutely," I replied. I understood he had his formal protocol to follow. I took his pen and clipboard and signed the release where he indicated.

Eric turned to the Captain and saluted, which the Captain returned. "You're very lucky, young man, not everyone gets this far. If you will follow me, I will release your two bags and escort you out," said the Captain. He looked down at Emilee and added, "And you, young lady, behave for your grandmother." He tapped her nose with his rough finger.

"Her name is Nahna!" Emilee replied with her little fists on her skinny eleven-year-old hips, her chin stuck out in defiance, which earned laughter from all of us.

My heart swelled to see how much she had grown. Eric was up for a visit last summer, however, it's been two years since I've seen my first grandchild. She was nearly up to my shoulder, and quite thin. I doubt she will be very tall, but maybe she got her height early, like I did. I was five foot four at the age of twelve, and only grew another inch. Emi's eyes were the same shade of light brown as her mother's, with flecks of gray and green. Her shoulder length hair was showing signs of rich golden chestnut, much like mine. Coincidentally, we both had had our very long hair cut in October, donating to Locks for Love.

I turned my attention to Eric, my first-born. He was now retired from the service, and still his fair hair is worn military cut, and I can definitely see the shades of pale brown and blond that it was when he was young. I did also notice a few patches of gray, and wondered how new that was. Eric and Jason were always such opposites. Eric was fair-haired and blue eyed, like his father; Jason dark haired and brown-green eyed like me. Eric preferred the heat of Florida, Jason gravitated to the north and the cooler climate, but looking at them together, there was no doubt they were brothers.

Standing beside the car while John put the two small carry-on bags in the back, I gave Eric another fierce hug. "I can't believe you're here. Oh my God, I've been so worried about you two!" The tears threatened again, but I did manage to keep them in check. "What about Beth?" I whispered, not wanting Emi to hear. Even though Eric and his wife had split up, I would have taken her in without a second thought.

"Her job is very important, not just to her, but to the entire county. She'll be fine. She sends her love and asks only that we keep Emi safe," Eric said.

Beth had made captain in the Fire Department last spring, after years being a paramedic, and worked hard now in public relations and emergency management. She'd been a very dedicated person for as long as I'd known her. She might not have come, but at least I have these two.

* * *

We arrived at four o'clock to a pleasantly toasty house, but John added more wood to the fire anyway. The winds outside have been slowly building all day, and I think we're in for another blast of snow. Eric and Emi were understandably tired and hungry, but when I offered hot showers before dinner, they both perked right up. John refueled and started the generator to pump the water, while I went over the basic water usage rules with our two new houseguests. Emi might be only eleven, but she was quite mature and understood that rules had reasons and were to be followed. Her parents have done a good job with her.

Emilee took her shower first and reveled in washing her hair for the first time in almost a week, which was how long their traveling took. Going by military stand-by was slow going and iffy to say the least. We gave her an extra five minutes and she was one squeaky clean and happy little girl when she came out of the steamy bathroom. In the last of her clean clothes, she sat down on the futon and promptly fell asleep.

Eric's shower didn't last quite as long, but he came out smiling.

"Oh, man, that felt good!" he sighed. "You don't know how to appreciate a hot shower until you can't get one!"

"Oh, yes I do," John snickered and offered to put their clothes in to wash.

Jason and Jacob would be over for dinner in another hour so I quickly started putting dinner together. At first I was going to do lasagna, but we were getting low on mozzarella cheese and I wanted to save that for pizzas, which were fast becoming a real treat. I decided on mock chicken Parmesan: canned chicken in a spaghetti sauce on fettuccini pasta.

* * *

"So where did you two go in such a rush?" Jason asked while he was helping Jacob take off his boots when they came over for dinner an hour later.

"Hey, bro!" Eric peered from the other room. Jason's head snapped around at the voice of his older brother. He scrambled to his feet and the two brothers hugged fiercely. They had always been close, being a bit over two years apart in age, but I hadn't realized how much they had missed each other.

"Mom, why didn't you tell me?" Jason asked, fighting his tears.

"I didn't know for sure. The message I got only mentioned a *package*. I thought it might be Eric when I was passed our code word, but I didn't want to get *your* hopes up too, in case I was wrong."

Jacob had finished taking off his boots by himself, and looked up at Eric. "I remember you, you're Uncle Eric." He reached up for a hug. My heart swelled. Not all autistic children shy away from physical contact, and Jacob is very affectionate.

Just then a sleepy Emilee wandered into the kitchen and spied her uncle and cousin, and rewarded us with another big smile from her.

"And you're Emilee," Jacob affirmed, and gave her a hug too. I think he sees he might have a playmate that is more his size.

* * *

Although we all understood that Eric and Emilee needed a few days of regular meals and much rest, we also have to discuss practical matters, like accommodations, and schooling for Emi.

"I would like you and Emi to stay here with us for a few days," I said to Eric. "After that, it would be more practical for you to move across the street with Jason. Don's house is much bigger. Why they needed four bedrooms, I've never understood, but it sure is convenient now." I glanced over at Jason. "Are you agreeable to them taking over the upper floor? With its two bedrooms and full bath, it would be perfect."

"Of course they can move in with us. Can you get us some more textbooks from the school?" Jason asked. "What grade are you in now?" he asked Emi.

"I'm in the fifth grade, but my teacher says I'm smart," she said, sitting up straight.

"I bet you are. Jacob is too, so I guess it runs in the family." I know Jason didn't want to boast, but Jacob, in only the third grade, had surpassed fifth grade math already. Before the event he was showing signs of having a photographic memory, even at nine years old.

By the end of the evening, it had been decided that Eric and Emilee would stay here for a week, and then move over across the road. Jason would continue the home schooling and include Emi in the classes, and I would try to get more books in higher grades from the school in Moose Creek.

Eric would soon need something to do, too, but that would be resolved when the time came. Meanwhile, I had my family here, we were together and we were all safe. It had been too long since I'd been this happy and content.

* * *

JOURNAL ENTRY: February 28

It's the last day of the month. By all accounts, it looks like March is coming in like a lion, so we should have an early spring after all. I hope so, anyway. I am so very tired of all this snow and cold.

Eric and Emilee will be moving over to Jason's this afternoon. Jason's, yes. I have to stop thinking of it as Don's house; he's gone. It saddens me, but it's the reality of this new life.

We've spent many hours, myself, John and Jason, trying to fill Eric in on all the events of the past five months so he understands the mood and attitudes of Moose Creek. New attitudes born from devastating events, horrific attacks, untreatable illness, and isolation, especially the isolation from all we knew. And the deaths. Some of us will never get over the losses.

In turn, Eric has relayed what he could of what happened down in Florida.

* * *

"It isn't much better down there, Mom. In fact, in some ways, it's been much worse. The gang violence is rampant; they're always fighting themselves or each other for territory or for the limited resources. There are shootings, executions and arsons every day, even in the wealthiest communities. Abby, Beth's older daughter," Eric explained to John, "moved back in to Beth's house to be with family and for the protection of the better neighborhood and also to protect her horse, Tint." He paused, taking a sip of tea, trying to maintain his composure. "In spite of the shooting lessons I gave her, she was attacked one day when Emi was in school. Tint was butchered in front of her, in broad daylight, and then Abby was repeatedly raped. When Beth home from work that night, she actually *begged* me to bring Emi up here, where she was sure it would be safer."

It took them eight days to make the trip, hopping one military transport to the next, moving northward in a jagged line, while being questioned at every stop until Eric put on his maroon beret and a jacket with his rank. Even retired, he retains the rank of Sargent First Class. At one checkpoint, the TSA tried to separate him and Emi, but the agent changed his mind quickly when Eric grabbed him by the throat and Emi gave him a karate kick to the groin. The biggest challenge came at Sawyer, when they were not getting back on a flight. They needed proof of family support to leave the terminal. They waited for almost three days.

* * *

As a celebration dinner for Eric and Emi's move to Jason's, we had pizza. I really wasn't joyous about their leaving here, but with so little good in our lives, a special event of this nature needs acknowledging. The kids watched the movie *Ice Age*, which I avoided because of the reminder of what smelled like an approaching storm.

As a parting gift, and because he needed his own weapon, I let Eric take the AR-15. If he ever went back to Florida, he would have to leave it behind anyway, so it was more of a loan. He also took the Smith & Wesson .357 revolver as a personal weapon. I prefer an automatic anyway. John had become very attached to the Mini-14 and it suited him.

When Jason and Jacob arrived for our pizza dinner, Jason had a surprise for us.

"You won't believe what I found in the basement!" Jason exclaimed. He set two six-packs of beer on the table. "Thank you, Uncle Don!"

John's eyes lit up, and Eric reached for a bottle opener. Even I had one.

CHAPTER TWENTY-EIGHT

I woke at my usual 7 A.M. I wonder how long the batteries in the clocks will last before I have to dig out the Big Ben wind-up clock from the drawer. From electric to batteries to manual, all in one easy step: a disaster, coming to a town near you. I put on my robe, smiling at the still sleeping John, and tiptoed out of the bedroom.

I knocked down the ashes in the stove and restarted the fire while a pot of water heated on the gas range. From this point on, any flame needed for the day would be taken from the cook stove to preserve the limited supply of matches. I had thousands, yes, but if I couldn't restock, it made them limited. I wonder if at some point, leaving a candle always burning would be our source of fire. That's a scary thought. Then I remembered I had several iron and flint type fire starters hanging in a pouch behind the stove. I never got proficient at using them, so I left them there. Learning to use them might make a good project for the kids.

I made coffee with the French press, and transferred the steamy, dark liquid to a different pot and set it on the stove to stay warm. I poured myself a mug full just as John came down the hall. I handed him my cup, but he set it down on the table and pulled me into a hug, nuzzling his sleepy face into my neck. Ah, this was the warm gentle hug like we would share after his massages on Eagle Beach. Those hugs always seemed to have an underlying, unspoken hunger. It seemed like a hundred years ago. He pulled back without letting go and kissed me. So many times I had yearned for that kiss in the past. I returned his kiss and deepened it with a sigh. The desire quickly grew, and without a word, we retreated to the bedroom.

* * *

A half an hour later, I rolled toward his warmth. "I think your coffee is getting cold," I said with a smile. He laughed, gave me a quick kiss, and we both got up and dressed for the day.

John poured us both a fresh cup of coffee, and then dumped his cold cup back into the pot to reheat. We no longer wasted anything. I set the griddle on the hot stove to fix toast, and started slicing bread while he opened the blinds on the glass door. Years ago I had Jason install the cell-style blinds on all the windows and the glass door. The cell forms an air barrier against the glass, keeping the hot air out in the summer, and the cold out in the winter. It was one of the most energy efficient things I've done for the house. Closing them at night is a must when it's so cold out.

"Houston, I think we have a problem," he muttered.

Problems we don't need, not after all we've been through. I moved to stand beside him, slipping my arm around his waist with my free hand and stared at the falling snow. I could barely see the barn through the veil of big, fluffy flakes falling straight down.

"I've seen snow like this only once before, back in March of 2002. It snowed for two days and then the wind blew for another two. Thirty-eight inches of snow brought Marquette County to a standstill." The memories of that time marched across my mind, and all that happened, some good, some not. "Come on, we need to plan our day."

We sat down at the table, toast forgotten until it started to burn. John turned it while I dug out two pads of paper and a couple of pens. He was buttering the toast and had the jam on the table when I came back from another quick errand—a trip to the cold pantry for batteries and the NOAA alert radio. I have no excuse for why I had forgotten we had this radio.

"Thank you, Marie," I said under my breath. I fed the AA batteries into the radio and turned it on.

In that tinny, computer generated voice, the announcement came: "The National Weather Service in Marquette has issued a Severe Blizzard Warning for the entire Lake Superior coastline of the Upper Peninsula from 6:00 A.M. until further notice; from Copper Harbor to Grand Marias to Whitefish Point; West winds will increase to twenty miles per hour and shift to the North by noon; winds will shift again to the North Northeast by 6:00 P.M.; Expect snowfall at the rate of up to two inches or more per hour, with wind gusts up to fifty miles per hour."

This was followed by the alert blast, and it started to repeat.

"Those North Northeast winds will dump us with lake effect snow, John. And I have never heard them say a warning was in effect until further notice! Never."

"Maybe they don't know how long it will last," he concluded.

"That's what worries me."

"We're okay, though, right?" He seemed worried.

"Absolutely! But there are a few things we have to do, and quickly." I took a sip of coffee, then a bite of toast. I was starting to like my own jam. John picked wild raspberry this time. "If this storm lasts a long time, and by the sounds of it, it will, we need to do all we normally would do over the next four to five days, in less than a day—today!" My mind was reeling with lists.

"Okay, tell me what to do." He had his pen ready to make his own list.

"Water is critical. I'll need you to gas up the gennie, and then refill the three five-gallon gas cans. One of them will go to Jason's, depending on what Don had left for gas, which I don't think was much, if any. After you do that, get the gennie going and fill the four five-gallon water containers, and the four big cooking pots that are out in the small shed. That should give us enough for several days." He nodded and jotted things down. "Once the water jugs are full, we'll need to do all the laundry." My mind was racing. "And flush both toilets and keep them flushed while the gennie is on."

"The chickens will need tending," John added. "I'll fill their water full, and the feeder. Will that last them a couple of days?"

"Yes, it should, thank you."

"I'll bring in extra wood and kindling, too. There's room behind the stove for about four days' worth if I stack it right," he said half to himself. I could see he understood the urgency.

"I'm going to start a double batch of bread, then go to the office while it's rising. The boys will need both loaves and I'll make ours later."

He frowned. "Why are you risking going into town?"

"Tomorrow is Food Bank day. I'm going to get ours early and make sure Anna knows about the storm. I'll get the boys' share and David's too." His frown persisted. "Don't worry," I said, touching his hand, "it looks about six inches out there. My car can handle it, no problem. I'll only be gone a half-hour. I promise."

While I put the bread together and spent ten minutes kneading it, we continued to talk, and John took all the notes.

"We'll need the snowshoes from the barn. They can stay in the pantry out of the way until we need them. Oh, and I might as well pre-grind some more wheat while the gennie is running all day, so the big electric grinder will have to come in from the shed too, but that can wait until I come back." I covered the bowl full of dough with a cloth and set it near the stove to rise. What else? What else? What am I missing? What am I forgetting?

* * *

The snow was deeper than six inches once I got out onto the main road, and I could see the plow coming in my direction. I pulled over and stopped, waiting until it was past. I wouldn't be able to see a thing in the cloud of snow it was kicking up anyway. It was hard enough to see through the falling snow.

* * *

"I didn't expect to see you here, Allexa," Anna said, already in the conference room filling food boxes while several people waited. I smiled at the few who had thought enough ahead to get their food early.

"I'm thinking like these folks and picking up early."

I helped Anna fill the last of the boxes, and soon the room was empty except for us. That's when I told her I needed four boxes for two people. She raised her eyebrows, but when I explained who I was picking up for, she nodded and pulled out more boxes.

"I managed to get a NOAA report this morning, Anna," I was trying hard to impress how grave this could be. "We're under a blizzard warning, no totals predicted, and no time frame on when it might end. I've never heard of that."

"I heard it too. It has me worried, but the town has come through everything that has been thrown at it so far. I have confidence we'll get through this, too." She helped me load the four boxes in my car. "Please try not to give into the temptation of going across the road to see your boys while it's still snowing, you might get lost!" She paused for a moment. "It's been said you can lose your way in ten feet during a bad blizzard."

And I instantly knew what I'd been forgetting! I stopped at Fram's before heading home, and caught Joe as he was locking the doors to go home to ride out the storm.

"Joe, I'll only be a minute." I headed back to the hardware department, past all the empty food shelves that stood like sentinels and reminders of more prosperous days. Thankfully I found what I needed and was back at the counter in less than two minutes.

He looked at my purchase with questioning eyes. "I'll put those on your tab. Now get out of here and go home!"

* * *

I was gone only forty-five minutes. Thankfully the plow had been by when it had. There was now almost as much snow on the road as before in that very short time. It was snowing hard and it was a struggle getting into the driveway through what felt like a foot of snow. Still grasping the steering wheel, I put my head on my hands after I had backed into the barn, and gave a sigh of relief. John tapped on the side window, startling me.

"Are you okay?"

"I'm really glad to be home. The roads are getting worse."

"You were late, and I was waiting to help with the boxes." He gave me that smile that always melts my insides. He had the sled ready, but it still took two trips to get it all in the house.

I did the next step on the bread, setting the dough into the loaf pans to rise again. The gennie was still running and John was almost done with the slow process of filling the water jugs. With so much to carry back in, we both went to the small shed to retrieve the cooking kettles, and get the electric grain grinder. The grinder could make five times the flour in half the time as a hand crank, which I did have, though rarely used. Right now, time was *not* on our side. While in the shed, I spotted the shower bucket I made and grabbed that too, just in case. John carried the box with the heavy grinder, and I carried the rest, five empty buckets and pots. It wouldn't be long and that storage shed would be inaccessible without a lot of digging, so I went back out while John continued with the water, and got an extra storage bucket of wheat berries and one of Basmati rice.

John still needed to bring in the wood, so I finished filling the four kettles we had brought in with water and setting two of them on the stove to heat. Finally, I filled a bucket and was on my way out to the coop, when John called out from the wood shed, "The chickens are taken care of!"

I nodded and went back into the house. The full bucket could go to one of the bathrooms. When John came in with that load of wood, I suggested we go over the notes.

"Let's see what's been done and what still needs doing, so we're not duplicating our efforts," I said, while we both sipped fresh cups of coffee.

Just then, Tufts decided to make an appearance, rubbing against first my legs then John's. After a scratch on the head, he went to see what offerings we had left for him in his feeding spot. I made a quick note. John raised an eyebrow in question.

I grinned. "I need to clean the litter box."

"All the water is done, so we start laundry now, right?" he asked. "I filled the gennie first, then all three gas cans, took water to the chickens and filled their auto-feeder full. On my way back I grabbed our snowshoes off the wall. The chicks left us six eggs by the way," he said.

Maybe I'll include some eggs with David and Jane's food box. We owe them a lot.

"Before the storm gets worse, I need to get the box next door," I said. I slipped the bread into the oven and set the timer. John wasn't happy about the thirty minutes or so it would take me to walk there, deliver and walk back. Neither was I, but it had to be done before dark. I promised to take a compass with me. "When I get back, we need to do something else…"

"What?"

"Lifelines. We need to run ropes between here and the boys, and here to the barn. I don't think we need it for the wood shed, since it's less than six feet from the edge of the house to the shed," I said, thinking of Anna's ten feet comment.

"Do we have that much rope?"

"I stopped at Fram's while in town and bought five hundred feet of clothesline. That should get from here to the boys. Maybe. I've never thought to measure it. Plus there's another three hundred feet in the barn that I stored last summer. We start with a line to the boys." I had thought there may come a time I would need to do a line to the barn, but it never occurred to me to run one across the road. In times past when this happened, we all would hunker down and wait out the storm.

* * *

It was hard shoeing through all that fresh snow, but I made it to David's in less than fifteen minutes, and started pounding on their door. He appeared with rifle in hand, which he quickly set aside when he saw it was me.

"Allexa! What are you doing out in this mess?"

"Don't worry, it's not my first choice of activity," I laughed. "I picked up all of our rations early." I handed him the big box, and I could see the relief on his face. "I added half a dozen eggs for you. We might be socked in for days."

"I know. I've been listening on the ham. Munising is already shut down with two feet in the last twelve hours. This will be one for the record books. If anyone is still keeping records, that is," he commented. "You better get back. And Allexa... thanks!"

At the top of his drive, I turned north. It's hard to get lost when out snowshoeing: you just follow your trail back the way you came. The exception is in a blizzard. My tracks made only ten minutes earlier were starting to fill in. I hurried, which was much easier to do towing an empty sled. The closer I got to home, the less I could see my trail, but I could still see an outline of the big, dark brown barn.

John was as relieved as I was when I made it to the back door. I knocked the snow out of the sled and handed it to him. I then stepped out of my snowshoes, sinking a foot deep in the fresh powder.

I warmed up by the stove, sipping on some soup John had thoughtfully heated. He prepped the food bank boxes, slipping them into large garbage bags to protect them from the constant falling snow. The bread was out of the oven, though not really cooled enough to bag, so I wrapped them in towels instead. I removed all the plastic wrapping from the new packs of clothesline, and loosened the starter ends. We would have to join them along the way. John waited until we were ready to leave before adding the one gas can to the sled that made it very heavy to drag through fresh, deep snow.

Outside, the snow was getting even thicker. I took a compass heading, and I knew the house was due east of here. John tied the rope to the bird feeder post right next to the door, and then wound it high around the closest tree—a tree that was barely visible only twenty feet away. We set out on our snowshoes in the direction I felt would lead us to my sons, unwinding the rope as we went, John pulling the heavy sled. We were never more than a foot or two from each other. Before we got to the large pines that marked the property edge, we stopped to attach the next rope. I'd used a special joining knot many times before, a Boy Scout square knot that got stronger the more tension it was under, deciding that would be the best one to use now. We were momentarily disoriented with the snow shrouding us in total whiteness. There was that instant internal panic of not knowing which way to go. I pulled out the compass to get us going again. A few more feet put us at the pine tree Don had planted ten years ago when they first moved in.

"See the tree, how big it's grown," danced across my memory and made me giggle sadly. Fortunately John couldn't hear me. From there we followed the grape arbor, trailing the rope behind us. Another stop to attach yet another segment of clothesline. I angled our approach to put us closer to the porch, and thirty feet later the gray house loomed in front of us. From there the going was more confident, and John attached the line to the banister on the steps. We breathed a sigh of relief, removed our snowshoes, and dragged the sled up the steps to the covered porch.

Eric opened the door when he heard us stomping the snow off our boots. "Mom! What are you two doing here? Don't you know it's snowing out?" He grinned and helped us inside.

"Very funny. Would you help John with those boxes, please?" I kicked off my boots in the kitchen and removed my snowy hat and gloves, leaving my coat on. We weren't going to be staying. I gave Jacob and Emilee hugs, and then turned to Jason. "Wood supply?"

"When I saw the snow this morning, we started hauling it in," he assured me. "This looks really bad, Mom."

"NOAA said a blizzard, two inches or more per hour, for an unknown length of time." I didn't hide my worry from my youngest son. He had to know the severity of this. "We brought this week's food rations for the four of you. I added a case of ramen, a dozen eggs, two jars of canned bacon, and a jar of corned beef. Oh, and two loaves of bread, still hot."

"We tied ropes as we came across," John said, "but—"

"But you need to stay here," I cut in. "Don't try coming over until the snow stops, which might be days. It's bad out there, really bad, and I do *not* want to worry that you might try taking the kids out in this!" I looked at both of my sons, sternly. "Promise me!"

I felt better when they both nodded.

"Moooom," Jason said, sounding exasperated, like he was the parent and I was the child.

"*Promise me!*"

Eric stepped in front of his brother. "We promise, Mom. We will not come across while the snow is still falling. Not unless it is an emergency." He looked sternly at his younger brother, taking the lead. Jason nodded, agreeing.

"Okay," I breathed. "Have you pumped water? How much gas do you have for the gennie? We only brought five gallons, so it will have to last."

"There's one container left. That gives us ten gallons. We *will* make it last, Mom," Jason said contritely.

"You've still got the FRS radio? We will be on from 9 A.M. until 10 A.M., from noon until one, and again at 5 P.M. until 6 P.M. Check in at least once a day, okay?"

They agreed.

"Something else..." I handed Eric the remaining hundred-foot clothesline package. "I want you to run this from the back porch to the wood pile. *Now* – before we leave. We'll wait."

Eric looked over at his younger brother. "Come on, Jay, she's right. Besides, they won't leave until we do this," he poked Jason in the ribs. This reminded me of when they were young boys. My boys are now men. When did that happen?

When they came back in, I said, "Just one more thing," Jason rolled his eyes. "I love you both," and I kissed each on the cheek. "See you in a few days."

As we put our boots back on, getting ready to leave, Jason came in with a package. "We were going to bring these for dinner, so you should take yours with you now." I nodded and tucked the package in my large pocket, giving him one more hug.

I didn't think the snow could come down any harder, but it did. The rope was truly a lifeline as it guided us back across the road. I'm not sure I could even see the compass. We literally pulled ourselves along until the big maple tree and then the bird feeder post came into sight. A foot away from there, the brown house came into view. Once inside, I collapsed from exhaustion. John was tired too. I could see it etched in his face.

"We still have some things that need to be done," I said and I pulled my list closer, "though I think we need a break, and something to eat. Shoeing is hard work!" I gave him a wan smile. "Soup or a sandwich?"

John picked out a jar of tomato soup, and set it to heat, while I made a single cheese sandwich to grill. We would split both. It wasn't good to eat too much and then do the heavy work that lay before us. The deck needed some shoveling so we could run the generator again, and one last safety-line needed to be run, to the barn. I would make sure we had a substantial dinner.

"All the laundry is done, Allex. Why the gennie?"

"We need showers, John. We've been working and sweating all day," I glanced at the battery operated wall clock, the one that had housed his Beretta. It was only 3 P.M., and with the heavy snow blotting out the sun it looked dark enough to be past dusk. "It might be days before we can have normal showers." I brought in that shower bucket only as a last resort. "If you shovel and get the gennie going again, I'll run the line to the barn. And don't give me that look!" I gave him my most confident smile. "The shoveling is too hard for me, and I'll not have you do *all* the work. Besides, I've walked that route in the blackest night. I'll be done before you."

We used paper plates for the sandwich, and burned them in the stove. The soup bowls would be washed later. We both put on lightweight dry clothes, and set to our tasks. John reluctantly started on the shoveling, while I donned my bright blue, pink and purple ski jacket, hat, gloves and snowshoes to make the short trek to the barn.

I tied one end of the fifty foot clothesline to the bird feeder post, aimed myself at the now invisible barn, and started walking. After a few minutes, I tripped and fell. The orange rod I used to mark the corner of the raised garden bed caught on my snowshoe. I freed my shoe, and then realized I had dropped the clothesline—the *white* clothesline which I now couldn't find. My heart stuttered. I was enveloped in a cocoon of furious white flakes, unable to see in any direction. I had a choice to make. The orange rod put me four feet from the garden fence, which would lead me to the barn, which still didn't get me back to the house. My alternative was to backtrack quickly, right now, before my trail filled in, get to the feeder post and get the line again. I opted for going back. The powder was deep so my trail was easier to follow, but only if I leaned over as I walked so I could see past the falling snow. Partway back, I found the end of the line I had dropped. I went the rest of the way back to reorient myself. I tied a loop on the free end of the rope and slipped it around my wrist. No more dropping it!

The second try was easier, having already broken the trail. I was extra cautious when I came to the disturbed area where I had fallen and stepped around the bed marker. I saw the fence and kept walking, only to be jerked to a halt. I had run out of rope. I removed the loop from my wrist, and slid it over the end of the first metal fence post. Following the ten feet of fencing was easy as the huge dark barn loomed over me, and I was once again thankful I had chosen dark brown siding instead of white. The sliding metal door groaned when I pushed it open and I stepped down into the gloom. I released the clips on my snowshoes, stepping out of them. The stress of the day caused my muscles to feel rubbery and they momentarily refused to work. Ignoring my fatigue, I used what little light there was to find my way to the shelf where I knew there was more rope. The laundry lines I had taken down a hundred years ago and checked off my winter prep list were right where I expected. These lines were much shorter, having been cut, but I didn't need much, only enough to reach the other rope.

After attaching it to the barn door handle, I stretched the new line over to the one hanging on the fence post and knotted them together, putting them both back up on the post, above the snow.

Back in the house, John was running the dryer. He hadn't yet showered.

"That took you a long time. Get lost?" he grinned, and I knew he had been worried. His smile turned to a grimace when I told him what happened.

"It's done now and there's no reason for us to go back out in this storm. Well, except to turn the gennie off, and I doubt either of us could lose our way on the deck," I tried hard to keep it light, but those few moments of being blinded by the snow, not knowing which way to go, really scared me. "I'll fold those clothes while you shower. Take whatever time you want, it'll be a few days before the next one!" I kissed his bald head and got the basket of clothes to fold.

* * *

"Oh, that really felt good," John said when he came out of the bathroom in clean clothes, freshly shaved too.

"Look what I found." I pulled out the package Jason had given me. "Tenderloin steaks!" It had been quite a while since we'd had fresh meat. Canned meat was fine, but not really the same. "I'm thinking mushroom gravy on basmati rice with the steaks. Does that appeal to you?" I grinned, knowing it would indeed be a hit.

I showered and washed my hair, taking my time, letting the hot water cascade down my back. Oh, how I missed the hot tub. To submerge myself in steamy water was now a distant memory, such an unreachable luxury. I wonder if I will ever have it running again. The thought saddened me, but over the past several months I'd gotten very philosophical about this new life. We were alive, we had food, we had heat, we had family, and we had each other. I could and would accept this all willingly, and let the old life go. I toweled off and put on fresh clothes. The gennie could run another half hour to finish drying the heavier clothes that had been air-drying near the stove. It was now 5 P.M. and it looked much, much later. The snow has so effectively obscured the sun it's hard to tell dusk from night.

* * *

With the generator off, it was so quiet. Quiet except for the howling winds outside; those forty to fifty miles-per-hour gusts had arrived.

The two oil lamps I set on the table cast a warm glow across our full plates. Another lamp was near the stove where the rest of the rice and gravy were staying warm, and a fourth lamp on the cook island, shining down the hallway.

As we sat down, John set a bottle of wine in the center of the table.

"Where did you find that?" I asked in a whisper, looking at the Earthquake label.

"In the wine rack where I'm guessing you put it," he said and opened it with a flourish. It was a great touch added to the meal. With soft light, the warmth of the stove, and the horrendous storm raging outside, it all made me feel cozy and secure. We toasted to getting done all we did without mishap.

"I do need to ask something…"

"What?" I prompted with a small smile.

"How did you know to run those ropes? You said this blizzard wasn't like anything you'd seen before." John set his wine glass down and cut a piece of meat.

I laughed. "Believe it or not, I saw it in a movie!" I took a forkful of rice and mushrooms, savoring the tastes and the warmth. "It was set in the 1800s. A young wife had been left alone when a blizzard happened. She tied a rope from the house to the barn to go get cow dung to burn."

"Cow dung?"

"Yes. The husband hadn't cut enough firewood before he left and she ran out. The movie stuck with me. When I started to burn wood for heat, I made sure I would never run out of firewood. And although I've never had to use the rope thing, it was part of the memory." I took another sip of the zinfandel and let it sit on my tongue for a pleasant moment before swallowing.

"Something else I wanted to ask," John said. "What will happen to the rope when the plow comes by?"

"They'll break it. It's strong, but not *that* strong," I said. "By the time the plows come, we won't need it anymore."

For an additional treat, we split a jar of canned peaches, some of what I put up two years ago. It had been a long and exhausting day and we both needed the extra calories of the sugar.

I washed the dishes quickly in some of the heated water from the stove and left them to air dry. It brought back memories of my time deep in the woods, pleasant ones this time. We closed the blinds to the storm outside, added wood to the stove and sat back down at the table.

Over a game of Obilqo, John asked me about the cost of supplies. When I asked why, he simply said he wondered why more people didn't do this.

"It's a question I've often asked myself." I set an odd shaped piece of wood in place and the tower toppled. John laughed and I groaned. "Yes, prepping costs money, eventually lots of money. If it's done over time, it's easier on the budget."

"How much do you figure you've gone through these past few months, money-wise?" he asked nonchalantly while he took a dowel piece and set it in the middle of the block I had placed as a base to start over.

"Probably a couple thousand dollars." I tried to sound casual, but it's a big chunk of money to me. "If you figure the average grocery budget might be a hundred dollars a week per person, and it's been almost five months, and there are now six of us. It adds up, and it's not just food, its supplies too." I set my piece down and looked at John. "I've been at this for a lot of years, John. I've sacrificed going on vacations so I could fill buckets of food and buy toothpaste, deodorant and canning seals, and those seventy-five rolls of toilet paper and soap. But it isn't only about food and toothpaste. I haven't gotten a new car so I could stock up on ammo. Let's face it: a new car wouldn't have helped us when the Wheelers came here."

"No, it wouldn't have," he said, deep in thought. "I still don't understand how you afforded all of this."

"I did a little at a time, John, a little at a time. Besides, buying bulk is cheaper. A twenty-five pound bag of wheat or rice is half the price per pound as opposed to buying a five- pound bag of the same item. I would check the bakery at Mack's every trip for empty frosting buckets, and when I could get a couple, I would clean them thoroughly and let them air dry for days. Then I would find something to fill them," I smiled. "One of the keys is to do something every trip or every week." I paused, thinking of a few odd looks I got in the checkout lines. "I was also careful to vary where I made larger purchases, to not raise suspicion." I chuckled. "One time I found a really good sale on rice and bought thirty pounds, which fills one bucket. The gal ringing me out said 'that's a lot of rice'. All I replied was 'yes it is,' and left it at that. I remembered who she was, and made sure I never went in her line again. Prepping becomes a way of life. It's a different kind of lifestyle, that's all. The way I look at it, I'm not spending money right now on groceries, I already did, so it's a wash," I answered, trying to reassure him with a smile.

"No, it's not a wash, Allex. If nothing had happened, you'd be feeding yourself, not five extra people. This is costing you a lot. I wish I could repay you somehow."

So that's what he was getting at. I waved it away with a flip of my hand and reminded him it was his turn to place a piece on the growing tower of wooden blocks. Inwardly I was hoping he'd drop the questions of cost, but I could tell it weighed heavily on his mind.

"Were you ever concerned you might be called a hoarder?" John asked with concern.

"No, because I'm not a hoarder. See, hoarding is a compulsion; stocking up is an activity," I explained. "My only compulsion is wanting to eat."

CHAPTER TWENTY-NINE

JOURNAL ENTRY: March 9

The snow came down all day on Tuesday, the fifth. It was a blinding whiteout most of the time, and then toward the evening it stopped. During the short respite of snow and wind, John took a bucket of water out to the chickens and was rewarded with eight eggs. Within an hour, though, the winds started up again, picking up the fallen snow and lashing it around into another whiteout condition that lasted two more days, piling drifts across the yard and across the road. It got cold, very cold, down into the teens during the day, and near zero at night.

* * *

"I really do have to bring more wood in now, there's no putting it off," John sighed.

"I know, perhaps we can make it go quicker though. We've got two slings, and—"

"No, I don't think it's good to expose both of us to this frigid cold," he said, blue eyes pleading with me.

"I understand, but if we work together," I said, holding up my hand when he tried to interrupt again. "By you bringing the wood into the cold room, taking the second sling to fill, while I take the full sling and stack the wood, and we keep switching, we can get this done in half the time and get *you* out of the bitter cold."

He smiled and kissed my nose. "You're so smart and logical."

We were done filling the space behind the stove in fifteen minutes.

* * *

The days went by slowly. I baked bread and pastries, fixed meals and read. John cleaned and oiled the guns and read. And we played games—two-handed solitaire, cribbage, dominos, tri-ominos, Obilqo, and we put jigsaw puzzles together, plus we planned this year's garden.

The boys called every day at noon on the FRS radio. Emilee is quite the chatterbox, always having something to tell her Nahna. Jacob is the silent one, and I'm used to that.

* * *

JOURNAL ENTRY: March 12

Today, three days after the snow and wind finally stopped and the sun came out. It's beautiful. The sun reflected off the pristine snow in a blinding display of sparkles. Sunglasses are a must now to prevent snow-blindness. Since Don and Nancy both wore glasses, there is no non-prescription eyewear anywhere in the house. I do have some cheap sunglasses stored out in the barn and in the car. As light sensitive as my eyes are and have been since a bout of Rubella when I was ten, I wear clip on sunglasses over sunglasses; nothing is dark enough for me when it's this bright out.

It was a strenuous walk out to the barn. The snow is deep and I sunk at least eight inches with every step. Thankfully, it's a short walk when I can see where I'm going. I remember the last walk during the blizzard when I fell.

I tried to pack down some of the snow in front of the barn so it wouldn't all fall inward when I opened the door. Once in, I was amazed at how deep the snow was against the doors. I had to shovel a "step" to get back out. I collected all the sunglasses from the storage drawers and the car, and I knew that Emi would lay claim to the Barbie sunglasses, while Jacob would want the Sponge Bob ones. I smiled at the fifty cent clearance price tags; fifty cents to save strain on their young eyes. There were standard sunglasses too. Eric and Jason won't have to deal with wearing Dora or Nemo specs. John got the standard pair from the car for his use.

John volunteered to shoe over to the boys and take them four pair of sunglasses and a sled. Having dragged a sled, full and empty, over a mile long driveway in deep snow when I lived deep in the woods, I knew how strenuous it was with weight. Those two youngsters together were well over a hundred pounds, very difficult to pull in one sled even a short distance. One in each sled would be easier, and I was anxious to see my family.

* * *

I planned an interesting dinner of sandwiches, canned coleslaw, macaroni salad, and apple pie for dessert. There were tuna sandwiches, egg salad, grilled cheese and corned beef with sauerkraut, all grilled if desired, heated or cold. I cut all the sandwiches into four pieces for sampling. Jacob was very happy with a grilled cheese sandwich and a juice box, with popcorn for his snack. We even invited David and Jane. It was a post-blizzard event, and everyone was happy to be out from under a blanket of snow.

Jane was amazed we had bread. "You *made* bread? Doesn't that take flour and yeast and other stuff? Where did you get it?"

"I've been baking bread since I was fifteen," I smiled at the thought of my first loaf. It came out perfectly. Since then, not all have been so pretty. "I did my winter stocking early in November, before the collapse, though I am starting to run low on flour now," I lied. I lied to protect our resources and so they would understand they could and *should* keep supplies on hand all the time. They need to be more proactive and not depend on others, and definitely not on us. Not for their supplies anyway.

I found my old personal DVD player and charged the battery the last time that the generator was running. My two beautiful grandchildren were being treated to a movie right now—*Finding Nemo*. They had to be quiet because the volume wouldn't go very high on the player. It was delightful to see the two of them together. They are so much alike, yet so different. Emilee is full of animation and quite a pistol. Jacob has fine, soft brown hair and eyes that are a deep shade of chocolate that often seemed so far away, but I knew he was looking at things we couldn't see. Sometimes it was difficult understanding him. Four years ago, he took a header off of his top bunk and knocked out his two front teeth. They eventually came back in, and seem to be too big for his mouth right now. He has the sweetest smile.

John followed me into the room and whispered, "Are we really running low on flour? Maybe we can cut back some, I know I can."

I cupped his face with one hand and stroked his beard. He was sweet to worry. "We're not that low. There's at least seventy-five pounds left, and mixing the white with fresh ground wheat will double that. It will last us months," I assured him. I would talk to him later about what and why I said that to Jane.

When David and Jane left, I handed her one of the four loaves I made earlier in the day and promised to teach her how to make bread when things got back to normal. No one wanted to think that normal might not come back.

The boys stayed a bit longer, and we shared a quart of apple cider I had canned two seasons ago. I even set a bottle of rum on the table if anyone wanted to spike their cider. We all did. Jason and Eric had theirs with ice chips while John and I had ours heated like a toddy. That was another thing I didn't want David and Jane to know: that we had alcohol. This is when I emphasized the need for keeping quiet about our supplies.

CHAPTER THIRTY

We woke up to an unbelievable fifty-five degrees! The air smelled gloriously like spring, but with an underlying chill from the snow on the ground. The chill didn't last long. During the day the temperature rose to sixty and as is so typical here, meltdown came fast and furious. We might have had a blizzard with nearly forty inches of snow only a week ago, and today there was less than a foot left on the ground. There is water and flooding and mud everywhere. I'm glad we didn't try to dig out the generator; it would have been a wasted effort. Two days of sunshine and all the snow on the deck is gone.

Neither John nor Eric, not even Jason for that matter, has ever seen such a fast transformation before. I have, almost every year of the seven I lived in the woods. I remember one year of snowshoeing out in the morning, and by afternoon, I could drive in; the roads were clear of snow except for shady areas. The temperatures that year had gone from thirty to eighty in one day. It was incredible.

We left the car in the barn. From past experience I knew that using the gravel drive while it was so wet would only create nasty ruts, something I didn't want to deal with.

* * *

By noon it was sixty-eight degrees and it hovered there for hours. With the snow melted from the deck, the wrought-iron patio furniture was once again exposed. After wiping the seats dry, John and I sat in the chairs, feet propped up on the hot tub, and enjoyed the sun and the warm air. It felt so normal, so right.

The biggest surprise came in the afternoon when the power came back on! Even though it was only on for two hours, it seemed like a miracle. We came back in for lunch, and I saw that the coffee pot was blinking. At first I didn't realize what it meant, and then it dawned on me. I opened the door to the breaker box and pushed the main switch back to its grid setting. The coffee maker was the one circuit that remained on the grid, as an indicator. The refrigerator started humming and it sounded like music. I wanted to walk through the house and turn on all the lights, but knew that was a bad idea. The grid must be very fragile now and too much usage would overload it. We smiled at each other and hugged for the longest time. Things were going back to normal.

* * *

JOURNAL ENTRY: March 11

Although the electricity was on for only two hours yesterday, it was a good sign. I needed to know more. I backed the new-to-me four-wheeler out of the makeshift lean-to and headed to town. John didn't even question me going alone, which seemed odd. I sincerely think that we are past the worst of any threats, though I still wore my Kel-Tec in the shoulder holster that now feels like a second skin.

I bundled up for the ride, even though the air temperature was again approaching sixty, and I drove along at a moderate thirty miles per hour, enjoying being outside in the sunshine and warm breezes.

* * *

"Good morning!" I greeted Anna, who gave me a big smile.

"You're in good spirits. You must have noticed our surprise yesterday."

"I certainly did. It was too short, but I'm supposing that it was a short run to test the circuits. Have you heard whether the power will be back to stay, and when?"

"Actually, I was on the phone the power company this morning," she said. "We should have full, regular power by this weekend!"

"Oh, my, that is such great news, Anna. I think we need to do some checking around town."

"You always seem to be one step ahead of me," she laughed. "Yes, we need everyone to shut down everything possible so that the surge is lessened."

"We'll have to go through all the vacant houses too and shut the breakers down completely."

"That was suggested too. We've got four days. They said they will throw the switch on Friday at noon."

Ken and Karen walked in where we were all gathered. Everyone was in a great mood, from the glorious weather I think. They were unaware of our short burst of power yesterday. Karen sank in the nearest chair when Anna made the announcement.

"Glory be!" Karen exclaimed with a sigh. "I can't wait to take an endless hot shower." We all laughed; we also understood.

"We do need to hit all the houses and camps and shut the mains off. You want to head that up, Ken?" I asked.

"You bet. Things here have been pretty quiet. We could use something to do."

"This reminds me," I said. "My oldest son Eric made his way up from Florida on military transports. He and my granddaughter are staying in Don's house with Jason." Ken sobered, remembering how hard I was hit with my brother's death. "He's retired military, Ken. He spent a lot of years in Special Ops. I think you might be able to use him in your new police department."

"Absolutely," he said without hesitation.

* * *

We spent another two hours going over maps, marking where we knew camps were and marking the on-grid ones. In town, going door-to-door seemed to be the most logical way to reach everyone within the town limits and still check all houses at the same time.

I volunteered for the town route and suggested that Jason and Eric team up, since nearly everyone in town knows Jason, and that John and I go together, since most know me. This way Jason could introduce his brother around town and I could introduce John. Strangers showing up at the door these days is not a good idea. After all that has happened, someone might get shot. Jacob and Emilee would spend a day at the school, in a real classroom. The kids need some socialization. John and I would also take the stretch of houses by Dawn and Guy. I knew that most of those neighbors were gone, and Dawn and Guy would know which ones, and could help identify which homes needed attention.

Ken would search out the camps with Lenny. Karen would take the houses around the inland lake, where they lived.

* * *

At first I couldn't find John. I thought he might have gone across the road to visit with the boys. I poured myself a glass of water and planned on sitting on the deck for a while. When I got to the door, John was already sitting on the deck and talking on his cellphone. When I opened the door, he hung up rather quickly and pulled the other chair closer to him.

"Your phone is working? I didn't think we were getting reception yet." I was curious who he had been talking to.

He looked a bit guilty, though it might have been my imagination. "I've tried to keep it charged. After the power yesterday, I thought I would try." He took my hand. "I just talked to my daughter," he grinned, his eyes damp.

"Oh, John, that's wonderful! How is she? And the rest? Your mom and sister?"

"Everyone is fine. They've all been worried about me and wonder when I can come home." He kissed my fingers, but suddenly my heart was stumbling. I couldn't keep out the thoughts that clouded my mind. Did he have a girlfriend waiting for him in North Carolina, or maybe even a wife he hadn't told me about? Did he want to go home to his *real* family? My insides lurched with a painful loss and I froze.

"I told them I *am* home, and that I would try to visit when things settled down."

* * *

"I can't believe we're out of coffee," John said, bewildered at the prospect of not having his morning dose of caffeine.

"I'm sure there's more. It's buried in the back of the bucket shed," I reassured him. "I thought I saw a bag in the cupboard yesterday."

"That bag is whole beans, and I don't want to have to start the gennie for a few seconds to grind them, assuming you have a grinder." He slumped in his chair.

On top of the woodstove, looking very much like a decoration is an antique coffee mill. Antique, yes, but it is still very functional. When I handed it to him he stared at it, then at me. I showed him what it was and how to use it.

"You never cease to amaze me with what you have thought of and have stocked," he said.

"I've always been fascinated by manual tools and with how our grandparents use to do things before all these electric gadgets came along. Sometimes the old tools come in handy!" I grinned. "I just hope I never get to the point of using the Sad Iron."

"What is a sad iron?" I took the odd looking hunk of cast iron off the shelf where I was using it as a bookend.

When I placed it in his hands, he exclaimed, "That's heavy!"

"They usually come in sets of two, with one handle," I unclipped the wood handle from it to show him. "They would stay on the woodstove, heating, until needed. Whoever was ironing that day would set up the ironing board next to the stove, clip the handle on and iron until that one got too cool, set it back on the stove, and clip on the next one. That way she could keep ironing, since there was always one being reheated."

"Why are they called 'sad' irons?"

"I know that kind of chore wouldn't make *me* very happy!" I laughed. "If I recall, 'sad' is an old word for solid, because some of the sad irons didn't have detachable handles."

While John played with the mill, adjusting the grind until he was satisfied with it, I made sugar cookies for the kids to take to school at noon. The coffee tasted extra good this morning.

* * *

Because all six of us were going into Moose Creek, we discussed taking the car. Jason thought it might be better if they took Don's four-wheel drive truck and John and I could take a four-wheeler. We would be hitting some muddy roads that the four-wheeler would handle better. He had a good point. I handed him the plastic container filled with cookies, reminding him I wanted the container back. It was one of those disposable ones, but *nothing* was disposable anymore.

By the time Eric and Jason met us at the township hall after getting the kids to school, plans had changed. Ken decided that it would be better if he and Eric teamed up, so they could get to know each other better. Jason and Lenny set out on foot checking up on the few businesses that were on their way to the heart of Moose Creek. Eric and Ken took Don's truck down Resort Road to check on the camps along there.

Anna, Karen, John and I discussed the best plan for the rest of the houses.

"I still think I'll take Lake Meade, I know most of the folks anyway," Karen said. "It's also a nice day for a walk." Even as she said that, I noticed she had several speed loaders in her pocket for her revolver. A couple of years ago, before she retired, we'd been talking weapons. She was supposed to carry an automatic like the rest of the troopers, however, she preferred her .38 revolver and could load it faster than any of the guys could change a magazine.

"Do you have a radio, Karen?" I asked, knowing that they only had one between them.

"Ken took it."

"These don't have much range, but they're better than nothing." I handed her an FRS unit. Jason had taken one with him, and John and I would keep the third. I gave the last one to Anna, so we could check in with her if necessary. We had been agreed to keep the first day short, working only four hours. The school would hold the kids until then.

Without other electrical interference, the radios worked rather well. John and I were on the road out of town where the houses were well spaced. Most of them on twenty, forty or eighty acres, and with rare exception were visible from the road. The first five we stopped at were empty. It was easy to find the circuit panel and pull the mains off, disconnecting the house from the grid. At the sixth house we found a dog on the front porch, lying by the front door, like he was waiting for his master to come home, long dead. I don't understand owners who will let their pets fend for themselves. I was angry when I stepped over the dog and shoved the door open. The stench hit me hard and I gagged. I guess the dog's master was home after all.

I turned back toward John. "Take a deep breath before you come in." I pulled my turtleneck over my nose. "There's a body in here somewhere."

John followed me in with a handkerchief over his nose. He headed for the back of the house. In the kitchen he found the circuit breaker panel, opened it, pulled the mains, and backtracked, grabbing my arm as he moved quickly. Once outside we both took deep gulps of fresh air. I took a notepad from my pocket and jotted down the address.

"Are you alright?" I asked John when I noted how pale he was.

He nodded.

"This won't be the last one, you know. I mean, I hope it is, but chances are there are more."

He nodded again, and revved up the ATV.

* * *

We covered fifteen more houses before we headed back to the township offices. By the solemn faces, I knew we weren't the only ones to have discovered bodies. Only Jason and Lenny had been spared. I'm sure that's because in the closer housing units of town, everyone kept tabs on each other.

"What's the total so far?" I asked.

"All the houses in the town proper have been covered. The power is completely off, and major appliances are unplugged. There were no unpleasant surprises," Lenny reported.

Ken looked down at his notes. "Eric and I covered twenty camps. Five had someone still living in them and the rest were vacant. We found two bodies, both older folks. I'm assuming they died of natural causes."

"I covered ten houses," Karen said. "Most were empty and no bodies, but I did run into some opposition. At the last house a few of the folks were not exactly friendly. One of them actually pointed a shotgun at me! I told them—from a distance—about the power, and then left."

Ken glanced down at his notes once more. "We've done almost eighty houses today, and found only three bodies." He folded his papers. "I'd say we've done rather well, all things considered. If The Jack had anything left, I'd suggest we go out for a beer. Since that's not the case, I'll see everyone here tomorrow morning at nine-thirty."

* * *

Back home, Emilee jabbered away about how nice the teachers were, how much fun she and Jacob had at school, and how everyone enjoyed the cookies that I had sent with them.

"Can we take more tomorrow? Dad says we're going again and earlier this time. All day school, just like at home."

I'm not sure if Emi was enjoying school itself or the attention of bringing treats for everyone.

"Sure, but we'll have to make the cookies tonight, Em, since there won't be time in the morning. How about we make oatmeal this time?"

"Yum!" she exclaimed, clapping her hands, which got Jacob clapping too. "Those are my favorite!"

* * *

JOURNAL ENTRY: March 13

The oatmeal cookie recipe made four dozen cookies, and I sent only two dozen with the kids. It's not good to have anyone get used to something that they can't always have. The kids were dropped off shortly after 9:15 A.M. School starting time has gotten very fluid with only a dozen students. Some showed up later, some not at all. I made a simple jelly sandwich for Emi, and sent a package of ramen for Jacob's lunch. The teachers were very used to Jacob's finicky eating, and happily boiled some water for his noodles so they could be sure he would eat.

* * *

The four of us were already at the township hall when Ken and Karen showed up. Anna was there when we arrived. Lenny didn't even show.

"Even though we knew we were doing something important, I think Lenny was really bored yesterday," Jason commented. "Or maybe he didn't want to face any bodies today. I have a feeling that when we branch out, that it becomes more of a possibility. I'm not sure that I want to either, though I'm willing to risk it to get the power back on and stable."

None of us want to find bodies, but better us than some children.

We teamed up differently this time: John, Jason and I comprised one team. Ken, Karen and Eric were on the other. The trouble Karen had yesterday shook her up pretty good. Ken wouldn't let her go alone again.

Our team headed for Guy and Dawn's place on two of our new four-wheelers. The road looked pretty good, only because no one had used it. With two of us on one machine, the weight bogged us down and we had a rough go of it for a stretch. Guy and Dawn's driveway was made of well-packed gravel. I breathed with relief when we got sure footing again.

"Guy? Dawn?" I called out as I was dismounting the ATV. The door opened quickly and Dawn came running out, grabbing me in a bear hug. The first thing I noticed as I hugged her in return was the gun stuck in the back of her jeans. This was a huge surprise because she was deathly afraid of guns. I stepped back, holding her by the shoulders.

"Okay, who are you and what have you done with my friend?" I laughed at her look of confusion. "The gun, Dawn, the gun."

"Oh, that. I took your advice and got over it," she grinned. "Turns out I'm a pretty good shot!"

"No," Guy added, "she's a damn excellent shot!"

Dawn beamed. She nearly wept with joy when I told her about the power coming back and why we were there.

"I'm hoping the two of you will come with us while we search your neighborhood to turn off the power, or at least tell us which neighbors are gone and which ones might still be around."

"That's easy," Guy said. "We're the only ones left on this end of Lake Meade. Everyone else left early on. Oh, there is one house you might want to avoid—the Cutters'. They stayed for a while, but around Christmas we heard two shots, spaced out. When there was no more smoke from their chimney, I figure it was a double suicide."

He described the house, and said that he would go there instead. John went with Guy to disconnect the houses to the south, while Jason, Dawn and I went to the north. The only thing we came across was more dead pets. I don't think I will ever become immune to the anger and sorrow I felt. From an early age, I was always more connected to animals than I was to people, and I would get emotionally distraught even *hearing* about the death of a beloved pet.

In slightly over an hour, we met back at their place, having disconnected fifteen empty houses.

"Don't forget to unplug your refrigerator and freezer on Friday morning!" I reminded them. "You certainly don't want the surge to short out anything. I doubt that we could get a repairman up here. With so many that we've managed to take offline, it shouldn't be a problem, however, *I'm* sure not taking the chance!"

"Mom, I'm sure you haven't forgotten it's my birthday today," Jason whispered after pulling me aside. I smiled; of course I remembered; I would never forget one of my sons' birthdays.

"I don't know if you had anything in mind, but could we invite Guy and Dawn, and Ken and Karen over?" He hesitated. "We've been searching Uncle Don's basement. There are cases and cases of his homemade beer still there down there," he said excitedly, "and a case of Nancy's wine too. If I could talk you into making a couple of pizzas, it could be a good way to celebrate getting the power back on."

How typically unselfish of him.

"Jason, it's your birthday, invite anyone you want." I tried to remember if there's enough mozzarella for two large pizzas; if not, there was always Parmesan.

* * *

When we all grouped again at the township hall, Eric had already collected the kids from the school. They played a game of tag in the near empty parking lot while the adults watched. Jason made his offer of beer and pizza to Ken and Karen, who quickly accepted.

* * *

"After watching those two kids playing, I just knew I had to share what we found," Karen said and paused to sip her cold beer. Jason had filled a cooler with snow from the north side of the barn, the side where the snow lasts the longest, and packed in a dozen brown bottles. A cold beer was the biggest treat of all. "Step outside with me for a minute, and bring the kids too."

We gathered outside and watched Karen open the back door of their truck. She mumbled something as she reached in, and then pulled out a Golden Retriever puppy!

"Happy Birthday, Jason!" Karen exclaimed with excitement.

CHAPTER THIRTY-ONE

JOURNAL ENTRY: March 14

A puppy! I'm glad the boys have it and not me. Tufts would probably run away from home! Jason has dealt with Amanda's Shih Tzu puppies before, so I'm not worried about the care. Jacob was a bit leery at first, but it being a puppy, it loved the attention, and it being a *dog*, seemed to know that Jacob was special. Emilee wants it for herself, of course. Now to find it food! I know we can pressure cook avian bones to the point of them being soft, and add it to other things, like rice. The boys have always enjoyed hunting, and spring is a good time to find grouse. It will be a win-win meal when they do. The humans get the breasts and the rest will be cooked down for the pup.

The puppy is about ten weeks old. The mother was bred a week before the event and gave birth shortly after New Year's. She really is a beautiful thing, pure bred, and likely would have gotten the owners a pretty penny. Things being like they are, however, they gave away two of the five pups, two died, and the fifth is now Jason's. In honor of the only other Golden we've known and loved, Jason named her Chivas. Kathy will be pleased, as the first Chivas was her dog. Maybe someday we will give Kathy and Bob one of Chivas' puppies. I'd like that.

The days have cooled back down and the nights are cold. With the bright sunshine during the day though, it's perfect weather for tapping trees and making maple syrup.

* * *

I was out digging in the small shed when John came looking for me.

"Are you looking for something in particular?" he asked peeking into the shed past the boxes that I had moved.

"You're just in time! Can you pull these boxes out so we can get this big one out?" I rapped on a plastic box.

He slid one of the other plastic boxes out first and set it on the soggy grass, then put two cardboard boxes on top of it, exactly like I would have done to keep the more fragile boxes dry. I pushed the larger one towards him and he pulled it out of my way.

"What's in here? It's not as heavy as it looks."

"Syrup making gear. Six sets of taps, buckets and tents, plus a brace and a selection of bits," I answered, wiping my hands on my jeans. "Have you ever made maple syrup?"

"Made it? No, but I've eaten it on pancakes," he grinned. He set the box aside and handed the other boxes back to me to put away.

* * *

I lined everything up on the counter and filled the sink with hot, soapy water, adding the taps to soak, and washing the tents first. They were small pieces of sheet metal, crimped in half to form a tent to keep debris, snow, and rain from falling in, and had curled edges on the bottom that would hold it onto the bucket. The buckets were galvanized pails with a hole near the top that hooks onto the tap.

"It's a simple setup, really," I explained to John. "We'll drill a hole in the tree at a slight angle, so the sap runs downward, two feet from the ground. We drive the tap in, let it run a couple of minutes to flush out the sawdust, and then attach the pail and tent. Tomorrow morning we will collect the sap and start boiling."

"That's it? I thought it would be more involved than that."

"Well, that's really only the first step. Once we collect a couple of gallons, and before boiling, we filter the clear sap to get any debris or bugs out of it, then it goes into a pot on the stove. When it cooks down, we keep adding more until it's condensed to a dark golden color. It will take about fifty gallons of sap to make one gallon of syrup."

He raised his eyebrows.

"It's worth it, trust me."

* * *

While we were setting the six taps, two to a tree, I told him a story about one of the locals.

"Charlie couldn't figure out why everyone else was having a great sap run and his was very little. He had done it all right. He measured up two feet and set the taps on the south side of the tree. It wasn't until the spring melt down when he found out his error. He had to get a stepladder to pull the taps that were six feet up from the ground. He had measured two feet up *from the snow*. We all had a good chuckle, and try not to remind him of that."

I showed John where I had set taps before that were now plugged with a branch from that tree, and sprayed with pruning seal.

"These old tapping spots are well healed, so we can drill as near them as we want, otherwise we'd have to move over a few inches."

"How do you know they're healed?"

"They must be. I haven't tapped them in four years," I said. "Besides, they're not weeping. One of the tapping traditions I like the best is the coffee made from fresh sap." I smiled at the thought of tomorrow morning. "It gives the coffee an interesting and pleasant taste. You'll like it."

* * *

JOURNAL ENTRY: March 15

I already let Anna know that I will not be on hand when the power comes back at noon. I really want to be at home with my family for this momentous occasion because it is a step back towards normalcy. It seems strange to consider electricity "momentous," and I feel certain that no one would have thought this way six months ago. Here we were, though, waiting for a light bulb to glow.

Last night we brought in one of the sap buckets, poured the contents into a pitcher and replaced the bucket on its tap-hook on the tree. The sap was slushy by the rapid cool-down from the drop in temperature of the night. By morning, though, it was completely melted and there was just enough for the French press.

* * *

John took a tentative sip of his coffee. The smile lit up his eyes first.

"Good, huh?" I asked.

"We get to do this every morning?" he asked.

"Every morning of tapping."

"Which is how long?"

"It will depend on the weather," I answered honestly. "Some years it will be three weeks, others only a week. We can collect sap until it starts to run cloudy, then we have to pull the taps or risk damaging the tree."

After we savored the flavorful coffee, we headed for the barn to uncover my old cooking stand, the one that I had used in the woods. Jason had made a custom cabinet for me that matched the cupboards in my kitchen. It was slightly smaller and just big enough to hold a twenty pound propane tank, and once the casters were installed it was as high as the counters and easy to work on. I had purchased a single gas burner and the necessary hoses and regulator to fit the tank, so Jason was able to size the opening in the top and everything could be contained inside. The top is unique; he made it a square trough. I had collected all kinds of rocks during my many walks and placed them within a bed of cement poured into this "trough." The first rocks that I placed were flat and set under the "feet" of the burner so it would be level. The rest were arranged to fit. There were rose quartz and white quartz, sand smoothed glass, stones with red veins, chunks of granite, and the glittery hematite and pieces with smooth holes worn from water constantly beating on one spot. All were selected carefully and they all were very special to me. Once the cement dried and hardened, my river rock tabletop served as a heat resistant countertop for cooking with propane. Now it's used only for cooking syrup.

"Why don't we use the gas stove in the kitchen?" John wanted to know.

"I did that. Once," I laughed. "Many years ago when I lived in Lower Michigan. The steam from cooking the sap down isn't normal steam. It's a sugary steam. I had a sticky coating over everything in the kitchen, including the ceiling. What a mess it was to clean up. From then on I cooked outside, and did only the final cooking and canning inside."

We set the cooking cabinet in the center of the barn after backing the car out. It didn't matter if the upper rafters got some of the sticky steam, and we needed the wind block that the barn would provide. John brought one of the full twenty pound tanks from the deck and I showed him how to hook it up. From then on, it would be his job to change the tank when needed. We should only go through two tanks, maybe three, and that depended on the length of the season.

When we broke for lunch at noon, we were rewarded with lights! I got my digital alarm clock from the bed-stand, plugged it into a kitchen socket, and set the time. This way we would instantly know if the power went out again for a period, but came back on; the clock would be blinking if that happened.

Having power was joyous, but we still had work to do. After some soup for lunch, back outside we went. John poured the contents of the six collection pails into five-gallon plastic buckets, and filled two of them. Ten gallons is a good first day! I strained enough of one into my largest cooking pot to fill it halfway, and set it to start heating. Remembering how I had two pots going out in the woods, over the wood fire, I asked John to bring one of the plastic buckets inside. I filled my next pot with the cold tree sap and set it on the cook stove.

"What about the steam?" he reminded me.

"This is just to take the chill off. It's easier to boil warm sap than it is cold. We'll take it out and add it to the big pot before it can come to a boil and start steaming." This was a lesson that I learned that first year in the woods, and made the cooking down go much faster.

* * *

I saw the boys, their children, and the puppy crossing the yard around five o'clock. Jason stopped to examine the pails on the trees, making some comments to Eric. I was about to say something to Jason about rationing when he set a six-pack of beer on the table. He produced a bottle of Zinfandel, so I figured I could remind him later.

"Uncle Don tapped his trees, didn't he?" Jason asked.

"Yes, so that equipment should be around somewhere. Maybe in their barn? I know he used the deep fryer burner for cooking. He would always set up the syrup stuff and his beer brewing in that screened shelter you built him." I visualized my brother sitting out there with a tarp dropped as a wind block and felt my throat tighten a bit. "Are you going to tap?"

"I think so. It'll give us something to do." Jason was getting bored. Eric would too, eventually. We all would in time.

I noticed the puppy sniffing around Tufts' food dish, so I moved it onto the table and sat back down. She scarfed up the pieces that had landed on the floor just when Tufts decided to make an appearance. We all watched with interest, and we wouldn't let either animal get hurt. The pup went to Tufts, sniffing with playful curiosity. Tufts hissed and Chivas stopped. The cat sat down where he was and so did the pup, but being a puppy, Chivas lasted five seconds sitting still and ventured closer to this big black furry thing. When she got too close, Tufts gave her a healthy swat on the nose with a clawless paw, and sent her scurrying to hide behind a table leg then Tufts slowly sauntered out of the room. I thought their first meeting went very well.

"Why don't you build something, Jason?" I commented. "Now that the power is back, I would think you'd be anxious to fire up your workshop."

His head came up sharply, and he turned toward the clock with its red digital numbers shining brightly, like he was seeing it for the first time.

"I forgot that today was the day. Yeah, maybe I'll make something..." he trailed off, lost in thought. He turned back, smiled, raised his beer and said, "To electricity!" He still had that faraway look in his eyes. Eric was preoccupied with his daughter. John was silent, staring out the window. Something felt very wrong with my family.

* * *

Later that evening after the boys had left John asked me if I missed going to work.

"In a way, yes, I do miss it. Massage is a calling to me. It's how I help people," I said, and then something occurred to me. "Are you asking for a massage?"

"Oh, no, that's not what I was getting at," he said with a hint of embarrassment. "I was thinking that with the power back on and things getting back to normal, you might be called back to the resort."

"That's always a possibility, though things *aren't* back to normal, John. We just have electricity back, that's all. We still have a gasoline shortage, and I don't know if there will be propane deliveries or not. There still isn't any food coming to Fram's. I doubt that Mack's has been fully restocked either." Something else occurred to me. "Do *you* miss going to work, John?"

I was afraid to hear his answer.

"Working at the mine, or rather, for Green-Way, had some advantages. I would get up, be driven to the mine, work a twelve-hour shift, be driven back. I ate dinner or breakfast and went to bed. The next day I did the same thing. Seven days a week, for six weeks straight. I never had to think about my day or what I had to do. It was always the same. I never had to think, so I had no worries." He had a shadow of sadness in his voice. "Of course when I was at the mine, I was always thinking about the job, what we were doing, what could happen a mile underground, and I was very good at what I did. Very good. They paid me exceedingly well for that. Sometimes I think they paid us so well because we had no other life. It was a way to keep us content—a big paycheck. The only break, the only thing I ever had to look forward to was you, once a week." He smiled at me, but there was pain there, in the back of his eyes.

* * *

JOURNAL ENTRY: March 16

Once again we brought in some slushy sap and made a small pot of coffee with it. Fresh maple sap with fresh ground coffee. It can't get any better than this. All this ran through my mind as we went through the process and the motions of plugging things back into the grid, setting the cell phones, the 4G, the Bluetooth, and the tablet on their chargers, powering up the satellite receiver on the TV and setting the clocks. How quickly we are reverting to those old ways. I felt saddened by this for some reason. I should be glad, shouldn't I? Things are on the way to being back to normal, right? Was I happy with the old normal? I think that I almost prefer my new normal. It isn't less stressful but I think I am happier, or at least more content in some ways. Maybe it's just that I was more needed.

It's Saturday, so no school for the kids. I called Jason on the phone. Wow, does that feel strange. I made arrangements for Emilee to come over while I make bread. She's ten and it's time she learned how. I'm hoping Jason never finds Nancy's electric bread maker! Some things are just better by hand. Another interesting revelation is that I keep mentally deferring to Jason as being in charge over there, where Eric is actually the older of the two. I wonder why I do that.

* * *

"So, Emi, did your mom ever make fresh bread?"

She stood there grinning in the blue denim apron her uncle had made me when he was a few years older than she is now. I had required both boys to take a home economics class when they entered high school. Jason chose to make *me* something in the sewing segment. My four "requirements" had served them well: home economics, drafting, typing and shop. They both could cook and do basic sewing, they both follow patterns and blueprints when building things, they learned do many basic household repairs, and typing. It's the way of the world with computers. Eric even called me one time from a training session while he was still in the military to thank me for making him take typing. Those were some wonderful memories for me.

"Only once, and she used the bread machine Grandpa Jim gave her," Emilee said wistfully, stirring the flour with her finger. "It tasted really good!"

She smiled, although I could tell she was thinking of her mom.

"Well, I'm going to show you how to make the same yummy bread without using a machine. Would you like that?"

I need to get her thoughts away from her mother, whom she might not see for a long time. When she nodded vigorously, I remembered how resilient young children were.

"First we put a cup of warm water in this big bowl. The water can't be too hot, and not too cold. Here, stick your finger in to feel the temperature. You did wash your hands didn't you?"

Looking down at my granddaughter, I couldn't help but think of a framed picture hanging on my wall of Emilee at the age of eight, set into a picture of me at the same age. Except for one picture being in color, the other in black and white, we looked like twins. It was uncanny.

"How does the water feel?" I asked.

"Warm, not hot," she answered. We added two teaspoons of sugar and the same of yeast, and then she stirred it, and we waited until it began to bubble and foam. Then she added a teaspoon of salt and a quarter cup of oil, measuring it all carefully. Next in was a quarter cup of instant milk and one cup of flour. I let her do all the stirring. I don't know how she got flour on her nose and on her chin, but there it was. My heart swelled. We added flour until she couldn't stir it anymore, and then I took over. Emi added flour a bit at a time while I stirred until the dough was stiff. I sprinkled some flour over the top and worked it into a sticky ball with my hand, while she put more flour on the countertop. I dumped the dough into that and scraped the bowl.

"Are you ready for the fun part?" I asked.

Her eyes got big. I started kneading it, first pushing it with the heel of my hands, then pulling it back with my fingers, and then I let her try. She got the hang of it pretty quickly. I was pleased.

"Keep going while I clean the bowl."

I washed the big bowl and put a splash of oil in it, while she punched and beat the bread dough. We put it into the bowl, turning it so the oil coated it, and then covered the big yellow bowl with a towel to rise.

Emi and I took a walk outside to watch John work on the syrup. I saw him quickly pocket his cellphone when we approached the barn.

He had collected and cooked down twenty gallons. The sap in the pot was turning darker all the time. I could tell he was excited over the prospect of making his first maple syrup. He promised a curious Emilee that he would explain the different rocks in the tabletop to her later, when he was done cooking. By the time Emi and I collected eggs, the bread was ready for folding into a loaf, and its second rise.

"Why does it take so long, Nahna?" Emilee asked.

"Good things take longer," I answered.

Another hour and the bread was ready for the oven. I set the timer for forty minutes just as John brought in the pot of golden syrup. I stirred it, watching it slide off the spoon.

"Almost ready!"

I set the pot on the stove, lighting the burner. It didn't take long for it to bubble, and I lowered the heat so it wouldn't scorch. It would be a small batch, but it was an important one. The excitement in the house was high with Emilee's first loaf of homemade bread and John's first batch of maple syrup and the accompanying delicious aromas—competing for our attention. The house smelled wonderful!

I slipped away to call Eric, sure he would want to be part of this. Everyone showed up a few minutes after I took the bread out of the oven.

"Oh, man, does it smell good in here!" Eric exclaimed when he walked in and hugged his daughter.

"Dad! I made bread! I really did, didn't I, Nahna?" Emilee looked over at me as she clung to her father.

"You sure did," I said. I cut the first slice of the hot bread, even though it was really still too hot. I portioned a couple of slices cut in half for us to dip into a bowl of John's maple syrup. Dessert before dinner! It was wonderful.

CHAPTER THIRTY-TWO

"I'm taking some time off, Anna. With the power back on, everyone is happy and things are getting back to normal. You don't need me anymore." I leaned back in my chair. "I'll file a final report today. You can send it to Tom or do whatever you want with it. I'm also officially resigning as your deputy."

I'm sure she conveniently forgot I was still sworn in from when she was down with the flu.

"Are you sure you want to do this, Allexa? I understand that this has been very stressful for you. It has for all of us. You've been a tremendous asset to the town and we won't forget all that you've done." She was quiet for a minute, as if trying to formulate the right words in her head for what she wanted to say. "You *will* be compensated, Allexa, I assure you."

"I don't care about that."

"I know you don't, but *I* do!"

"I really have other things I need to do now, Anna."

This was hard to explain and it wasn't coming out the way that I had wanted. I needed to not worry about everyone in Moose Creek. I needed to talk to my sister and my friends. I needed to plant flowers and tomatoes. I needed to get my life back. I needed a lot of things I felt I was losing my grip on.

"You don't have to explain yourself to me. I will accept your resignation as my deputy, and don't you dare try to resign from being emergency manager. That one I will *not* accept."

"Deal."

I turned back to my computer to do a final report. I wanted to go home.

* * *

JOURNAL ENTRY: March 19

The weather has been staying in the high fifties during the day, and drying the ground out nicely. I hauled out my tumbler composter from under the cistern platform. Although with the power back on, I have the washing machine available anytime I needed it, I had kept in the back of my mind that the composter would make a good manual washing device, and one of these days, I intended to find out if it could work. Even not using it for clothes, I could see using it to wash blankets and big items, since the capacity is three times that of the washing machine. Maybe I'll try it for the bedspread soon, instead of going to the Laundromat.

The sap has been running really good, a constant flow instead of a fast drip. The weather is perfect for collecting sap. From each of the six taps, we've collected almost two gallons, twice a day, from the big, mature trees. In only two days of constant boiling we have enough for a gallon of fresh syrup. Although the work has been tedious and continuous, it certainly was not hard.

* * *

I had just set a loaf of cheesy bread to its final rise when John came in.

"You want to check this batch? I'm thinking it's getting close to being ready," John asked. He really has been pleased with having something to do and learning something new at the same time. We walked out to the barn, steam rolling out of the big doors in fragrant clouds.

I stirred the dark golden liquid with the big spoon and let it run off of the edge. "Yes, very close. You're getting a good eye for this. Keep it cooking while I get the jars prepped and the canner heating. It shouldn't take too long. I'll let you know when I'm ready."

A half hour later, we were ladling hot, deep golden syrup into pint jars, fixing them with a sterilized lid and ring. Five jars were submerged into the boiling water bath and timed for ten minutes. I lifted them out and John set them on a folded towel to cool. Then we started on the next five jars.

"Now that's a beautiful day's work!" I said, hooking my arm into his to admire the ten pint jars of the deep amber liquid, all perfectly sealed and lined up on the counter. I rested my head comfortably against his shoulder.

"Do we need to do more?" he asked.

"Not unless you want to. This should last us a while. Jason is doing his own, so we don't need to provide for them. We could pull the taps, now."

He nodded tiredly.

I got the small wagon from the garden, and armed with a hammer and a near empty can of pruning seal (another hole in my preps), we started at the furthest tree. We removed the tent, then the bucket, emptying any sap into the five-gallon pail for tomorrow's final coffee, and put everything in the wagon. Next came pulling the tap out, which John did while I searched for just the right stick to plug the hole. I jammed the stick as far as I could and broke it off. John used the hammer to drive it in. A quick spray of sealant and we moved to the next tree. The last bucket to come down reinforced John's desire to stop syruping. The bucket had two inches of milky fluid in the bottom proving *this* tree at least, was done.

I dumped it on the ground. It really didn't surprise me though. The temperature had climbed into the high fifties for several days now. The removal process took less than fifteen minutes, and I still had to wash everything so it could be stored for next year.

I told John I wanted to make something special with that first small batch that he had made. There was about a cup left.

I melted two sticks of precious butter, plus a half-cup of evaporated milk in a pot. I now had only four pounds of butter left from the ten that I had in the freezer back in October. A sobering thought. Then I added the cup of maple syrup to the pot, a half-cup of brown sugar, and two cups of graham cracker crumbs that I found in the back of the cupboard, sealed in a glass jar. I cooked that at a boil for five minutes. Next I opened one of the jars of canned crackers, using the club crackers. I lined a 9x13 inch pan with the crackers, then poured one-third the cooked mixture over them. Then another layer of crackers, another third of the mixture. One more layer of crackers, using all of that one jar. I took a chocolate bar that I had been hiding and grated it into a bowl. I made sure that the final third of the mixture was hot, spread it over the top and sprinkled the chocolate over the surface. The heat softened the chocolate to the right consistency. Then I set the pan in the pantry to chill.

"What did you just make?" John asked with a fascinated look on his face.

I grinned. "Maple cracker bars! You are going to be amazed how good they are!"

"But you used a whole jar of crackers."

"Yes, John, and this is the reason I stored up what I did. All the canning I did, all the work I went through, has been to provide things for myself and my family. Things that might not be available when the time came to need them. That's what prepping is all about, hon. Having what you need, when you need it. It might be tomatoes or ready-made soup. It might be aspirin and Band-Aids, or it might be rope or crackers. It might even be something I forgot."

"I doubt that you've forgotten anything," he said, putting his arms around me for one of those special hugs that I've come to love.

* * *

Later that evening everyone enjoyed the sugary treat, and *none* of it was going to the school!

* * *

JOURNAL ENTRY: March 20

The chilly nights have quickly given way to more moderate temperatures in the fifties, which means open windows to me, and fresh air for sleeping. Listening to the woods wake up in the spring is very special. The night birds come back, the animals rustle around in the leaves looking for food. I was very excited to hear geese honking high above us this morning, and I almost wept with joy to hear the very distinctive call of the Hermit Thrush looking for his mate.

This morning's fifty-two degrees rose to sixty-five degrees by noon and I knew how I wanted to spend the day - washing curtains and hanging them in the sunshine! John helped me sort through the coils of rope stacked on a shelf. After the blizzard was over, we retrieved all the ropes, carefully rewinding them, tying them individually and hoping that we wouldn't need them for a long time.

* * *

"You don't know how this makes me feel! I love the way things smell when they have dried outside." There was only room for four fifteen-foot lines, but it was enough.

"Since you'll be spending the afternoon washing curtains, you don't mind if I take the four-wheeler out for a ride, do you?" John asked, pulling the last clothesline tight.

"No, of course not," I replied, though I was disappointed that I wouldn't have the extra set of hands for some of the other work I had in mind.

I took down all of the curtains in the kitchen and dining room, and set them to wash. Then I started washing the windows. Months' worth of wood smoke was evident as I sprayed on the window cleaner, watching it drip in dirty streaks. I had to wash each one twice, and now they're sparkling. When I got to the glass door wall, I also had to clean the track that was full of mud and birdseed. No wonder it was getting hard to move!

When the first load of curtains was waving on the clothesline, I put the next load in from the bedroom and hallway. Since this room was the furthest from the woodstove, the windows weren't quite as dirty, but still needed cleaning. As each window was cleaned, I left it open to help air the house out.

Trying to be systematic, I moved the dining table, swept and mopped under it, moved it back and did the same to the rest of the room in preparation of hanging the clean window coverings back up. For some reason I felt an urgency to clean, or maybe it was just the warm breezes that was spurring me on. With the power readily available now, I vacuumed the bedroom and as a last thought, stripped the bed and washed those sheets too. We might even get fresh pillowcases tonight!

When the sheets finally went on the line, and since all the curtains were back on the windows, I began cleaning up the yard from the winter, a very harsh winter in more ways than one. I stopped, leaned on the rake, and pulled my cloth hanky out of a pocket to wipe away the tears as memories bombarded me. I tamped down the emotions and lifted my face into the sun, welcoming its heat.

* * *

With all the curtains cleaned and back up, windows washed, floors cleaned, even freshly sun-dried sheets back on the bed, I sat down in my rocker with a sigh of satisfaction. It was then I realized it was almost six o'clock, and John was still not home.

The kids would be over for dinner soon. It was our Wednesday spaghetti night, and I had yet to put it together. I found a jar of pork shreds for meat, and two jars of sauce that I made last summer, a pound of linguini instead of my usual angel-hair and a package of noodles for Jacob. My arms were full when I walked out of the pantry, and almost bumped into John. My heart leaped. I was so glad to see him.

"Did you have a good ride?" I asked, though I really wanted to tell him that I was getting worried.

"Yes, I did. It was a beautiful day. Let me help with that," he said, taking two of the jars from me.

As we set everything down on the work island, he said, "The house looks great, nothing like fresh air."

I wanted to scream. It was burning in me to know where he had been all this time. Just then the kids came in.

FINALE

The power has been back on for a full week now. It's been easy to get used to again… water when we want it, lights in any room, the refrigerator making ice, coffee ready before we get up, clothes washed and dried in the same day. The Internet was back on too, and I spent way too much time catching up on the groups, reading news, and sending emails. It sure felt good. Watching TV at night still feels surreal and mystical. In reality, my life will never be the same ever again, no matter how free the power is or how much is now stocked in the grocery stores. Our lives have been changed, damaged, for some beyond repair. We've starved, we've killed, some have been killed.

No, we will never be the same.

I woke during the night with my heart pounding and I was gasping for breath. It was only the result of a bad dream. I snuggled closer to John for comfort, and found he wasn't there. The sheets were cold, so I knew he had been up for some time. I got up and wandered toward a softly glowing light in the other room. He was standing by the deck door, staring out into the darkness. I wonder what's on his mind?

* * *

I leaned against the doorway to watch John with his sweat pants slung low on his hips, barefoot and shirtless.

"I can feel when you come near me, you know," he said, without turning from the window. "I don't have to see you to know you're there." The small battery operated lantern cast a soft glow and his shadow bounced off the opposite wall. I waited until he turned around.

"Are you okay, John?" I asked softly.

"I couldn't sleep and didn't want to disturb you."

It didn't escape me that he hadn't answered my question.

"Why don't you go back to bed, Allex? I'll be there in a minute," he promised.

I turned and went back to bed. A few minutes later I felt him shift under the covers and he curled himself around me, holding me snug against him. We both finally fell asleep.

* * *

We made love that morning. It was sweet and gentle and… sad. John slipped out of bed and I heard the shower start. I turned over and wept. All I could think of were the unexplained hours away from home, the quickly hung up phone calls when I came near, and most of all his growing distance. Before the water went off, I used the second bath to rinse my face and use eye-drops, hoping to conceal the redness from my tears. I slipped on my usual morning sweatpants and t-shirt, both now too baggy on me.

I was already pouring a cup of coffee when he came out, dressed in jeans and a deep green hoodie. I turned to him. "You're leaving, aren't you?" I asked, making more of a statement than a question. My hands were shaking and the coffee sloshed. I set the cup down on the table.

"I got a message from Green-Way. They're starting up operations again, and I have to report back."

He crossed the room to me. I backed up. "Allex…" his voice caught, pleading in that sweet, charming North Carolina drawl that I've gotten so use to, clawing at my heart.

"Why can't you stay here and still work for them?"

"They don't work that way." He ran his hands over his bald head in that oh so familiar way, and I lost it. The tears streamed down my face. He stepped closer, using his thumb to wipe away the tears on my cheek. I blinked hard, sending a fresh cascade down my wet face. Were those tears I saw in his eyes? I couldn't tell.

"If you have to go, John, then just go." I was surprised the words came out. I hadn't seen his duffle bag already packed by the door. I wanted to reach out, to hold him and keep him from leaving me. But I can't force him to stay. I can't make him love me. My hands hung limp at my sides, twitching, aching to touch him, to hold him here. I wanted to beg him to stay. I stood silent. Pride stopped me.

John picked up the duffle bag and walked out.

I stood at the door, hidden by the curtain, and watched him walk down the road, the duffle slung across his broad shoulders, a sob escaping from my throat with every step he took away from me. How could he do this to me? To us? Did the past three months mean nothing to him? He *had* told me, tried to warn me so long ago, that he wouldn't get emotionally tied to anyone ever again, because he always left. *Always.*

On uncertain legs I went into the bathroom, hoping to find some relief under a hot shower. There on the dryer, all neatly folded, were the clothes that I had given him that first day; sweatpants, t-shirts and socks, with the Beretta sitting on top.

He wasn't coming back.

My world shattered. My life shattered. Then my heart shattered. My legs collapsed and I slid to the floor, and everything around me went dark.

THE JOURNAL:

Ash Fall

Book Two

PROLOGUE

The cool, wet spring, with muddy roads and soggy lawns, eventually gave way to the more pleasant warm breezes of the approaching summer. As the long slope down to the small spring-fed creek dried out, the wildflower seed Allexa had strewn about last fall took root, and a rainbow of color began to dot the landscape. With the warm gusts of wind and warmer sunshine, it was just too tempting. Allexa set aside the rototiller and took her glass of iced tea to sit by the creek, hoping to straighten out her chaotic thoughts.

All the tragic events of the harsh winter paled next to her loneliness. The months of being without power, the sickness that had swept through her town of Moose Creek, even the fires and shootings she could and had dealt with. Though the loss of her brother was difficult, she could visit his grave if she wanted to. John was a different matter. He was out there, somewhere. And she missed him fiercely. Letting out a sigh, she rehashed that last day in her mind. Pride had kept Allexa from begging John to stay with her. Pride had kept her from telling him how much she loved him, needed him. Pride had watched him walk away, six weeks ago.

Eric, her oldest son, had found her collapsed in the bathroom, her cat Tufts curled up tightly against her chest. Eric had come across the road to borrow something that was quickly forgotten when he found her too still form lying on the cold tile floor. A cool, wet towel to her face, much to Tufts' chagrin, had brought her around, enough to tell her firstborn that John had left, and wasn't coming back. Eric and his younger brother, Jason, wanted to hunt John down, make him see reason, or at least get a reason, for his abrupt departure but Allexa had told them no. If he wanted to come back, he would; if not, then he wouldn't. She was resigned to that fact. She didn't like it. She felt the pain of loss every day, but facts were facts: he was gone, had chosen to leave her, with no explanation. She had taken him in after the massive earthquakes had crippled the country, shared with him, loved him and he had left her when recovery began. She remembered a quote from what seemed like so long ago: Never make someone a priority in your life who makes you an option in theirs. Right now, she felt like an option.

Allexa referred to April as Apathy April, to remind herself of the mental and emotional hole she had been in. The month wasn't all bad: Amanda had returned. Her daughter-in-law had come to the house early in April, wondering if Allexa knew where Jason and Jacob were. After staying in Marquette with her friends during the worst of the winter months, she had first gone to their home on the Dam Road, only to find it vacant and winterized, the power turned off and the house hauntingly empty. Allexa told her all that had happened that spring, with the death of Jason's uncle and aunt, with the arrival of Eric and Emilee, ending with how the two brothers and their children now lived across the street in their uncles house. The reunion between husband and wife was strained, as was to be expected. Jason had felt abandoned by his wife of ten years and her return, though welcomed, was a reminder that he had spent all those harsh months alone caring for their young autistic son. Jacob, on the other hand, was ecstatic to see his mommy. After a few days, the three returned to the house on the Dam Road, leaving the new golden retriever puppy, Chivas, with Eric and Emilee, who continued to live in the big house alone.

CHAPTER ONE

"Mom? Where are you?" Eric called out from the direction of the garden.

"Down here by the creek. I'll be right up." I scooped a handful of cold spring water and splashed my face then dabbed the moisture off with my ever present cloth hanky, and made my way back up the hill, taking deep cleansing breaths as I went. I had gotten very good at hiding my pain from my family. They had their own grief to deal with; they didn't need mine too. I greeted my son and granddaughter with a sincere smile, and gave each of them a hug once I made it to the top of the hill.

"Did you come over to help me work, Emilee?" I teased my son's eleven-year-old little girl.

"No, Nahna, but Dad says I should if you really need me to," she said, shrugging her thin pre-teen shoulders.

"That's good to know. When I really need help, like for weeding, I'll call you." I laughed when she groaned at the thought of weeding. "What's up, Eric?"

Since he and Jason no longer shared my brother's house across the road, there was more than enough work and upkeep for Eric to stay busy, so I didn't see him all that often.

"Jason and I were talking this morning about foraging, and I was wondering what might be coming up soon. I know the cattail flowers are a ways off yet. I haven't even seen any shoots."

I remembered the first time I fixed him that delicacy and he ate most of the plateful!

"They won't be ready for another month or six weeks, but I was just noticing the fiddleheads starting by the creek. These are too young yet, we'll give them a day or two and we can start picking. Ramps might be ready, though. Want to take a ride?" The wild leek patch wasn't far, less than four miles, though we were still restricting gas usage. With their high miles per gallon, the four-wheelers with which we had been gifted were perfect for a short trip such as this.

Although Moose Creek had power restored two months ago, we were still struggling. My contact at the County Emergency Management office, Tom White, came through for us again with a tanker of regular gas, though it wasn't free. Limited supplies and limited availability from the refineries had jumped the price of gasoline to a whopping twenty dollars per gallon. We no longer rationed the gas at Fram's, the only gas station in Moose Creek. At that price, it was self-regulated. No one made a casual trip to Marquette anymore. Those with vans or mini-vans offered shopping rides for a share in the cost of gas. Food was still coming in to our new food bank, however with the grocery stores in Marquette being restocked, that was coming to an end soon. I was told we had one more delivery and then we were on our own. Again.

The series of earthquakes that ripped the country in half along the New Madrid fault line last November left many small towns and communities floundering. There were few deliveries between the East and West Coasts: little food, less fuel, and diverted electricity. Moose Creek suffered greatly, and though we made it to the other side, it was not without great cost and deep personal suffering.

* * *

"Give me a half hour to finish tilling the garden and to clean up, and we'll go," I told my eager granddaughter.

"Mom, I can finish that if you want," Eric offered. My boys knew there were times I needed to do my own hard work and keep my mind and hands busy.

"No need, but thanks. Since it was tilled up in the fall, it's an easy walk through, and I'll do it again anyway." I was looking forward to getting the garden planted, though without a nursery to fall back on for plants, I couldn't risk planting too early and having the tender house grown seedlings killed by a late frost. Planting was still a few weeks away.

Eric and Emilee arrived on the four-wheeler left for Jason. No one touched the deep metallic blue machine parked in the lean-to that was John's. With tools and cloth bags secure in the milk crate basket on the back of my camouflage painted machine, I led the way to the ramp patch, a few miles down the road.

* * *

"Wow, Nahna, look at all the pretty flowers!" Emi said, turning circles to view the patches of the Dutchman's Britches, little flowers that looked like upside down white bleeding hearts, mixed in with the brilliant yellow of the low growing Marsh Marigolds, and my favorite, the tiny fragrant Spring Beauties, with their mix of pink and white and striped. There was even the occasional False Solomon's Seal, a tall stalk of delicate white blossoms.

"Yes, they are very pretty, Emi. Maybe we'll pick a small bouquet before we leave. First, let me show you how to identify what we came for: food!" I'd been collecting ramps to supplement my meals for many years, and only found out a few years ago that the greens were just as tasty, making the entire plant edible.

The long oval leaves with a pale rosy base were easy to spot, and abundant, though many of the bulbs were too small and immature to harvest. "Guess we're a bit early for the ramps, but we can still gather the leaves. If we cut them off with these scissors, Emi, the bulb will keep growing and make more leaves." I handed her a pair of left handed scissors and one of the three cloth bags I had stuck in my carrier, and let her work on her own. Of my two sons, Jason was left-handed while Eric was right-handed. However, both of my grandchildren were lefties, as are their mothers, and my mother. With that genetic propensity, I made sure I had adequate tools for either. Eric and I used pocketknives to harvest our share of the delicate, tasty leaves. I even found a few bulbs that were large enough, and would add a zing to our meal later.

After collecting two full bags of ramp leaves, we walked over to the low wetlands near the river, looking for fiddleheads.

"Like these, Nahna?" Emilee had carefully snipped off a tightly curled fern stalk, and held it up for approval.

"That's just perfect. Let's see if we can find twelve of them."

"Why only twelve, Mom?" Eric asked.

"That gives us four each. I want to see how you and Emi like them and react to them before we pick a lot. No sense in over picking if you can't or won't eat them. We might as well let them mature. The mature ferns are not only lovely to look at, they offer shade that helps keep moisture in the forest floor and protection for small animals," I replied. It had taken many hours of study to understand our delicate woodland ecology, and I refused to upset it needlessly.

Pan-fried Brookies caught earlier in the day and a big pot of ramp greens, along with our daily fresh bread, made for a wonderful dinner. I missed having Jason and Jacob here with us, especially at meals.

* * *

JOURNAL ENTRY: May 1

I spent a few minutes on the computer tonight and printed out my Fall Prep/ Chore list. It's past time I reverse the process and turn everything back on. It seems like such a very long time ago that I was wrapping up hoses for winter and turning the outside water off. Of all the chores, I dislike that one the most. I doubt that will ever change. It's the first one I need to do though, because so many other things depend on having that water available.

Next will be turning the cistern over and hooking up all the gutters again, and that's Jason's chore. Then I need to make any repairs to the fencing. I need to put the flower boxes up on the railings, and run all the hoses. And, and, and...

So much to do.

* * *

CHAPTER TWO

The world is run by those who show up. It was time I stopped hiding and showed up, not that I had any interest in running the world, but I did feel somewhat helpful in running Moose Creek.

I still stopped in to the office once a week, mostly to just to touch base with Anna and to keep up on the latest news in town. Otherwise, I was keeping a low profile. My emergency management position with the township was never meant to be a round the clock job as it ended up these past six months. I was physically, mentally, and emotionally drained from all that had been thrust upon me. I really didn't feel like socializing and there were so many things to do at home with summer just around the corner.

I parked my four-wheeler between another ATV and an unfamiliar small gray car in the town hall parking lot. The township was given eighteen semi-new machines after we defeated a mob of escaped prisoners. The prisoners had stolen the four-wheelers and started a pillaging rampage that ended here, with us killing all of them. A grateful county and dealership told us to keep the vehicles.

"Hi, Anna, is anything new or interesting going on?" I asked as I walked into her office, not knocking and not noticing she wasn't alone. "Oh, I'm sorry! I didn't realize you were busy. I'll come back later."

"It's okay, Allexa, please come in." She was all smiles and professional. "I'd like you to meet our newest resident, Dr. Mark Robbins."

I smiled and offered my hand. "Doctor, welcome to Moose Creek." I couldn't help noticing his unusually dark blue eyes, fringed with dark lashes, and the way his chestnut brown hair curled around the collar of his hunter green Polo shirt. He was right out of *GQ*.

"Allexa Smeth is our Emergency Manager, Doctor, and has been invaluable to the survival of Moose Creek these past few months," Anna continued.

"My pleasure," he said, his voice deep and soft, and he held my handshake just a bit too long.

"A new member of our community? We sure can use you." I smiled again and pulled my hand back. "What's your specialty?"

"I was a trauma/ER doctor in Saginaw," he replied. "After the collapse, I saw way too much of the cruelty man was capable of, and the damage he can inflict. So I escaped." He grimaced, and though a very real shadow clouded his deep eyes enhancing the blue, it still seemed a well-rehearsed explanation, and there was an uncomfortable moment. Anna cleared her throat.

"I'm glad you're here, Allexa. I've got something for you," she said, opening the top drawer of the large desk. She pulled something out and handed it to me.

I looked at the long white envelope in my hand. It was windowed and had my name on what looked like a check. "What's this, Anna?"

"Your paycheck for the last six months. I wish it were more, but it's all I could get out of the Board. And don't you dare try to give it back," Anna replied. I had to stifle a smile because that's exactly what I was thinking of doing.

"Fine," I said, folding the envelope and sticking it in the back pocket of my well-worn jeans. I felt grubby next to Anna with her neat as a pin hairstyle and pressed powder blue pants suit, and the doctor in his chinos and polo shirt. "I'll talk with you later," I said to Anna, and turned to acknowledge her guest with a nod. "Doctor." I made to leave, feeling very awkward.

"Allexa, wait!"

I turned back to face Anna, eyebrows raised in question.

"I was hoping you would give us some help here. We need to find the doctor someplace to stay temporarily, then a place to live, and some suitable office space. You're the problem solver, what would you suggest?" Anna asked.

"Well," I said, leaning against the doorjamb, still feeling unkempt even though my baggy shirt was one of my best, "there's no shortage of motel rooms. For temporary housing, I'd suggest the Inn since it has dining facilities. The green house just across the road, Anna, is it still vacant?" She nodded. "It would take some work. The upstairs is a private residence, and that lower level could be converted to an office for the doctor, *and* it's centrally located." I turned to the handsome man sitting by Anna's desk. "It would be comfortable, just not luxurious, as long as you don't mind living and working in the same space."

Anna knew all this, and probably had thought of it herself, which made me wonder why she was asking me.

"It's what I would expect, and it would be more convenient for attending to any patients, day or night," he agreed. "How long would it take to get it ready?"

I looked back at Anna. "I can have Jason stop over later and look at the place and give an estimate. He will want to meet with Dr. Robbins to know what he has in mind." I had absolutely no idea where we would come up with the equipment that would be needed to furnish a functioning medical office, however that wasn't my problem. "I'll talk to him when I get home."

"Is this Jason your husband?" the doctor asked.

I smiled. "No, I'm not married. Jason is my son."

"Allexa, why don't you take the doctor over to the Inn, show him where it is and give him a quick tour of the town while you're at it?" She smiled innocently. I had the feeling she was playing matchmaker. How could I politely tell her—and him—I wasn't interested?

* * *

"Perhaps we should start with the house, Dr. Robbins," I offered, as we walked to the parking lot. "It's just across the street here, and you might want to see it before you start thinking about repairs or remodeling."

"Mark."

"Excuse me?"

"Please, call me Mark." He flashed a toothy white smile at me.

"Fine, Mark it is. I'm sure the few things needing attention on the residential level aren't anything Jason can't handle. I'd guess maybe a week, you'll have to talk to him about his schedule," I commented as we made the quick tour of the house. "It sure does need a good cleaning though," I added.

"Anyone you could recommend for that?" Mark asked politely.

"Let me ask around," I replied, though I knew my daughter-in-law Amanda was very good at cleaning and she needed the work.

The office area, which was at street level and a definite attraction for a doctor's office, would need a great deal of remodeling. I needed to ask Anna who was going to pay for all of this.

* * *

I had Dr. Robbins park his car, that same gray compact, at the Inn, and climb on the ATV with me, instantly feeling it to be a mistake. I could feel his warm breath on the back of my neck and the nearness of his very male body. The four block tour took less than ten minutes, even stopping to point out places of interest: the post office, the ball field, the school, two churches and a bar. Moose Creek was four blocks square and didn't have a traffic light, just four stop signs that most ignored. The main road, County Road 695, ended there. The joke in town was if you were there, it was either intentional or you were lost. There was no driving through; you had to turn around and go back to go anywhere else. This one way in had served us well when dealing with the gang of prisoners we called The Wheelers, named so from the four-wheelers they rode in on.

After our short tour, I got Dr. Robbins checked into the Inn, and told him we would be in touch when Jason needed to talk with him.

"Allex, please stay and have dinner with me," Mark asked, smiling warmly, showing an obvious personal interest. I really hate being called Allex. "It's been a long time since I've met a beautiful *and* intelligent woman. I'd like to know you better."

"That's very flattering, Mark, however I must decline," I said politely. "And the name is Allexa." I retreated quickly before I would have to explain that I was still suffering from a badly broken heart and that only one person could get away with calling me Allex and it wasn't him. How did I tell a very attractive man he didn't interest me? That I felt numb inside? Easy—I didn't. I ran.

* * *

Since I was already in town, and to save gas, I drove the short distance over to the Dam Road to talk to Jason about the renovation of the new doctor's house. I hugged my grandson Jacob and he went back to his room to play.

Jason was enthused about getting some carpentry work. Work of any sort was still hard to come by. "A doctor in town? That's awesome, Mom!"

"Amanda," I said to Jason's wife, "how would you like a job cleaning? I know you're a marvelous housekeeper, and I think you would be perfect for getting that place ready for the doctor to move in. He might even hire you for an on-going position."

"Oh, Mom, that would be great, thank you," Amanda instantly replied.

"I'm sure the doctor would like to move in as soon as possible. Can you meet with him tomorrow about the details?"

"Sure. From what you've said, the living quarters might not take much, just some upgrading, *if* I can find the supplies."

* * *

It was a beautiful night; the temperature was in the low sixties, there was only a slight warm breeze, a perfect night for sitting outside—before the mosquitoes wake up. The full moon rose in the darkened sky. Not the white shiny orb of winter, a dull yellow tinged with orange, as though there was something high in the upper atmosphere filtering the reflection. I watched as some random dark wisps of clouds made their way across the face in a jagged dance, to eventually obscure the moon itself into a smudge of light hanging low in the night.

* * *

Regular chores still needed to be done. I found that out a long time ago while living deep in the woods. Unlike in the woods, here I had even more to do: chickens needed tending, the garden would need attention once it was planted, all the yard work, stacking wood, laundry and housework fell on me alone, once again. I'd done it all by myself before; I know I could do it again. Right now, laundry was waiting.

After I sorted out the clothes, I started with the heavy stuff first, since it would take the longest to dry on the clotheslines outside. I checked pockets as each thing went in the machine. That's when I found that envelope from Anna. I had completely forgotten about it. I added soap and turned the water on, thankful for the convenience of on demand power to pump the well.

I poured myself a fresh cup of coffee, opened the envelope, and almost choked on that first sip! The township had deemed my past services as the Emergency Manager for Moose Creek were worthy of a thousand dollars per month! After the usual taxes, I was looking at a check of almost five thousand dollars. I was stunned. My mind started racing on what I could use that money for. First would be resupplying all the food and supplies I had used over the winter; or maybe a small solar array, or even a greenhouse. This was going to take some careful planning. I started a list, my thoughts whirling with possibilities.

* * *

At noon, Jason, Amanda and I met Dr. Robbins at the house he was to occupy. Jason had turned on the power and the water first, so there was electricity and he could test the plumbing. Amanda had thought to bring cleaners, disinfectants, a mop and bucket, a vacuum cleaner and dust rags, and while Jason and the doctor went room to room discussing what needed fixing or replacing, she started cleaning in the living room. With only that room, a small kitchen, bathroom and two bedrooms, it wouldn't take her long. I excused myself, and went across the street to talk to Anna.

"So how did last night go?" Anna asked with a grin, tapping her manicured fingers together. I looked at her confused. "With the good doctor? I could tell right off that he's interested in you!" She leaned back in her brown leather chair, expecting some juicy gossip.

"We toured the house across the street, and then I gave him a tour of town, which you know takes all of ten minutes. I made sure he was checked in to the Inn, and then, Anna," I leaned on her desk with both hands, "I refused his dinner invitation and went home." She froze. "Please, do *not* try match making. Let it go."

"I'm sorry. I thought maybe after John left you might ..." she let that trail off.

"Business, Madam Supervisor," I retreated to hold up the doorjamb with my shoulder. "Who is paying for the repairs and remodeling of the doctor's new residence?" Back on formal footing, she stiffened some.

"The township is leasing the house to Dr. Robbins for a dollar. He's responsible for all the work at making the office functional beyond structural. We'll pick up the tab for any repairs to the residence. Repairs, not esthetic replacement. Anything beyond repairs is on his tab." Her quick answer confirmed my suspicion that she had already selected that place for the new doctor and pulling me into the situation was an unwelcomed bit of strategy.

"That sounds reasonable," I responded. Satisfied, I went back across the road, fairly certain Anna would leave my personal life alone now.

* * *

I took the sandwich I made for dinner to the TV room, and flipped on the news. I couldn't believe half of the political diatribe that was spouted, while other events needed no glossing over, like the frequency of severe tremors along fault lines. I turned on the computer and logged into the National Earthquake site. The minor movements rarely made the news; however, the swarms could be a red flag of something bigger coming. I had my settings to show all activity, no matter how slight. Most of what I read centered out west, away from the New Madrid. I breathed a sigh of relief and finished my sandwich.

CHAPTER THREE

I added a quart of gas to the rototiller and made a couple more passes to the garden, churning up the soil, releasing a heady earthy scent, then walked it back into the barn and shut it off. The chickens would scratch around in the freshly turned soil and even out some of the ruts; the rest I would rake.

Part of last fall's preps was getting new fencing and more posts. It had been covered with a tarp and stored under the cistern until needed, which was now. I knew I needed to redo the chickens' yard and buying the material early would save me money on the price increase. Little did I know at the time that there would be a *horrendous* increase in price, and a definite lack of availability. I thanked my stars that I did what I did back then. I believed in having whatever was needed *before* it was needed. I had preached that on my Internet groups, and lived by my words. If I hadn't, I would not be able to do the necessary fencing now.

By creating a second enclosed yard, I would be able to seed one and close it off while the chickens were confined to the first one. Once there was adequate grass growing, I would switch the gates, plant the first yard, and then continue with that method all summer. Keeping them fed was going to take some ingenuity. No more running to the feed store. We might have power restored, and gas in our tanks, but things were definitely *not* back to normal, and they may never be.

I had just taken down all the old fencing when I saw the pale green car cruise slowly down the road. I didn't think much more about it. Not until I felt that stirring, that feeling of someone being near. I straightened up, squaring my shoulders, my heart thudding hard in my chest.

"I can feel when you come near me, you know. I don't have to see you to know you're there," I said as I turned slowly. John was standing just outside the garden at the entrance gate.

The emotions that surged through my body almost caused me to sway: the joy, happiness, sadness, anger and relief, all conflicting, all hitting me at once. I could not have stayed where I was if I wanted to. I was drawn to him like that proverbial moth to the flame and I offered no resistance. I opened the gate and stepped out, closing it behind me.

"You left me," I stated simply.

"I'm back."

"Are you so sure I'll take you back?"

"No."

The admission startled me.

"Where have you been?"

"It doesn't matter."

What an odd conversation this was.

"I've missed you," my voice broke on the words. I remained steady, almost defiant.

"I couldn't stay away any longer," John confessed, and reached out for me. I slid comfortably into his arms. We stood there, just holding each other, for the longest time. Then I let go and backed away.

"I'm still angry at you."

"You should be. I'm mad at me too. Can we talk?" John asked. I don't think I ever saw him so unsure in the two years I'd known him.

"Have a seat at the picnic table. I'll get us some iced tea," I said. I took my time getting our drinks. I found a tray, set the glasses filled with ice cubes, added the sugar bowl, wondering if he took his cold tea as sweet tea like many southerners do, then I placed a small pitcher filled with golden herbal tea in the center.

* * *

The wooden picnic table that nestled between the tall maple trees was my birthday present from Jason last year and was well shaded with the newly sprouting leaves. The sun was streaming through and dappled the pine boards with splashes of muted green. I intentionally set the tray to the side as I didn't want anything obstructing my view of John. I could see he had put a little weight back on, and his face was less pale, like he had been spending some time in the sun. He looked wonderful to me. I silently poured some tea into each glass and set one glass in front of myself, allowing him to take his own. I took a tentative sip, mostly to quench my too dry throat. There was a time when the ensuing silence would have been companionable. Now it was awkward, with each of us waiting for the other to say something.

John set a ring of car keys on the table between us. "These are for you."

"What do you mean?" I asked, only glancing at the keys.

"I bought you a new car. Well it's not new-new, but the newest one I could get. Automotive manufacturing has shut down." He pointed over his shoulder to the minty green SUV. "And before you say anything, I know you need a new car and that you haven't gotten one because of all the money you sank into your preps. Preps that kept not only you and your family alive this past winter, but me too. This is my way of saying thank you, Allex."

"We'll discuss this later," I said, leaving the keys untouched. "Talk to me, John. Why did you leave like you did? It was such a shock." All the pain of watching him walk away came rushing back, bruising my still broken heart.

He ran his hands from his forehead back across his bald head, a gesture that was undoubtedly unconscious and that was also so him. I stifled my sob by taking another sip of tea.

"I knew if I didn't just leave, I wouldn't be able to, and I had to go back. There were things I needed to do and get." He rolled the cold glass between his hands and set it back down again. "See, Green-Way pays me very well and I wanted to buy you this car," he waved his hand toward the driveway. "There are so many things I'd like to give you and I can't without working." There was a plea in his voice.

"I told you before you don't have to pay me back anything! I don't want the car, I don't want anything." *Just you*, I added silently. "It's been six weeks since you left. Where have you been? Why haven't you at least called?" I really wasn't sure I was ready for his answers.

"When I got back to the house on Eagle Beach, most of the guys were already there, acting like not much had happened. Steve was cooking breakfasts, Sandy was cooking dinners, and the routine was so easy to fall into. *I* was different." He paused, finally taking a drink of his tea, no sugar. *I'll remember that.*

"I don't think you ever met Simon, our liaison to the Green-Way home office. He noticed the change in me, and when he found out I had spent those four harsh months here in Moose Creek, and with you, he immediately sent me home to my daughter's for a two-week rotation. I don't know if he thought that it would help get you 'out of my system' or what, but it didn't. If anything, going back to my daughter's, seeing my mom and sister, it just made me miss you all the more." He started to reach across the table; instead, he stopped and picked up his glass again. I could understand needing to keep the hands busy; I really wanted to touch him too.

"I made up my mind then that I would work the mine, for as much money as I could make, only if I can have you, too..." he hesitated. "That is, if you'll have me back, Allex. If you don't want me back, I'll ask for a transfer someplace far from here." His eyes told of the sadness he felt at the prospect of leaving here.

"Don't want you?" I snorted. "Of course I want you, John. I've been miserable without you. I don't want you here out of some kind of obligation though." When he started to interrupt, I held up my hand to stop him. "Do you *want* to be here? Do you want to be with *me*? And will you promise to not leave like that again?"

He stood up from the table, and came around to my side, taking my hand and pulling me into his arms again. "Yes, Allex, I want to be here, with you. I... I..."

"Spit it out, John, I can take it."

"I must confess that this scares me spit-less. I love you, Allex. I won't ever leave you again."

Love me? He'd never told me that before. I kissed him lightly, and then sighed when he pulled me even closer.

"What shift are you on? When do you have to report back in?"

"I'm on rotation." He grinned. "The two weeks to see my daughter was out of sequence. So when I got back I worked only two more weeks to be back in sync with my crew. This is our normal time off, so they don't expect me back for another ten days."

Ten days. My heart was tripping over itself with the prospect.

* * *

Inside the house, John looked around.

"Something's different," he observed. "You painted. It's blue now instead of green. It looks good."

"A few weeks ago I decided I needed to make some changes." I took a deep breath. He should hear the truth. "Everything reminded me of you. I had to do something so I could move on. I repainted the TV room too, and the bedroom. I rearranged the furniture, replaced some light fixtures. A few changes helped pull me out of the deep hole I was in."

His face fell when he grasped what I was saying. "I'm so sorry to have put you through all of this, Allex I really am, and I hope in time you will forgive me."

I hope so, too, I thought silently.

* * *

Tufts meowing in the hallway roused me from a deep and restful sleep. I stretched and felt the body next to mine. I rolled to my side and smiled into John's sleepy blue eyes.

"Good morning," he said and kissed me lightly. I snuggled closer to him, my head on his shoulder, ignoring Tufts' protests. Yes, it was a very good morning.

* * *

Over coffee and toast with jam, we discussed the day. Some things just would not wait. I needed to finish the fencing, and two of us working on it would make it go much quicker. What would take me all day should only take the two of us a few hours. Then I needed to rake out the garden and add the last of the commercial lime. Every winter, I've added all the wood ash I gathered from the wood stove to help balance the acidic soil in the garden. I found myself wondering if it would be enough when the lime ran out.

We finished the new fences, and while John made the gate, I inspected the perimeter fencing for winter damage and made a few repairs. When I did the original fence, I started with two-foot chicken wire at the bottom because it was easier to handle by myself. I buried six inches into the ground to keep any animals from digging under, and then attached the remaining eighteen inches to the posts I had set every eight feet. Once done, I ran four foot fencing above the shorter fence, overlapping it only slightly, and attaching the two together with small zip ties. I loved zip ties; however, they did break and needed to be replaced occasionally. I had a good stock of them, now I was thinking I should use wire, if I could find any. There were things I had not thought of to stock up on.

We had an easy lunch of egg salad sandwiches and tomato soup while planning out the rest of the afternoon.

"What's next on the agenda?" John asked. It was good to see him enthused about this kind of work.

"Well, the wire around the top of the fence needs to be tightened up, and then the electric fence charger reinstalled so we can attach those wires. I really don't want to do any work in the garden until it's protected from the animals."

"Makes sense," he replied, eying all the foot high tomato plants sitting in front of the windows.

"Before planting the garden, I want to rake out and plant one of the new yards for the chickens. I'm thinking of planting vetch or clover. I've got seed for both. I was going to do a 'green manure' planting for the garden and never got around to it."

"Why not seed some of both?" he questioned. "That way they would get a little variety."

I smiled. It was good to have him back.

"Good idea, John, we can do that."

* * *

John pulled the tiller back into the garden and walked it into the first chicken yard. I was really happy he volunteered to do that, since the ground in that area hadn't been broken in years. I dug around in the metal trashcan where I kept all my seeds, found what I needed, and mixed a cup full of the ground cover. It might take a month or six weeks for it to grow enough, and the sooner it was planted the sooner the chickens would have something healthy and natural to eat and I could cut back on the remaining feed. I was worried about how I was going to keep them fed this next winter. It was definitely worthy of a family discussion at some point.

"How are the chickens laying, Allex?" John asked as he put the tiller away.

"The eight hens are giving five to six eggs each day, sometimes only four, though. Someone is slowing down." I frowned.

The oldest of the *girls*, two black Astralorpes, were now five years old. Their seven offspring were three years old. It was time to renew the flock. As noisy as he could be, I was glad I kept the one rooster.

John chuckled. "What are you thinking? I can see those wheels turning."

"I'm thinking we need to stop eating eggs for a week and collect enough to fill the incubator, and then hatch out a new flock."

"Why does it not surprise me that you have an incubator?" He reached out and gave me a hug. "Where is it? I'll get it down for you."

I put the lightweight incubator box and the egg-turner in the house to be washed later, and went back to the garden. John had already started the raking, which was another thing that would be done much quicker with two of us. I hand spread the seed around the inner yard, and grabbed a second rake. We worked silently side by side for another hour. As delighted as I was that so much was done today, it was time to stop and clean up. My lower back was feeling the strain.

* * *

After my shower, I slipped on a casual t-shirt dress that was cool on my legs and made me feel more feminine. Feeling feminine was not something I had worried about for the past several weeks.

While John showered, I washed and sterilized the incubator, and set it aside. It would be started with the first eggs tomorrow. Jason and I experimented one year and realized we had a better hatching rate if the incubator was started immediately, rather than waiting until it was full. That also let the chicks hatch out over a period of time instead of all at once.

* * *

JOURNAL ENTRY: May 5

It's been a long and hot day, with temperatures into the 80's. For dinner I mixed up a cold macaroni and tuna salad, using rehydrated celery and red sweet peppers, canned peas, and the first of the fresh onions from the garden I planted last fall in the raised beds. We drank the last bottle of white wine from the shelf, one of Nancy's stash. I think I will use some of my paycheck from the township to replace the wine supply. Maybe I should look for wine making supplies instead.

* * *

"I think we should plant the garden today," I mentioned to John over our morning coffee. "The ground is ready. We can do the seeds and the potatoes, but I'd rather wait another week or two for the plants."

He looked at me over his cup.

"That is, if you want to help."

"Allex, of course I want to help. I will do whatever you want me to do, to be part of *here* and part of your life again." He said it with such sincerity that I believed him. "What are we planting?"

"I still have the layout we worked on earlier," I said softly. "It's a good plan and utilizes the space well."

I took a sip, remembering how I changed a few things after he left. I wasn't going to plant the collards he wanted, or the okra.

"We can do the first row of green beans, peas, pea pods, cucumbers, and the carrots, beets, turnips, collards and of course lettuce," I read off the list.

He grinned at that, knowing how much I love salads. The memory danced across my mind of him having the opportunity to buy anything he wanted at the bulk food store and chose to buy lettuce, for me.

"I have enough trellises in place to do three plantings of the peas and pea pods," I said. "By planting every three weeks we can have a continuous harvest of those. I know shell peas take so much room to get so little, but they're so good and I really like them. We can put them against the chickens' fence. When the second sowing is producing, the first will be pulled up and replanted. The cucumbers can manage on the same trellis. I'll plant half the width, wait until it starts flowering, then plant the other half. This way we can have fresh cukes and peas well into October."

John nodded.

"Green beans will be done similarly, for a different reason," I explained to John. "Beans are usually quite prolific, and as much as we will need to feed all of us, they will likely still overproduce. I have only so much time for canning, and I don't want to be needlessly overwhelmed. The beans will be planted in three stages, giving us plenty to eat, without having bushels full all at once."

It crossed my mind then that I should teach all of my family how to can.

"I think we should do a small patch of corn, too. Four rows maybe six or eight feet long. They should ripen all at once, no way around that, so we will have some to eat and a few dozen to can."

"Why four rows?" John asked. "And is there really enough room for everything?"

"For pollination four rows is the minimum. When we do that spot, it might be more, maybe five rows. It will have to wait a day or two though. Those seeds need to soak at least overnight. We will double up certain things. The winter squash, like pumpkins and acorn, can be planted right with the corn, so yes, there's room." I could already taste the crunch of those golden kernels.

"You have all the seeds you need?"

"When I bought my heirloom seeds a year ago, I bought way more than I knew I could use in one year. I have plenty." I answered. My coffee was getting cold. I got up to retrieve the pot for us. "I've been into town only twice in the last few weeks, and there was very little available. It seems everyone is planting a garden this year and that's a good thing!"

A thought kicked across my mind. I needed to talk to Anna. While John got started with the last of the raking, and after promising I wouldn't be long, I made a quick trip into Moose Creek.

* * *

"You want to do what?" Anna asked curiously.

"I think the town needs its own community garden," I repeated. "That acre next to Bradley's house would be perfect. Everyone can walk to it, and it's in full sun. I think Bradley would be pleased." He was one we lost to the flu epidemic that decimated the town this past spring. "I can donate *some* seed; others will have to come up with seed too. I'll even help lay it out. It can be done in personal plots, or all as one. That will be up to the townsfolk. Anna, the town has to feed itself," I said, remembering all too well how the town nearly starved to death this past winter.

"I agree. What do you suggest we do?"

"First we have to find someone with a tractor that can plow and disc the land. Once that's done, we'll get Carolyn involved and plan it out."

Carolyn was our local minister, and she was pivotal in keeping The Stone Soup Kitchen functioning, and keeping the people united during our very dark time. I just knew she would do it again. Being a minister fit her well; she had a kind and loving soul.

"Okay, let me work on it. What are you doing today?" Anna asked.

"I'm going back home and plant *my* garden!" I stopped when I got to the door. "Oh, and Anna, John is back." I left her stunned with my announcement. I know I smirked all the way home.

* * *

The day was long, hot and productive. With both of us working, we got half of the garden planted. In another week or two we can put in a good portion of the plants I had growing in the house that were staying protected from a possible late frost. Two weeks after that the rest of the seeds could go in along with the second planting of vegetable seeds we did today.

Being self-sufficient is part of being prepared, an important part, and that need was growing stronger in me. I'd always tried to heed those feelings, and it usually served me well. Something was tweaking my alert system. I didn't know what it was, but I'd listen, although it was likely just memories of this past winter and worrying about shortages. I wish I could easily resupply everything we used over the winter. I don't think that will be possible though.

CHAPTER FOUR

Keith Kay stopped by this morning to see if I was still interested in fire wood.

"Of course I am!" I readily agreed. "And you saved me from having to track you down, Keith."

We'd been friends a long time and he had furnished my stove wood for many years. Having it cut, split and delivered saved me a great deal of time that I could spend on other things, including the garden.

"Unfortunately, the price has gone up, Allexa. It's the cost of gas for the splitter machine and diesel for this hog of a truck," he said, pointing a thumb at the large red dump truck parked in my driveway.

"I understand, Keith, the cost of everything has gone up. When can you bring the first load?" I asked. I was delighted when he said later that day. It gave me peace of mind to get all my winter wood done early in the season. I had acres of wood I could harvest, and cutting wood was very time consuming. We used a lot of wood last winter for staying warm and cooking, and we needed every piece we could store.

"So how did you do this winter, Keith? How's Carron? I didn't see either of you at the food bank at the township hall," I asked.

"The wife is fine and it's thanks to her that we made it," Keith said. "She did a lot of canning last fall. I must admit, though, I got real tired of tomatoes and green beans." He laughed. "But we didn't starve, and I did manage to get a deer or two, which helped, and the swamp was abundant with rabbit. Of course staying warm wasn't a problem."

I imagined not; he must have years of wood stacked in his yard.

* * *

After Keith left, John and I emptied the woodshed of the remaining two face cord that we didn't burn over the winter and I stacked it on the pallets nearest the house for the first burn in the fall.

"Aren't you putting any on that other set of pallets?" he asked, looking toward the small brown barn that I used for storing canning jars and equipment. Under the clothesline attached to the short sloping roof were three empty wooden pallets.

"Yes, I have longer range plans for that spot though. There are a couple of trees down by the creek that fell during a wind storm that still need to be cut up, and one that has already been bolted," I explained. "It will be very green wood and need longer seasoning so I want to keep it separate. Once we get the shed full, you can cut up the trees whenever you want, *if* you want."

I so appreciated the work he was helping me with and I certainly didn't want to take advantage of him, plus I didn't want to wear him out. My heart tugged at the thought of him going back to work soon.

John grinned at me. "It's been awhile since I've used a chain saw. It might be fun."

Fun? I smiled, bemused. I don't think he understood how many trees there were, and that cutting was only the first step. The bolts then need to be hauled up near the pallets, much easier now with the four-wheelers, and then there was the splitting and stacking. It was all hot, sweaty work, and black fly season was approaching, not to mention the ticks and the mosquitoes, another reason I liked to get the firewood done early.

* * *

It was always a shock to get that first load of wood dumped in the yard. Keith showed up later in afternoon with a trailer loaded instead of the dump truck. John gaped at the pile.

"Is all that going to fit into that small shed?" he mumbled. The 8x8x8 shed held a full ten face cord of stacked wood.

"Actually, this will only fill it halfway," I said.

He looked skeptical. On my own, it would take me a week to stack this much wood, re-splitting what I needed to. Keith had a commercial splitter, so it only did standard cuts for a wood stove. Having a wood *cook* stove, my wood requirement was slightly different. I need smaller, just not shorter, pieces. About half of this wood would need to be split again. I really didn't mind. I felt like I was doing more of the process myself this way. Of course having a gas log splitter helped a great deal.

I explained to John about the various sizes while we sorted through the pile nearest the wood shed, tossing pieces in that direction. Then we stepped over the wood now inside the shed and I started lining up hunks of the wood on the floor in a particular fashion, explaining why as I went.

"Even though the shed has sides that could hold the wood in place, I don't want to put the physical pressure on the boards. By stacking as if it were a freestanding rick, we get the same amount in, without possible damage to the building. Last thing we need is a collapsed shed in the middle of winter." I showed him how turning the end pieces sideways every other row gave a stable foundation for the next row, and how by using a piece that had a flat side kept the wood from rolling. Whole, un-split logs could be stacked in the middle, not on the ends. It was all very similar to how we had just done the pallet stacking, only on a larger scale. There was also a need to pitch the rows slightly backward, to prevent the row from falling forward. I once had a stack of wood fall and narrowly missed getting my legs buried in logs. I had listened to that inner voice and moved out of the way only seconds before getting crushed.

Once the area immediately in front of the shed was cleared of logs, I showed John where the log splitter was, a big, shiny, red twenty-seven-ton splitter. John's eyes got big, and his grin got bigger. Men just loved these kinds of toys. We pushed and pulled it into place, and then I remembered that over at Don's was a handy device for moving things like this around: a ball-to-hitch caddy. Maybe we'd use it to put it back when we're done. We worked for hours, and then called it quits. I was exhausted and my back ached. I'm sure John was tired too, though he wasn't admitting it.

* * *

"Have you been able to replace any of the stuff we used up this past winter?" John casually asked over dinner.

"Not yet. Most of the food we used came from the garden. I'll start canning when the garden starts producing." I was being nonchalant about it, and I didn't want to worry him. Gardens are very iffy things. "I haven't been to town to see about the basic staples like flour, rice and pasta."

"Is there anything you would do differently?"

Even though what I had done all these years had served all of us very well, there was definitely more I'd like to do, and the question got me thinking.

"As a matter of fact, I'd like to take a break from the physical work tomorrow, and go shopping. I just got a big check from the township—a belated paycheck for the past several months. I need to cash it."

"I'm sure whatever they paid you doesn't come close to what you gave in return." John smiled at me sincerely, knowing how many times I made trips into Moose Creek, sometimes under adverse conditions, to offer my knowledge and help to the community as emergency manager of the township.

"I told Anna I didn't want it. She insisted, and I must admit I can use the money. It will sure make me feel better if I can replace some of the supplies we used up, especially what I gave to the Stone Soup Kitchen."

The volunteer soup kitchen may have been my idea, and I may have secretly donated buckets of rice and beans to it; it was Pastor Carolyn who kept it going and the town folk that made it successful.

"Do we have a shopping list?" he asked, and I felt a warm rush at the we part. I was happy and content that John was back and I think he felt the same. I just wondered how long it would last this time.

"Not really. It shouldn't take much to come up with one though," I said. "Maybe we can work on that tonight?"

"It will be interesting for me to see what you've used," he said, and I was gifted with one of those lopsided smiles that made me feel warm inside. "So," he continued, "what would you do differently? Or maybe a better question is, what would you liked to have had to make things easier?"

I thought for a minute. "Well, I think a second means of power would have been helpful. Maybe a solar array with a bank of batteries, that's really pricey though," I said wistfully. There were a few residents that had set up huge solar panels a year or two ago. The systems were for usage and feeding back to the power company, not for energy storage. They depended on the sun for daytime power, and then went back on the grid power at night, which meant they had no evening power this past winter. A large bank of batteries being charged during the sunny days would ensure electricity to use at night.

"Yeah, having solar sure would have been nice," I said. "Not having to get dressed to start up the generator would have been much more convenient and Jacob could've watched TV anytime he wanted."

We both remembered how angry I got at Jason the time he ran the gennie just for his son's cartoons, wasting precious and limited gas.

"Anything else?" John prompted.

I gazed out the window thoughtfully. "A greenhouse," I smiled, lost in the thought.

"A what?"

"A greenhouse. A glass room where we could start plants for the summer garden, and grow fresh things for us to eat even in the middle of winter. Of course, we'd have to figure out a way to supplement the heating when there was no sun. I think that's a minor issue, considering a structure like that is way too expensive to even think about."

I sighed wistfully. A greenhouse had long been a pipe dream of mine. I could envision a large addition, with an aquaponic pond at one end for humidity and irrigation using nutrient rich fish-water, a warm, humid room with growing plants to spend time in while the snow swirled outside. I shook myself mentally. It wasn't gonna happen.

"I suppose you could put a solar array on the greenhouse to help heat it," John continued, tying the two things together. Interesting thought.

* * *

JOURNAL ENTRY: May 8

John has been back with me for only a few days, and there is something we still have to address, and soon: Eric and Jason. Both of my sons are really protective now, and they are still mad at John for leaving like he did. I need to fix that. I went over to talk with Eric first, finding him sitting on the front porch, whittling.

* * *

Eric didn't waste any time letting me know he watches the house. "Looks like you've got company, Mom."

I jumped in with both feet and said, "John is back."

That stopped Eric short. He looked at me, those deep blue eyes showing concern, waiting for me to continue. It hadn't taken long for my oldest and I to get back to the silent communication we had shared while he was growing up.

"He wants back in my life, our lives. I'm accepting his return, Eric, and I want you and Jason to accept it too." I paused while I chose my words carefully. "He felt he had to leave in order to do some things that would allow him to come back on a more equal footing." Still only silence from Eric. "I've been so happy these last few days. I'm glad he's back."

Eric finally smiled. "That's what I've been waiting to hear, Mom. If it makes you happy again, then I will welcome his being here." He got up and gave me a hug and I knew everything would be all right. Now I had to tell Jason.

* * *

Leaving John at home, I drove my new car out to the Dam Road to see Jason. He had been working daily on the remodeling of the doctor's new quarters and I wasn't sure where I would find him. His truck wasn't at the doctor's office when I drove past, so he had to be home.

I pulled into his driveway off the rutted stone and dirt road. The county trucks weren't wasting the limited diesel fuel on grading residential roads and the quarter mile was rather bumpy. Jason stepped out of his workshop, shotgun in hand.

"Sorry, Mom, I didn't recognize the car," he said, leaning the rifle against the doorframe. "New wheels?"

"Actually, yes." It was a great lead in, as I had hoped. "An apology gift from… John." Jason's head snapped up at the name. "He's back. I'm happy he's back. I might even forgive him for leaving," I smiled.

"And he gave you a new Subaru to say he's sorry? Wow." He ran his hand over the shiny pale green fender. "Can I have the old one?"

I laughed. This was going easier than I thought. "You and Amanda have a gas efficient car. I might give the '01 to Eric so he doesn't have to always use the big pickup." We chatted for a few more minutes and I asked how the doctor's project was coming along.

"I'm just about done with the residence. I have a few pieces of trim to finish staining and install in the bathroom, and then I'll move down to the office. Amanda is there now cleaning. He's moving in tomorrow." Jason took a deep breath. "Mom, thank you. We both really needed this work, and not just for the money. Amanda was getting really depressed not having anything to do. Dr. Mark has hired her to clean every week now. Her spirit has really picked up."

"You two were perfect for the job, Jason." I smiled at him, gave him a hug and told him dinner was at my place tonight, for everyone to welcome John back.

* * *

JOURNAL ENTRY: May 8

Beef has gotten outrageously expensive, just like gas. At $15 per pound for ground round, we don't have it anymore. I still have some canned, though since it's already cooked, it's good for only certain dishes. Now that we have power again, most of the deer Eric recently took is curing in the second refrigerator out in the barn. Of the remainder, twenty five percent has gone to the Soup Kitchen, and a haunch to Bob and Kathy, whom Eric has grown very fond of. Tonight I showed John where the venison is and asked him to cut off a big chunk for me to grind into burgers.

* * *

I mixed the freshly ground meat with some fresh chopped ramp bulbs, herbs, seasonings, a cup of oatmeal and two eggs, and shaped the mixture into five large patties and two smaller ones. It filled the plate nicely. I wrapped a towel around it and set it in the refrigerator for the flavors to blend.

The bread I started before going to see Jason was ready to form into buns, with enough left over for one loaf of bread. I covered that with a towel to rise and started the oven warming to bake.

"What would you like with the burgers tonight, John, potato salad, macaroni salad, three bean salad or veggies?" He was sitting at the table watching me, chin on his hand, lost in thought.

"Can we do a potato salad *and* a macaroni salad? I remember Emilee doesn't like the macaroni, and Jacob won't eat the potato salad."

I smiled that he did remember those little things about the kids. Then I reminded myself it hadn't really been that long ago.

"Sure, let's go get what we need from the pantry." I took a basket that was hanging on the wall and started for the back room. Though there was still a decent amount of food on the shelves, the supply was down by a good fifty percent.

John looked at the empty shelves, with a solemn expression. "These shelves used to be so full."

"Using the food is why it was there in the first place," I reminded him. "I'll replenish the stock from the garden." I was trying to reassure myself as much as him. I handed him the basket, then loaded it with a quart of canned potatoes, dried corn, a box of macaroni, a can of ripe olives and a jar of peas.

"This basket is new, isn't it?"

"Yes, I made it a few weeks ago while the tree branches and bark were still supple with sap. It gave me something to do." *To help me stop thinking about you.* "Oh, by the way, Eric has gotten very good at making beer. Don kept very detailed notes on the process and the results. When I was there earlier, I noticed he had a fresh batch going, which means he recently bottled. I hope he remembers to bring some tonight."

* * *

Even with grilled venison burgers on fresh buns, potato salad, macaroni salad and chilled, foamy pale ale, dinner still started out a bit strained. By the time I cleared away the dishes, the mood was lighter and it was like John had never left.

* * *

With the birds singing right outside the window, I woke earlier than usual. As I lay there in a sleepy glow, I could hear the singsong of the robins hopping from branch to branch, and the two-note lament of the chick-a-dee. Somewhere in the nearby underbrush by the creek was a hermit thrush calling to his mate with the crystal like song that to me is the most beautiful sound in the woods. I smiled, and nudged John.

"Let's go fishing!" I whispered in his ear. He instantly came awake.

* * *

Breakfast was quick. While he made the coffee and toast, I got two fishing poles out of the barn, and my tackle box. I hadn't been fishing with John before, and his enthusiasm told me it was a good way to start the day. With a thermos full of coffee and several pieces of toast wrapped in a cloth napkin, we headed out on one of the four-wheelers.

"Where are we going?" John asked from behind me.

"There's a bend in the Snake River that's good for trout." I called back to him. This was also the same area that I took Eric and Emilee ramp picking, so we could get some greens too. If we were lucky, dinner would be all fresh caught or foraged.

In less than five minutes, we were heading down a little used and crumbling asphalt road, shaded and overgrown with massive trees. The non-existent shoulders dipping low into swampy areas were rich with decay. We came to a two-lane concrete bridge, sporting faded graffiti so old it was spray painted by teenagers who now were grandparents. The Snake River churned below us.

"Are there snakes in the river?" John asked nervously.

"Not at all. It's named that because it snakes through the land, turning back on itself several times." I had spent some time when I first moved up here, learning the history behind the names of the rivers, streams and lakes, and why roads and settlements were called what they were.

I left the green, brown and tan camouflage painted four-wheeler parked on the stone bridge and peered over the edge. John handed me a tin mug of coffee and a slice of buttered toast. Even as generous as I was using the butter over the harsh winter months, feeding six of us did not deplete the twelve pounds I had started with in the freezer last November. John's toast was smothered in one of my jams. I definitely would have to make more this summer.

"That looks like a good pocket right there," John commented, pointing with his toast. An errant crumb fell, hitting the surface. It was immediately snatched up, and a flicker of tail followed the rainbow scaled body as the trout dove for deeper water. He laughed gleefully. Further downstream, fog rose off the moving water as it went from deep shade to new sunlight. The shallow wisps looked like ethereal wraiths, disappearing into nothingness as the heat of the day grew.

I handed John a pole and took one for myself and slipped a small piece of crust from my toast onto the ready hook, then cast over the edge of the bridge.

"Trout won't bite on bread," John announced. I just looked at him as I got a hit.

I shrugged. "My daddy always said to feed the fish what they want to eat." I played the fish a bit then reeled in a nice sized rainbow. "Grab the net, will you? We're kind of high over the water and I don't want to lose this beauty." I caught another one and John caught three more. Our toast gone, we switched to flies, but they were done biting for the morning. It was 10:30, still early in the day, and we had other things to do.

"Let's pick a few ramps to cook with these tonight," I suggested and we filled a small cloth bag I had sewn for collecting wild edibles. I used to use plastic grocery bags; those were now a thing of the past.

We had five fish and a bag full of wild greens, all fresh, all healthy and best of all, free for the taking. We would eat well and leave the stored food for another day.

* * *

We gutted the fish, giving the entrails to the hungry chickens. I had thought of just burying it in the garden for fertilizer, but the chickens provide plenty of that when they're fed well. Washed and packaged in a well-worn baggie, the fish sat chilling in the humming refrigerator. John and I split a jar of soup for lunch, and after cleaning up, we headed to town for shopping. Hoping the trip would be successful, I had talked Eric into lending me the pickup truck for a few hours.

* * *

As much as I love to shop, especially for prep items, going from store to store was depressing. There was so little available, and what was on the shelves was either useless or outrageously expensive. People had finally seen the benefits of clothesline and clothespins, evident by the empty shelf space, making me grateful I still had plenty of both. Ammo, of course, was not available at any price. Word was out the government had purchased all reserves, and then shut down the manufacturing plants.

We did, however, find soap and shampoo, deodorant and toothpaste. They were all at hyper-inflated prices, even so, I felt we should replenish those supplies.

"Do you really want to pay ten dollars for a two dollar bottle of shampoo?" John asked me.

"No, I don't want to, but I'm going to," I replied simply, placing four bottles in our cart. "Look at it this way, twenty years ago, that two dollar bottle of shampoo was only fifty cents. What's the difference? We need it, it's available, and we can buy it. Besides, some day it might become a barter item. Twenty years from now, there may be no shampoo at any cost. We just don't know." He looked sullen, and accepted it.

One of the items on my list there seemed to be plenty of—children's clothes. I found this sad. To me it meant there weren't many children left. I picked up generic pants, shorts and t-shirts in a variety of sizes for both Emilee and Jacob. Emilee's clothes could be passed down to Jacob, and as she grew, Emi would fit into some of mine. I could alter what I had to, to fit her if needed. I added socks and underwear for each child. I was surprised to find adult socks—thick heavy, winter socks. Then I realized this was leftover stock. There was nothing lightweight for the warmer months. I wondered out loud if the clothing mills were shut down too.

"When I was down in Indiana with my daughter and my mom, the news was that all industrial plants had been closed. I heard that only once, so I don't know how accurate it is," John piped in. My thought was that sound bite probably got silenced and so did the newscaster.

From there we went to the bulk food store. The gal at the front desk recognized us from previous trips, and allowed us in.

"Do we have a purchase limit?" I asked. "We're paying cash today."

She raised her eyebrows. The township always used a chit from the county emergency management office, and never had to pay, we also had to take whatever was sent. I don't think they got many that paid cash.

"No limit, unless marked on the shelf. We're happy to help Moose Creek," she answered. We had gotten quite the reputation after the Wheeler fight. I didn't correct her assumption that the supplies were for the Stone Soup Kitchen, which had also developed a following and had been mimicked across the Upper Peninsula.

Out of earshot, John stopped me. "Shouldn't we tell her it's for us, not the town?"

"Some of it *will be* for the town and the Kitchen, John, I just don't know what they will need yet," I replied in all honesty. "Besides, we're replacing what I gave them. I think that's fair."

As we moved down the aisles, I noticed that almost everything was marked "limit of one". We wheeled the cart up and down each aisle, carefully selecting items, some in bulk that I could re-can into smaller jars like mushrooms and nuts and crackers, some in everyday size, no longer packaged in four or six units as they once were. John went back to the entrance to get another cart for the big items. The flour had a limit of only one fifty-pound bag, and the same for rice. I was happy with anything. There was also a limit on the twenty-five-pound bags of sugar and salt, and I felt better knowing some of it was going directly to the Soup Kitchen. The dried beans were emptied out and pasta had no limit. The shelf for oil was empty save for two five-gallon containers of canola oil, and though not my choice, it was better than nothing. Remembering the first fish fry the Stone Soup Kitchen held where they grilled the fish because there was no oil to fry, I took both jugs of oil. I avoided canned vegetables since I would be canning all the produce from the garden, and hopefully so would the town residents. I then reconsidered and took two #10 cans of mixed vegetables that would also go to the Kitchen; then took two more cans for us. Something flickered across my mind, and I went back for a large can of spaghetti sauce. The Kitchen will put it to good use at some point. Our last stop was for hard cheeses. I had read on the Internet how to wax them to make them last longer. It was worth a try. I was dismayed to see only one small wedge of Parmesan. I would ration it deeply.

"Do you see what I see?" John whispered to me. My mouth watered at the sight of a small ham sitting in the cooler. It would make a wonderful celebration dinner for our family.

Checking out, I was stunned at the total. My windfall was dwindling fast. At least I had replaced some of the basics we had used up or given away over the winter. I had hoped we could restock all at once. I guess I would have to do it slowly, just like I did in the first place. Some of my fears of being so short were assuaged, though there was still more to get. There would always be still more to get, however, this was a decent start.

The last stop was at a well-guarded liquor store. The AR-15 carrying soldier at the door dressed in casual camouflage checked our IDs. Mine was the official Emergency Management badge I carry with me all the time now, and since John only had an out of state driver's license, he was stopped.

"Hey, I'm only her grunt, they didn't give me the fancy ID," he told the young man with a straight face. The soldier cracked a stony smile and let him pass.

I hid my chuckle beneath a cough, remembering all the times I had called John my bodyguard.

We were in luck. There had just been a delivery of inexpensive Michigan wines— "inexpensive" now being twenty dollars per bottle instead of eight. I calculated how much I had left and selected a case of wine, several bottles of liquor, and a cube of cola. Jason would be ecstatic to have a rum and cola again. Providing for my children, even though they were adults now, has always been in the forefront of my mind when prepping. The two bottles of whiskey and vodka could be very useful medicinally.

John talked with the clerk at the counter, who then accepted the cash handed to him. He carefully counted it out, smiled and slipped some of it in his pocket. Another guard stood quietly to the side, alert and intent. John said something else to the clerk that I couldn't hear. A stock boy came from the back pushing a dolly, loaded with double my order. I gave John a questioning look. With the slightest shake of his head, I knew not to say anything. The boxes just fit in the back of the truck. As we walked out, John dutifully slipped the stock boy and the guards some folded bills. I hadn't planned on John paying for any of this. There are now some things I don't argue with him about, and this was one, besides, I still needed to refill the drums of gas.

"What was all that about, John?" I questioned once we were alone again.

"Graft. It's the new old way of doing business."

The borrowed pickup truck was well packed when we made the long drive home to Moose Creek. I did well suppressing how giddy I felt over what we accomplished, even though we were a long way from where I was last fall in supplies.

JOURNAL ENTRY: May 10

With the fresh eggs I collected this morning, the incubator was full. I placed the last of the eggs tip down, refilled the lower trough with more water and turned it back on to warm. The automatic egg turner hummed in its slow motion travel, slightly shifting all the brown and tan eggs, just like a broody hen would do, a full rotation every twelve hours. I replaced the thermostat at an angle I could read through the window in the top of the lid. The heat needed to be warm and steady. Opening the top to check the temperature would let too much heated air escape. Hopefully in three weeks we'll have forty baby chicks. I contemplated how to divide the hatchlings up.

"Why will you divide them at all, and to whom?" John asked a very valid question.

"Jason will get his choice first, of course," I said. John nodded, understanding that my sons always came first with me. "I also want to give some to the community to raise for their own eggs." I sighed. "I love my town, John; however, I can't do it all for them. They have to take care of themselves."

"You give more to this town than anyone else," he replied. "So, how many are you keeping for here?"

"It's going to depend on how many are hens. If out of the forty chicks half are hens, I think Jason having six and the community having a dozen, and each get one rooster, that would be fair. That would leave *us* with roosters to butcher and a couple of hens to barter." When he looked like he was going to protest, I put my hand on his arm to silence him. "We already have laying hens. This would give everyone an early start, the chicks will need a full summer and fall of growing to survive the winter. I think I'll start a second batch of eggs as soon as these hatch. Those will be for us to replenish the layers, and more for the freezer."

"You're a generous person, Allex. Moose Creek is lucky to have you. And so am I." I was rewarded with one of his special smiles and a loving kiss.

* * *

JOURNAL ENTRY: May 10

We spent most of the day putting yesterday's purchases away. Some needed repacking, some I set aside to go to the Stone Soup Kitchen, and some got left in the middle of the room. The bulk rice went into the buckets we emptied over the winter and then were stored back in the food shed. The pasta refilled the empty spaces on the shelves that were so full last fall. With the extra flour, I needed another large metal trashcan, the easiest and most convenient way to store bulk flour.

* * *

"I need to make another trip, John. Do you want to go with me, or would you like a day to relax?" I had been working him pretty hard, occupying all his vacation time. "I want to get the metal cans before there aren't any, and I completely forgot about spices. Herbs I can grow, just not spices like cinnamon, pepper, and nutmeg."

"If you don't mind, I think I'll stay here," he said, stretching like his back ached.

"That's okay, enjoy your day off." Marquette wasn't nearly as dangerous now as it was over the winter, as long as I didn't venture downtown. I gave him a hug, and left in my shiny new car.

* * *

My first stop was the big-box hardware store for the trashcans. I was surprised to see so many in stock. I selected two thirty-gallon ones, knowing they would just barely fit in the hatch of the car, and only if I lowered the back seats. When I couldn't find lids for them, I was forced to take the twenty-gallon instead, and got three. There would always be a use for them. Being in a hardware store made me think about Jason.

What was once a common practice now seemed new and foreign. I called him on my little used cellphone, told him I was at the hardware store in town, and asked him if there was anything he needed.

He thanked me, and told me he had an ongoing list, and most of it he needed to pick out himself.

Next stop was Mack's for the spices. We had been so accustomed to just going to any grocery store and getting anything we want. The world became a small place with the advent of international shipping. Exotic things like allspice, nutmeg, peppercorns, cinnamon sticks, cloves and paprika were once extremely expensive and hard to get. That had all changed and we got spoiled. I knew the seasonings were in the baking aisle and I wandered in that direction, going through the bakery section first. Two young women were in a deep discussion, and my curiosity got the better of me. They both appeared to be in their mid-thirties, both blondes. One might have been a true blonde; the other had dark roots that were showing noticeably. Well dressed, thin and attractive, they each had the look of being a trophy wife at some point. Now, they were just young and scared. I made a pretense of checking out the donuts so I could eavesdrop.

When I finally got the gist of their conversation—the lack of decent bread, and what there was, was now ten dollars per loaf—I couldn't resist. I asked them why they didn't just make their own bread.

"*Make* bread? No one does that anymore," one of them said in a huff.

"Don't you have a neighbor or someone who could teach you?" I suggested. Once I said that, I knew I was interfering and moved away. Their lack of basic cooking skills was really none of my business.

In the baking aisle, the spices were where they always had been. I found one ounce jars of peppercorns and whole cloves, plus a larger container of cinnamon sticks. There was no whole allspice or nutmeg to be found, not even a space for it. All of the pre-ground spices were gone so I was out of luck for the paprika I wanted. Then I remembered what paprika was: ground red peppers plus some cayenne pepper to zing it up. I could make my own!

The meat section had very few items, most of it now being kept behind glass in the butcher case. At twenty dollars per pound for a steak, there was a sharp rise in theft. There were a few small chickens, some cut up, and some left whole, also behind the glass. There was no seafood at all, not one shrimp, which wasn't a surprise.

The produce section fared only a little better. No one was trying to steal; there wasn't much to be had anyway. There was a pile of sad and bruised red apples emitting just a hint of sour over-ripeness, cabbages wrapped in plastic, a few limp carrots and a bin of papery onions. The stock boy, Andy, whom I've known for years, saw me and gave me a hug. Not a normal thing, and these days, we were losing those we knew at such a rate it was heartwarming to see a familiar face.

"We're really hoping to have a better selection later in the season after the local farms and gardens have some time to produce a crop, though I doubt there will ever be scrap again for the chickens," Andy admitted. That didn't surprise me, as people were finally learning not to be wasteful.

"Andy, I really appreciate all that you guys have done for me in the past by giving me the old produce for my chickens and I really do understand. I'll manage."

There was a local dairy still in production, so I checked out that department too. John loved cottage cheese as much as I did, and I was thrilled to find some in the cooler. I got us each a carton. Next to it was sour cream and butter, all with limits posted. I still had some butter, although it was one of those things I really had the anxious need to keep plenty of, and who knew when I'd make it back to town? I got the posted limit of two of both.

I was delighted to see Marie at her register, and put the few items on the conveyor. When she looked up, I smiled and her face just lit up.

"Hey, girlfriend!" Marie greeted me. "It's so good to see you. I've thought about you, wondering how you're doing."

We chatted for a few minutes. I asked how her cousin and his son were doing, and was pleased that all was well. It was nice to catch up. I took my bag and headed to the parking lot, remembering another time, and I shuddered with the memory, while unconsciously feeling for the reassuring weight of the Kel Tec in my shoulder holster.

* * *

Watching the news in the evening was disturbing. There had been several large earthquakes on the West Coast, thankfully with minimal damage. The Ring of Fire, the area that circles the Pacific Ocean Basin, had been unusually active and violent. There were more quakes along the coast of South America, too. In one small town in Chile, there was a mine cave-in as a result of the 6.2 quake that rocked the countryside. I shuddered and John tightened his arm around me, knowing what I was thinking. He assured me that it was a completely different kind of mine than the one here, and that he was perfectly safe down in the tunnels. Nothing would ever completely convince me of that.

CHAPTER FIVE

Over a light dinner of chicken Marsala on linguini pasta, one of John's favorites from this past winter, we talked more, knowing he had to go back to work tomorrow afternoon.

"I remember you saying when one of the other guys moved his wife up here and rented a house, Green-Way cut his pay because they then considered him a 'local' employee." John nodded, mopping his plate with a crust of fresh Italian bread. "Will that happen to you if you stay with me?"

"Yes, and I'm ready to accept that. What I can't accept is not seeing you, not holding you." He pushed his plate aside. "Besides, Sven is really mad at me, because *he* can't see you either, for *his* weekly massage." Sven was the big Swede I also saw at Eagle Beach. "This way you can go there."

I thought about this for a few moments. "I have an idea."

We took our iced tea out to the back deck and sat at the black wrought-iron bistro set. Shaded by the numerous trees on the hill, and buffered from any noise by the house, the deck was quiet, peaceful and secluded. I took John's hand across the small table.

"Before you say anything, I want you to listen to what I'm going to suggest. There's nothing I want more than to have you with me all the time. I also know you have to work, and so do I. I know you well enough to know that the money you earn is important to you. If your pay is cut, it will take that much longer for you to earn enough for whatever it is you want to do."

"Are you saying you don't want me to stay here?"

"Goodness, no! I never want you to leave me again. Just hear me out, John. If you stay here, we would hardly see each other anyway, because of your hours." If I recalled correctly, they worked twelve hours a day, seven days a week for six weeks, changing from days to nights midway, and then got two weeks' rest.

"If you stay at Eagle Beach during your six weeks of work, you keep your pay rate. You take your rotation here with me for those two weeks. I'll start coming back to give you massages, so we *will* see each other, and I'd like you to spend your shift change here with me, it's only a few hours, I know, but it's better than nothing. Very soon I'm going to get busy with work too, though just for the summer." His expression was so unreadable. "Do you think this might work?"

"So, I stay at the Green-Way house, and come here during shift change, not missing any work, and then spend my two weeks off here? And you resume coming to do massages? Sven will be happy about that..." he muttered. "That's more time than the other guys get with their wives and family. We'll make it work." He gave me one of those smiles that tell me everything is all right.

* * *

JOURNAL ENTRY: May 13

The news tonight had a long story about the first bridge to be rebuilt across the Mississippi. It is a four-lane bridge that will allow limited traffic to resume. Auto ferries have been pulled out of storage and have been shuttling cars and semi-trucks across the big rivers for two months now, but it's a slow route. The new bridge will greatly improve the delivery system.

The film footage of this new bridge couldn't hide the surrounding devastation from the quakes that rocked our country last fall. Much of that damage is still apparent and likely will be for a long time to come.

* * *

We were just finishing our morning coffee that John insisted on making with the French press like he had done most of the winter when Keith Kay drove up with the next load of wood for my winter supply. He carefully backed the long trailer across the lawn, stopping short of the log-splitter we had left in front of the half-filled woodshed. After unlatching the metal doors on the back, the hydraulics lifted the trailer, spilling the heavy load of wood. Keith drove out slowly, while the cut wood continued to tumble out, leaving another huge mound. John frowned; I was delighted. I retrieved some cash from a drawer, and handed it over to Keith, who left happy to not have to extend me credit this time.

"Why the frown?" I asked, puzzled at John's expression.

"I'm leaving in a few hours," he stated. "Promise me you won't do all this wood by yourself."

"I can't promise you that. Look, I've been doing these chores for years before you came along. I really don't mind." He still had that look etched on his tanned face. "Tell you what, I promise I will ask one of the boys to give me a hand, how's that?" It seemed to satisfy him.

It was a sad day for me, knowing John was leaving; however, at least I knew what was coming this time. Until then we had the day to ourselves. After that, even though I would be alone again, knowing he would be back lightened my heart. I drove him back to the Eagle Beach house around 5:00 P.M., just before the other guys from his team were due to show up after their long flights back to Marquette.

CHAPTER SIX

"I know this doesn't exactly fall into emergency management, Allexa, however, I was hoping you might give me some ideas," Anna said from behind her desk.

"About what?"

"The school, more specifically, the teachers."

"I know we only have ten students left and just the two teachers now. Is there a problem?" I asked. I thought I would have heard about it before now from Eric or Emilee. Emi loves the smaller classes and has taken a real liking to her teacher, Joelle Maki.

"Not really a problem, Allexa. I want to make sure they get paid somehow. Only, a check won't cover what they're doing, and besides, most of the school funding is from the state and that's been stopped." Anna frowned, wrinkling her forehead.

"Emi really likes Joelle to the point of sharing her lunch every day she's there." When Anna gave me a quizzical look, I continued, "I pack Emilee a sandwich and two cookies every day she goes to school. She's been giving half of her sandwich to Joelle. She said her teacher is always hungry and that she can 'hear her tummy rumble.'" I thought a moment about that. "What if each child brings in some food, once a week, for the teachers as a payment? Or maybe we could suggest the teachers get invited to dinner, like the ministers of old?" I suggested. "When the gardens and orchards are full, I'm sure fresh veggies and fruits would be appreciated."

"I think that's a great idea, Allexa. If just once a week, each child brought in two lunches, both teachers would be fed every day." Anna smiled. "I have a meeting with Joelle and with Sheila Lehman this afternoon. I'll get their view on it. You know some of the kids won't be able to do this. I know all the families are having a rough go of it."

"It's worth asking opinions on. Maybe Joelle and Sheila will have a suggestion of their own to offer."

* * *

JOURNAL ENTRY: May 16

Early this morning I went to the ramp patch for some greens to go with dinner, and it occurred to me I could be canning this stuff for a delicious addition to a winter meal. I cut for only a few minutes when I was attacked by a swarm of hungry mosquitos. It must have been a new hatching since they were very small. I dropped my bag and bolted to the car for the head-net I keep in the car box. Thankfully I was wearing long sleeves and always wear gloves to protect my hands. Those vicious little devils were angry they couldn't get to my face or neck, and were about to drive me nuts buzzing around my head. I kept cutting the greens until the bag was full even though the bulbs are still a bit too small to dig up.

I soaked the ramps, and then I lined the pint jars up on the work island and started chopping, picking out any stray bits of grass or twigs that I missed during the washing process and started filling the jars. After the first one I remembered I would need boiling water for filling the jars and set the big kettle on the stove, filled with fresh spring water. With the jars full, I had ten pints, not quite a full canner, and it was a good start. It's seventy minutes once the canner comes up to pressure, and I decided as soon as I could turn the heat off for it to cool down, I would go back for another, fuller batch. Besides, I had packed my dinner greens in the jars and needed more for tonight. Today would be a very productive day, and I smiled to myself at the surprise everyone will get when I add these luscious greens to a rice pilaf at Thanksgiving or Christmas this winter. That's part of prepping: doing, gathering, preserving in season for a later time.

* * *

I was just finishing a third batch of canning ramps this morning, when Jason showed up carrying a scroll, which turned out to be blueprints he had drawn on what appeared to be art paper from the school. I remember the huge rolls on paper cutters in our class when I was young, and doing a six-foot long mural of exotic birds. It's odd what can trigger a memory. When the boys were in high school, the curriculum was very lax. They could take anything they wanted, *with* parental approval that is. I insisted they each take four classes: Shop, Home Economics and Cooking, Drafting and Typing. After that they had free choice. They have both thanked me for those classes. Each of those four classes were practical, useful and functional, and both Eric and Jason still use the skills they learned. Jason had the knack and could have been an architect, instead choosing to use his talents for hands-on building.

He unrolled the wide paper across the picnic table, anchoring the edges with a few rocks from the driveway. I looked over his shoulder at the drawings. He did a really nice job of lying out an 'L' shaped room.

"What do you think, Mom?"

"What is it?"

"Your new greenhouse," he said proudly. I was dumbfounded. "John asked me to draw up some plans for your approval. I guess he figured I would know what you wanted."

"You better start with some explaining, because I don't know what this is about, Jason." My eyes roamed over the sketches, admiring the sharp angles and the steep pitch of glass that would easily shed snow.

"Mom, John has contracted me to build you a greenhouse. It's going to be so much more. Look," he said, pointing to a spot on the sheet, "this is the basic growing area, which faces south and wraps around the end of the house, here is the fish pond at the apex of the 'L' where it's more accessible to both growing areas, and over here is the window herb garden...right next to the summer kitchen and the second wood cook stove."

Summer kitchen?

"And mounted on this side will be the solar panels and battery bank that will run the lights and pumps for the fish." He straightened up and smiled, like I had known this all along. "Oh, I almost forgot. This side runs far enough along the front of the house to encompass the door in the back pantry, so you have access to the greenhouse without going outside."

I was stunned. What had John done now?

"And when did all this sneaking around behind my back take place?" As soon as I asked, I knew. John had hours of free time when I went shopping that second day, enough time to involve my son in his spending plans. No wonder he was so quick to hang onto his higher pay rate. This was going to cost a bundle!

Jason pulled me along by the arm until we were standing at the proposed corner of the house. He paced out one direction, then the other. It looked huge to me. It was only eight feet wide, and wouldn't seem so large once closed in. He stopped by the exit door near the pantry.

"I had forgotten your well is so close..." He frowned in thought. "Say...I can do a small addition, like a mudroom, to enclose the well here. We need an airlock room anyway for bringing wood in for the cook stove." He smiled broadly. "And I can even hook up the hand pump to operate alongside the electric pump. That way, if we lose power again in the winter, you don't have to run the generator for water unless you want to."

I was more than stunned now, I was on the verge of believing I was getting a greenhouse, a summer kitchen and a well house, all rolled into one.

"When do you plan on starting?" I murmured breathlessly.

"As soon as I make up a parts and lumber list and can dig the footings." I know Jason was just as excited about doing this as I was. He has always loved a challenge and this certainly will put him to the test.

Later I sat down in the kitchen with a cup of fresh raspberry leaf tea, mulling over this new development. It would have been so much easier on us this past winter if we had had this greenhouse.

* * *

Jason was back this morning with the power auger to start the footings. He sure isn't wasting any time.

"Oh, I forgot to mention it yesterday. We're also doing something about the deck."

"Wha 's wrong with my deck? I like it just the way it is."

"Mom you've mentioned enclosing it a number of times. I thought you might at least like   over it. I thought a slanted roof to match what's there, and to do it all in lig ls. That way it's sheltered, and you still get ninety percent of the sun effect.   , this was an important part of the project to John. He said he got tired of sh ing out the generator last winter." Jason grinned. He knew I would cave if it was for John. "The roof will only be a two day project and…" He looked sheepish, "I've already ordered the new trusses and the panels, so you're stuck with it." Sheltering the generator *did* make sense.

* * *

While Jason was working on the footings for the greenhouse, I got started on splitting and stacking the rest of the wood. I worked my usual hour on it, and then took an hour break to do something in the garden. It was a beautiful day, and the sun beating down on my back felt wonderfully comforting as I weeded around the new seedlings. Digging up the rich soil, I made the decision to put in some of the plants. I felt confident there wouldn't be a frost again until fall. The rest of the afternoon, I divided my time between stacking wood and planting tomatoes. By the time dinner ca   ound, I was exhausted. I made a quick quiche of ramp greens and fresh o   ushrooms, and sat down to watch the news. I almost wish I hadn't. I guess it's b   er to know then to hide from the world.

There was a 6.4 quake in the Baja and a 7.8 further south on the coast of Mexico in a sleepy little village that is now gone. It was leveled. Two hours after those quakes, one hit in Puget Sound, sending a mini-tsunami over the break wall and flooding Pike Street.

Just before I went to bed at 11:00 P.M., the power went out.

CHAPTER SEVEN

Except for making my tea on the gas stove, I really hadn't noticed that the power was still out until it came back on around noon. It's so easy to get used to it being on and almost as easy when it goes out. This was short lived and overnight, many were likely unaffected by the outage. It made me wonder if this was going to be a regular thing.

Jason stopped by to take a few measurements, and then headed to town for supplies, saying he'd be back in a day or two when the footings had set.

* * *

It was late afternoon when I heard unfamiliar voices out in the yard, and stepped outside to investigate. What I saw surprised me: A family walking down the road, the woman pushing a stroller and a tall man pulling a small wagon. When the man saw me, he stopped, said something to the woman, and then approached halfway up my gravel drive.

"Excuse me, ma'am. My name is Max Johnson, and this is my wife Lydia and our three kids," he said, pointing back to the family behind him. "We're from Harvey and trying to get to our hunting camp on the Mulligan. My car broke down in Marquette a week ago and we've been on foot ever since. I've been doing odd jobs for food and water along the way. I know once we get to camp everything will be fine. I'm sorry, I'm rambling. It's just that it's been two days since we've eaten and it's been a very long, hot morning." Max paused, looking down and embarrassed. "Is there any work I can help you with for even a little food?"

Anyone who was familiar with the Mulligan Truck Trail referred to it just as the Mulligan, so I felt certain this man's story was true. He stayed a respectful distance away, and his family stayed even further. They understood there were boundaries to uphold.

I ventured down the drive to where he stood.

"I'm Allexa, and I could use a hand stacking wood. First I'll get you and your family something to eat. It won't be much though. Why don't you all come under the shade of the tree where it's a little cooler? You can use the picnic table."

I went inside, calculating how much I wanted to help. I set a large pot of water on the stove to heat, and measured in three cups of regular grain rice, adding a couple of seasoning packets for flavor.

"If you're thirsty, there's a water faucet next to the garden," I said once I stepped back outside. "I'm sure you understand that I can't invite you inside for security reasons. The world is different now, so please don't be offended."

"We're not offended at all! I really appreciate just being able to sit in the shade without someone running us off," Max said. I was sure that had happened more than once to them. Their clothes were a bit old, and worn and dirty from days on the road.

Not wanting to use my personal glass bowls outside for people I didn't know, I went searching in the barn for disposable ware from my catering days. I came out with a large black plastic bowl with a thin clear lid, and some plastic forks and spoons. It would have to do.

The three cups of rice once cooked expanded enough to fill the bowl, with some extra broth sinking to the bottom. I set it on the wooden picnic table along with the plastic spoons and forks. Lydia had the two older children washed their hands in the cold water of the faucet before eating while the infant in the yellow and white stroller slept quietly on.

They all crowded around the bowl and spooned the warm rice into their mouths with gusto, making me wonder if it had really been only two days since they'd eaten or whether it had been longer.

The bowl wasn't empty, but it looked like they were done eating. Lydia started talking first. She looked to be in her mid-thirties, with dull blue eyes and natural blond hair now matted and uncombed. She wore sensible walking shoes, jeans and a printed V-necked T-shirt covered by a gray sweater. I noticed that the sweater was buttoned wrong.

"This little angel is Jessica and she turned six last week," Lydia stoked her daughter's dirty brown hair. "This little guy is Aaron. He's two." Aaron promptly sneezed, and then coughed a very lung-y, raspy wheeze. I backed up further toward the tree I was standing near.

"The baby is Sara. She's been such a good little girl, not complaining or crying, but then she's only six months old and they usually sleep all day anyway." Lydia pulled the soiled pink blanket down so I could see the child. The baby's skin was a darkening mottled gray, and it was immediately obvious to me that she was dead, and had been for days. My stomach twisted. The mother was either in deep denial, ignorant or crazy. Perhaps all three, which made her dangerous.

I looked at this wayward family more carefully. They hadn't looked sick at first, but now I spotted how listless and lethargic they all were.

"Cute baby," I said. "Excuse me," and I retreated into the house. In the bathroom, I washed my hands with the hottest water I could stand, then doused them with peroxide, thankful I hadn't touched anyone, but wondering if the distance was enough.

From the kitchen window, I saw Emilee bounding down the well-worn grass path on the way here, and moved quickly to intercept her.

"I'm sorry, Emi, this is not a good time for you to visit."

"Why not, Nahna? There's new people here," she protested.

"Don't argue with me!" I knew I was too harsh with her. "I'll be over tomorrow to explain. For right now, you and your dad stay home, you understand?" She nodded and sullenly went back to their house.

* * *

"You're welcome to stay the night on the lawn," I said as the sun was setting. I placed the plastic lid to the bowl on the table for Lydia to put on.

"I promised to help with the wood," Max protested weakly.

"And I do appreciate that. I really don't need the help. Consider the meal a gift, my Christian gift to a family in need in a world gone crazy." I smiled and returned to the house, after locking the barn up.

What was I going to do?

* * *

I slept fitfully, knowing I might have been exposed to whatever sickness this hapless family carried with them.

When I looked outside the next morning, they were gone. It was as if they'd never been there.

I took the remaining half-gallon of bleach from the pantry, and doused the water faucet and the garden hose. Then I poured the rest of it over the picnic table and the seats, any place I could think they may have touched. I didn't know if it would help, but it sure wouldn't hurt.

Then I called our law enforcement, Ken and Karen.

* * *

"We didn't see anyone on the road coming here," Ken stated.

"They probably left at first light, or during the night," I replied through the facemask.

"Well, we'll take a cruise along the route to the Mulligan and see if we can spot them. I'm not sure what we can do, Allexa," Karen said.

"You can warn others along the way not to get near them!"

After they left, I called Tom White in Marquette.

"Well, hi, Allexa," he answered. "You might not believe this, but I was going to call you today."

"About what? A new outbreak of some virus?" I know I sounded snarky and I didn't care.

"How did you know? I just got the reports this morning from the MEs office. There have been several cases of flu similar to the one last winter, and all of them have been along County Road 695, moving toward Moose Creek."

"Tom, they were here and I've been exposed."

"They? They who?" he asked.

"It's a family, Tom. They were on the way to their camp when their car broke down and they've been walking. Apparently they've been spreading this along the way," I slouched in my seat, my head pounding. "They were here, at my house. Max and Lydia Johnson, along with three kids. The baby is dead and they keep pushing it in a stroller. The two-year-old is bad-sick, and the rest look...I dunno, just ill."

"How were you exposed, Alex?" Tom asked gently.

"I was near them before I realized they were sick," I admitted. "I've washed well and sanitized everything they touched, I don't know if that's enough though. How is it spread, do they know yet?"

"No, they don't. The ME said if it's like the last one, it's airborne and with a very short incubation. Have you been in to see Dr. Robbins yet?"

"No, that's my next call, though I doubt he can do anything either." When I hung up, I washed my hands again, and sprayed the phone.

With gloves and a mask firmly in place, Mark met me outside by the picnic table. I explained to him everything that had happened and he listened solemnly.

"So you were exposed twenty-four hours ago?" he asked.

"Yes, about that. It was mid-afternoon when they showed up."

"I talked with the ME after you called me. They're getting a quick handle on this virus, Allexa. There *are* survivors," Mark said with an air of hope. "Although the virus is fast, about twelve hours, and deadly if you get it, it's also very hard to become infected. So far it's hit only small children and those with weak immune systems. How are you feeling right now?" he asked as he listened to my lungs, flashed the penlight in my eyes and looked down my throat.

"Other than tired from not sleeping and a headache from worrying, I feel fine," I answered.

"No sore throat? Any coughing?"

"No, nothing."

"I would say you escaped catching this nasty bug. You're very lucky. Maybe next time you won't be so trusting," he admonished me as he removed his mask and gloves to prove that he wasn't concerned with me being contagious.

* * *

"We found the family, Allexa," Karen said. She sat down in my kitchen for a cup of coffee. "We were a bit late tracking them down."

"What do you mean *late*?" I asked, setting down a plate of scones.

"The father, Maxwell Johnson, was sitting on the cabin porch with a gun in his lap when we arrived, almost like he was waiting for us. We kept our distance. He knew all along that the baby was dead, and that the boy, Aaron, was really sick. He said he expected the girl to get worse quickly. So he shot the two and buried all three children while his wife was asleep," Karen said matter-of-factly. "The two older children were his from a previous marriage, but the baby was Lydia's first child. He also knew that Lydia was well past the curve of sanity over the baby, so he killed her too. Right after he told us all that, he shot himself."

I was stunned at the news, although not really surprised. The world had indeed gone insane.

CHAPTER EIGHT

It was my day to see John and Sven for their massages. I needed John's comfort, however, I just couldn't tell him about the recent events involving being exposed to the flu. So I kept it to myself, like I did so much.

It had only been a week, and it was good to see John, until I remembered I was mad at him for covertly deciding on all these building projects without discussing them with me first. I set my massage table up in the open hall, just like I'd been doing for almost two years, and waited, quietly seething. When he came around the corner, his face split with a genuine smile, and then it froze when he saw I was angry. Instinctively, he must have known the source of my ire.

"Honey, I wanted to surprise you," he pleaded as he enveloped me with his muscular arms. "And yes, I also knew you would protest." He looked around and, seeing we were alone in the room, he gently kissed me. That's all it took for me to forgive him.

"The plans really are incredible and Jason already has the footings in," I said as I spread some oil on his back and began to knead his tight muscles. "I've got some of the plants set in the garden too, mostly they're just acclimating to being outside." I told him about what I had planted, and intentionally left out any details about the pile of wood that was dwindling steadily.

When the hour was over, John laid some cash down on the side table.

"I don't feel right about you paying me, John, you're already doing way too much for me as it is!" I folded the table and put it back in its black canvas carrier.

"This is your work, Allex. You work—you get paid, simple and no arguments." He was quite adamant, so I folded the cash and slipped it into my pocket. The Resort hadn't started up yet, and I did still have expenses, especially with gas at twenty dollars per gallon. John carried the table to the car for me and loaded it in the back.

I wrapped my arms around his neck and he slid his around my waist. It was our hug time, just like always.

"Next week is shift change," he reminded me. "Can you pick me up around nine in the morning?"

* * *

The morning began with clear blue skies and just a hint of coolness that was refreshing to work in.

The garden called to me. I took the hoe from its corner in the barn and worked on the first row, digging away at the weeds that were already starting to grow. I still needed the markers to show me where some of the rows were. The beans and peas had popped through the soil and were starting on their second and third leaves already so they were easy to work around.

By noon, I had half the garden done. I also felt a new chill in the air and noticed some dark clouds forming over Lake Superior. We needed the rain. With such deep, sandy soil that drained away quickly, we always needed the rain.

Jason had come by yesterday and showed Eric how to put the gutters and drain spouts back up on the barn eaves, and together they turned the cistern over and readied it for summer usage. If these distant clouds did produce rain for us, at least we could start collecting again.

Within minutes, the sky turned very dark and I felt a few drops of cold rain hit my face. The gray and black clouds were roiling low overhead. Just as I was putting the hoe away, there was an earsplitting crack of thunder simultaneous to a jagged streak of lightning and the sky poured out hail. Large icy balls the size of quarters pounded the ground, bouncing in all directions. It was stunning in its beauty and fury and I stood just inside the barn, mesmerized, as a thick carpet of ice started forming. From inside the metal barn, the noise was deafening and I pulled myself out of my reverie when I realized that ice was pounding away at the tender seedlings in my garden!

I grabbed a tarp and headed out into the downpour, quickly covering my head from the onslaught. Ice beat down on my arms, stinging the exposed flesh with every strike.

My tray of unplanted seedlings was taking a beating. I covered them with the tarp while dragging them closer to the plants already in the ground. The ten by twelve foot plastic tarp didn't cover much. I squatted next to a tomato cage, pulling the tray closer and trying to spread the covering to protect more ground. The hail continued to pound on my back the whole time.

It was over in minutes. I stood, shook the ice off the tarp, and surveyed the loss. Stunned was the only word that fit. The hailstorm had lasted maybe five minutes, however, the destruction wiped out two weeks of new plant growth, eighty percent of the newly planted seedlings, and weeks of work.

* * *

"Mom! Mom! Where are you?" Eric yelled as he came running across the road.

"In the garden," I called out.

He came to a halt at the fence and just stared at all the ice, piled up like small Ping-Pong balls. The winds had come out of the north, depositing much of the hail along the inside of the southern fence line.

He stepped carefully around the damaged plants. "I've never seen hail this big."

"Me neither," I sighed.

"What are we going to do?" he said as it sunk in what this meant.

"We're going to replant, that's what. First we're going to get this ice off the plants so it doesn't give them freezer burn," I said with a confidence I really didn't feel, and we started raking the balls of ice away from the damaged plants, piling them in the pathways.

"I have an idea, Mom, but it has to be done quickly and it won't wait until tomorrow."

The idea he came up with didn't surprise me, but it did impress me. He took a Master Gardening class in Florida and although some things were different here because of the climate, some things just don't change.

He set a pile of sticks he collected to one side, most of them about two feet long.

"I've heard this works, Mom, and now is a good time to try it out." Eric was trying to splice and tape some of the plants he felt might survive.

He started to break some of the long sticks into six inch pieces. Very gently he straightened out some of the broken tomato plants and splinted them in place with two sticks and wrapped it with some of my plant tape, then loosely tied the entire plant to one of the longer sticks he shoved into the ground, propping it up.

"If the outer cambium layer is still partially intact it will continue to feed the plant from the roots, growing and healing the broken layers," Eric said. "At least that's the theory. It's worth a shot."

He managed to repair ten of the plants. Whether or not they survived was the question we wouldn't have an answer to for at least a week.

* * *

JOURNAL ENTRY: May 24

With the temperature back into the low eighties, the hail from yesterday has completely melted and now I need to fix the damage done and replant what I can.

My back is sore and bruised from the hailstones. My arms are worse. I never thought hail could be sharp, but it is and I have small cuts and large black and blue bruises where there was exposed flesh.

I hurt, but the work still needs to be done.

* * *

I planted two more rows of beans in and around the sprouts that were broken and still alive. Beans are very hardy; even so I lost a lot. The tomato and pepper plants took the biggest hit. Of the three dozen I grew indoors, I had already planted twenty of them, only the six I managed to protect are left, plus what was in the tray. Fourteen irreplaceable food sources are gone unless Eric's quick thinking works.

Had this been another time, I would have just gone to the nursery and bought more. There is no nursery now; it's one of those businesses that have remained closed. These twenty-two plants will have to be tended carefully and guarded. Hopefully they will produce well.

The only fortunate part was many of the seeds had not come up yet, so they were saved from the brutality that befell the rest of the garden. The sprouted seeds that were destroyed are fast growers so a replanting will still give us a crop. Using extra seed could hurt us in the long run though. I'll have to designate a few extra plants for saving seed to replace the additional used.

I suppose I should go into town and see how Bradley's Backyard fared, however I need to tend my own first.

* * *

"What hail storm?" Anna asked, looking bewildered.

"Two days ago, Anna! Quarter sized hail! Are you saying you didn't get that here? You're only five miles from me." I sat down abruptly. "That's amazing. My garden was severely damaged and you're telling me that Bradley's Backyard just got a light watering?"

"That's all, Allexa. I guess we should consider ourselves lucky that it hasn't been planted yet. The town is going to depend on the food that the community garden produces." She looked away, embarrassed by what she just said. I depend on what I grow too.

"Don't worry about it, Anna. I did get to replant some of it. We'll be fine." *I hope.*

Maybe it wasn't so strange after all that Moose Creek didn't get any hail. The wind currents from Lake Superior shifted directions and changed all the time. During the winter there might be a heavy squall of snow just down the road and I would only be getting flurries. The Big Lake was something we just couldn't second guess.

We needed to plant more and there was only so much room in my garden space. Maybe Eric could clear away some of Nancy's flowers and plant something over there.

* * *

JOURNAL ENTRY: May 28

This week has really passed quickly. I've finished getting the remaining plants in the garden, and have delighted in seeing more new green sprouts everywhere. The green beans I covered and saved from the hail damage are now four inches high, while the special red foot long beans I bought last fall have barely broken ground. The heirloom honey and cream corn was well soaked before going in the ground, so it only took a week for it to come up and the rows are so obvious now, I can take down the yellow marker tape. The last minute decision to put in potatoes has paid off with new leaves pushing up. Each day there's something new to see, and it always makes me smile in spite of how much was lost.

I picked John up at 9:00 A.M. so we could spend some time together before he reported back for his change to night shift. It's only for a few hours, but it's better than nothing and I'm anxious for him to see the progress Jason has made.

* * *

John wanted to see the garden first and it gave me a good way to break the news to him about how much we lost.

"Why didn't you tell me sooner about this, Allex?"

"It happened right after the last time I was over to Eagle Beach. There wasn't any reason to call and burden you with the news," I said. "Besides, there wasn't anything you could do and I've managed to get everything replanted." He looked really concerned.

"Don't worry, we will have enough."

* * *

John was impressed with Jason's progress. "This is incredible, Jason, you work really fast." The footings cured quickly in the dry heat, allowing Jason to start on the walls as soon as the lumber arrived. Most construction yards in the area had been very slow, so they filled the order within a few days. The outside walls were only four feet high to allow the steep pitch of the glass roof.

"Once the walls were up and insulated I installed the plumbing," Jason said. "The floor is in removable segments in case we have to get to the pipes for some reason. And everything is raised on triple joists to hold the weight of soil and the fish tank. You can see the markings on the floor of where things are going to go, John. What do you think?"

"It's really amazing, Jason," John repeated. "I'm impressed."

"It won't take long to finish once I can get the glass. I'm having trouble finding a local glass company that's still in business. What I would like are long, triple paned sheets of glass. Each one to be two feet wide by four feet long and there needs to be a lot of them. I think it's safer to have lots of smaller sections in case something breaks. Like I said, I'm not having much luck, so I might have to rethink this."

Jason had already explained this to me, nevertheless, he delighted in rehashing it with John. It's a guy thing, I think.

"I'll build the growing boxes in place next, while I'm thinking out the glass thing. Each box will be high enough for working in while standing up, almost level to the exterior walls, with lots of storage underneath." He pulled out the rumpled blueprints to show John. "All the solar equipment has arrived, including the batteries, however, I won't put it in until after the place is weather tight. Since wiring is next on the agenda, I might ask Eric to build the boxes. The fish tank should be here tomorrow." He made it sound like a big aquarium when it was actually a five hundred gallon *pond*.

I was really proud of what Jason had accomplished, and in such a short time. John was astounded.

"Oh, and the deck is done," he announced proudly as he led us around the back of the house to show John the new roof. "Eric and I worked at the supports and trusses. That took two days, and then I left Eric to do all the panels on his own while I kept on the greenhouse." The roof made me smile. Following the lines of the house pitch, the new roof sloped over the deck, hot tub and generator, and extended two feet over the edge. The opaque white panels allowed the sun to shine through and seemed to enhance the light.

I nudged John and said, "No more shoveling the generator out from under a foot of snow." He grinned.

"What about the exhaust from the gennie?" John asked.

"It's vented over here," Jason said. "I attached a dryer hose to the muffler, reduced it to a PVC pipe, and it goes up here and out the roof." He tapped the white plastic pipe in the corner. John nodded in appreciation. We talked more about the project, and then Jason said he had some things to do at home and left. This was prearranged. John would be here today for only a few hours and I wanted some private time with him, so I had asked Jason to take the afternoon off.

3:00 P.M. came way too quickly, and I took John back to Eagle Beach so he could change and catch a ride with the guys back to the mine for their late shift. I would see him in another week for his regular massage.

It surprised me that he didn't notice the pile of firewood was almost gone.

CHAPTER NINE

I had managed to do that last load of wood with very little help from either Eric or Jason, and without so much as a splinter, until today. I had nosed the wheelbarrow into the woodshed to unload, and stepped around it to start stacking, when my shoe caught on some bark debris. I tripped, bouncing off the stacked wood and falling against the sharp metal rails that hold the wheel on the cart.

The gash on my left shin was pretty bad and I couldn't ignore the severity of it when I saw blood welling from the new wound. It wasn't long, moments really, and the blood started to run down my leg, soaking my foot and the bark chips. I limped into the house, leaving a trail of large red drops across the kitchen floor as I headed to the bathroom. I grabbed a couple of clean rags from under the sink, and then set my leg on the edge of the marble basin where I could wash it with the cool running water. It was really bad and wouldn't stop bleeding. I sighed with impatience at the thought of having to seek medical help. I wrapped the rag towels around my shin, securing them with an elastic bandage, and grabbed my wallet and keys. As I headed to the door, I stopped long enough to get one of the few plastic garbage bags I had left. I wasn't about to get my shiny new car all bloody. I hoped the new doctor was in his office. Sitting sideways in the driver's seat, I pulled the plastic bag over my foot and up to my knee before getting fully in, thinking that should contain any wayward droplets.

* * *

I pulled into Mark Robbins' office parking lot just as he was coming out, and locking up.

He leaned on the driver's door. "What a pleasant surprise, Allexa. What brings you into town?"

"Well, I kind of cut myself, and thought you better take a look at it," I tried hard to be nonchalant about a gash I knew was going to need stitches.

His expression changed to concern as he opened the car door for me. I swung my injured leg out first, and he went pale when the plastic bag slid off, revealing towels completely soaked with blood.

"What happened? Never mind, let's get you inside first." Mark hurried to unlock the door as I limped behind him. He ushered me into an exam room, turning on lights as he went. When he helped me up onto the table, I noticed how warm his hands were. The other thing I noticed was that I was actually feeling lightheaded. I could *not* have lost that much blood so it must be shock.

He slipped on a pair of surgical gloves, which for some strange reason made me feel better. As he started to cut away the towels and bandage, he started to talk.

"So, what happened, Allex? Sorry, Allexa." He was completely professional as he irrigated the wound after dropping the blood soaked towels into a small metal trashcan. Inwardly I was pleased he remembered my preference on my name.

"I tripped, that's all. It was just in the wrong direction. I feel foolish," I confessed. "I fell against a wheelbarrow and the metal rails are calf high. It was full of wood, and didn't give—however...I did."

"When was your last tetanus shot?" he asked, not even looking up.

"Five, maybe six years ago. I try to get them regularly, considering where and how I live. Ouch!" He didn't warn me before poking me with a needle. "What was that?"

"Just something to numb the skin. You *will* need stitches. Are you allergic to anything?" He finally looked up at me. It might have been my imagination, but he seemed angry.

"Yes, I'm allergic to penicillin and codeine. They make me sick to my stomach. Are you mad at me for some reason?" His hands stilled and he looked at me again, and then turned to retrieve two sterile packs of sutures, that looked just like what I had in my med-kit.

"In the few weeks I've been here, I've gotten to know the people in the town. Interesting folks and they love to talk." He paused. "Do you know how much they think of you? How much they depend on you?" His back stiffened. "This is a serious injury, *Allexa*. What would have happened if I weren't here to stitch you up? You shouldn't be so careless!" He ripped one of the packages open with unnecessary force.

"Well, *doctor*, I guess I would have butterflied it closed, or stitched it up myself, or called one of our capable paramedics!" I knew I was getting defensive, who did he think he was? And now that I think about it, I didn't understand why I was so hostile toward him, except maybe because I *did* find him attractive, and I felt somehow disloyal to John because of it. Anyway, we glared at each other for a moment, and then he started to laugh.

"You're a tough one. I bet you *would* try to do your own stitches! I apologize for my gruffness, it was uncalled for. It's just that most accidents can be avoided." His voice softened. "You might not want to watch this. On the other hand, maybe you do." He grinned at me and I smiled back, the tense moment gone. I leaned back on the table and let him work. The cut was deeper than I thought. It took six internal stitches and ten external to close up the gash.

"I'm normally quite cautious when it comes to my physical safety," I sighed. "It was the very last of the wood to stack, and then I was going to clean up all the bark that had come loose. Maybe next time I'll clean up as I go."

"What do you use the wood for?" Mark asked casually. Finished with the last of the stitches, he started to bandage my leg.

"Heat and cooking in the winter," I replied with a smile, thinking of all the wonderful meals I'd fixed on that stove over the years. I then explained to him about the stove and gave a brief history of it in my life.

"All done." He reached out his hand to help me sit up. "I still need to give you a tetanus booster. I've also got a Z-Pak of antibiotics for you. Do you want pain meds?" Interesting that he asked, rather than just assumed I would want pain pills.

"No, I'm pretty good with pain," I snickered. Then I paused, knowing having a few pain pills on hand might not be a bad idea. "On second thought, maybe just a few in case it gets too bad."

"Okay. I'm going to give you a couple of sleeping pills for the night. The next few days are going to be very uncomfortable and you'll need the rest." I saw him unlock another cabinet, remove some packets, then lock it up again. Even in a small town like this, it was best to keep narcotics under lock and key.

"And as for the town, they shouldn't depend on me so much. That makes me really uncomfortable. I was trained for short term disasters or problems, not for *this*," I flipped my hand toward the township hall. "Not for problems that last for months and months. I'm not that strong, Doc." I could feel the tears prickle behind my eyes. It must be adrenaline shock.

"But you are," Mark said softly.

I slid off the exam table and finally had a chance to look around the office to admire my son's handiwork. "Jason did a nice job with the rooms," I commented, changing the subject.

"Nice? He's a wizard. It was a delight to explain what I needed and he just went to work. He was done in half the time it would have taken a whole crew." The good doctor was obviously impressed. "And the upstairs looks even better. Would you like a tour?" he offered.

"I think I'll take a rain-check." When he looked disappointed, I added: "I'd rather not tackle the stairs with fresh stitches."

"Of course not, what was I thinking?" He laughed, and then got serious. "What is your home situation?"

"Excuse me?" I'm not sure what he meant.

"Are there many stairs to deal with? Can you move your sleeping to the first floor? Is there someone to check on you?"

"Ah, I see. It's all one level once I get up the three steps to the door. My older son lives just across the road. I'll let him know about my little mishap." I hobbled toward the door. "Thanks for seeing me so quickly, Mark. It's good to have you in town. What do I owe you?"

"We'll discuss that another time." He smiled gently and walked me to the car.

I'm not sure I liked being in his debt; then again I *was* glad he was here.

CHAPTER TEN

I woke this morning to the faint sounds of peeping and realized I had baby chicks hatching! It's an exciting thing to watch as they force their way out of the shell. As much as I get tempted to help, I know the baby chicks need to do this for survival. I checked on their progress, disappointed that John wasn't here to witness this event, so I sent him a text with the news.

Not all of the eggs have hatched, because they were started at different times, spread out over several days, and so far so good. I'm hoping for a good turnout. It will be hard to tell for sure the sex of the chicks for a few weeks, and they are all active and look healthy.

* * *

I called Eric as soon as I had dressed for the day. "We have chicks hatching! Do you and Emi want to come over and watch?"

Eric used to have chickens down in Florida and showed me an old-time trick for sexing baby chicks by holding the chick in cupped hands, with the chick on its back: a female stays there, passive, while a male will struggle to right itself. It's looking like we have more hens than roosters. I was pleased.

I then had Eric retrieve a large cardboard box from the barn that would be their temporary home for the first week. Spread with old newspapers and a lamp positioned overhead, they would be cozy and protected. In a few days I'd have him get the brooder cage down and sterilize it. The chicks would stay in there for a month, letting them acclimate to the older hens. They grow really fast and will be able to defend themselves quickly. In a month, Jason can take his pick, and I will keep some and then offer the rest to the town. As soon as all the chicks finish hatching, I'll start another batch right away. With three dozen eggs in the refrigerator, it will be easy to start saving new eggs without restricting our own egg usage.

* * *

The same urgency about hatching more eggs hit me as I surveyed the garden. The first row of greens beans that survived the hail storm are several inches tall now and the second row is pushing up through the soil. Although I had told John I would do a wide staggering of plantings, I feel the need to plant the rest right away. It might be a foolish mistake. The worst that could happen was I had a lot of work all at once to can them for the winter. It also occurred to me that I should plant a crop of something for the chickens' winter feed.

* * *

I limped into Anna's office and sat down across from her. I had already driven by the new community garden to check on the progress and noted that it had been plowed several times. Two teenagers were raking the ground level and were followed by others planting something.

"Bradley's Back Yard is really taking shape, Anna. I see it's being planted now. That's great!" I winced when I bumped my shin into her desk.

She sighed. "What did you do now?"

"Just a small cut. Mark stitched it up for me. It's fine."

"Stitches? How many?"

"Sixteen," I murmured under my breath.

"Sixteen stitches is *not* a small cut! You have to be more careful, Allexa," Anna admonished.

"Why is everyone getting pissed at me for an accident?" I retorted.

"Because we need you, and you of all people should know how even the smallest of injuries can be major in these times."

She was right, of course; things were still bad. The only thing that had changed from six months ago was we'd had our power restored and the outside air was now warm instead of bitterly cold. We were still short on food, we were still short on medical supplies, and we still lacked many of the normal things that we were used to for civilized living. *And* our safe little community was still in danger from those who would take what little we had.

I looked down at my bandaged leg. It was a harsh reminder, and I looked up at her, contrite. I admit it was hard. I know I'm a stubborn person. "Okay, Anna, I agree to be more careful." For some reason that left a bitter taste in my mouth. "Aside from that, Anna, the people of Moose Creek need to rely more on themselves and less on me. I can't always help them! I need to be helping myself and my family right now. Besides," I looked her straight in those soft gray eyes, "long term disaster planning is not part of my job description. I may know a lot about prepping and food storage, except that's personal prepping, not mass prepping." I leaned back and stared at the white and black speckled ceiling tiles for a minute, the silence pounding in my ears. "You know I will do whatever I can for Moose Creek, however, it might not be enough, Anna, not without everyone pitching in. There are no more free rides. We will need *every* person helping."

She was startled to hear that, although I think she understood what I was getting at. We lost a lot of people in the past seven months, and I hope those that were left were strong and were survivors.

* * *

I cut away the gauze bandages to inspect the wound. It sure looked nasty, though I didn't see any signs of infection. The antibiotics and pain meds Mark gave me were safely stored away in my medical bag. If I didn't use them then they would be available for someone truly in need of them. However, I also didn't want to risk an infection myself. I went outside to the herb garden and plucked off several leaves from the comfrey plant to make a poultice.

In one of the boxes I have for medical supplies, I had stored several poultice bags. They are just new washcloths folded in half and sewn on two sides, leaving a pocket. I used white for these so they could be boiled and bleached. When I pulled two out, I spotted the red washcloths, also washed and stored in zipper bags to keep them sanitary. Mostly for children, it was discussed that cloths already red in color would be less traumatizing if saturated with blood. I smiled, knowing several adults who would need the red cloths too. Though I've never had to use them, there were at least a dozen in the box, and a couple in my medical bag.

I tore the comfrey leaves into pieces and stuffed them into the white bag, setting the bag into a shallow bowl. I poured boiling water over the bag and let it sit for several minutes to release the healing oils. Wringing the cloth gently, I captured the water in the same bowl. It would make a good infusion for a second application. I set the timer for a half hour, got my current book, and a notepad and pen. I set my injured leg to rest on a second chair and covered the wound with the now warm poultice. It instantly felt soothing. I read maybe five minutes, then set the book aside and started making notes. I know I've got a few extra bean seeds I can give to the community garden, just not as much as I planned since I had to replant what was destroyed.

* * *

It occurred to me that I hadn't received any calls from my clients at The Resort. In the past I've always had at least one busy week in May before things picked up in June, so I gave the gate a call this morning. I was startled and disturbed to discover that The Resort was not opening this year, not until things normalized in the country. I suppose that made sense, since most of the members were scattered across the nation, however, it also meant that the recovery wasn't going as well as the government was telling us, not if the wealthy were so restricted.

* * *

I was washing dishes while the bread was rising and heard engine sounds getting closer and closer. Eric had decided to cut our lawns with my brother's riding mower. I stopped him just as he was starting on mine.

"I don't want the front part cut, Eric." The desperation and near panic in my voice caught his attention.

"You weren't here yet when the neatly plowed roads and driveway attracted the attention of that gang, and it's what got your uncle and his wife killed. I don't want us to look too lived in."

Visions of that day sent a chill up my spine. I've tried hard to block out the sight of Don on his porch, falling backward from the impact of the .223, and of the red blossom on Nancy's yellow shirt, her heart ripped apart by the next bullet, while we watched helplessly from this side of the road.

"That's over, Mom," he assured me. "Things are getting back to normal now."

"Don't be lulled into a false sense of security, Eric. Things are *not* back to the way they were, and they may never be that way again." Maybe I was overreacting. Still, it had to be said. "Eric, listen to me. The only thing that is back to normal is having the electricity on, and even that we can't be sure of. It could go out again any minute. Food is outrageously expensive *when* it's available; gas prices have gone through the roof; and any city of over a hundred thousand is still under martial law. You think that's *normal*?"

He cast his eyes down and away.

"Tell you what. Why don't you cut the grass near the house and the side yard? That will help keep the bugs and ticks down."

My brother's yard was well hidden from view with lots of mature trees and underbrush, so keeping it cut was now Eric's decision.

"Besides, gas is too expensive, and cutting the grass is wasteful." That point he didn't argue with. After he was done cutting, I raked up all the clippings to mulch down the garden; the extra nitrogen would also help build the soil.

* * *

"I don't know what to do, Mom," Jason said. "I'm thinking we might be better off scrounging around some of the vacant houses and salvaging windows for the greenhouse. In fact, that definitely would be better. It would give us more options for the ventilation."

I was delighted at how quickly Jason worked once he got started on the greenhouse. He laid the entire area under the floor with heavy plastic and stones to keep any weeds from growing up through the slatted wooden floor. The joists were strengthened to handle the weight of the water for the fish tank and the tons of soil needed for the growing boxes, and then covered with closely spaced decking to allow any water spillage to seep down. It might be chilly on the feet in the winter; then again, maybe not. We just don't know yet.

"I'm holding off doing any more on the area around the grow boxes on the south side until the dirt is delivered, which should be this afternoon," Jason told me. "I figure it will be a lot easier shoveling the dirt 'through' the wall as opposed to walking one wheelbarrow at a time through the door just to fill up the boxes."

He's so smart. It's a very logical order of doing things, and I told him so.

"We'll use as much of the load of the composted black dirt as we need for the six, twelve inch-deep 4x4 beds, and the rest we'll bank against the wall from the outside to insulate against the snow."

"There's certainly no hurry on the fish pond, but what's the plan?" I was more than curious, and wanted to make sure I had some input this time. I looked over at the new pond sitting empty in the corner.

"I don't want to wait too long, because finding some aquatic plants might be difficult. Once we have them though, I'll need to do something with them."

"I think if we put some rocks in the pond on one side, we can use them to wire the plants in place until they can take root," I suggested. "And although the fish won't have any predators to hide from, like eagles or geese, I'd like to have maybe some driftwood for a more natural habitat."

"That would solve a problem that's been bothering me. I think I'll ask Eric to gather up some large rocks, then a couple of buckets of creek bottom. The fish will need a sand and gravel bed if we want them to spawn. Any thoughts on what kind of plants you want?"

"I think I'd like some cattails and water lilies, maybe some marsh marigolds." Just those three plants would add a great deal to the new pond, in both habitat and color.

"Those should be easy enough to find. The cattails and marigolds are just down the road, and I know a spot on McKenna's Bay where I've seen lilies."

I could see his mind drifting away with plans, and knew better than to interrupt his creative moments. Besides, I had bread to bake.

* * *

JOURNAL ENTRY: June 3

The news tonight just reaffirmed in my mind that things were not going well in the rest of the country. There were more riots in the cities that are still under Martial Law and heavy curfews. Refugees from the mid-sized cities of 150,000 are invading the countryside and farms looking for food and relief from the violence, only to bring the violence with them. And new diseases are emerging, some flu-like viruses, some bacterial and highly communicable.

CHAPTER ELEVEN

I pulled into the parking lot at Eagle Beach at 7:50 A.M. This was the start of the morning massages for John and now Sven, too. Inwardly, I was thankful it was a cool morning so my wearing long pants to hide the stitches on my shin didn't seem unusual.

I was ready at eight o'clock sharp, and Sven took the first massage. Even though I know John waits so he can sneak in a kiss or two, he really needs to get some sleep. Those night shifts are brutal.

"Only two more weeks and I go on rotation," John murmured into my ear as we hugged after his massage was over.

"I'm definitely looking forward to it," I grinned. "Now, you get some sleep and I'll see you next week."

* * *

I took what seeds I felt I could spare and a mesh bag of old potatoes that I had extra and left for town around noon. Most people would have tossed out these shriveled up spuds, with the dark brown skin all wrinkled and the long white eyes poking out. I had let these grow intentionally from what I dug up last fall. I haven't bought seed potatoes in years, always perpetuating my own. I planted all I had room for in the garden, so the rest could go to the community garden. Now I needed to find Pastor Carolyn.

* * *

Cruising by the community garden first on my four-wheeler, I spotted her with a hoe, hacking away at the soil. Other members of the church were there too, diligently marking rows with strips of cloth.

"Hi, Carolyn," I said, announcing my presence so I didn't startle her. She was now our most senior member in the town. We had lost most of the elderly to the flu that rampaged through Moose Creek last winter.

"Allexa, good to see you!" She leaned on the hoe, seeming to be grateful for the break. "What do you think of our garden? Come to help out?" Her usually bouncy gray curls sagged under the heat and sweat. She, too, seemed to sag under the blazing sun and bright blue sky.

"In a manner of speaking, yes I have. I brought you a bag of seed potatoes and some seeds. There's rutabaga, kohlrabi, radish, collards, and carrots." I handed the bags to her, and her eyes smiled. Carolyn and I have a history of quiet collaboration from last winter. She knows I will do whatever I can to help, but I have a limit and I don't want any credit.

"These are all I can spare, and I wanted you to have them as soon as possible. They need time to germinate, and we never seem to have enough of that. There won't be any second chances with the garden." Time and fate have had a way of going against us lately. A worried cloud passed over her face and was gone just as quickly.

"How are you feeling, Pastor? You look...extra tired." I reverted to her formal title so she would understand my concern. "Maybe it's time you had a checkup from our new doctor."

"Fiddlesticks! I'm fine. I *am* tired though, and hot. Maybe it's time for me to take a break and let the youngsters work for a while." She leaned the hoe against a nearby fence where other tools were lined up. It was interesting to me to see how we have stepped back to a time where there was an unspoken trust. Those tools would still be there in the days to come; no one would even consider moving them, except to work in the garden. Theft and crime in our town had come to a halt, leaving our new law enforcement team, Ken and Karen, without much to do. Eric and Lenny were backup deputies, and were even less needed.

Carolyn sat down in the shade with a bottle of water, and I turned my attention to the remaining workers to show them how to maximize the handful of sprouting spuds. We dug four long trenches and watered. Then I selected one of the potatoes, pulled my pocketknife out, and cut it in four pieces, leaving one or two eyes on each piece. I had one of the young girls place them in a trench, cut side down, eighteen inches apart. Once they got the gist of it, I took Carolyn home on my four-wheeler so she wouldn't have to walk. I did *not* like the ashen color of her skin.

Since I was right next door, I decided to pay a visit to Bob and Kathy. It had been too long since I'd seen them and I felt like I hadn't been a very good friend.

"There you are," I called out to Kathy when I found her hard at work in her raised bed garden.

She looked up from the troweling and gave me a bright smile. "Hey! Good to see you, my friend." She wiped her hands on her ragged jeans, something she never would have done before, and gave me a hug.

"What are you planting, Kath?" I asked, surveying the eight beds laid out in a spoke design. The hub was multi-tiered and filled with perennial herbs, and the paths were packed with faded bark chip.

"I'm putting in the usual veggies, just a lot more of them. This bed will be all carrots, and that one I've already put in the potatoes. Another will have green beans if I can find the seed. There's the rutabaga, peppers and summer greens," she said as we walked the circle. "And peas. I'm still debating on the squash; it was a wasted effort last year."

"Are the tomatoes on the deck in the earth boxes?"

"Yes. Once the power came back on steady, I started some seeds in my hydroponic herb unit. The tomato and pepper plants are a lot smaller than what I normally start with, I'm just glad I have some."

"That's the one thing lacking in the community garden right now: tomatoes! I sure hope someone else has tried to grow something on their own." I paused, and then turned to her. "I've missed seeing you and Bob. Maybe the four of us can get together soon?"

"Four? Is John back?" Kathy asked excitedly.

"Yes, just not full time. He's still working the mine and staying on Eagle Beach, and we see each other as often as our schedules allow. It seems to be working."

* * *

I was going to do some laundry when I got home, except the power was out again. This was becoming more and more frequent.

* * *

A visit from Joshua Beals was the last thing I expected. The young man is only twenty-one, tall and lanky, with a laid-back attitude toward life and a ready smile. If he were forty years older, I would liken him to a hardworking hippie. I hadn't ever visited his place, but I knew he and his grandmother loved to garden and I assumed that had sustained them in their solitude.

"Joshua, how nice to see you," I said, smiling. Neither he nor his grandmother had been seen for the entire winter. "It's good to know you are still with us." I gave him another big smile and a hug.

"It was a rough winter, Miss Allexa, but we made it." Like everyone else, he had lost some weight, and had a haunted look in his dark eyes.

"How's Martha?" His grandmother preferred to be called by her first name, even by her own grandchild.

"Truthfully, she's been better," he replied. "Actually, that's why I'm here..." I waited for him to continue, since I had no idea what he meant. "I stopped to see the new doctor, and asked him to come out to check her over. Martha refuses to leave the farm. Anyway, he said he would and when I asked him how much, he said he wouldn't charge us anything at all."

I instantly knew part of the problem: the Beals would look at that as charity. They were very proud and would never accept Mark's generosity.

"I told him we would pay," Joshua said, "though it would have to be in barter, so I offered him a goat."

"I didn't know you had goats," I said, just picturing Mark with a goat and I stifled a snicker.

"Doctor Mark said he didn't need or want a goat. He said maybe I could trade it to you for something he *did* want. He said if you accepted the goat, then he would consider having been paid. Will you take Matilda?" Joshua pleaded.

I couldn't imagine what Mark had in mind, however, if this was the only way they would accept his visit, I knew I must.

"Of course, Joshua, I accept the goat in payment for Doctor Mark. You might have to hold her for me while I can figure something out for her. And you might have to give me a few tips on how to care for her." He looked so relieved. "What other animals do you have?"

"Well, we still have Bossy. I know that's a stupid name for a cow. Martha thought it was a good joke. Bossy's been giving us enough milk to drink and make cheese. Would you like to do some trading?" There was an undeniable eagerness in his voice.

"I would be happy to. What do you need?" I suddenly had visions of a new Moose Creek economy.

"Martha has been too weak to make bread. Do you know how or know someone who does? I miss my sandwiches. And I lost my last chicken to a coyote a few weeks ago. Do you know anyone with chickens?"

"You've come to the right place, Joshua. Would you like some iced tea?"

* * *

We sat down at the picnic table and discussed "prices."

"I have eggs and just hatched some chicks. How many chickens do you think you could use, Joshua?"

"Um, I-I don't know," he stammered. "I hadn't thought that far since I didn't think anyone would be willing to give any up."

"Would six hens and a rooster do for now?" The relief that flooded his face was magical. "Of course, the chicks are less than a week old, so you can't take them just yet. I'll trade you a dozen eggs for a gallon of milk for now, and every week until the new hens start producing. Would that be okay?"

His head bobbed in speechless agreement.

"Now, how would you like a loaf of fresh bread for some of your cheese?"

"You make bread too?" he asked in wonder.

"Every few days. My family loves bread." I laughed. "I do have one small request, Joshua. I need you to keep Matilda. I agree that she's now mine, except I really don't have the space or the time to take care of a goat. Will you do that?"

I had seen the sorrow in his eyes when he talked about giving up his goat, which I suspected was more of a pet, and I knew he would do it to get his aging grandmother the help she needed.

He swallowed hard. Emotions didn't come easy to this young man. He nodded compliance once more.

"Great! That sure helps me out, Joshua, thank you." I stood and held out my hand to seal the deal.

It's an extra bonus that his farm is less than a mile away. I sent him home with a dozen eggs, a loaf of fresh bread, and a promise from him of returning in a day or two with a gallon of milk and a pound of cheese. He took the "credit" reluctantly. He's a good young man with very firm morals.

I felt buoyed for the first time weeks. We were establishing something meaningful for the community now.

* * *

All this encouraging news was darkened by tonight's newscast and the report of more quakes on the West Coast, including three in Yellowstone.

CHAPTER TWELVE

When I was weeding the herb bed, I plucked a handful of chive flowers. Those sweet smelling purple flowers have quite the zing to them. Most people don't realize they're edible fresh or dried and make a charming garnish.

Emilee came skipping across the road as I finished weeding. Even though traffic is non-existent now, she still stopped and looked both ways before starting across. She makes me smile and watching her lifted my spirits.

"What are you doing, Nahna?" She stuck her nose down into the chive flowers. "Oh, they smell pretty!"

"Yes, they do. They are also tasty." Emi's eyes brightened. Unlike her cousin Jacob, Emi is willing to try almost any new food. I picked one up and held it out to her. "Do you want to try one?" When she reached for it I added, "Be careful, they have a strong peppery taste."

She popped it in her mouth and started to chew. The expression that flooded her scrunched up face was priceless and I had to laugh.

"It's okay if you want to spit it out," I told her. She didn't. She grimaced and swallowed it.

"I don't think I want another one, Nahna. The taste isn't bad, but there's so much of it, it makes my mouth burn." She made another face that got me laughing again.

"There's some sweet tea in the refrigerator, Emi. Why don't you get us each a glass?"

She bounded away quickly into the house. I dreaded the thought of Emilee's mother asking Eric to bring her back to Florida.

Neither of the kids attends school every day now, and Wednesday was Emilee's day off. The only children who went every day are the ones who lived right in town and could walk the few blocks. Gas was just too limited to take one child to school and the buses used too much diesel.

Just as Emilee brought us two glasses of tea, I saw Eric heading our way. "Emi, you might want to get another glass for your dad," I suggested.

Eric sat down at the picnic table and propped his chin in his hands, elbows on the surface, a position I've come to recognize. "Hi, Mom."

"What's on your mind, son?" I smiled and he grinned.

"I want to ask you about using your four-wheeler and the wagon a couple of times each week. I've been talking to a few of the other parents, and we'd like to get a kind of carpool going for getting the kids to school as cheaply as possible. I know I could fit three kids in that garden cart you use, the heavy duty one that attaches to the ATV. I could pick up the other two kids on my way in, and then one of the other parents would bring everyone home."

"Kids in the garden cart isn't exactly the safest means of transportation, Eric," I cautioned. "You need to come up with something better." Although the ATV *would* be the most cost efficient.

* * *

JOURNAL ENTRY: June 7

The last of the chicks hatched out this morning. After candling the four remaining eggs with a strong flashlight, I could see the shells were empty. We set forty eggs and thirty-six hatchings is a very good turnout.

With Eric's method of guessing the sex, it appears we have twenty-four hens and twelve roosters. If Jason takes six hens plus a rooster, and Joshua takes the same, I can give the community twelve hens and a rooster. That leaves me with nine to butcher.

I washed out the incubator and sterilized it with a spritz of bleach, and set it in the sun to dry. Tomorrow I start collecting eggs again.

* * *

"Good morning, Miss Allexa," Joshua said, smiling at me. "I've brought you two gallons of milk and a pound of cheese, just like I promised."

"Thank you, Joshua, but that should be only one gallon of milk," I reminded him.

"Well, the extra gallon is for the kids. I know Jason's little boy will want some too, once he tastes it." Joshua beamed. "It's real good milk."

"I'm sure it is. Have you tried making butter yet?" I asked, knowing my supply was getting low.

"No." He looked down at the ground. "I don't know how," he confessed.

"Wait right here."

When I returned, I handed him a book on making dairy products. "I've collected these 'how-to' books for years, thinking that someday someone might need the knowledge. I think that time is now."

"Gosh, thanks, Miss Allexa!" he said, already getting lost in the pages. I left him thumbing through the book while I put the milk and cheese away. I broke off a small bit of cheese and tasted it. It was a little bland, but it was indeed cheese and creamy rich.

"Do you have enough salt to make your cheeses?" I asked.

"Oh, we haven't had salt in months so I've learned to make things without it," he said, still scanning the pages of the dairy book.

"Wait right there a moment."

I retrieved two one-pound boxes of salt from the storage shed and placed them on the wooden table in front of him. His look shifted from surprise to delight and finally to disappointed resignation, all in a matter of a few seconds.

"Joshua," I said sternly, "you're going to accept this salt as a gift from me. And don't argue with me! Our bodies *need* salt, and don't function properly without it. In fact, this could be a contributing factor to Martha not feeling well."

"Yes, ma'am," he replied politely in a very humbled voice.

CHAPTER THIRTEEN

I got home from the office early in the afternoon, to find Jason and Eric unloading large panes of glass from the pickup truck.

"Where did you find all those?" I asked, watching them stack at least a dozen sliding glass doors near the unfinished greenhouse.

"I got the list of abandoned houses from Ken and Karen," Eric said. "We were real careful, Mom, and took only what we could use, and then boarded up the openings. There was one house where we got most of these. It looked made of glass. The roof was caved in, so we just took what was there."

"It didn't take us long, maybe two days, to get all I'll need to finish this up," Jason piped in. "I'll have to redesign some of the braces, so we tried to stick with all glass doors, sizes I know will fit, at least width wise. And they're tempered glass, which is what I would have ordered. I'll just need to add more cross members to the joists."

"While he's doing that, I'm going to start pumping water up from the creek to fill the fish pond," Eric chimed in. "I've already got the gravel and sand ready to go in, and a couple of rocks. I'll finish that up, set the pump, and then help him with the higher windows."

"We need to start at the top and work down. If there are any adjustments to make, it'll be easier to do at ground level. We should have this all closed in by tomorrow, Mom," Jason said proudly.

I surveyed the new structure, speechless. In the southeast corner sat the fishpond, just waiting for water to bring it to life. Around it, Jason had built benches that were functional as stabilizers for the heavy plastic edge of the pond itself; it would also add a place to sit to enjoy the room. Along the south and southwest wall, the six grow boxes were filled with rich black soil, begging to be planted. As of yet, the storage space underneath was empty, and I hadn't decided if I wanted doors or to just leave it open.

In the northeast corner sat the extra wood cook stove that had been sitting in storage ever since I got it from a Resort member. It was resting on a brick hearth;

however, it hadn't been installed yet. There was time for that, it was only June and we wouldn't need heat in here until October at the earliest.

So much had been done in so little time. I couldn't wait for John to see this!

* * *

Right after lunch, Emilee and I took a walk down the road toward the small swampy area that formed the front yard of the abandoned house next door. Doreen never came back to reclaim it. In time, the house might be occupied again, so I had made it off limits to my sons' scavenging. I'd really like to see Jason and Amanda move in there so they could be closer to us, but I doubted that was going to happen any time soon.

"What are we looking for again, Nahna?" Emi asked, skipping down the road, slightly ahead of me.

"We need some water flowers for the new fish pond," I answered. "I want those yellow flowers over there," I said, pointing to the Marsh Marigolds. "Those should be easy to dig up, and we need to take a lot of the dirt around them so they feel at home in the new pond." I planned on wrapping the root ball in old pantyhose to contain the dirt while it set in the water.

We climbed down the gentle slope to the damp ground and surveyed what was available. The marigolds grew prolifically at the edges of ditches and swamps, as long as they had some dirt to hold on to. The cattails would tolerate deeper water, but seemed to prefer a damp soil. We were in luck today. It hadn't rained in a few days so we weren't going to get too soggy digging up what I wanted.

"These are really pretty, Nahna," Emilee chattered. She dug the shovel around the clump of yellow-gold blossoms. She stomped her foot on the blade's shoulder a little hard and was rewarded with a squirt of muddy water up her tanned bare legs.

I laughed. "Maybe a bit slower won't cause such a splash." She shrugged and lifted the clump into a waiting bucket.

"How many do we need?" she asked.

"There are several flowers in each clump, so just one will do, dear. We'll need at least six of the cattails."

We dug and lifted, moved and carried for more than a half hour. The little wagon we had brought with us was full.

"This doesn't look like very much, Nahna," Emi observed.

"Uncle Jason knows where there are some water lilies, so he will be getting the rest of what we will plant. You did good, Emilee, and didn't even complain about getting the muddy water on yourself. I'm proud of you."

"Well, it's only water and dirt," she said, dismissing any girly revulsion. She's a tough one.

CHAPTER FOURTEEN

I was just starting to get something put together for dinner when I heard Emilee screaming my name and sobbing.

"Nahna! Dad's hurt real bad!" she cried out to me, running into the kitchen. "Some bad men came in the yard and hit him. He yelled at me to run. Then he fell on the ground."

I pushed her into the living room. "Stay here!"

Before I could even get to the side door where my shotgun was, a strange young man burst through the door. The screen was no match for the violent rage that etched his pale young face, and he literally ripped it to shreds. He was well over six feet tall, lean and large with curly black hair and black eyes. His eyes swept the room, coming to rest on me.

"What do you want?" I yelled at him as I backed away. He growled and lunged at me.

He struck me hard with his fist on the left side of my face and I instantly tasted the coppery blood that started to fill my mouth when the soft inside tissue mashed against my teeth. I staggered against the counter next to the hall, grabbing the nearest thing and swinging it in his direction. The heavy flashlight made a satisfying crunch when it connected with his nose and slowed him enough for me to flee down the hall and out of his reach. My foremost thought was to distract him away from my granddaughter.

A few feet from the next doorway, on the right side of the hall, hung my Dirk. A million thoughts ran through my head as my brain registered what my eyes were seeing. I remembered when I bought that sword five years ago from a local knife smith. With an overall length of twenty-three inches, the dagger shaped blade was a full sixteen inches and hefty in weight yet perfectly balanced. When I showed it to my brother, he insisted on putting a razor sharp edge on it for me. Hanging at an angle, it rested in its decorative wooden scabbard. I reached out and grabbed the hilt, sending the polished wooden sheath clattering to the tiled floor. The hair on my neck twitched and I could feel the guy getting closer. I took two more long steps then pivoted low, the blood pounding in my ears. With both hands now holding the heavy weapon, I braced myself, putting my weight and my fear into the force, aiming for the vulnerable spot just below the sternum. Whoever this monster was, he impaled himself on the blade as he came at me. I was a good twelve inches shorter than him and the blade entered low. His thin black t-shirt and soft pink skin offered no resistance to the sharp blade and it slid in easily. I used his surprise to my advantage and angled the sharp steel upward, slicing an opening six inches wide, ripping through any organs that were missed by the first impact.

His hot and sticky blood gushed over my hands as I pushed the blade even deeper, and his frozen look of surprise changed to anguish, and then the light went out of his dark, menacing eyes. He fell, pulling me down with him.

I struggled to get him off of me, and managed to liberate one of my legs. I kicked and shoved with my foot, rolling him enough to free myself from his dead weight. Emilee screamed again, this time in pain.

Anger now raging through me, I put my foot on the unmoving chest, pulled the Dirk free and raced to the living room, the still warm blood dripping from the blade.

When I made it into the kitchen, another man, slightly smaller than the first one, was dragging Emilee by her ponytail.

"Let. Her. Go!" I screamed at him, my chest heaving as I struggled for breath. He sneered at me and turned toward the door, right into the brushed steel barrel of Eric's .357 Smith and Wesson.

"No one hurts my kid!" Eric growled through clenched teeth.

My son didn't even hesitate. He stuck the gun under the guy's chin and pulled the trigger, scattering pinkish gray brains, hair, and bits of white bone on my ceiling.

"Don't worry, Mom, I'll help you clean up," Eric said calmly. I could see the seething hatred and fury in his dark blue eyes.

He knelt and clutched his daughter. "You did real good, Emi. You did exactly what I told you to do and now you're safe." He kissed her temple as she sobbed. "Shhh, shhh, Emi, we're okay now. They're gone and we're safe again." He looked up at me, seeing my blood soaked shirt and the dripping blade in my hand for the first time.

"Mom? Are you okay?" he whispered, worry filling his eyes.

"Yeah. What about you?" I managed to get out before I started shaking uncontrollably, dropping the Dirk to the floor.

"I'm thinking a couple of bruised ribs where they kicked me," Eric said.

"Dad, I think I'm going to be sick," Emi whimpered.

"Into the bathroom, quick," Eric said, ushering his little girl past me.

My own stomach lurched as I stared at the body on my kitchen floor. I hurried to the sink and spewed bile, blood and iced tea into the drain. I coughed and went into dry heaves. Pulling a steadying breath, I rinsed my mouth to rid myself of the foul taste.

"I think Dr. Mark should look you over," I said to Eric after he brought Emilee out of the bathroom. She was pale and shaky.

Her lip quivered, and she averted her eyes from the corpse on the floor. "Can I sit in the other room, Dad?"

He gently held her by the shoulders. "Yes, in a minute. First you need to look at this. I know it'll be hard, but look at this bad man. He was truly evil, and this is what we do to evil people, Emilee. Can you do this for me?" She nodded, looked at the cooling form lying on the floor, and then started to cry.

* * *

Mark stood just inside the door, taking in the scene of the pooled congealing blood and the splattered goo that was once brains. "My God! What happened here?" he exclaimed.

"We don't know who these guys are or where they came from," Ken said, "and it seems that they were trying to steal Emilee." He paused, wiping his hand over his damp face. "There were two other children in the back of their van, tied and gagged, but alive."

"Who has the worst injuries?" Mark asked, shaking off the shock of the violent aftermath.

"I think Eric's ribs are broken," I said. Mark looked over at me and I could see the concern in his face. "The blood isn't mine," I said, answering his unasked question, and my stomach felt queasy again.

"Take care of the kids first, Doc, I'll wait," Eric said flatly. Mark nodded at Eric and followed Ken into the living room, where Karen was trying to soothe the two other children.

* * *

"The kids are deeply shaken, and thankfully there are no injuries other than a few bruises," Mark informed us after examining the children. "They're very lucky." He looked over at my son and then back at me. "Eric, take off your shirt please and let me see those ribs."

Eric couldn't pick his arms up above his head. Fortunately, he was wearing a buttoned shirt, and once unfastened, we slid it down his arms. He was covered in bruises; the worst were on his back where the hardest kicks landed.

"Emi was weeding along the grape vines toward the road and I was working on the new compost patch by the porch when the van pulled into the driveway all the way to the house," he told us, wincing while Mark gently felt around the ribs. "They didn't say a word. They just got out, walked up to me and sucker punched me. That's when I yelled at Emi to run. She's fast." He grinned. "Those

5K races she's done with me paid off." Eric coughed and moaned. "She was long out of reach when the first guy took off after her, then the second one started to kick me when I tried getting up. I pretended like I had passed out, and he took off, following his partner over here. I figured if they were leaving me alone, it was Emilee they were after, and that was *not* going to happen." He coughed again and almost passed out.

"Stop talking, Eric," Mark ordered. "That makes you breathe harder. I can feel two possibly broken ribs. I'd like to take an x-ray to be sure that's all it is."

Mark turned to me. "And now for you."

"Like I said, this blood isn't mine. It belongs to the guy in the hallway." Everyone turned in that direction. "Don't worry, he's not going anywhere. And I would like him out of my house as soon as possible!"

"Well, Allexa, some of the blood *is* yours," Mark said, lowering his voice. "Apparently you haven't looked in a mirror. You've got a nasty cut on your lip and a rather large contusion on your cheek. Open your mouth and let me look."

My jaw was feeling pretty stiff and it was difficult to open very wide. Mark put on fresh surgical gloves and swabbed the inside of my left cheek with a gauze pad. I was shocked to see how much blood covered it. After two more swabbings, the pads were barely pink.

"Ouch!" I yelled when he wiped my face and lip with some chilled saline.

"Ouch? That's coming from the woman who wants to do her own stitches? Sissy." He smiled and wiped again. I knew he was trying to keep things light in a very serious situation, so I swallowed my next moan, though I couldn't mask the flinch.

"Cold compresses on the face and lip for the next forty-eight hours. I don't think the lip will need stitches." Mark pulled off the gloves and tossed them in a plastic bag he had used for the bloody bandages.

"As for these two," he straightened, looking down at the floor. "I pronounce time of death," he glanced at the clock, "at 5:30 P.M. for this one, and make it 5:28 P.M. for the one down the hall." Ken jotted down the times in his notebook.

"Cause of death?" Ken asked. We all looked at him as though he was kidding.

"I don't think the coroner will accept *stupidity*" Mark grumbled, "so make it a gunshot wound for this one, and..." He looked at me and said, "You did say he impaled himself, right?"

"More or less," I responded.

"Close enough. Blood loss from a self-inflicted wound for the one in the hallway," Mark concluded.

"Lenny and Jason are on the way to help move the bodies," Ken said. "I say we just leave them in the back of the van for now. By the way, when we got the children out of the back, I noticed the license plate was missing. The idiots had just tossed it inside and it was under the blanket used for the kids. I've already called it in for an ID."

* * *

"Emilee, while Dr. Mark has your dad at the office, I need to start cleaning in here, and get cleaned up myself," I said to the still shaken little girl. I just can't wrap my brain around what might have happened.

Her little lip quivered again. "Don't leave me alone, Nahna."

"I won't, sweetie, I promise. We are all safe and I don't want you to be afraid," I told her. "I'm going to show you how we can lock the doors and be safe, and still get fresh air in here, okay?" She nodded, tears glistening on her brown eyelashes. The day was still warm and the house now harbored strange and unpleasant odors. I wanted some windows open to air the place out.

We locked and bolted the back door, then opened that window to let in some air. The deck door had the same type of door set up, and Emi did that one once I showed her how to lock the window preventing it from opening any further. There would be no ventilation through the glass door, and that was ok. And since the larger window hadn't been replaced yet from the shoot-out with the Wheeler gang, we skipped that one and opened a window in the hall, fitting a rod in at the top.

"Do you feel better now, enough for me to take a quick shower and change clothes?" I asked her. I couldn't wait to get out of these bloody clothes, even though I would have to change yet again once I cleaned up the mess. The bodies were now gone, however, there was so much blood everywhere!

"Yes, Nahna. You look really bad so a shower should help," Emilee replied in a grown up voice.

I chuckled over that until I looked in the mirror. My face was swelling and already showing signs of bruising; there were dark streaks of dried blood flowing down my neck and arms; and how that much blood got in my hair I'll never know. I removed my clothes with shaky hands, depositing the soiled garments in the washer. I would rather have burned them, but many things are irreplaceable now, so they'd get washed.

The hot water stung my face as I stepped into the shower. I didn't care. I rinsed and washed, then rinsed again, watching the red water swirl down the drain. I washed my hair again and again until the water ran clear.

* * *

"Eric has one fractured rib and lots of deep bruising, although nothing that would endanger his life," Mark told me when he brought Eric back after taking the x-rays. "I also think he should spend the night here, or you there, in case any problems crop up. Both of you need watching for the night."

"Why do I need watching?" I asked.

"There's always a chance of a concussion, and that's also why I can't give you anything for the pain that might make you drowsy. I'm sorry. As much as you need to rest, you have to do it naturally, not with chemicals. I don't want you sleeping so deeply that you can't wake up, Allexa," he explained further. "Eric would be better off sleeping reclined, not flat on his back. The ribs are going to be very painful for the next few weeks."

"I know. I cracked two ribs a few years ago and could barely breathe for three months. Emilee will keep an eye on him," I smiled. "Thank you, Mark, for all you've done today. It's good to have you around."

"I'll be back in the morning to check on you. Now try to get some rest." His deep blue eyes roamed over me, filled with sadness and compassion.

Just then Chivas came bounding into the room, skidding to a halt at Eric's feet. She looked up at her master, cocked her head and sat down. She pushed his hand with her nose, then licked him gently and settled down at his feet. She may be a young pup, but I think she knew that something was very wrong.

* * *

"I can't thank you enough for helping me clean up last night, Amanda," I said, giving her a gentle hug. The gentleness was for me; I ached all over! I was relieved when she showed up after the bodies were removed to help me clean and put the house back to rights.

"Anything else we can do?" she asked, her big brown eyes sweeping over me with such sadness. Jason was so quiet I almost forgot he was there.

"Yes, there is. Knock it off!" Amanda and Jason both looked startled. "Yes, my face is bruised and it hurts. I got slugged! And the rest of me aches because that weirdo *fell* on me! Otherwise I'm fine, okay?" I crossed my arms defiantly. "Go check on your brother, he's the one with the broken bones." I gave them a forced smile and shooed them out the door.

I was glad to finally be alone. The emptiness left behind when the adrenaline finally dissipates in the system can be overwhelming. I could feel myself starting to shake, and those darn tears were prickling behind my eyelids, threatening to escape in a body-wracking sob.

I heard a car pull up in the driveway. My sob-fest would have to wait.

* * *

Mark shined a light in my eyes. "How are you feeling this morning? Any headaches? Nausea?" He gently probed the developing bruise. "How did you sleep?"

"If you stop asking questions, I'll answer!" I protested then laughed. Laughter was better than the tears that were still threatening. "No headaches, no nausea, except when I think about those scumbags touching my granddaughter! And I slept restlessly; I ache everywhere. I think I'm going to soak in a hot tub tonight."

"How are you feeling emotionally, Allexa?" Mark asked gently, obviously concerned. "It isn't every day you kill someone."

"Is this a professional visit, doctor, with all the confidentiality in place?"

He looked at me for a moment, the concern back in his eyes, and then said, "Yes, of course."

"Okay." I took a deep breath. "I'm familiar with how adrenaline reacts in the body during stress or extreme fear. It gives us the strength to do things otherwise difficult, if not impossible."

"That pretty much sums it up."

"That can be physical strength or emotional strength, and I think I had a jolt of both yesterday. The rebound effect, that adrenaline dump, has left me shaky and on the edge of tears," I said. "But...this isn't the first time I've had to kill a person, Mark, and I certainly don't want to think that it's going to get easier."

"What happened, Allex?" he asked in a whisper.

I told him all about Bill Harris and the events that led up to my shooting him last December. When I was finished, I wiped my eyes, embarrassed.

"What did Jason say after that happened?" Mark asked.

"I haven't told anyone this, not even John," I replied. "Only my brother knew, and Ken and Karen." All the dark emotion I'd been harboring slowly drained out of me. It was good to unburden the memory.

"You've kept all this bottled up inside for months? You're stronger than I gave you credit for."

"Well, I don't *feel* strong," I snapped. "I feel weak and vulnerable. I feel stupid and girly for wanting to cry."

He laughed. "You *are* a girl though, a very nice one I might add. If you want to cry, then cry, Allexa. You're experiencing a form of PTSD, post-traumatic stress disorder, and that doesn't go away overnight. In the ER back in Saginaw, I've seen seasoned cops fall apart after a shooting. Don't be hard on yourself, just feel those emotions, whether it's anger, regret or guilt, and you should go through all of those feelings, just feel them, know it's normal, and then let it go."

Mark reached toward me, hesitated, and then with one finger, lifted my chin so my eyes met his. "Now that I know, if you ever need to talk, don't hesitate to call. Okay?"

"Okay."

He looked at me for a minute and stood. "This might be unprofessional of me, but I think you need this." He wrapped his arms around me for a very satisfying hug and I leaned into his strength.

* * *

"We ran the plates, and the van was stolen in Wisconsin. No surprise there. Identifying these two pieces of trash was easy; they both had wallets," Karen said when she stopped over to give me an update. She shook her head in disbelief.

"The big guy, the one who, ahem, died of blood loss, was a registered pedophile. The other one was clean, no record at all, though I'm guessing he had just never been caught."

"What about the children?"

"There are two very relieved and thankful parents in Crystal Falls. The children are brother and sister by the way, ten and eleven years old," Karen answered. "From what we can piece together, and it's all speculation mind you, is that these two stole the van, crossed over the state line in a small town to avoid the checkpoints, and headed to another small town to…hunt. They grabbed the two kids at a park yesterday morning." She sipped the coffee I set down in front of her. "We figure they were looking for a quiet, remote spot to… finish whatever they had planned when they spotted Emilee and couldn't resist taking one more." I could hear the disgust in her voice.

"Those children must have been terrified," I mumbled, my breath not filling my lungs.

"Yeah, they're going to have nightmares for a long time."

CHAPTER FIFTEEN

"Hey sleepy head," John teased. It was almost ten o'clock and I had finally fallen into a deep sleep only a few hours earlier. "I was worried when you didn't pick me up for rotation."

I turned to face him and the smile on his face instantly disappeared.

"My God, Allex, what happened to you?" John asked, sitting down on the edge of the bed. He trailed his rough fingers down my cheek and across my swollen lower lip.

"We had a bit of trouble, John. Day before yesterday, two guys tried to kidnap Emilee."

His hand stilled. "Is she all right?"

"Yes, she's fine. That little girl is a real trooper." I smiled, and then winced. "Eric has several bruised and fractured ribs, and I got beat up, but we fared better than the other two." I took his hand in mine. "I killed a man, John, stabbed him."

"You stabbed someone to death?" he asked in disbelief.

"Actually, I disemboweled him," I said with a forced matter-of-factness. I'd been dealing with these events, and I didn't want to lose my tenuous reign of control by getting too emotional.

He brushed a stray lock of hair out of my eyes with a tender touch, while examining the purple bruise on my face.

"Remind me to never piss you off," he said softly, then gave me one of his special smiles, and I smiled back.

"I doubt you would ever attack me or hurt my family in any way, so you're safe. I can be a real mother bear when someone I love is threatened." I leaned into him, resting my forehead on his chest. "Will you hold me please?"

John stood, stripped his clothes off, and slid beneath the covers. He wrapped his strong arms around me, spooning his body to mine. His body heat soothed my aching muscles; his presence soothed my aching soul. We both drifted off to sleep.

* * *

"Time to get up, John," I said, nudging him gently. His blue eyes opened with a smile, and then the smile faded when he again took in my bruised and swollen face.

"I was hoping this was just a bad dream," he said as he reached out to my face, dropping his hand before making contact.

"It will be all healed in no time, so don't worry about it."

"It's one o'clock in the afternoon. The boys will be here soon," I told him. "We have something very special planned."

"Do I have time for a shower?" John asked.

* * *

"We need to collect fish and water lilies for the pond," Jason was explaining to John over a late cup of coffee. "Eric and I decided it would be a nice day to include a family picnic down at McKenna's Bay into our gathering session. I know we can all use a pleasant diversion."

In view of the recent events, we were all keeping the children closely watched, though Ken and Karen tried to reassure us this was an isolated incident.

"What kind of fish are you trying to catch?" John asked.

"I'm thinking perch. Even though they can be aggressive, they would be less so with their own species. That's why I think one type would be best to stick with," Jason said. "Of course, goldfish would be best, though I doubt something like that would be available. Goldfish are another type of carp, and the hardiest in captivity."

"Too bad we can't find some catfish," John lamented.

"While we're waiting for Eric and Emilee," Jason said, "I'd like to show you what we've done so far, John." Jason gave me a quick smile, and the three of us went to look at the finished greenhouse.

John stopped about ten feet from the protruding edge of the new structure and stared.

"Come on, just wait to you see the inside," I said, tugging on his hand.

Over the past few days, when I had the time and the energy, I had sorted out the gardening stuff in the barn, knowing much of it could be better used in here. Hanging from the wall was now an assortment of trowels, forks and other gardening tools, watering cans and a basket full of odds and ends. Jason had attached hooks to the upper exposed beams, which allowed me to hang pots. Although the pots were still empty, I could visualize vining tomatoes spilling out with juicy red fruit for us to enjoy during the winter, maybe even some flowers to brighten the room.

"What's the matter, John?" I said. "You're not saying anything."

"I'm...I'm speechless! This is just wonderful, Allex. I can see now why you wanted it." John turned to Jason. "You are a magician, Jason. I would never have believed so much could be done in so little time." He turned slowly in a circle, stopping to look at the fishpond. "That is just beautiful. How are the plants staying in place?"

"That was Mom's idea," Jason told him. "We put large rocks in the bottom for the fish habitat, and wired the cattail roots to them. The Marsh Marigolds are almost a floating island. There are some rocks built higher there. We put several rocks in the bottom of a pair of pantyhose along with the flower clump. So far the mesh of the pantyhose is keeping the dirt in place. It's resting on the top of the rock pile, unsecured, like a floating island." He grinned at the solution we had come up with.

We were all silent for a moment, listening to the water cascading into the pond from the little figurine perched on the side.

"Where did you get that?" John asked, taking in the statue of the miner panning for gold. The water was pumped up a tube to just behind the miner's feet, and then it ran over the pan and back down into the pond, ever circulating.

"I've had that for over twenty years. It's part of my favorite birdbath. I guess I've always wanted a miner in my life," I said, smiling up at John. "All this wouldn't have been possible without you, you know, so you have the place of honor—guarding the fish tank." We all laughed at that.

"And I see that you came up with a solution to the glass, too, Jason. Where did you get it?"

"They are all glass doors we removed from vacant houses. I then took them apart to use singly. There's one double hung window at either end that can open for heat ventilation when needed. I'm just glad we got all of it hung before Eric got hurt. I never would have been able to put those high pieces in place by myself," Jason replied, just as Eric and Emi came across the road.

* * *

Over at McKenna's Bay, John joined Jason and a bruised and slow moving Eric catching minnows with a seining net, while Amanda and I moved one of the picnic tables closer to the shore so we could watch Emi and Jacob play in the cold water. It might be well into June, however, the lake water here heated slowly.

"Jacob is so happy to have someone to play with," Amanda remarked. "Most of the kids in the school are older, and even if Jacob is academically equal, he's too young to play the way they do and would rather play alone or with just one other. I worry about him, Mom."

"I know, Amanda, we all do. I remember reading that many of these problems and quirks he has right now are just a stage that he'll grow out of in time," I tried to reassure her, just as Jacob started splashing Emilee, like a normal little boy would do to his cousin.

I watched the three men in my life, thankful we were all together. Not everyone was so lucky. They were off to the side now, near the lily pads. Jason had retrieved my scuba mask from the shed before we left, and had it on now. He reached down and felt the stalk of a plant, then took a deep breath, submerging into the cold water. A moment later he surfaced, took another breath and went under again. This time when he came up he had the bulb root in hand. I would have at least one pink lily in my new pond. Then, surprising me, John took the mask and repeated the dive, retrieving yet another lily for me. Eric stood off to the side, I'm sure to not be in the path of any jostling, although he was the one son who shared my love of scuba diving. I knew it must be hard for him to only watch.

* * *

The bucket of little fish was dumped into a long, flat pan so we could check them over. Both Eric and Jason grew up fishing so were able to quickly identify and separate the species. With the discarded fish returned to the lake and fresh water in the bucket, the dozen little perch and the deep pink lilies were taken to their new home in my greenhouse.

CHAPTER SIXTEEN

"Oh," I stated flatly, stunned by John's announcement.

"It's only for a few days, I promise. I really want to see my daughter and my mom. Please understand, Allex," John pleaded.

"Oh, John, I *do* understand, really. It's just that this is so unexpected. I'm being selfish for wanting you here with me for all of your spare time. Perhaps a visit down south should be worked into each rotation," I suggested.

"That's a good idea, but maybe every other rotation would be enough," he stopped pacing and sat down across from me, searching my face. "The bruise is already turning yellowish, and your lip is almost healed." He grinned, and leaned forward to kiss the other side of my mouth. "By the time I come back, you'll be good as new."

"Which brings up, when are you leaving?" I asked, not hiding my disappointment.

"I think on Friday and come back on Tuesday, which will still leave us another six days before I have to report back in. Is that okay with you?"

I reached across the polished wooden table and took his rough hand in mine. "John, you don't need my permission. Part of our arrangement here is that we both have lives to live; lives that don't always include the other. We both know that and accepted that right from the beginning. Yes, I will be here waiting for you when you come back." Then I smiled at him and saw the relief in his blue eyes.

"Right now, I need to see Dr. Mark to get the stiches removed from my shin. Do you want to come with me?"

* * *

"I'm glad I caught you in, Mark. Do you have time to take these stitches out?" I asked when I walked into the new medical clinic, interrupting his paperwork.

"Yes, of course," Mark replied a touch too curtly when he saw I wasn't alone.

"John, this is Mark Robbins, our new doctor in town," I made the introductions, noticing how Mark and John eyed each other warily, or maybe it was hostilely.

"Come into the exam room, Allexa, and have a seat." He turned to John and dismissively said, "This will only take a few minutes."

John got that stony look on his face that I'd come to recognize as him seething, as Mark closed the door.

"Is that my competition, Allexa?" Mark asked. He wiped the area of the stitches with some alcohol and set out tweezers and fine-nosed scissors, not looking at me.

"Yes it is, and would you please open the door," I stated bluntly.

He looked up at me in surprise. "Yes, of course."

Once the door was opened, I could see John sitting stiffly in full view, and I invited him into the room with us. He crossed his arms over his chest and leaned against the doorjamb to watch.

"This healed very nicely, Allexa. Did you do anything special to the wound?" Mark commented as he snipped and tugged each stitch out.

"I used comfrey poultices on it every day. They were very soothing and I think helped to prevent any infection."

"Interesting. Well, you still need to be more careful about injuring yourself," Mark stated, to which John grunted in agreement. "Now, let's look at that face." He gently probed my cheek for any tenderness. "Have you been doing the same poultices on your cheek?"

"Yes, except I've made them chilled instead of warm, to help with the swelling."

"Well, it's done wonders. I wouldn't have expected this to be so well-healed so soon after taking a punch to the mouth," Mark cast a quick accusatory glance over to John. "The lip will take a few more days though." He put his instruments in a metal pan and dropped the gauze with the stitches in the trash.

I looked from one man to the other and almost laughed. The posturing was so amusing to me, however, I knew if I laughed out loud it would only make the situation worse. I got down from the table and reached for John's hand, turning back to the doctor.

"Thank you, doctor, I appreciate your concern. I'll be in touch."

* * *

"Maybe I should stay here instead of going to Indiana," John said as we were setting the table for dinner.

I was stunned for the second time today, only this time I understood. "You're jealous of the doctor, aren't you? That's flattering, John, really," I said, smiling at the thought.

"He's a good looking man," John commented.

"So are you," I replied simply.

"He's a professional."

"So are you."

"And he's educated."

"So are you," I replied once more.

"You're attracted to him," John muttered.

"No. I find him attractive, yes, but I'm not attracted to him. I'm attracted to *you*. Isn't that obvious by now, John?"

He looked at me, with sadness in his eyes. "I still think I should stay here."

"I don't think I've ever given you any reason to not trust me, John. I will be here when you return. I love you. Isn't that enough?"

* * *

"Is there any part of your restocking that you haven't done yet?" John asked me, admiring the recent additions to the pantry shelves. The newly filled canning jars twinkled in the filtered afternoon light. After doing all the ramps, I started on the fish that Jason and Eric had been bringing me. Eric had even managed to snare some rabbits from the wooded back acreage. We ate fresh what we wanted and I canned the rest for later. I'd even taken the smaller, softer rabbit bones and pressure canned them for dog and cat food. There was no waste, not anymore.

"I think the only thing I haven't been able to get started on is the fuel. The propane tank is good, we used very little over the winter since the furnace never ran, so it only fueled the water heater. The drums of gas are almost empty because of using the generator," I said with a frown. "It's going to cost a small fortune for a hundred gallons of gas. Once I start back to work at the Resort, I should be able to refill it a little at a time."

"Let me do that for you," John offered. "For *us*."

"No, John, that's too much money," I protested.

He took me by the shoulders, making me face him. "I want to do this, Allexa, for you, for me, for the family you care so much about. I don't want you worried or stressed out that something isn't done that *could* be," he insisted. "I owe you so much. Please, let me do this."

"You called me Allexa, not Allex. You must be very adamant about this, John. Okay, you win," I relented. "Besides, if I don't agree, you'll just go behind my back and have one of the boys do it anyway."

He laughed, giving me a big hug. "Thank you, Allex. It means a great deal to me to contribute."

* * *

JOURNAL ENTRY: June 14

The news tonight was filled with the increase in earthquake swarms along the West Coast, along with new volcanic activity in Mexico. The pictures of all the upheaval are frightening.

* * *

"I'll be back in five days," John said, holding me tight.

"You better be," I replied with a smile I didn't feel. I hated seeing him leave so early.

He tossed his overnight bag into the front seat of the Green-Way truck he still had, and headed for Sawyer Airport.

Trying not to worry about John, I spent some time in the greenhouse, enjoying the coziness, the smell of fresh dirt, and the gurgling sound of the water as the pump moved it around, constantly aerating it so the new fish could breathe. The solar array on the house was functioning perfectly, providing power to the greenhouse during the day as well as charging the six batteries, and the batteries powered the pumps at night. It was none too soon; the power went out this morning and hasn't come back on yet.

I picked up a handful of soil and let it sift through my fingers, deciding then that there was no real reason to wait on trying my hand at indoor growing.

I raked the surface smooth in the first grow box, then dug a very shallow trench and watered it. From my stash of seeds I selected some radish and sprinkled them in the groove, covered them and watered again. I decided on a row of green beans too.

There was one narrower box near the cook stove that I had decided would be for herbs and that became my project for the day.

Back at the raised beds by the garden, I dug up some oregano, tarragon and chives, and moved them into the greenhouse, nestling them into the soil. This would also be a good place for the rosemary bush that I had to move indoors every winter. I was sure it would flourish being in soil instead of a pot. The four foot tall Bay Laurel tree would be perfect next to the fishpond. I was told I'd never be able to grow a Bay tree up here; it was just too cold. Now here it was, almost five years old and thriving, giving me those tangy leaves to spice up my soups and stews. I decided against moving any spearmint indoors. It's very hardy outdoors and spreads well; too well.

I dug into the seed bucket again, and found some basil, dill and parsley seeds. Those three annuals were the herbs I used the most, and the thought of having them all year long was so enticing, I just had to get some planted. All of those had already sprouted out in the garden, and would give all of us plenty of fresh herbs all summer, with some for drying, but I wanted them indoors too. I had to admit that in part, it was because I wanted to see things green and growing during the winter.

The last perennial herb to transplant was the thyme. I dug a large chunk of creeping thyme from near the back steps to the deck and replanted it in one of the hanging baskets, positioning the new plant so its tendrils were already draped over the edge of the black plastic pot.

I gave everything one more watering and, satisfied with the day's work, closed the door and went inside. John had only been gone a few hours and already the house felt so empty.

CHAPTER SEVENTEEN

Moose Creek was not a wealthy community in terms of money, but it was rich in diversity. People there were do-it-yourselfers and artists of all kinds.

With the abundance of rural land, many had taken to the woods to live and do their crafts. Whether it was pottery or woodworking, the isolation of the area allowed anyone who wished to work long hours without disturbing neighbors. Furniture derived from steamed and bent saplings or delicately carved burls were always available at local craft shows along with hand thrown pottery or wall hangings of birch bark. Somewhere out in our woods there was a blacksmith who was known to forge the most intricately twisted wrought iron utensils.

As independent as these artisans were, I'd found they leaned to being independent in only their craft. They still needed to buy groceries, gas for their cars and obtain dental work for the children they birthed at home. Very few of them had gardens, choosing instead to devote their time to making beautiful things to sell. Even fewer stocked their pantries to make it through the harsh and snowy winters, which I found very confusing.

When the earthquake hit down south, splitting our country in half and interrupting the supply lines, I think many of them must have headed to the larger cities. Either that or they died. No matter what it was that drove them out of their homes, most of them were now gone.

I found that particularly sad. I really thought they were the types of people who would survive without society. I was wrong.

* * *

"Where in the world did you find that?" I asked Jason. He was cutting a T1-11 sheet of wood and proceeded to nail it to the outside of the greenhouse.

"I went to see Toivo and Sharron hoping to get some milled wood suitable for siding," Jason said. "The place is empty, though, Mom. Eerily empty. Like they just went out for a walk in the woods and didn't come back. Their truck is gone.

The icebox was cleaned out, and there are still canned goods on the shelf. It looks like they froze and burst. There are clothes still hanging in the closets." He paused for a minute, searching for words. I knew this must be difficult for him since Toivo was a good friend of his and they shared a love of wood craft.

"Anyway, I looked around and found two sheets of this," he pointed to the rough wood siding, "and since it matches your house, I took it. I did leave them a note, just in case they come back. Oh, and in their workshop, I found stain that's a reasonable match to your siding. It won't be long and this addition will look like it was always here." He smiled at that. He took great pride in his work and especially how he could blend something into an existing structure.

"I think my greatest find was sandpaper!" Jason said excitedly. "Sharron must have resupplied their stock just before everything shut down, which would have made sense since they usually wintered in."

I'd known Toivo and Sharron for years before Jason came to live up here. While Toivo built beautiful furniture and cabinets, it was Sharron that brought it all to life with the finishing touches of baby-smooth sanding and glowing stains.

"I'm saddened that they're gone," I said. "Maybe we should be starting our own list, Jason, of places you've searched that appear empty. If the owners are still gone come next Fall, more things might be salvageable. I know Sharron was a canner and she might have left behind some jars or equipment that the community can use."

* * *

Lately I have spent most of my time out in the garden, coaxing the little plants to grow. The weather had been cooperating, perfect even, for growing things. The hailstorm that damaged my new seedlings had been mostly forgotten, and things were now flourishing.

"Mom!" Eric called out, clearly excited about something.

"I'm out in the garden," I answered.

"I found the most amazing thing today!"

The foraging my two sons had been doing had taken on a life of its own in the way of friendly competition. I just wished they didn't venture into possibly dangerous situations alone.

"What did you find today?" I asked, bemused by his enthusiasm. When he unveiled a window, currently leaning in the bed of the pickup truck, I found myself just as excited. It was almost identical in size to the one that was shot out during the Wheeler fight, the one that was still boarded up. I was stunned with the thought of having light back in my dining room!

"Oh my! Wherever did you find it?"

"I took Emi over to Joshua's to see the animals and spotted a house down the road not too far from his farm. I asked him about it, thinking I might find some manual tools. The place has been empty for two years. Joshua and I did a bit of browsing," Eric said, and then Joshua got out of the pickup.

He tipped his head in my direction. "Afternoon, Miss Allexa."

"It's nice to see you, Joshua." I smiled at him and then turned back to Eric. "Where's Emilee?"

"Oh, she's still with Martha. I'm not sure who is watching who, but they're getting along right nicely. There's no need to worry about her," Joshua answered first.

"I needed Joshua's help to get the window out and now back in. We might need your help too, Mom. You game?"

* * *

We worked the next hour or so removing the plywood that boarded up the opening, cleaning out the splintered wood, and then lifting the new window into place. I held the window steady from the outside, Joshua fitted and shifted the frame, and then Eric secured the new window in place. A small filler piece of siding was needed, and with a dab of the stain Jason had brought back from Toivo's, the window was done.

"You don't know how happy this makes me," I sighed, giving both young men a hug. I tested the window's lock and then slid the filthy glass open. While I cleaned the dirt and cobwebs from the corners, Eric installed the screen so once again there was airflow.

"I think I'd better get Joshua back to his chores and retrieve my daughter. Martha probably has her mucking out stalls by now," Eric laughed.

* * *

JOURNAL ENTRY: June 18

We're now on day three of no power. I think I'll give Tom White a call in the morning. Many of the townspeople equate electricity to normalcy. It's a way of life and they don't want to be without.

* * *

"Eric, have you taught Emilee how to shoot yet? If not, I think it would be a good idea. She'll be twelve next month."

"Yes I have, but we had to leave the mini-rifle I had for her in Florida," Eric said. "You wouldn't happen to have one, would you? You seem to have everything else."

"No, I don't. I do have a small .22 handgun. It's a Berretta Bobcat, a five shot automatic, although the slide is a bit stiff. Maybe you or John can loosen that."

"Speaking of John, when is he coming back?" Eric asked.

I smiled. "He's due back tomorrow."

I know he'd been gone for longer stretches when he was working, though it felt different when my mind knew he was hundreds of miles away, and not just ten or twenty.

"I'll go get the gun for Emilee."

All handguns in the house were kept loaded and ready for use, safeties on. I released the magazine and racked the slide to eject the chambered round, and then placed the gun on the table in front of Eric.

"I hate to say this, Mom, but that's really cute," he said laughing, picking up the palm-sized weapon.

"I know, that's why I bought it. We both know that a .22 is just as deadly as a .38 or a 9mm when it hits its target, and one should never underestimate the power of a weapon just because of its size!" I grinned. "Maybe I can give this to Emi as a birthday present next month?"

"She would love it, guaranteed."

* * *

Jason stopped by this afternoon to see if I had any work for him. Eric was still there, and was just itching for his brother to notice the new window. He didn't have to wait long.

"Okay, Eric, you win," Jason said, punching his older brother in the arm. "Your halo just got a bit shinier. Where did you find it?" While Eric relayed the tale about his find, it occurred to me that the halo reference was about how these two were trying to please their mom, and it made me smile.

CHAPTER EIGHTEEN

When the phone rings at seven in the morning, it's never good news.

My heart sank at John's news. "Your flight's been cancelled? Why?"

"I'm not sure. I think it's because the plane wasn't full. It's the economics of fuel usage. Don't worry; I'm on the next flight tomorrow morning." John's soft North Carolina accent was filled with anxiety.

I pouted. "Maybe you *should* have stayed here."

"I *will* get back!" John insisted.

I didn't want to worry him with words that the power had been out as long as he'd been gone, and that my contact in Marquette wasn't answering his phone.

* * *

JOURNAL ENTRY: JUNE 19

I waited and waited all day, and still no word from John. Tom White still isn't answering his phone either.

* * *

When the phone did ring, it startled me, and I lunged for it.

"Allexa? This is MaryEllen in Midway," a soft, sad voice said.

"What can I do for you, MaryEllen?" I asked, disappointed it wasn't John. I knew who MaryEllen was; her husband was one of the casualties in the shootout that took place in Midway with the Wheeler gang, just before they came here and killed my brother.

"I'm sorry to bother you," she said, "but I really don't know who else to ask."

"What is it you need? Perhaps I can direct you to the right person."

"That's just it...there *isn't* a 'right person,'" MaryEllen wailed. "I want to get out of here, Allexa. There's no food and I can't grow any. Charley's dead and

I'm completely alone. "I want to get to one of the relocation centers in Marquette, however, I don't have gas for the truck. I'm not even sure it still runs. Can you find someone to give me a lift to town?"

"I'll see what I can do." I took down her phone number, promising to find someone going that direction who could give her a ride.

How sad. Even when someone survived the initial disaster and then the weather, it didn't mean they were guaranteed to survive the new way of life that had been thrust upon them.

* * *

JOURNAL ENTRY: June 20

It's been five days since the power went out, just one more thing to worry about. The first two days I ran the generator a few hours each day, just like I did last fall, and for the same reasons: to keep the freezers going and to pump water.

Today, though, I took the venison out of the extra fridge and started canning it. Like always, the meaty bones went into a big pot to make soup, except this time the chunks of meat were canned separately for stew instead of ground. We can*not* lose any meat; it's too valuable. I processed the meat all day and into the night.

CHAPTER NINETEEN

"Jason, we can't all go over to Bob and Kathy's at the same time and leave these two houses *and* the garden unprotected," I protested.

"Mom, it's your birthday. Can't you loosen up just for once?"

"No, I can't. Besides, I need to stay here, just in case..."

Jason frowned. "I know, Mom, just in case John comes back." He let out a big sigh. "I suppose we could have everyone come here. Would that be okay?"

* * *

At four o'clock, people started showing up. Somehow I thought it would be just the boys, Bob and Kathy, maybe Guy and Dawn. Soon, Anna was here, and Pastor Carolyn, Dr. Mark, Joshua and Martha, plus Ken and Karen and a few more. It seemed that half the town turned out for my birthday.

Bob and Kathy had loaded up two long banquet tables from the church into Bob's pickup truck, under the supervision of Carolyn of course, and now were setting them up around the side yard, which Eric had freshly mowed. Thankfully the power had come back on during the night and Jason ran an extension cord over to the tables to keep the hot food hot.

Kathy shoved a glass in my hand and filled it with a deep ruby liquid. I took a sip. Wine was a real treat. What I had was rationed for special occasions and I didn't feel this qualified.

"If you won't come to the party, the party comes to you." She grinned. "Happy birthday, my friend!" She gave me a fierce hug. Just then Chivas came bounding across the road. To my surprise and delight, she stopped at the edge of the road, and actually looked both ways before launching into a full speed run, right to Kathy. Eric must be doing some serious training with that dog.

"Thank you," I replied to my best friend, returning her smile. "I really didn't expect so many people."

One of the tables was filling up with potluck dishes and serving utensils. Lawn chairs sprouted up all over the yard as more people arrived. Kathy was now so engrossed with the puppy that it was easy for me to mingle.

I sought out Pastor Carolyn to give her MaryEllen's request. Perhaps she would know someone going to town soon.

"As a matter of fact, I'm heading there tomorrow to do some parish work at the hospital. I'll take her in. It's sad to see so many leaving this town, Allexa. Last count on Sunday was only twenty people. How can we survive with so few?"

"I don't know, Carolyn, maybe it will be easier with fewer." I shrugged my shoulders and moved off.

"Can I steal a minute or two of your time, Allexa?" Dr. Mark asked, most pleasantly, when I reached where he was sitting.

"Of course, Mark, and thank you for coming to my party." I looked around and continued, "I am overwhelmed by this turnout!" There really weren't too many vehicles parked on the road, as many had doubled or tripled up on rides to save gas.

"Um, where's John?" Mark asked casually.

"I'm not sure," I answered. "He's overdue."

"How did you know about Martha?" he asked suddenly.

I truly was confused. "What do you mean?" I asked, sitting down at the picnic table.

"My initial exam of her indicated progressing heart failure. Not unusual for someone her age, but she also had dizziness, mental confusion and muscle cramps that seemed to be something else, something I couldn't verify without blood work."

At first I didn't know what he was getting at, and then it struck me. "It was the salt, wasn't it?"

"Yes, it was a Renin secretion and it completely got past me! What made you think of it?"

"Joshua brought over some milk and cheese. We're trading my eggs and bread for his dairy," I explained. "When I tasted the cheese it was bland. I asked him about it and he said they had run out of salt months earlier and he was now making the cheese without it. I know that salt is a very important mineral to the human body. Most of the time we get too much of it in all the processed foods we eat, but most of us haven't had any of those foods for almost eight months. It was a wild guess that that just might have something to do with what was ailing Martha, and if it wasn't, they still needed it."

"Well, Allexa, that little observation likely saved Martha's life, or at the very least, gave her a few more years." Mark gave me a curious smile. "Just look at her, she's doing fine now." Martha was a whirlwind of activity, helping set out the food, socializing, and apparently having a good time.

318

"While we're on the subject of Martha, I've been meaning to ask you what is this business about Joshua's goat?" I asked. "I neither need nor want a goat, however, I had to accept it or they wouldn't have let you come out to examine Martha." I crossed my arms over my chest and waited for him to answer. When he didn't say anything, I went on. "So what is it you want to barter with me for your payment from the Beals?"

"I'll think of something. First I'd like to ask you something else, but a bit more privately, if you don't mind," Mark requested. "Can we walk a bit?"

I stood without saying anything, wondering what was on his mind.

Further down the driveway, he asked, "How are you dealing with the events of the attack, Allexa?"

"There are times I get a bit shaky and my stomach gets queasy when I see the bodies and blood in my head. Then I get angry that this happened. I haven't felt the regret or the guilt yet, though I *have* felt a level of remorse that it happened at all. This is much like what I felt after the Harris incident." I stopped and looked at the man beside me. "Normal so far, doc?" I offered a tentative smile.

He gave me a warm smile in return, his eyes searching my face. "You're dealing with this remarkably well, Allexa. PTSD can be very difficult." We had walked all the way down the back loop of the driveway during our chat, and had just turned to walk back, when Mark stopped short.

"That must be your new greenhouse! Amanda has told me about it. Can I see it, please?" he asked enthusiastically, completely changing the subject.

"Absolutely. It's not completely finished inside, though. I'm still adding a few touches." I opened the door and stepped in, Mark followed too close behind me.

I showed him what I had planted in the herb beds, giving them a light watering as I explained the "whys" of what I had done. In the next grow bed the radish was now three inches tall and showing signs of thickening into bulbs. The green beans I planted at the same time were pushing through the soil, which greatly pleased me.

"The fish pond," he stated simply, gazing at the gurgling water. The lilies had survived the transplant, though they were looking a bit peaked. Mark's focus lingered on the statue of the miner in the corner as I tossed the fish a handful of breadcrumbs from a bowl I'm keeping there for the kids. The little fish splashed as they snatched the food floating on the surface.

"Over in these two grow boxes I plan on a couple of tomatoes and pepper plants that I'll dig up in the fall. I'd like to see how long I can keep them producing." I turned to see if Mark was listening, and he was so close I bumped into him. He gently held my shoulders, pulling me closer, looked longingly into my eyes and then lowered his mouth to mine for a gentle but searing kiss. My traitorous body responded instantly and I leaned into him, returning the passionate kiss. I bunched his shirt in my fists to keep myself from exploring his muscular chest.

I stepped back, breaking the contact. We were both breathing hard.

"What am I doing?" I said aloud and I pushed against his hard body, fleeing out the door.

* * *

"Are you okay?" Kathy asked, giving me an odd look.

"I'm fine," I replied too quickly. Looking for a diversion, I spotted the food table. There were bowls of pasta salad and baked beans, deviled eggs I'm sure came from Martha, and cookies. "I'm surprised at all this food, Kath. How are people managing this?" Before she could reply, Eric and Emilee came across the road, pulling a wagon loaded with chilled beer. He's obviously been busy brewing!

* * *

Everyone had left and the yard was cleaned up by eight o'clock. I was once again left alone.

It's the Summer Solstice, the longest day of the year. The sun was hanging low in the fading blue sky, and still had more than an hour before setting. I took my final glass of wine to the greenhouse and sat by the pond, letting the bubbling water soothe my jangled nerves. I did not want to think about Mark's kiss or how it had affected me. I had told John I wasn't attracted to the doctor...

I hadn't lied to John. I had lied to myself.

CHAPTER TWENTY

I had just poured my first cup of coffee when I heard a truck pull into the driveway. Curious, I stepped outside, after slipping the Kel Tec into my pocket.

The white truck with the green logo had just come to a stop. I stood on the bottom step, clutching my coffee cup. John was back!

He wearily got out of the cab and walked around to the back, grabbing his bag. When he headed toward the house, he finally looked up and saw me standing there.

I set my cup down on the step, and he dropped his battered bag where he was standing.

"You look tired," I said, breaking the silence.

"I am," John replied. "I've been driving for almost twenty-four hours." He took several long steps and reached out for me, crushing me against his chest.

"I've been so worried, John," I whimpered, wrapping my arms around his neck.

"It's been a nightmare clusterfuck," he said, with just an edge of anger. "Is there more coffee?"

John never swore anymore, so I knew this had to have been a very frustrating time for him. When I was seeing him and Sven at the Eagle Beach house, the other miners from his crew were always around and trying to unwind from the day. The language got very rough at times. It was just the way it was and I tended to ignore it. Now, John always was careful of what he said since Emilee or Jacob might be around.

"After I talked to you on Tuesday, I waited at the Louisville airport for the next flight. I slept on the bench nearest the departure gate so I wouldn't miss the loading call," John told me. "Late that night, there was a full plane and we finally made it to Green Bay. That's when everything fell apart." He ran his hands across his bald head, and the familiar gesture warmed my heart. "The power went out across four states, and I was stuck in the airport with a dead cellphone and no electricity to recharge it."

"The power was out here too, until yesterday," I said, not wanting to interrupt his story. I wanted to know what took him so long to get back.

"Without electricity to run everything, no planes could land—or take off." He took a sip of coffee, closing his eyes in appreciation. "They kept telling us it wouldn't be long, it wouldn't be long, but nothing changed. I finally decided I'd be better off renting a car and driving back to Sawyer, but the rental agencies couldn't run without power either." He looked at me in exasperation. "How did things run smoothly before there was such dependence on electricity? Everyone seems incapable of making a decision without a blasted computer in front of them!"

"The disadvantages of progress. What did you do?"

"I flagged down a taxi, one of those minivan units and paid the guy cash to drive me to Sawyer so I could get the truck. I was exhausted and slept for a couple of hours while he drove. When we hit the Wisconsin-Michigan border, there was a four-hour wait to get passed through the checkpoint. Then it was another hour to get through the inspection and questioning."

I'd made the trip by car before, from Moose Creek to Green Bay, and knew how long it could be under normal conditions. Now things were far from normal, and may never be again.

"I also don't have a car-charger for the phone, so I couldn't call. Larry offered his phone, however, I don't know your number. It's programmed in so I never bothered to memorize it, and I couldn't retrieve it without it being on! Do you know how frustrating that is?" He finished his coffee and I poured him another cup.

"Traffic was bad. It wasn't until we hit Escanaba that I realized without power none of the traffic lights were working. I will say that most everyone was being polite and cautious at all the intersections, although there were still accidents that blocked many of the roads. The delays were maddening!

"It was hours before we pulled into Sawyer, and then I couldn't get out of the lot because the automated toll booth didn't work, and there was no one around at five in the morning."

"How did you finally get out?"

"It's a truck. I drove over the curb." John grinned. "I really wish I could have called to let you know I was on my way, Allex. I didn't want you to worry."

"I was *very* worried, John. You're back now, and that's what counts." I was very relieved that he was back safely.

"I missed your birthday," he lamented. "I have something for you, but I want to do this right and I'm exhausted. Do you mind waiting just a few hours more?"

John took a long hot shower, and then slept for six hours.

While he was sleeping, I made a fresh batch of bread—cheesy tomato, his favorite. Then I got a jar of chicken and diced it, along with some hard boiled eggs and onions fresh from the garden, mixing it all with homemade mayonnaise to make chicken salad sandwiches for when he woke up. I knew he had to be hungry.

* * *

"Oh, that really hit the spot! I didn't realize how hungry I was," John said, finishing off a second sandwich and one of the beers Eric had left behind.

"I really am relieved you're back, John. I've missed you," I said. "How was the visit with your daughter? Christine, right? And your mom? I imagine they were disappointed it was so short."

"Yes, they were, and they were very understanding about it."

I couldn't help but think he looked nervous about something and it filled me with trepidation. Maybe I didn't want to know, yet I had to.

"What's the matter, John?" I asked quietly, reaching for his hand as he drummed his fingers on the table.

He stood up suddenly and started pacing. Then he stopped in front of me, knelt down so we were eye to eye. He looked like he had just swallowed a lemon wedge. Sideways.

"Will you marry me?" he asked, producing a small ring box.

I was stunned. How many times had I thought about hearing those words? And now, was filled with doubt. I smiled to cover the chaos in my thoughts.

"John...I-I love you and there is no one I'd rather be with than you...except, well, we've both been married before, and we both know it didn't work. That piece of paper seems to say it's okay to stop trying. Then complacency sets in and relationships fall apart. Without that legality, we continue to try and work on being a good partner. Let's give this some more thought." He looked crestfallen. "With all the pain and chaos going on, I need *some*thing to stay the same, John. We're together and we have such a good thing going, why change it?"

Just then Emilee burst through the door and threw herself at John.

"Grandpa John! You're back!" she squealed, giving him a hug. "Nahna's been very worried about you. She hasn't said so, but I know she has, I can tell."

John slipped the ring box back in his pocket.

* * *

"I want you to see what progress I've made with the greenhouse, John," I told him over morning coffee.

"Sure," he said quietly. He rinsed his cup and put it in the sink.

John had been very distracted and distant since yesterday. He was leaving this afternoon for the Green-Way house so he can get the needed sleep to be up at four o'clock tomorrow morning, when they all readied themselves for the first morning shift.

We took the outside path to the greenhouse. The warm late morning breeze lifted my hair away from my face and dried the sweat from my neck. It was going to be a splendid day.

"Wow, you've been busy," John commented as he looked around at all the new plants and sprouts.

"You like it?" I asked. I really want him to feel part of this, and not just because he paid for it.

"I love it," he replied, turning to me. "And I love *you*. I think you're right too. We don't need vows to be happy and together."

"Thank you, John. I knew you'd understand once you thought about it. It's not to say we can't change our minds in the future, just that right now I do feel this is best." I gave him a long hug.

"Let's go look at the main garden. Things are really coming up now. I've got good feelings about this year's garden, and I think there will be plenty to can even after feeding all of us over the next few months."

Just when we opened the electrified garden gate, a roll of thunder sounded off to the west.

"Guess I won't have to water today," I laughed. So much for a splendid weather day.

* * *

While out in the garden area, John let the chickens out into their second yard. The seeding of the two yards was working really well, even though one of the younger hens had found a way to sneak past the gate and get into yard that was still growing. We left the gates open so they could get back under cover when the rain started.

The overhead clouds were bunching quickly in ever darkening clusters, and more thunder met us. When the first flash of lightning cracked across the sky, we headed back to the house.

* * *

"It's time for me to go…" John looked longingly at me. "I seem to be always saying that, don't I?"

"You've always come back, and that's what counts," I replied and gave him a quick kiss. He climbed in the truck just as the sky opened and the warm rain pounded the dry ground.

CHAPTER TWENTY-ONE

It's been twenty-four hours and the rain hasn't stopped. The cistern started overflowing yesterday evening and now the chickens' second yard is a quagmire. In the garden I've left deep holes where I've stepped with my mud-boots. I don't dare touch any of the plants for fear of spreading any water-borne diseases. It will take days to dry out, once the rain finally stops.

* * *

"Allexa! Tom here. I see you've called several times," Tom White said apologetically.

"Gosh, Tom, I was getting worried when I couldn't reach you!" I replied, thinking of when I couldn't reach Liz only to find out she had died!

"You weren't the only one," he said. "Actually, I've been in the hospital for a couple of stents."

I was stunned. "Are you okay now?"

"I'm doing much better. They just extended my warranty," he joked. "What was it you wanted?"

I had to think back to when I was trying to reach him. "Oh, the power had gone off and was out for days. I was wondering why and when it would be back. It's back on now though," I answered. "This keeps happening, Tom. Is it going to be a regular thing? I just want to know what we need to be ready for."

"Unfortunately it just might be." I could hear him moving papers around. "You know that Marquette produces its own power, however, all the surrounding towns get supplied from outside the city and Moose Creek gets fed from Wisconsin."

"Yes, I know, and that's why our power was cut all last winter," I said, remembering how devastating that was to our town. "*Is* it going to be a regular thing?" I asked again.

"Yes," Tom admitted. "The edict has come down that the small towns will go on a rotational power cut. They're still trying to figure out a schedule that will be workable for the power companies and not too hard on the communities."

"Workable schedule? Like being without power for five days straight? That doesn't sound fair and it *will* be hard on the communities!"

"Every other day is too hard on the transfer relays. The next outage for you is tomorrow and will last three days," Tom answered. "Then it will be back on for three days. They're going to give that a try and see how everyone copes."

"I guess I'd better let everyone know," I replied, exasperated.

* * *

JOURNAL ENTRY: June 26

The rain continues to swamp the garden. Noticing how the water collects where I've walked, I'm now digging trenches to draw the water away from the wilting plants. Too much water is as bad as too little.

At the risk of damaging the plants, I dug up six tomato plants, two pepper plants and an eggplant, moving them into the greenhouse, trying hard to not touch the tender leaves. At least their water-logged roots will have a chance to dry out some. I can always plant them back in the garden later.

Jason stopped over today and helped me string the few grow lights I use for my indoor plants during the winter.

* * *

"I don't know if this will help, Mom, but it certainly won't hurt," he professed as he finished suspending the last of the five lights and then plugged them in. A soft glow pushed back some of the darkness of the rain soaked sunlight.

"I'm really tired of the rain," Jason complained, sitting at the kitchen table while Jacob watched cartoons.

"Where's Amanda?" I was hesitant to ask.

"She's gone shopping. Today was payday, and we need groceries," he replied.

I frowned. "Oh, Jason, that's just not safe." Changing the subject, I said, "I wanted to talk to you about another project. I'd like another woodshed built next to the greenhouse. That stove will get plenty of use this winter keeping the plants warm, and I don't want to haul wood that far. Besides, we'll need all that's been put up for the stove in the house."

"That makes sense. How big do you want it?" he asked. I think he's looking for more work and that's fine with me.

"Well, if you put it against the house it can't be too tall or it will block the bedroom window. And if it's against the greenhouse, it can't be any higher than your four-foot structure wall, or it will block the glass. Do you have any suggestions?"

"Why not put it against the full wall where the stove is? I can still make it eight foot tall, making it easier to stack wood in, and if I make it still eight feet long, at only four feet deep, it won't be so obtrusive. Of course it will hold only half the wood as the other shed, although you won't need as much with the solar heating. It will be easier to rotate, too."

"I like that idea! How long will it take and can you start as soon as the rain stops?" I gave him a couple hundred dollars for materials and his labor, and left myself a note to call Keith Kay for more wood.

* * *

I heard Jason pull into the driveway, and quickly opened the door as he made the sloshing dash from car to house, trying not to get too wet. It was still raining.

"I need a huge favor, Mom, and before you say 'I told you so,' I'll admit how right you were." He slumped into the wooden kitchen chair.

"Well, that's nice to hear, Jason, but what are you talking about?"

"Amanda. She went shopping yesterday, and spent almost five hundred dollars on groceries. She said it really didn't buy much," he looked down, embarrassed.

"What happened, Jason?"

"After shopping she went to see Lori, and you know how she loses track of time. She thought it had only been a few minutes, except she was inside for over an hour. When she went to leave, the hatch was open on the car and all the groceries were gone." He choked on those last words. "She didn't even *lock* the car!" He was on the verge of tears. Money was not worth much anymore and work was very scarce, so to lose all that was devastating.

"Where's Amanda now?" I asked quietly, feeling so sorry for my son.

"She's at home, alternating between crying and being depressed. She didn't want to come with me. Actually, she didn't want to face you, because she knows how much you have tried to warn us about security." Jason finally looked up at me, tears brimming beneath his green eyes.

"What is it you want from me, Jason?" I asked, promising myself that I would not be harsh on them, that I would not be judgmental. I reminded myself that we all make mistakes.

"I'm not even sure if we can replace what was taken," he said, "but can I borrow some money?"

"I'm just glad she wasn't hurt—or worse," I said.

I sat back down at the table, and set some bills in front of him: six one hundred dollar bills. I normally didn't keep that kind of cash on hand, but John had been very generous when he paid for his massages, giving me way more than he should. Even Sven had been paying more.

"Here's the five hundred, and extra to put gas in the car." I spread the bills out a little so he could see what was there. "There is one condition, Jason, and that is Amanda must promise that she will *never* go into town alone again! Is that clear?"

* * *

JOURNAL ENTRY: June 28

The rain has finally stopped! Five days of a steady downpour has been devastating to the garden. I don't know if it will recover.

I emptied the rain gauge every day. Some days there was one inch; some days there were three inches; total was eight inches. After the first day I had to move it closer to the house since I was squishing across the sodden lawn to get to it.

My little creek down the hill is beyond swollen, it's way over the banks and the bridge is underwater. I can't get within ten feet of either. I'm afraid the soggy land will loosen the shallow tree roots near the creek, and the trees will topple in the first wind. At least that will give us more firewood.

* * *

I stopped in town to see Anna. It was very slow going on the main road with so much water running across the asphalt. I'd never seen it this bad, not even the year we had six inches of rain that mixed with feet of melting snow during spring meltdown.

"The rain was hell on my garden," I commented as I sat down across from her. "How's Bradley's Backyard doing?" The community garden had quickly adopted the nickname.

Anna frowned. "It's ruined. At least it looks it right now. A lot of sunny days will help dry it out. And everyone is praying that our fast draining sandy soil will come through for us. So basically, it's too early to tell, but it looks bad," she replied with exasperation. "You're the gardener, why don't you stop and take a look?"

"I'll do that, though there isn't anything I can do to help, Anna. Everyone who has a garden is in the same boat. It's going to be another lean winter, I'm afraid." I sat back in my chair. "You know, this is why our grandparents and great-grandparents stocked up for a year or two. They knew there might be a lost crop at some point. There was always, or *should* always, be enough to get a family through a bad season."

This was a harsh reality that had been lost over the generations. It had been too easy to go to the grocery stores and get whatever we wanted, whenever we wanted. Since the New Madrid earthquake last November, all that had changed and most people were having a hard time adjusting to this new life.

* * *

JOURNAL ENTRY: June 30

The recent batch of eggs has now started hatching. I don't have high hopes of a good outcome, considering the five days without power during the beginning of incubation. Although I was careful to roll the eggs every morning and every night just like the egg turner would do, the heat was inconsistent and may have damaged the growth, in spite of the blanket I kept over it. So far there are six new baby chicks. The next few days will tell us a lot.

* * *

The hatching was complete, however, there were only fifteen baby chicks. A very poor outcome for all the work, but it was better than nothing.

The news for the past week had glossed over the swarms of earthquakes along the Caribbean rift. Experts, though, when one could find a station that would air the commentary, say the swarms verify that the mantle is shifting. Nothing to be concerned about they say, as it might take decades or millennium to move enough to be a problem.

* * *

"I'm glad to see you today, Joshua. How is Martha doing?"

"She's doing very well, thank you, Miss Allexa. Here's your milk. I'll have more cheese next week, *and* I have a surprise for you," he said, producing a small bowl.

I lifted the cover to find butter!

"This is wonderful, Joshua! Was it very difficult?"

"Not really. That book you lent me was great help. I thought you should have some of the first batch. Martha insisted we used some on her biscuits. It came out real good, even if I do say so myself." He beamed with pride.

"Well, thank you, and I have a surprise for you, too. How would you like to take your chicks home today?"

His face lit up. "Are they big enough already?"

"They're almost a month old, so yes. They will still need to be kept warm, especially at night, but they're ready to go."

I found a small cardboard box in the barn while Joshua picked six chicks. He had a good eye as he selected all hens. I looked over the brood and gently grabbed two more that I was fairly certain were roosters.

"Miss Allexa, our agreement was for seven, not eight," he protested.

"I know; this extra one is insurance. Besides, I just hatched more," I told him. "If this extra one is a rooster, then in two months you can have a fresh chicken dinner." I could tell that appealed to him.

* * *

During dinner of scrambled eggs on toast with some of Joshua's fresh butter, I watched the news, dumbstruck that no one had said anything. Maybe no one in Moose Creek knew that the Turks and Caicos Islands were hit by a 9.2 earthquake during the night and were now — gone!

The Islands covered one hundred seventy square miles with a population in excess of thirty thousand people and it was now all under water. The Caribbean Mantle that was slipping slid, and quickly. Details were still few. So far it was known that the quakes struck at around two o'clock in the morning while most of the population was asleep and consequently were crushed in the collapsing buildings that were shaken to rubble. Within a half hour a second quake hit; an aftershock of 9.2, which was the mantle sliding, taking the small islands underwater. The people didn't stand a chance. If they weren't crushed, they were drowned.

The earthquake warning system sent out a tsunami warning, however, with it being in the middle of the night, very few were made aware. With that much displacement of land into the ocean the circular tsunami was monstrous. With nothing in its way, a wall of blue-green seawater one hundred feet high bashed the shores of Haiti and the Dominican Republic first, obliterating the northern shoreline of those two tropical countries. The same wall took longer to hit Cuba so had more distance to grow and it swallowed the southeastern end of that island, devouring Guantanamo and the Guantanamo Bay U.S. Naval Station along with several small villages inland.

To the north of the epicenter the devastation was just as bad. Although the tsunami wasn't quite as high, a ninety foot wall was enough to wipe clean some of those very small islands, carrying the debris of buildings and bodies onward to the Florida Keys assaulting Key West with a fast moving twenty-five foot high putrid wave of destruction.

It had been eighteen hours since the first quake struck and news footage was just starting to come in. In the past I had found that the early coverage was the most complete and accurate, since the government controlled media hadn't had time to filter the information yet.

As daylight was breaking, the news helicopters had taken to the air, hoping to out-scoop each other. Rather than the usual running commentary, some of the footage was accompanied by reverent silence, punctuated occasionally with an audible intake of breath or a heartfelt sob. Bodies by the thousands floated in the churning muddy waters, pushed and pulled by lumber and walls that were once homes and businesses, symbols of lost life. Occasionally there would be a small animal, a dog or a parrot perched on a floating mattress, otherwise, no life was visible. The destruction was complete.

The worse was seeing the telltale fins of the circling sharks; blue sharks, Great White and tiger, mako and hammerhead, they'd all come to feast at the expense of mankind. They showed a scene where the shark opened its gapping mouth to claim a foot or an arm, only to find it wasn't attached to anything more, a small prize. More than once that fin emerged within the wreckage only to take something unidentifiable below the surface. I'd no doubt those scenes would be cut from the official news releases.

I sat back, my mind reeling from this latest catastrophe, the balance of my sandwich forgotten. What was going on with our world? It was no longer local issues, or even national ones. It was becoming worldwide. A whole Earth calamity.

* * *

July 4
In years past, Moose Creek had put on a small Fourth of July parade. The parade would begin with a Color Guard, consisting of local representatives of the Army, Navy, Air Force and National Guard, retired or active, in full uniform, proudly displaying the American Flag.

There would be the usual fire department truck, showing off the newest pumper or hook and ladder truck, and last year the EMS was proudly driving its new state of the art ambulance. One year Keith Kay put a dozen whole logs on his logging truck and had a few of the local women dressed in jeans and matching red plaid shirts sit on the cut trees and wave to the watching masses, calling them his "Lumber Jills."

For many years, Kathy and I would host a "pirate ship," which was really just a flatbed trailer with a pole sporting a tattered bed sheet. We dressed up as pirates and had a grand time tossing out candy and Mardi Gras beads to the eagerly waiting hands of the little kids.

We would all slowly drive around the two square blocks of town, entertaining the hundreds of people who would come to watch. I never did figure out where they came from or why. It was a fun afternoon that ended with us having a potluck dinner back at Bob and Kathy's lakeside house, and perhaps an evening cruise around Lake Meade on their pontoon boat.

No pirate ship this year; no throngs of visitors; no parade.

CHAPTER TWENTY-TWO

I was just finishing my afternoon weeding when a Green-Way truck pulled into the driveway and Steve got out.

"Hey, Allexa," he said way too softly.

"What's wrong, Steve?" I asked, my heart starting to race. He rarely stopped to visit and he never, ever came in a company truck. I was immediately alarmed.

"There's...there's been an accident at the mine."

I think my heart actually stopped beating for a moment. I swayed, seeing white spots before my eyes. I don't know where the term "blacked out" came from; the few times I've been close, everything went bright white first. Steve grabbed my arm to keep me from falling.

"There's been a cave-in, Allexa. John is on the inside," there was a definite catch in his voice. John was well-liked by all the local workers for Green-Way, not just me.

"Is he..." I just couldn't say the word...dead.

"No one knows the condition of any of the men. The cave-in happened about two hours ago, and it's bad, Allexa, really bad." Steve turned away from me and looked up at the azure sky, taking a couple of deep breaths. "Your emergency management territory covers the mine," he said, turning back to me, having collected himself. "They want you there. Simon was sent to get you. I came along because we're friends and because of John."

"How soon can you be ready to leave, ma'am?" Simon, a seasoned miner and the Green-Way liaison, asked. I hadn't even seen him get out of the truck.

"Give me five minutes," I replied, wiping my muddy hands on my already dirty jeans.

I grabbed an empty backpack from the bedroom closet and started to fill it: two pairs of socks, underwear, two t-shirts, one dark green and the other pale beige. I could wear the same jeans for a week if I had to. I looked down at that thought and changed into clean clothes. I have small emergency kits already made up with soap, toothpaste, a toothbrush, deodorant and a comb. I grabbed one from the pantry, and let out a sob remembering the last time I needed one and that was for John when he first came to me last December. I washed my hands and splashed cold water on my face, trying to calm myself.

My cellphone went in a pocket and the charger went into the backpack. I had to call Eric about watching the house, however, I could do that on the way. I slipped into the leather shoulder holster and secured the Kel Tec, putting on a lightweight jacket to conceal the weapon. Having done that, I went back to the closet and selected a heavier jacket for later. It might be July, but the nights were still cool, especially up on the Plains where the mine was.

I gave Tufts a quick ear scratch, plus a pet down his silky black head, and I was out the door. I tossed the pack to Steve and headed to the barn.

On one of the large wooden storage shelves behind another box, was a small box with a new pair of jungle boots. I could put them on in the truck.

Out of the back seat in my car, I got my pink hard hat that said "Emergency Manager – Moose Creek TWP."

I was ready. It took me six minutes.

* * *

I've been to the mine before for introduction tours. We all had to wear the provided ill-fitting hard hats and ridiculous, but effective, steel toed caps over our shoes that clattered like tap shoes with every step. My jungle boots had built in steel toes, and my pink hard hat would make me highly visible. They weren't going to keep me safely somewhere else.

The ride up to the mine seemed to take an extra long amount of time, although I knew it was still only twenty-five minutes.

The huge metal gates rolled open as the white and green truck drove up to the manned guard shack. Security was very tight around the mine, and always had been, considering the controversy from the onset. Many people just did not want this kind of a mine in our community. Simon spoke quickly to the guard on duty, and we passed through in seconds.

When I was there before, we were required to park in a certain area, where chocks were provided for each vehicle, a safety procedure. This time however, Simon bypassed the near empty parking area and drove straight to the portal, a yawning maw that was the entrance to the mine itself.

Overhead, the sky was a deep blue and the sun beat down hot, the beauty of the day cloaking the tragedy that was unfolding somewhere beneath our feet. Waves of heat pulsed from the new asphalt road, releasing a sick stench of petroleum tar. I grabbed my pink hard hat and slid out of the truck, following Simon into the mine entrance.

Simon made the introduction. "Allexa Smeth, this is Roger Boyle, the mine supervisor." I extended my hand and returned Roger's firm handshake. He glanced at my hard hat and offered a suppressed grin.

"At least you won't be hard to find," he said, turning back to what he'd been doing.

"Would you care to bring me up to date, Mr. Boyle?" I said with an intended edge to my voice. I was *not* going to let him use my being a female to dismiss me from the loop. It did get his attention.

"Certainly," he said with a restrained sigh. "You will forgive my lack of protocol. This is a very serious situation."

"I'm very well aware of how serious this is, Roger. I'm here to help however I can," I replied, softening my voice. I looked around at the cavernous entrance. The ceiling was a good twenty feet high and the width was slightly more, perhaps thirty feet. A hundred feet in, the floor began to slope and it veered off to the left. When I had been there before that slope was plunged into darkness, lit only by the headlights of the vehicles descending into the bowels of the mine. Now, however, I could see shadows from unseen lights. I also noticed a drop in the temperature even just twenty feet inside, and wondered how low it dropped further in.

Boyle led me over to a large map fastened to the smoothed rock wall. Overhead lights bolted into the rock pushed back the gloom. It was a two-dimensional map of a three-dimensional series of tunnels that led ever downward.

"It looks like a gerbil tunnel," I commented, which earned a sincere chuckle from the supervisor.

"We've learned a lot from those little animals," he said. "They too have constant switch-backs and widened passing areas. The cave-in is here," he said, pointing to an area two switchbacks in, "and it runs, we *think*, to here." It was a large area that was blocked, maybe fifty feet.

"Do you know what happened?" I asked, unable to tear my view from the map.

"No, we don't. It's still too early. However, we do know a few things." He moved away from the map, glanced from my pink hat down to my feet. "Steel toes?" he asked. When I nodded, he started walking deeper into the mine.

My heartbeat picked up a couple of notches, matching my increased claustrophobic breathing as we descended and lost visual contact with natural light.

"This happened close to shift change, so the day crew was on their way to the surface. The night crew was still on top. We don't let that many men below at the same time for obvious safety reasons. Plus, there aren't enough pods for that many."

"How many life pods are there?" I asked. "I've done the tours," I added when he glanced back at me.

"There are currently four. The life pods are constructed of the hardest material available and designed to withstand incredible weight. They're large enough to hold twelve men, and are supplied with food, water and air to keep them alive for twelve hours, which is why they are placed at every turnout. One man alone could conceivably last six days. We're not going to test that though."

We had arrived at another map, and lots of activity, and a wall of smashed rocks.

"Okay, what we know is this. The crew was approximately here when rock started shifting overhead," he pointed at the new map. "Some of the guys tried to make it out, although most of them got caught and are likely dead. Only two made it out and they've given us what intel we have so far. The rest headed further back in just before the ceiling let go. We don't know how many made it to a safer area. There are twelve men possibly alive, and within range of two pods, here and here," he pointed again. "From what we can estimate, there's at least fifty feet of solid rock between here and open space. We just don't know until we can drill through the blockage. At least then we can pump in some O_2."

"How far in have you drilled?" I asked. I would need to go topside soon; I was starting to feel dizzy.

"We've made it twenty feet. That's ten feet per hour. It will be another three hours before we can assess when we can start serious rock removal."

"Where are the two that made it out?" I asked. I already knew John wasn't one of them, but it wouldn't hurt to ask them some questions.

"In the infirmary. They were pretty banged up," Roger answered just as the lights flickered and went out.

I closed my eyes, willing myself to stay calm while I reached in my pocket for the Maglite. Once I switched it on I felt better. Other lights were coming on now, mainly from the dirty and chipped helmets of the workers.

"You should consider getting one," Roger commented as he turned on his own helmet light. He led the way topside.

"It's in my bag," I replied. "I didn't think I would need it just yet."

"While you're getting it, you might want to leave your weapon there. It's against company rules for there to be any firearms on the premises." It surprised me that he was aware of my holster.

"The world has changed, Mr. Boyle," I countered.

"Not here it hasn't," he stated flatly.

"As you wish."

* * *

Once back at the mine entrance, I breathed deeply, gulping in the fresh, warm air. Roger turned me over to one of the night shift guys who led me to the infirmary in search of the two very lucky miners who escaped the avalanche of rocks.

* * *

"Good afternoon, Allexa," Dr. Mark greeted me. "John's down under, isn't he? How are you holding up?" His voice had softened and his eyes were filled with concern.

"I'm hanging in there, Doc." I gave him a wan smile. "I guess I'm still in shock over all that has happened, and until we know for sure the…condition of those still trapped, I'm not going to borrow trouble. I'd like to see the two guys that escaped, if I may." I realized quickly that I shouldn't have been shocked that Mark was there. He was the only doctor in the township and he was likely the first one called. Still, it was the first time we'd seen each other since my birthday and the greenhouse kiss, and it was a bit unnerving.

I removed my hard hat and set it on one of the vacant padded chrome chairs that served as a waiting room.

"They were badly battered by the rocks. Travis has a concussion and Paul dislocated his shoulder. These guys are incredibly muscular and it was difficult getting the humerus back in its socket," Mark told me. "Last time I checked they were both sleeping. Pain is exhausting."

I moved the curtain back and was shocked by the sight of the two young men, still dirty from the rock dust, lying motionless on two of the six blue cots.

"Mark, would you mind if I washed their faces? I'll be very careful. Being clean sometimes works wonders." Once I got an approving nod from the doctor, I got a couple of towels from an overhead cupboard and a small bowl of warm water. I sat down on the edge of Paul's bed and dampened the towel. I wiped the dirt from his chin, then cheeks. When I removed the sooty smudges from his forehead he opened his eyes.

"Hi, Paul. How are you feeling?" I asked softly, still moving the wet cloth across his dirty skin.

"I hurt everywhere, Allexa. Have they…?" He closed his eyes again.

"No, they're still drilling a hole, trying to get some air in there. It hasn't been long." The water was getting muddy. "Paul, did you see John at all?"

"I didn't see him, no, but he always brings up the rear, making sure everyone else is out." He coughed and groaned in pain.

If John was at the end of the group, that was very good news. It meant he was away from the rockslide.

"You rest now. I'll let the doctor know you're awake." I swayed when I stood, relief flooding me. I informed Mark that one of his patients was conscious, and moved to the other one, having refreshed the steel bowl with clean water.

Travis didn't just have a concussion, he had massive bruises and cuts on his face and scalp. I dabbed gently, not wanting to add to his pain.

"You do that rather well, Allexa. You should have been a nurse," Mark whispered in my ear as I finished washing Travis. "Thank you, I haven't had time to clean them up. I can see Travis needs a bit more attention to those cuts. Will you assist me?"

"I'm really not qualified, Mark."

"You've got compassion and a gentle touch. That's all the skills you need right now," Mark replied. We worked silently together, washing and dressing the wounds that were uncovered.

By the time we were done, more than an hour had passed, and the need to get back was strong. I found my backpack beside the first desk at the portal. Knowing the switch I needed to make, I went back to the infirmary.

"Mind if I leave this here, Mark? I'd feel better if I knew this was in safe hands." I removed my light jacket, exposing the shoulder holster. I slipped it off, wrapped the straps around the gun, and buried it in the bottom of the pack.

"Leave it behind the desk," he said noncommittally. I'd never asked him his view on guns and wondered if he was anti-weapon.

"Does this bother you?"

"I've seen too many gunshot wounds to be pro-gun, Allexa, although I do see the necessity of them in this new era," he stated simply. "Your pack will be safe here."

* * *

Roger met me partway down the first ramp. "I was just coming to find you, Allexa. We've broken through! The blockage seems to be only twenty-five feet, not the fifty we first thought."

"That's good news! I'm assuming it also means less to clear out," I responded.

"Absolutely. We should be cutting recovery time in half, depending on what we find along the way." He glanced over at me. "Are you squeamish? This might not be pretty. In fact, it's likely to be quite unpleasant at times. Can you handle that?"

"I think she'll be fine, she's tough," Mark commented, coming up behind us. "Gray just got here so I left him to tend our two patients, and to get ready for more." He looked over at Boyle and said, "Thanks for keeping me up on the progress; those radios are very handy."

"Which reminds me, Allexa, here's yours," Roger handed me a small walkie-talkie type device to clip on my belt.

* * *

Just as the three of us arrived at the site, there was some frantic activity feeding a long device in through the newly drilled hole.

"What are they doing, Roger?" I asked.

"The pipe that's going in right now is to hold the opening intact and to protect the camera that will go in next," he replied. "The camera is infrared and will let us see any heat signatures, which means live bodies. Next will be an actual light so we can look around for other victims. Hooked to the camera is a series of microphones, both to send and receive. If there is anyone within range, we will have communication."

The first images on the monitor that came back from the camera were not encouraging, not until the camera scanned the cavernous room on zoom. That's when we were able to see several inert forms further down the passage. A sigh of relief was felt by all. There were men still alive! When there was no verbal response from inside, the light was sent in and the camera was switched off infrared. There were no visible bodies in the immediate area.

"That isn't necessarily good," Roger informed us. "The rest could be buried under the rock. On the other hand, some may have made it to the pod in that area that appears to be buried. We'll pipe in some music while we work on this side."

"Music? Why music?" I asked, shivering, not from scene, but from the cold that was seeping into my bones. I hadn't realized how low the temperature would be this far from the surface.

"If any of the men wake up, they'll know a rescue is underway. They all know the risks; they also know we will do everything and anything we can to get them out in case of a cave-in. Music is the sign. It will give them hope, knowing we're here and busy trying to get them out."

"What now?" asked Mark.

"Now we start digging. We've got some incredible machines capable of picking up boulders. The larger ones will be moved out on trucks one at a time; smaller ones will fill a truck first then be removed." Roger looked over the map and the wall of debris, slowly pacing the length of the fallen rock. "We'll start here," he said half to us, mostly to the work crew, pointing to an area to one side. He turned back to Mark and me and said, "The objective will be to make a man-sized tunnel that will allow us to get the survivors out of there as quickly as possible. It's going to be a slow and dangerous process, and I can't let you stay right here."

I started to protest, but he stopped me.

"There are monitors being set up at the entrance of the portal. You can watch everything from there," he said. "I'm also asking both of you to stay nearby in case you're needed." Without waiting for us to agree, Roger led us out of the chilly gloom.

* * *

I walked around in the fading sunlight, just a few feet outside of the portal entrance, trying to get warm. The temperatures had been in the low eighties all day, except we had spent several hours two hundred feet below the surface at forty-five degrees, and I was still chilled.

"I'm going back to the office for a few minutes," Mark said. "Can I bring you anything back?"

"Yes, if you don't mind, I'd like my heavier jacket, thanks." I couldn't keep my eyes off the monitors once they were set up. One twenty-five-inch screen gave us a view of the inside, where the men were trapped, and another was a long view of the work in progress.

As I stood there watching the sun touch the horizon, a sentry insulated from the harsh work below, I realized I was indeed alone. There were no reporters, no family members waiting for word of their loved ones, no one. These men had no family to worry over them or to grieve if they didn't come out. Even Steve, as much as he cared for this crew under his roof, had gone. I was left here, the only one to weep or cheer.

* * *

I slipped into the jacket Mark brought when he returned and took the offered bottle of water, and we waited. Dusk morphed into a purple twilight and then into the blackness of midnight. We watched as small, fist sized rocks were scooped out of a hole, only to be replaced by larger ones. The progress was maddeningly slow.

* * *

I woke to the morning sun warming the back of my head and a heavy blanket draped around me. I sat up, pushing off the now too warm cover and looked at the monitors. It was as if nothing had changed, until I saw someone come *out* of the new hole!

I grabbed my hardhat and hurried down to the excavation site, making it just in time for a quick briefing.

During the night, the hole had been widened to three feet in diameter, big enough for someone on this side to crawl through and inspect the damage and the victims on the other.

* * *

"I thought it would take a lot longer to get inside," I said to Roger as I came up behind him, partly to make my presence known and to not startle anyone.

"We got lucky, very lucky. We ran into a long pocket of plain gravel and made a lot of headway in a short time."

Simon had been the first one in.

"There are five survivors, three of them badly injured," he glanced my way then looked away just as quickly. That told me John wasn't one of the five. "Though the pod is intact, the door is partially buried, so I don't know if anyone made it inside. The overhead looks fairly stable, and I want to get those five out as quickly as possible. We'll need a couple of stretchers and volunteers to go in."

Every member of the mining crew stepped forward, even Mark.

"Sorry, doctor, you can't go in there," Roger Boyle stated. "We can't risk you being hurt and you're needed on this side much more than in there. Adam has trauma training and will stabilize each man before sending him out to you. Now let's get those men out of there!"

The four volunteers went in that tiny hole, each dragging something with him: lights, ropes, medical supplies, water and several dark green canvas bundles that I found out were trauma stretchers.

"The flexible stretcher allows the patient to be restrained. If they come to and start flailing about while being extracted, they could panic and hurt themselves or get wedged," Mark explained.

More lights appeared on the monitors as the crew worked quickly. The black and white screen was somewhat fuzzy and it was impossible to tell who was doing what unless you knew each of the participants. They were all about five foot ten inches tall and slender in build. Many of the workers I was familiar with were taller, bigger. These four were selected for the obvious reason that they could get into smaller places.

I watched the gray screen as bottled water was passed to each of the men, two of which were now on their feet and as they moved about I recognized Sven!

* * *

The first of the mummy-wrapped injured men was being pulled from the rock. I moved off to the side to not be in the way while Mark went into action assessing the carnage. A second, then the third one appeared, each moved further up the tunnel.

"I can't tell much while they're still restrained, so I'm moving them to the infirmary," Mark announced to Roger. Then he turned to me, gave one of my hands a squeeze and said, "Good luck." He knew I would be staying until John came out, one way or another.

I was half expecting the two uninjured men to come out next; however, they elected to stay behind to help dig out the life pod. Every shovel full of the rocky cold dirt they moved was replaced by double from the sliding rock and gravel, slowing the progress even more.

I lost track of time as I watched the screens flicker with movement. Eventually the two uninjured miners crawled through the opening and emerged, dirty and tired. Two more volunteers went in.

"Sven!" I called to him. He turned with a big smile on his Swedish face and gave me a hug.

"Don't you worry, we'll get John out," he reassured me, knowing my first concern was for John.

"Are you sure he's in the pod?" I was near breathless with anticipation.

"I saw him go in, he and Bradley. He was pushing the boy into the pod and we were all set to follow when more rock slid, pushing the door shut, so we ran the other way," the big Swede explained. "If rescue didn't start so quickly, we would have gone further in to the next pod and waited." His face darkened. "There were so many that were caught. I could hear them screaming. It didn't last long. I can still hear them here," he tapped his head and visibly shuddered.

"Paul and Travis made it out ahead of the slide," I told him, knowing it would be good news that he needed. I was rewarded with another genuine smile. "They're in the infirmary. I think Dr. Robbins would like to check you over too. Wait right here a minute and I'll go with you."

I moved up next to Roger and got his attention. "Can you spare me for fifteen minutes? I'd like to walk Sven over to the infirmary," I told him.

"Sure. I doubt there will be anything major happening here for another hour or more. And Allexa, get something to eat, you look pale," Roger replied. I turned to leave, when he caught my arm, and lowered his voice. "Thanks for being here. I know the guys appreciate seeing that someone cares."

* * *

At the portal, I was shocked to see the bright sun so low in the sky. I had been down there for hours, no wonder I was so chilled. My stomach gurgled to remind me that I also hadn't eaten all day.

Sven stopped when we stepped into the waning sunshine and lifted his dirty face to the light.

"Every time I go down, I understand anything can happen. It doesn't seem to be a real possibility until we're actually faced with not coming back out." He stood there for another moment, silently soaking in the sun. I could see the tears dampening his face, glistening in the fading daylight. I slipped my small hand into his rough big one and gave a gentle squeeze.

* * *

Mark was nowhere in sight when I opened the door to the medical facility, so I suggested to Sven that he wait while I got us something to eat from the kitchen.

When I brought a tray back loaded with sandwiches and sealed coffee cups, Sven had disappeared. I set the tray on the desk and opened one of the coffees. The hot brown liquid released a fragrant steam that made my mouth water. The aroma apparently wafted around the room, as Mark peeked from the other side of a curtain.

"Is one of those for me, I hope?" He smiled. Something wasn't right.

"Absolutely. There's even a sandwich with your name on it," I replied. "What's wrong, Mark?"

He slumped down in the over-padded chair behind the worn desk and reached for a Styrofoam cup. He took a sip, then another, and said, "I just lost one of the men. He had massive internal injuries that I just can't deal with here. Although, I don't know if it would have made any difference if we were in a fully equipped hospital." He looked up at me, then to the clock on the wall behind me, and jotted something down in a file.

"I'm so sorry, Mark," I laid my hand over his. I just didn't know how to comfort someone who had seen so much death. "Where's Sven? I brought him some lunch too. I'm sure he's hungry after this ordeal."

Mark raised his dark blue eyes to meet mine. The sorrow there made those eyes even darker. "I'm sorry, Allexa."

At first I didn't understand what he was saying, and then it hit me. "Sven? Sven was hurt? He was *fine* when I left him here. He had even stayed to help dig the others out! This can't be...." The words caught in my throat and I pushed away from the desk, spilling my coffee.

Mark moved away from chair to stand in front of me. His arms gently circled my shoulders.

"When I heard the door close, it must have been you leaving. I came out and found Sven slumped on the floor, blood pouring from his mouth. Gray and I got him onto one of the cots; however, he was already hemorrhaging badly. Before he died, Allexa, he asked me to tell you thank you for being his friend." Mark's voice quivered with emotion, and his embrace tightened.

My radio beeped. I grabbed my hardhat and ran for the mine entrance. I came up behind Roger just in time to see the monitor flicker to life.

"I had them move things around down there so we had a better view of what's going on," he said. "They've managed to get most of the rock away from the pod door, but there's a big one wedged tight. Simon feels if it's moved it will create another cave-in."

"Can they get the door open?"

"We sent in a hydraulic crowbar. If nothing else it will peel the door open like a can of sardines. We *will* get them out tonight, I promise you that," he was adamant and that was reassuring.

My stomach gurgled.

"I thought I said for you to eat."

"I forgot," I replied, just as Mark showed up with the tray of sandwiches and coffee.

"Eat," Mark commanded, shoving half of a ham and cheese on rye sandwich into my hand, and setting a fresh cup of coffee down in front of me.

* * *

The screech of tearing metal poured out of the three-foot hole and filled the cavernous room, waking me from a fitful slumber. I don't know how long I slept. My coffee was now icy cold.

My hands started shaking as the door to the yellow life pod slowly opened. A dark haired young man stumbled out, followed closely by John!

Simon appeared first, climbing out of the large hole in the wall of rock and stone. He reached behind him and took the arm of the next one, helping a very shaky Bradley climb down the pile of debris. John emerged next. He was filthy, and his jacket was torn; he was clutching his left hand to his chest and I could see it was bandaged. He looked wonderful to me. He scrambled down the rocks and looked up. I smiled at him, my chin quivering and tears of joy brimming unshed in my eyes.

He drew me into his arms and whispered, "You're here."

I laughed as the tears spilled over. "Where else would I be?"

We walked up the long slope into the breaking sunlight of a new day.

He stopped, much as Sven had done, and breathed in the warm summer air, relief swimming over his face as he marveled at his freedom.

"I do need to give you a quick check over, John," Mark said following us out. "I guess the protocol is for you to clean up and leave your gear here, is that right?"

John nodded. He looked so tired. "Actually, I'd like to shower first, if you don't mind, Doc."

"Did you take any blows to your body or head?" Mark asked. He looked as weary as John did.

"No, just my wrist got jammed when the door was slammed shut," John replied.

"Then I don't see any harm in showering first. I'll be in the infirmary when you're ready." Mark backed away and I walked with John to the metal building that held the barracks so he could clean up.

* * *

When John came out of the low steel building, I was waiting on the wooden steps. He was dressed in a black t-shirt and a dark green sweater, jeans and brown loafers. He sat down next to me.

"How long have you been here?" he asked, picking at the chipping paint on the wobbly railing.

"Ever since they came for me. It's been three days," I told him. "I could probably use a shower myself."

* * *

Mark had fallen asleep at the desk, his dark curly hair half covering his closed eyes. I gently prodded to wake him, and he sat up with a start. I set a cup of coffee down in front of him and he sighed with appreciation. John and I sat on the other side of the small desk, sipping our brew, waiting for the doctor to fully wake.

"Sorry about that," Mark apologized, addressing John. "It's been a long night, and much longer for you. Let's check you out. I've already discharged Bradley. He's a scared, but tough kid. He'll be fine. He owes you a great deal, John. He said if you hadn't pushed him into the pod, he likely would have been crushed."

When Mark started to open the exam curtains, I stopped in my tracks, afraid of what else might still be back there. He noticed my hesitancy.

"Gray has been busy...housekeeping," he said with a double meaning meant for me. "You're welcome to come into the exam room, if you wish, Allexa, and if John doesn't mind."

Mark checked John's wrist, rewrapped it, and took vitals, pronouncing him fit to leave.

"I would like to x-ray the wrist though. There don't seem to be any serious breaks, though there might be a hairline fracture." Mark looked at the wall clock. "It's 10:30. Can you meet me at my office in town around three o'clock? It won't take long."

* * *

"Can we just sit here for a while?" John asked, basking in the late afternoon sun. "Maybe even have dinner outside?" He laid his left arm on the bistro table, the wrist now splinted to prevent any movement after our visit to Dr. Mark's office in Moose Creek.

"Whatever you want," I replied, curling my fingers with his. "Dinner is only egg salad macaroni with fresh green beans."

"Considering the tasteless MRE type food in the pod, anything you fix, no matter how simple, will taste gourmet. And I need to thank Eric for the beer. You just can't imagine..." the thought trailed away as he closed his eyes and finished off the pale ale Eric had brought over earlier to welcome John back.

CHAPTER TWENTY-THREE

"Allex, I'm still on shift! I *have* to go back," John stated. "I've no doubt that they will overlook that I wasn't at Eagle Beach last night, considering what's happened, but rules are rules. Besides, it won't be for long."

"What do you mean, *it won't be for long*?" I questioned. "There's still two weeks before rotation. Today would have been shift change and you'd be on nights tomorrow."

From across the wooden kitchen table, he held my hand. "I'm going to quit, Allex. I can't do this anymore. The last cave-in I was trapped in was while I was married. When I insisted on going back to work, my wife left me." He paused. "Not only will I not risk losing *you*, I'm getting too old for the risks. My heart just isn't in it anymore."

"Are you really sure you want to do this, John?"

"No doubts in my mind at all. I just need to go back long enough to collect my hazard bonus." He smiled. "Any injury sustained during a cave-in automatically doubles the bonus, and Mark has the x-ray to prove this wrist is fractured."

"They pay you a bonus for being trapped by a landslide of rock?" I snorted. "It would never be enough to cover what you endured."

When he told me how much it was, I was shocked, and now understood why he wanted it. He had earned every dime.

"When will you be back?" I asked. Having John sleeping beside me last night had been *my* bonus, and I really didn't want him to leave again so soon.

"In a couple of days," he answered. "There's paperwork to do and I need to collect all of my stuff from the house. And I need to say goodbye to those left, and to Steve and Sandy. They've been good to all of us and I'd like to leave them something. They may be out of a job soon," John went on. "This was a *very* serious accident, Allex. There will be a skeleton crew clearing the debris and recovering bodies, and after that, the mine will close for a lengthy investigation. While that is going on, the rest of my crew will be sent home, and the shift that was still topside will be reassigned to different location. This is going to cost the mine millions."

"Millions? Of dollars? I don't understand."

"Every man that was lost, all fourteen of them, had a life insurance policy worth one million dollars," John stated flatly. "It will be given to whomever they had designated. Not that it will ever replace the life, but their families should be okay."

* * *

After John left to return to Eagle Beach and start his packing, I went to the office to see Anna, hoping she had some further news for me.

"Do you have your phone turned off?" she asked me as soon as I sat in the brown leather chair next to her big desk.

"Oh, I guess I forgot to turn it back on, sorry. I didn't want anything to disturb John last night," I said, reaching in my pocket for my phone. I switched it back on and saw six messages waiting for me.

"I understand. How's he doing?"

"Better. After being underground for over forty-eight hours, he didn't want to go inside last night. In fact, I think he would have slept on the grass if I had agreed," I laughed. "So, I know it's early, but is there any news from the mine about the cause?"

"I think it's going to take a long time to be sure, Allexa. They won't even start looking for answers until the shaft is cleared and all the bodies are recovered. The speculation is it might have had something to do with the rumblings some of the survivors reported. That's just rumor right now," Anna hastened to add. "Hard to believe we could have an earthquake around here."

* * *

JOURNAL ENTRY: July 10

I took a leisurely walk this morning along our short and crumbling road. I've been trying very hard to notice any changes, anything different every time I pass an area. It's been a warm and wet summer so far and the road weeds are producing in abundance. Pale purple asters are peeking out from under the yellow tansies. The wild redtop grass, thin tawny brown stalks with elongated seed heads, are now four feet tall. Had it been a *normal* time, the county would have been by already to cut them away from the road. Now they are crowding the asphalt, vying for space with the shorter, less mature wild wheat. I had an idea that this might solve an ongoing problem.

* * *

Emilee came bouncing across the driveway as only an almost twelve-year-old little girl can do. "What are you doing, Nahna?"

"I'm so glad you're here, Emi, I was just about to come looking for you." I smiled down at her. She'd grown at least six inches in the past few months. "How would you like to help me collect feed for the chickens?" I asked her.

She had that skeptical expression on her face that I've come to recognize as the "are you serious?" look.

We got two pair of scissors and the small wagon and walked back down the road where I had just been.

"See these seed heads?" I asked and Emi nodded. "These are called redtop and the chickens will find them very tasty this winter. They have plenty to eat right now, with grass and bugs, however, when it snows again, they're going to get hungry and we have to make sure they have something to eat or they won't give us any eggs!"

At this she smiled. She loved collecting the fresh eggs as much as she loved eating them. Just then she swatted at a mosquito.

"First, we're going to pick some bug dope," I announced, and plucked some leaves from the nearest tansy plant. "Crush them in your hand like this, and then rub it on your arms and legs. It will keep the bugs away. I'll do the back of your neck." I hope she remembered this trick in the future. There would be no more sprays or lotions from the store.

I showed her how to bunch a handful of the Redtop, like a bouquet, then cut just below her fist. It wasn't long, maybe a half an hour, and the little wagon was full. We spread the seed heads on the picnic table for extra drying and went the other direction down the road to collect more.

"Aren't these a pretty blue, Nahna?" Emilee joyfully pointed to a tall stalk with odd looking and distinct cornflower blue blossoms.

"Good eye, Emi. Those are chicory. The flowers are pretty, yes. What makes this plant special is the root." With the spade I had brought with me, I dug down and loosened the still damp soil around the plant, then gave a steady pull.

"What will you use that for?" she asked.

"I'm going to roast it, then grind it to make coffee for Grandpa John." I knew our coffee supplies wouldn't last forever and I hadn't seen even one can in any grocery store. I set the chicory root aside and we finished filling the wagon with more seed heads. By the end of the afternoon, we were both tired and ready to quit.

"There's a lot of food here for the chickens. I hope they appreciate all the work we just did and give us lots of eggs." Emi was so insistent that I didn't have the heart to tell her that all we collected would last only a few days. Our work had only just begun! Thankfully, I also knew to make the seed go even further; we could soak it and grow sprouts first, tripling the feed content.

* * *

JOURNAL ENTRY: July 12

Working on picking grains for the chickens yesterday reminded me of grains for us. I haven't seen any bags of wheat berries or barley at any store we've been to, although there has been flour. With all the bread I've been baking for everyone, I'm going through a great deal of that. Jason, Eric and Joshua all get a loaf every week, and of course we use at least one loaf too. I've even been giving Mark a loaf as a barter payment for the medical treatment he's extended to us. That's five, sometimes six loaves every week. I've tried to mix it up some by making pita and tortillas. Most everyone still prefers something they can slice.

* * *

"I don't like being this low on flour," I grumbled as I scraped the bottom of the bin I store it in.

Eric had stopped over after dropping Emilee and Chivas off at Jason's for a play and swim day. Amada wanted to take Jacob swimming at Lake Meade and thought it would be nice if he had some company. I know she also misses her little Shih-Tzu dog and she won't talk about what happened to it.

"I'm not doing anything for the next few hours, Mom. Do you want to go into town and do some grocery shopping, see if we can find any?" Eric offered.

"That would be great! Let me wash up and I'll be ready." I sure could use a break, and we'd all agreed that we would never, ever go into town alone anymore.

I pulled some cash out of the envelope in my drawer and noticed something strange: there was a lot more in there than there should have been. I wonder if John was adding more when I wasn't looking? I wasn't in a position to question that right now. Inflation had gotten mind-boggling. Although the government was saying the inflation rate was at a plateau, they had manipulated the figures by removing the high priced items, like gas, food and medication, from the calculation. The average citizen still couldn't buy or even find enough food for his family, and everyday medications just didn't exist anymore. Then again, anyone who needed daily doses of anything from blood pressure meds to insulin were all dead now.

I took five hundred dollars. These days, five hundred only bought what fifty did just a year ago. I took five hundred more, and closed the drawer.

* * *

"Where to?" Eric asked as he pulled out onto County Road 695 in my new car. I wondered if he wanted the trip just so he could drive the sleek, smooth riding vehicle instead of the pickup truck.

"Let's start at the bulk food store. They seem to always have *something* I can use," I answered. "And I'd like to stop at the hardware and check on batteries." As an afterthought I asked, "Did you remember to bring your military ID, Eric?"

He gave me that "of course I did" look and said, "Do you think I'll need it?"

"I just don't know when we will need what. They change the rules all the time, that's all, and it's better to be prepared than be refused entry into somewhere we want to go."

* * *

The parking lot for the bulk food store was nearly empty of cars. It looked as though the place was closed, until I saw someone being let out the front doors. Eric opened the door for me, and we were stopped by two guards in the glassed-in room where the carts were kept.

"Identification, please," one of the very military looking men stated briskly.

I handed over my Emergency Management badge to the first guard, while the second one patted me down. I had left my Kel Tec in the car under the seat, although I still had the shoulder holster on. The guard stepped back.

Eric handed over his military ID card. The first guard looked at it quickly, and came to attention, saluting him with a sharp "Sir!" I was right; the guards were active military, which I found both interesting and disturbing. Eric returned the salute and we were passed through the next set of doors and into the quiet store. I grabbed a cart and wiped it down with an alcohol wipe. Illness was and may always be a big concern wherever there were groups of people.

Nowhere did I see the woman who usually greeted us, which confirmed in my mind that if the military was protecting the food supplies it meant the government had taken control of it. This may now mean that my position meant little, while Eric's meant more.

"Where do you want to start?" Eric asked, looking around at the massive building. The shelves were six feet tall and mostly empty in certain aisles, fuller in others. There were no extra-large boxes of breakfast cereals, no candy, and no bags of salty snacks in that first lane that was meant to attract impulse buying. In the baking section we did find fifty pound bags of flour, limited to one per person.

"I'll be right back, Mom. I forgot my cart," Eric grinned as he returned to the front of the store.

It had been over a month since his ribs were injured and though he was healing well, he was also wisely being cautious. We both lifted the heavy bags, one into each cart. At that time, I slipped him half of my cash to pay for his cartload.

I was glad I took the extra money. The cost of flour was now ten times what it used to be!

We wandered up and down each aisle, our footfalls echoing in the stillness. It felt like we were the only people in the store, though I could hear hushed voices coming from somewhere.

I took a large can of spaghetti sauce for the Stone Soup Kitchen and two ten-pound bags of pasta which still had no limits. I put a twenty-five pound bag of rice in Eric's cart and two big cans labeled *meat stew*. I wondered what kind of meat it was. As an afterthought, I put two bags of pasta into Eric's cart, too. We each took a five-pound canister of oatmeal. I'd have to repackage those into smaller, more useful sizes; however, it was minor extra work for what we were getting.

We passed up the eggs in the cooler. I refused to take something we didn't need and that we could provide for ourselves.

When we came to the cleaning section, I was pleased that there was dishwashing liquid and clothes soap! Again, there was a limit, and we were only allowed two each.

The very last aisle was where frozen foods used to be. The oversized chrome and glass freezers were silent, emptied of everything and turned off. In the center bunker, there was locally made cheese from the sole dairy still in operation. Joshua was doing very well at making cheese, but he hadn't yet been able to master all the varieties. I put a five-pound block of Jacob's favorite American cheese in my cart, happy to pay the fifty dollar price tag.

I scanned each of our carts, and satisfied that we were well under our limited funds, we headed for the checkout.

My cart came to $380, and there wasn't that much there. Eric paid $350, even after selecting a tempting mega-bag of potato chips that was kept behind the counter.

"Do we still want to go to the hardware store, Mom?" Eric asked me when we were loading everything into the back of the small car, taking up most of the room.

"I'd like to, however, we can't leave the car unguarded," I said. "Let me think a moment..."

I mulled over the situation as Eric drove across the highway to the other store.

"Stop back here, away from the other cars," I said, "and let me drive. I'll drop you off at the front, and I'll keep moving to be less of a target and so no one can see in the back." I gave him the remainder of my cash. He was in the store only a few minutes and I pulled up to the curb for him to get in, then I got in motion again.

"Nothing. There are no batteries of any kind or any size available. Period."

"It was just a chance, Eric. We'll manage." I thought of losing power again, and that battery operated lamp sitting dark on Anna's desk at the township hall.

CHAPTER TWENTY-FOUR

The day began on a glorious note. The sky was sapphire blue without a single cloud, and the golden sun shone, almost too brightly. Although the thermometer read eighty-five degrees, the light breeze coming down from the north brought a coolness that made the day spectacular.

"Allex, can you pick me up? I'm packed and ready to leave here," John announced.

"I'll be there within a half hour," I replied jubilantly. He was coming home, and this time to stay. I hoped.

* * *

"This is all you have, John? One duffle bag and two boxes?"

"I always travel light," he replied. "There have been times when we would leave on rotation, only to get notice while at home that we were being moved or laid off and someone else would be sent to pack up what we had left behind. Many of us got used to staying semi-packed, even if we were in one location for two or three years," he explained. "That happened to me while I was working in Alaska. I was there for five years and had settled in. Then *wham*! We were sent somewhere else while I was in Indiana with Christine. They shipped me twelve boxes, ten of which I would have left behind if I had known."

"It doesn't matter. We'll find or make anything else you might need." I couldn't help but be enthused; not only was he coming to stay, he would also now be out of danger.

"Is all your paperwork done?" I asked, knowing how important it was to him to leave on a good note with this company that had treated him so well.

"Yes. It isn't unusual for someone to resign after a mining accident, so the home office was one step ahead of me. My final paycheck and my bonus were already processed and just waiting for a keystroke to be deposited in my account, although I did insist that half of my bonus was in cash. It's all done, Allex. I'm officially unemployed," John said with such enthusiasm that it made me laugh. "Oh, and Simon will be by later for me to sign my final disclosure papers."

* * *

"Is John around?" Simon asked, stepping down from the Green-Way van.

"He's across the road talking with my son, I'll call him," I said.

"Not just yet, Allexa, there's something I need to discuss with you first, and I'd rather do it privately. It will be your choice to share it with John or not." Simon had a very strange look on his face, almost embarrassed.

"Okay, Simon. What is it?" We sat down at the weathering picnic table.

"This is for you," he said, sliding an envelope toward me.

"What is it?" I asked, picking it up.

"It's a letter, from Sven. And yes, I've read it; it was part of our agreement. I have letters on file from most of the men, including John, whose letter will now be destroyed. One of Green-Way's most valuable assets in their employees is the lack of family ties.

"I don't know how well you knew Sven. He came to the States after both of his parents died in an automobile accident. He was an only child; there are no siblings. He never married, and had no children. He was a brilliant electrician and Green-Way recruited him quickly. Even though Sven enjoyed his work and liked his teammates, he was also very alone. Each new place we would send him, he would find a person he liked, someone that he could talk to. Someone who was kind to him or treated him like a friend and made him feel a little less lonely. You were that person for him here. It explains it all in the letter: he felt you genuinely liked him as a person and that meant everything to him...so he made you his beneficiary." At that Simon handed me another envelope, this one with a check window.

"Are you saying Sven left me his life insurance?" I whispered.

"Open it," Simon said with a smile.

I tore the flap and gasped. I had never seen a check for a million dollars before, and it had my name on it.

"I do need you to sign this agreement that you won't sue the mine for anything beyond this." He handed me a pen and a clipboard. I scanned the agreement quickly, and absently signed where he indicated.

I was having just a bit of a problem breathing when I saw John cutting across Eric's lawn, coming this way.

"I think I'll keep this for a surprise," I said, and folded the two envelopes, tucking them into my back pocket.

"Simon!" John greeted his friend and now former boss. "I didn't see you pull in, or I would have come back sooner."

"Not a problem, John. I was having a pleasant chat with Allexa," Simon stood to shake John's offered hand. He shifted the sheets on the clipboard, turning the one I had just signed face down, and offering the same pen to John, who quickly scribbled his name. Simon then handed John a very thick envelope.

"We're all going to miss you, John. You were the best foreman Green-Way has ever had," he said sincerely, adding, "Good luck to you, to both of you."

John turned to me as Simon backed the big white and green van out of the driveway and said, "I think we should celebrate!"

"I agree. What would you like to do, John? This is your 'freedom' day."

"It's still early. I say we go into Marquette and buy some steaks, no matter how much they cost! And maybe even find a bottle of champagne while we're at it." He laughed and gave me a fierce bear hug. I'd never seen him so happy. It was like the weight of the world had been lifted from his shoulders.

* * *

The shelves at Mack's were just as lean and empty as they were the last time I was there and that same cloying rotten scent hung over the fresh food like a sticky cloud. We wandered the vacant aisles quietly, John's jubilant mood somewhat subdued, until we came to the meat counter.

Fresh steaks were being stocked behind the polished glass while we watched. My mouth actually started to water. I hadn't had a beef steak in many months and the sight of the juicy red meat made me hungry.

"How much are those?" John asked the butcher. I was shocked that the prices had gone up yet again when he told us.

"I'll take *all* of them!" John said with gusto, and laughed.

The butcher wrapped the fifteen steaks and personally carried them to the front to a waiting cashier, where John paid with eight one hundred dollar bills.

My mind did a quick calculation. Meat was now forty-five dollars per pound! Inflation was out of control and spiraling higher with every passing hour.

"Where's Marie?" I asked the cashier, wondering where my friend was.

"She hasn't been here in more than a month, just stopped showing up," the young blonde woman replied with a shrug.

John stopped just before the automatic doors opened, and turned back to the wide-eyed cashier. "Wine! Do you carry wine?"

"All alcohol is now controlled by the State. The only place it's available is over on Washington," she replied, eyeing John warily. No one spent money like this anymore. No one *had* money like this anymore.

We stepped out into the warm afternoon air, John carrying the heavy package. I scanned the parking lot, and withdrew my Kel Tec from its hiding place under my left arm when I saw one person in the distance, leaning casually against a car. Holding the 9mm automatic pointed skyward, I walked a half of a step in front of John until we reached the car. He set the meat in the back seat in a cooler we had brought, and got in behind the wheel, locking his door. I walked around to the passenger side, opened the door, slid in quickly, locking my side, and holstering my gun.

I smiled at John and said, "I got to be *your* bodyguard for a change!"

Just then the first attack came; someone tried to open the locked doors. I heard pounding on the windows as John slammed the car into gear and peeled out of the near empty parking lot. I looked back and saw four people stomping around where the car had just been. They must have been waiting for us.

Our humanity was cycling through phases. The first was and likely would always be denial of whatever the circumstances were. No matter how obvious the situation may be, nearly everyone tried to justify the undesirable away, ignoring what was right in front of them. The next phase was panic, when there was a rush to get everything possible, whether it was food, water or a flat screen TV, there was mass buying and inevitably the digression to stealing. That was what had happened last fall after the earthquakes. When all the supplies were finally gone, people settled into an acceptance because they had no choice. When a recovery of sorts began with the return of electricity and the minor restocking of grocery shelves, there was rejoicing that all was well again, shutting out the fact that it was *not* all well again; they were just being spoon-fed what would keep them calm and compliant. The next step was also inevitable: the anger that normalcy was being denied them, and that anger resulted in violence, as we witnessed today.

* * *

The State controlled store was the same one we had been to before, only with different guards, older, wiser ones. We submitted our ID, and were patted down. The guard found my holster, though I had wisely left my weapon in the car again.

"You didn't think I would be foolish enough to bring it in, did you?" I said calmly as he blocked our way. "We're here to *buy*, nothing else."

He did a quick check on my emergency management ID, letting us in when the counter man recognized us, likely from the large graft John had left before.

We selected four bottles of relatively inexpensive champagne that now cost fifty dollars per bottle. With the hundred dollar bill that disappeared into the proprietor's pocket, and two fifties that found their way to the guards, this was getting to be a mind boggling shopping trip!

Locked in the car once more, we both broke into a nervous laugh.

"Oh, let's not do this again," I hiccupped nervously, putting my Kel Tec back in the leather holster.

"Deal!" John agreed.

* * *

"So how do you want to celebrate, John?" I asked, putting the steaks and the champagne in the refrigerator. It was the last of our "on" days for power;

tomorrow started three days of "off." I'd been making ice to help keep things cool during those no electricity times. I just hoped it was enough to keep everything from spoiling.

"Tonight, I'd like just the two of us, Allex, and tomorrow I'd like to have a small party," he replied, slipping his arms around my waist. "Let's stick one of those bottles in the freezer to chill it down fast."

"Who would you like to invite tomorrow?"

"I'd like the boys to join us, of course, and Bob and Kathy, and Guy and Dawn."

"Guy and Dawn went downstate to see Guy's sister and won't be back for another week or two," I informed him. Inviting Bob and Kathy was no surprise to me as John had gotten quite fond of those two. "A small party is good!" Then something occurred to me. "Tomorrow is also Jacob's birthday. Is a double celebration okay with you?"

"Of course it is. I just want to share some time with our friends and family." He looked thoughtful before going on. "Is there anything I can do for a present for Jacob?"

* * *

For dinner, we grilled two of the steaks and ate by candlelight on the newly sheltered deck, sipping champagne well into the balmy night.

"Next year we screen in this area!" John said when the mosquitoes started swarming and we had to move inside.

Sometime around midnight the power went out as scheduled. We were asleep long before it happened.

CHAPTER TWENTY-FIVE

"You know what would have gone really good with those wonderful steaks last night, John? Fresh mushrooms!" I exclaimed.

"I doubt if the grocery has any, Allex," he laughed.

"Maybe not, but it's the right season, and I know where we can pick all the wild ones we want," I replied, visions of luscious golden orange Chanterelles fried in butter dancing across my mind.

With Eric, Emilee, John and I crowded into the car, Chivas curled up in the hatch with our picking buckets, we set off. The first stop was to Bob and Kathy to see if they wanted to go with us on our foraging jaunt. In the years past, Kathy and I had always done this together.

"I'm really not much of a mushroom picker," Bob said, declining our invitation. "Kath is the gatherer. I've a few things to do around here anyway. We both would be delighted to join you for dinner tonight."

It was a snug fit, but Kathy sat in the back seat with Emi between her and Eric for the drive up to the Snake River Plains, to our favorite mushroom patch.

When we arrived, the four of us adults spread out some to search for that sometimes elusive orange mushroom, with Emilee staying close to either me or Eric.

We wandered through the low growth of wild blueberry bushes, hanging heavy with unripened fruit and the tall, spindly Juneberry bushes, searching the more open spaces of heavy ground moss.

When Kathy shouted "Mother lode!" we all congregated in the one spot under a scraggly jack-pine tree, so John, Eric and Emi could see what we were all looking for and how to spot them. The little mushrooms popped up underneath the soft gray-green moss that grew abundantly in the sandy, acidic soil, and it was easy to miss them. Even Chivas came to investigate the excitement. She was being good, not venturing too far from Eric, enjoying the freedom like only a growing puppy can.

We picked that area clean and wandered away again, each searching the ground, yet also keeping in visual contact with everyone else. It was very easy to get disoriented, even lost, when following the fairy rings in that terrain. Kathy and I had had that happen in the past, and it was why we always had a compass and a whistle with us at all times.

The picking was very good after all that rain we had and the moss was soft underfoot instead of the crunchy soil we so often find, and we moved about soundlessly. My bucket was nearly half full of beautiful, large mushrooms after just a half hour of searching. When I stood to stretch, I saw the stranger who had approached the area quietly.

"Eric," I said, alerting him as he harvested mushrooms only a few yards away.

He gave a whistle for the wandering dog, just as a shot rang out, and we heard Chivas yelp in pain.

Eric dropped his bucket and sprinted the hundred yards toward the shooter. Emi started too, until I grabbed her arm.

"Stay here with Kathy!" I commanded, dropping my bucket too, running after my son, John close on my heels.

Eric jumped over a fallen log and made a running tackle just as the guy was raising his rifle again. He brought him down with a hard and very audible thump; the shot went high and wild.

I knelt beside the golden retriever puppy, stroking her nose as I cried with angry tears. Her left rear flank was bent at an awkward angle and she was bleeding from a small hole, her golden fur staining red with wet blood. Chivas lifted her head to lick my hand, her eyes glowing with pain.

Eric had pulled the guy to his feet by his tattered plaid shirt. "You shot my dog!" he snarled.

"It's a dog," the guy stated in calm contempt, his scraggly hair framing his dirty face, his dark eyes vacant. "Dogs are animals and all animals are *food* now."

I could almost see the waves of anger and hatred rolling off of my son.

Eric's lip curled. "Then I guess that applies to you too, then. Food." The guy's black eyes focused and widened, just as Eric pulled his pistol and shot him. The impact of the .357 ripped his throat out and blasted the body back a dozen feet, now unmoving and half under a low hanging broken tree limb.

"Nobody hurts my kid, and nobody hurts my dog!" he spat out, and turned toward us. He holstered his gun with ease, though he was breathing hard.

I was stunned at what had just happened, however, it was the way of the new world we lived in and I let it pass. We left the body where it landed.

"She's still alive, Eric, hurt but alive. I don't think anything vital was hit," I said. "We need to get her to Mark." I pulled off the light jacket I was wearing to hide my shoulder holster and wrapped it around Chivas' back legs to contain the bleeding.

Eric dug his hands down into the spongy gray ground cover to get underneath Chivas' body, then lifted her gently, cradling her against his chest to begin the long walk back to the car.

John inspected the human body with disinterest and retrieved the fallen rifle.

Kathy and Emilee were holding all the partially filled buckets, waiting hand in hand as we made our way back to them. Emilee started crying when she saw the injured puppy and the blood seeping through my jacket.

I took Emilee aside as the others kept walking, Kathy in the lead.

"Emi, listen to me. Chivas is hurt, but she's alive and we will do everything we can to keep her that way, you understand? I know you're very upset, we all are. You need to be brave for your dad and for Chivas. Chivas knows when you're sad and that makes her sad. We don't want that right now, okay?" Emi nodded, and wiped her tears with the back of her small hand, and we both hurried to catch up with the long strides of the others.

"Where did that guy come from?" John bellowed. "I didn't hear any vehicles."

"During one of our wanderings last year, Allexa and I kind of got lost," Kathy said. "While trying to get back to the road, we came across two separate camps. We gave them a wide berth when it was obvious someone was living there. Maybe he was from one of those."

"Maybe he felt *we* were the trespassers," I commented.

With her great sense of direction, Kathy had us back to the car in five minutes.

Eric sat in the hatch so he would have enough room to cradle the dog comfortably and to keep Emi from seeing how much pain Chivas was in.

John eased the car over the dirt and gravel two-track, and once back on the newly paved main road, he took the curves easy and the straight stretches fast. Within twenty minutes we were pulling into Dr. Robbins' parking lot. I jumped out first and went inside, while John helped Eric out of the back of the car.

"Mark! I'm so glad you're here. There's been a shooting accident," I panted, the adrenaline coursing through my veins.

Mark grabbed my hands to steady them. "Deep breath now. Tell me what happened." He searched my pain-filled eyes. "Not one of the children...?" he choked out.

Just then Eric came in holding a very still Chivas.

"I'm not a veterinarian!" Mark protested. Eric laid the dog on the metal examining table anyway.

"Mark, please!" I pleaded. "Bleeding is bleeding! Can you stop it?"

He looked from me to Eric to John to Chivas and back to me. "She's your dog, Eric?" Eric nodded. "Then you stay to keep her calm. Allexa, I need you to assist me." Mark looked at John and said nothing. John slipped out the door to wait with Emi and Kathy.

Mark listened to various points along Chivas' body with his stethoscope, determining that the dog was indeed still alive and breathing. He handed surgical masks and gloves to us and after he pulled on his own sterile gloves and mask, lined up alcohol, sutures, gauze, other instruments and some needles on a sterile tray. Removing my jacket from the dog, he surveyed the damaged leg and muttered a curse under his breath, then starting to clean the area.

"I hope you caught who did this," he said gravely.

In a very calm and stoic tone, Eric repeated, "No one hurts my kid and no one hurts my dog."

Mark's hands stilled for a second and he shared a knowing glance with me, recalling the last person that had tried to hurt Eric's kid, and the messy results.

"I'm going to give her a shot for the pain and to numb the area so I can probe for the bullet," he said. "About how much does she weigh?" he asked, then calculated the dose for a small child.

"I'll need at least one x-ray to see how far the bullet went in. We'll have to shave her first." When he turned on the electric shears, nothing happened.

"Today is an off day for the power," I stated flatly and proceeded to clip Chivas' silky fur as short as possible with a pair of scissors. "Did you know that the scissors were invented by Leonardo da Vinci?" I said as a matter of conversation, which got incredulous looks from both men standing there. "Just a piece of trivia," I commented from behind my mask, "Although there is some evidence to support the idea that the ancient Egyptians had scissors centuries earlier."

Mark angled the portable x-ray machine and scanned the area, watching the results from the attached digital screen, thankful it had its own battery backup.

"It appears that the bullet went clean through. That's the good news. The bad news is it looks like an artery has been nicked and that's why the bleeding won't stop."

He swabbed the area again, and asked for a retractor, which I laid in his hand. He stretched the wound open, and I handed him a sponge to soak up the blood. We worked silently for perhaps twenty minutes. He put tiny dissolving stitches in to close the hole in the small canine artery, while I kept the area visible by cleaning the pooling blood. When he removed the original retractor, I handed him the remaining suture for him to close the ragged wound.

Eric just stood by Chivas' head, stroking her soft fur, crooning softly to her.

I used some of the alcohol to clean up the drying blood on Chivas' fur, more for my granddaughter's sake. Mark bandaged and then wrapped the leg immobile after checking to make sure the fragile bone wasn't broken or dislocated. The odd angle I saw it at was apparently an illusion of the odd shape of a dog's hind leg.

"My first non-human surgery and I think the patient is going to be just fine," Mark said, breathing a sigh of relief. "Last thing to do is a shot of antibiotic, and you can take her home," he said, giving her the hypo. The entire process took just over an hour and I was exhausted!

When we each removed the mask and gloves we were wearing, Eric broke into the biggest grin I've seen on him in a long time.

"Thank you, Dr. Robbins." He gave Mark a handshake and a surprise hug. Eric turned to me and smiled, then his face collapsed and he started to sob. I put my arms around him and just held on.

"Okay, I didn't expect that," Eric said after his crying jag. He sniffed, and gave his tear-streaked face a splash of cold water from the sink in the exam room before going to face his daughter.

Eric gently lifted Chivas, who was now sleeping, from the table and walked out, holding her carefully in his strong and loving arms.

"Thank you so much, Mark. I know this wasn't something that you would normally do, but—"

"But these aren't normal times, are they, Allexa?" He smiled back. "Someday we need to discuss your medical career; you did exceptionally well."

* * *

Kathy lived only a few minutes from the clinic, so she walked home after she reassured John that her and Bob would be over later for dinner.

John drove up Eric's drive and got as close to the house as possible. While John unlocked the house door with Eric's keys, Eric carried Chivas up the stairs with Emilee trailing behind.

"I'll be back soon with the garden cart, Eric. You can use it to bring Chivas over tonight," John offered. It went without saying that the dog would come to the celebration.

"I can do that, Grandpa John!" Emilee jumped up. Sensing she needed to contribute, we had her come back with us to get the green metal cart.

I got one of the disposable emergency blankets from the box on top of the outside refrigerator and laid it in the wagon. Emilee said it wasn't soft enough for her dog, so I found an old blanket too. We walked across the street together, but she insisted on pulling the heavy wagon by herself.

* * *

"I've got a quick errand to run," John announced when I got back home. I saw that he had pulled one of the still wrapped steaks out of the refrigerator, and one of the small bottles of ice I was using to keep things cold and then placed them in one of my cloth shopping bags. I'd learned not to question him, especially not over this, since it was his generosity that bought those steaks in the first place. I also had a feeling I knew what his errand was.

It had been a long, hot and emotional day, and I desperately needed a shower. I started up the generator to power the well pump and stepped into a cascade of hot, pulsating water. I washed my hair, finding bits of gray moss and wondered how it got there, then remembered many of the jack-pine tree branches we all had to duck under had lacey moss growing on them. I scrubbed my face hoping to rid myself of the cloying stench of blood that clung to my every pore. Satisfied that I didn't stink anymore, I rinsed and stepped out of the shower. I decided on a cream colored short-sleeved top and a long brown printed skirt for the occasion and stepped into my well-worn sandals.

I had just pulled the four large sirloin steaks out of the cooler to cut them in half as John and I had discussed we would do, when he pulled into the driveway. All of the steaks were thick cut and half of any one of the steaks would be ample meat for one person. I set them on a platter, sprinkling them with garlic salt and fresh ground pepper, and then put them back in the cooler. The day was still very warm.

"I hear the generator running," John said, smiling at me. "Good, I need a shower, too." He kissed me on the nose and headed for the bathroom before our guests started to arrive.

* * *

It was around six o'clock when I heard Bob and Kathy pull in. They both were still sparkling from a recent dip in the lake, an advantage of living right on Lake Meade.

"I brought a dish to share for dinner," Kathy grinned. From that look on her face I knew it had to be something special.

"Okay, what did you do now?" I teased, and lifted the cover to expose a Chanterelle Risotto, one of our favorite dishes to fix with the fresh wild mushrooms. The other favorite was a white sauce pizza drowned in sautéed orange mushrooms. Maybe that would be tomorrow night, I thought. I took a deep sniff of the risotto, and covered the dish back up.

Jason, Amanda and Jacob arrived a few minutes later and we all sat out under the boughs of the maple trees that graced my front yard with cooling shade. When a familiar compact car arrived next, I knew my suspicions were correct. John had gone back into town, paid Dr. Mark for his services with a pricey steak, and invited him to join us tonight. Those two just might get to be friends someday. Would that be a dilemma for me at some point?

Ten minutes later, Eric and Emilee started across the freshly mowed lawn. Eric was pulling the green garden cart with a drowsy Chivas sprawled over the blankets, and Emilee was pulling the small plastic cart loaded down with an ice chest filled with Eric's latest brewing.

The main topic for the evening was of course our adventure up on the Plains and Chivas' injury. Mark reminded Eric that he would be by tomorrow to check on the puppy and to change her bandages. There were many questions for John about the mining accident, which he couldn't answer because of the disclosure he'd signed yesterday.

"Has anyone heard any more about the Caribbean earthquakes and tsunami?" I asked.

"For as major of an event that it was, Allexa, and so recent, the news is just down to a trickle," Bob answered in frustration. "And most of it is just a rehash, with very little footage, mostly what the island *used* to look like! It's as if they don't want us to know what's going on."

"I'd like to say that's the new world we live in, Bob, however, it isn't. The media and the government have been doing that to us for years."

Out of the corner of my eye, I saw my big black kitty cautiously approaching the wagon where Chivas lay resting. I'd been letting him out during the day to hunt for birds and mice, hoping to keep his dry food needs to a minimum. He sniffed at the puppy's paw dangling over the lowered edge, and then smoothly leaped, landing deftly on the blanket. Tufts examined the bandages, and then in a surprising move, licked Chivas' face, which caused the pup to breathe a sigh. The cat curled up next to the dog and rested his big black head on the golden shoulder of the injured canine.

In spite of the somewhat depressing conversation, it was a wonderful evening. The risotto was delicious and John grilled the steaks to perfection. There was enough chilled champagne for everyone who wanted it, and the rest had icy beer.

* * *

"I have a present for you, Jacob," John announced just after dinner.

"What is it, Grandpa John?" Jacob looped his arm through John's in a positive sign of affection. So many autistic children shy away from physical contact, thankfully, that wasn't one of Jacob's issues.

"Well, maybe you should open it," John said, and handed Jacob a small package wrapped in old newspaper and tied with string.

Jacob squealed with delight when he held the book John had given him. It was an alphabet book in Swedish that John said had belonged to Sven when he was a child.

Seeing that book reminded me of the check hiding in my drawer.

* * *

JOURNAL ENTRY: July 15

I saw Mark's little compact car across the road at Eric's this afternoon. I'm guessing he was checking on Chivas. I must admit I find it very admirable that he would follow up on a puppy surgery. Chivas means a great deal to all of us. She's become a sign of hope and a normalizing future.

CHAPTER TWENTY-SIX

"John, look at that!" I pointed to the sky where thousands of birds were in flight. It was early in the day and we were working in the garden. He was picking green beans for our dinner and I was tending the sprawling tomato plants.

He looked up, as mesmerized by the sight as I was. I was used to seeing the geese in long Vs going north in the spring and south in the fall, but the geese were greatly outnumbered by the lower flying birds. It was difficult to separate the species, though I caught flickers of red and blue and yellow amongst the darker browns and blacks of the highflying flocks. It seemed that the cardinals and bluebirds, which were rare this far north, had joined their cousins in a strange mass migration.

I felt a distinct rumble under my feet. John had already stopped and straightened up, looking around.

"What was that?" I said out loud.

The movement in the ground was more of a vibration, like a really heavy truck had just gone by even though there are no trucks anymore.

He looked worried. "I don't know, but it felt like an explosion. Distant, but definitely an explosion." I will always trust what he says in that realm; he was the expert when it came to explosives and the Earth moving. "It was much like what I felt just before the cave-in." His confession surprised me. I'd never asked him about the mining accident, and I never would.

"Should I be worried too?" I asked. He glanced at me. "I can see the concern written all over your face, John."

"I think for now awareness is prudent, especially of anything unusual. It might be cause for concern, it might not," he stated a bit too quickly. He was right though; ignoring something out of the ordinary would not be wise, considering our situation. And this mass flight of birds was definitely out of the ordinary.

I paused, my hands still holding a wayward branch, heavy with green tomatoes. "What do you think it was, John?"

He looked around again before answering me. I knew he was choosing his words carefully.

"I really do feel it was an explosion of some kind...it felt very odd to me and it felt deep, maybe far away. I just don't know, Allex, maybe another earthquake." Then he frowned. "Maybe you should give Tom a call."

"I will, maybe later. Information is slow to move around these days so he won't know anything for a day or so, even if it is something important." I brushed it off and tried to forget about it, but that rumbling underfoot kept creeping into my thoughts the rest of the morning.

* * *

Dinner was finished, dishes were washed and put away, and we were taking a leisurely walk down the quiet road when the next rumble hit us. I could hear my wind chimes clattering several hundred feet away and the chickens sent up a raucous clucking. I swayed slightly on my feet and clung to John's arm.

"John..." I said with an unasked question.

"That was a quake, Allex."

"Maybe I *should* try to reach Tom," I thought out loud.

Just then my cellphone vibrated and the ringtone started: "Hall of the Mountain King", a melancholy dirge of doom. It was Tom White. Uh-oh. I unhooked the phone from my belt.

"Yes, Tom?" I answered quickly, switching to the speaker so John could hear, too.

"Did you feel it?"

"Yes. Was it an earthquake somewhere?"

"How did you know? No, it doesn't matter. It just came across the EM fax line. There was a major quake in Yellowstone this morning, a 7.4, and I'd say everyone is worried."

Just then I felt another more intense vibration under my feet. I reached out for John, not wanting to feel the panic that was rising inside me.

"Tom! I just felt another one! That's the third one today."

There was a long pause on his end. I could hear something printing in the background. "Third? Hold on, another fax is coming in." He had set the phone down, leaving the line open, and I heard him swear. It wasn't a good sound.

"Allex, I gotta go. The Yellowstone Caldera just erupted! I know that's bad, though I don't really know what it's going to mean to us here in the UP." There was an edge to his voice that I'd never heard before, one of disbelief, maybe even of panic.

"Tom, wait! *I* know what it will mean," I needed to keep him on the line for some weather information. "Tom, can you get us some wind projections for the next few days from the weather service?"

"Yes, but what good will that do us?"

"It will tell us how much time we have..." I left the rest unsaid.

"What do you mean? Time for what?" He rightfully sounded confused... and worried.

"Just find out and call me back. Quickly, Tom, quickly!" I hung up.

John was staring at me. I don't know when I've felt so scared and I couldn't hold back the tears that were raging inside of me. He pulled me into his arms and held me tight. We stood like that until I caught my breath and the shaking subsided.

John was very serious and even he looked scared, something I've never seen before. "Okay, so tell me what you meant, Allex, about how much time we have."

"If the caldera has erupted we could be faced with a cascading effect plus a massive ash cloud, depending on the wind." I took a deep breath as I picked up my walking speed back to the house. "That ash could kill everything that breathes: plants, animals...us."

He stopped walking, bringing me to an abrupt halt. I tugged on his hand. "Come on, John, we've got work to do." It was only 6:30 P.M., plenty of daylight left.

* * *

My next phone calls were to Eric, Jason, and Anna, in that order.

"Anna, don't talk, just listen, okay?" I said as soon as she picked up her phone at home.

"Okay, Allexa, I'm listening."

"I need you to arrange a town meeting for first thing in the morning, say around nine o'clock. Make this a mandatory meeting for everyone, and I do mean *everyone*, no exceptions! I'll need a screen and a VCR." I stopped for a moment to collect my thoughts; my mind was racing.

"What's going on, Allexa?" Anna asked, and I could hear the worry in her quiet voice.

"There were at least two earthquakes at Yellowstone today, one this morning and another just a bit ago." I took a breath before going on. "Then the caldera that's below most of the park erupted, Anna. It's the largest known subterranean volcano."

"That's way out in Montana," she protested.

"It's mostly in Wyoming, but that's irrelevant. Regardless of where it is, it's huge and it's to our west. The ash cloud it has produced *will* come this way. It's just a matter of how soon. Now, please, Anna, just do it. I'll see you in the morning," I said, hanging up.

* * *

Eric and Emilee arrived first, of course, and I gave them a quick rundown of what was going on.

"Nahna, I'm scared," Emi said with a quivering lip.

"That's okay, honey, sometimes it's helpful to be scared. It means you're aware of what might be a bad situation, and that makes it easier to deal with," I answered her, knowing I wasn't going to sugar coat anything.

"What does this mean to us, Mom? And what do you want us to do?" Eric asked in his calm voice. I could see the anxiety in his clear blue eyes.

"So I don't repeat myself, we'll wait until Jason and Amanda get here," I said. "You can start by driving each car up to Fram's and topping off the tanks, okay?" I tossed him my keys.

I turned to John. "You know where I keep the cash pouch? Will you get it for Eric?" He nodded.

"How much?"

"All of it! Come tomorrow, cash might be worthless."

That stunned all of them, even Emi.

* * *

By the time Eric returned from filling the second vehicle, his double tank pickup truck, Jason and Amanda had arrived, so we had a family conference. Just as we all sat down at the kitchen table, my phone rang. I set in on the table on speaker.

"What have you found out, Tom?"

"Right now the winds are coming from the northwest, as usual," he said. "With the hotter air building up from the eruption, the National Weather Service is expecting that to shift, pushing further north, and bringing us the northern edge of the ash cloud." I could tell by his calm voice he was reading. "So, does this mean what I think it does, Allexa?" he asked.

"Tom, I have you on speaker phone," I warned him. "My family is here and I want you to listen to what I'm going to tell them, it might help you too." I took a sip of water from the glass John had just handed me. "The winds coming northwest would push the ash cloud below us. A straight west wind could still take the cloud past us. However, a southwest current will very likely bring that cloud right to us, and the ash cloud is fine particles of pumice, which will turn to a thick sludge once it comes into contact with water. That isn't as much of a problem as the fine shards of rock falling. It would be like breathing *glass!*"

All the information I had read in the past few years about what-ifs slammed to the forefront. I needed to get to my notes.

"This is all speculation so far, of course. *Anything* can change, but I'm not going to bet our lives on it. We have to start making plans and getting certain things done, and as quickly as possible," I told them.

"How much time do we have, Allexa?" Tom asked quietly, voicing everyone's concern.

"That will depend on how fast the wind is. Three or four days would be my guess, maybe less. I'm not an expert, so I just don't know. Tom, if you can, please stay on top of the weather and keep me updated. I've got notes somewhere on someone else's speculation, plus an old video that was done by one of the PBS stations as a fictionalized documentary. I'm going to play it for the township tomorrow morning."

"What are we going to do to get ready for the worst case, Mom?" Jason asked.

"Think about what this will do. The cloud of ash will be just that: ash, and not breathable. Any living thing will suffocate trying to breathe that air unfiltered. Going outside at any time will require wearing a mask, no exceptions. All the wild animals are likely to die. It's not the same as nuclear fallout. This *is* survivable. The first thing we need to do is think about everything that will ready us to stay indoors for an extended period of time. I'm talking perhaps weeks, not just days." I looked at the stunned faces of my family. "As the ash falls and accumulates, it will smother everything else: plants, fish, and trees."

"What about our garden, Nahna?" Emilee asked, with a touch of anger.

"We're going to dig up as much as we can and put it in the greenhouse. Maybe we can save some of it," I told her. "We have to work as fast as we can. There's so much to do."

I moved closer to the phone. "Tom, it might be good for you to stock as much food and water as you can and stay home with your wife and son."

Tom was slow to respond. "They...they both died in that last round of flu, so I guess I'll stay here," he said in a soft monotone.

"Oh, I'm so sorry, Tom, I didn't know." My heart ached for my friend. "You should still gather as much as you can, Tom, the city will need your guidance." With that, he disconnected.

My family sat in stunned silence. I don't know what was going through their minds. I just knew that mine was in chaos.

"Okay, here is our first plan of action. We need all of the vehicles filled with gas; Eric has already started on that. We need to dig up as many plants from the garden as we can and get them into the greenhouse. We use pots, buckets, anything, just get them indoors." I thought hard, my mind racing. "Jason, there is more chicken wire out behind the garden. Will you close in under the grow boxes? We need to move the chickens too, plus their barrels of feed."

"Okay. What else, Mom?" Jason asked.

"Amanda, you three need to move back across the street. I think we have to circle the wagons," I laughed nervously. "Besides, the food is here, and once the cloud hits, there will be no moving about. Do you understand what I'm saying?" She nodded. I know that neither of them was anxious to leave their house yet again.

"I think that's enough for tonight. If any of you have any concerns about something, please speak up and share. I think between all of us we just might come up with a solution."

"I think I can handle filling the cars, Mom," Amanda said. "I can pack the stuff we'll need when we get home tonight."

"I've already done Mom's car and the truck, so it's just your car and Mom's old car and the gas cans," Eric said, handing her the cash pouch.

When Eric mentioned the gas cans, those empty drums in the barn burned in my vision. "Oh, I wonder if we have time to fill those drums!" I exclaimed in frustration.

Jason and John exchanged a quick look.

"Ah, Mom," Jason said, "they're full. John and I filled them when you and Eric were shopping the other day. We wanted to surprise you, but I think you should know now so you don't have to worry about that."

I spun around to look at John.

"But you said I could," he pleaded.

"Yes, I did, and thank you," I hugged him fiercely.

The rest of us started digging up the delicate plants in the garden as soon as Amanda left, taking Jacob with her for the ride. With the first batch of tomatoes and beans, I stayed in the greenhouse, quickly replanting what I could into the grow boxes to make more floor space for whatever else they brought in. They brought in pepper plants and cabbage, kale and chard. The root crops like beets and potatoes couldn't be moved. I would have to start over with those.

It was dark by the time we were done digging and moving, and Amanda had filled their car and my old car.

"I'll do the cages tomorrow, Mom," Jason said, "I need some of my tools to make things go quicker."

"Get some rest, everyone, and thank you," I said as my family started to leave. "I'll see you all at the township building at nine o'clock sharp!"

"Why do we have to watch the video, Mom?" Jason asked.

"Because you need to see what everyone else will, to understand the importance of what we're doing and what's possibly going to happen. Before you say you can watch it later, I also need you there to help me answer questions, okay?" Jason nodded, and he and Amanda took Jacob home.

I slumped in the wooden kitchen chair, exhausted. John came up from behind, set a glass in front of me. I tasted the amber liquid that slid around the ice cubes: the reserve stock of my spiced rum. It glided down my throat and I sighed as John started rubbing my shoulders.

"Do you really think this cloud will reach us and that all this we're doing is necessary, Allex?" he asked, digging his thumbs into my tight neck muscles.

"I'm hoping with all my heart that all this frantic work is for nothing, John, and that the ash cloud passes us by. What if it doesn't go south of us? What if it goes even more north and puts us in the center of it? We just can't take the risk of being caught unprepared. Our very lives may depend on what we do in the next few days." I closed my eyes to the weary tears I felt building.

"Let's see if we can catch some news. Maybe it will give us a better idea of what to expect," John suggested.

The footage that was being shown started clear and ended with heavy static and a blurry picture. After the first quake this morning, the park was evacuated of the few visitors. The second quake prompted the staff to make a hasty exit. For some of them it was too late. They did provide enough information to explain what had happened.

"I'm standing about a mile from Yellowstone Lake, up on the rise near Park Point," the disembodied voice stated. A park ranger was using his phone camera to show the panorama. The multi-acre lake shimmered and sloshed just as the second quake hit and the camera jiggled when the ranger lost his footing. Once steady again, the picture cleared and the ranger resumed speaking. "Holy shit!" he exclaimed. "The lake is…it's disappearing! Let's get out of here!"

A very tired looking young woman came on the screen. Simone Johnston, a geologist specializing in seismology according to the banner on the bottom of the screen, moved a few papers on her desk before looking up.

"From what we've been able to piece together from the readings that come into our office automatically and this video you just watched from the brave but foolish park ranger, the second quake, a 9.7 on the Richter Scale, opened a massive fissure here," she said, pointing to a chart, "and in a matter of seconds, that fissure emptied billions of gallons of water down into the molten lava, creating an explosion that went beyond our instruments. What it did, in short, was to waken this simmering subterranean volcano." She looked right at the camera and said, "It's no longer subterranean. We now have an active, make that a *very* active, thirty mile-wide volcano that continues to grow and spew lava at an alarming rate. With each belch, it builds the volcanic height, giving the smoke and ash it produces longer range." With that, the picture cut back to the newsroom.

John turned the TV off. "Let's go to bed. It's going to be a very long day tomorrow."

* * *

I left John sleeping and went back to the greenhouse to plant more seedlings into the grow boxes. There were only so many pots I'd saved over the years and those needed to be reserved for the plants that would have to stay in them, like the corn! I had to remember to dig that up tomorrow.

Several small pots held the delicate sprouts of the purple pod pole bean. At first I wasn't sure what to do with them since we couldn't do trellises in the shallow boxes. I decided to move them out of the containers and into one of the many hanging pots; if they couldn't climb up then they'd have to climb down.

Two hours later I slid into bed, completely exhausted, and fell instantly into a deep, troubled sleep.

CHAPTER TWENTY-SEVEN

I slipped the old VCR tape into the player and hit pause. The room was full, but it wasn't standing room only. There just weren't that many of us left. I wasn't sure if that was good or bad anymore.

"I'm glad so many of you could be here this morning," Anna stated solemnly as the room quieted down. "As I understand it, time is short right now, so I'm turning this over to Allexa Smeth." With that she moved to the back and leaned against the wall.

"I'm sure by now everyone has heard that there were several earthquakes in Yellowstone Park yesterday," I began. "While that in itself isn't unusual, the magnitude of those quakes is, and what has resulted is what has our attention today. I know everyone has heard about the caldera that is below Yellowstone: heated rock and lava. It has been that way for millions of years and we've been told that it could stay just like that for a million more." I looked at the crowd; my friends, my family, they were all watching me with grave faces. I was inwardly pleased to see Pastor Carolyn and Dr. Mark. They would both be needed in the coming days and weeks and they need to be fully informed.

"Late yesterday, one of the stronger quakes ripped open the bottom of the Yellowstone Lake, the largest lake in the park," I looked down at my notes, "in the southeast corner of the park that had a depth ranging from 140 feet to almost 400 feet. That's a lot of water and that rip dumped billions and billions of gallons of icy forty-one degree water into the smoldering lava, which created an explosion of steam that sent a hundred million tons of pumice, rock and ash a hundred thousand feet straight up. In turn, that opened the caldera even wider. It was an explosion equal to one thousand Hiroshima bombs.

"The report I got this morning states that there is now a mega-volcano that is at least thirty miles wide, continuously spewing lava and ash and it's still growing. The caldera is estimated to be thirty-seven miles long, eighteen miles wide and seven miles deep. That's just an estimate. It took only twenty minutes, and there is now nothing left within a one *hundred* mile radius of the initial site, and that keeps expanding as more and more pockets erupt."

"Just twenty minutes? How?" Lenny asked.

"It's called a pyroclastic cloud, Lenny," I answered. "Super-heated gas moving at almost five hundred miles per hour sucked out all the oxygen and replaced it with ungodly heat and gases miles in front of the actual cloud. Everything living died instantly: plants, animals, and people, all gone.

"I have a fictionalized docudrama on what might happen in such an event. It's only about forty-five minutes long. I first want to say, this is probably the most serious single thing that we have faced as a community. An eruption of this magnitude puts tons of steam, hydrogen chloride, hydrogen fluoride, sulfur dioxide and pulverized rock and pumice, ten to twenty miles up into the air, and then it comes down. It comes down as acid rain, dust, and those pulverized fine shards of rock falling that look like ash will be like breathing glass."

I hit play.

* * *

When the short movie ended, the room erupted into a buzz of murmuring voices.

"What does this mean to us, Allexa?" someone asked from the back of the room.

"The ash cloud is coming this way," I said flatly. "This cloud is huge and it's getting bigger all the time as more eruptions happen. It will take four days to hit New York and it will be east of the Mississippi and *here* in less than forty-eight hours if the winds stay as they are. The jet stream is being affected because of the height of the heated cloud, so it keeps moving and the forecasters are having trouble projecting the path. Too much of a shift, and those forty-eight hours could become twenty-four. That's why time is of the essence. We just don't know when it will arrive."

"So what do we do?"

"I think it best for everyone to stay together. It will be easier to secure one or two places than ten. The hotel would be ideal. There are a dozen rooms for sleeping, multiple bathrooms, and space to find some privacy, too." I caught the pastor's attention. "Pastor Carolyn, if the Stone Soup facilities could be moved into the hotel kitchens that would help a great deal." She nodded.

"All of those working on Bradley's Backyard garden should dig up your plants and get them indoors. Put them in pots, buckets, anything to bring them out of the ash and to keep them alive. They just might live long enough to feed you.

"Animals need to come in, too," I made eye contact with Joshua. "If you've got pets, or chickens, sheep, goats, *any* animal will die if left outside when this cloud hits. The key will be to not breathe this ash, and for most that will mean not going outside, not even opening windows. If there is a reason to be out, wear a mask." I reached to my left and set a box on the table. "There are fifty surgical masks in here. I want everyone to take one and another one for someone you know isn't here."

"Is anything else going to happen?" Amanda asked, her face furrowed in a deep frown.

"The sulfur dioxide and sulfuric acid in the upper atmosphere will start to reflect the sun's radiation and at the same time it will absorb the heat radiated by the Earth, so our temperatures will start to cool. Since the temperature might drop twenty degrees or more, we might even break our own records and have snow in August." I smiled, but few found it funny.

"How long will we have to stay inside?" Anna asked.

"I don't know," I answered honestly. "It could be a week or two weeks or two months. I just can't answer that, Anna. This won't affect just us. That cloud will circle the globe, maybe for years."

* * *

"How is it you have boxes of surgical masks, Allexa?" Mark asked as everyone was leaving.

"Because I'm paranoid, Mark," I said flippantly and with a shrug. Then I got serious. "Please be careful. We're going to need you."

* * *

"What do we need to do now, Mom?" Jason asked, pacing in my kitchen.

"There are two boxes of heavy clear plastic in the barn, lower left shelf. Each box is eight feet wide by one hundred feet long, if I remember right. One box should be plenty to wrap the deck area. The ash isn't like radioactive fallout. We don't need to be as air tight, though we do need to keep the ash out of the generator's air intake. It could be very important mentally to be able to 'step outside' on occasion once we're confined and the deck would be a nice place to go," I responded. "I think the second box should be used to wrap the porch across the street, for the same reasons." I looked around. "By the way, where is Amanda?"

"She took Jacob back home. I came over with Eric. She'll be here later," Jason replied.

I can't worry about her right now.

"What do you want *me* to do, Allex?" John asked.

I thought for a moment. So much was running through my brain.

"Fish! All the fish will die once the ash starts falling. It would be good if we had a different kind of protein to eat. I know how to can fish, and it can also be smoked."

"I don't think I should waste precious time fishing, Allex," he replied with a snort.

"Agreed, you're the best one here to dynamite fish," I said with a big grin. "Once the three of you wrap the deck and the porch, I think you should do mass fishing. It shouldn't take long to bomb a section of McKenna's Bay and net all the dead fish. I'll do the rest."

"Sure, that can be done, but I need certain materials, Allex," John reminded me.

"I do reloading, John. I'm sure I have whatever you need," Jason piped in. "Good call, Mom, and I know just the place we can set the charge."

"If you could start filling the hot tub first, John, I'd appreciate it. Even though it would have been nice to have a hot soak, I haven't filled it yet because the power has been so erratic; however it's a perfect place to store water. I'll bring all of the full gas cans to the deck so we don't have to go to the barn for a while."

While others were busy doing these tasks, I sat for a moment and started a list of more things for us to do. Antsy, I pushed the paper aside and got my small plastic garden wagon to move the gas cans. At forty pounds per five-gallon can, they were too heavy for me to carry more than one, unless I used the wagon. Two trips and I had that done, less than ten minutes. I went back to the list.

I could hear my three men out on the deck working quickly at installing the plastic sheeting. A peek confirmed that Eric was unrolling and unfolding the long sheet, while John held it in place and taut against the wooden supports for the new roof as best he could with his fractured wrist tightly bandaged, while Jason used his power stapler to make short work of securing it. The garden hose snaked under the sheeting and I heard it splashing into the big blue speckled tub.

Unlike being isolated this past winter, when I could still get out to the sheds for a bucket of this or that, I wouldn't have that easy access for a while. I needed some of that food indoors, and *now*.

In the food shed, I pulled out two buckets of rice, two of mixed beans, and two more of hard winter wheat.

"Emi, would you bring back the garden cart for me, please?" I asked. Happy to have something to do, she scampered across the road and was back in just a few minutes.

"What are we doing now, Nahna?" Her big eyes held such concern it made my heart hurt.

"I know you're going to need food over there, so you and I are going to fill this cart," I told her. I set a bucket of rice and one of beans in the cart. We got three empty canning jar boxes from the shed and went to the back pantry.

"Let's pick what you want to eat. How about chicken soup?" I suggested. She nodded vigorously. As I handed her jars filled with food, she placed them into the waiting old and battered brown cardboard boxes. When we were done, there was a box of soup, one of veggies and another with meat. I picked up a box of pint jars and set them in her waiting arms.

"Is that too heavy?" I asked.

"I'm strong, Nahna, I can carry this," she insisted, so I set a very lightweight case of oriental noodles on top for Jacob, and picking up the other two cases, we went back to the kitchen.

With three cases of food and two buckets of grains and beans, the cart was too heavy for her to pull. Emilee needed to be helpful, this I understood. I took the two buckets out.

"You take these cases back to your house, Em, and just set them on the ground, then come back for the buckets." By the time she had everything unloaded from the wagon, the guys would be moving over there to wrap the porch and they could move the heavy containers up the steps and into the house.

* * *

"Just so you know, Mom, when I was out at the garden getting the chicken wire for Jason, I also started draining the cistern so we could turn it over," Eric announced.

I closed my eyes briefly in relief. "I had forgotten about it! Once that ash starts falling it will turn any water to sludge! Thank you for remembering."

With both the porch and the deck wrapped in a shroud of transparent plastic, Jason was ready to start on closing in the bottoms of the grow boxes. He had already made short doors for access, which he attached first. While Eric was busy building a couple of nesting boxes, John and Jason placed and secured the chicken wire.

The power was still on so I was staying ahead of laundry, doing as much as possible.

Emilee had been assigned the task of catching the baby chicks and putting them in one of the cat carriers I kept. A few of the hens were amiable to being picked up, so she put them in the second carrier and took them to the greenhouse.

Everyone was working smoothly, and we were almost finished when Amanda pulled into the driveway. She'd been gone a long time.

"Whew!" she said. "I'm glad that's all done."

"What is it you've been doing?" I asked cautiously.

She looked at me in surprise. "Moving. Jacob and I packed up all his things and brought them over. I put them in his room at Eric's. Then we packed things for me and Jason, and all the food we have and put that there too."

I'd been so occupied here I hadn't noticed her across the road. I felt embarrassed.

"I made sure everything was unplugged or turned off at our house. Jason still needs to do the rest. I don't know if he wants to drain the pipes or not, but I'm pretty sure I remembered the rest."

"I'm impressed, Amanda, you've done a lot today." I gave her a quick hug.

"Well, you did say we don't have much time. I don't need anything else from there, so I'm going back across the road and start organizing Jacob's room. Are we all having dinner here tonight?" she stood and stretched.

"Of course we are. Seven o'clock."

* * *

At three o'clock, the guys set out for McKenna's Bay. At 4:30 they returned with two thirty-gallon tubs filled with fish! I'm going to be very, very busy canning the next couple of days.

"Oh, Mom, you should have seen it, it was fantastic!" Jason exclaimed. "John mixed up some things, stuffed it into a coffee can, rigged up a detonator and *BOOM!* Water geysered up everywhere! Fish went flying through the air and then dead fish started floating up to the surface, *thousands* of them! It was awesome!"

Eric chortled. "Jason was having a good time."

"We took the skiff out and just scooped them out of the water with the long handled net. They were so heavy, we would fill a tub and then take it back to shore.

"I will never look at fishing the same way again! John, you're the man!" Jason clapped John on the shoulder and walked away smiling.

"I think you guys should get those tubs into the refrigerator in the barn," I reminded them. "And then go take a shower!" I playfully wrinkled my nose at them.

* * *

While Amanda cleared the dishes from the table and set them in hot soapy water, I pulled out my list.

"So far we've wrapped the two decks and moved as much into the greenhouse as will fit. Hmmm, Jason, when you wired your Uncle Don's generator, did he have you build a shelter for it? I've never even noticed."

"You haven't noticed because I hung lattice around the underside of the small porch where it sits. It can be heard though not seen. Why?"

"If it's just lattice, you will have to plastic that too, to keep the ash out of the air intake. Is it vented?"

"No, it isn't." He frowned. "It didn't need to be. We'll figure something out, won't we, Eric?"

"Okay, that's something that will have to be taken care of by the end of tomorrow," I said. "That's our goal: tomorrow. Everything that is outside needs to be finished no later than tomorrow afternoon. During the worst of the cloud, all of you will be isolated there, and us here. Emi and I packed up some food, and I want you to take more with you."

"We won't be coming here for dinners?" Amanda asked with sad eyes.

"Not for maybe a week. It might be okay to come across wearing masks and eye protection, I don't know. I don't think Jacob will take well to stuff on his face." It was something both Jason and Amanda understood.

"So, we've got the chickens in their new home, but we still need the other bale of straw and their feed. I'll do that tomorrow. Gas cans are on the enclosed deck for the generator. Amanda, did you fill the gas cans from Eric's while you were filling the cars?"

"I filled the cans in the back of the old car. Were those the ones, Eric?"

"Yep, and I already moved them down to the generator area, Mom," he replied.

"Excellent! I'm proud of all of you. We'll start cleaning the rest of the fish in the morning, I've got enough done to get started on the canning." I turned to John. "I need to make a quick run into town tonight and drop some things off at the Soup Kitchen."

"More, Allex? Haven't you done enough for them already?" he said in exasperation. "The more you do for them, the more they expect, you know."

"You're right, but when Eric and I went shopping, some of it was meant for them, I just haven't had the time to take it over. We got four ten-pound bags of pasta: three for here and one for them. The kitchen gets just one, plus the large can of spaghetti sauce and a bag of rice. The rest is for us. We'll need it all." I could see he didn't really agree with me, however, it was something he knew I was compelled to do.

"Help me load these few things up, John and then take a ride with me." I turned to my sons. "You've still got some daylight left, will you two gut the fish? I'll start canning when we get back."

* * *

"Carolyn?" I called out, my voice echoing in the stillness of the empty Stone Soup Kitchen. "Where is everyone? I thought they would be moving the Kitchen?"

"Good evening, Allexa," Carolyn said in a way too calm of a voice. "Walk with me, please. You, too John." We set the boxes down on a table in the church basement and followed Pastor Carolyn as she started up the street toward Bradley's Backyard. I don't think I'd ever seen her look so...peaceful.

"What's going on, Pastor?" I asked, reverting back to her title. "Why isn't everyone getting ready?" We had been so busy at home, doing so many different things, I just couldn't figure out why the town wasn't doing the same.

"After that meeting this morning, we had another one at the church," she gave me one of her famous beatific smiles. "The consensus is we will accept what comes." She stopped. "Everyone is tired, Allexa. Tired of fighting, tired of running, tired of being frightened all the time. Oh, we're not going to roll over and die, but what good will all this preparation be if the cloud misses us? Or even if it hits us?" Carolyn took my hand. "Everyone is grateful for what you've done, for all of your efforts and caring. Most are ready to let go and let God. You should try it sometime."

I was bewildered. And I knew that there was nothing more for me to do there.

* * *

"It's their choice, Allex," John reminded me. "This is not something you can force on them, you know that."

"Yes, John, you're right. It's just...I don't know. I thought I knew these people, and I don't, not at all." I stood up and paced across the deck. I ran my hand down the tight sheet of plastic that now covered all the edges, sealing us in.

"Are they right and I'm wrong?"

"I don't think it's a matter of who's right or who's wrong, Allex. It comes back to them making a choice that is best for them. You and the boys are making the choice that is best for you." John paused as if he had more to say.

"I know you, John, you have something to say, and I have a bad feeling that I'm not going to like it." I sat back down on the wrought iron chair and took his big, rough hands in mine. "What is it?"

He pulled his hands free and rubbed them across his face and over his bald head. "I've watched how you and those two fine young men work together. You're so close to them, and they adore you, you know. I envy you that. The three of you are so strong and you think alike. I can see Emilee taking after Eric in this." He smiled. "Even Amanda has come around. She's a good woman. All of you are survivors, and I think that's what bothers you about the town. You feel like they are giving up." John trailed his fingers down my cheek. "It saddens me that my daughter Christine isn't as strong, Allex. She believes that the government will always be there; always take care of the big problems; won't let anything happen to 'the people.' I've failed her in that respect." He took a deep breath before continuing. "I have to make a choice too, Allex. I have to see if I can reach my daughter, to protect her from what's coming."

I felt as if I'd been hit in the chest with a very large hammer.

"You're leaving?" I squeaked out.

"I'll be back, I promise. I have to try and get to her, bring her back here," he said. "If I leave first thing in the morning, I could be in Indiana early on Friday. It's a twenty-four hour drive, I've done it before."

"John, the ash cloud...it could beat you there!"

"If it were your boys, you know you would try to save them."

"Yes, I would." I looked down at our hands, fingers entwined. A single tear escaped as I centered on being practical. "There are things to get ready for your trip, and I need to fill the canner with fish. Then let's make the most of tonight."

CHAPTER TWENTY-EIGHT

We got up early to finish John's travel preparations.

"I think it's best if I left before Eric and Jason know I'm going. They're not going to be happy with me," John said quietly.

"Well, I'm not very happy with you either, but I'd be more worried about Emilee." My lip quivered. I couldn't help it. "It's her birthday today, John, and she loves you." The tears leaked down my cheek.

I had boiled a dozen eggs last night and they were well chilled now. I set them in a plastic baggie, and then into an old blue cooler, along with two loaves of bread and a couple cans of tuna, and a can opener. I had put two one gallon containers of water in the cooler first, one was frozen and would keep everything chilled for at least a day, and once thawed, John could drink it when the other gallon of water was gone. Then I filled a thermos with coffee.

"You might need to bribe your way through checkpoints, John," I said and handed him the cash pouch. "And don't leave the Beretta behind this time. Take an extra box of ammo, too. The road is going to be a dangerous place."

"I have cash, you keep this." He handed the pouch back to me. "I think I will take the Beretta with me. Funny how I feel much safer with it."

We stepped outside.

"I think I should take your old car," John said.

"No, you take the new one. It's more reliable and gets better gas mileage. Just make sure you bring it back to me." I tried to smile, but it was difficult. We loaded an old sleeping bag, his duffle, the cooler and one extra can of gas into the hatch.

"This may seem strange, just trust me," I said and handed him two packages of pantyhose, receiving a very quizzical look.

"There was a TV special years ago about when Mt. Saint Helen's erupted in 1980. One of the issues the locals had to deal with concerning the constant rain of ash was that it kept plugging up the air filters in the vehicles. They solved it by stretching pantyhose over the intake. The ash couldn't get through the fine weave. If you get caught in the cloud John, put one of these on the car before the filter plugs." I was trying very hard to stay calm, stay even, though I felt neither. "And here are three of the newer face masks. They also have an eye shield. Not only can the ash damage the lungs, it can also damage your eyes. There's one for your trip down if needed and one for each of you to come back. And please be careful with your wrist, it's far from healed."

* * *

The car was fully packed and by 6:00 A.M. John was ready to leave. We stood awkwardly by the car, neither of us wanting to be the first to say goodbye.

"I want you to know I believe the town is wrong. I believe you, and I believe *in* you, Allex, and that's why I have to do this," John said.

"I don't want you to go, John," I choked out. "Please, don't leave me, not again. I'm afraid if you leave this time I'll never see you again."

"I love you, Allex, but I have to." He wrapped his arms around me, and held me for the longest time. "I'll be back in a week, I promise." He kissed me and drove away.

Ironically, he was dressed in jeans and his deep green hoodie, exactly what he was wearing when he left me last March.

* * *

I crawled back into bed and wrapped myself around his pillow, drowning myself in his scent, and wept until I was dry and numb. Then calm came over me and I knew John wasn't coming back this time.

I had just finished showering and dressing for the second time this morning, when I heard the voices outside.

"Gosh, Mom, with your car gone we thought you'd gone somewhere or we would have been quieter," Jason said with a sheepish grin. "Did John go somewhere?"

"Yes, he had something to do," I dodged. "What's on the agenda for today?" I asked as I looked at the two double batches, twenty-eight pints, of fish I had stayed up to can last night.

"I thought we should go over your list again and see if there's anything we've missed," Eric said. "I know we need to flip the cistern, and that should take no time at all. Then what?"

"We really need to get those fish cleaned," I said. I set out some cups and poured freshly brewed coffee. Neither of the boys used sugar. Eric had taken a liking to some of Joshua's fresh milk, so I set a small pitcher of it on the table. I picked my cup up and my hands trembled just a bit.

"Let's take a walk around the house and yard. Maybe something that we're forgetting will shout at us," I suggested. I knew that I needed to keep moving, stay focused, or my thin veneer of control might shatter.

Behind the big metal barn, Jason quickly climbed the permanent wooden ladder that was attached to the cistern platform, so he could check the remaining water level.

"Stand back!" he shouted down at us, hefting up one side of the big cattle tank that served as the collection pool, pouring the remnants out over the edge. The few remaining gallons of rainwater splashed heavily onto the ground. Using balance and counter-balance, Jason walked the tank backward and then lowered it, upside down.

"While I was up there, I noticed some blackberries ripening," Jason said. "Maybe Emilee would like to pick some later, Eric. Give her something to do."

It was becoming obvious to all of us that once we had done all we could, it would be difficult to just sit around and wait. We needed to stay busy. I doubted that would be a problem, at least for the next few days.

The three of us finished walking around the back side of the garden, through lush knee high weeds and undergrowth and then we passed under the fruit trees, laden with developing apples and cherries that likely would never ripen. Stopping at the house to replenish our coffee, we checked the list I had started yesterday.

"There's still the other bale of straw to move and the metal can of chicken scratch. I didn't get around to doing that yet, but I will," I said, looking over the list. "And a birthday party to plan," I smiled at Eric. "Has Emi mentioned what she might want for dinner?"

"Pizza is her favorite," Eric grinned. "I think she understands that presents are going to be few if any. The attention might make up for it."

"I still plan on giving her the Bobcat handgun, if that's alright with you."

"She'll love it, Mom. Is there anything else we can do or give her?"

"Well, you can give her a box of ammo and the little holster that fits the gun. I used it as an ankle holster, though it's adaptable to a belt."

"Will John be back in time, Mom?" Eric asked, searching my face.

"No."

I stood and moved to the door, my sons remained silent.

"Let's check the greenhouse, see if anything strikes us there." I was one step in front of the boys, when I turned. "Don had turned that old shed into a smoke house, didn't he? Can you get it fired up? We should smoke some of this fish we have. I'll can two more batches today, though I think over fifty jars of fish should be enough. Maybe Amanda and Emilee can help me clean the rest of them."

"We need to bring in wood for both stoves!" I commented as we neared the new building and I saw the newly constructed woodshed. "Wait a minute... when did you two fill this wood-shed?" It had completely slipped my mind. I had called Keith for the delivery, and I didn't remember seeing the pile of split wood. I know I had lots on my mind at the time, but it would have been hard to miss.

"Keith came by the morning of the mine accident," Eric told me. "Jason and I got it all stacked before you got back. I paid Keith from the pouch. I hope you don't mind."

"Not at all," I replied, bewildered that I hadn't noticed this major chore being done. "Thank you for taking care of it."

"Why do we need to bring in wood now, Mom? It's July!" Jason said.

"If the temperatures drop significantly from the ash cloud blocking the sun, it's going to get cold. I don't want any of us out unless absolutely necessary. And that reminds me, we need to lower the tarps, too, to keep the ash off the wood."

* * *

The greenhouse was crowded, and it was a good crowded. There was green tumbling from the hanging baskets and lots of green in the boxes as the plants acclimated to their new home. The chickens started up a welcoming clucking when we walked in. I threw them a handful of grain and they clustered around it, cackling in pleasure. Jason changed the water in the adult pen, while Eric watered the baby chicks in the other.

I sprinkled some pellets on the surface of the fishpond and smiled at the splashes the little fish made as they gobbled up the food. My eyes rested on the statue in the corner: the bearded gold miner, with water endlessly cascading over his sluice pan. I turned away, only to be confronted by my silent sons.

"What's going on, Mom?" Eric asked first.

"Where did John go?" Jason asked next.

They weren't going to let me slide on this. I sat down on the bench that surrounded the gurgling fishpond.

"He left. He went to Indiana to get his daughter. He said he'd be back in a week, and I have to believe that, though I have my doubts."

Both boys just stood there, still silent. I have to remind myself to stop calling them boys; they are grown men with their own families.

"Well, Mom, you have us, and you know we aren't going anywhere," Eric said, taking my hand and pulling me to my feet. We had a group hug that made me laugh.

"We haven't done that since...I don't remember," I said.

"And don't tell anyone, Mom, or we'll lose our badass status!" Jason quipped.

I took a deep breath and looked at the two of them, so different yet so much alike. Jason, with his dark hair and green/brown eyes; Eric with his clear blue eyes and lighter hair that was now speckled with early gray; yet they were both hard working and compassionate men.

"You're right, I have my family and that's what counts the most. Now, let's get the rest of this stuff done in case that damn cloud shows up early!"

"Mom, before we get started, I wanted to mention that while I was up turning the cistern, I saw several deer close by and moving, heading north, just like the birds," Jason said. "I think Eric and I should take a few hours and do some hunting. A couple of deer hanging in the barn could really help out."

"Excellent idea, just be back in time for Emi's birthday dinner," I reminded them. "Much of this I can do myself, if the girls will help gut the fish."

* * *

We set up work with boards across two sawhorses near the outside faucet. One tub was set to the side to catch the heads and guts of the fish, while the other was partially filled with water to wash the gutted fish. We separated the fish by size. The largest would get smoked, the smallest set aside for us to eat in the next couple of days, and the rest would be canned.

Amanda really caught onto the method of filleting the fish with scales and those were the ones we would use for upcoming meals. The three of us worked quickly and efficiently, finishing our task in less than two hours, while Jacob quietly watched a cartoon movie.

As the next batch of fish pressure canned on the stove, I gazed out over the yard, my thoughts still in turmoil. John had left me again. Why didn't I feel worse? I didn't want to think that I was getting used to his abrupt departures, or maybe I was. Or maybe it was because at least I had some warning this time. Or maybe I was numb to it because I just didn't care anymore. The disappointment, the pain, it was just too much to bear time and time again.

My eyes rested on the herb garden. Even with fresh herbs now in the greenhouse, I should harvest and dry what I could from the raised beds. They would just die in a few days anyway.

I gathered a basket full of oregano and tied it in bunches to hang from the beams in the kitchen. Then I did parsley and sage the same way. The chives don't dry well in that manner, so I got the dehydrator out of the shed and plugged it in. The light oniony scent quickly filled the room so I moved it onto the deck. I lined up several glass jars on the counter to hold the herbs once they dried.

I finished washing and sorting out the remaining fish. A half tub full of the larger ones was ready for the smokehouse, and it looked like enough for a dinner with one more batch in the canner. I was starting to feel fatigued, and there was still so much to do.

I started the dough for the pizza and set it to rise.

The little Bobcat pistol lay on the table, magazine to the side, empty of shells. I took a soft cloth and wiped it down with gun oil. It glistened in the sunlight shifting through the window, a light breeze coming through the opened screen ruffled the papers it sat on.

* * *

I walked across the road to finalize the party plans with Amanda and was met at the bottom of the porch steps by an energetic Emilee.

"Nahna, Dad did the funniest thing this morning," Emilee said. "He made a litter box for Chivas on the porch! Instead of sand, he filled it with grass. He dug up some of the lawn. Good thing my Mom isn't here, she'd have a fit if she saw that!" she giggled.

"He made a litter box for the dog? This I need to see." I followed Emi up the stairs where I saw a two foot by four foot box that looked about eight inches deep, filled with a layer of freshly harvested chunks of lawn, and it dawned on me how useful that would be.

"I think your dad is a very smart man, Emi. What a clever solution! Chivas will need a place to go, you know, pee, and she's still too weak to go down the steps. Besides, once we all have to stay inside, it will be the only place she *can* pee."

I gave her a hug. "Oh, and happy birthday. You're now twelve years old, almost a teenager," I said, realizing how much time had gone by since I had been in Florida to witness her birth.

"Thank you, Nahna," she said quietly. "I know it can't be special, not like other birthdays, because of what's coming." Emi shrugged her little shoulders.

"We will make it as special as we can for you," I promised her. "How would you like pizza for dinner tonight?"

"Yay! I love pizza! Can we have pepperoni on it?" Emi was all smiles now, anticipating a special dinner in her honor.

"I think I still have some left," I assured her, thinking of the venison pepperoni I had made.

I saw my two sons making their way across the creek carrying what looked like a deer between them, so I hurried out to greet them and offer some help.

They had cut down a small tree and after tying the deer's legs together, ran the poles between the feet and then hoisted it across their shoulders. They were carrying a great deal of weight like that.

With his ribs still not completely healed from the altercation a month ago, Eric was soon struggling as he tried coming up the steep hill. They had just stopped to set down the carcass when I met up with them, at which point I took over for Eric to finish bringing the fresh meat up the incline. We got the deer hung in the barn and I was thankful they had already gutted the animal.

"That didn't take long! This is great," I said, beaming at my two hunters as they made short work of skinning the animal.

"I'm just sorry we only got one, Mom. We'll go out again another time," Eric assured me.

* * *

Everyone gathered in the kitchen around six o'clock for dinner. Everyone except John, and his absence was a glaring reminder of the approaching storm.

Eric had told Amanda, Emilee and Jacob that Grandpa John had gone on a trip far away and might be gone for a long time.

"I like Grandpa John. Did he die, Nahna?" Jacob asked in the innocence of an autistic child.

"Oh, no, Jacob, he didn't die! He just had to go see someone who lives a long way away. He said he would be back, but we don't know when." I tried to reassure my grandson. Maybe I was trying to reassure myself. It didn't work on me—I hope it worked on everyone else.

After dinner I brought out a plateful of muffins I had made earlier and put a single candle in the middle one and we all sang happy birthday to our beaming and budding young lady.

"I have a present for you, Emi," I announced. I handed her a box wrapped in Christmas paper, which made her laugh.

Her eyes got very wide and I thought she was going to burst at the seams when she saw the little gun.

"Oh, Nahna, my very own gun..." she said breathlessly. "It's so small, is it real?"

"Definitely very real, but you will need lessons from your dad before you're allowed to shoot it, okay?"

She nodded vigorously, then her Uncle Jason gave her a box of ammo, and Eric gave his daughter the holster, attached to one of her own belts, which pleased her greatly. Amanda presented her with a necklace, a reminder that she was still a girl. Jacob being Jacob surprised us all by giving Emi a hand drawn birthday card. He gave her a hug and a kiss on the cheek, and then went to read one of his new books.

* * *

After our great family night, we got back to business.

"We still need to get the fish smoking and I have another batch of fish for the canner," I commented. "This needs to be done tonight. I know we're putting in long hours and I, for one, am feeling the strain in the way of fatigue."

"We are too, Mom. I think that's why I had such a hard time getting up the hill," Eric said.

"Well, we're not done yet. In another couple of days we will have a deer to butcher and that might mean pulling an all-nighter," I warned them. "Fatigue can do strange things, so we need one person to keep us on track. Amanda, while the three of us are cutting and canning meat, can you be the one to watch the kids, fix our meals, and keep us focused?"

She looked doubtful. "Sure. I guess so."

"You will be the one adult that can sleep. We might be able to figure out a shift of sorts, once these two understand the meat canning process," I said, "but none of us can get much more than a catnap until the meat is done. We just can't risk losing it."

Before everyone left for the night, I reminded them that this was the last day of grid power for three days, and to all take showers, baths and to do laundry.

I settled down to watch some news after I took my shower. The final load of laundry tumbled in the dryer.

"...the reports that have filtered in, we now know that the 9.6 earthquake and the subsequent volcanic eruptions in Yellowstone were felt as far east as Washington, D.C. and as far north as areas in Ontario, Canada.

"No reports yet on how far the eruption of the Valles Caldera in New Mexico was felt. The Valles Caldera, centered in the Jemes Mountains, has been dormant for millions of years and was considered to be a non-threat. The eruption this morning is believed to have been triggered by the Yellowstone eruptions. Government officials are suggesting caution when venturing outdoors, and recommend that those with breathing disorders remain indoors until the possible ash cloud passes.

"On a brighter note, the Detroit Tigers take on the Yankees tomorrow in a home game..."

I turned the TV off. How could they discuss *baseball* at a time like this? I shook my head in disbelief. *Caution when venturing outdoors?* That was unbelievable. People were going to die. Maybe a *lot* of people.

CHAPTER TWENTY-NINE

JOURNAL ENTRY: July 20

It looked like fog, hanging quiet and heavy in the tops of the trees; a slowly moving, shifting mass. It hung there, silently obscuring the morning sun. I wasn't really quite sure if *it* had begun or not. It wasn't what I had expected, but then, what *did* I expect? I called the boys on the FRS radio to let them know that I thought it had started.

The ash cloud settled lower in the branches, filtering more and more of the sunlight until it touched the ground and the shroud was complete. Fine ash and pumice, like motes of dust, gathered on the pavement, only much more deadly than the benign dust it mimicked. A light breeze sprung up and quickly became a brisk wind that lashed at the growing piles of death. The wind pushed first one way and then another, scattering the ash in ever moving tendrils that resembled snakes darting in a confused dance back and forth across the pavement. The wind picked up a handful and swirled it tornado-like down the road, dropping it in another drift.

I was watching the growing gloom in abstract fascination from within the safety of the house when I saw Mark pulling into the driveway across the road late in the afternoon. It was a bad time to make a house call on a dog. I could see he was wearing a mask of some sort though.

Forty-some minutes later I heard knocking on the glass door.

"Mark," I said through the glass, "come around to the greenhouse so you can shake the ash off." He nodded, and I moved through the house to let him in the back way. The ash had been falling for over six hours now.

He stepped into the greenhouse entrance Jason had made to enclose the hand pump on the well. Only then did he remove his hooded jacket then his facemask and goggles, shaking the ash off. I opened the door that led into the warm and humid growing room.

"Mark, you've picked a bad day to come visiting," I commented, as I hung his jacket on a shaker-peg.

"Allexa, we need to talk," he replied quite ominously.

I poured two cups of coffee and we sat at the kitchen table.

"Why are you out and about, Mark? You of all people know how dangerous this first wave of ash might be! We all love Chivas and appreciate your concern for her, but a house call for a dog is not worth risking your life."

He smiled at me and sipped his coffee. "That's just like you, to think of someone else first." Mark set his cup down. "I didn't come to see the dog, I came to see you."

"I'm not sick. And I haven't injured myself again either. So why are you really here?" I sat back, crossing my arms over my chest.

"John came to see me yesterday morning. Damn early I must add!"

"And?"

"And he told me about the last visit the two of you had in town, with Pastor Carolyn. John thought I should know so I could watch the town people and be ready. He believed, *believes*, in the facts you presented to the town, and it made him angry that they were just going to ignore your warnings. I must tell you that is one man I do *not* want angry at *me*!" Mark chuckled.

"Yes, I was very disturbed by their attitude. Fortunately, I don't think everyone thinks that way."

"Well, too many of them do...or did." Mark frowned.

"What do you mean *did*?" I asked, my alarms ringing, and my heartbeat picking up. "Have some of them come back around?" I asked hopefully.

Mark rubbed his hands over his face. "Do you have anything stronger than coffee?" he asked me.

"What's your choice? I have a small variety of alcohol, and not much of that," my breathing was short. I wanted to hear what he had to say, although he needed time and perhaps fortification.

"Bourbon?"

I retrieved the bottle from the back pantry and poured him two fingers in a short glass. He took a sip, then with eyes closed tossed the rest back and set the glass down.

"By any chance do you have some ice?" he asked, gasping from the alcohol's impact.

It was only the first day of the three-day shut off from power. I took a bowl from the silent freezer and dropped three ice cubes in his glass. After he poured more bourbon over the ice, he went on. "Allex, it was horrifying to watch, and I felt so helpless. Within a half hour of the ash cloud's appearance this morning, entire families were walking to or from the church singing hymns. It didn't take long, and the youngest grabbed his throat and screamed. His mother dropped to his side and then crumpled herself. I couldn't even get near them. Then others screamed and fell to the ground. They dropped like flies, Allex! I know it must have been agonizing, and at least it was quick. They just couldn't breathe. The ash lacerated their lungs with a single intake. The rest couldn't get inside fast enough. If they had breathed outside, they were already doomed." Mark stared at his drink.

"How many, Mark?" I asked in a hushed voice. This had to be incredibly hard on a man dedicated to healing.

"At least twenty..." He took a swallow of the amber liquid sloshing around in his glass, his hands trembling.

Twenty? My God, there were only maybe thirty left in the whole town! I was beyond astonished they could be so reckless, so *stupid*.

"That was today, this morning." Mark gathered his thoughts and his composure. "When John stopped by yesterday, he also told me what *he* was doing, where he was going. I tried to talk him out of it, Allex, but he was very insistent. He also asked me to do something for him," he took another sip from his drink, stalling.

"He said he'd be back in a week...he isn't coming back at all, is he?" I blurted out.

"No, he isn't. At least it's very doubtful," Mark confessed. "He said he has to try to reach his daughter. He thinks he will be stopped at some point and not be able to make it back here. There is also a strong chance he will be killed along the way."

I breathed in gulps, keeping my feelings silent by wrapping my heart in a cool, dark blanket.

"He told me that he asked you to marry him," Mark stated, "and that you said no. He didn't tell you this, but he thinks your turning him down has something to do with *me*, Allex. He knows that I have...feelings for you, and that you might return those feelings, even if you deny it now. So he asked me, made me promise, that if and when the clouds got here, that I would come to you, to keep you company during the bad times that are sure to be ahead of us."

"He wants you to *live* here? Mark, moving about is going to be extremely difficult. If you stay here, how can you help the town, the people?" I pressed, even though I was wrought with confusion that John would just pass me over to another man.

"Allex, there's no one left to help! Those few that didn't succumb to this first wave are hunkered down and playing it safe. They don't need me right now. John felt that you might," Mark searched my face. "Do you? Will you?"

"I...I don't know, Mark," I told him honestly. "I do know you can't go back out in this, not yet anyway."

I made up the futon couch for Mark, and in the deepening summer twilight, I sought solace in a dreamless sleep.

* * *

JOURNAL ENTRY: July 21

My mind adjusted quickly when I couldn't see the red numbers of the digital clock on my nightstand. The grid power is out, so coffee will have to be made manually.

The air temp is still mild and not yet affected by the cloud that is hovering around us.

* * *

I slipped on a t-shirt and flannel pants and made my way to the kitchen.

I boiled some water and pulled out the French press, thinking about John, wondering where he was now. Those thoughts didn't last long when Mark came into the kitchen on his way to the bathroom. Burgundy and gray checked lounging pants hung low on his narrow hips, emphasizing his muscular and *bare* chest; a chest sprinkled with dark, curly hair that trailed down over a flat abdomen, forming a V that disappeared below the waistband.

I couldn't help but stare. He was a very good-looking man. When I realized he had stopped moving, my eyes flashed up to his smiling face.

"Good morning, Allex," Mark grinned, and moved past me.

If the heat I felt was any indication over my embarrassment, my face must be flushed bright crimson.

"Good morning," I mumbled, and went back to fixing coffee with shaky hands. The desire I had felt shocked me.

* * *

"We need some ground rules, Mark," I said as we sat at the table, coffee in hand and muffins in the center of the distance between us.

"Do we?" he asked, another grin forming on his perfect lips. He took a bite of a blueberry muffin. "These are very good, Allex."

"Yes, we do, and the first rule is you can't walk around half naked. Please put a shirt on."

He chuckled and went into the other room, returning while pulling a gray t-shirt over his head.

"That better?"

"Yes, thank you." I said, looking away from his intense blue eyes. When had they gotten so dark? "I believe in being honest, Mark, so I'm going to admit that I find you very attractive," I held up my hand as he tried to interrupt, "however, you can't expect me just to switch my affections from John to you because he *might* not be coming back. He's been gone less than three days!"

"You're absolutely right, Allex. It was unfair of me to be so obvious," Mark admitted. "I promise to control myself. When you come to me, it will be because you *want* to."

We fell into an uneasy silence as I poured more coffee.

"The muffins really are very good. John said you're an incredible cook," Mark said, moving on to a safer subject.

"Thank you. I tried to bake ahead knowing the power would be out for a few days. The stove is gas, and can be used with just a match, however, the oven needs electricity to stay on," I informed him, babbling. "During the cooler months it isn't an issue, since our... my...heat comes from that cook stove over there." I pointed to my wood burner, stumbling over my words.

Mark glanced over his shoulder. "Why don't you use it now?"

"It would make it too hot in here. However, it might be a good time to try the summer kitchen out. That will be my project for the day." I smiled at his confusion. "You passed the other cook stove when you came into the greenhouse," I said, relaxing some as I explained one of the functions of my homestead. "Jason designed the greenhouse to have multiple functions. That cook stove burns wood too, and will only heat up that room not the house, plus the plants love the heat. If it gets too hot, it can be vented. During the cold months, it will add the needed heat to supplement the passive solar. I suppose I could run the generator to use the gas oven, but I'm looking forward to trying the summer kitchen out."

"I wonder just how much passive solar will be available from here out, Allex," he thought out loud.

It didn't slip by me that he'd taken to calling me Allex instead of Allexa. I also noticed that I didn't really mind.

"It could become a problem. We'll deal with it when it comes along." A thought rumbled through my mind. "I see another problem approaching, Mark."

"What's that?"

"Explaining you to my family across the road."

"Already taken care of, Allex. Yes, I checked on the puppy while I was there, and she's doing very well, by the way, but my main reason was to talk to your sons. Another suggestion that John made."

"You told them you were staying here? Before I knew?" I stood, angry at the implication.

"Please, Allex, it wasn't like that," Mark said. "John said you don't keep anything from your sons, but some of it coming from me might be easier. On you and on them. He wanted me to tell them it was his idea, so they would accept it better. Was he wrong?"

"I don't know, Mark. I just feel like so much control of my life has been taken away from me." I sat back down. "How did they take it?"

"Although he wasn't against me being here, Eric wasn't sure it was a good idea. Jason is all for it. I guess we just have to make the best of it and wait."

* * *

I had decided to leave the t-shirt on and just add a pair of jeans when I spotted the money pouch on my dresser where I had tossed it the morning John left. Thinking it would be better to put it back in my drawer, I moved it, only to discover what it had been hiding for the last two days: another envelope, a folded piece of paper, and the ring box.

I opened the box to find a beautiful diamond and emerald ring set in yellow gold, but no wedding band. When John proposed I never did see it. I closed the box and set it aside.

The folded sheet was a simple note:

Allexa,

I know I said I will be back in a week, but if I'm not back in two weeks, I didn't make it and I want you to move on.

The doctor is a good man.

Don't forget me,

John

I set the note aside, my heart heavy with the grief I knew was coming, and picked up the other envelope. It was thick and heavy, and inside it was filled with one hundred dollar bills. John had left behind a great deal of his hazard bonus.

I swept all of it into the drawer and closed it, then finished getting dressed.

* * *

Tufts made a rare appearance and followed me out to the greenhouse. I thought about what Eric had done for Chivas and wished I had done something like that for my cat. Maybe I still could.

"I need to get some things from the barn. I'll be back in a few minutes," I told Mark, as I pulled on the thin white papery biohazard suit that would protect my skin. I pulled the hood up and secured it, adding the tight fitting goggles and surgical respirator, and then gloves.

"It still amazes me what you have on hand, Allex. When you get back in, you'll have to tell me why," Mark said.

The small anteroom was beginning to feel like an airlock, and maybe that was what we *should* think of it as.

* * *

In the barn, I found the old litter box that had a crack in the bottom. Useless as a litter box now, I had been using it for weeding or moving plants. I rummaged in the corner where I kept all the gardening stuff, hoping to find a bag of potting soil, and then remembered there were still two buckets full of fresh soil in the greenhouse. I found the bag of grass seed I used for the chickens' yard and set it aside. I found a rake and shovel and after pushing aside an inch of ash, I dug up a big chunk of lawn. I took it all back with me.

"May I inquire what you're planning on doing?" Mark asked, looking at everything I had brought in.

"I had forgotten that Tufts might want some fresh grass to chew on or just to sit in. Hopefully this will satisfy him," I replied. Before removing my protective gear, I pumped some water into a bucket and rinsed the clinging gray ash from the blades of grass.

With the grass in the center of the flat plastic pan, fresh dirt piled around it sprinkled with seed and then watered, I set it on the floor. If Tufts takes to it, great, if not, it was something to do that kept my mind off the note hidden in my dresser.

My white bio-suit hung next to Mark's hooded jacket. Masks and goggles in a small pail on the floor. Protection needs to be always available, always ready. Something we would have to work on more.

* * *

"I thought we were going to start up that other stove?" Mark said.

"We will. I think we need to talk some first. You need to know why I do what I do, why I have what I have, and why I feel this way," I answered. There are things that were so clear to me, but others just didn't understand. "Plus I have a few questions about yesterday, though I've been hesitant to ask."

"Ask away," Mark said. I knew his smile wouldn't last long when I start asking questions.

"All those people who died yesterday, where are they? What did you do with them?" And as I suspected, Mark's good mood vanished.

"The town handyman, Pete, and I moved them into the nearest house," he said, a shadow passing over his face. "We couldn't just leave them lying in the street for wild animals to desecrate them. I wasn't thinking at the time that the wild animals are just as susceptible to the ravages of this ash as we are. The thought made both of us want to move the bodies to safety anyway."

"So Pete wasn't one of the victims, that's good. I like Pete, he's a good man," I paused. "Who else made it? Who is left alive?"

He looked at me, sorrow filling his very being.

"Pastor Carolyn was the only one to stay inside, Allex, along with your friends, Bob and Kathy. The very young, the very old, all of them went quickly if they weren't wearing protective gear. I still don't understand why they did this. Such a waste!"

"Who is still alive, Mark?"

"When I left Pete, Lenny took over helping him. I didn't see anyone else moving around."

"My friends, Bob and Kathy, you actually saw them?"

"Yes, they were helping Pastor Carolyn in the Stone Soup Kitchen. Even inside they were wearing their masks," he reached for my hand. "They were smart enough to heed your warning. I know I'm glad I did."

So many gone. I closed my eyes and pictured Pastor Carolyn the last time I saw her. She looked so peaceful, so ready to accept whatever came. Well, her god sent her this and it almost killed her.

"So now it's your turn, Allex," Mark said. "How is it you seem to have whatever someone needs?"

I gave him a sad smile. "I've long felt there would be a disaster that I needed to live through. The bio-suits, and boxes of masks and gloves? I thought it would be for a flu pandemic of some kind. I never, ever pictured what we have here." I swept my arm out, parting the curtains from the window beside the polished table. The view was dismal: everything was coated in gray and black ash. It clung to the leaves on the trees and bushes, the green almost completely obscured. It covered the yellow pine picnic table where we had sat not two days ago. It coated the black asphalt road. And it was still coming down, drifting silently, smothering the life out of anything living.

"I didn't stop there, Mark, oh no, not me. I worried about *everything*, not just a pandemic flu. I studied and researched. I knew that so many things that could happen likely wouldn't. I still got ready in case, just in case, an invasion or nuke or economic collapse *did* come at us! And all that research told me that we would need the same things no matter what it was that finally took us down: shelter, heat, food, water and security." I turned as I paced, facing this man *my* man had chosen for me. My breathing was getting labored. I knew I had to continue, I had to get my emerging dark thoughts out or I would burst.

"By the way, even after feeding so many this past winter I still have close to five years of food out in the sheds. At least another ton of wheat waiting to be ground into flour so I can keep making bread for my family; another ton of rice and other grains; freeze dried this and that; soaps and shampoo; coffee? Eventually we'll run out, but not for a long time! And books…books that tell me how to do what I don't know how to do already." I could feel the tears welling up, spilling over. "And for what, Mark? *For what*? So I could watch my friends and family die? This, this *ash* could kill us all! If not today or tomorrow, then next year! Did I save us just so we could watch the world end in a slow painful death?"

I was standing near the glass door. I reached for the handle to open it, to let the ash in, to let death in, when I felt Mark's arms wrap around me from behind, pulling me away.

"No, Allex, no!" he said into my ear, holding me against his hard chest.

I struggled, and then I let out a sob, and turned in his arms. I laid my head against him and circled his trim waist with my arms, trembling.

Mark held me secure until I stopped.

"What brought this on, Allex? Something I said?"

I dragged myself from his warmth and retrieved John's note from my room. I laid the note on the table and pushed it toward Mark. After he read it and set it down again, he pulled me back into his embrace, holding me close and tight.

"It's going to be a long two weeks," he whispered to no one.

CHAPTER THIRTY

We stood there, holding each other, my head against his chest, his chin resting on top of my head. After the failed relationships I've had, all I've desired is for a man to hold me like he wanted to, and to kiss me like he meant it. I had that with John; would I find that with Mark?

"So my strong and independent Allex has a vulnerable side?" Mark chuckled softly.

"Please don't tell anyone. It'll ruin my image." I smiled up and him and moved away, pulling up my shields once again.

"Do you think we should go into Moose Creek to see if they need help to... to...bury the bodies?"

"We could, if you want," Mark said. "We would have to take your car, mine was running really rough by the time I pulled in yesterday."

"Rough? Ah, the ash likely clogged up your air filter. We can fix that," I said to a surprised doctor. "Would you like one of the bio-suits? They're really easy to get in and out of and surprisingly easy to move around in, too."

"And just how many extras do you have?" he asked with a smirk.

"None are extra," I said with a straight face, and then smiled. "I stored a dozen of various sizes." I got the bin of medical supplies out of the closet and retrieved a packaged suit for him, along with one of the one-piece masks.

"Please understand, Mark, I don't mean to be rude, but how much do you know about your car? Can you find your air filter? Sometimes they're not so obvious."

"No offense taken. I wasn't always a doctor, Allex, I think I can remove the filter, and not even need a scalpel," he joked.

"Okay, let's suit up and take a look." I grabbed a package of pantyhose on the way out the door.

Mark popped the hood, and undid the cover to the air filter. He handed the dirty and clogged device to me. I tapped it hard several times against the nearest tree, loosening an amazing amount of ash, and gave it back to him. Once the cover was on again, I fitted the panty hose over the cover, tying the legs into a knot and out of the way.

Mark stared at me and shook his head. He took several boxes out of the back seat, handing me a couple and took an armload himself.

"Did you put *pantyhose* on my car?" he asked, aghast, once we were back in the house.

"The fine mesh will keep the ash out of the filter, and will be easier to clean," I said with a grin, and then changed the subject. "What's in the boxes?"

"I couldn't very well leave all my medical supplies and instruments unguarded in my office, could I? Most of it is pharmaceuticals that need a cool place. Any suggestions?"

"Better to have them here, yes." I agreed. "You can store what you need to in the refrigerator. Right now it's only cool anyway." While he unloaded those two boxes into the silent appliance, I retrieved another jug of ice from the upright freezer, and put the melted one back in.

"One of the things I do, and I need you to do too, is rotate the ice blocks when we don't have power, and to make sure there is always ice freezing when we do." It was one of those many things I didn't even think about anymore, I just did it.

"I can do that, Allex, anything to make your work a little easier," Mark said. "When we come back, or in the next few days, if you don't mind, I'd like to look over what you might have in the way of medical supplies. That's another thing I can take completely off your hands, the doctoring."

When I looked alarmed, he added, "There will be times when I'll need your help, you've already proven to be an excellent assistant."

My FRS crackled.

"Mom, are you receiving?" Jason asked.

"Yes, Jason, I'm here," I answered quickly. "Anything wrong?"

"No, I just wanted to warn you that I'm on my way over. I have something to show you and I need some things from the barn. Out."

I certainly didn't mind delaying what we had to do.

* * *

As I watched Jason approach I chuckled. My youngest son's inventiveness never ceases to amaze me. He was holding an umbrella that had a heavy, clear plastic bag draped over it. The bag came down to his knees.

Without me even suggesting it, Jason came to the greenhouse door and shook his umbrella suit a second time, and then stepped into the humid heat and removed his facemask.

"So what do you think of my idea?" He grinned at me. "Good morning, Doctor," he said, acknowledging Mark.

"Very clever, Jason, and I'm glad to see you wearing the mask too. What made you think of this?"

"I'm trying to rig something for Jacob. When I tried the mask on him, he freaked," Jason frowned. "I do have some ideas; maybe making a bubble for him to sit in the wagon, I'm just not sure. Do you have any extra umbrellas I can use to make my contraption for the others?"

"Of course. I'll get them."

When I returned with three umbrellas, it was obvious Mark and Jason had been in a deep discussion.

"Mom, I think Dr. Mark is right, and that Eric and I should go with you two into town. It's the least we can do, and we can get the task done that much quicker," Jason stated, and he wasn't going to take 'no' for an answer.

"Fine. In fact, I think it *is* a good idea. I'll get two more suits," I said, going back to rummage through the tub of medical supplies.

"We will need more room than your little compact for the four of us, Mark, so I'm going to rig my car air filter the same way. We should be ready to leave as soon as the boys come back," I said, "and while I do that, you might want to look through my little black bag, and make whatever changes you feel appropriate. I didn't see one in everything you brought in." I handed him my very stuffed black purse.

"Doctors don't carry little black bags anymore, Allex."

"Well, times they are a'changing, Doctor," I grinned, heading out the door.

* * *

The four of us, suited up, gloved and masked with the eye shield units, drove into a ghost town: downtown Moose Creek. The ash dust streaked across the road and settled in the church parking lot. We parked near the home Mark indicated housed our departed citizens.

It was eerie and way too quiet, until I heard the rumble of machinery. The four of us walked up the main street following the noise, and as we approached the cemetery, I could see Pete on the bulldozer, digging up the baseball field next to it. He was wearing a long sleeved red shirt with the cuffs tucked into rubber dishwashing gloves, covered by gray leather work gloves. When he saw us approaching, he stopped. His face was covered with one of the surgical masks I had handed out, plus a diving mask for his eyes; odd looking, but effective.

"Pete," I called out so he would know who we were. I imagine we looked as odd to him as he did to us.

"Allexa?" he said, climbing down from the machinery. "I'm so glad you're here!" He pulled me into an awkward hug.

"Are you doing this all alone, Pete?" Eric asked.

"Lenny went home to rest and to get something to eat. I thought I would get this part done. There's no room left in the cemetery, Allex, in case you're wondering. I'm just about finished here."

"Pete, we've come to help. Eric, Jason, Dr. Mark and I, we will help you bury everyone," I said. "If there is an open bed pickup truck, we can start loading the... people."

He tossed Jason the keys to the black township truck parked next to the ball field. While Jason drove, the three of us walked the two deserted blocks.

* * *

It was a heart-wrenching task. The agony or surprise etched upon the faces of the townspeople was almost too much for me to bear. The seven children were the hardest. I picked up a small child that was perhaps five years old; he weighed next to nothing and was stiffening with rigor mortis. I wrapped him gently in a sheet and laid him in the back of the truck, trying not to look at his innocent face.

We would not just dump these people into a hole. I went searching for more sheets and found more bodies.

"Mark, could you come in here please?" I called out to the doctor. Eric and Jason were making quick work of this unpleasant task, wrapping each person then moving them to the truck. The bed sheets were very effective body bags.

"Oh," he said when he saw the two people on the bed, forever frozen in lasting embrace.

"Can you tell what they died from?" I asked from behind my mask.

"At this point, I don't think it matters much, does it?" he sounded bitter. "It wasn't the ash though. It appears to be suicide." He reached into a pocket and retrieved the man's wallet, slipping it into the bag we had been collecting IDs in. Some of the victims didn't have wallets or purses, and it was getting increasingly difficult to recognize faces. It was July and it was still warm; rigor wasn't the only thing we had to worry about. I searched the next house for more sheets.

* * *

We had all twenty-two people laid in the bed of the truck and Jason drove slowly to the new gravesite. I wanted to rip off my mask to get some fresh air, although I knew there *wasn't* any fresh air, not here anyway.

Lenny had returned by the time we arrived with our grisly load. One at a time, we moved the sheet wrapped bodies into the mass grave, laying them side by side in a final defiant stance against the cloud of deadly ash. Death shrouds of flowered sheets and striped, bold colors and bleached white; everyone was given the tender dignity they deserved as we laid them to rest.

The five of us stood silent while Eric recited the Lord's Prayer. Then Pete climbed back onto the growling bulldozer and finished the burial. This was the part I couldn't watch.

* * *

"Mom," Jason said, "it's too late in the day for me to make more of my umbrellas for all of us to come here, so why don't you and Dr. Mark come over to us for dinner? Amanda and I will cook up the rest of the fish."

"Thank you, Jason. I don't know if I'm up to it."

"I think that's an excellent idea, Jason," Mark cut in. "We'll be over in an hour."

"Allex," he said, running his hands down my arms, "you need something to take your mind off of what we did today. In fact, we *all* need a diversion, and I think visiting your family is the best thing I could prescribe."

I looked down at the floor before answering. "You're right, I tend to hide when I'm upset and that's not good. I'm going to start the generator so we can take showers first. Even though I know we were well covered, I still feel... contaminated."

While the generator was running for the second shower, I refilled a couple of buckets of water and washed our morning coffee cups. The lack of dishes made me realized we had skipped lunch. I felt like I wasn't being much of a hostess and decided I would make an extra nice dinner tomorrow.

* * *

Amanda had fried the fish that didn't make it to the smoker and served it with home canned corn and green beans. Emilee had made her first solo loaf of bread, which delighted me.

"I'm so proud of you, Emi! This tastes wonderful," I told her.

"Dad wants me to learn something new now," Emi replied. "I think I'd like to try something sweet."

"Maybe tomorrow we can make sweet rolls, would you like that?"

She gave me a big smile and nodded, just as her father came up from the basement with a pitcher of freshly brewed beer.

"I had this cooling when the power went out, so it's ready to drink, just not real cold."

Not being a drinker, Amanda had some coffee, while Eric, Jason, Mark and I enjoyed a second pitcher of beer.

* * *

Night was quickly approaching when Mark and I walked home. The heaviness of the ever present cloud darkened the air even further and I held onto his hand as we navigated through the dim light, more for him than for me; I knew the way in total darkness.

"I think I had a bit too much of Eric's beer!" I exclaimed, rubbing my temples to ease the growing headache. "Plus it's been a long, long day. I'm turning in. Good night, Mark." I turned to leave, when he stopped me.

"You might have that vulnerable side, Allex, but when it counts, you do what needs to be done, I admire that. With you as an example, it's no wonder your sons have turned out so well." He pulled me into his arms for a brief hug, and we headed to different rooms.

I tossed and turned for a couple of hours, not being able to rid myself of the vision in my head of bodies lined up at the bottom of a deep, dark hole, laying there in pink and flowered sheets.

Dressed in sweat pants and a t-shirt, I went into the TV room where Mark slept on the futon. I laid down on the edge so I was just barely touching him. The comfort of another person seeped into my bones. He turned on his side and draped a protective arm over me. And I slept.

* * *

I stretched, and then remembered where I was. I moved slowly to not waken Mark.

"Don't leave, Allex, this feels good," he said sleepily, pulling me back against him.

I lay back down, snuggling into the covers. Yes, it felt very good.

"Don't wiggle like that! It's disturbing," he groaned in frustration.

I froze. Any movement on my part might be interpreted as an invitation on his part. I stood up quickly, and embarrassed, I headed for the kitchen to make coffee.

* * *

With the water boiling for coffee, I washed my face and got dressed, trying to compose myself.

"Mark, I'm sorry…"

"Stop! No apologies, Allex. Look, I'm not even going to ask why you crawled in bed with me during the night, because I know why." He faced me now, with concern and sympathy etched on his tanned face. "Yesterday was a very traumatic day for all of us. Human contact can be a good remedy for soothing that stress. I know there wasn't anything else you were seeking, Allex, but you have to understand that my desire for you is real. I can't and I won't deny that, and being together like this and alone is…difficult. So until you want *me* the same way I want you, I think it best if you stayed out of my bed."

I couldn't help it, and I started laughing. A moment later, Mark was laughing too.

"Mark, you need to understand that I'm a touch-oriented person. I've been a massage therapist for over twenty-five years; I have a need to touch and be touched. John was right, he knew I wouldn't do well without company, without someone to give me a hug when I needed it," I said seriously, searching his face. "And you're right, that's why I came to you this morning. I needed that contact."

"I do understand that, Allex," he smiled gently at me. "Do you need a hug now?"

I nodded. He reached for me and I laid my head on his shoulder, inhaling his scent. Closing my eyes, I could feel myself relax as the heat of his arms warmed my back and his own unique musky scent warmed my heart and soul.

Mark's unshaven jaw was so close to me I could feel the roughness as I pulled back a slight bit. Without thinking what was about to happen, I touched his lips with mine. His response was instant. His hold tightened and loosened at the same time as the strength and depth of the kiss changed. It felt as if he was drawing something out of me, demanding a raw passion I hadn't experienced before, not even with John. I plunged forward, out of control.

My breathing came in ragged gasps when I stepped back, breaking the contact.

"Whoa," Mark said his breath as erratic as mine. "Ever since that first kiss on your birthday, I haven't been able to get our chemistry out of my mind, Allex. This time, this was different, way more powerful. What are we going to do now?"

"Nothing, Mark." I released my hold of him. "I needed that kiss and I think you did too. I also need to wait that full two weeks before we...well, before we explore our feelings any further. I couldn't live with myself otherwise."

"It's going to be a long nine days, Allex," Mark sighed. "No crawling in bed with me, and no more kisses either. Maybe we should limit the hugs too." He sat hard into the kitchen chair, clearly shaken.

"Okay, doctor, I will restrain myself," I snickered as I worked the French press and made our morning brew.

While Mark munched on another muffin, I noticed my black medical bag sitting on the side bar.

"Have you had a chance to look through the medical bag yet? I think you should adjust what you prefer is in it so you don't have any surprises at an inopportune moment."

"Not yet, but there's no time like the present." He pulled the bag to sit in front of him, and started going through the exterior pockets first. "This is a purse isn't it? A woman's purse? This might ruin my image you know, especially with the brass studs on all the pockets.

"First end pocket, band aids; second end pocket, eye dropper, Neosporin and Darvocet?" He set the pill bottle aside. "A good idea, I want to replace it with fresh though. "Front pockets: individual alcohol wipes; gloves in a baggie and surgical masks in plastic baggie." He looked up at me. "That's a good idea to have them on the outside and immediately available."

He unzipped the main compartment and removed everything from inside the bag. The stethoscope, ace bandages, surgical items and finger blood pressure machine, plus all the miscellaneous things I tucked in there were all laid out.

"What's with the red wash cloths?"

"It came from a discussion that it might be easier on a child when wiping blood," I explained. "If the cloth is already red, seeing blood will be less traumatic."

"Interesting idea, I'll have to remember that," Mark mumbled. "All this is remarkable. What's with the shoelaces?"

"A tourniquet or a sling," I replied.

"They would work in a pinch," he allowed. "And certainly takes up little room."

"Is there anything missing, doctor?"

"Very little, Allex, I'm impressed." Mark sat back in his chair, reaching for his now cold coffee.

"'Very little'..." I probed. "What's missing, Mark?" I really wanted to know. I had worked hard on that kit.

"It needs updated pain-killers and hypodermics, and that's about it."

"Hypos are just not something I had available to me, sorry."

"Don't apologize, Allex. If this was all I had available to me, I'd be well prepared for most situations. You did very well." He smiled broadly, getting up for the coffee pot. "By the way, where did you get the surgical items, the sutures, clamps and scalpels?"

"The Internet. You can find just about anything if you keep looking long enough," I answered and then I thought I would save the military field medic bag for another time.

* * *

At noon my FRS squawked.

"Mom, are you there?"

"Yes, Eric, I'm here."

"I'm sending Emilee over for her next baking lesson," he replied. "She'll be coming to the greenhouse door; out."

I watched out the large recently replaced picture window until I saw Emilee crossing the road. She had white garbage bags on each leg and carried a shorter version of Jason's umbrella bubble. Once inside the outer room, she shook the remaining gray ash dust off her smiley-face umbrella and stepped into the greenhouse, and only then did she pull down her facemask.

"Dad and Uncle Jason have been very strict with me about how I dress when I come over here, Nahna. They can be a real pain in the butt!"

"You have to do what they say, Emi. It's for your own good. Don't worry, though, this won't last forever."

"How much longer, Nahna?" she asked, clearly exasperated with all the extra precautions she was now required to do.

"I have no idea, Em, no one does."

* * *

We made up a basic batch of bread dough, adding several eggs to the mix plus a tablespoon of cinnamon. I looked on and supervised while Emilee mixed the additional items into her now familiar recipe for bread, and I let her knead the dough without my help.

"This feels different, Nahna."

"It's because of the eggs, Emi, they add a different texture." She'd been an excellent student and that reminded me of teaching the boys to cook when they were younger. Neither one had been very interested in baking though. And now having her to teach was a delight, plus it was keeping my mind off of Mark.

While it was on the first rise, I had her pick out what she wanted to put in her sweet rolls.

"They must have sugar and more cinnamon and nuts and raisins! And some of that white frosting stuff!"

"That white frosting stuff is a powdered sugar glaze," I instructed her as we collected all the items from the back pantry and lined them up on my butcher-block topped mobile work island.

After the short first rise was done, we rolled the dough out, filled it with her selection of nuts and raisins plus more cinnamon sugar. Emi's little hands had some trouble rolling the dough so we each took an end. She cut the dough, placed the sweet spirals close together on a cookie sheet and then draped it with a light cloth towel.

"Just another half hour of the dough rising, Emi, and we can bake!" She squealed with delight. I punched the pre-heat button on the stove, and then remembered we didn't have power back yet.

"I guess we need the generator."

"If you show me how, Allex, I can be doing that for you," Mark offered.

I got a wave of deja vu and mentally heard John making the same offer last December. I smiled to cover my memories and led Mark out to the deck.

* * *

An hour later the house was overflowing with the sugary sweet aroma of fresh baking. As much as I steered away from sweets, this luscious scent was making me hungry.

"Oh, my, that smells wonderful," Mark announced as he returned from sitting on the deck, reading.

Emilee beamed. "Would you like to try one, Dr. Robbins?"

"I would love to share one with you and your Nahna. We certainly don't want to hog them all! You need to take most of them back home with you," Mark teased her, as he cut one of the confections into three pieces, placing the biggest piece in front of me.

"I think you like Nahna," Emilee announced, embarrassing Mark. Shyness was never one of Emilee's drawbacks.

He looked up and smiled. "Yes, I like your Nahna very much," he replied, looking at me from beneath his long, dark lashes.

"Well, I know she likes you, too. I can tell," Emi stated quite matter-of-factly. "She gets all quiet when you're around, like she used to do with Grandpa John before he left us."

The room was suddenly quiet.

"I think it's time to get you back home, Emi, so you can share your goodies while they're still warm," I told her.

I wrapped the remaining sweet rolls in a sackcloth towel, then into one of the few remaining white plastic shopping bags, and then into one of the cloth bags that we'd been using to send things back and forth.

Instead of her bag-leggings, I put Emilee into one of the small bio-suits. She still needed her facemask and the umbrella. She was more protected, and looked and acted more grown up now.

"Eric, are you listening?" I asked over the FRS radio.

"I'm here," he replied.

"I'm sending Emi back across."

Just as she made it to the road, a red pickup truck came careening out of nowhere. Emilee fell to the ground just as the truck passed her and kept going. Moments later I heard a loud crash.

"Mark!" I yelled, slipping on the eye-shield facemask and running out the door, forgetting the rest of the protective wear.

I knelt down beside my granddaughter.

"Emi," I said gently. She looked at me through the plastic umbrella with tears in her eyes. "Are you hurt?"

"No, Nahna, but that bad truck scared me, a *lot*. Dad taught me to watch everything when I crossed a road, and when I saw that truck coming I waited. When it got closer and I knew it wasn't slowing down and it was too close to me, I jumped back and I tripped and fell."

I hadn't seen them arrive, but Eric and Mark were suddenly both there, kneeling in the gray dust. Eric was both angry and distraught, as he hugged his little girl, fire showed in his blue eyes.

"Do you feel any pain anywhere, Emilee?" Mark asked gently.

"No, but I think I squashed some of the sweet rolls."

"Did the truck hit you Emi?" Eric wanted to know.

"No, Dad, I jumped out of the way like you told me to do. You said if I ever thought I was in danger, to listen to myself and to move out of the away. That was right, wasn't it?"

"You did good, Bug. You did real good," Eric reassured her, using his baby-name for her.

All the time they were talking, Mark was tenderly feeling her legs and arms for any broken bones. He gave me a smile with the slightest shake of his head, sending a slight dusting of ashes cascading over his eye shield.

"No broken bones for you, young lady!" he announced. "As for those damaged sweet rolls, perhaps I should examine them further?" Mark's joke got Emi giggling as he helped her stand.

"Eric, are you armed?" I asked and he nodded yes. "I think you and Mark should check the crash site for survivors."

I walked Emi back to their house, remaining on the porch since I was still covered in ash.

"Is she okay, Mom?" Jason asked worriedly once Amanda had taken Emi into the house.

"As far as Mark can tell, yes. I'm worried about Eric though. He's so angry. I'm going to the crash site to make sure he doesn't do anything…unnecessary."

The red pickup truck was lying half in the ditch, half around the "curve-in-the-road" sign near the end of the road. Steam rose from the ruptured radiator, and the smell of gas was prevalent even with the mask covering my nose.

Mark and Eric were kneeling beside something in the dust-covered grass. A body. I came to a halt a few yards away, and walked up slowly to not startle my agitated son.

Mark looked up first, and stood. He stopped me short of the scene.

"Leave him be for a few moments, Allex," Mark suggested. "When we got here, this guy was half out of the truck, thrown out by the impact is my guess. I saw too many of these kind of accidents down in Saginaw." That cloud passed over his eyes again, and was quickly gone. "He was struggling for breath. The ash is my guess, so either way he was already dead. I asked Eric to end the suffering." He looked over where Eric was still kneeling.

"He's an interesting young man, Allex. In anger or protecting his loved ones, he has no remorse, but euthanizing another human being, he couldn't do it. Once I told him I believed there was no malice behind the near accident and that it was quite likely the old man was in panic not being able to breathe and that he probably didn't even see Emi, Eric's whole demeanor changed."

I came up behind my son and laid a hand on his shoulder.

"Come, Eric. This gas is about to go."

The three of us quickly lifted the crash victim into the bed of the pickup truck. Mark removed the elderly man's wallet from his denim jacket, while Eric said a prayer.

We were halfway back down the silt covered asphalt road when the truck exploded into a funeral pyre.

* * *

"Will this tragedy ever end, Mark?" I slumped in the wooden chair, a finger of rum left in my glass. The bagged blocks of ice I had made while the power was on were almost gone, but there was still enough to chip for cooling a drink. "It seems that every time things start to even out a bit, something else happens to throw us off balance again."

"It does seem to be never ending, doesn't it," he replied. "How are you holding up, Allex?"

I gazed at the man across the table from me. "I'm getting weary, doctor. How about you?"

"I've had more practice," he said with a smile that didn't reach his eyes. "I will say I'm eating better than I have in the past. What was it you fixed for us? It was wonderful," he said, deftly changing the subject.

"I call it mock chicken Parmesan. Just a jar of home canned chicken reheated in my own spaghetti sauce, with a few extra herbs and then topped with Parmesan cheese. I used pasta this time. If you prefer rice, we can have that next time."

"I think it was perfect just the way it is, and thank you." This time the smile did reach his eyes, just as the power flickered on.

"Power wasn't due back on until midnight! Maybe we can catch some news." I left the dishes on the table and turned on the TV. We could have the TV on with the generator any time we wanted, however, the cable satellite, as well as the cellphone tower, needed power too and that had to come from the grid.

"...And on the national front, the ash cloud from the new volcano, Mount Yellowstone, is slowly moving out across the Atlantic Ocean, much to the relief of everyone affected. Officials are saying that by listening to the staff at FEMA and the CDC, and following the instructions of your local emergency services, the injury total has been kept to a minimum," the young blonde newscaster said with a confident smile. The camera shook, distorting the live broadcast, and a new face appeared.

"Don't believe this political media crap! It's all lies! My name is Dustin Abernathy, and I'm a doctor at the Montrose Medical Clinic. I lived in Cleveland, Ohio when the cloud hit and I watched thousands die in just a few hours! Tens of thousands! You have to know the truth! People are still dying and they're dying because our government is lying to them about how to deal with this Drifting Death! Stay inside, everyone, don't breathe the ash cloud! It will kill you by slicing your lungs to shreds! Protect yourself!" In the background, the blonde reporter was being restrained by a man with a surgical mask covering half of his face. A shot was heard over the screams of that young newscaster, and Dr. Abernathy slumped across the polished glass podium. The screen went blank.

We sat there momentarily stunned. Mark grabbed the remote and changed channels. A jittery camera shot rolled across the TV as we watched mobs of people running in the streets, only to be indiscriminately mowed down by automatic gunfire from the gas-masked swat teams billeted behind armor plating. Buildings were burning behind and around the mob, but also behind the shooters, the raging fires being a great equalizer. The camera panned the crowd again in time to catch the explosion from a building a block behind the protesters. The concussion was so great that everyone stumbled or fell. The only narration came from the screams of the people and the sound of rapid gunfire. This screen went blank too.

"My God, what is happening out there?" Mark whispered.

CHAPTER THIRTY-ONE

"General Marlow," a strange, gruff voice answered.

"I'm looking for Tom White. Did I dial the wrong number?" I asked, knowing I hadn't. My suspicious nature was suddenly alive and screaming.

"Mr. White has been relieved of command. Who is this?" General Marlow asked impatiently.

Relieved of command by the military? What was going on in Marquette? Something was very, very wrong.

"Oh, the military has come to help? That's wonderful!" I lied, trying to buy some time while I thought. Mark gave me the strangest look and I put my finger to my lips to shush him.

"What is your location, ma'am? I'll send someone to assist you." The general's voice was now soft and patronizing, and it sent all of my alarms blaring.

"Great! I'm alone in a house on Bluff Street," I said, lying again. "Can you hear me?" All the while I was randomly punching numbers on the cell phone to create interference. I disconnected quickly, hoping there wasn't time for a trace.

"What was that all about, Allex?" Mark asked.

"Tom has been relieved of command as Emergency Manager...by the *military*," I told him. "They wanted my location to 'assist' us. This is very wrong and very bad."

I hadn't talked to Anna since the video presentation. I could only hope that she was hunkering down. I speed dialed her home, relieved when she answered on the first ring.

"Anna, we have a problem."

"What now, Allexa?" she asked wearily.

"The military has taken over the emergency management office in Marquette. Tom has been 'relieved of command' by a General Marlow," I told her, repeating what I relayed to Mark. "I really, really believe it's in our best interest to sever all communications with the county, Anna. Can you get to the office and put a repeating message on the automatic voicemail, something to the effect that most here have died and the rest are relocating to Marquette? That should lead them away from us."

"Normally I would say I think you're overreacting, but you haven't led us wrong yet." She sighed and said something to someone in the background. "I'll get to the office immediately. Oh, and Allexa, Pete told me what your family did for the town. Thank you." She hung up.

Mark was looking more and more confused, and just a touch worried.

"A military takeover is likely to mean rounding up the remaining citizens for relocating into detention camps, confiscating all food supplies for redistribution, disarming everyone *and* separating families," I told him bluntly. "I certainly don't want that to happen with us here, do you?"

"No, of course not, Allex, and from what we saw on the TV last night, I think that could be what would happen," Mark agreed.

"It also means that with Tom gone I no longer have access to information. We are truly on our own," I said, staring out the window at the continuing ash fall, though it did seem to be less than yesterday.

"What do we do now?"

"We go on with our lives," I said with a sad smile. "I think we will be ignored for now."

At least I hoped so.

* * *

As prearranged, Eric and Jason arrived at 9:30 to start the butchering of the deer they had shot a few days ago that was still hanging in the barn.

"The good news is with the power back on, we won't be under such a crunch," I told them. "Still, we should work as quickly as possible, just in case the power goes out again. I need you two to cut the deer up into quarters. Bring one in, and put the other three in the refrigerator out there. Mark and I will bring in the supplies."

I handed Eric an old sheet to cover the meat from the ash while they were bringing it in. It was still coming down steadily, just not as thick as before. I was taking that as a good sign that it might be starting to let up.

"What supplies do we need, Allex? And where are they?" Mark asked. John knew where everything was and I was feeling just a touch impatient that Mark didn't. But then, he wasn't John. John left. John always left, and this time he wasn't coming back.

"Everything is out in the small brown shed," I answered, reminding myself that he was trying, really trying, to help. "We'll need jars, seals, canners and cooking kettles. I'll hand them out to you since I know what to look for. I think this will be a good time to use the second pantry entrance. There's too much to walk all the way around to the greenhouse."

* * *

The big double stacker pressure canner sat on the stove. I filled one of the cooking kettles with water and set it to heat for cooking the bones and the scrap. Mark and I pushed the work island and the utility table together and draped it with a sheet of plastic I keep with the canning stuff. It's easy to wash and sterilize. We set out cutting boards, knives and bowls.

"This looks like you've done this a time or two before, Allex," Mark commented laughing.

"Once or twice, yeah," I grinned back. "Once we get in a rhythm the work goes smoothly. When there's enough cleaned meat for me to work with, the boys will continue to butcher and I'll start canning."

"What do you want me to do? I really do want to learn so I can help," Mark said sincerely.

I was so accustomed to doing so much by myself it was hard to let the tasks go. I knew I must though.

"While they're cutting the deer up, we need to start washing the jars, and this table will need to be wiped down with bleach. Take your pick." Soon I was washing jars and Mark had the table sanitized. Then he offered to sharpen all the knives, while I fed the chickens and watered the plants out in the greenhouse, a daily chore.

The four of us worked steadily for hours, sometimes quietly, sometimes talking.

"So what brought you to Moose Creek, Dr. Mark?" Eric asked innocently as he sliced a large piece of red meat away from a bone.

Mark had been slicing meat for jerky with surgical precision. His hands stilled. I could see the battle going on inside him on what to say.

"I was an ER doctor down in Saginaw. It was work I loved. It was very gratifying to help so many. It became my whole world after my wife and son were killed in a car accident. That was many years ago that they died," he paused, placing the slices in a bowl and took another large piece of meat. "When the quakes hit last fall and society started to crumble, I was even more needed. But it wasn't the same, so I left. I just got in my car and started driving."

"Why here? Why Moose Creek?"

"This is where I ran out of gas," Mark chuckled, and he continued to cut, with a quick glance at me.

* * *

At six o'clock, just as we were cleaning up, having done two quarters, the FRS squawked.

"Jason, are you still at Mom's?" Amanda's voice came over the small radio.

"Yep, we're just cleaning up now," he answered, pushing the button to respond.

"I was wondering when you would be back for dinner."

Jason looked at the three of us before answering his wife.

"You guys can go ahead. I can't leave the canner, I have to finish," I said to them.

"I'll walk over with them and bring back our dinner. How's that, Allex?" Mark offered, washing his glove-covered hands of the blood.

"I'll set the jerky cuts to marinade overnight and you two can dry them in the smoke house tomorrow, okay?" I stated, filling another pint jar with pieces of meat. "I'll see you two tomorrow morning. Get some rest, we're only half done," I reminded them wearily. I gave Mark a dozen eggs to deliver to Amanda.

* * *

Mark returned a half hour later just as I was emptying the canner and getting ready for the next double batch of venison.

"Eric insisted I sample his latest brew," Mark said to explain his tardiness as he set the protective cloth bag on the counter. "Dinner is two beers and some kind of chicken casserole, for which Amanda apologized. I think she's tired of casseroles."

"I can see I'll have to teach Emilee to make tortilla bread. That should give Amanda something new to work with!"

"You can make tortillas?" Mark asked in awe.

I nodded. "And tacos, English muffins, bagels and pita. If it's bread-like, I can make it," I boasted, suddenly feeling shy about my skills.

"How's the canning coming?"

"Last batch for today is coming up to pressure. That will give us twenty-eight jars of meat, a good day of work. We should get the same tomorrow, plus all the soup stock and the jerky. This will give us a nice protein base. I won't be able to can the soup for two more days. Once cooked it needs to cool so I can remove the floating tallow, and then remove the bones and dice up the meat. Only then will it be ready to can. It's a long process," I said. "I think having this extra food is worth the work."

"What kind of flavoring do you use for the jerky?" He was very inquisitive tonight.

"The marinade is a blend of my own apple cider vinegar, soy sauce and teriyaki sauce, plus some water to thin it down enough to cover what's in the bowl. In fact, let's do that right now." I got the gallon-sized containers of soy and teriyaki out of the cold pantry.

I went to the greenhouse to retrieve sprouted garlic and some chives. Once chopped they were added to the three gallon marinating pail with the cup of soy sauce, half cup of teriyaki, and a half cup of vinegar. The meat was added in small batches to make sure it was well coated. I set it in the humming refrigerator for the night.

We finally sat down to enjoy Amanda's chicken casserole and Eric's beer. I was exhausted.

* * *

At 9:30 the next morning Eric and Jason entered the barn and brought both remaining quarters of the deer back to the house to save the additional trip later. Mark and I were up early to get everything ready for another long day.

"Amanda made us pancakes for breakfast, Mom, so we're not hungry. I sure could use another cup of coffee though," Eric said, when I offered them some toast.

"She's been digging around in the basement in Aunt Nancy's food storage and found a sealed canning jar labeled 'pancake mix,'" Jason said. "With some of Nancy's jam smeared on top it was awesome!"

"Yeah, I think I ate too much," Eric said, pouring himself a cup of coffee.

"I'm very glad Amanda is comfortable enough to go exploring," I commented, pleased that she would take the initiative. "Nancy did a lot of canning, too. I'm surprised there's much left."

"Mom," Jason gave me one of "those" looks. "We ate over *here* a lot last winter, in case you forgot."

"You're right," I admitted. "It's time to get to work and finish this up. Mark already re-sanitized the table and sharpened all the knives. I washed and stored the two cases of meat from yesterday and have more jars ready for today's canning. Anything else?"

"Just one thing, Mom," Eric added. "On our way here we noticed that the ash in the air is significantly less. Do you think it's stopped?"

I gazed out the glass door into the yard. It was still covered in a thick blanket of gray and darker gray. The fence around the garden looked like a lacy web of clingy soot with every crevice of the chicken wire packed full of ash and more ash. Trees were now bending under the weight of it, coating the now invisible tender green leaves. Some were bending so low they looked as though they were ready to snap; maybe they would. The ground was cloaked with more of the monotonous color. Everything, literally *everything*, was the same dull, muted, ugly gray, even the sky. But Eric was right, what was drifting in the air was noticeably less.

"It does look less, yes. I sure hope its stopping! Maybe because we're on the northern edge it will stop sooner. I just don't know, and now there's no way to find out," I said to my sons.

"What do you mean?" Jason questioned as he set a freshly washed hindquarter on the table and began dis-jointing it.

"I apologize for not telling you yesterday. When I called Tom White in Marquette, someone else answered the phone: a general. The military has moved in, and they're rounding everyone up," I cast my eyes down.

"*What?*" they both said.

"He thinks I was in the city, if he believed me that is." I looked at the three men around me. "Moose Creek is too insignificant to matter, and I'm fairly certain we will be left alone. To be on the safe side, Anna left a message on the township phone that should misdirect any interest."

Eric had been listening intently.

"Mom, do you want me to contact Captain Andrews at Sawyer?" Eric said. "See if I can get more details?" He looked at Mark and said, "That's the captain that

I had contact with while waiting for my mom to come and vouch for us when we showed up unexpectedly last winter."

"I don't think that's a good idea, Eric. I'd rather not bring any attention to us at all," I replied. "Plus we don't know if Andrews is even still there. An inquiry might only be another red flag. Let's just wait and see on this one. Besides, we have work to do." With that, we got back to cutting up meat.

By the end of the evening, I had processed another twenty-eight jars of venison, half of which we had ground first. Instead of more jerky, we had ground that too, mixing it with the commercial seasonings, and made sausage for the smoker. We had also cut several nice steaks from the rump that I seasoned and that we would cook in a few days.

"I don't know about you, Jason, but I'm beat," Eric admitted to his younger brother. "What do you say that we load this meat in the smoker tomorrow? Can we leave the jerky marinating? And I know the sausage should flavor cure a bit before smoking."

"Yes, just put it all in the refrigerator," I said. There was very little I kept in there anyway.

"Are you going to make a neck roast again, Mom?" Jason asked with a grin. "Mark, she has this secret way of stuffing and cooking a venison neck roast that is just incredible."

"Yeah, maybe Mark can get the secret from her," Eric punched his brother in the arm.

"Okay, neck roast it is. Tomorrow?" I offered, feeling a bit embarrassed that they are recognizing Mark's place with me.

After those two had left and it was quiet again, I deboned the neck roast, seasoned it, and let it chill down in the refrigerator until tomorrow when I would stuff it with fresh bread, canned ramp greens and mushrooms. There really wasn't any secret.

* * *

JOURNAL ENTRY: July 25

Twenty-one quarts, three batches, of venison soup that was heavy on the meat, are lined up on the counter and still cooling. It is only six o'clock in the evening and I am already tired.

I know the extra food and meat, could mean everything to us in the future, but I'm burning out. So much feels futile.

Mark and I walked the marinating jerky and the sausage over to the boys for them to load up the smoker. It wasn't much physical exercise, but it was good to get out of the house.

* * *

CHAPTER THIRTY-TWO

"I know you're tired of cutting and canning venison, Mom, but we might not have this opportunity again for a long time," Eric insisted. "Jason and I are going out again. We'll be back in a few hours or sooner."

I couldn't argue with his logic. This ash cloud might very well kill off the entire local herd of deer, moose and elk, not to mention all the smaller animals.

The grid power was still on, so I busied myself with mundane chores, like laundry and puttering in the greenhouse.

I was folding clothes on the large dining room table when I heard a rifle shot.

"Sounds like they got something," Mark commented. "Are you ready for more work, Allex?"

"He did have a point, Mark. Our protein availability may be..." and then I heard several shots, and then a few more. "There's trouble!" I said, racing for the greenhouse to put on my bio-suit coveralls. I grabbed my hunter orange knit cap so I could be easily seen by my sons, and my Mini-14 rifle. I checked to make sure it was loaded, and I took an extra loaded magazine from its hiding place in the clock and I was out the pantry exit.

I raced down the hill toward the now sluggish creek, its normally clear spring fed water muddied with volcanic pumice, and I heard another report, and then another. My breathing was labored behind the bio-mask as I lurched up the other side.

I wasn't expecting the scene I stumbled into. At least twenty deer lay scattered over a two acre area, some of them struggling to move, others not even trying, still others already dead. That wasn't what made my blood run cold. It was the wolves circling my sons! Eric was attempting to stand while Jason stood, aiming with one hand, the rifle butt tucked in his armpit and helping his brother with the other.

"Eric! Get up! You're too much of a target on the ground! Get up!" Jason yelled.

Another wolf lowered his head, slowly moving forward, its teeth bared. Wolves were majestic, and this one was a prime specimen. His thick dark gray and black coat bristled as he stalked closer; tufts of dark brown rippled across his haunches as he moved and its black speckled pink lips revealing long and deadly fangs. I leveled my .223 at him and pulled the trigger. The male leaped sideways from the impact and fell. The three other wolves stopped but did not retreat.

I ran to join the fight. There wasn't anything I wouldn't do to protect my children, even if they were grown, maybe especially now that they *are* grown. No, that wasn't right either. My level of protectiveness knows no age limit, no boundaries.

I could see that Jason was getting fatigued from the dual task.

"You shoot, I'll get Eric standing!" I told him, and laid my rifle down beside Eric, who had stopped in a sitting position. His left foot was bloody and the bio suit was ripped to shreds below the knee.

"I'm going to get under your arms, Eric, you'll have to push with your right foot, okay?" He nodded, obviously in a great deal of pain. "Now, push!" and with that he staggered upright as I lifted. I led him over to a broken tree so he could hold on, keeping upright, while I retrieved both of our rifles.

Another shot rang out as Jason took down another, then another. The last wolf turned and loped away.

I went back to the tree. Eric was looking very pale. His teeth were clenched in pain and his breath came in shallow gasps. I looked at the tears in his skin from the wolf's teeth. It looked really bad. I took off one of my shoes and pulled off my sock. I cut it down both sides to the toe to give me one long piece and tied it just below his knee, hoping to slow the loss of blood.

"We need to get him back to the house. NOW!" I yelled at Jason. I took both of our rifles and slung them across my back, Jason doing the same with his. I found a long, sturdy branch that Jason and I could both hold onto in front of us, while Eric sat on it and held onto our shoulders. With the weight evenly distributed and with us being able to move forward instead of sideways, we cleared the earthen rise and descended to the creek quickly. Going up the other side was more difficult and we stumbled, and Eric cried out in pain. It was agonizing for me to hear.

"Mom, I'm going to pick him up fireman-style, and I need you to push me from behind, so I don't lose my balance," Jason said, tossing aside the pole. It was slow, but steady, and soon we were at the top. Only a few more yards and we'd be at the house.

The glass door opened and Mark ran out, putting his mask on. Jason let Eric slide off his shoulders while Mark guided him to the ground. He grabbed Eric around the chest from behind and lifted, while I kept his injured foot from dragging on the ground and we moved him quickly into the house.

I swept all the laundry off the table, letting it drop to the floor, and we laid Eric down.

"What happened?" Mark asked as he began to cut away the bloodstained bio-suit. I ran a sink full of warm water and got an armload of towels from the bathroom.

"There is a small herd of deer just beyond the second rise that is struggling. Some have already died, most are just lying there, barely breathing," Jason explained. "We didn't even have to shoot, but Eric wanted to be humane. We could have just walked up to them and slit their throats. As soon as Eric made the belly cut to dress out the deer, the first wolf showed up. We didn't hear it and I saw it only after, while I was looking for the next deer to shoot. Before I could even raise my rifle, the wolf was on Eric, dragging him away by the foot, and Eric was kicking and screaming. I had to get real close to shoot or risk hitting Eric," Jason sobbed. "Then the others showed up. I started picking them off, but honestly? I was scared and shaking. I know I missed a few." He paced, stopping to rip off his suit.

"Eric had set his rifle against a log when he started gutting, and he was dragged too far to reach it. After I shot that one, Eric crawled back to the deer, maybe to get his rifle, maybe for his knife, I don't know, they just started coming at us. I had to get Eric standing or they would have killed him. That's when you showed up, Mom."

Mark had finished cutting away the pant leg, and then the laces on the boot, removing it as gently as possible. Eric still moaned.

"Allex, get his sock off then wash the area so I can see," Mark directed me as he opened the refrigerator. He opened two of his medical boxes, pulling a couple of vials from each and two syringes. He filled one and injected it into Eric's arm.

"A pain killer," he explained. "It should put him out for an hour while I do what I can." He injected more into the calf, above the mangle tissue. Eric was soon asleep.

"I need light, lots of light," Mark said. "And this table just won't do, it's too wide. What else can we use?"

"How about my massage table? I can raise the legs some on it. It's vinyl so we can sanitize it, and there's padding so he'll be more comfortable, plus it's only thirty-two inches wide," I said, stroking Eric's cheek while a tear slid down mine.

I set up my table, adjusting the legs to give the maximum height, one that Mark was comfortable with, and then I wiped it down with bleach and draped it with a clean sheet. We set up side tables for his instruments, positioning what extra lights and lamps we had around the foot area. It took less than fifteen minutes. We moved Eric carefully; the dead weight took the three of us without dropping him.

Mark began. He put my son's leg back together from the horrific wolf attack. The bite marks were deep and would leave scars. I handed clamps and retractors, wiped the flowing blood from Eric's calf and the sweat from Mark's forehead so it wouldn't drip into his eyes and blind him.

"Number six suture," he said, his eyes not moving from his task. I searched and handed over what I found. Slowly, ever so slowly, the bleeding lessened, and eventually stopped. The internal wounds were closed, and the external lacerations were closed with drainage tubes installed.

An hour after he had begun, Dr. Mark took off his surgical mask and gloves, tossing them into the trashcan.

"We're done. Now it's up to him," he announced. He sat back on the stool and closed his eyes. "Thank you, both of you," he looked at me, then to Jason, then back to me. "I think he's going to be fine. He might limp a little, but he still has a foot, thanks to those boots."

Jason let out a sob, as did I.

"He might need blood, though. Do you know your blood types?" Mark asked.

"I'm 0-positive," I said. "Both Eric and Jason are A-negative."

"I guess that leaves you to donate, Jason," Mark said.

"Anything. Take as much as you need," Jason responded.

"Hold on..." I said, looking out toward the barn in the dimming light. "We have company." The wolves had followed the blood scent.

"How did so many wolves survive the ash fall?" Mark said, clearly frustrated and not just a little frightened.

"Wolves are highly intelligent, Dr. Mark. If they sensed a problem, they would have hidden in their dens until the threat subsided. By the time it passed, they would have been really hungry, starving. With us harvesting the deer, it would have sent the blood scent in the air, activating the blood lust. That could be why they attacked," Jason concluded.

"We need to take them out, Mom, or they will never leave us alone," he continued, getting off the table where he was ready to donate blood to his brother. "I have to call Amanda."

Soon I could hear him talking to his wife, gently and then forcibly, telling her they all needed to stay inside until he got there, and to not be concerned about the gunfire they would soon hear.

I slapped a freshly filled magazine into my rifle and chambered a round. Jason had done the same and was waiting at the deck door. I slid the glass door open just enough to get the barrel out, and aimed carefully. I killed one of the wolves and began laying down distraction fire while Jason went out the door and up the ladder to a more advantageous spot on the roof.

Of the remaining canines that had followed us, we killed them all. As much as I hated killing such beautiful wild animals, this was a matter of them or us so it had to be them.

* * *

Dusk was closing in quickly. Jason had to return across the street and soon. Mark took a pint of blood from Jason, and then we moved Eric on to the futon and made him as comfortable as possible. In the waning daylight, I stood just outside the greenhouse door, watching for any movement while my youngest son made it safely across the road and onto the porch. He gave me a flash of the porch light to let me know he was once again inside, and I retreated into the safety of the house.

Mark had worked quickly to set up an IV drip that would deliver Jason's lifesaving blood into Eric's depleted veins.

I was drained; totally exhausted. I looked in on Eric before I settled into the hard wooden chair at the kitchen table and looked around. I weakly stood up again, gathered the bloody sheets that still lay on the tables and stuffed them in the washer, setting the dial to hot. Then I collapsed the massage table and pushed it to the side. After that, I went to bed. Mark stayed at Eric's side for most of the night.

At some point during the dark of the morning hours, Mark slid into bed with me. I felt the hardness of his chest press against my back as his arm slid around my waist. His breathing slowed and he fell quickly and soundly asleep.

* * *

JOURNAL ENTRY: July 27

The wind was howling this morning so loudly it woke me early. Mark was still sleeping when I checked on Eric. They both were sleeping peacefully.

I made some coffee and stood at the glass door, watching the wind whip the dust around anything vertical. The gray ash shimmered in the approaching morning, which is now just a lightening of the sky with no sunlight to be seen. Our new false dawn. I noticed yesterday when I touched the ash it crumbled to a fine powder and I can't help wondering if that's good or bad.

* * *

"Penny for your thoughts," Mark whispered from behind me. "On second thought, make that a dime. Inflation you know."

"I read a post-apocalyptic book a long time ago, *Earth Abides*, where pennies actually became more valuable than any other coin because they could be pounded into arrow heads. Of course, that's when pennies were still made of copper." I turned to face Mark and smiled at him. "Have I thanked you yet for saving my son's life?"

"No need, Allex. He's a fine young man and deserving of anything I can do for him," he replied. "And about last night..."

"Shush, Mark, where else would you have slept?" Our eyes locked and a moment of understanding passed between us.

"Anything moving out there?" he asked with concern.

"Nothing but a furious wind. I suppose once it gets light enough, Jason and I should move those wolf carcasses so they don't attract anything else. I really hated killing those animals, Mark."

"I could tell," Mark said, putting his arm around my shoulders.

* * *

"Mom?" Eric called out from the other room, with a faint moan.

"Mark, he's awake," I called down the hall to where he was getting dressed, and then hurried to Eric's bedside.

"Don't try getting up," I said, as he struggled to sit upright. "How are you feeling?"

"Like I've been chewed on and spit out," he chuckled then winced. "My foot really hurts. Is it still there?" he asked, swallowing hard, his tone quite serious.

"Last time I looked it was still attached," Mark said from the doorway. "Unless you've undone all my fancy stitches during the night." He sat down on the edge of the futon couch and pulled the stethoscope from his pocket. He listened to Eric breathe, and then took his blood pressure.

"I just need to change these bandages and I'll be done here," Mark continued while he cut away the bloody gauze. "Are you getting hungry, Eric? You can have anything you want. Well, anything your mom has, that is, and I think she's pretty well stocked from what I can tell."

"Anything? Let me think." Eric leaned back into the pillows, mostly to avoid seeing what the doctor uncovered. I think. "I've got a taste for hash browns, a couple of eggs, maybe some corned beef and toast with butter."

"I'll get right on it." I smiled down at Eric, hoping that his appetite was indeed that good.

"Make that two orders, Allexa, if you don't mind," Mark said. Just then the lights went out, leaving the room in a soft semi-darkness.

I reached for the propane lantern hanging just around the corner, lit it, and placed it on a ceiling hook near the futon. The bright light illuminated the room sufficiently for Mark to continue changing the bandages.

"You know, Eric, I've been meaning to ask your mother what all these hooks in the ceiling everywhere are for. Now I don't have to look dumb," he jokingly confided in a rather loud stage whisper.

* * *

As I collected jars from the pantry to make breakfast, Mark joined me.

"Allex, I didn't want to say anything in front of Eric, at least not yet, but the wound is looking infected."

"You've got antibiotics don't you?"

"Yes, and I'll start him on a Z-pack immediately. I was wondering if you had whatever it was you made a poultice from, the one you used on yourself?"

"The comfrey. Yes, I dug some up. It's in the greenhouse. Here, you take these," I said, pushing the jars into his arms. "I'll be right back."

I plucked several leaves from the wilted plant I had potted that now sat beside the fishpond. I gave it some water and hurried back to the kitchen. This growing room may be the best thing I've ever had!

I tore the leaves and stuffed them into a poultice bag, set the bag into a glass bowl and then poured boiling water over all of it to infuse.

"It'll take about twenty minutes to cool enough, and for the infusion to create enough liquid for the next treatment," I informed Mark. "How bad is it?"

"Not very. I want to catch it quickly though."

* * *

"Unless you've got a pair of crutches hidden away somewhere, we need to figure out a way for Eric to move around. I really don't want him putting any weight on that foot for at least a week," Mark commented as he set the table for us.

"When I twisted my ankle last December and needed to stay off of it, I used these chairs with casters to get around," I told him. "Maybe Jason can come up with something better."

When it was time, we helped Eric stand and got him into the office chair, and then rolled him over to the one step up into the kitchen, where the bungee chair waited. From there he was able to move around on his own. The first destination was to the bathroom, after I removed all the rugs.

* * *

"Not exactly hash browns," Eric said, "but crisp fried taters are just as good! Thanks, Mom, this is wonderful! And as good as those pancakes were this is better." He scooped another forkful into his mouth.

"I agree, Allex, this is great!" Mark chimed in, mopping up some egg yolk with his toast.

"I'm glad you both are enjoying this so much, just don't get used to it," I replied. "This is a special breakfast. Eric needs to regain his strength and we all missed dinner yesterday. None of us can afford to miss many calories."

Just then, the FRS crackled.

"Nahna, are you there?" Emilee asked.

"Yes, we're here."

"I want to see my dad!" She sounded like she'd been crying. "Can I come over? Uncle Jason said it's up to you."

Before answering, I looked out the window. The wind was still blowing hard. It looked like a sand storm out there, except gray.

"I think the wind is blowing too hard, Emi, maybe in a little while. I promise to watch the wind and let you know when I think it's safe, okay?"

"Yes, Nahna," she sounded very down. "Can I talk to Dad?"

I handed the radio over to Eric, and started clearing the dishes.

* * *

At noon, Jason called and said he was walking Emilee over. I did note that the wind had died down considerably in that short of time.

"Jason, we need to attach the garden cart trailer to the four-wheeler and get those wolves out of here," I said.

"That's partly why I came over with Emi." He sat down at the table after Emi and Eric had retreated to the front room. "We should do that soon."

"I also need to know Eric's limitations, Doc," Jason said. "His bedroom is downstairs, but most of the living area is carpeted."

"I don't think he should be doing walking of any kind for at least a week, unless we can devise some crutches for him to keep his weight completely off that foot," Mark replied.

"That's what I thought you might say. Which brings up the other reason I wanted to talk to you two," Jason went on. "I think I can make some crutches from a couple of saplings. I need a certain kind of wood—wood that I saw where the deer herd is." He looked over at me. "Mom, there should always be two of us going into the woods now, I know this. Will you go with me this afternoon? I feel really bad about Eric's injury. If I had been paying more attention, I would have seen that wolf before it got so close. I want to make it up to him."

"Of course, Jason," I said, patting his hand. "I'm glad you brought up the need for us to always stay in pairs now. This reminds me, back to the garden cart, any suggestions on where to dump them?"

"Yeah, there's that logging road on the other side of 695 that I think would be far enough so we're not in danger. I also think that should be our first priority."

* * *

After Jason rigged the four-wheeler with the needed filtration on the intake manifold, he drove it back across the road and attached the garden cart.

We lifted each wolf into the cart as best as possible. They were stiff in death and didn't fit well, being such huge animals. We could get only two bodies at a time in the trailer and made three trips to dispose of them.

During the ride we kicked up a great deal of dust and ash on the back road, but it appeared that the wind had moved much of it away in the more open areas. Where to, I didn't know and at that point, I didn't care. It was gone and we could see bare ground again in many areas.

419

Still, when it came time for us to look for suitable wood for Jason's project, we went fully suited and fully armed.

We walked among the deer herd. It was sad to see so many dead animals and so much wasted food. There had been no feeding from other predators, that was obvious, and the wolves we had shot after the attack were still lying there.

"Mom, this one is still breathing!" Jason called out, his voice semi-muffled from behind the mask. He was kneeling beside a big doe, her brown and tan hide scarcely moving with labored breaths.

"Are you thinking what I'm thinking?" I knelt down, and put my hand on the deer, feeling her warmth.

"Let me select the wood I need for the crutches and then we can use it to move her back to the barn."

I watched the area while Jason cut down three saplings and removed all the small leafy branches. There wasn't any movement anywhere in the forest, save us.

To not alarm those back in the house, Jason slit the deer's throat to end her life. I silently thanked her for the nourishment she would give my family, and all the while I kept my hand on her, to calm her spirit as it left.

Jason quickly gutted her and we tied her to the travois he had fashioned. While Jason pulled and dragged on the poles, I kept watch on all sides so we wouldn't be ambushed. At the top of the rise, we switched places, and I pulled our burden down the slope. Once across the muddy creek, Jason climbed the hill alone to get the four-wheeler.

"This will make the trip up the hill much easier. I don't know why we didn't think of it sooner," he said as we lifted the deer into the waiting cart.

* * *

"I thought you were just going for the wood Jason needed, Allex!" Mark said impatiently. "Not to do more hunting."

"Mark, please, she was dying anyway. Should we have just let her die in agony? And if we put her out of her misery, it would have been a huge waste to not harvest the meat," I said, defending what we had done.

"My mom's right, Doc," Eric said as he rolled into the kitchen with Emi behind him, pushing the chair. "It doesn't make my foot feel any better, but it does make *me* feel better knowing we have that extra food now."

Mark sighed. "I can see I'm out numbered!" He stalked away, still angry. I heard the door open and close going to the greenhouse.

"What's Uncle Jason doing, Nahna?" Emi asked, leaning on her father's arm.

"He's removing the hide, Em." I looked at Eric. "It was a real pistol hoisting that carcass up! Next time we leave the pulleys in place." I hoped I could divert the questions, as I knew Jason was also stripping the bark off the saplings. Jason wanted to surprise Eric with the new crutches so we were keeping it as secret as possible. I think Eric knew anyway.

* * *

Although it was fine to have rested in the seasoning an extra day, the neck roast from the last deer needed to be cooked soon, especially now with the power off and no refrigeration. I laid out the boned meat on the countertop and spread out my mixture of bread, chopped mushrooms and canned ramp greens. Rolling it as tight as I could, I tied it with butcher twine and set it in a roasting pan. With the power off, the gas oven wouldn't work, so it was either start the generator and run it for a couple of hours, or test out the stove in the greenhouse. It might also be a good time to make amends with the doctor.

He was sitting on the bench beside the fishpond, the water barely trickling down through the gold miner's outstretched pan.

"Mark, can we talk?" Although he knew he wasn't alone from the sound of the door opening, I wanted him to know it was me.

He turned and stood. "I was so worried, Allex. You two were gone too long! I was afraid something had happened to you," he reached out and I moved into his arms, welcoming the chance to comfort him. I wondered who was comforting whom.

"I'm sorry you worried, Mark. I can't promise it won't happen again, but I'll find a way to make it better," I said, looking up into those pain-filled deep blue eyes.

I don't know who moved first, and maybe it doesn't matter, but the kiss was soul deep and I clung to him as he held me tight.

"I can't lose you, Allex, not now that I've just found you," he whispered, his lips brushing my temple.

* * *

The greenhouse stove worked fine, though it did require closer tending. The kitchen stove is cast-iron while the other one is thinner metal sheeting and didn't hold the heat as well. Having to constantly tend the fire also gave Mark and I some needed alone time, to decide on how to handle our new, evolving relationship.

Jason left the trailer attached to the four-wheeler and drove it home, returning with yet another surprise: a bubble unit for the cart and in the bubble sat a delighted Jacob and a nervous Chivas.

The puppy was happy to escape the strange carriage, and roamed around the house, limping and sniffing everything. As if on cue, Tufts emerged from under the bed and sat in the middle of the kitchen, waiting for Chivas to find him. When the pup came skidding to a halt in front of the cat, Tufts lifted a clawless paw and tapped Chivas on the nose gently. I still find it strange how they have become such friends.

* * *

It was good to have the entire family together for dinner. It seemed like a long time, although it really had only been a few days. So much had happened in that time, my head—and heart—were in such a spin.

"Nahna, I know you're taking good care of my dad, but I think he needs me, so I want to stay here until he's ready to come home," Emilee announced.

"Are you sure, Miss Emilee?" asked Mark, in his best doctor voice. "I work my medical staff pretty hard, especially the caretakers." He did manage to keep a straight face, even though the rest of us didn't.

At first Emi looked shocked, then she smiled and said, "You're teasing me aren't you, Dr. Mark?"

"Yes, I am," he laughed, and pulled a quarter out of her ear, much to her delight.

"Of course you can stay here, Emi," I said. "How much longer do you think Eric will be laid up, Mark?"

"At least a week. Depending on how his leg looks in the morning, I think he can go back home tomorrow, especially since his sleeping quarters don't involve any steps," Mark answered.

* * *

"I know how awkward this is for you Allex, and I promise to restrain myself," Mark promised as I started dousing the bedroom lights for the night.

"I won't deny it's awkward, Mark." I smiled. "I don't think there's much choice, and we *can* be adult about this."

"Yeah, that's what I'm afraid of," he said with a sigh.

* * *

"Are you two ready to go home?" Mark asked our two houseguests.

"I know I am. Mom, do you mind if I take a shower here first?" Eric answered as he rolled into the kitchen on the green and black bungee chair.

"I'll start the generator," Mark offered.

The power had been out for a couple of days now, and I had a bad feeling it was going to be out for a while this time. Maybe Moose Creek was back to being a casualty to the needs of the many outweighing the needs of the few, and with the military now in control, I had no way of finding out.

"Emi, while your dad is getting cleaned up, I want to show you how to pick the medicine leaves so you can do this at home," I said, and took Emilee out to the greenhouse and showed her the comfrey plant.

"It's really important that you never hurt the plant, and that means you take only the outer leaves, never ever from the middle, okay? And we never use metal to cut the leaf, no scissors, no knife," I emphasized, and she nodded seriously. "We're going to take two big leaves today, and maybe only one tomorrow. It will depend on what Dr. Mark says when he changes the bandages later."

She put the leaf I pinched off into a baggie, and then I had her pinch one too. The baggie went into her pocket for later, and she guarded it carefully. I mused how quickly she'd grown up in this harsh new world we live in.

* * *

I pulled the car out of the barn and as close to the house as I could get. Mark and I helped Eric down the steps and into the back seat. I put the lightweight bungee chair in the back, and drove across the street and up close to the porch, while Mark and Emi walked our well-worn path.

"Here's the chair for Eric," I said to Jason when he met me on the porch. He had pulled back a section of the heavy plastic to make an entrance, and a brisk breeze flapped it erratically until he managed to secure it.

"I got the crutches made last night, Mom. He's going to love them," Jason boasted. "Now all we have to do is figure out how to get him up these steps!" My brother's porch was graced by ten steep steps. It was going to be a challenge.

"You could try that over the shoulder fireman's carry again," I suggested, however, Eric opted for butt-scooting up each step instead. I think it saved his dignity.

Amanda had already laid out an early lunch of Emi's fresh bread, home canned chicken made into spreadable sandwich filling and pork and beans heated on the gas stove.

"I want a ride!" Jacob insisted when he saw his uncle sitting in what he felt was *his* chair.

"Maybe later, Jacob, when Uncle Eric is getting his bandages changed, okay? Right now he needs the chair because he can't walk," Amanda explained.

"We picked some comfrey leaves earlier, and I'd like to show Emilee how to prepare them to make a poultice," I said, excusing us from the lunch table.

"Now we tear the leaf in pieces and put it in this washcloth bag," I said.

"Tearing it not cutting it, right, Nahna?" she observed.

"That's right. The metal is bad for the healing juices in the plant," I further explained. "Now take the bag and set it in a glass or ceramic bowl, and cover it with boiling water."

"It's kind of like making tea! My mom used to make tea like this," she said wistfully.

"It's very much like a tea. When the water has cooled and it's been soaking for about a half hour, then it's ready. Now let's finish our lunch while this cools."

* * *

The consensus was that lunch was wonderful and the only thing missing was potato chips.

"I'll never have chips again, will I, Dad?" Emi frowned. He looked at me, raising his golden eyebrows in question.

"One of these days, Emi, when we can grow potatoes again, we'll make some chips and French fries too!"

I hope I can make good on my promise.

"Well, I think I need to check my patient here, so we can get back home soon. It looks like rain is on the way," Mark said, leading Eric away from the table and grabbing his — my — little black bag.

Emilee watched in fascination as Mark cut the bandages away to reveal the red and swollen tissue, speckled with black stitches.

"Oh gross, Dad!" she made a face, but stayed by her father's side, staring at the massive injuries.

"Yes, Emi, I know it looks bad, but it's really healing quite well. Here, lay your hand on it gently," Mark guided her little hand to a rather red area. "How does it feel? Cool or hot?"

"Neither really, maybe cooler than hotter," she scrunched up her face in thought.

"Very good! If it was hot, that would mean it was infected, which of course is bad news. Is that poultice ready? I think you can do a couple of treatments today, and then I'll be over to bandage it later."

I took the bowl over where Eric was resting, and showed Emi how to gently squeeze out the excess liquid, noting how it had turned green.

"You let it sit on the wound for a half hour, while the good stuff from the plant soaks into the skin, and then put the poultice back in the bowl to soak up more medicine. Wait one hour, and repeat. You can do that until all the green liquid is gone, or until your dad has had enough nursing." I smiled at the two.

Mark gave Eric a single Darvocet for the pain that would also allow him to sleep.

* * *

At one o'clock, I stood at the glass door, watching the dark clouds form in the distance over Lake Superior. This was an angry stormy sky, not the sullen gray skies we'd had for the last nine days.

"I think we're really lucky, maybe even in the top one percent of the luckiest people in the entire state," I said, thinking out loud. "We've got plenty of food and water, sturdy shelter and heat if we need it, several different ways of cooking or heating our food, hot showers, too. We're relatively safe from all that's going on out there in the world. And even though Eric was badly injured, he's *alive*. We're *all* alive, and healthy, and together." I felt Mark standing behind me, and welcomed his arms around my waist as he pressed his chest to my back. "John's not coming back, is he?"

"No, he isn't," Mark stated ever so quietly.

"I think I've known that all along, I just didn't want to face it. I don't know why it isn't as painful this time. He's left me so many times in the last few months, and each time he came back, only to leave again. And every time he left he broke my heart all over again.

"I've been thinking about the note he left," I continued, leaning ever so lightly into Mark's comforting embrace. "John and I knew each other a long time before he came to stay with me last winter. We were close friends, not lovers, not until he moved in. I thought that would make our relationship strong. He kept leaving me anyway. I think he asked me to wait two weeks for his return that he knew would never come, so you and I could get to know each other first, before we became intimate. In his own way he was looking out for us."

The ominous black clouds rolled chaotically across the heavy sky. Thunder boomed in the distance and then closer. A flash of lightning split the sky with an ear-shattering crack, and the rain started coming down in torrents.

I turned within the circle of Mark's arms, reaching up to thread my fingers through his dark curly hair, and pulled him down so I could reach his lips and asked, "Are you going to leave me too?"

"No, I'm not," Marked kissed me with a depth that left me breathless.

I pulled back from the embrace and smiling said, "Good, because my heart can't take any more."

I took his hand and led him to my room, where we undressed each other painfully slow. Sliding under the covers with him, his skin was so hot it left a blazing trail where it touched me.

We spent the rest of the afternoon talking and kissing, loving and exploring, and even napping a little wrapped tightly against each other. For a moment I thought how John was tender and gentle, and while Mark could be tender and gentle too, he was also passionate and playful and exciting. Then John slipped to the back of my mind, and to the back of my heart.

The storm outside raged on, pounding against roof and against the windows in a relentless quest for entrance.

Hours later, I reached for my robe hanging nearby.

"And just where do you think you're going?" Mark reached out grabbing my belt in a vain attempt to pull me back to the bed.

"I don't know about you, but I'm starving!" I smiled down at him, laughing, really laughing for the first time in what felt like forever. I playfully swatted his hand away and stepped out of his reach.

In the kitchen, I was drawn to the glass door again. The rain was pelting the lawn just as hard as it had been for the last few hours, but I didn't seem to mind it as much, and the sky wasn't as gloomy even though it was just as dark.

Mark came up beside me, slipping his arm around my waist and pulling me possessively closer to his side. "So what's for dinner?"

"What would you like? I was thinking something with pasta."

He looked quizzically in my eyes. "You seem to be glowing, Allex, absolutely glowing. I do hope I've had something to do with that."

I laughed. "You've had *everything* to do with that, doctor." I gentled my voice and said "I feel...happy, Mark, content and...at peace."

* * *

While we had the generator going for much needed showers, I tried the TV and actually found a news channel.

"...*Latest on the seismic activity along the Ring of Fire has indicated an increase not only in the number of tremors, but the force. In the past five days, there was a 6.9 on the Richter scale quake off shore in Northern California; a 6.1 in Japan; and both Peru and Chile suffered 6.3 quakes, the Chile quake caused a tsunami warning to be issued. Geologists and scientists are still unsure what this might mean.*

"*Meteorologists say the ash cloud that has blanketed much of the U.S. should be passing out of the region in the next few days, and some are already experiencing clear skies again.*

"*In other news, the rioting in Detroit, Chicago and other major cities has escalated today with the announcement of the imminent collapse of the dollar.*" The anchorman looked at the camera and said, "*Spend it while you can!*"

Then the screen went dark.

I almost laughed thinking of all that money in my drawer that was now totally worthless. Maybe I should frame that check, to prove I was once a millionaire.

CHAPTER THIRTY-THREE

JOURNAL ENTRY: July 29

It was incredibly gorgeous out this morning. The thunderstorms had moved out during the night and the day blossomed with blue skies! Not quite as rich of a blue that I've seen here in the past, but blue is blue and it filled me with joy.

* * *

"I need to talk to the boys today about the deer hanging in the barn," I said to Mark while we sipped our morning coffee and munched on toast. Mark had become very fond of my blueberry jam, and it almost dripped off the edge of his bread.

"What about the deer? And that is a deer *you* helped Jason harvest, don't forget about that. It's as much yours as it is his."

"Yes, I know." I took the hand of this man across from me, a man I'd come to love very quickly. "And that's why I want to give it away."

He looked stunned, then he grinned. "That's my girl!"

* * *

"Are you sure about this, Mom?" Eric asked while Mark was bandaging his foot and calf.

"I'm absolutely sure. We already have so much to be thankful for that I want to share the goodness my heart feels."

Jason had been quietly listening to us, not saying anything, just watching us closely. "Who do you want to give it to?" he finally asked.

"That's a good question. We have so many friends that could use the extra food, who do *you* want to give some to?"

Emilee was the first to make a suggestion when she blurted out, "Joshua and Martha! They're nice." I wrote that down even though I already knew everyone they were going to suggest.

"And Bob and Kathy, Ken and Karen," Eric added.

"How about Pete and Lenny?" Mark suggested. "They've been so busy with...things, I'm sure they haven't had time to hunt."

"I'd like some to go to Anna and George. Anna has been a good friend. Oh, and Pastor Carolyn, too."

"Mom, I think your list is just about all that are left in Moose Creek," Amanda commented. She was right. Most everyone else had gone to town, or had died.

"That we know of, Amanda. There still might be some at camps or in the woods, but they must be taking care of themselves or we would have heard from them."

"Maybe you should take some of the smoked fish too," Jason suggested, getting into generous mood we were all feeling. "Not too much though. Amanda likes it."

"So when are you going to do this?" Eric asked.

"Just as soon as we get that deer cut up into sections. Jason, when will you have time to come over and help us cut and portion out?"

"In an hour?"

* * *

Mark and I set the tables up one more time for butchering. I covered the two tables with the sheet of plastic and Mark sanitized it with spritzes of bleach and wiped it down. I set out the knives and he sharpened them.

"Did you notice how chilly it was when we walked back from the boys'?" Mark asked.

"Yes. I think it was mostly from the storm, though soon it will be from the ash cloud in the upper atmosphere. Although one could be deceived by the current blue sky, the sun is being blocked."

"I meant to ask you about that, if you had a theory on why we suddenly have a blue sky?" he asked, setting down a freshly honed knife.

"Well, the cloud is moving from west to east, so we got it first. As it keeps moving east, it will come back around after covering Asia, but they won't get the fallout we did. So right now we're on the back side of it, although it will catch up to itself before long. Or at least that's how I understand it."

* * *

"So how do you want this divided, Mom?" Jason asked. "We normally cut it into four quarters, however, we need more than that this time."

"We'll need six sections. Your family should get a nice haunch, something to eat fresh over the next week," I said. "So, there are two shoulders, two hinds, two hind shanks, and all the ribs plus the front shanks. The ribs and front shanks I'll cook and can. *We* need to keep some too," I said when they looked at me. "So what we have left are two shoulders, two hind shanks and one hind, that's five sections."

"Plus some fish," Jason added.

"Plus some fish, yes. Not too many though, not if Amanda likes them," I said. "I've noticed she doesn't eat much of the venison, and she needs protein too."

We set to work.

It went quickly since we were just separating the sections, not cutting the meat up, that would be left up to the others. Thankful I had kept all the plastic grocery bags over the years, we wrapped each section and tied the handles closed. Because all the awkward bones had been disjointed, all of it fit into one cooler, where I also placed a thawing ice pack. That should be sufficient while we made the deliveries.

The first stop was to Joshua and Martha since they were closest.

"Joshua, how good to see you!" I gave the young man a hug.

"Oh, Miss Allexa, how nice of you to come by," he smiled at me and shook Mark's hand.

"I thought while we were here I would see how Martha is doing," Mark said, holding up his new little black bag.

Joshua's whole demeanor shifted.

"Martha…Martha passed away in her sleep last week," he stated quietly. "I know I should have told you, but there didn't seem to be any point. I knew there was nothing that could be done. *She* knew she was dying soon. She told me so."

There was a sadness in his eyes that tugged at my heart.

"I buried her in her flower garden, just like she told me she wanted. I hope that was okay," Joshua said, taking a deep breath.

"I think that was a lovely gesture, Joshua," I told him sincerely. "And I'm so very sorry for your loss. Martha was a good woman."

"How are the animals?" Mark asked, quick to change the subject.

"Right well, I think. They seemed to like living in the garage, but I think they're even happier to be back outside," Joshua replied. He looked at me with a sudden frightened look. "They'll be okay, now won't they, Miss Allexa? Being outside I mean."

"They should be fine. The ash cloud has passed for now. A cloud will be back, though it will be one in the higher atmosphere, and shouldn't hurt them," I replied. "You still need to keep watch, and if the ash returns, get the animals inside quickly."

"In the garage?" Mark asked.

DEBORAH D. MOORE

"I moved the truck out and filled the garage with straw bedding and hay, and even moved in the cage with the baby chicks. That way I could tend and water everyone without me going outside," Joshua explained.

"That was brilliant, Joshua," Mark complimented him.

"Now, for the next reason we stopped over," I continued on, knowing we had lots to do today, "is to bring you some fresh venison. We managed to harvest one last deer before they all succumbed to the ash, and we wanted to share it with our friends. I also brought a dozen eggs, on Emilee's suggestion and some smoked fish from Jason." I selected one of the hind shanks from the cooler, since now it was for only one person and three of the fish.

"That's right generous of you Miss Allexa! I do appreciate it. I'll have to hide it from Bossy, she gets upset when she smells me cooking red meat," he said in all seriousness.

* * *

Our next stop was to Ken and Karen, since we were trying to keep the deliveries in order of where everyone lived.

As we pulled into their driveway, Ken stepped out with a shotgun, and then lowered it when he saw it was us.

"What a nice surprise!" Karen said from behind him. She came forward and gave me a hug, whispering, "Where's John?"

"John left and went back to Indiana to be with his daughter," I said so all could hear. I didn't feel like explaining my new relationship with the doctor, so I changed the subject. "We were able to harvest two deer since the eruption, and the second one we want to share." Mark opened the cooler that sat in the hatch, and brought out a shoulder section, which he handed over to Ken.

"I also have something extra for you," I said with a grin, and handed Karen a baggie filled with ground coffee.

Her eyes got wide and moist as she accepted the gift.

"We have other stops to make, so we can't stay," I told them. I gave Karen a parting hug, and I slipped something into her hand and gave her a wink. She returned the big smile when she saw the mini-bottle of whiskey, and I think she was touched that I remembered she liked adding it to her coffee.

* * *

Anna and George were next on the list, and likewise we were initially met with a loaded gun. After gladly accepting our gift, I asked Anna if she'd heard anything from the county offices.

"Not a word. Although there have been two calls that came in to the office, no messages were left. So I'm hoping your ruse was successful! It would be good if they just left us alone. Although..." she looked pensive, "one of these days we'll all run out of food and we'll have to seek help."

430

"Well, let's hope we can keep that from happening, Anna." We said our goodbyes and headed over to Pete's house.

* * *

"I'm surprised we weren't met with weapons drawn," I joked when Lenny answered the door.

"No need to. Pete had the car in his sites from upstairs before you got within a half block!" Lenny laughed. "Of course we both recognized your car, Allexa. What can we do for you?" he asked, as Pete approached from behind.

"Remember that venison shoulder you brought me last December?" I asked, and when he nodded, I went on. "I've come to return the favor." Mark handed him the second shoulder section.

His big pale blue eyes, magnified by his thick glasses, swam with grateful tears.

"What goes around comes around, Lenny," I said with a smile as I remembered that cold and snowy day so many months ago.

"Oh, and here's an extra gift," Mark said, extending a plastic quart jar filled with rice and a bag of dried macaroni into Pete's hands.

* * *

I intentionally made Bob and Kathy our last stop, so we could spend some time with them.

"Pastor Carolyn! How good to see you. I didn't expect to run into you here!" I gave her a hug. She looked…hollow, and sad.

"Bob and Kathy were kind to take me in after…after the horrible mistake I made," she said, on the edge of tears. "Oh, how I rue the day I didn't listen to you!"

"Pastor," Mark said softly, "every one of those people made their own decision. It wasn't your doing and certainly not your fault." He placed his hand tenderly on her shoulder to emphasize his remarks.

"We've come bearing gifts!" I said, hoping to change the somber mood. "Mark, would you bring the cooler over here please?"

We had settled ourselves on their deck overlooking Lake Meade. Even though it was a little cool, it felt good to sit in the sun and breathe fresh air without fear.

Kathy pulled her chair closer to mine and whispered, "What's up with you two? And where's John?"

I whispered back to her, "John left, *again*. Mark has moved in." Which got a shocked look from her, just as Mark came back, carrying a much lighter cooler.

"Allex and Jason went out after the attack and harvested one more deer. We've been making the rounds all day sharing it," Mark stated.

"Attack?"

"What happened?"

"Who attacked you?"

The questions came from all three of them.

"Jason and Eric were out hunting and were attacked by a band of wolves," I told them. "Eric was badly injured, but Mark saved him. He performed some fancy surgery—on my massage table! Instead of losing his foot, Eric is well on his way to recovery." I looked over at Mark with love and gratitude.

"Anyway, two days later, Jason and I went back out and found one deer still alive in the herd. It was a joint decision that we would share that meat with our friends," I announced. "And here is your share. There is a hind shank we were going to offer to Carolyn and the rump to the two of you. Since she's here, we'll leave it all with you."

"That's a lot of meat, Allexa," Bob said, stunned.

"I hate to sound corny, but that's what friends are for!" I told him.

While Bob was retrieving a bottle of wine from his dwindling cellar, Kathy and I put the venison in their refrigerator, along with the melting block of ice, and a bag of smoked fish.

"How's Carolyn doing, Kathy, seriously?" I asked in private.

"Not well. She really does blame herself for all those people dying," Kathy said grimly. "We had to physically restrain her from going out to join them when she heard the screams. It was awful." She set five wine glasses on a tray and turned to me. "What's with the doctor and what the hell happened to John?"

"John decided he needed to be with his daughter, so he went home. Before he did, he asked Mark to take care of me," I said, still not believing all that had happened. "So he moved in, and before you ask and I know you will, yes, we're sharing a bed now." I've always been honest with my friend, and it was good to share that with her.

"Well, you look absolutely radiant, so he must be good for you!" She gave me a brief hug and we joined the others on the deck.

* * *

Back at home, I stood at the glass door watching the blue sky fade and the ash move in again.

Our reprieve was over.

"It's starting again?" Mark asked from behind me.

"It looks that way. There must have been more eruptions," I said sadly.

"Should we call the boys?"

"They'll notice and do what needs to be done," I replied. I couldn't take my eyes from the scene outside.

Like before, the ash came down gently at first, and then it changed. The dark gray flakes got larger and denser. Soon the sky was gone and there was nothing to see but ash falling.

THE JOURNAL:

Crimson skies

Book Three

PROLOGUE

The nation was brought to its knees in early November with the devastating earthquake that ripped the country apart at the New Madrid fault line. Thousands of lives were lost and the actual count would never truly be known. When the shipping lines were completely cut off from west to east, everyone felt the impact, especially small towns like Moose Creek. The final blow came when the power was cut in the middle of winter. Allexa Smeth was activated in her once quiet role of township emergency manager. Nothing would ever be the same for her again.

Spring brought relief from many problems that plagued Moose Creek during that long and cold winter; gardens were planted; children went back to school; life resumed. But Mother Nature wasn't done.

The New Madrid earthquake was devastating, but the quake that woke up the seething caldera beneath Yellowstone National Park was massive, and the results were nothing short of catastrophic. The ash clouds that drifted across the country killed hundreds of thousands of humans and animals alike, in a matter of a week.

Allexa's heart ached when John left again and he knew that would happen. He also knew that Dr. Mark Robbins was secretly in love with Allexa, and asked him to stay with her during the dark time ahead.

Allexa Smeth was once again struggling to save what was left of her family and her town.

CHAPTER ONE

I woke early, depressed that the ash from the Yellowstone eruption has moved back in. While I was in the kitchen making coffee, I was startled by the bright sunlight coming through the glass door. Apparently the ash clouds last night were a fluke or very small, either way I was delighted to see the sun shining.

* * *

"What an amazing day it is!" Mark proclaimed with unbridled enthusiasm, looking out the door to admire the bright sun. He was suddenly somber. I turned to him, questioning his unusual silence.

"Marry me," he stated in all seriousness. "I know it seems sudden…"

"Yes."

"…but it's not sudden to me. I—what did you say?"

"I said yes, Mark. I'll marry you. Conditional on your answer to two questions: Do you love me? And will you promise to never leave me?"

Mark took my hands and searched my face. "Yes, Allex, I love you deeply, so much so it surprises me. As for leaving you, it will be 'until death do us part.'"

I grinned with excitement. "Then yes, let's get married."

"I do need to ask, Allex, why me? You turned John down, after all you two had been through together."

I didn't need to think about my answer. "I believe that as much as I loved John, and I still do, John is a wanderer. I'm still not sure why he asked me, because he knows he always leaves—always. Some part of me felt he asked out of gratitude for taking him in last winter, and that's not a good reason to get married. I knew deep in my soul it wasn't a forever thing, and I want forever. With you it's different. We *will* have a life together. Does that make sense?"

"Perfectly! When shall we do this?"

"Let's go and talk to Pastor Carolyn tomorrow, if that's okay with you," I replied. "Tonight we celebrate." I kissed the man that would become my husband. "Oh, and we need to tell the boys."

* * *

"Your m-mother and I...h-have made a decision," Mark stuttered.

"Mark asked me to marry him and I said yes," I finished.

Both Eric and Jason looked shocked, but not as shocked as Amanda.

"Well, say something!" I said, aghast and somewhat offended at their silence.

"Isn't this rather sudden, Mom?" Jason said. "I mean, you haven't known each other very long, and have dated for what, two weeks?"

"We've known each other for three months and you can't call living in the same house dating. The world has changed, or haven't you three noticed? I'm going to grab onto this happiness I've found with Mark," I said, disappointed at their reaction.

"What if John comes back?" Amanda asked in a small voice.

So that's what this was about. "If John comes back, which I don't think he will, then he'll find out that his leaving had consequences. I love Mark and he loves me, and we're getting married. Now, do you three want to help us plan a wedding?"

Eric stepped forward on his crutches and gave me a hug, while extending his hand to Mark. "If you're happy, Mom, then we're happy!"

CHAPTER TWO

"It does feel like we're moving fast on this, doesn't it?" Mark commented over our lunch of soup.

"Having second thoughts?" I asked, worried that he might be trying to back out.

"Oh, no, not at all!" He set his spoon down, stood and coaxed me into his arms. "It's overwhelming, you know? It's all happening so quickly."

"I know it is, Mark, and this new world is very tenuous. I want every bit of happiness we can find, and I want to hold on to it. We don't know what tomorrow will bring, and I don't want to miss a bit of today!" I stroked his smooth cheek with my palm. "Would you rather wait a week or maybe a month?"

"No! I want you as my wife, now if I could. I want *you* to be sure," he said.

"Oh, I'm sure. If you're finished with lunch, let's go talk to Pastor Carolyn."

* * *

It was another beautiful day with clear skies and a steady temperature around seventy-five degrees, a good ten degrees cooler than normal. We even drove with the windows down.

As I got closer into Moose Creek, something felt different...off. I couldn't quite put my finger on it until we saw the military truck turning the corner several blocks ahead of us. Fortunately it was heading in the same direction and turned away, out of sight.

"I'm guessing that's not a good thing to see," Mark commented.

"Not as far as I'm concerned it isn't!" I made a quick right turn, pulling into Bob and Kathy's long hidden driveway. I stopped in front of their large storage barn and parked. Normally I'd pull closer to the house, but I wanted to make sure the car wasn't visible from the road and the huge building hid it well.

"Follow me," I said to Mark, edging my way along the side of their house where it was sheltered with shrubs. I moved quickly along the emerging wall of the walk out basement and was soon looking at their screened in lower deck with the upper deck facing the lake. We were in luck; they were sitting up there enjoying the day.

"Hey up there!" I called out, and Kathy peered over the side.

"What are you doing down there? Why didn't you come to the front door?" she questioned.

"Because we've got company! Is this door open?"

"No, I'll be right down though." She backtracked through the house and came out near us, unlocking the glass door, and then unlocking the screen so we could come in.

Bob was right behind her looking worried. "Who is the company, Allexa?" he asked.

"The military!" I said once we were inside. "We were coming here to see Carolyn when we saw a truck turn up Dutch Street. Once they turned I pulled in here and parked up near the barn."

"I wonder where they were going, or what they're looking for," Bob wondered out loud.

"My guess is they're looking for survivors, maybe to help, but maybe to take them to the 'Relocation Center.' Either way, I don't want to be found, at least not until we know for sure."

"But we really came to see Carolyn," Mark told them. "Is she around?"

"She's spending some alone time at her house at the top of the driveway. I guess we can be a bit overwhelming at times," Kathy chuckled. "Is it something important? We can go get her if you want."

"Well, *we* think it's important," I said, smiling. "Go ahead, Mark, tell them."

My two friends turned to him.

"Allex has agreed to marry me," Mark announced. "We want Carolyn to do us the honors."

Bob looked shocked, and Kathy was all grins. "Oh, that is just wonderful! When is this going to happen?" she asked.

"As soon as we can make all the arrangements, but we're thinking Thursday."

"That's three days away!" Kathy exclaimed.

"I know, we would rather it be this afternoon, but August second is the day we decided on."

Mark and I had discussed that John asked me to wait two weeks for his return, and though we were both sure he wasn't coming back, and it wouldn't matter if he did, it was a symbolic gesture. August 2nd was the end of the two weeks. I didn't feel the need to share that with Bob and Kathy just yet.

"That's not what I meant," she laughed. "Three more days is really soon. Is that enough time to do everything? To get all the preparations done? What about a dress? And a reception? And that means food. Are you sending out invitations? Oh, my." She dropped down into a chair. "What can I do to help?"

I had to laugh. Kathy is the most organized person I've ever met, however, she likes having time to make everything just right.

I took my friend's hand. "Kathy, we don't need much. We would like our friends to be with us that afternoon, to witness our joining. After Carolyn performs the ceremony, we'll have an early supper. That's all."

"That's all? What about food? What about a gift?" she was more nervous about this than I was.

"No gifts. Your presence is our present," I told her. When I saw she had that look of determination on her face that I've come to know, I said, "Look, if you want something to do, make a dish to pass. And come early to help me set up and then get dressed. Okay?" That seemed to satisfy her.

We left the car beside the barn while we walked up to Carolyn's house. It was an impressive log house to begin with, shining with its deep glow of amber stain, now even more so with the addition of a matching garage and loft apartment, all attached by an enclosed two-story glass breezeway. All of that space and she lived alone. I never understood the need for all those rooms. She answered on the first ring.

"What an unexpected surprise! Come in, Allexa, Mark. What can I do for you?" She was now in her best pastoral mode.

I got right to the point. "Well, Pastor, Mark and I want to be married and we would like you to perform the ceremony for us. This Thursday at four o'clock in the afternoon. We will be providing a buffet dinner afterward. Will this fit in your schedule?" I asked with a slight snicker, knowing she probably didn't have much going on.

She smiled broadly at us. "It would be my honor and my pleasure." Mark and I were holding hands, so she took hold of our free hands, completing a circle. "This is wonderful, Allexa, it gives me hope for a future; a future I haven't been too sure about lately."

* * *

"I think I heard that military truck drive past while we were in with Carolyn," Mark mentioned on our walk back down the driveway to the car.

"I heard it too, so it's probably safe to leave. Damn! I hate being so paranoid. They might want a head count to send some supplies in," I sighed.

"You don't really believe that, do you?" he said to me.

"No, I don't," I sighed. "Sometimes it pays to be paranoid." I started the car and backed up. "I'd like to stop and see Pete and Lenny, tell them about the wedding. Is that okay with you?"

"Of course." Mark leaned over and gave me a quick kiss. "They're our friends, part of *our* circle."

* * *

Pete's white and maroon bungalow sat on a corner lot and was only a block away so we saw the smoke immediately. I pulled in on the side street, where we saw the overturned grill, wood chips spilling out, singeing the brown grass. No one answered our calls, so we got some water from the rain barrel and doused the fire.

"What do you think happened, Allex?" Mark asked absentmindedly as we left Moose Creek.

"I'm not sure. Did you see any food on the ground?" I asked.

"No, I could smell that something had been cooking though," he answered.

"Same here, and it smelled like meat cooking, perhaps some of that venison." I thought for a few moments, driving slowly by the burnt out shell of the Shoreline Treasures building that had succumbed to arson last December.

I then passed Fram's store. It was closed, windows boarded over. I had talked with Joe only a week ago and recalled that he was considering moving to his camp deep in the woods to ride out the ash cloud.

"It's only a theory, however, it's possible that when the military truck came back through, they smelled the cooking too and followed the scent to Pete's. I know it's a stretch, but I think there was a struggle and they forced Pete and Lenny to go with them back to Marquette. And that whoever was in that truck took the food. It would be like Lenny to leave us a clue like the overturned grill, so we knew they didn't go willingly," I said.

"Let's run your theory by Eric. He's the one with the military experience." Mark looked sullen, worried, and a bit frightened. "I think we need to be very cautious, Allex."

"I agree, but I'm not going to let this interfere with our wedding!"

* * *

"Well," Eric said, his foot propped up on a pillow, "I think Mom might be right about this, Doc, but I don't understand it. This isn't a thing the military would usually do. Why would they *force* help on someone who is obviously not in need of help? Unless..." he paused while thinking. "Unless it isn't about helping them. Maybe they looked at Pete and Lenny as being a threat somehow, and they were sent out to eliminate threats."

"Now that's a scary thought," I said to Eric. "What if they consider *anyone* not in their control a threat? That would mean rounding *everyone* up. What threat could a handful of loners be?"

Jason looked at me and laughed. "Say, Mom, you have a copy of *Red Dawn*?"

"Sure, but why..." Thinking about the movie I answered my own question. "Point made, Jason. Thank you. The military — or whoever is really in control — is afraid the lone wolves might start a rebellion against their power." I shook my head. "Don't they and *we* have enough to worry about without this, too?" I stood and started pacing.

"I suggest we limit outdoor activities for a week or so, let them look around town, see no one else is there and maybe they'll go away," Eric said. "We'll keep the kids inside, or limit their play area. Same for Chivas, she's still recovering and has adapted well to the grass box. Oh, and have you noticed that she hasn't barked? I've been working with her on that."

"Well, weather permitting I still want to have the wedding outside. Other than that, Eric, I agree; we need to keep a low profile until we know what they want."

CHAPTER THREE

JOURNAL ENTRY: July 31

Clouds have moved back in, though they're high and thin. It looks like a normal summer day, except for the chill in the air.

* * *

"I think it's time to move the chickens back into their coop," I told the boys and Mark over our lunch strategy meeting. They had come over, one at a time, practicing some stealth maneuvers Eric was teaching his brother.

"We can do that, but any reason why?" Jason asked, munching on half of an egg salad sandwich.

"It's starting to smell in there," I said. "And they need more space and fresh air. Speaking of the chickens, I've got a dozen eggs I'd like you to take back with you for Amanda to make deviled eggs for the wedding dinner."

"Do you want us to mingle the chicks in with the adults? I think they're big enough now," Eric said. He'd raised lots of chicks down in Florida so I trust his decision.

"That would be fine, and it would save us having to figure out a means of separating them. And before anyone asks, I know the roosters are a noise threat, so I think you should butcher them. There are several males in the baby chick batch to replace the breeding stock, so we should be okay."

The chickens definitely looked happier out in their yards, scratching and pecking away at the grass that was uncovered by the windstorm that passed through a few days ago. Not enough ash had fallen during the brief downpour to matter.

While Eric and Jason were instructing Mark on the art of killing and butchering a chicken, I rummaged around in the barn for a box I knew contained some vases. I had seen some wildflowers on the hill that had survived the ash and thought they would be a nice addition to the tables for our celebration in two days. Two days.

* * *

JOURNAL ENTRY: August 1

Last night we were able to get one channel on the TV for ten minutes. News and weather seem to be considered as one lately, as the death toll comes to light. The loss of life has been horrendous, close to seventy percent of the population. Europe and Asia were largely spared, as the deadly shards hidden in the ash fell quickly and are now gone from the cloud.

The comment was also made that those above the forty-fifth parallel were spared the worst of the fallout. Spared? If we were spared, with as bad as it was here, it must have been unimaginable elsewhere. I guess we've been lucky that the first cloud lasted only a week and not more.

We will all, though, face a sunless, cold future, for perhaps two years, maybe more, hopefully less.

CHAPTER FOUR

JOURNAL ENTRY: August 2

The gray and dismal clouds we've been having for the past two days moved out before noon and left us with a beautiful blue sky, sunshine and a pleasant seventy-five degrees.

* * *

"Are you getting nervous, Mark?" I asked my intended over a light lunch that he had barely touched.

"A little," he replied, pushing his plate aside. "Aren't you?"

"Somewhat, yes, although I'm more nervous for the reception than the wedding. I've never been surer of a decision than I am about marrying you," I said with a sincere smile.

"I think you were born to entertain, Allex," Mark snorted. "In three days you have put together a party for a dozen people and done most of the cooking, too."

"Oh, that's not true, Mark. Kathy is doing a dish, plus something else she won't tell me about. Amanda is making several dishes, and Emilee is trying her hand at making mini-sweet rolls for desert," I reminded him. "I'm left with making the bread rolls and a spaghetti salad. That's all. That does remind me that I need to do the next step with those rolls or they won't be done in time." I set our bowls in the sink full of warm, soapy water after scraping the bread crusts into a bowl for the chickens.

"While you do that, would you like me to take care of the chickens?" Mark asked, nuzzling the back of my neck.

Now that the birds were back out in their coop, it was a bit more time consuming to haul water out to them. Having them in the greenhouse for their daily feeding and watering was convenient though it was nice to have the increasing odor away from the house again.

"That would be wonderful, thank you." I really did have more things to do. The least of all was to choose a dress to wear.

I set the bread on the next rise and then filled a pot of water to cook the pasta for the spaghetti salad. I decided on using multi-shaped pasta to make it fun: bow ties, penne, spirals, and shells, whatever I could find. I knew it would be limited because of not having certain fresh things like green onions, cukes, green pepper and cherry tomatoes, though I doubted anyone would notice that there were only sliced black olives, canned tomatoes, and rehydrated onions with the pasta.

After I drained the cooked pasta, I drenched it with my remaining half bottle of Italian dressing and added the few extras. It would have to do.

The rolls were formed and on the final rise, so I took a shower and started getting ready. Kathy and Bob arrived early so Kathy could help with any last minute things, and Bob kept a nervous Mark occupied.

"Have you decided on a dress, Allexa?" Kathy asked, flipping through my closet.

"I was thinking about this one." I pulled a hanger out from the back of the half bath door. It was a soft sage green, with a long skirt, long sleeves, and a deep V neckline. It was plain, but I thought it lovely and wearing it made me feel good.

"Oh! That is very pretty, Allexa! I don't think I've seen it before. When did you get it?"

"Actually, it's sort of new. I bought it last year because it just called to me. It was a size too small then, so it's hung the closet. Now that I've lost almost thirty pounds since November, it fits perfectly, even a bit loosely. I know it's rather plain, but I love the color."

"I think it will be perfect," Kathy said. "Can I pick out earrings for you?"

I agreed. She selected two pairs for my double piercing: one of simple gold chains and the other long and sparkling.

"What about wedding rings, Allex?" she asked.

"I hadn't given it much thought," I said, and a touch of panic hit me until a memory slid to the front of my thoughts. "I have an idea." I opened a glass box on my dresser. "This box was specially made by a stained glass artist the year my mother died," I explained to Kathy. "He inlaid dried Bleeding Heart flowers that were picked from the plant my father gave my mother for their twenty-fifth wedding anniversary." I opened the box to reveal my parents' wedding bands. "I know Mother's ring fits me, perhaps Dad's will fit Mark."

"What a lovely gesture," Kathy said, taking the rings from me. "Don't worry, I won't lose them. I want to polish them up." She left me to finish combing my hair.

* * *

At 3:30, our guests started arriving. Amanda took over arranging things on the food table, while Kathy kept me in the greenhouse so Mark could shower and change clothes.

"Keeping Mark and I apart is silly, Kathy! We've been living together for the last two weeks," I said, pacing, and then sitting on the bench by the fishpond, the water gurgling happily from the full batteries. There has fortunately been enough sunlight that the solar panels have kept the batteries charged.

"Tough!" she said. "Stay here. I have something for you I need to get from the car." She left, leaving the door open. The breeze it brought in was welcomed and it helped to soothe my growing anxiety.

When she returned, she had a bouquet of flowers! It was made up of a hodgepodge of baby's breath, zinnia in bright yellow, wild ox-eyed daisies, blue forget-me-nots, and a single rose. The combination was stunning, and I almost cried over her thoughtfulness.

At four o'clock sharp, she let me out of the greenhouse to greet my guests and my soon to be husband.

* * *

"You look stunning," Mark said as he took my hand and walked with me to where our friends and family waited with Pastor Carolyn.

When we said our vows, Mark added some of his own. "And I promise to never, ever leave you. It's until death do us part. Now that I've said that in front of everyone, you will have to believe me."

When Carolyn called for rings, Mark looked panic stricken.

"Don't worry, Mark, we got it covered. I hope yours fits," I whispered to him. Jacob walked up to Carolyn and held out his hands. The newly polished gold rings sparkled in the sunlight.

"Anything you would like to say about these rings, Allexa?" Carolyn asked.

I turned to my new husband and said, "These are my parents' wedding rings. I think they would be very pleased that you and I are now going to wear them." I slid my father's ring onto Mark's finger to find a perfect fit. He took the other ring from Jacob and placed it on my finger.

"I now pronounce you man and wife," Pastor Carolyn announced proudly.

* * *

"It was all lovely, though I hadn't expected for us to make such a big deal over getting married," I confessed to Mark as we accepted a glass of wine from Bob.

"I think it was just enough, Allex," Mark said, giving me yet another kiss. "Your family and friends wanted this, and who are we to deny them?"

Right before we were ready to start our buffet feast, which included a wedding cake Kathy had made and decorated with fresh nasturtiums, a vehicle was heard coming down the road. The military Humvee came to a stop across from our group.

Both the driver's door and the passenger side opened at the same time. The driver stepped out, holding a rifle, while the passenger walked around the vehicle and came up to us.

"Good afternoon, everyone, I'm Captain Andrews of the United States Army," he introduced himself. "This looks like a celebration of some sort."

"It's a wedding, Captain. Can we help you?" I said, noting something about him was familiar.

"Congratulations to the happy couple," he said. "I've come to Moose Creek to see if there is anyone who needs assistance in relocating to Marquette."

"I don't think there is anyone left in Moose Creek, Captain. I believe any survivors have already moved to town," Anna said.

"What about everyone here?" he asked calmly.

"We're fine, Captain. We don't require any help," Bob said. "Are you going to force us to leave our homes?"

Captain Andrews looked at each one, lingering on Emilee, and then said, "No. I'm not interested in stressing our already overloaded system."

During this brief conversation, Eric and Jason came from the house across the street, carrying a case of Eric's latest brew. When they saw we had visitors, they quietly set the beer down and advanced slowly. Even limping, Eric was silent in his stealth.

The driver of the Humvee had been standing a few feet from the vehicle, far enough for Eric and his brother to approach from either side. In one swift act, Jason held a knife to the young soldier's throat while clamping his other hand over his mouth. During that same move, on the other side, Eric relieved the now prone young man of his M4 carbine rifle.

With the rifle tucked under his right armpit, and a crutch under his left, Eric advanced silently until he was within range, and touched the barrel of the rifle to the Captain's ribs. Captain Andrews froze.

"Sargent Rush, I presume." The captain turned his head slowly.

"Sir," Eric stated, not moving the rifle, and yet acknowledging the officer's recognition.

"I'm not here to make trouble, Sargent," Captain Andrews said. "Can you lower that weapon?"

"No sir, not yet. Mom, will you relieve the captain of his service weapon?"

I could tell Eric was in a different mental zone. I strode forward and took the gun from his service holster and backed away, out of reach, and set the Beretta M9 on the table.

"It appears as if you were right, none of you need my assistance," Captain Andrews said, smiling. "If you're wondering how I knew it was you, son, I recognized your daughter from your stay at Sawyer this past winter."

"Captain, *are* you going to force us to go to Marquette?" I asked.

"No, ma'am, I'm not. My orders were to clear out Moose Creek. It's obvious to me that you're not *in* Moose Creek," he replied with a friendly grin.

"Okay. Then would you care to join us for dinner?"

"That's generous of you. Thank you, I think we will. May I turn around now, Sargent?" he asked. Eric stepped back, still holding the rifle level.

When the captain saw his driver face down on the ground, he chuckled. "A green recruit. Can he get up now?"

As the young man stood, he asked, "How did you get the drop on me so easily?"

"Too much time spent in The Sandbox," Eric replied.

"Ma'am, you will get no trouble from us, I promise. Will you ask your son to lower that weapon? It doesn't help the digestion having a high powered rifle aimed at you, especially when it's in the hands of a trained sniper," the captain said. "Sargent, after you arrived last February, I did some inquiries on your service record." He looked at Eric's crutch. "What happened to your leg?"

Mark, who had been silent this entire time, now spoke up. "A wolf tried to include Eric in his dinner plans. Eric disagreed with the menu."

"His foot and calf were mangled pretty badly, but Mark put him back together," I said. "We eliminated the threat—all of them," I said as steely as I could and with as much implication as I could manage.

"You're a doctor?" The captain's attention was now focused on Mark, who responded only by nodding. "We sure could use you in the city. Please consider joining us."

"I'm needed here, but thank you for the invitation," Mark said coldly and politely.

The captain had been eating from a plate put in front of him, even sipped from the cup of beer set beside him by a silent Amanda.

"Captain Andrews, what happened to our two friends in Moose Creek that were forced to leave a few days ago?" I said accusingly.

"I'm sorry, I don't know anything about that," he said calmly, and took another sip from his still full cup. "I can tell you have a competent and well-rounded group here: military expertise, hunters, a minister, a doctor, and some excellent cooks," he took another sip of beer. "A fine brew-master, too. If you decide you want to relocate, you would be more than welcomed. You have some highly desirable talents. We could really use you, but we won't force you. If you decide to stay here, we will let you be."

This alarmed me for some reason.

"Can we discuss this option among ourselves and get back to you? In say a week?"

"Yes, I will need a week to pack," Anna said. I looked at her sharply.

"Same here," Carolyn chimed in.

He smiled. "I think that can be easily arranged." He stood and moved away from the table. "Thank you very much for your hospitality, but we must be going. When you're ready you can reach me by calling 911, dispatch will find me."

They drove off without even asking for their weapons back.

* * *

"Anna, Carolyn, do you really want to go to Marquette?" I asked, shocked.

"Of course not," Anna said. "However, if he thinks some of us *do* want to be relocated, he might give us that full week before coming back."

"Mom," Jason spoke up, "do you believe him? That they will let the rest of us be?"

"No I don't," I said, taking a deep breath. "We may have bought a few days, however, we need to get out of here before he comes back with enough troops to *take* us."

"Where will we go?" Amanda asked with a frown.

"I don't know."

* * *

The festive mood of the afternoon wedding was completely doused by Army Captain James Andrews' visit.

"Mom," Eric limped forward, "are we really leaving here?"

"I don't know what we should do," I said. I looked at my guests, my friends, my family. Were they still looking to me to answer their questions, give them guidance? This time I really felt I was out of my realm.

"I've never known you to run from anything before," Jason said, sitting down across from me. "Why do you think we should leave?"

"That's a good question, son. I don't want to leave. I'm happy here." I smiled at my husband of an hour. "However, I fear for what — or who — may come after us. While Captain Andrews seems sincere, I don't know if we can or should trust him. Eric, you spent a few days with him, what are your thoughts?"

"I take him for an honest man. I think he will do his best to keep his word, and if the situation changes, I believe he will inform us first. I can't say exactly why I feel that, but I do," Eric answered. He lowered himself into a seat next to Emilee and picked up the captain's gun, ejecting the magazine. "Nice gun. Beretta M9, 92A1, fifteen plus one rounds, double-stacked magazine. Would you mind if I kept this, Mom? That revolver is only a five shot. This one makes me feel right at home." He grinned when I nodded.

"Tell you what. Let's not make any decisions tonight," I said. "We can regroup in the morning and discuss this over breakfast," at which point Mark gave a quiet cough. "Make that lunch, around noon." Everyone laughed and I blushed.

CHAPTER FIVE

I felt the warm presence at my back, curling around me, nuzzling my neck. I turned into the embrace.

"Good morning, wife," Mark said with a sleepy smile, placing a gentle kiss on my mouth.

"Good morning, husband," I replied with a heartfelt grin. A twelve-hour honeymoon wasn't much. However, I was optimistic that we had many years ahead of us to make up for it.

An hour later I slipped out of bed and started a pot of coffee, noticing how late in the morning it was. While the coffee brewed, I started the generator to take a shower.

"If that shower stall were bigger, I'd join you," Mark said seductively from the other side of the glassed in enclosure, startling me.

"You're insatiable," I teased, turning the water off. He handed me a towel when I emerged, then stepped into the stall himself and turned the water back on.

There was now just an hour before everyone would return for this conference on what to do. Last night before everyone left, we forgot to discuss who would bring what if anything, but sandwiches were always good to have. I opened two jars of the recently canned fish to make a tuna-like sandwich spread. I mashed the processed fish, adding some chopped onion, homemade mayo, and a few dashes of Worcestershire sauce. Once more it struck me that this might be the last of that pungent sauce and I better go easy on it. I covered the bowl and set it in the refrigerator, which had begun cooling when the gennie was started. Mark's pharmaceuticals and narcotics needed the cooling too, though the air temperature was decidedly lower than normal, and soon keeping things chilled wouldn't be an issue.

* * *

Since the air was chilly for early August, having dropped from yesterday's balmy temperature, we all sat or stood around in the house at the kitchen table instead of the picnic table outside.

"Has anyone come up with any ideas?" I asked bluntly.

"George and I have decided that we really *are* going to Marquette," Anna announced.

"Why, Anna?" We'd become close over the past year and it pained me to hear her decision.

"As much as we love this town, Allexa, we can't stay without food and supplies, and we're almost out. The garden we started was completely destroyed by the ash, and the hunting, well, the animals are all dead," Anna lamented. "I'll leave you in charge, if it will make any difference, but there's really no one left that we know of that will acknowledge any form of Moose Creek government."

"When are you leaving?" I asked quietly.

"We figure we'll stretch it out a few days," she chuckled. "When we do leave, George wants to leave his rifle and shotgun here with you. I do believe you were right before, when you said all weapons would be confiscated once we arrived in town. Why give them any more? Besides, we might want them back some day." Anna smiled wistfully.

"I'm going too," Pastor Carolyn announced. "I have no congregation any longer, so no reason to stay here. Besides, I'm getting too old to stay by myself. Maybe I can do some good in town in the few years I have left. Allexa," her voice quivered, "you've been an inspiration to the town. I wish more had listened to you. I will miss you."

A lump formed in my throat.

"Well, you aren't getting rid of *us* so easily," Bob said, breaking an awkward moment. "Kath and I are with you, whatever you decide to do."

"Which brings up, Mom, what *are* you going to do?" Jason asked. "Because you know we're with you a hundred percent, no matter what."

I looked at all these faces, my family and my friends, as they looked at me, waiting. What was I going to say? Mark and I hadn't discussed this last night and I couldn't very well make a decision without his input. We were now one.

"Mark, what do you want to do?" I asked, turning to him as he sat beside me. "There are few patients for you to attend to. Do you think you might get bored?"

"Actually Allex, I was thinking if I could get some books on animal physiology I could be a part-time veterinarian," he responded. "And I could teach the kids biology and anatomy."

"You've obviously been giving this more thought than I have," I confessed. "I want to stay. This is our home and I don't like the thought of being run off my land." I turned to my two sons and their families. "If that's okay with you."

They nudged one another and grinned.

"We were betting you would say that! Yes, Mom, it's okay with us," Jason said.

I looked around the room. Joshua was hanging around the back, near the door. Ken stood behind his wife, Karen, who was sipping her fresh coffee and eating a quarter of a sandwich.

"Joshua, are you leaving or staying?" I asked, though I was fairly sure of his decision. Even at the young age of twenty, Joshua was very mature and dedicated.

"Well, Miss Allexa, I have given it some thought, and it didn't take much to realize that if I left, Bossy and Matilda would miss me. If I took them too, they would likely get butchered for food," he stumbled on those words. "So I'm staying, though I would like to move."

"Move where, Joshua?" I asked. I didn't like the idea of him moving further away, even to protect his animals.

"Actually, I was thinking about one of these vacant houses on this road," he replied, shyly, looking down at his feet. "I've only got five acres where I am, and I know I could claim more. The truth is, I don't like being so alone. I miss Martha."

"I think it's a good idea for you to move here, Joshua! I'd rather you were closer to us anyway," I answered. He looked pleased at this. "There are two places, one on either side of here that might work fine for you. I'm sure that between all of us, we could get you moved quickly."

I hadn't heard from David and Jane to my south for several months. That property had a lot of cleared area that might be suitable for grazing, plus a creek and an apple orchard in need of care. I decided to ask the boys check it over.

This was turning out better than I expected, though there was still a matter of our law enforcement couple. I didn't have to wait long.

"I think this might solve a dilemma for us too, Allexa," Ken said.

"Yeah," Karen interrupted her husband. "As much as we like our house, we don't like being so isolated from everyone, not now. Quite frankly, Allexa, over the last six months or so, we have come to feel like part of this family. So is there one of the empty houses we can occupy?"

This confession stunned me. I'd always liked these two, and I know that the hard times we'd shared tend to bond people, but I didn't know they felt this way.

"I know the perfect place." I smiled, thinking of the fairly new house on the other side of where I'd like to put Joshua, past the curve. It was also the first house at that end of the short road and would be the first line of defense.

This line of thought brought to mind a book I have on long-term survival. I'd have to pull that out later and reread it—maybe it would give me some hints on what more we could do to protect ourselves.

"I'm really sad that you've decided to leave, though I understand," I said, looking at Anna, George, and Carolyn. "Our lives aren't going to be easy. Anna, if it's all right with you, I'd like to go with you to the township office to call Captain Andrews. It might help me take the pulse of the city as to our situation, and the reliability of the captain's word."

* * *

It was later in the afternoon, after everyone else had left, that Eric, Jason, Joshua, Mark and I, walked down to the house where David and Jane had lived. They had been silent all winter until the situation with the Wheelers had come up, and then they disappeared from our lives. I called out to them as we approached the small house. No one answered and there was no sign of their many dogs either. Eric took the front door, while Jason took the back. Neither door was locked and the place was indeed vacant.

While those two checked for any signs of leakage from the pipes, Joshua roamed from room to room, I checked closets, and Mark walked around outside. After fifteen minutes, we all met back in the front room, now much cleaner than the last time I saw it and eerily quiet.

"No sign of any water leaks, Mom. In fact, David had pulled all the breakers in the power box. He must have drained the pipes too: there isn't any water in any of the traps or toilet, not even in the water heater," Eric announced.

"The closets are empty of clothes, and so are the cupboards. I noticed too that all the Ham radio equipment is still here. Maybe we can figure out how to work it. It's my opinion they moved out and don't plan on coming back." I turned to Joshua, "What do you think of the place?"

"I think it's right cozy, Miss Allexa. I like it. I'd like to look at those two outbuildings to see if they might be suitable for Bossy and Matilda."

"Mark, did you see anything interesting?" I asked once the three young men had left to inspect the barns.

"It's a nice place, Allex. There are fruit trees out there that could use some care if they've lived through the ash," Mark replied. "Let's take another look."

* * *

There was a clearing in what should be full sun that looked like it had been a vegetable garden at some point in the past. It was close to the creek that the properties shared; that could be used for supplemental watering. This was a well thought out location, and it wouldn't take much to get it functional again, if we were we to have enough sun to start growing things again.

"These are apple trees, Mark, and it looks like a few cherries too," I commented as we walked among the now mostly leafless dwarf trees. "Eric took Master Gardening in Florida and I took it too when I lived in Brighton. I still have my books, so I think we should be able to help this orchard come back to a productive life with some much needed pruning!"

Thoughts of apple pies, and cider and vinegar were racing through my head!

"You lived downstate?" Mark said, eyeing me. "I didn't know that."

"There are lots of things you don't know about me, dear. I'm not hiding anything though."

We had come back around to the front of the house where the other three were waiting for us.

"What do you think, Joshua? Think Bossy and Matilda could live here?" I asked.

"Oh, yes, Miss Allexa! That barn is much like what they have now and it even has a section that would be good for the chickens. I think that other building could be fixed up to be my own little dairy!" It was obvious that Joshua was excited with the prospect of the move.

On the short walk back home, we discussed getting Amanda over to give it a good cleaning and an airing out. Jason would work on the generator, fixing it if need be, while Eric and Joshua started moving any remaining hay and feed for the animals before moving the animals themselves.

"With all of us involved, how long do you think this should take?" I asked to no one in particular.

"Two, maybe three days," Eric said, still leaning heavily on his crutches.

"I really don't have much to move," Joshua admitted shyly.

"I can help you pack up the dishes and kitchen stuff you'll need," I offered. "What's the matter, Joshua?" I asked when I saw him wipe his eyes.

He swallowed hard. "I'm...I'm just not use to everyone being so kind to me."

"Do you remember what Karen said, about being family? Well, I think you have been welcomed into being part of *this* family, Joshua," Mark stated. "I understand being overwhelmed with it. I'm feeling the same way."

* * *

I met Anna at the township office around noon to make the call to Captain Andrews.

"Anna, I want you to know how much your friendship has meant to me these past months," I said to her before we made the call.

"The feeling is mutual. I know we haven't always seen eye to eye, though I do respect your views and opinions," she replied. "You have to admit that I was right about one thing though..."

"What was that?"

"You and the doctor."

"Yes, you were definitely right about us." I chuckled. "Now, let's get this over with."

I dialed 911 and told the dispatcher that Captain Andrews was expecting my call. He hesitated oddly, before responding with a sharp, "Yes, ma'am."

The captain came on the line rather quickly. "Andrews."

"Captain, this is Allexa Smeth in Moose Creek," I said, turning on the speaker so Anna could hear the exchange.

"I was doubtful that I would hear from you, Ms. Smeth, and I'm delighted you've changed your mind." His voice sounded too cheery to me.

"Oh, *I* haven't changed my mind, sir, but I want to make arrangements for several others. The township supervisor and her husband wish to come to

Marquette, along with our pastor. The pastor will need someplace to stay, and Anna and George have family they can go to."

"I see. It's always helpful to us when we don't have to do a placement. When would you like me to send someone for them?" He sounded disappointed.

"No need to send anyone, Captain, they will drive themselves in on Monday," I ventured, looking over at Anna who nodded her head at me.

There was a pause on his end. "There is a checkpoint on the edge of town. I will notify them of the arrival. Please understand there will be some necessary processing before they are allowed to move into any housing," he said. "It should only take a few hours. And would you get word to her that she should bring whatever food she has as a gift of sorts for her family? It will help out until the rations can be adjusted."

"I'm right here, Captain. I will be sure to do that," Anna answered.

"I have a question or two for you, Captain," I pressed.

"Yes, Ms. Smeth?"

"First, are we allowed into town to shop? And next, I would like your word again that we will be left alone out here." I reminded him of what he promised.

"Yes, ma'am, you have my word that you will be left alone. As for shopping, I will have to get back to you on that. What few shipments we have gotten in are needed for those under our care," he replied. At least he didn't say no.

I hung up the phone.

"I hope he's a man of his word, Allexa," Anna said. "We will stop by on our way in to say goodbye."

CHAPTER SIX

JOURNAL ENTRY: August 5

It was a busy day! All of us pitched in to get Joshua and the animals moved into their new home. Amanda had already done the cleaning, and said it was easy and it looked as if Jane had cleaned before leaving.

* * *

"It really was just a wipe down to get rid of the dust, then mopping and vacuuming," Amanda said. "Jason had the generator going to test it out, so I washed all the curtains and hung them back up on the windows to dry. The place is ready." She smiled in satisfaction. "I'm glad there was something I could do to help. Some days I feel so useless."

Our biggest challenge was getting old Bossy onto a trailer for the move. She did *not* want to get in there. With Joshua on one side and Matilda on the other, Bossy eventually relented and made the trip to her new home. She immediately took to grazing under the apple trees, as did Matilda.

"I don't know how to thank everyone, Miss Allexa," Joshua mumbled, looking embarrassed.

"There's no need, Joshua. We're all happy to have you here. You're the first step in us establishing a new community," I said to him. "It's like the phoenix that rises from the ashes: we will rise too, one wing at a time."

* * *

Anna, George and Carolyn stopped by this afternoon on their way into Marquette.

"I don't know if you will be allowed to communicate with us, but if you get the chance, Anna, please leave me a message at the township. I'd like to know how you're doing. I'll check the answering machine every Friday." I hugged her goodbye.

"Here are my rifles and the shotgun," George said, laying three weapons on the table. "I'm going to keep this old .22 revolver. The firing pin is messed up, so it's no good, and I thought it might be interesting to see what becomes of it when we go through their processing procedure." He gave me a wink. I think George understood more than he was letting on.

"Here are the keys to the pickup truck," he went on. "It's yours if you need it, and don't forget it takes diesel."

Carolyn already had tears in her eyes, and her hug was long and surprisingly strong.

"I think this time it *is* good to 'let go and let God'," she said, tears trickling down her heavily lined cheeks.

"Yes it is, Pastor. I hope to see you again," I said in all honesty.

"Well, if I see Him first, I'll put in a good word for you," she said.

The three got into Anna's car and left.

* * *

"I feel as if I've lost a large piece of myself," I commented to Mark over a simple dinner of pasta served with a thickened venison soup and fresh bread.

"I understand, Allex. They've been a large and important part of your life for a long time. Well, maybe not a long time, but definitely during an important time of your life," Mark said.

* * *

I harvested the first of the green beans from the greenhouse, the ones I planted in early June. They were small and thin and I wanted us to have the very first of what was produced. I felt selfish that I didn't want to share with my sons, not yet anyway, so I kept the beans a secret until dinner.

"Where did you get fresh beans, Allex?" Mark said with obvious joy when I set his plate in front of him.

"These are the first of what I planted back just before my birthday. I know they're small, but I wanted us to have some first. I think they go well with the spiced beef stew on fresh pasta, one of my favorite recipes from *A Prepper's Cookbook: 20 Years of Cooking in the Woods*."

I smiled. I know I was still trying to impress Mark, or maybe it was more wanting to please him now. I lit the slender white candles on the table and turned on the battery CD player for some soft music.

He poured some wine in my glass, then in his. The love I saw in his eyes took my breath away.

The song "Waiting For a Girl Like You" came on. Mark stood and took my hand, pulling me into his arms for a very romantic slow dance and I knew I had made the right decision to marry him.

* * *

Jason grinned. "We hit the jackpot, Mom."

"Big time!" Eric slapped his brother's shoulder. "If this works the way I think it will, that is."

"What are you two talking about? And where have you been now?"

I knew they had gone off on one of their scavenging jaunts, and they don't tell me where until they're back. I've tried to explain that wasn't a good practice.

"We decided to check out the Sportsman Club down near Blind Belly Road," Jason said. "I doubted we find any ammo or weapons, which we didn't, but we found targets. Boxes and boxes of metal targets, you know the kind that pivot or spin when hit?" He paused for effect. "They're bulletproof, Mom."

"From my understanding," Eric went on, "they will withstand a small caliber bullet, anything under a .38, like a .22. However, if we layer them, they might stop armor-piercing rounds such as a .45 pistol shot, or a rifle in 5.56 or 7.62. Since the targets are only one-eight inch thick, it might take four or more to make them effective, but we've got lots to play with."

"I thought we could make a sandwich-board with two, creating a sort of bulletproof vest, but they're too heavy for that," Jason said. "If the layering works, I can build us protection to shoot from behind. I think certain windows that we might use to fire from can be made much safer!"

"And after we test out how many are required to withstand armor-piercing rounds, I'd like to make a protected crow's nest up on the roof," Eric said.

These two never cease to amaze me.

* * *

Late in the afternoon I heard some commotion outside only to find out the boys had finished their target testing and Eric was hauling lumber and some of the heavy metal sheets up on to the roof. They hammered away for an hour then came down.

"I'm not quite done, Mom, but do you want to see your latest addition?"

"Not really, Eric," I replied. "The need for what you're doing is a reminder of how much danger we're still in, and I really don't want to think about that right now."

"Oh, okay." He sounded disappointed. "I'm leaving the ladder here for now, at least until we finish. After that, if it's alright, Jason thinks we should build a permanent ladder on this side of the house too."

I reached out and took his hand. "Eric, I really do understand the need, and I think what you've come up with is ingenious, but I'm tired. I'll look at it another time."

CHAPTER SEVEN

JOURNAL ENTRY: August 10

We spent the morning working in both the greenhouse and in the garden. The garden is alive, barely, not flourishing like it should. However, there hasn't been any regular sunshine in weeks, with the exception of a few days surrounding our wedding, a brief respite from the dreariness. The solar panels in the greenhouse are working out very well. Even ambient light recharges the batteries that keep the pond and the lights going.

The high ash cloud is now circling the world, a band that is allowing only filtered sunlight to the northern hemisphere. Without Internet or television it's impossible to know if South America is helping with the food shortage, or how they are affected.

* * *

At two o'clock, Mark and I drove to the township hall to see if there was a message from Anna. I was delighted to see a light blinking on the answering machine.

"We need to start the generator to listen to this call," I said to Mark. "Let me show you where the switch is, in case you ever need to use it."

We went through the hall into meeting room where we had done the food distribution last winter and from there into the maintenance area. In Pete's office everything was neatly labeled and I quickly found the switch that turned on the whisper quiet generator that ran on propane.

"Let's hope there is enough gas left so we can at least listen. If not, we'll take the machine back to the house with us."

"Allexa," Anna's voice came over the speaker, "it's Thursday and we just arrived at my sister's house. This has been a horrible experience! The three-hour processing has taken three days! Right after we got there, we were immediately separated and questioned. Interrogated is more like it. I don't know where Carolyn is. I haven't seen her since we got here.

"George told me later that they took the gun, as expected, but kept demanding to know where his ammunition was. When he told them he'd used it all hunting rabbits, they laughed at him and pointed the empty gun at his head and pulled the trigger! And they took away George's pocketknife, the one his father gave him for his sixteenth birthday fifty years ago. I'm not sure if that made George sad or angry.

"That night we got our suitcases back. Of course they had gone through them. It looked like they had dumped it all out then stuffed it back in. Oh, and my jewelry case is gone.

"That place is nasty, Allexa. It's dirty, smelly, and overcrowded. We each got one bottle of water a day, plus a bowl of rice and one slice of bread. That's it! One skimpy meal per day. I kept trying to tell them we had family to go to, but they wouldn't listen.

"And the nighttime. Lord, have mercy! We could hear things...hitting, beatings, crying, and other things I don't even want think about. We huddled in a corner, hands over our ears, but even that didn't keep out the sound of the rats scurrying around.

"We finally just up and walked out this morning when no one was watching. Even though the car keys had been taken from us, I had a spare in one of those magnetic boxes, so we did get the car back. The box of food we had for my sister was gone, and most of the gas had been siphoned out.

"I never expected to be treated this way! If you ever talk to that Captain Andrews again, don't trust him! He lied to us. The city is in shambles and I'm so worried about Carolyn."

I was stunned.

Just then a military Humvee sped by on the main street, going out of town, followed shortly by Kathy's red convertible. With the top down it was easy to see that she wasn't in the car, but two soldiers were, and they looked like they were having a great time.

"Mark, go shut the generator off, and hurry!" I said. I unplugged the answering machine and wrapped the cord around it. I stuck it in the back seat of the car before Mark rejoined me. As soon as he got in, I headed for Bob and Kathy's house down the road.

That car was Kathy's baby and she would never ever let someone take it! Something was very wrong.

* * *

The front door to the house stood open. I pulled my Kel-Tec from the shoulder holster and edged along the garage, trying to stay out of direct sight of the foyer. Once alongside the door, I peeked in and almost lost it. There was so much blood!

"Mark! Help me here!" I called out, and stepped inside.

Bob was in the living room, sitting in a kitchen chair, tied tightly with what looked like a clothesline. His head was down, his chin resting above the ropes that were used. I could see a bullet hole in the middle of his forehead.

It was deathly silent. I put my gun away and followed the red streaks on the floor to the kitchen, where Kathy had dragged herself and lay in a pool of wet blood. I gently turned her over. Her face had been battered and her lip was split. Her red hair was smeared with the deeper red of congealing blood oozing from a cut on her scalp. Her jeans were pulled half off and still clung to one foot.

Mark quickly knelt down opposite me and searched for a pulse.

"She's still alive," he reassured me. "Bob is dead."

I stood shakily, and noticed that all the cupboards were opened and everything had been pulled out and thrown on the floor.

"Allex! Pull yourself together and get her a blanket, a sheet, anything!" Mark commanded.

I looked at him for a second, then ran to their bedroom and yanked off the top blanket from the bed. I stopped in the bathroom long enough to grab a couple of big towels.

"Can you help her, Mark?" I asked, freeing her foot from the bloody and torn jeans, and then tucked one of the towels between her legs where most of the blood was coming from. It was obvious she had been raped, brutally, and perhaps repeatedly.

"I hope so. We need to get her back to the house where I can examine her better. Help me wrap her in this blanket and get her to the car," Mark was so calm, so business-like.

"What about Bob?" I asked, my eyes pleading for any scrap of hope.

"There's nothing we can do for him. He's gone, Allex. Let's just concentrate on Kathy."

We lifted her as tenderly as possible and laid her in the back of my car. I put another blanket over her and we sped home.

* * *

I hurried into the house to set up my massage table to lay Kathy on so Mark would have a higher surface to work on, like we did for the surgery on Eric's foot after the wolf attack. After covering the table with a clean sheet, I helped Mark bring her in.

Redheads tend to have pale skin, and Kathy was no exception, and her skin was taking on a translucent look. She was losing a lot of blood.

I started the generator and set up lights for Mark to work, and then moved the table closer for his instruments. A quick spritz of bleach water on the wood, then a bleached sackcloth towel and we now had a sterile surface for his instruments.

As we gently removed the blanket she was wrapped in to give Mark access to her injuries, I draped another in its place to keep her warm. Then I began to carefully wipe the blood from her face and hair so Mark could see those injuries too.

She moaned. Her eyes widened in fright and she tried sitting up.

"Kathy!" I threw my body across her, facing her so she could see me. "You're safe. We're here. You're safe," I kept repeating. She fell back against the table and sobbed.

"You're hurt, and Mark needs to examine you to see how bad it is, okay? Can you tell me what happened?"

I needed to distract her while Mark worked.

"Bob was out in the barn when the Humvee pulled into the driveway and four guys jumped out, weapons drawn. From the house, I could see Bob grab his rifle. One of those guys shot first and caught him in the knee, and he managed to shoot back before going down. I'm sure he hit one of them before another shot hit his shoulder." She winced when Mark removed the towel.

"I saw them come toward the house, so I locked the door and hid in a closet. I didn't know what else to do, Allexa. Bob wouldn't teach me how to use a gun," she said, tears running down her face.

I grabbed a couple of kitchen towels and tucked them under her head like a pillow.

"Can she have some water?" I asked Mark and he nodded. I filled a glass from the kitchen sink and added one of Jacob's straws, bending it so Kathy wouldn't have to sit up. I gave her a sip, and then continued washing her face and the hair around the laceration on her scalp, sending fresh blood oozing out.

"What happened next, Kath?" I urged to keep her talking.

"I heard a lot of banging around in the kitchen. I think when they couldn't find any food they got pissed and started looking everywhere." She let out another sob. "That's when they found me in the closet."

"The first one hit me, really hard, and he was on me." She shut her eyes tight. "He raped me, Allexa." She gripped my hand so hard my fingers went numb.

"The others went out and dragged Bob in. When that first one forced me into the living room, they had tied Bob to a chair. They," she breathed hard, crying harder, "they made him watch while they all took turns raping me, hitting me. Then the fat one put a hand gun to Bob's head and shot him!" she wailed. "The fat guy told me to shut up and hit me with that gun. I don't remember anything else."

"You did good, Kath, you did real good," I said, comforting her as bet I could. "You rest now."

* * *

"What do you think, Mark?" I asked quietly, even though I was sure Kathy was out.

"The injuries are extensive, Allex." He looked up at me with sorrow in his blue eyes. "I'm a trauma doctor, not a gynecologist, and that's what she needs to repair the damage."

"Stay with her, I'll be back shortly," I said, leaving the house. I could feel the anger surging through me as I hurried across the road.

Eric looked at me with questions in his eyes. He instantly knew something was wrong.

"Is Don's landline phone still working?" I asked.

"Yes," he said. "I unplugged it and hid it so Emi wouldn't be tempted to call her mother."

"I need it. *Now!*"

Within moments, Eric had retrieved the bright red desk unit and plugged it in. I dialed 911.

"Put Andrews on the line, now!" I snarled into the receiver. The dispatcher said not a word, and put me through.

"Andrews," the Captain sighed.

"You promised to leave us alone!" I spat at him.

"Ms. Smeth. Yes, I did, and I will," he replied.

"Then why did you send those men to terrorize us this afternoon?" I yelled, getting even angrier.

"What are you talking about?" He actually sounded perplexed.

"Four of your soldiers rode into Moose Creek today in a Hummer, shot and killed one of my friends, raped his wife, and ransacked their house!" I started breathing hard. "Are you going to deny sending them?"

"Who did they kill, Allexa?" Captain Andrews asked quietly.

"Bob, the big guy," I said, my voice cracking. "Kathy is in really bad shape. Mark is doing all he can, but he's not a gynecologist, and that's what she needs. She needs surgery to repair the damage they did to her." I paused for a moment. "She might die, Captain."

"Do you know who these four were?"

"No, though one of them was wounded, and Kathy described one as fat. Oh, and they stole her red convertible; it's going to be hard to miss."

"I'll get back to you," he said with controlled anger and hung up.

"Bob is dead, Mom?" Eric looked at me in disbelief.

"Yes, and Kathy is dying," I sobbed.

* * *

We've learned to leave at least one of the boys at the house across the road. If ever there was a need for defense, two directions were better than one. Eric followed me home, while Jason stayed.

"She's sleeping," Mark told me when I arrived back at the house. "I gave her a light sedative, against my better judgment. I've no doubt that blow to the head has

467

resulted in a concussion, and she shouldn't have any drugs, but it might be a moot point if we can't stop the bleeding and replace some of the blood she's lost."

"Can we donate?" I asked.

"It would be too risky without knowing everyone's type," he replied.

"The boys are A-negative, I'm O-positive, and Kathy is AB-positive," I remarked immediately.

Mark looked startled and said, "I'm not even going to question how it is you know her blood type, but yes, we can do a transfusion from all three of you if need be since she is a universal receiver. That will buy us some time."

Mark set up the equipment and Eric went first so he could relieve Jason.

Jason had finished donating his pint when we saw flashing strobe lights in the dimming twilight coming down the road, preceded by a military Humvee. Jason and I both grabbed our rifles and stepped out.

Captain Andrews emerged from the driver's side of the Hummer, and a pretty, short, blonde haired woman got out of the source of the flashing lights: an ambulance. She was dressed in wrinkled scrubs and carried a large medical bag.

"Allexa, this is Dr. Denise Streiner, the gynecologist you asked for." Andrews looked at the rifles in our hands. "Believe me, I understand your wariness, but you won't need those."

"Dr. Streiner, please come this way." I looked at Captain Andrews briefly and snarled, "You stay here."

When we got inside, I introduced the doctor to my husband.

"Mark, this is Dr. Denise Streiner, a gynecologist. Dr. Streiner, my husband, Dr. Mark Robbins. And this is—"

"Oh, Kathy!" Dr. Streiner rushed to her side. "Kathy is one of my patients. What happened to her?"

I explained as briefly as I could what Kathy had told me, Mark adding that she'd received two pints of blood.

"How did you type?" Dr. Streiner asked.

"For whatever reason, my wife knows everyone's blood type. Kathy is AB-positive, and she was given A-negative," Mark replied.

While Dr. Streiner added her instruments to the examining table, I took the opportunity to explain.

"Kathy and I would go together to the blood center to donate. I'm the second most common type; she's the second most *uncommon*. It seemed worth remembering. My head gets filled with all sorts of trivial data."

Kathy blinked her eyes open and saw Dr. Streiner.

"Denise?" she whispered.

"I'm here, Kathy. Don't worry, I'll take care of you." Denise blinked back some tears, though her voice never wavered.

The two doctors scrubbed as best as they could in the kitchen sink, and then I assisted them with sterile gloves and tied masks to their faces. At that point, I left them to do what they could and stepped outside to confront Captain Andrews.

He must have recognized the determined scowl on my face.

"Before you lay into me, Ms. Smeth, I did not send those men here, and I didn't even know about this situation until you called," he scowled right back.

Eric arrived, coming up quietly behind our visitor.

"Hello, Sargent Rush," the captain said. "Your mother hides her expressions well, though I did see a flicker of eye movement that told me someone was behind me, and I assumed that if I didn't hear the approach, it must be you." He turned to face Eric.

"Capt..." Eric started, then looked confused. "Sir, may I ask what's going on? Even when field promotions were common, a captain doesn't generally make the leap to colonel in a week."

"You have an exceptionally observant son, Ms. Smeth," Colonel Andrews said turning back to me. "Can we sit somewhere?"

"I'd like you to listen to something first, *Colonel*, while we sit." I retrieved the answering machine from the back seat of my car, and led the way to the greenhouse.

After plugging it in, I hit the play button, and Anna's voice spoke:

"Allexa, it's Thursday and we just arrived at my sister's house. This has been a horrible experience! The three-hour processing has taken three days! Right after we got there, we were immediately separated and questioned. Interrogated is more like it. I don't know where Carolyn is, I haven't seen her since we got here."

The colonel listened silently while the recording continued.

"Adding in your deception about your rank, you now know why I'm so upset and why none of us trust you. We are not your enemy, Colonel, though it would appear that you are ours. Would you care to explain yourself?"

"Understand, ma'am, that I owe no one an explanation, except for my superior officers. However, for some reason this little community is tied to a bigger problem, not as a cause, mind you, but as a target."

"A target? Why would we be anyone's target?" For a moment I forgot that I was so angry with him.

"I don't know. It's just one piece of a very complicated puzzle." The colonel stood and paced for a moment, looking intently at the flourishing vegetables in the grow boxes. He sat down again on the bench by the water pond.

"I was sent to Sawyer because of a growing and festering hole of corruption that had been reported within a month or so of the first earthquake last fall. I decided to come in 'undercover' as it were, as a lower ranking officer. I mean to find the head of this and dispose of it. I'm being stalled and I don't know where to dig, since I'm not from around here. I'm old school military, ma'am, and I don't tolerate this kind of corruption, the kind you're experiencing firsthand."

"I see," I mumbled. "How can we help?"

The colonel smiled. "Thank you, but I don't know if you can. That being said, this current event will give me an opportunity to shake things up a bit."

"I don't understand," I said. "How?"

"Finding an injured soldier and a red convertible should be fairly easy. One or both of those will lead me to the others that participated. Once I have them, I will execute them if need be, one at a time, until I have the information I require."

"Execute, as in kill?" I asked, astonished over his casualness.

He looked at me in surprise. "From what I've heard, Ms. Smeth, this town has done its share of dispatching its enemies, quickly and without remorse. Do you have a problem with my method?"

"No, actually, I don't, Colonel. I thought there would be more legality you were required to follow."

"Not anymore, Ma'am, not anymore. We did up until Yellowstone, but now I get to take the gloves off. Anything goes," he replied stonily. "I *will* get to the bottom of this, and when I do, the punishment will be swift and severe. Count on it!"

Eric stepped into the greenhouse. "Mom, Mark wants you inside." I hurried into the house, leaving the colonel listening to the soothing sounds of the waterfall.

* * *

Both Mark and Denise were rinsing their instruments in the sink, their masks down, hands still gloved.

"How is she?" I asked, approaching the table.

"Denise did some very interesting surgery!"

"Her uterus is horribly shredded; that's what was bleeding so profusely. I tied it off at the juncture above to stop the bleeding. I need a regular operating room to finish removing it safely," Dr. Streiner said. "Once that's done, Kathy should be fine, but she will have to stay in the hospital for a few days."

"Thank you, doctor."

The ambulance driver and Eric brought the gurney in, and transferred the inert Kathy, strapping her down for the drive into town.

"I'm going in to assist with the surgery, Allex," Mark announced

"No!" I placed my hand on his arm. "You promised to never leave me, remember? If you go, they may not let you come back!"

"I will guarantee his safety, Ms. Smeth, and I will personally bring him back in the morning," Colonel Andrews said from the doorway.

"Allex, I know so little about gynecology. I could learn a lot from Dr. Streiner. Knowledge that someday may help me save you, Emilee, or Amanda. I'm a doctor, Allex, this is what I do. Please don't make me choose, because I *would* choose you," my husband pleaded with me. I removed my hand from his arm.

"You're right, Mark, this is you and I won't make that demand of you out of my own fear." I kissed him lightly and turned to the colonel. "You better keep your word on this!"

* * *

JOURNAL ENTRY: August 11

It's hard to believe that we've been married only nine days and how quickly I have become accustomed to having Mark by my side. Without his presence I slept poorly and fidgeted all night. This morning finds me restless and bleary eyed, anxious for his return.

All of what Col. Andrews told me yesterday keeps running through my mind and little of it makes sense. I understand him investigating this kind of a problem from a lesser rank; many will open up to someone closer to their own status. For this I can forgive him, though it isn't my place to bestow forgiveness to anyone.

What still doesn't make any sense is why anyone would be trying to hurt us. This is a small town, we haven't harmed anyone, well at least no one that didn't try to harm us first, and then that was just self-defense.

I don't get it.

* * *

While I was pouring a second cup of coffee, Emilee came bounding across the road. She seems to be getting taller every day.

"Nahna, Dad just had a phone call! He says you need to come over right now," Emilee relayed in a very grownup, matter-of-fact tone.

* * *

"Yes, Col. Andrews?" I kept my voice level when I returned his call. Dispatch had saved the phone number from yesterday, so it's now our means of communication. I don't mind, it's better than going to the township hall to make a call.

"I thought you would like to know things have moved quickly," he said. "I have all four culprits in custody and they can't stop talking."

"What have you learned and where is my husband?"

"Dr. Robbins is assisting in a second surgery this morning. Another rape victim came into the ER during the night, a victim of the same attackers. We picked the guys up a couple of hours ago. Your friend should be awake soon and I need her to identify these men. It would help her to have you here." The actual request was left unasked.

"Do I get the same safe passage?"

"Of course. In fact, I will meet you at the security gate myself." He sounded relieved. "One hour?"

* * *

"No, Eric, you *cannot* come with me!" I said to my son. "I will *not* risk any of you being detained. If the colonel is still lying, then he has Mark and me and we will find a way to escape. Do not argue with me! Besides, I need you and Jason to take care of Bob. We can't leave him in the house, tied to a chair."

"You're right, Mom. We'll take care of it. Please be careful."

* * *

I waited a hundred yards from the rusting security gate on County Road 695, until I saw the colonel walking up to the single guard, then I drove forward.

"Always so cautious, Ms. Smeth?" Colonel Andrews asked, smiling. He lifted the gate so I could drive my car through.

"Yes, Sir, I am, and I think I have every right to be. I want to see my husband."

"If you follow me, we will go directly to the hospital. There you can see Dr. Robbins and your friend," he replied, handing me a security clearance badge, his smile gone.

* * *

We rode the elevator up to the sixth floor of the quiet hospital in strained silence. There were few visitors and fewer patients, since all elective surgery was cancelled and only the direst of illnesses or injuries were admitted, a necessity with the lack of doctors and nurses.

Stepping out of the tiny elevator, I breathed the relieved sigh of a claustrophobic. Then the smells assaulted me: disinfectants couldn't hide the odors of urine and feces and blood that wafted through the halls.

"This way to the surgical lounge," Col. Andrews said, leading the way. When we approached the double doors, they opened and Dr. Streiner stepped out. Her face froze when she saw me.

"I will leave you here, Ms. Smeth, while I make arrangements for you to see Kathy," Col. Andrews said, and he left.

"Dr. Streiner, how is Kathy doing?" I asked when she emerged from a set of nondescript double doors.

"I removed her uterus. It was damaged beyond repair, but I know Kathy had no interest in having children. There were other injuries as well, though none life threatening." She looked solemnly at me. "She's lucky you found her so quickly or she would have bled to death within an hour. For all of that, she's doing well, but I'd still like to keep her a few days for observation."

"Where is Mark?" I asked, glancing behind her.

"He did amazingly well for not having much OB/GYN training." She avoided my question.

"Where is he?" I asked again.

"You should really consider encouraging him to stay here, where he would be more useful."

There was something about her stance, her tone, and a look in her eye. There was a smug hostility I didn't like. She was more of Mark's professional equal than I was and I felt jealousy rising within me. I tamped it down and took another approach.

"Denise, I know Mark is an amazing man, and I know he's handsome, and charming and kind. He's a really good person. But he's *my* husband." I could have said more, lots more, but I didn't.

She looked away. "Am I that obvious?"

I smiled in understanding. "He has the same effect on me."

"He must love you a great deal, Allexa. You're all he would talk about," she admitted. "But I *will* take him away from you. You're just a mousey little farmer and he's a brilliant doctor. You don't deserve him." Denise lifted her chin. "He'll be out in a minute," and she stepped toward the double doors, sneering at me. I was shocked by her verbal attack and I was trying very hard to ignore the insults she just lashed at me.

The swinging doors opened and Mark stepped out. His somber expression faded when he saw me and he took me in his arms for a long, embarrassing kiss.

"Ahem," Denise cleared her throat. "Excuse me. Let's look in on our patient." She turned away from our blatant display of affection.

We walked down the hall to the elevators and rode in silence to the floor Kathy's room was on, which was marginally cleaner and by far less noxious in odor. She lay against the crisp white pillow, her freshly washed red hair fanned out like a flaming halo. She opened her eyes and smiled.

"Hi, Allexa," she said sleepily. I sat down next to her on the bed and took her hand, tears threatening behind my lids.

"Hi to you too," I said softly. "You look better than the last time I saw you."

"Well, that wouldn't be hard to do," came the retort I expected from my gal pal of many years. "I was a mess." Now the tears formed in *her* eyes. "I owe you one, my friend. I understand I owe you many. If you hadn't come by when you did…"

"If she hadn't, we wouldn't have caught the men responsible," Colonel Andrews said from across the room. None of us had seen him waiting there in the shadows when we walked in. "Do you feel up to making a visual confirmation on these scumbags?"

"The sooner the better, Colonel." Kathy saluted the colonel from her bed and he laughed.

Mark and I rode with Kathy in the ambulance that took her and a wheelchair to the National Guard Armory where the men were being held under heavy guard.

Colonel Andrews pulled in beside us as we were settling her in the chair.

"Please follow me," he said, walking briskly around the outside of the squat red brick building along a broken cement path to what looked like the parade grounds.

The ride was a bit bumpy for her, and Kathy winced. I stopped Mark from pushing only once.

"Are you okay, Kath?"

"Let's get this over with," she replied, and we kept going until we hit the open field, where four young men were standing in front of a brick wall, handcuffed and shackled.

Against the red brick building stood a squad of a dozen soldiers at parade rest. Sheltered and semi-hidden by the gloomy shadows, they were there as security and as witnesses.

"Ma'am, do you recognize any of these men?" the colonel asked Kathy formally.

"Yes, I do. I recognize all of them as the men who attacked my husband, raped me, and that fat one on the end is the one who shot my husband in the head," Kathy replied calmly, with tears streaming down her still bruised and swollen face.

"Corporal Jones, do you have anything to say?" Colonel Andrews addressed the first man. The answer was silence. "Then for the charges of rape, accessory to murder, theft, and for behavior unbecoming a member of the military, I sentence you to death."

Colonel Andrews went through the same charges with Corporals Carter and Griffin. When he got to Sargent Streeters, he added the charge of first-degree murder.

"Do any of you wish for a blindfold?" he asked. The one named Griffin said yes. "Tough, you can't have one, close your eyes," the colonel replied harshly.

Colonel James Andrews pulled his service revolver, and shot each one of them in the head from a short distance.

Mark was shocked by the execution; I was expecting it. I'm not sure about Kathy, but she didn't protest.

"Doctor, can you confirm death for me?" Andrews requested. Mark pulled a surgical glove from his pocket and after slipping it on, felt for a pulse on each of the soldiers lying in the brown grass.

"You were quite effective, sir. May we leave now?" Mark asked flatly.

"Thank you, and yes, please return Ms. Kathy to the hospital," Colonel Andrews replied, and then turned to me. "I would like to talk to you further. If you'll ride with me we can talk."

"No," Mark interjected immediately. "She stays with me. If you want to talk to her, you will talk to *us*. You can either come back to our car or we will rejoin you here, but we will *not* be separated!"

"As you wish, Doctor. I will wait for you here."

We helped Kathy back into the wheelchair and pushed through the ER doors, only to be met by Dr. Streiner. She beamed at Mark, but her smile for me was less than friendly.

"I can see you're getting ready to leave. This has been a pleasure, Mark. I've got some surgery scheduled in a couple of days I think you will find interesting. I'll give you a call and let you know the times," Denise said, offering her hand.

"Don't bother, Dr. Streiner," Mark said stiffly sliding his hands into his pockets in obvious rebuff. "I have no intention of ever working with you again." Denise looked like she'd been slapped. "I heard every word you said to my wife outside the surgical suite. You insulted her, and you insulted me and the integrity of my marriage. I don't care if I ever see you again, and I'm certainly not going to be caught alone with you under any circumstance." With that, Mark turned his back to her and we walked arm in arm to the parking lot.

Before getting into the car, Mark took me in his arms and hugged me tight. "You're twice the lady she is and you have a class that she doesn't even know exists. I'm proud of the way you handled her," he kissed me soundly then said "And I can't wait until we get home!" His lascivious grin made me laugh and forget all about Denise Streiner.

* * *

Colonel Andrews was leaning against his vehicle, a dull brown Humvee, when we pulled back into the parking lot.

"Join me for a late lunch? There's a nice little restaurant around the corner," he offered.

"There are restaurants open?" I asked in surprise.

"Not many, but we *are* trying to bring some normalcy back to the town," he confirmed as we walked the short distance.

We settled into a booth and the men ordered sandwiches while I ordered a large salad and a bottle of water.

"I feel I owe you an apology about earlier," the colonel said, "I know it was a shock, but the word will spread quickly about the executions. Those who are taking liberties with the populace need to understand that they are being hunted down and the punishment is swift and severe. I have limited control over the civilians, but I have full authority over the military, and that includes all branches."

"What about General Marlow? Doesn't he outrank you?" I asked.

"Ah, now that is a good question. I've been doing some digging, as I mentioned, and his records are evasive." The colonel wiped his fingers on a red and white checkered napkin. "But that's not what I wanted to talk to you about. As a gesture of good will, what can I offer you or do for you?"

I didn't need to think twice. "Power. Can you get the electricity restored to us?"

"That's it? Just electricity? Done! It should be back on in the morning," he smiled in relief. "Anything else?"

"Well, I did ask before about shopping..." I reminded him. Mark was sitting quietly, his sandwich finished.

"You must understand prices have gone up a great deal. What is it you want to look for? I'm assuming food."

"Yes, there are certain supplies I'd like to replenish, and I'd also like some normal things, too. I'd like to see Emilee in a dress that fits, or at least a skirt, and Jacob needs shoes. Is the fabric store open? Material would be good to have." I turned to Mark. "What would you get if you could?"

"Other than to replace the medical supplies that we've used recently, I can't think of anything I need that I don't already have." He smiled at me warmly.

"Feed!" I thought suddenly. "Is Lamb Z Divey open?"

"I'm not familiar with the place. What is it?" Andrews asked.

"It's an animal feed store," I said. "There is an old song: "Mares eat oats; does eat oats, and little lambs eat ivy.' The store name is a play on that: lambs eat ivy — 'Lamb Z Divey.' The animals need hay. The chickens need feed and straw, oh, and cat food and dog food too!"

"I know what we need," Mark said, "Flour! This sandwich was a treat, but Allex makes incredible bread, much better than this, and she needs flour."

"This will cost a great deal, you understand," Colonel Andrews warned. "Inflation has skyrocketed, and there are no more credit cards. Debit cards are taken, only because it's an instant transfer from a bank account."

"So the banks are operating?" I asked, thinking about a very large check sitting in my dresser drawer. There was also a matter of the cash John had left. I didn't know how much was there as I had never counted it.

"Yes, only nine in the morning until noon."

"So can we come in to shop?"

"Yes, I will make the arrangements. When would you like to do this?" he took out a notebook and jotted something down.

"Since tomorrow is Sunday, how about Monday and Tuesday? That will give us time to make our lists," I suggested.

"*Two* days?"

"Yes, I'd like to do it in shifts. I know all of us would like the freedom of doing a normal thing, but if you haven't found who is behind all the attacks and corruption, we're still at risk and we can't leave the houses without protection."

"That makes sense. Monday and Tuesday it is."

* * *

That night as we snuggled under the covers, Mark said, "You continue to amaze me, Allex. We have this golden opportunity to get things, and you think of everyone else except yourself. Isn't there anything you want?"

"Yes. I want to see smiles on everyone's faces! I want the satisfaction of knowing the animals are going to make it through the next winter. And I want to spend all the money I have before it's not worth anything."

CHAPTER EIGHT

I dropped all the bundles of cash on the kitchen table in front of a very surprised Mark.

"Where did you get all of this?" he asked in awe.

"John gave it to me when he left. I haven't bothered to count it. It's been sitting in my drawer since I found it along with that note that said he was leaving. I think we should take stock of what we have, don't you?"

Since the cash was still bundled neatly in groups of fifty-dollar bills, twenty bills to a bundle, the counting went quickly. John had left behind $28,000.

"Where did he get that much cash, Allex?"

"Remember the mining accident? He got hazard pay, and that fractured wrist doubled the benefit. I remember him saying that he requested half of it in cash, the other half going into his account," I looked at the stacks on the table. "I never asked him how much he was given as it wasn't any of my business, and considering that we spent some of it, and how much is left over, and that he took some with him, I'm going to guess it was one hundred thousand dollars, with fifty thousand in cash," I ventured.

Mark leaned back in his chair and let out a deep breath.

"Even with the hyperinflation, this is still a great deal of money, Allex!"

"Yes, it is. There's something else I need to share with you." I slid the envelope with Sven's check in it toward him. "Before you open that, I want you to know that I'm still not comfortable with having received this. Even after Simon explained the reasons, I'm still in shock by it."

Mark looked at me as he opened the envelope and pulled out the check. He looked back at me sharply, then back at the check.

"A million dollars?" he gasped. Inside was also a short note from Sven that I hadn't seen. He unfolded the piece of paper.

"I haven't read that yet, Mark. What does it say?"

Allexa,

If you're reading this, then I'm dead. Thank you for being a true friend to me while I was alive. I know this must be a shock to you, but other than my teammates, you're the only person I really know here.

Sven

"For being his friend he left you a million dollars?" Mark asked, still disbelieving.

"It's the life insurance they all had. Simon explained when he gave that to me, that Sven wanted someone to benefit from his death, and since he had no family, I guess that was me." I stood and reached for the coffee pot.

"I remember how hard you took his death, Allex," Mark said gently. "You really liked him, didn't you?"

"Yes I did. He was a good person, kind and gentle, and he had an odd sense of humor that always made me laugh. I'm not going to cash it, Mark. No matter how much we need it, it just doesn't feel right to me. I only wanted you to know about it." I poured us a refill. "So, let's start making a shopping list! I doubt we will be spending all of this cash, but if we do, we do."

* * *

With the power restored, TV and Internet were available too. How much we have missed about what's been going on is frightening.

The earthquakes in Yellowstone and the new volcano not only haven't subsided, they've spread out, creating a longer and more dangerous breach along the Continental Divide. The Great Divide begins in Alaska and crosses into the Yukon, zigzags south through Canada, and continues into northwestern Montana. From there, it snakes across Wyoming into Colorado and crosses New Mexico into South America. It hasn't affected the entire Divide, at least not yet, but much of what is west of there, Washington State, Oregon, Idaho, Nevada, Utah, Arizona and especially California, have become very unstable. Refugees from all those states are heading east, and overwhelming the limited resources along the way.

Maybe having the news again isn't such a good idea. I just can't sleep with the images of the rioting running around in my head.

* * *

The morning sun shone through the cloud and ash cover like a great silver smudge in the sky. There was no blue to be seen, only endless grays in varying depths. I was delighted and thankful to have the power back on to keep the greenhouse functioning. Even though there are ground crops still alive in the garden, there is no way of knowing if they will produce any kind of a harvest. The plants we have saved in the greenhouse may be our only source of fresh food for many months.

The dismal sky could not dampen my excitement of going into town, with guaranteed safety, and having the means to buy what we needed if it was available. The good mood was contagious when I explained to the others what we were going to do.

"Because we still need to keep the houses guarded, we will have to go to town in shifts. We also have two days to do what we need to do."

"Allex thinks we should draw lots to see who goes when," Mark said. "Personally, I think she should make the decision herself."

"Makes sense to me," Ken said, "as long as we all get to go, what difference does it make? Besides, we don't have anything to spend, so it doesn't matter to us."

"That brings up something else," I said. "And I really don't want any argument with this. John left a lot of money with me, and we are *all* going to have a share in it. There are things we need to purchase first because they are critical to our needs, like animal feed and medical supplies, but we will all get a certain amount to spend however we want."

Joshua looked like he was ready to protest.

"Joshua, your animals are critical food producers. You will not argue with me! In fact, I would like you and Jason to be on today's team, and go to Lamb Z Divey's first and get as much hay and straw as you can get on that flatbed trailer, plus chicken feed, and dog and cat food."

"Yes, Ms. Allexa, that does make sense," Joshua said.

"Mark and I will be going on both days," I said firmly, and no one disagreed. "I think Amanda and Jacob should come today too. That leaves Eric, Ken, and Karen here to protect the houses. Tomorrow, Eric, Emi, Ken and Karen come in with us, again in two separate vehicles. Any questions?" I intentionally chose Amanda to go in on the first day because of her love of shopping, and being on the first 'team' will make her happy. I want everyone happy.

* * *

At the security gate our passes were waiting, like Colonel Andrews had promised. Mine and Mark's had our names on them, while the others had 'visitor' printed, along with the date. I noted that Mark's and mine also lacked a date, but didn't say anything. I made a mental note to ask the colonel about that another time.

Jason and Joshua headed to Lakeshore Drive to follow the loop around Marquette to avoid traffic with the trailer. All of us had charged our cellphones during the night knowing it was imperative to stay in touch, and Jason was to call if they had any problems or to let us know when they were done. Before we had left home, I gave Jason five thousand dollars, and I hoped it would be enough.

"I think we should meet up at Presque Isle Park for lunch when you two are loaded up," I said to Jason and Joshua. "It will give us a chance to see what restaurants are open that we can get something for a picnic. It might be difficult hauling that trailer around, and it will need to be guarded at all times."

* * *

In Walstroms, Amanda and Jacob went one direction while Mark and I went another. There were plenty of people in the store pushing empty carts, though there were few in the checkout lines. Maybe it was just a place to be instead of cooped up at home.

"I really don't like the way people are looking at us," Amanda commented when we crossed paths in the shoe department. "Have you noticed that very few have anything in their carts?"

"You might have answered your own concern," Mark observed. "We're unusual. We're buying, therefore we must have money. I think perhaps we should stay together from now on."

This surprised me some and it also pleased me that Mark was seeing things around him from a different view. He'd arrived in town from Saginaw very disillusioned, even afraid of humanity, only to be lulled into the false security of Moose Creek. I was inwardly relieved that he isn't hiding from reality.

Amanda had several things for Jacob: shoes, socks, underwear, and a couple of new toys and books, and also some clothes for herself and Jason. She was being very cautious about what she was selecting and I asked her why.

"Have you seen the price tags? I would never buy Jacob shoes for a hundred dollars, even though he's already growing out of this last pair!"

"Then while we're here, you should get the next two sizes up," I suggested. "Boots too." She stared at me. "I can pay for it, Amanda. Get them," I insisted. "Look, all this money might not be worth anything at all in another week. We need to spend it while we can."

* * *

Mark and I added OTC items like peroxide, alcohol, bandages and Band-Aids to our cart. At the pharmacy, he presented his medical identification, and was able to purchase sutures, syringes, and some heavier drugs like morphine and antibiotics, even though we had to pay for them immediately. Aspirin, cough syrup, and other pain relievers were in short supply, so we got a few bottles of each, all at outrageously inflated prices.

At the checkout, I took a deep breath and handed over almost a thousand dollars for what we had carefully selected, and that was above the two thousand for Mark's medical purchases. It made me wonder how much the food was going to be.

While we were loading the car with our purchases, Jason called.

"We're done, Mom. I'm almost afraid to tell you how much this cost us," he said.

"Don't worry about it, Jason. I'm thankful we can do this. I need to stop at the food warehouse for flour before we leave this end of town. We'll see you at the fountain at Presque Isle in about a half hour or so."

We set out for the quick grocery stop and finding a take-out place.

* * *

When Mark pulled up to the fountain, I saw Joshua sitting on top of the bales of hay with a shotgun in his hands. Jason was there too, his .308 aimed at a dozen guys crowded around the trailer.

"Stop here, Mark!" I ordered, quickly called Colonel Andrews, and explained our situation.

"If you can hold out for a few minutes, Ms. Smeth, I'll send a few troops," the colonel said before hanging up.

The National Guard Armory was only a few blocks away, and two Humvees arrived just in time. The soldiers poured out of the military vehicles, much to the dismay of the assailants, who scattered quickly.

It felt odd to have the immediate area sealed off by our military protectors as I set two large pizzas on the picnic table.

"VIP treatment, Mom?" Jason chuckled as he cut up a slice of pepperoni pizza for Jacob and helped himself to a slice.

"I guess..." I mumbled. "I will have to thank the Colonel. I really didn't expect this kind of trouble, though I suppose it shouldn't be that much of a surprise. We're spending a great deal of money, and that was bound to attract attention."

We switched vehicles, putting our purchases in the back of the pickup truck with the bags of dog and cat food. Jason, Joshua and Amanda went to do some casual shopping with the extra money that I gave each of them, while Mark and I took Jacob home. The ever present gloom made it look later than it was. That night, Jason told me about their excursion to Lamb Z Divy's.

"The straw was twenty dollars and hay was thirty dollars a bale *and* they look like short bales. We got as many of hay as we could, which Joshua says should last six months for Bossy and Matilda, if not longer. I got only twenty of the straw, since that's only bedding. I thought about extra straw, but the trailer wouldn't hold any more and the hay was more important. Anyway, we bought ten bags each of the chicken feed and corn, plus the dog and cat food. It all came to over four thousand dollars, Mom," Jason apologized.

"It's worth it, Jason. The animals are now fed until spring," I reassured him. "Besides, next week all of that might cost twice as much, if it's even available."

* * *

Ken and Karen drove over at ten o'clock. We had already discussed they should take the Moose Creek Law Enforcement car. It might give them an edge in a tight spot.

With Eric and Emilee in our car we all stopped at the gate for passes. I was surprised to find Colonel Andrews waiting for us.

"I should have called before you came all the way in. My apologies," he said. "I'm afraid I must ask you to not shop today. You created quite a stir yesterday and the news spread like wildfire about all the money you spent. I can't guarantee your safety. The rumor is you're going to buy up what little food is available."

I was stunned.

"Doesn't us spending money help the economy of the people still here?" I asked. "What if we don't buy any food? Only clothes and other stuff?"

Andrews hesitated.

"Are there any garage sales or resale shops? Spending at those would help those people directly. Please, Colonel, just a few hours. The two children are growing so fast."

"Colonel Andrews?" Emilee piped up from the back seat. "Can I get an ice cream cone before we have to go back home?"

"Only if you let me buy it for you," he relented, smiling at her.

* * *

At home, we sorted through the bags of clothes we bought at a couple of yard sales. One place in particular had a table full of girl's clothes that fit Emi. The woman told me her daughter had died in the last bout of flu. She seemed drained of emotions, yet so sad. I made a deal with her and I thought she was going to cry when I bought all the clothes for three hundred dollars. Another stop had some jeans that would fit Emi next year. Another deal, another happy person. Though that was it for shopping.

* * *

JOURNAL ENTRY: August 19

The power has been back on for one week, so I took the chance and filled and started up the hot tub. Eric carefully sliced the plastic sheeting in two places, folding the covering on top and out of the way. It could be repaired later, but for now I wanted to gaze out over my woods like everything was normal.

* * *

I tipped the lid over, removed my robe, and slid into the hot, steaming water. I know I sighed out loud. I sat with my eyes closed for several minutes, relishing the heat and the pulsing liquid surrounding me. The sun was beginning to set, though still above the horizon. I looked out over the creek valley and a movement caught my attention. Bright hunter orange flickered in the light breeze; a marker Eric had left for a hunting blind two years ago, now tattered by time.

I watched the slight movement of the plastic tape wrapped around a mid-sized tree, and my vision also caught a movement to my left, then another to my right: a slow, creeping, stealthy movement, like leaves and twigs shifting in the wind. The longer I concentrated, the more I could make out the expertly camouflaged shapes of humans when they moved.

I stood, letting the water slide off my naked body. I moved deliberately, stepping out of the tub and picking up a towel I had laid across a chair. There was no further movement, not until I reached for my robe and I caught the slight advance.

I opened the door and stepped inside. I casually dropped the blinds over the picture window and that's when I broke into a run.

I grabbed the FRS radio and hit speak.

"Hey, boys, the west is looking a bit active, there might be some storm clouds branching out. It looks like rain could be here really soon. You might want to get those two sheets off the line," I said calmly, knowing they would understand the code: that I'd seen two hostiles.

"Thanks, Mom, we'll get the laundry in," Eric responded with another code, an acknowledgement of my message.

"What is that all about, Allex?" Mark asked as I hurriedly pulled on some clothes.

"We've got at least two people approaching from the woods, heavily camouflaged."

"Maybe they're lost," he ventured.

"Mark, no one comes in like that, clad in ghillie suits, unless they mean to take us by surprise, and surprise is *not* friendly." I picked up my M-14 and checked the magazine. "I know you don't like guns, so if you're not going to use one, please stay out of the way." I looked at his startled expression. "Mark, I don't want you hurt in any way. We need you. *I* need you." I gave him a quick kiss.

He laid his hand on my shoulder. "I understand, Allex. Is there anything I *can* do to help?"

"Yes, you can watch out the back window and look for any movement. Let me know if you see anything, anything at all."

Eric quickly made his way across the road in his limping gait, his AR15 held in both hands. Without stopping to talk, he climbed the construction ladder that was still in the front of the house from when he was working on the roof. Fortunately it was out of sight from the invaders coming from the back. Maybe we should leave it there.

Eric, Jason, and I had discussed different possibilities and the codes we would use in the event our radio signal was being intercepted. Any attack from the west was coming from the woods, and whoever it was would have to descend into the creek valley before making the final assault. That's when they would be the most vulnerable and when Eric's sniper talents would be the most logical to utilize.

Meanwhile, Jason would guard Amanda and the kids by getting them into the basement, then perching himself in an upstairs window that had been recently reinforced with the metal targets to protect the shooter. He had an excellent view of the street and three sides of the house.

I had the position of taking out anyone that made it past Eric. I knelt down beside the picture window in the living room and slid open the recently redesigned window panel. Eric had replaced the six twelve inch square panels of glass that decorated the sides of the larger pane. The new reflective one-way mirrors provided a good view without being seen, and the two lower ones slid open to provide a spot to insert a rifle barrel. I would never again question their foraging! Mark stood behind one side of the large window, watching. It was comforting to have a second pair of eyes.

We didn't wait for long. A shot rang out from overhead, and I saw a body tumble down the hill into the creek. Seconds later another shot, but I couldn't see where it landed. I heard a dull *thump* as a round hit the side of the house. A muffled shot came next and I saw a camo clad body fly backward from *this* side! Somehow one of them had made it across the creek and came up from the south, concealed by the hill and the southern end of the house, though not concealed from Jason. This was followed by a barely audible "Fall back!" and we saw three more stand to retreat, which was then followed by three more shots.

Then we waited again.

Mark looked over at me. "Are we just going to sit here?"

"Yes. It could be a ruse. We wait until Eric comes down. This is his forte, so his decision. I know it isn't easy, but we're up against professionals and we can't afford to make mistakes. Fortunately, we have our own professional sitting on the roof, and he's highly motivated."

Ten minutes later we could hear quiet movement overhead, and then heard the rattle of Eric descending the metal ladder.

"Good shot, bro," Eric said into the FRS to his brother.

"No problem," Jason responded.

I turned to Mark to explain, but Eric beat me to it.

"That is my signal to Jason to keep watching, and his that he understands," he said.

"What if those men are still alive?" Mark asked, still looking a bit pale.

I had to stifle my smile when Eric raised an eyebrow and said, "Doubtful. I will check when we recon and collect weapons."

After ten minutes and no movement at all, Mark, Eric, and I went to check on those that were shot, while Jason stood guard on the side of the hill. There were five on the west side of the creek, one of whom had tumbled and was lying half in the water. We pulled him out first.

"He's dead," Mark announced after looking for a pulse.

Eric handed me the M-4 that was lying alongside the body and yanked the dog tags from around his neck, which I pocketed.

The next three were also dead. I knelt beside the body of the fourth one and pushed to turn him over. As I did, his arm came free and he jabbed at me with a very wicked looking knife. The blade sliced into the soft tissue of my upper arm as I tumbled backward. At first there was no pain, no sensations at all, and then it built like a blazing fire. Eric was closest and he shoved the barrel of his AR15 into the gunshot wound that was bleeding profusely on the soldier's other shoulder. The pain must have been intense; the soldier's eyes rolled back in his head and he slumped.

"Allex!" Mark screamed. He was only a few steps away, though it felt like a mile to me. I've been hurt before, but nothing like this. My vision swam and I closed my eyes to block the sudden vertigo.

* * *

I woke on my back, staring at the ceiling tiles in the kitchen, thinking I needed to repaint soon. I closed my eyes again and thought that was stupid, I had just painted a few months ago after John left. Then it all came rushing back and my eyes flew open. I tried to sit up.

"Easy, Allex, you don't want to rip the stitches," Mark said quietly. It soothed my mind to know he was here.

I took a couple of deep breaths and opened my eyes yet again, focusing on Mark's smiling yet serious handsome face. I smiled back.

"That's better. Let me help you sit up," Mark slipped his strong arm under my shoulders and lifted me. My left arm was bandaged almost to my elbow and it ached fiercely.

"Oh, we ruined my shirt!" I lamented. "I really liked this one." Again, I thought that was a stupid thing to think.

"Well, it's good to see Mom is back," Jason joked, and then got serious again. "How are you feeling?"

I looked around the room. Mark, Jason, Eric, Ken, and Karen were all there, looking afraid.

"I guess I should have kicked him over instead of pushed, huh?" I tried to smile. "Where is he? I hope you didn't bring him in the house!"

"No, Mom, Ken has him tied to a tree," Eric replied. "Mark insisted on treating his gunshot wound, though agreed to do it without any painkillers."

I looked at my husband, and he shrugged. "We've already called Colonel Andrews and he's on his way," Mark said, flicking his little penlight in my eyes.

"His dog tags say his name is Ken Krause, and that he's from a Virginia battalion," Eric informed me. "I did manage to get a few things out of him before he clammed up. His CO is General Marlow."

"That's interesting..."

DEBORAH D. MOORE

Two vehicles pulled into the driveway. Colonel Andrews got out of the Hummer, and two uniformed soldiers got out of the canvas-covered transport.

Colonel Andrews let himself into the kitchen like a regular visitor.

"Ma'am, are you okay?" he asked, then turned to Mark. "How is she, Doctor?" He turned again, to Eric this time, "What happened?"

I looked at the worried man in front of me. "I'm okay, though my arm hurts like hell."

"The stab wound was long but not deep, and not life-threatening. I put in ten internal stitches, and twenty external," Mark reported. "If she hadn't moved, she would have been hit in the chest and died. This soldier was looking for a kill."

Eric reported the events up to and including the preliminary interrogation. He handed Colonel Andrews a fist full of dog tags, saying, "We're keeping the weapons, sir, especially the knife. My mother has earned the right to keep it."

"No argument there, son." He looked at me, somber and apologetic. "Allexa, I'm really sorry this has happened. I'm very close to catching the head of this mess. It *will* be over soon, I promise."

After his men put the bodies in the back of the transport truck, and shackled the prisoner in the Hummer, with one standing guard, the colonel came back into the house.

"May I speak to the two of you privately?" he asked. The others stepped outside, leaving Mark and I with the colonel.

"I believe this General Marlow is deeply involved. He was the only one I told that Kathy had been released from the hospital and was coming *here* to recuperate," he informed us, "and for some reason he wants her dead. I think he was behind the first attack too, and was only half successful when she lived. I'm not sure how *you* tie in, Ma'am." He paced the floor a bit, while we waited for him to continue.

"Where is Kathy really?" I asked.

"She's in the hospital under a false name."

"Can I see her?"

"Perhaps tomorrow," he said as he walked out the door.

* * *

Mark changed my bandages before we settled in for the night. The bleeding had stopped, and my upper arm was swollen and ungodly sore. I just wanted to sleep.

* * *

We rode the elevator to the eighth floor of the hospital and stepped out into silence. The overhead lights flickered in the ever-present dimness.

"No one knows Kathy's here, and no one except Andrews knows *we're* here. I think I'm safe," I said to Mark. "Andrews said he'd meet us in the waiting room. Why don't you find him, while I sit with Kath a bit? See you in a few minutes."

I gave Mark a quick kiss and a reassuring smile and slipped into Kathy's private room, where she was lying quietly in her bed. I started over to her when something made contact with the back of my head and everything faded.

When I came to, my arms were held fast to the arms of a chair with surgical tape and Dr. Denise Streiner was throwing water in my face.

"Oh, come on, I didn't hit you that hard. Wake up!" she snarled at me.

I opened my eyes and saw the scalpel in her hand. She gave me a vicious grin when I recognized my peril.

"That's better," she said, pacing nervously around the room. "And don't bother yelling, no one will hear you anyway."

"How did you know Kathy was here? No one was supposed to have that information except the colonel." I noted Dr. Streiner's rumpled smock and disheveled blonde hair.

"Don't be silly, I work here. *All* information about *all* patients is mine for the asking," she stated as though I was stupid. "I popped in to say hello to the new patient and guess what? It was Kathy, hiding out. She thought I was in on the deception."

"What do you want from me, Denise?"

She laughed. "Your husband of course. With you out of the way, he will be free to come to me."

"You kill me and he will hate you forever," I spat.

"Oh, *I'm* not going to kill you, General Marlow will do that. I might hurt you a little though. See, he wants Kathy out of the picture and I want you out. Of course, he wants you dead too, for what you did to his brother, and we're helping each other here." Her explanation made little sense.

"But you *saved* Kathy," I said, watching her circle my chair.

"Yeah, I did, but I took it back. Ever do that as a kid? Take back something once you realized you shouldn't have done it?" Her voice rose and fell in the cadence of a mad person.

"What do you mean?" I looked over at Kathy.

"Don't worry, it was painless. I gave her a little overdose of morphine, that's all. She slipped away quietly," Denise said, shrugging her shoulders.

"You killed her?" I gasped, a sob escaping from my throat.

"I had to! She was the last one who could expose Marlow." She sat down on the end of the bed, shifting the scalpel from one hand to the other. "See, Hank Marlow isn't really a general. He's just a bottom-rung sergeant, but when his unit was wiped out from the flu and he lived, he promoted himself. No one knew the difference. No one except Bob and Kathy. Bob used to do Hank's taxes, so it was only a matter of time that he would be found out." She smiled happily, insanely.

"That's all taken care of now. Of course, now you know too, and that won't matter once Hank gets here."

"I know why you want me dead, Denise, but why does Marlow?" I didn't know if keeping her talking would make any difference, but I had to try. "If I'm going to die, at least tell me why."

She jumped down from the bed in anger, her knuckles going white as she gripped the knife tightly. "Why? You killed his brother, that's why! After all the trouble he went through to get his brother on that prison work crew last winter, you killed him. He's really pissed at you for that, you know. His brother was supposed to slip away and stay hidden for a few days, and he went on that little escapade instead," Dr. Streiner growled at me. "I wonder what's keeping him?"

"*Little escapade*? Those men killed and brutalized dozens of people! Including *my* own brother!" I threw back at her.

"Whatever." She walked over to me and looked at the bandages on my arm. "Aw, does that hurt?" She squeezed my arm.

"AHHH!" I moaned out loud and she walked away, ignoring me.

"Where *is* he? I can't wait around all day! I have surgery in a half hour!" She looked at her watch. "I guess I'll have to kill you myself."

"You're insane; you know that, don't you?"

"Maybe a little, but some comfort from that hunky husband of yours and I'll be just fine! Maybe I'll mess up that nice skin of yours first. Mark won't like you all scarred up." She nicked my left cheek with the tip of the blade and I felt the blood run. She came at me again and drew a line down my jaw with surgical precision. I could feel the blood start to drip. I moaned from the pain, then I kicked at her with my foot, and scooted the chair backwards.

"Ouch! Now stop that!" she screamed at me.

The door burst open. "Thank you for the confession, Dr. Streiner," Colonel Andrews said, his gun aimed at her. "Marlow is already in custody and now that little speech of yours ties up all my loose ends perfectly."

Denise rushed him with the razor sharp knife. He side stepped her easily, grabbed her wrist, and disarmed her.

Mark was right behind the colonel and fell to his knees to cover me with his own body. He quickly cut the tape to free me and I sank into his embrace, my face bleeding all over his pale blue shirt.

"She's insane! She killed Kathy with an overdose of morphine!" I sobbed into Mark's chest.

"You're bleeding again," Mark observed. The gauze covering my new stitches was turning a bright red to match my blouse where I was dripping more crimson blood.

"She squeezed my arm, and then cut me!"

"What a bitch," Mark glared at Dr. Streiner, who was now handcuffed to a very burly MP. "Come with me to the nurse's station and I'll fix it, and then we're going home."

* * *

At the nurse's station, Mark washed my cuts with chilled saline, and then butterflied the one on my cheek closed.

"The one on your chin I'm afraid will take some stitches."

He had such sadness in his eyes I thought Streiner might be right, and the scars would offend him. He asked the nurse to get him a hypo to numb the skin and a number 00 dissolving suture.

"I'm going to put in a sub-dermal woven stitch. The scar will never show." And he kissed the other side of my mouth. I realized that Streiner was wrong, very wrong, and so was I. Mark was not the kind of man that would let a scar detract from his feelings.

CHAPTER NINE

"Ms. Smeth, I'm sorry it's taken so long to get back to you," Colonel Andrews apologized. "The city is in chaos with a new outbreak of this deadly flu, and I've been busier than a one armed paper hanger. However, we do need to finish up some loose ends. Kathy's body will be released from the morgue this afternoon, and I'm assuming you would like to take care of the burial."

"Yes, of course." I let out a long, controlled breath. "I'll have Jason dig another grave with the township backhoe."

"Better make that two," he said gently. "Yesterday we found Pastor Carolyn sleeping on a park bench. The coroner said she died peacefully."

A quiet sob slipped out from me.

"I will bring them to you myself," he offered.

* * *

It was a short funeral, as Kathy would have preferred, and I know Carolyn was with her God now and didn't care. Carolyn was buried with her congregation and Kathy was laid to rest next to her husband in the new cemetery that was once the township baseball field. Eric said the Lord's Prayer while leaning heavily on his walking staff, and I found that in spite of all the misery and heartache I've had to deal with, I still had more tears to shed.

* * *

"I didn't know your friends very well, Allexa, but I did admire their spunk, both of them. Because I feel a great deal of responsibility for these deaths, I took the liberty of providing for a modest wake," Colonel Andrews said, leaning against the hearse he drove that was now parked in front of my house. "Plus, I'd like to bring you up to date on all the events."

From the front seat he retrieved a large, heavy cardboard box and handed it to Jason, while he carried a pizza-warming box into the house. The colonel and the ten members of our little settlement gathered around the kitchen table and nibbled away at the four extra-large pizzas. To my surprise, the heavy brown box contained several bottles of liquor and wine.

"I wasn't sure what everyone preferred so I opted for a variety," he said, setting a bottle of Jack Daniel's on the table, then a bottle of Gray Goose, Captain Morgan Private Stock and Famous Grouse, along with two bottles of red wine and two of white.

Karen was quick to get the glasses down off the rack and poured herself two fingers of the whiskey. I handed her the bowl of ice cubes, and she plunked one into her glass and sighed.

"First, let me say I share your grief. You lost some good people." Colonel Andrews took a sip of his vodka on the rocks. "I move around a lot and consequently don't get to make many friends." He looked over at me and Mark. "I feel that you've become my friends, and I hope in time you will feel the same."

"I will admit, Colonel, I was unsure of you to begin with, but yes, I think we can be friends," I said.

"Thank you, and please, call me Jim," he said, settling into one of the wooden chairs. "Now I can tell you that I had my suspicions about Streiner and had bugged the hospital room, and if I had any idea that she was homicidal, I would never have left her alone in that room with Kathy. I definitely underestimated how unbalanced she was. Please forgive me."

"What's to become of her?" Mark asked, tightening his arm around me.

"She's made it easy for us. She had a second hypodermic hidden in her smock that was perhaps meant for you, Allexa." I shivered, remembering the scalpel. "While she was handcuffed to a chair waiting for transport to the jail, she injected herself with enough morphine to kill *two* people. By keeping her hand concealed in her pocket, no one knew what she was doing until it was too late. It must have taken her a lot to force that needle through several layers of clothing and into her thigh."

"Dr. Streiner is *dead*?" Mark gasped. "What a waste. She was an excellent surgeon."

"Mark," I asked gently, hoping he would understand why I needed to know, "you worked closely with her, did you have any idea that Dr. Streiner was insane?"

"Insane? No. But I did see right off that she was unbalanced. There is something you need to understand about doctors in general, myself included. We all have egos that surpass the average person. I would say that comes from the education we've gained and the knowledge of what we are capable of doing. That ego, though, varies greatly in each physician, depending on their own background and self-image. Personally, my medical ego has been humbled enough that I have a decent grasp on reality; at least I'd like to think so. Plus I had loving parents that raised me well, and I've always had a firm confidence in my sexuality. Denise

Streiner, on the other hand, had a very poor self-image of herself as a woman, so her whole being became focused as a doctor, which resulted in her personality being… top heavy, so to speak. She used that side of herself to get whatever she wanted, and when she couldn't get it, or rather couldn't get *me*, her reality started to slip. It was only a matter of time until her shell cracked, and that happened when she was faced with prison and her license being stripped from her. Her entire identity was being a doctor. With that gone, she was nothing," Mark replied, settling back with a glass of scotch on the rocks.

"What other news do you have you can share, Jim?" I prodded, wanting to get my thoughts away from that insane doctor, while absently fingering the itchy stiches where she had cut me. "Anything on the relocation center?"

"Ah, yes. I fired everyone and re-staffed it with military personnel. At the same time, we moved all the unattached men to a different location, the single women to another, and the families stayed at the arena. I think things will run much smoother now, and I am keeping a close eye on it. The military really is here to help. Rape and abuse is not part of our agenda." He took another sip of Gray Goose. "Oh, and you will be pleased to know that Tom White is now back in his office. He's really quite efficient."

"That's great. I'll have to give him a call. Thank you, Jim, it seems you are getting things turned back around," I said.

"Mr. White also asked me to deliver a message to you. He said the offer still stands. Does that mean anything to you, Allexa?"

"Yes, it does," I laughed. "He offered me a job as his assistant. Each time he asks, I turn him down," I added when I felt Mark tense beside me.

"I see. Well, even without you, I've no doubt Tom will get that office running smoothly again. Now if we can just get a handle on this new virus. It keeps cropping up every four or five months, and the medical examiner's office is so short staffed they can't get ahead. It's the same one that's been around, with slight mutations each time. It's still attacking the very young, the very old or those with suppressed immune systems, which seems to be a growing sector from the limited diets lately."

"What's the incubation timetable?" Mark asked.

"Quick, maybe twelve hours, sometimes longer; it depends on the person."

"Wow that is quick. Mortality rate?"

Jim hesitated. "About seventy-five percent. There are some with a natural immunity, and there's no rhyme or reason behind that. There have been a few that have recovered, but that's small in numbers."

"Has it been verified how it's spread?"

"That's the tricky part. It seems the delivery varies. It's airborne, yet it can also be transmitted by touch, so multiple methods of protection are being observed."

"I guess we all stay out of Marquette now," I murmured.

"What's going to happen to Marlow?" Eric asked.

Colonel Andrews looked at Eric with a weighty gaze, noting there was no rank attached to Marlow's name, and then took sip of his drink. "Hank Marlow is sitting in a jail cell, waiting for his court martial. I assure you, the trial will be just as swift as the one for his minions. He will then be executed for treason." Another sip. "Much of our breakthrough came from that soldier you captured, Ken Krause. It seems Marlow filled him and a handful of others with a great deal of propaganda regarding Moose Creek and your group in particular, Allexa. Krause was told you were a band of terrorists bent on taking over Marquette, and that you had slaughtered a convoy of humanitarians bringing Moose Creek much needed aid last winter."

That revelation left everyone speechless.

"When I explained to him the truth behind the lies, he actually wept, and he sends his deepest apologies. I can't fault him for following orders, so I'm sending him back to Virginia," the colonel finished. "I wish I could kill Marlow twice for all the sorrow he's caused, but one execution will have to do."

The colonel went back to his vehicle and pulled a heavy box from the back seat. "I almost forgot, here are those books you were interested in, Doctor."

"Books?"

"The ones on animals. I had someone familiar with the University library get as many books on veterinary medicine and animal physiology as he could find. Hope they're useful."

Mark's eyes glowed as he accepted the box.

It was late in the evening when everyone left, and the artificial darkness hung like a dirty curtain in the approaching dusk.

CHAPTER TEN

The next earthquake to rock the nation hit around noon and was felt all the way up the East Coast. The Florida Keys, precarious as they were, were the first to go. Aerial videos taken by a tourist on a plane ride out of Marathon Key captured the swaying Seven Mile Bridge as the pylons buckled and collapsed, snapping the long concrete bridge into several pieces and sending afternoon travelers to the bottom of the blue-green ocean.

The speculation for now is that movement from the Puerto Rico Trench was responsible for dislocating the delicate subterranean structure that held Florida afloat.

"Picture, if you will, a two-story dollhouse made of toothpicks, and someone bumped the table," one seismologist explained. "Florida sits on a bed of coral, and coral is porous and therefore fragile. One nudge of the table could easily push it off its foundation."

The bump was recorded at 7.8 on the Richter scale, followed an hour later by a powerful aftershock. The 8.2 aftershock that hit Florida was recorded at 1:15 in the afternoon and quickly downgraded to an 8.0. In the process, everything from Fort Lauderdale to Naples and south of Alligator Alley was now covered with several feet of seawater, putting half of the Everglades completely underwater. News crew helicopters recorded a mass stampede of alligators, large snakes, panthers, and other wildlife heading for drier land. In Miami, the only buildings visible were those over four stories tall, which included most of the vacation hotels along the Atlantic. Rescue efforts were underway for those lucky enough to have been in or made it to the upper floors. The resulting fast moving tsunami wiped the crowded beaches clean on what was a clear and sunny day. There had been no estimates on the death toll.

* * *

I turned the television off and we sat there watching the glow of the plasma screen fade. Neither of us spoke for a long time.

"Do you believe in God, Mark?"

"I was raised within a church, so my belief is there, yes. However, it's hard to comprehend how a merciful being would allow such merciless things to happen." He tightened his hold on me, and shuddered into my neck. "Why do you ask?"

"Well, we've been married all of three weeks and though we have known of each other for four months, I really don't know much about you, or you about me."

"True, but I know you're a good person, Allexa. You've got strong morals and a deep sense of right and wrong, all of which you've passed on to those young men across the street. How you did that on your own makes you a remarkable woman. And the most important thing I know is that I love you." He smiled and kissed me gently. I sighed and snuggled closer.

"Do *you* believe in God?" Mark asked.

"I don't know, Mark. I did at one time, but I have such doubts now," I answered honestly. "There are so many beautiful things on this planet that it's hard not to want some greater being to thank. Yet..." I hesitated, "yet I believe most bad things that happen are a result of our own fault. Why would a creator of such beautiful things destroy what He's built? What would be the purpose?

"All of these horrific earthquakes and disasters in the past year can't be just natural happenings can they? Did man trigger these events with fracking and mining and nuclear testing? I think for some it's easier to have a belief in God so there's someone to *blame* for the bad things. It's typical human arrogance to not take responsibility for our actions.

"It took me a long time to come to terms with myself and my responsibilities with this life I have. If I do something wrong or that causes pain, I accept that, even if only to myself. I don't shift the blame onto anyone if indeed it was something I did. And that's what I believe is at the core: someone has done something at some point in time to set off a chain reaction. I think when I got to that understanding is when I lost faith. There was no one left to blame, or to thank, except myself or another human, not some mystical unseen entity."

"Then you don't think it's only Mother Nature rebelling?"

"Giving credence to a Mother Nature is acknowledging yet another entity that has more control than you do. It's like blaming Mother Nature for wiping out your house with a flood, and then rebuilding on the same flood plain, only to get wiped out again. Blame Mother Nature instead of moving to a safer place. So no, Mother Nature isn't rebelling; the Earth is reacting not acting. Rebelling is a conscious act. When someone cuts a tree down, is the tree rebelling by falling on them? No, the person either cut the tree wrong, or failed to get out of the way."

* * *

DEBORAH D. MOORE

JOURNAL ENTRY: August 25

The aftershocks continue. The most recent was a 7.5, and with the subterranean infrastructure already shattered, the damage was the worse yet. From Orlando to Tampa Bay a rift has formed five miles wide, closing off any overland relief efforts for the devastated lower half of Florida. There is no solid ground for helicopters to land on and all rescues are now done by boat. The airboats that once populated only the Everglades are currently the main mode of transportation between the smatterings of tiny islands that now exist. The trapped population has turned near vicious in their quest for a spot on any passing boat, often capsizing the vessels of several good Samaritans and spilling their frightened human cargo into the muddy, predator infested waters.

With more than fifty percent of Florida uninhabitable now and covered with varying depths of saltwater, the fresh water mammals, reptiles, and avian life have all fled to higher ground looking for a new habitat and…food.

The exodus of the mass and aging population of Florida into Georgia and Alabama is now creating an overload on services and supplies in those states. The movement of people from the West Coast to the eastern side of the Continental Divide continues to overwhelm the government agencies in the Midwest. The only states not being invaded by our own population are those with extreme winter weather.

For as difficult as our lives are now, I continue to be thankful for where we live.

CHAPTER ELEVEN

"Allexa, I want to keep you updated on this virus," Tom White said when I answered my phone that was ringing with "The Hall of the Mountain King" dirge. Was it really only ten months ago I got that call from Liz Anderson with the same ring tone?

"Colonel Andrews said it was getting worse, Tom."

"Yes, it's like a ghost town here. Of course, with the price of gas, there's little traffic anyway." I could hear the familiar shuffle of papers and smiled to myself, thinking of more normal times. "The hospital is triaging in the lobby, there's so many. There's little they can do except keep everyone as comfortable as possible. They either fight it and live, or fight it and die."

"Where are they putting everyone?"

He sighed, loudly. "The elderly that come in are moved one floor up. The mortality rate is really high with anyone over sixty-five, almost ninety percent. That floor has the most service elevators available for…body removal. Children have the next floor to accommodate parents staying with them. The parents are often sick and given a bed too. The staff is trying to keep families together, it makes for easier identification."

I could hear the pain in his voice.

"How are *you* feeling, Tom?" I asked, knowing his wife and young son died in the first sweep of this virus late last winter.

"A bit rundown, tired, not eating right; you know, normal," he chuckled. "I'm also staying isolated, though, so I should be fine. Which is actually one of the reasons I called. I think it advisable for your group to stay out of Marquette. And before you deny anything, I know some of you have snuck into town and hit the yard sales. Word gets around," he added before I could protest.

"I understand, Tom. I will make sure everyone knows we're under self-imposed quarantine. You do know that some of our forays have been to spread some money around," I replied. "I'm surprised the economy has lasted this long and I'd rather scatter this cash while we can and others can take advantage of what little value it has left."

"I understand what you've been doing, and that's why I want you to stop. You're a good person, Allex, and no one wants anything to happen to you."

* * *

We finally had a break in the ever-present depressing ash-cloud cover. The sun came out and warmed the air to a delightful seventy degrees. I took the opportunity to hang sheets out on the clothesline and to work in the garden some.

"Do you think there will be much of a harvest, Mom?" Eric asked as he worked the hoe down the rows of stunted corn.

"Certainly not what we might hope for, and since those ears are forming so well, we might get a few to eat. Most will have to be saved for planting next year, though. And when you're done hoeing, don't forget to knock the stalks against each other." I went back to weeding the peas.

"Do you really think that helps pollinate them?"

"Sure can't hurt."

While the garden in the yard looks paltry for September, it had a decent head start before the ash fall hit. We might get some corn and peas. The root crops, potatoes, beets, and rutabaga are doing much better than I expected. What is really going to sustain us this winter are the greenhouse crops. The green beans are close to picking at a mature size and will keep producing for another six weeks. After that, I'll replant and maybe we will have fresh beans all winter. The bin I had set aside for compost now holds potatoes that might give Jacob his fries and Emilee her chips.

CHAPTER TWELVE

"Mom," Eric said, bursting in the back door, "you're not going to believe this, but we just came from the Resort and it's like the ash never touched it!"

"There was no one at the gate, so we cut the chain and went in," Jason cut in. "I thought we might be able to find some old manual tools at the compound, but what we found was even better...deer. A lot of deer. And moose, turkeys, and geese. I'm guessing all the stampeding we witnessed in July was the animals heading to safer ground."

"That's incredible," I said with awe. "We must have truly been on the very edge of the cloud, and that's why it moved away so quickly." My mind was reeling with possibilities. "Did you find any people?"

"There wasn't anyone at the compound, though we did see a smoke signature that might be from Mathers Lake. We didn't check it out, because we thought you might like to go with us for that," Jason said.

"We did, however, do some harvesting," Eric grinned. In the back of the pick-up truck was a six-point buck and two wild turkeys.

The thought of fresh meat made my mouth water. I also thought of all the lives that could have been saved by moving just ten miles north.

"What's all the commotion?" Mark asked, emerging from the sheltered deck where he spends his time reading. He's been engrossed in all the books Jim had dropped off last week, and I know he's thrilled with the new knowledge he's gaining on taking care of the animals.

"My boys have outdone themselves this time, Mark. Look!" I pointed to the harvest.

"Jason and I were talking it over on our way back, and we think this deserves a celebration," Eric said.

"I know this is a bit early, but what about a Thanksgiving dinner?" I suggested. "Even though Thanksgiving is almost two months away, we really don't know what the weather is going to be like. The roads may be impassable by then. Plus, every day should be a day of giving thanks."

That sobered the mood a bit, remembering we no longer had snowplows to keep the roads open and once the snow fell we could be completely isolated for months.

It was decided that in a few days, we would invite Colonel Andrews and Tom White out for dinner. Meanwhile the boys needed to hang and cure the deer and I needed to clean some birds. From past experience, I know that the quicker the cleaning is done, the easier it is.

Dressing the turkey was easy since it's just a big chicken, though I wanted to save the organs and the neck for making gravy. I boiled a big pot of water, dipped the bird, ripped the feathers off of it and gutted it in less than an hour. After setting it in the outside refrigerator, I called Amanda and Emilee over to help with the second one.

We set up the sawhorses and boards like when we cleaned all the fish in July. My thoughts momentarily drifted to John and how his demolition expertise got us a hundred pounds of fish in a very short time.

I dipped the bird again, and then let those two de-feather it for the experience.

"That wasn't so hard, Nahna, but it sure was messy," Emi announced.

Next I opened the body cavity and pulled out all the organs, separating the ones I could use and scrapping the rest. The heart and giblet would be added to the turkey broth for gravy, and the liver would make a delicate liver pâté.

Amanda had the job of using my propane torch to singe off the hair-feathers from the now naked turkeys. I washed the birds in cold water and set them back in the refrigerator. By then, Eric and Jason, along with a curious Mark, had finished skinning and hanging the deer.

"Mom," Eric whispered to me, "Mark wants to autopsy the next deer."

I laughed. Mark certainly gets into his work, and it makes sense to for him to see the internal workings of different animals.

* * *

"What can I do for you, Allexa?" Colonel Andrews said, and I could hear a smile in his voice.

"I'd like to do something for *you*, Jim. How would you like to come out here on Friday for dinner? We have some exciting news to share and my sons have managed to supply us with fresh meat that we would also like to share."

"Fresh meat? I thought all the animals died in the ash fall."

"Apparently not, Jim, and that's part of the good news."

"I would be delighted to come to dinner, and thank you for thinking of me, Allexa," Jim said.

"I'm inviting Tom White also. You might want to touch base with him in case he wants to share a ride."

As much as I would have liked to invite Anna and George, I had no idea where they were. Nor about their exposure to this virus, and I can't risk my family getting infected.

It was only Monday, and I felt our small group shouldn't have to wait to do some celebrating. I decided we should have venison steaks for dinner tonight and save the two turkeys for Friday. I called Amanda over to give me a hand.

"What can I help you with, Mom?"

"I need you to do an errand for me," I replied. "Would you take Jacob and Emilee for a walk down the road to tell Ken and Karen and Joshua about dinner tonight? That would sure help my timing out."

"Of course! I think the kids could use some diversion; they're both getting fidgety."

"What would you normally do with Jacob about now?"

"We would go to the beach," Amanda said wistfully. "It's too cold though."

I filed this in my brain, wondering if the boys could come up with a solution. After all, Emi and Jacob are *their* children.

* * *

With the days growing shorter all the time, and the false dusk coming early, we gathered at six o'clock for dinner. Along with the venison steaks, I had fixed a large bowl of rice with canned ramp greens. Then I surprised Jacob with a plateful of French fries, which got me a big hug.

"Thank you, Nahna! I love fries and I love you!" Jacob exclaimed, dipping a fry into some catsup.

"You're welcome, Jacob. You do know this is a treat, right? We don't have enough potatoes to make fries all the time, but this is a special day."

"I know, Nahna. I hope we can have more special days!" He gave a fry to Emi, who had been eying the plate.

"And here's something for you, Emi." I set down a bowl filled with lightly salted homemade potato chips. Her eyes got huge and teary. She picked one up and took a crunchy bite, sighing with obvious contentment. Then she gave one to Jacob, and passed the bowl around so others could have some too. It didn't surprise me that everyone took only one.

* * *

"That was delightful, Allexa," Karen commented while sipping on a glass of Eric's latest beer, a dark ale. "I think we've all missed fresh meat."

"Oh, yes, Miss Allexa, it was a wonderful change from dried fish and cheese," Joshua chimed in. He's been quietly working at making his new home more comfortable for him and his animals so we haven't seen much of him lately.

"How are things coming along, Joshua?" Mark asked. "Is the barn big enough for your cow and goat?"

"Oh, yes, Dr. Mark. The girls are right happy in their new home. I think because they are still together. The baby chicks are growing bigger every day and are always underfoot, but they never get stepped on. Bossy and Matilda are real careful around them."

That seemed to be the cue for Chivas and Tufts to appear from the living room where they'd been napping, and were now on the hunt for table scraps. Eric pushed back his chair to tend to the animals, giving them separate bowls of dry food with some meat scraps and rice poured on top. The two pets were doing well on the limited diet.

"While we are all here," I announced, "on Friday we're doing another bigger dinner, with company. To truly celebrate our thanks for Eric and Jason finding a source of fresh meat, we're doing a Thanksgiving dinner early and we've invited Colonel Andrews and Tom White to join us."

"What's on the menu, Allexa?" Ken asked, taking another roll from the near empty basket.

"Turkey with all the trimmings and a stuffed venison neck roast is what I have planned. The meat won't last much longer even in the fridge. I think we should eat as much fresh as possible, and then we'll set up to can what's left. Since it's their deer, Eric and Jason will cut the meat up and deliver it. That way each household has the option of how they want to cook it, or to freeze it if that's your choice."

"Other than the meat, what else is planned, Mom?" Jason asked.

"I think it would be nice for Emi to do dessert," Eric said before I could answer. "She's getting real good at making sweet things." My granddaughter beamed at the compliment.

"Then an Emi-dessert it is. I'll make rolls and figure out some veggies. If anyone thinks of a dish they'd like to make let me know. The less I have to do the better," I said, absentmindedly cradling my still very sore arm.

***

"You were awfully quiet at dinner, Mark," I said while we snuggled under the covers later that night.

"Sometimes I get overwhelmed by the family dynamics, that's all," he confessed. "It still amazes me how Eric and Jason treat you as a friend as well as their mother. The interaction is so smooth and natural, and rare."

"It isn't rare to us; it's the way we've always been with each other. I was young when I had them and I guess we grew up together. Although I maintained being the 'mom', I also treated them as mini-adults, and with respect. I hoped it would forge a deep bond between us, one I never had with my parents."

"Really? As stable as you are, I would have thought you had a great upbringing," he responded, sliding his hand down my hip.

"I didn't have a bad childhood, but there were many things in the way I grew up that I set out to change with my own children, and affection was at the top of the list."

"Well, I would say it worked, because those two young men adore you and would do anything for you."

* * *

"Do those stitches itch, Allex? You keep fingering them," Mark asked, pouring me a cup of coffee.

"As a matter of fact they do. When can you take them out?"

"Well, since it's been two weeks. I think I can take them out now, and I'll take the ones out of your arm while I'm at it." He cupped my chin gently, tilting my head for a better look.

The slice along my jaw Dr. Streiner made with her scalpel was a grim reminder of what she did to me...and to Kathy. The sooner the stitches came out, the sooner I could forget about her, though it would be a long time before I forgot about Kathy's death.

With tweezers and thin scissors, Mark snipped and tugged the few stitches out one at a time.

"You have remarkable healing, Allex. These could have come out days ago." He kissed the fine scar. "And the scar is so faint it won't be noticeable at all once the redness fades."

"I've got good genes, and a good doctor," I smiled up at him.

"Perhaps. I think it has a lot to do with your health, and maybe your happiness, which I'll be happy to take some credit for." He kissed me deeply and I silently decided he was right.

CHAPTER THIRTEEN

Jason and Amanda came over early to help bring in chairs and set the table. With all the extra guests coming we set the three tables up in a "U" shape to have enough seating space.

"I wish we had some table decorations that would be suitable," I lamented.

"Let me see what I can do," Amanda offered. She finished setting the table, then left.

I set the rolls for the second rise and basted the turkeys again. They were small, maybe ten pounds each, and both fit into one large roasting pan. They were now a golden brown and the scents coming from the meat and the stuffing were heavenly.

I saw Amanda coming back across the road, but she veered off toward the barn and I lost sight of her. Even from this distance I could see that determined look she gets, and I knew not to interfere.

Ten minutes later, she came in, carrying a basket, set it in the center of the large table, and proceeded to pull things out. Shortly she stepped back, to reveal what she'd been doing.

"What do you think, Mom?" She beamed at her handiwork. On the table was the basket, with branches of hops and bittersweet artfully spilling from it.

"That is stunning, Amanda! I know you must have gotten the hops from down in the gully, but where did you find the bittersweet?" The papery pale green hops contrasted perfectly with the orange berries.

"They were in the basement, in a box marked 'Fall Decorations.' Aunt Nancy was really organized. Do you like it?"

"I love it. Thank you so much for doing this." I was feeling an unexpected tearing over her thoughtfulness and gave her a quick hug.

Just then, Mark came in with an armload of firewood.

"It smells fantastic in here!" he gushed. "Is there anything I can do to help?"

"As a matter of fact, you can help me drain the turkeys. My arm is still too sore to lift much."

"Is it very painful? Maybe you're doing too much."

"I'm fine, I just don't want to stress it." I gave him a quick kiss, and then retrieved a pot we could use for the juices that would become gravy.

At 3:30 the rolls came out of the cook stove oven as the military Hummer pulled into the driveway. The boys took that as their cue to bring the family over, and soon Ken, Karen and Joshua arrived. I'd say no one wanted to be late for our early Thanksgiving dinner.

"The bar is open. Thanks to the colonel's generosity during Kathy and Carolyn's wake, we still have plenty of alcohol." I motioned everyone to the side counter. Soon I heard the tinkle of ice cubes filling glasses, and friendly chatter among my guests.

With everyone milling about, it gave me time to pull Amanda aside so we could set the food out. Two golden brown turkeys took center stage, and were flanked by a bowl of steaming stuffing, a pot of rich gravy and a large casserole of fresh green beans. On the dining table were a basket of hot rolls and two platters of deviled eggs.

* * *

Tom belched. "That was incredible, Allex. I can't remember the last time I ate so much. I'm stuffed!"

"But there's dessert," Emilee protested. She'd been keeping her sweets a secret, even from me.

"I'm sure all we need is a few minutes for dinner to settle, Emi," I said to her. Her enthusiasm with baking has been a source of pride for me.

"So, Eric," the colonel remarked, "where did you manage to harvest our dinner? I really thought all the wild animals were gone."

"We thought so too, Colonel, but Jason wanted to check out the private resort north of here for tools, and we surprised a flock of turkeys in the road."

"The resort is a private club that holds over thirty thousand acres in wildlife refuge," I added. "Most of the animals there are accustomed to humans and to being fed. I'm surprised, too, that there is wildlife still there. I know the place pretty well; it's where I've worked for the last eighteen years."

"After we gave the compound where all the cabins are a cursory check to make sure no one was there, we went back to the field where we last saw the turkeys. Fresh food was more important than more tools," Jason continued. "There was a nice buck under the apple tree, grazing right along with the birds. Since Eric can shoot double skeet, he took the birds that took wing when I shot the buck." They both grinned. "We make a good team."

"As they were leaving, they noticed smoke above the trees in the direction of Mathers Lake, which is one of the residential areas not owned by the resort." The guests were now rapt with attention. "More people means survivors. I think we should investigate. Jim, Tom, what do you think?"

Tom was quick to reply. "The city services are stretched to the limit, Allex, we really can't take any more in."

"Tom, I appreciate your concern, but anyone up there won't need help. I'm sure they're doing just fine. I was thinking more along the lines of a trade route. They've got lakes untouched by the ash for fishing and herds of animals."

"And what do we have to trade?" Amanda asked.

"A doctor," I smiled at my husband. "And limited dairy products; and beer. There could be more, and until we find out what they need or want it's hard to speculate."

Colonel Andrews had been really quiet during this conversation up until now.

"When do you plan on going there, Allex? I'd like to come along as extra security. In fact, I'd like to bring a few of my most trusted soldiers. Only a few, mind you; you don't know what may be waiting for you."

"I think Jim has a valid point, Allex. I know I would feel better with him along," Mark stated. "Especially if you plan on trading me."

"I would never trade *you*, Mark," I took his hand in mind. "Only some of your services." I grinned.

"So when is this expedition planned for?" Tom asked.

Just then, Emilee stood and declared she was still hungry and wanted dessert. She went over to the counter where under a towel, she had hidden her treat.

"It's a focaccia," she announced. "It's got brown sugar and cinnamon on the top and rhubarb and raspberry jam in the middle."

Eric did the honors of slicing it like a pizza, giving everyone a crusty piece.

CHAPTER FOURTEEN

"Mom, where's Dr. Mark? Jacob is really sick!" Eric said, bursting in the side door.

"On the deck, I'll get him." I turned to find Mark already coming in the back door.

"What's wrong with Jacob?" Mark asked, grabbing his doctor bag and followed Eric and me out the door.

"He says his tummy hurts real bad, like he has to poop," Eric replied as we hurried across the brown grass. "I remember when I had appendicitis I thought I had bad gas."

Mark gave me a sideways glance. I knew that look to mean something serious.

Jacob was curled up on his side on the couch in the living room, crying. It broke my heart to hear him in such pain.

"Hey there, big guy," Mark sat down next to him. "Where does it hurt?"

"I'm *not* a big guy, I'm a little guy," Jacob whimpered. "It hurts here." He pointed at his belly button region.

"Okay, let me see, Jacob," Mark's voice was gentle and kind. Jacob moved his hands, and Mark examined his skin on the lower right side, feeling around. "That was good. We're going to go over to Nahna's house and I'm going to make you feel better. Is that okay with you?" Jacob nodded through dark, wet lashes.

"Jason, wrap him up in a blanket and bring him over—quickly. Carry him, don't use the wagon. I don't think he could stand the jostling." Mark turned to me and said, "I'm almost certain it's his appendix; his belly is swollen and distended. I hope it hasn't ruptured yet! We need to do surgery immediately."

We?

* * *

I quickly set up the massage table that had been used more for medical purposes than massages lately. I spritzed the vinyl down with bleach and wiped it with one of the sterile washcloths I've started to keep handy. I even laid out a few of the red cloths, though I doubted we would need them.

While Mark set up the table with his surgical tools, I brought the two standing lamps that we had used for Eric's surgery, and made sure they had the brightest bulbs possible. The table was ready with sheets and blankets when Jason arrived carrying a very sick Jacob and laid him down on the fresh linens.

"Okay, my little guy, I have to give you a shot. I know you don't like shots—I don't like them either—but it will make the pain go away," Mark said softly. "I want you to watch your daddy and not me. That's good." Mark injected the anesthesia, and soon, Jacob was asleep.

I helped Mark glove and gown and then did my own. I tied his mask, then my own, then one on Jason.

"Jason, you can stay, though you might not want to watch this," Mark warned my son. He began to work by swabbing Jacob's belly with the povidone-iodine solution.

The delicate work took less than a half hour, and was completed before the organ ruptured. Mark had worked very quickly.

When Mark finished the stitches and pulled his mask down, Jason let out a sob of relief.

"Will he need blood?" I asked.

"No, there really was very little loss. I'd like to keep him here and sedated until the morning. Jason, he's a lucky little boy. Good thing you caught this so quickly. You're staying, right?"

"Of course I am, but I need to let Amanda know he's going to be alright." Jason swallowed hard. "Thank you, Doctor, thank you!" He turned away before we could see his tears of relief.

While my grandson slept peacefully on the surgical table, I made up the futon for him, and put a mattress on the floor for Jason.

I wrapped my arms around my husband's neck. "Thank you for saving him. He would have died if you hadn't been here." Mark tightened his grip on me and sighed heavily.

"I won't say this in front of Jason, but it was touch and go there for a few minutes. It almost ruptured, and then we might have lost him. In a surgical suite, it would have been different, with all the equipment to wash out the poisons that would have resulted in peritonitis. We don't have that luxury anymore."

With limited supplies, we've gotten into the practice of immediately re-sterilizing everything; we never knew when it might be needed again. The scalpels were boiled and the sheets were washed in bleach. I folded up the table and put the lights away. What would we have done if there wasn't any power? I know we have the generator, but what will we do when there is no more gas?

Weary as we both were, we sat with Jason for an hour when he returned.

* * *

"Our emergency surgery yesterday has got me thinking about my medical bag," Mark commented over a second cup of coffee. Jason and a sleepy Jacob had left less than an hour ago.

"What about your bag? I thought you said it was sufficient."

"Oh, it is, for most situations. However, if we couldn't get someone back here and I had to do an emergency procedure wherever we were, I wouldn't have enough. I need a bigger bag." He looked thoughtfully into his cup. "Do you have a backpack or something similar?"

"I think it's time to bring out the medic kit." I went to the front pantry to retrieve the large, stuffed pack and set it on the table, watching Mark's quizzical look turn into a grin.

"You never cease to amaze me, Allex. How did you come by this? Never mind, it doesn't matter." He started unzipping pockets and opening Velcro pouches.

"I know you'll want to make changes, add some things, and remove some. Let me know what I can do." It was like watching a kid opening presents.

He opened everything. Some of the items he put back in after examining, others he spread out on the table. One of the first things he set off to the side was a package of more scalpels.

"Why are you leaving out the extra scalpels?" I asked.

"I'm not going to leave them out; however, I don't trust the packaging and want to re-sterilize everything possible: scalpels, forceps, and clamps, everything metal." He looked up. "You don't mind do you? It's not that I don't trust what you've purchased, it's just…caution."

"Of course I don't mind, Mark. Do whatever you feel needs to be done. Is the bag going to be big enough now?"

"Oh, yes! This will hold four times what the purse held," he said. "I don't want to do away with the black bag, Allex, I've gotten rather attached to it. However, this will definitely be more practical in the long run. So I have to ask: where did you get this?"

"It was one of those items that caught my attention while I was doing some online shopping a year or so ago. I had already set up the purse thing, but that duffle really called to me. It wasn't cheap, but now I'm glad I got it. And you won't have to be embarrassed about hauling around a purse."

"Hey, that's not just any purse, that's a bad-ass, brass-studded purse!" Mark joked.

I got out one of my larger cooking pots, and filled it with filtered water, setting it to boil so the new instruments could be sterilized. Once the pot was filled, I boiled it for a half hour and then let it cool. I gloved and removed the items with some tongs I had also set in the boiling water and laid everything out on a bleached towel. Mark joined me in repackaging the instruments, and then he found room for them in his new duffle.

CHAPTER FIFTEEN

Colonel Andrews arrived promptly at 10:00 A.M. with six young and not so young men and women as part of his trusted core group. I was a bit nervous at first with having agreed to this escort, however, all of his group, himself included, were dressed in civilian clothes to not be so obvious to anyone we came across.

"Good morning, Jim."

"Good morning, Ms. Smeth," he smiled back. "Where's the doctor?"

"He'll be here in a few minutes. He had to perform an emergency appendectomy on Jacob two days ago, and wanted to check him over before we all left."

"The little guy alright?" he sounded alarmed.

"He is now, but Jason and Amanda will be staying behind today, along with Joshua and Emilee."

"Sanders, you and Perkins stay here for additional guard duty. Go across to that house and introduce yourselves, then make yourselves invisible." Colonel Andrews turned back to me, "Any objections, ma'am?"

"None at all, and thank you," I said.

"Let me introduce you to the rest of my crew. They are all hand-picked for their expertise and loyalty. Step forward with name and rank!"

The first one stepped forward. "Specialist Tony Ramirez."

"Specialist Carol Midler."

"Corporal Chuck Wilders."

"Sargent Jones."

The colonel didn't hide his grin very well as he addressed the last one. "Come on, Jones, you might as well get it over with."

She gave him a very un-military glare and said "Sargent Rayn Jones."

"All of it."

Her eyes straight ahead, she repeated, "Sargent Rayn Bow Jones, ma'am."

Even as I smiled at the name, I couldn't draw my eyes away from this exotic beauty. She stood about five feet three, petite and well-muscled, and had silky short cropped hair that was so dark brown it was almost black. Her skin was the color of caramelized honey and her eyes were an unusual translucent gray with the slightest tilt. I could tell Eric was caught by her stunning looks, too.

"That's an unusual name, Sargent Jones. Is there a story behind it?" I smiled at her, hoping to put her at ease. She glanced at her superior officer who gave her the slightest nod of his head.

"Yes, ma'am," she replied with a sigh. "My grandparents are Egyptian, Native American, Caucasian, and Japanese. Black, red, white and yellow: a rainbow. My parents were hippies. They couldn't resist."

"Well, I think your heritage is a remarkable blend. You're a beautiful young lady. And apparently my son thinks so too." I turned to Eric. "Stop staring at her!" They both blushed.

"Well, now that we've got that over with, shall we get going?" Colonel Andrews said when Mark joined us.

"Did I miss something?"

"I'll tell you later," I whispered to him.

* * *

The drive up to the gate that marked the entrance to the resort property was only fifteen minutes, but that was only half of the journey. From the gate to the compound was another five miles, though we wouldn't be going in that direction once inside, at least not yet.

"The chain has been put back in place, Mom, but there's no lock this time," Eric commented.

"Maybe they're expecting a return visit," I thought out loud as the first Hummer nudged the gate open and we passed through.

A quarter of a mile in, another road veered off to the right heading toward Mathers Lake, and a few hundred yards from there was another gate. The Hummers came to a stop and we all got out.

The colonel looked at the chain and locks carefully, and then swung the gate open.

"It wasn't locked," he stated.

A shot rang out, and all the military hit the ground and rolled behind the trucks. Mark and I dashed behind an open truck door. Another shot, clearly a warning.

I was starting to get pissed off. "Stop shooting at us! We haven't done anything to you!"

"Allexa?" came a voice from behind a cluster of bushes. As he peered out, the sun glinted off his thick glasses.

"*Lenny?*" I stepped out from the protection of the heavy truck. Mark grabbed my arm but I shook him off.

Lenny made his way toward the road, rifle lowered. "I didn't know it was you. What are you doing here?"

"Oh, Lenny!" I stepped closer to him. "We thought you and Pete had been taken by those rogue soldiers, maybe even killed! I'm so glad to see you!" It was hard to contain my excitement. Our friends were alive! "What happened back there?"

"Well, we heard those soldiers coming back. They sure weren't being very quiet. We had just put that venison on to cook, so we covered it and hid behind the next house over, where the tree line starts. I guess they could smell the meat cooking, because they zeroed right in on us. They went through the house, then took the meat and kicked over the grill."

"Oh, we thought maybe you did that, to let us know you didn't go willingly," Mark said.

"Nope. We left it like that in case they came back though. We saw you come and put out the fire. Once you left, we went back to the house, got our rifles where we had hidden them, and came up here."

"I'm so glad you're safe, Lenny. Where's Pete?" I asked.

"He's inside at the compound. He's really sick — got some kind of infection."

"Maybe I can help," Mark offered.

"That would be great, only..." Lenny hesitated, "...it's a pretty tight group that's here now, and the head guy doesn't like strangers. He's got real strict rules about that."

"He sounds like the person we want to talk with then. Will you take us to him?" I asked.

All of us got back into the vehicles, and followed Lenny down the twisting dirt road. A mile later he turned left, and shortly after that I could see the water of Mathers Lake shimmering ahead. There were a few cottages along the ragged shoreline, but mostly larger, year-round structures. It was very secluded, and a few lucky souls had found a perfect retreat.

I hadn't thought before to ask Jim how well armed his men were, though it seemed prudent to do so now before we stopped.

"Each one has their M-4, plus two side arms and various knives, and trust me, they know how to use all of them," he informed me. "And you?"

"I have a 9mm Kel-Tec in my shoulder holster and Mr. Krause's knife in my boot," I replied. "I'm not sure what Ken and Karen are carrying, though I'm sure it's substantial."

Lenny pulled up to one of the nicer houses, a log A-frame with a wide porch, with several trucks parked in front. The colonel twisted the steering wheel and backed up, facing outward. The other driver did the same; a quick escape maneuver. Everyone emerged at once, and we waited while Lenny went inside. Only a few moments passed before a young, dark haired man appeared in the doorway. He looked in his mid to late thirties, fit and well fed.

"Good morning. I'm Arthur Collins. I run this place, what can I do for you?" His voice was soft, firm and held little emotion. "Before you go on, understand we do not welcome visitors here. Leonard has violated our security and will be dealt with for that."

"Good morning. I'm Allexa Smeth, from Moose Creek. This is my husband, Dr. Mark Robbins; my friend Jim Andrews, and a few of our group," I stated, intentionally not informing him of Eric being my son, though Lenny knew this. "I understand you have one of our friends here, Pete, and that he's quite ill. My husband would like to see him, and treat him if he can. And before you punish Lenny, understand he knows us, and he knows we mean no harm to your group whatsoever. Besides, we already knew you were here."

"I will take that into consideration." He turned to Mark. "What kind of doctor are you?"

"An M.D., general practice." Mark kept his voice calm, though I could tell he was nervous.

Collins nodded and looked back at me. "You couldn't have known Pete was injured until you arrived, so I'm asking again: why are you here?"

I had anticipated this question when we first decided to make contact.

"Honestly, we wanted to make contact with other survivors," I said. "Plus, we were wondering if you were interested in establishing some kind of trade between our two groups."

"What do you want from us?"

"Only the right to hunt and fish occasionally without being challenged, plus anything you might be interested in trading," I shrugged my shoulders.

"What do you have for us in return?" His questions were disturbingly blunt.

"We have a small beer brewery established, limited dairy products, and of course the medical services. I'm also willing to discuss what other needs there may be. Unless we talk, we can't know what the other has and is willing to part with." I was so tempted to cross my arms, but the body language might be misinterpreted. This was not a stupid man we were dealing with.

"Okay, Doctor, you can treat Peter. The rest of you must stay here."

"That's not acceptable, Collins. My wife is also my nurse, and I don't go anywhere without my own personal bodyguard." Mark stood his ground, crossing his arms.

Arthur stood on the porch and stared at Mark for a moment, his eyes dark with anger at being defied. He went inside without a word. Moments later, Lenny came back out, looking nervous.

"Okay, Doc, you, Allexa and one other can come with me. I'll take you to Pete."

"Jim, pick one," Mark said quietly.

"Mr. Wilders, you've just become a bodyguard. Forget you have a rank while you're here, son, these folks have twitchy fingers. I'll be right here," the colonel said quietly with his back to the house, then turned and casually leaned against the nearest Hummer.

Lenny led the way down a well-worn gravel and pine needle path to one of the smaller cottages, and walked right in.

"Boy, Art was really pissed when he came back in! He doesn't like being stood up to," he said, going to one of the back rooms and opening the door. The rank, sick smell hit me hard. Mark flinched then ignored it, though I saw a flash of anger in his eyes.

Pete was lying on the messy bed, eyes closed and his left arm on top of the covers. Even from the doorway I could see the wound seeping yellowish fluid.

"Hey, Pete," Lenny said softly to his friend. "I've brought some help. Dr. Mark is here to fix your arm." Pete's eyes fluttered open and he smiled at us.

"Dr. Mark, Allexa, it's good to see you. Do you really think you can fix this scratch? It hurts." Pete's breathing was labored.

"What did you do to it, Pete?" Mark asked, sitting down in the nearby wooden chair and opening his new medical bag. I automatically moved an end table closer so he could set things out. I was getting good at anticipating his needs.

"We were climbing over some fences and I got scratched pretty deep by the barbed wire. I washed it out with the water in my drinking bottle, but we don't have any medicine to put on things like this. I did try to keep it cleaned and covered, and it still got infected."

"Lenny, do you have a couple of clean towels? And some water, preferably sterile; maybe some you boiled then didn't use?" I asked of him.

Mark cut Pete's shirtsleeve up and back to expose the rest of the swollen, red skin. Multiple weeping lesions were centered on a deep purple gash, with long red tracks leading up the arm.

"Pete, I'm not going to lie to you. This looks really bad. It's gone into septicemia and it's dumping poison into your system," Mark stated bluntly. "I'm going to give you a shot that will numb your arm, and then I'm going to drain as much of this pus as I can. Do you understand?" Pete nodded.

Mark stood and looked at me, saying "Double gloves, N-99 masks." He looked deep into my eyes. "Do *you* understand?" I nodded. It was going to get very messy.

Lenny returned with a stack of towels and a pitcher of water. I told him he didn't want to watch, and he left. I got out two peri bottles that I had put into the new pack yesterday, filled them with the water and set them on the table. The angled spouts would let me dispense the water without getting in the way. Mark was right; this bigger pack was much needed.

Once the anesthetic took effect, I put three towels under Pete's arm and Mark wiped the arm down with povidone-iodine solution, and then sliced into it, sending a spurt of noxious yellow fluid into the first layer of towels, which I removed.

"Squirt the water slowly into the wound. I need it constantly irrigated while I probe," he said through his mask. More water, more probing, more towels.

"Ah! Just as I suspected." Mark triumphantly held up a metal barb with the forceps and dropped it on the table. We continued to irrigate until the fluid changed colors from the sickly yellow to a pale blood pink. After wiping the skin dry, Mark applied several butterfly bandages, and some ointment, then I wrapped the arm in gauze and taped it.

"Pete, the wound wouldn't heal because there was a piece of the metal imbedded in your arm. It should do better now. I didn't stitch it closed, because it needs to drain."

"Thank you, Dr. Mark. It already feels less swollen."

"It is. We drained a lot out. I'm leaving you a Z-Pak of antibiotics. Four pills today, three tomorrow, two and then one. You should be better by then." Mark stood, pulling off his gloves and mask. "And Pete, you were damn lucky we came when we did. The next step would have been amputation to your shoulder, if you weren't already dead."

I left my mask and gloves on while I bundled up all the towels we'd used and stuffed them into a cloth hamper bag.

We had been at it for almost an hour. Corporal Wilders was understandably relieved to see us and the three of us walked back to the vehicles.

"How is the patient doing, Doctor?" Collins asked from his seat on the porch, his feet up on the railing. The false casualness was no doubt meant to be distracting.

"I removed a piece of barbed wire from his arm, drained and irrigated the wound, and left him with some antibiotics. He should be fine in a few days, but he will need stitches to close the wound. Lenny can bring him to my office next Monday."

"There's a bundle of towels we used that should be washed and sterilized immediately — or burned. Pete also needs a shower, clean clothes, and clean bed linens. And, Lenny, open the damn windows!"

"I've made a few decisions while you were busy." Arthur dropped his feet to the deck and stood. "We'll come to your homes and see what you have that we may want. We certainly don't need more people here to take care of, but you, Doctor, can stay."

"I think you misunderstood our offer, Art. I can call you Art, can't I?" I tried not to snarl at him, though it was difficult. "We don't need anyone to 'take care' of us, and *none* of us are staying here. If, and it's now a doubtful *if*, we decide to do some bartering with you, it will be a mutual exchange, and will be done in town, not at any residence, and under full guard."

Who did he think he was?

"I think *you* misunderstand, Ms. Smeth, we need a doctor. We're keeping him, and you, if it makes him happy."

"Now you listen to me you arrogant, pompous dictator! There is no way I'm staying here under any conditions. I am fed up with your authoritarian bullshit and I'm leaving. Now!" Mark spat out, and turned his back on Collins.

All of our personnel pulled up their rifles, chambering a shot, and every one of them was pointed at the porch. Collins froze.

"Ms. Smeth, my apologies," Collins called out. "Please understand that for this small band of people to survive, someone has had to be in charge. It's been much easier for one person to make the rules and make the decisions. That's been me. These men and women trust me to do what's best for them. Perhaps I was a bit…hasty." He stepped down from the porch and approached us. The soldiers closed in and Eric stepped in front of us, preventing Collins from getting any closer.

"I think Ms. Smeth, you and I have something in common." He glanced at those protecting me, us, and gave me a chilling smile. He looked at Mark and said, "I assume Leonard knows where your office is. I will have him bring Peter to you on Monday at noon." He climbed the stairs and went into the house without looking back.

Mark and I climbed into the nearest Hummer, Colonel Andrews slid in behind the steering wheel, and Corporal Wilders and Specialist Ramirez hung one-armed onto the sides, keeping their guns trained on the empty porch. The other vehicle duplicated our action, and we left as one.

* * *

"What was that all about, Allex?" Mark asked, pouring me a splash of spiced rum. My hands shook slightly as I took it. "What could *you* possibly have in common with Arthur Collins?"

It was late afternoon now, and darker than normal as the heavy clouds moved back in.

"Nothing," I said a bit too quickly, a bit too sharply. I stood by the picture window and watched Eric and Rayn at the picnic table, laughing and talking, like a couple in new-love. I was happy for him; everybody needs somebody. The other soldiers were playing Frisbee with Chivas on the front lawn. Everything looked peaceful, normal. The encounter with Collins had shaken me deeply.

"If I may," Colonel Andrews said, pouring a similar drink for himself. "I think Collins looks at the command structure here as similar to his own. What he doesn't know, and doesn't need to know, is that this is a family, with a matriarch at the helm. The loyalty here runs much deeper, because it runs on love and respect. His group runs on fear."

Mark looked from Jim to me, waiting for more.

"He all but accused me of being a dictator!" I protested.

"Allex, honey, you're certainly no dictator, but you *are* in charge. Besides, you were the first one to speak introducing yourself and the rest of us. I think being in charge was a natural assumption on his part. Why didn't you mention that you're the Emergency Manager?"

"I'll answer that, if you don't mind," Jim said. "It was obvious from the start that there was going to be a distrust of anything government, whether it was local or military. After all, that's why *we* came in civvies. I think it was wise and prudent for Allexa to not mention her official title, just as she failed to mention Eric's relationship. He could have been used against us."

I slumped down into the nearest chair. "I hope I didn't screw things up by insisting we go there. I don't like this Collins. He makes me nervous, and I don't think we should trust him, no matter how fast he back peddled under your show of force."

"Well, I will agree with you on the trust part, ma'am," Jim said. "He's got a lot to make up for in my book. I think it's a wait and see what his next move is."

"I'm sure glad you were with us, Jim. And please stop calling me ma'am. It makes me feel old."

CHAPTER SIXTEEN

"Well, good morning, Sargent Jones," I said, wondering what she was doing here. "This is a pleasant surprise. What can I do for you?"

"Good morning, ma'am, Doctor," Rayn acknowledged Mark over my shoulder. "Colonel Andrews sent us to accompany you to your office for the visit from the Mathers Lake guys. Before you say anything, he told me you would protest and to ignore you." She had the decency to look embarrassed.

I laughed. "He's right, I would protest, and I appreciate the concern. I was considering asking Eric to come with us." Rayn's gray eyes flashed at the mention of Eric. "I'm guessing you wouldn't mind if he joined us."

"That would be great!" She grinned. "In fact, Perky and I were talking it over, and he suggested much the same. I think he really misses his dog, and he wants some more play time with Chivas, so he volunteered to switch places with Eric."

"Perky?"

"Sorry, Corporal Ansell Perkins. Our group calls him Perky since he seems to always be in a good mood."

"And it would give you more time with Eric," I commented, and she blushed. "That's okay, Rayn, I know my son is an attractive young man. Quite frankly, I think the two of you make a good pair." Her eyes widened at my admission.

"Thank you, ma'am. In the short time I've known Eric, I...I've grown quite fond of him and I would like the chance to know him better," she admitted.

"Then go across the road and get him while we finish getting ready."

"That didn't take long for them to zero in on each other!" Mark laughed. "You don't think they may be moving too fast?"

"Mark, when did we meet? How long have we been married? Times have changed drastically."

Mark opened the locked doors to the clinic at 11:45 A.M. It was a little dusty inside, so I quickly gave everything a wipe down while he set his medical bag on the portable tray in the exam room.

"I'm still not sure why you didn't bring the bigger bag. Won't we be needing more supplies for you to do the stitches?" I asked.

"I'm not doing stitches today," Mark said. "It never did need any and I did enough butterflies that it should have begun knitting. If it hasn't, nothing will help."

"Then why this appointment?"

He smiled down at me. "I thought you would appreciate the time alone with Lenny and Pete away from Collins. Don't you have questions for them? I know I sure do."

"I know you're a smart man, but I had no idea you were also so devious!" I grinned. "I hope they come alone."

"With Eric and Rayn outside, even if they have guards, only those two will be allowed in. We will still have time to get some answers."

I heard the rumble of a truck out front. Pete climbed out of the passenger side holding his arm, and Lenny got out from behind the wheel, making a show of leaving his rifle on the dashboard.

"How are you doing, Pete?" I asked when he walked in. He looked better than the last time we saw him.

"My arm still hurts, but it's a lot better, thanks." He turned to Mark. "And thank you again, Doctor. I don't know how to repay you."

Mark cut the soiled bandages off of Pete's arm to reveal the wound. The red striations were gone and the swollen tissue had lost most of the puffiness, though it still had a strange look to it.

"It's definitely better, Pete, but something is not quite right," Mark said. "I want to do an x-ray scan of it." Having power back at our house also meant power was on in the town, even though there wasn't anyone to use it. Mark flipped a switch and the imaging machine came to life with a hum. "There are times I love technology! Look here, Allex, I missed a piece. That barbed wire fencing must have been really old, Pete, when it scratched you and broke off, it also broke into pieces."

"Is that why it still hurts?"

"Yes, those antibiotics helped with the infection, but this would have started festering again soon, and you would have been right back where you started. We will repeat the procedure, which will be it will be quicker and easier this time knowing what we're after."

Pete lay down on the exam table, and Mark gave him another local anesthetic. We gloved and masked and I swabbed the area. Mark made a small incision in the center of the dark tissue. This time there was only blood and not the rank fluids from deep infection. I kept it rinsed away.

Mark dislodged another small piece of metal and I irrigated again. The scanner was pulled over to the table and Mark watched the screen, focusing on the open wound.

"I'd say we got it all this time!" he said triumphantly. "Since you still have the antibiotics in your system, I'm only going to give you a booster shot, no more pills." Four tight little stitches later, and we were done.

I dabbed some precious antibiotic cream on the stitches, then a couple of gauze pads, and wrapped it all with an ace bandage.

The four of us sat in the tiny waiting room to talk.

"How have you been treated up there?" I asked both Lenny and Pete.

"Oh, it hasn't been bad, Allexa," Lenny said. "Collins has some rules with hard punishments, and once you understand everything, it's fine. It's hard work, but at least we're fed and safe."

"Yeah," Pete said. "If you don't break his rules, and do your job, you're left alone."

"Do you want to stay there?" I had to ask. I inwardly cringed at the thought of them being held against their will.

"I'm okay with it," Lenny said, and Pete nodded.

"My turn," Mark stood to talk. "How many are up there? And why does Collins want me so bad?"

Lenny took a deep breath. "There are twenty of us, including six women and a handful of kids. Four of the women are pregnant. I'm guessing he wants you for them."

I was stunned.

Mark was delighted. "Babies? That's wonderful!" He started pacing. "I need to think some things through. Lenny, are you and Pete free to come and go from there?"

"Or can we get messages in to you or Collins? Maybe leave them at the gate?" I added before either of them could answer.

"I think messages would be good, and the gate is the perfect spot, inside the guard shack. That way Collins won't be as concerned about breaching security, and he can preview any messages going in or out, which will give him the control he needs," Lenny replied. He'd caught on quick to Collins' personality.

"Great. We'll leave a message on Friday morning. And we will come back on Monday morning to pick up a reply," Mark said.

"If Dr. Mark is needed for an emergency or if Collins wants to talk to us before Monday." I said, "either one of you are to come for us, but *no one* else. Make sure Collins understands that. We have our own security to uphold."

* * *

"I want to set up some kind of hospital, Allex," Mark blurted out once we were alone back at home. "In town, so our home won't be compromised. My clinic office is much too small to handle more than one or two people at a time, and not set up for overnight stays."

I could feel love and concern battling inside me for this man I married. "You want someplace to care long term, don't you? I can tell you're worried about those pregnant women."

"Yes." Mark pulled me close. "I know *we* will never have children, but the thought of bringing new lives into the world is exciting to me! And even though women have been giving birth for millennia, they've also been dying in the process. Saving lives is why I became a doctor."

"You're a good man, Mark. It's one of the reasons I love you. Now, tell me what you will need in this new hospital, and I'll see what I can come up with."

CHAPTER SEVENTEEN

We had spent the last three days looking at empty houses in Moose Creek. There was always something that didn't work, and I was starting to feel discouraged.

"Maybe we should stick to the main road, Allex," Mark suggested with a trace of disappointment in his voice.

"Good idea and most of them are, or were, businesses." I frowned. "Wait a minute; I think we're overlooking the obvious. Park at the clinic."

I led Mark to the large house next door to the clinic. It was a two-story wooden structure with a wide covered porch that was once a clothing boutique. The main floor had a large open room, just past the enclosed foyer. Behind what was once the sales floor were two rooms that may have been a fitting room or office space. A bathroom in between the two rooms serviced the building. The north end of the main room opened to a tiny and functional kitchen, and a staircase that led upstairs took up a corner, opposite the woodstove.

Mark looked into all the rooms, and then returned to the main area. He turned slowly in a complete circle and looked up.

"Allex, I think this is perfect. Or could be perfect with some minor alterations," he said.

He draped his arm around my shoulders and turned me as he described the vision he was seeing in his head.

"The foyer is fine. All it needs are a couple of chairs and a desk. In this open area, picture four, maybe six twin beds, much like a hospital ward. If we can devise curtains or a screen of some sort, that would be great, though not really necessary. The back two rooms could be used as a surgery and an office. A functioning kitchen is helpful to feed whatever patients there may be. And upstairs would be private space for us. When there are patients we would need to stay overnight." The more he talked the more enthused he became.

"Are you sure we need all this?"

"There are ten of us in our extended family, Allex, and another twenty at Mathers Lake. Eventually, yes, we might need a four to six bed facility. The fact that it's right next to the clinic means I don't have to move any equipment." He searched my face. "I really want this."

"Then let's get Jason over here and see what he thinks. First we need to write a note to Collins and get it over to the gate."

"Mr. Collins," I typed while Mark dictated, "we have made the decision to expand my clinic capabilities by opening a field hospital next door to it. I will be offering my medical services to anyone in need. That includes all those who live at Mathers Lake under your protection.

"We had hoped to establish a cordial, if not friendly, relationship with your community, though our initial contact indicates that will be not impossible, but difficult. Perhaps that will improve with time.

"The new facilities will be closed, locked, and unmanned until needed. There will also be no drugs stored on the premises. When the facility is in use, it will be guarded by an armed force.

"If I'm needed, please send either Lenny or Pete. Anyone else that shows up at our home will be considered hostile and dealt with accordingly."

"I think that's really good, Mark. It's an offering, without letting on we know about the pregnant women. That might get Lenny in trouble, and it sets a few rules. I like it! And I suggest we send Eric and Rayn to deliver it."

"Why not us?"

"Collins knows a message is coming," I said. "I don't want to walk into a trap. He will think twice about trying to kidnap two armed messengers. Besides, he wants *us* not them."

"Agreed. I sure wish I could have made a direct offer of prenatal care though," Mark said wistfully. "Although that would have given away that Lenny gave us information. I hope he's not such an egomaniac that he would jeopardize those unborn babies."

* * *

"Did you have any problems with the drop, Eric?" I asked when he and Rayn returned.

"None whatsoever, Mom. It sure is nice to work with someone who knows what they're doing." He grinned. "While I kept the truck and the guard shack door covered, Rayn went in and cleared the room. She left the envelope on the desk, and we backed out together."

"Excellent. On Monday I'd like the two of you to check to see if we have a response."

CHAPTER EIGHTEEN

While Emilee, Jacob, and Karen stayed with Joshua on the pretense of caring for the animals, the rest of us went into Moose Creek to check over the house that Mark wanted as a hospital.

"The plumbing is old, but it looks fine and I can't see any leaks," Jason announced after climbing out from the crawlspace.

"What about the wiring?" I asked.

"Impossible to tell without ripping walls down, though I found a circuit panel instead of a fuse box, which is a good sign. Perhaps it was upgraded when the previous business came in," he ventured.

"So what's our next step here? I'm sure Mark wants to get this operational as quickly as possible," I commented.

"If there's one thing I learned in the ER down in Saginaw, it's to expect the unexpected and to never depend on having time 'tomorrow' to get ready for something today. So yes, what can we do to get started?" Mark said.

"Fortunately the place is absolutely empty. We can start cleaning while you guys hunt down furniture. I'm sure there is an abundance of beds in this empty town. In fact," I hesitated only a moment before continuing, "The house on Eagle Beach has all *new* beds, most of them singles, and there should be at least a dozen of them.

"Amanda, you and I can start sweeping and mopping, and then washing walls and windows while they're gone. Once we get everything washed down, including the bathrooms and kitchen, we can go through some of the houses nearby for sheets and blankets." I instantly had a vision of collecting floral sheets as funeral shrouds for all those people that had died in the ash fall a couple of months ago, and gave an involuntary shudder.

"You okay, Mom?" Amanda asked.

"I'm fine, dear, just a distant memory, that's all."

* * *

Four hours later, the guys returned with six twin bed frames and three box springs.

"Once we get the frames reassembled and set in place, we'll go back for the rest." Mark was beaming. "That place is a treasure trove, Allex. There are sheets and blankets still in the closets, and towels in the bathrooms. Do you want us to take those too?"

"That would be great and would save us some time. All of it will have to be washed anyway, so no need to box it carefully. On second thought, Mark, leave the linens. Amanda and I will go back for those. You four will have a full truck as it is."

* * *

I took a moment to watch the wave action on Lake Superior. The water lapped gently at the shoreline, leaving a gray film of wet ash mixed with seaweed and sand. Still, it was peaceful and reminded me of better times, but something was missing. Then it dawned on me: there were no seagulls; no birds of any kind, and it saddened me.

I crossed the threshold into the Eagle Beach house; the house where John and his co-workers had lived. The house where I had spent many hours giving John a weekly massage; the house where I fell in love with him. I felt my heart twist into a tight knot, and I acknowledged to myself that I still loved him, different than what I feel for Mark, but the feelings were still there. I let out an involuntary sob, and felt Amanda's hand on my shoulder.

"Dr. Mark is a good man, Mom. You did the right thing, you know." How did she know the turmoil I was feeling?

"Yes, I know," I whispered. I took a deep breath, and I swear I could smell John's presence. "Let's get this over with."

We piled twelve sets of sheets on the large wooden dining room table, and then all the pillowcases that were in the closets. Next were as many blankets as we could find. We emptied the other closets of bath towels, washcloths and kitchen towels, plus laundry soap, dish soap and even hand soap.

"It's going to take forever to wash all this!" Amanda exclaimed.

"We'll take it to the Laundromat at Fram's and be done in no time," I replied as we stuffed all of it into the back of my car.

* * *

"So who is up for a little B & E?" I asked, and all four men stopped what they were doing to stare at me. "We have to get into the Laundromat."

Ken let out a chuckle and said, "I can help with that."

* * *

"Now don't tell the guys how easy this was," Ken said, producing a ring of keys and letting us in the front door. "As the Moose Creek law, I have keys to all the businesses."

"Your secret is safe with us, Ken. Can you jimmy the coin boxes on the machines? We can keep feeding the coins back in that way without much damage. We'll need to have all the machines going and I don't have that much change."

"No problem, and I'm sure Joe would understand." He popped the front cover off all the washers and dryers, revealing a multitude of quarters for our use. Then he slipped the key off his ring and handed it to me. "Lock up when you're done."

Amanda and I loaded half of the blankets into the triple washers and the sheets and pillowcases into the regular washers. The rest of the blankets and the towels would have to wait until tomorrow. It was getting late and everyone was tired.

* * *

"This looks great, Mark." Four of the beds were lined up in two rows, box springs and mattresses in place. "Where did you get the desk and chairs for the foyer?"

"We thought it appropriate to use furniture from the township offices, Mom," Jason answered. "There's one in the smaller back room, too. We also took one of the file cabinets. Don't worry though, we placed all of the files in a couple of boxes."

I wandered from the front to the back and between the beds. "Didn't you bring back six beds? Where are the other two?"

"We took them upstairs for when we need to stay overnight. These four fit perfectly," Mark said.

"This is shaping up faster than I thought it would," I said.

"Yes," Mark replied. "It's amazing, isn't it? Now all we need now are curtains between the beds."

"We have an idea for that." Jason and Eric both grinned.

* * *

Amanda and I went back into town to the Laundromat to finish drying and folding the first load of sheets while the last load was washing.

"Where are we going to store all of this?" Amanda asked as we brought in stacks of neatly folded sheets, blankets, and towels.

"I'm not sure. For now we will leave them sitting on the bed here. It will be a reminder that we need to have Jason or Eric build some shelves."

"What about a couple of dressers? There's got to be some around somewhere."

"Great idea; that would solve the problem without additional work on their part," I concluded. "I think you and I are capable of finding the dressers, even if we can't move them without a truck. Speaking of which, I saw the guys leave this morning in the truck, do you know where they went?"

"Um, y-yeah, I thought you knew they were going into M-Marquette," she stammered.

"What? No, I didn't know! What are they doing? They know we've been restricted from drawing attention by spending more money." I was now concerned for my son's safety.

"I think they had permission from the colonel. Rayn and Ansell came out together, and Jason, Eric, and Rayn went back into town for some supplies to build the privacy curtains for Dr. Mark." She looked downcast. "I hope I haven't gotten them into trouble."

"No, I can't expect them to check with me for every move they make. Between the three of them I'm sure they'll be fine," I said, thinking of Rayn's military clearance.

"I wanted to tell you that Jason has been so much happier these past couple of days having something challenging to do. It gets boring, just sitting around," she confessed. "I could tell he's really excited about the plan they've come up with. He said you're going to love it."

* * *

When I got back home I asked Mark if he knew what my sons were up to.

"Not exactly, but Eric stopped in while you were in the shower this morning, and asked for some money. I figured it was fine since it was for construction of the hospital and I took it out of the pouch. Was that okay?"

"Of course it's okay, that money is for all of us to use. I'm surprised you didn't tell me, that's all."

Mark hugged me close, and all my doubts melted away. "I think those boys of yours love to surprise you and hope you'll be pleased. I'm happy that they've taken such an active interest in fixing the hospital."

CHAPTER NINETEEN

"Mark, while you guys hunt up a couple of dressers for the hospital, Amanda, Emi, Jacob, and I need to finish harvesting what little is left in the garden."

"It doesn't look like there's much there, Allex."

"That's because what has survived is in the ground. There are still potatoes, beets, carrots, turnips, rutabagas, and onions. Those are the few things that weren't affected by the ash. Although I'm not expecting a really good harvest because of the colder temperatures, there will be some. I highly doubt it's going to get any warmer for them to grow more, so we might as well get them out."

"You're the gardener," Mark said amiably. "So how many dressers do you think we will need?"

"I would say one for each bed. That way we can store extra sheets right there, and the patients will have a drawer for their stuff. That is, *if* you have patients." I took his hands in mine. "I hope your expectations aren't too high, Mark. In fact, wouldn't it be great to *not* have patients?"

"Yes, it would, but I still can't get those pregnant women out of my head. I want to be in the position to help them if they ask," he responded.

* * *

"This is going to be fun, Nahna!"

"I sure think so too, Emi. Finding the food we planted months ago is thrilling to me." I smiled at her. She'd grown another inch at least.

Jacob had the job of retrieving the various vegetables we dug up and putting them into the plastic wagon. I started with the potatoes, showing Emi how to spot where they might be and how to dig with the claw tool so as not to bruise them.

"Why is that important, Nahna?" she asked, wiping the dirt off a big spud and handing it to Jacob.

"The more bruised or damaged they are, the harder they are to store," I answered. "However, any badly bruised ones we'll eat right away by making French fries and potato chips!" That got Jacob's attention, as I knew it would.

"Can we have French fries for dinner tonight?" he asked.

"I think that's a great idea, Jacob." Amanda was working quietly by herself digging carrots. She put the orange tubers in a basket after cutting the tops off and made a neat pile of the greens. At the end of each row, regardless of how few or how many greens there were, she tossed them over the fence into the chicken yard for them to eat. I was pleased how everyone had learned that we don't waste anything.

"You might want to put on some gloves, Amanda," I mentioned to her when she got ready to work on the row of beets. "Once you cut the greens they bleed red and will stain your hands."

"It's too bad we can't use the stain somehow."

I felt like slapping my hand to my head!

"We can! Oh, Amanda, I'm so glad you thought of that. I had completely forgotten," I said. "Instead of giving those to the chickens, put them in a bucket. We'll cut them up and cover them with hot water. In two days we will have deep red water that we can use to stain branches for making baskets!"

"Is there anything else that will give us a stain?" she asked with enthusiasm.

"Yes," I answered, "the skins off the onions will produce a pale yellow or tan coloring, but those have to be done as we use the onions, not now."

Everyone seemed to work with a new zest and we were finished by early afternoon. We lined up our harvest in front of the barn. All the soil had been carefully brushed from each vegetable and then laid out on a tarp to dry, which was part of the curing process for all except the carrots. A gentle warm wind dried them quickly and we turned everything over to finish.

Once done, we carefully piled the potatoes into three bushel baskets for storage in the cold pantry. The rutabagas and turnips filled another. I sighed inwardly with relief and satisfaction that we were able to harvest so much. It would make the coming winter much easier.

"What do we do with the onions?" Emi asked as she eyed the full basket.

"This is going to seem kind of silly, and it's a trick I learned a long time ago, back when your dad and Uncle Jason were quite young. I'll be right back." I went into the house to find my stash of pantyhose.

"You're right, that looks pretty silly," Amanda agreed when I dropped a handful of onions down into one of the legs, and then attached a twist-tie. I added another handful of onions, and another twist-tie.

"Okay, Emi, Jacob, it's your job to fill this with onions! When you're done, we will hang this in the pantry. Whenever we need onions, we cut the bottom segment off. *But*," I added, "we don't throw away the nylon, we will put it in a bag or maybe another stocking. Then we can use all those pieces to stuff toys with, soft toys that will then be completely washable."

Amanda looked perplexed. "What are we going to do with soft toys, Mom?"

"Give them to babies." I smiled.

CHAPTER TWENTY

"I'm sorry, Mom, there wasn't any message in the guard shack again," Eric told me. He and Jason had gone together. Much to Eric's disappointment, Rayn hadn't come out this afternoon to go with him. I insisted that there were always two of them, and that they were always heavily armed whenever they went near Mathers Lake.

Last week Eric and Rayn had gone out on Monday, only to discover our first note had been picked up, and nothing left in its place.

"Maybe he didn't have anything to say," Mark suggested.

"We did have the time to stop at the hospital for the final touches on our project," Jason grinned. "Want to see what we've been up to?"

* * *

The first thing I noticed when we pulled up to the old boutique building was the sign.

Mark was speechless, as he looked up at the four by eight sheet of plywood mounted over the front door that read "Moose Creek General Hospital."

Jason beamed. "We put the second coat of sealer over the paint yesterday, but it wasn't dry enough to put up until today."

"That's only the first part," Eric said. He opened the front doors for us. "Doctor, Mom, your wish has been our command," he joked as we entered.

The inside had been completely transformed by the installation of rails and curtains separating the beds.

I looked up in amazement, realizing what they had done.

"That looks like PVC pipe! And those are shower hooks." I then fingered the sturdy material that hung there, several inches off the floor. "Is this..."

"Yep, shower curtains!" Jason blurted out. "We were really surprised to find them, but I guess anyone buying shower curtains now were getting the cheapest available, and these cloth ones were expensive. We needed eight for each side of the room, so we had to get three different colors. I hope that's okay. And we weren't too sure about how high off the floor they should be so we guessed."

"What do you think, Doc?" Eric asked pensively.

Mark had been silent since we walked into his new hospital. He swallowed hard and his eyes glistened. He cleared his throat. "I'm not sure what to say. This is…it's wonderful. No, not just wonderful, it's fantastic!"

"There's one more thing Jason insisted on doing, and that's what took us so long. Follow me." Eric led us to the back room we had decided on as the examination room and surgery.

There, in the center of the room was my old massage table that I hadn't used in years. They must have found it out in the barn. Against the inside wall was a new, deep, stainless steel sink set into a cabinet with a white countertop and glistening faucets.

"Eric reminded me how you scrubbed up right in the exam room next door when you took care of Chivas. I thought you would like a sink, with hot water, in here too," Jason said.

Eric eyed his brother. "Aren't you forgetting one more detail?"

Jason smiled and flipped a switch next to the door. Three rows of bright lights illuminated the room. "They are on a dimmer in the event you don't need this much light," he said, turning the lighting down to a glow.

I left Mark's side to hug my two sons, and Mark was right behind me and hugged them too.

"I admire how much you can get done in such a short time, Jason," Mark complimented him. "It's been only nine days since we began this project. You work really fast. All the plumbing, wiring, rails and the sign… the sign is remarkable and not something I was expecting."

"I must admit having Eric helping sure sped things up. He must have learned a thing or two watching me," he chided his brother.

"Hey there, little brother, respect your elders and remember who's older," Eric kidded back.

* * *

We decided to have an open house for the hospital in a few days and invite our new friends from Marquette, Jim and his merry band of soldiers, and to extend an invite to the Mathers Lake crew as well.

"Do you think Collins will come?" I asked.

"I don't know, maybe out of curiosity," Mark answered, "but I think we should try. We won't get anywhere if we keep ignoring each other."

"How much of an open house should we do?" I kept thinking of additional food. It was getting more and more scarce.

"I've got a batch of beer almost ready, Mom," Eric said. "I'm sure we can come up with a couple dozen juice glasses to serve it in. I doubt we want to make it look like we have a lot."

"That's a good idea, Eric. Joshua dropped off a nice chunk of cheese this morning, and I can make some saltine-like crackers," I thought out loud. "I think that's where we stop though."

"As much as I like the colonel and his crew, why are you including them in this?" Amanda asked.

"That's easy," Jason said. "It's a show of force. The more people Collins thinks we have, the less likely he will think about attacking us."

CHAPTER TWENTY-ONE

"I was noticing how dark the sky was to the west last night," I commented to Mark as we had our morning tea. "It looks like we might get some rain today."

"Perhaps," he replied. "Something looks different with these clouds though." Mark opened the door and stepped outside into the cool morning air. He moved to the center of the lawn and turned in a slow circle, like he was sniffing the air, and then he came back in.

"Last night's clouds were the Mammatus clouds, heavy with impending rain, right?" Mark asked me and I nodded, remembering the popcorn look with the dark underbellies. "These are more of a shelf or wall cloud formation with stratus fractus mixed in. A very odd combination, *and* I smell ozone, lots and lots of ozone. We're in for a really big storm."

I almost laughed, but he was so serious. "You sound like a weatherman."

He looked up from his tea and smiled at me. "One summer in college I signed on to a storm chaser crew out west. It was an exciting vacation, and I learned a great deal about the weather and storms, especially tornadoes. The thing I learned the most that year was that I did *not* want to be a meteorologist—too dangerous! That's when I decided to become a doctor, and I've kept in touch as a hobby."

"You amaze me," I said. "So you think this will be a bad storm? We should let the kids know in case they had made plans to do outdoor things."

"That's a good idea."

* * *

We have our drill for preparing for storms; it just changes somewhat depending on whether it's rain or snow. Anything loose in the yard was pulled into the barn or put into the fenced garden. The chickens were confined to their interior yard and we gave them extra feed and fresh water and then collected the few eggs they had left us.

"Will the greenhouse be okay?" Mark asked while we circled the house, looking for anything that could be destructive if caught by a strong wind and turned into a projectile.

"I don't know. The glass panes are triple thick door panels and are really strong, though nothing will stand up to a tree falling on it," I said. "I think I should take down the solar panel, just to be safe. I sure don't want to lose it in a high wind. It's one of those totally irreplaceable items."

"Can I do that for you?" Mark asked. "Sometimes I don't feel very useful."

I stopped and looked at him. "You're kidding, right? Not useful? Besides being the only doctor within thirty miles, and the only veterinarian, you are also now our weatherman. We wouldn't know how severe this storm might be without you. Sure, I knew rain was on the way, but you have spurred us on to prepare for something worse." I kissed his cheek. "Jason showed me how to do this already. I need a ladder, a wrench, and a screwdriver."

I slid open the window adjacent to the solar panel. Jason had purposely put in an access for this reason. I reached up and loosened a few bolts, bringing the delicate panel inside, handing it to Mark. Using the screwdriver, I undid the wires so the panel didn't dangle. Mark set the panel safely on the floor and out of the way.

"I remember my first visit to this greenhouse," Mark said, smiling.

"So do I," I blushed, "and that first kiss shook me to my core, Mark. Everything I felt in that moment made me doubt...everything. And that's not a bad thing, look where we are now."

* * *

It was early afternoon and we were walking across the road. The wind picked up to a stiff breeze, sending more of the tangy ozone smell our way. I always loved that scent when I was a young girl in the city. I think the years of smog dimmed that greatly, except for here, where we have very little pollution.

Amanda opened the door for us. "Come on in! It's sure getting chilly out there."

"We've already battened down the hatches, and thought you should be aware of the storm that might be coming this way," I said after giving her a hug. "Where is everyone?"

"Jason and Eric took the kids and Chivas into Moose Creek to play on the playground equipment at Diggers Park. What storm?" Just then a loud rumble of thunder shook the house. "Oh!" she said.

"I'm sure that will send them back in a hurry," Mark commented. "Let's check around outside and put things away, okay? We'll help you."

When we were tucking the last of the lawn chairs under the porch, Jason pulled into the driveway. Chivas was the first one out and she scrambled up the porch steps whining to get inside, Jacob and Emilee right behind her.

"Wow, that thunder made my hair stick out!" Emi said, wide eyed once inside. "Static electricity," Mark mumbled.

"Why don't you two see if Joshua needs any help with the animals, and then make sure Ken and Karen know about the storm, although I think there's little doubt now," I told my sons, after another rumble of thunder was heard.

"Keep the kids and Chivas inside, though I doubt you could get that dog to go out right now," I laughed. "Amanda, do you need any help with the lamps in case we lose power?" She shook her head. "We're going back home to wait this out. I'm sure Jason and Eric will be back before the rain starts."

* * *

"The static electricity Emi felt has me concerned," Mark said while I lined the kerosene lamps up on the table, along with matches and a flashlight. I try not to use the flashlights since the batteries are limited and there's no replacing them.

"Why?"

"An electrical discharge doesn't happen alone, it's usually associated with lightning, which we didn't have. It's probably nothing, but something to watch," he paced over to look out the door again. This time there was a huge jagged streak of brilliant white light across the sky, followed a few seconds later by a loud crack of thunder. "That was really close, maybe five miles. This storm has developed fast." He continued to watch out the door.

I sighed with relief when I saw the silver SUV return and the boys make a dash into their house.

The thunder and lightning continued. Sometimes the flashes were wide, jagged streaks; sometimes they filled the sky like page-lightning does. The rumbling was almost constant now and started getting on my nerves.

"Why doesn't the thunder let up when the lightning stops? It's been over two hours of non-stop noise!"

"I'm not sure, Allex. Remember, this is only a hobby of mine." Mark put his arms around me for a comforting hug, as a bolt struck across the next rise over and the simultaneous thunder sent two hanging wine glasses shattering to the floor.

"Where is the rain?" I asked no one in particular as I got the broom and dustpan to clean up the glass. When I was dumping the shards in the trash, the first pellets hit the sliding glass door.

"Well, there's your rain, except its frozen. Hail. That comes from the upper atmosphere. If the wind currents are moving so fast that they're picking up moisture from Lake Superior and thrusting it high enough to freeze, and we're still not getting any rain, that could mean the lower cloud bands are too dry, yet the winds are really strong — tornado strong. I never saw anything like this when I was storm chasing."

The hail pounded the ground in a sheet of white ice. Quarter sized balls of ice bounced on the steps and pinged off the glass. Another bolt of lightning streaked across the sky, then another and another. I had never seen so many hits of lightning all at once and the thunder was deafening. I shivered.

"Here, I think this is a good occasion," Mark said, as he put a glass in my hand. He clinked his glass against mine and I sipped the dark liquid. Private Stock rum slid down my throat and heated my chest, easing my breathing.

"I don't know what's going on, Allex, though I will admit to being scared. My guess would be there is some kind of very high disturbance happening that is causing this extreme weather."

I laughed nervously. "Some kind of very high disturbance? You mean like an ash cloud from a super volcano circling the Earth? An ash cloud that's already killed possibly millions of people? Is that all?" I downed the drink and held the glass out for more. A tear slid down my cheek. "I'm sorry, Mark, I'm not scared; I'm terrified!"

* * *

JOURNAL ENTRY: October 3

With all the thunder pounding my ears and the brilliant flashes of lightning illuminating the house, I hardly slept last night. Even with little to no rain, this storm has been brutal and relentless.

* * *

"How do you feel this morning?" Mark asked me. He was sitting at the table, cradling his shaggy head in his large hands.

"Exhausted!" I poured us each a cup of coffee instead of tea. "I figured we could use the caffeine," I responded to his questioning look.

"I'm not complaining," he said, inhaling the scent of the dark brew. "I know we're rationing ourselves to make it last longer, but I still miss it."

"So do I, but it isn't just us, there are six other adults leaning on our storage, and we all have to make certain sacrifices."

"Allex," Mark said, looking serious, "do you think we will ever get back to a normal life? I mean a life like two years ago, where we had jobs and paychecks and could go to the store for whatever we wanted, like coffee."

"I don't know," I answered him honestly. "I would like to think that eventually, the Earth will stop its rumblings and movement, and commerce can start back up again. Maybe with limited trading, that will get things going again."

"What do you miss the most?"

"Oranges," I said wistfully. "With the two rifts that have divided the country into thirds, maybe being in the third with Florida that will happen someday, even though there's only half of Florida left."

* * *

I took a bucket of fresh water out to the chickens and refilled their food dispenser. They were all huddled in one corner of the coop, obviously frightened. I doubt we will get many eggs until this storm passes.

* * *

"I got hit by a few drops of rain just now," I told Mark as I hung up my jacket. The sky was still dark with rolling clouds. It was only noon, though it looked like nine at night. We were both watching the rain increase when a bolt of lightning hit the cellular tower a half-mile away. The simultaneous crack of thunder shook the entire house.

"Wow! That was close." Mark shivered.

"I think that was the end of our phone service." I picked up my cell phone from the computer desk and turned it on. "It says 'searching for service.' Yep, the tower was hit, and I really doubt there will be anyone out to fix it this time." I shut the phone off out of habit and left it on the desk.

"I guess the bright side is that metal structure is a good lightning rod; as long as it's standing we are probably safe from a direct hit," Mark concluded.

* * *

"Do you notice anything, Allex?" Mark asked.

"The thunder isn't as loud," I replied, amazed at the quiet that really wasn't quiet.

"I'm going to venture that the storm is moving on," he said, looking out the glass door. "It looks to be moving right over Marquette. I hope they're ready. A three day lightning storm is hard on the nerves."

I was washing the morning dishes when there was a pounding on the back door.

"Pete! Come in," I said, opening the door and putting away the gun I automatically grabbed when I heard the knocking.

"Is the doctor here?" he asked.

Mark came out from taking a shower. "What is it, Pete? Is one of the women in labor?" he asked anxiously.

"No, but Collins has been hurt," Pete said. "During that lightning storm, he was out checking on the dogs when a tree was hit and split down the middle. Half of it landed on him. We think his leg is broken, maybe an arm too."

"When did this happen?" Mark asked, finger combing his wet hair.

"This morning. He didn't want us to bring him in, said you probably wouldn't treat him considering the way he acted before," Pete said. "I told him you weren't like that. He still protested, and now that he's unconscious he can't say no."

537

"Where is he?" I asked.

"We made a stretcher and put him in the back of a pickup, the only one with a cap. I didn't think it would help any if he got soaked by the rain."

"Yes, but *where* is he, Pete?"

"They're at the clinic. We came in two vehicles because you said you didn't want anyone but me or Lenny coming here, right?"

"Who else is there, Pete?" I asked calmly.

"Just Adam, who's driving, Collins, and Claire, that's Collins' wife," he told us.

I thrust the medic bag at Pete and turned to Mark. "Go with Pete. I'll get Eric and be right behind you," I said. "Your first patient! Do you need me to bring anything else?"

"No, I think I've got what I need," Mark said, retrieving a box from the refrigerator that contained pharmaceuticals.

* * *

I pulled into the clinic's gravel parking lot between two pick-up trucks. They had lifted Collins out of the back and were headed indoors, followed by a very pregnant woman.

"You must be Claire," I said to the young, dark haired woman. "I'm Allexa, the doctor's wife...and nurse. Please, sit. Mark will do everything he can for Art. Trust me on that." With that, I went into the exam room and shooed Adam and Pete out.

"Thank you, dear, it was getting crowded in here," Mark said. He turned on the scanner while I cut the fabric of Collins' pants up the outside to the waistband, folding open the material so Mark had full view of the injuries.

"You're being awfully neat with that," he commented.

"Hopefully his wife, or someone, can repair the pants to a useable condition," I replied.

I put on a mask and handed Mark one. We both washed our hands up to the elbow, and dried. I held each glove while he slid his hands in and then I did the same.

Mark positioned the digital scanner and peered into the tiny screen.

"I see two breaks. One a simple fracture to the tibia; another simple fracture to the fibula. They are both out of alignment. I'll have to set them here so I can check it with the scan." He moved the machine over. "Now let's look at the arm."

"Which one?" I asked. Then I noticed blood on the left side. "With the blood, I would guess a compound fracture?"

Mark moved the machine along the arm. "Excellent, Allex. Compound fracture of the ulna. Cut the sleeve off and let's take a look."

As I carefully cut the material away, a jagged bone was exposed, protruding from the red and bloody skin on the lower arm.

"It looks like a clean break. Lucky for him." Mark selected a vial and a hypodermic needle, and administered a sedative. "I don't want him waking up while we're setting these bones."

I swabbed down the area with alcohol, and while I held the upper arm stable, Mark pulled and forced the exposed bone back under the flesh, maneuvering it into place. He then rechecked the setting with the scanner and, once satisfied, stitched the cut and splinted the arm. I wrapped and taped it closed.

We followed similar procedures with the two breaks in the leg, with Mark checking the alignment of the bones carefully.

"Too bad we don't have any plaster to make a cast," Mark commented as we wrapped the leg.

"Would papier-mâché work?" I thought of making light bulb puppets with the boys, and those were quite hard.

He looked at me and grinned. "Yes, it might. We'll worry about that after Mr. Collins regains consciousness though."

We emerged from the exam/surgery room after an hour and a half, and we were both exhausted.

"Mrs. Collins, Art suffered two simple breaks in his left leg and a compound fracture in his lower left arm. All three fractures have been set and he should heal completely," Mark said, sitting next to her. "We're going to move him next door now into the new hospital where I'd like to keep him under observation for a day or two, if that's alright. You're welcome to stay with him."

"Thank you so much, Dr. Robbins. We didn't know what else to do, except come here," Claire sniffled.

"You did the right thing. I told your husband my services would be available to everyone, and that included him. That also includes you, Claire. While you're here, perhaps tomorrow, I'd like to give you a prenatal exam. How far along are you?"

"Oh, not far, maybe five months." She placed her hand on her very large belly. "He's going to be a big boy!"

* * *

Even though the new hospital is next door to the clinic, it's still over a hundred feet away, so they loaded the still unconscious Art back into the truck and drove over. I drove over first, with a reluctant Claire, to make up the bed.

"Claire, please don't be so nervous around us. We're not your enemy."

"I do want to believe that, but Art said..." she hesitated, "he said you helped Pete because you knew him, and that you want to come and take our food."

"That's not true, Claire. Yes, we would like to hunt and fish, however, the deer will eventually come back to our area, so it's not a necessity for us. Knowing there was another group of people so close was encouraging to us and we just wanted to reach out and see if we could be friends. I think our arrival took Art by surprise and made him nervous."

"That's what Pete and Lenny said."

Once they had Collins settled in the bed, I made up the other one for Claire, all the while listening to the conversation.

"Pete," Mark said, "you know that Art and Claire are perfectly safe here with us, though I'm not convinced that the opposite would be true. Why don't you and Adam go on home and get some sleep. Come back around noon, Art should be awake by then."

Claire said something to Adam that I couldn't hear, and after that they left.

"It's getting late, Mark, are you hungry?" I asked.

"Yes, I sure am."

"Then I'm going to run home and put something together for all of us. I should be back in a half hour, after I check a few things in this kitchen."

The kitchen was small, and held a gas stove, a refrigerator I could hear humming, and a few cupboards. I opened a drawer next to the sink, to find a note:

Mom, I washed all the dishes, silverware and pots. I turned the refrigerator on to make ice and wiped out the stove. Love, Amanda.

Bless her thoughtful heart! There were two pots, one fry pan, and a tea kettle, with several mismatched bowls and plates. I wouldn't need to bring anything from home except food.

* * *

"What did you bring us?" Mark asked, peering over my shoulder where I was heating some water on the stove.

"I thought I would keep it simple and make some rice with chicken soup. Art should be able to eat that when he wakes up, shouldn't he?"

"Definitely the rice and broth, and if he can keep that down, he can have some chicken. Claire can have whatever she wants." Mark looked pensive.

"What's on your mind, Mark?" I asked, slicing some bread.

"It's Claire. She says she's about five months, but she looks like she should have delivered last month. Unless it's twins, and even if it were, she shouldn't be this big yet. I think she's comfortable enough with us now that she'll agree to a simple exam tomorrow. I hope."

I ladled out some rice into three bowls, topping it with a scoop of chicken soup, and set a plate of bread in the center of the table that graced a corner of the tiny kitchen.

"Claire, if you're hungry, I've made some soup for us," I said. Her eyes lit up and I knew she had to be really hungry.

She wolfed down the soup and sopped up the rest with bread.

"That was wonderful, Allexa, thank you! I haven't had rice in a year and the only things any of us can make are biscuits and cornbread, and we're not very good at that," she confessed as she yawned.

"I think it's time you get some sleep," Mark said to her as he finished his meal.

I made up a bowl of soup and two slices of bread for Eric. He was still on guard duty in the foyer.

"Thanks, Mom, I was getting really hungry out here."

"I know you sleep lightly, Eric, so if you want to lock up tight and take a nap, do so. I don't think we'll have any trouble tonight." I made my way upstairs where Mark was already fast asleep.

CHAPTER TWENTY-TWO

Because of the pounding rain overhead, I couldn't hear the raised voices below us until I heard that one word all mothers respond to.

"Mom!" Eric yelled up the stairs. "Doc! Mr. Collins is awake."

Mark and I had both slept in sweatpants and a t-shirt, so we rushed down the stairs barefoot and alarmed. We skidded to a stop when we saw both Eric and Claire restraining a very upset Art Collins.

"What am I doing here? What have you done to me?" he bellowed.

Mark crossed his arms over his chest and calmly stared at his patient. "Well, Mr. Collins, it seems that you had a tree fall on you and break several of your bones. Your friends and your wife thought it prudent to seek medical help to set said broken bones, which I did last night. As to where you are, you're in the Moose Creek General Hospital. Any other questions?"

Collins slumped back down on the bed and glared at us. He closed his eyes as a wave of pain hit him.

"Where are you feeling the pain, Art?" Mark responded with concern.

"My arm, it burns," he said through clenched teeth.

"That's a good sign, actually. Your arm had a compound fracture, which means it was broken in half and part of it broke through the muscle and skin. You have strong arms, so it was a bit of a struggle pushing the bone back in place. Some pain indicates the healing process has begun," Mark explained. "The one thing I can't check for is internal injuries. If you feel any discomfort anywhere other than your left arm or your left shin, you need to tell me."

"Am I a prisoner here?"

"Of course not. However, I would strongly advise you stay another day for observation. Sometimes injuries don't show up immediately."

Collins grimaced in pain again.

"Would you like something for the pain?" Mark asked gently. When Collins reluctantly nodded, he went upstairs where we had left the med kit.

"This needs to be taken with food. Are you hungry? Think you can handle some soup?" Mark asked, his tone all business again.

I warmed up the chicken soup and strained it into a bowl of rice. Mark and Eric got Collins sitting up and Claire stacked some pillows behind him. I handed her the bowl so she could feed him, but he took the spoon from her and fed himself while she held the bowl.

He closed his eyes, in contentment or exhaustion, I couldn't tell which, and when he opened them again, he looked at me and said, "Thank you, that was actually good. We haven't had rice at the compound for a long time. Is that one of the things you might be willing to trade?"

"Perhaps," I answered, and I carried the empty bowl back to the kitchen smiling.

When I came back into the room, Mark had given Collins a pill and they had lowered him back to a resting position.

"That's Darvocet you took. It will ease the pain and it will also make you sleep, which is what you need now," Mark instructed.

"Look, Doc, I apologize," Collins struggled with the words. "I really didn't think you would help any of us. You truly have no reason to."

"Yes, I do have a reason, Mr. Collins, it's called the Hippocratic Oath, and I believe in it with my very soul. So yes, I will help any of you, all of you, whenever you need it. It will be on my terms though," Mark stated, almost angry.

"And what are your terms?" Collins yawned, becoming drowsy from the pain medication.

"I don't know yet," he said. "I hadn't given it much thought before because I wasn't sure if I'd see any of you here. I'll let you know. Meanwhile, rest."

Collins quickly fell into a deep sleep.

"Eric, I think I should get Ken or Karen to relieve you," I said. "Even with Mr. Collins' change of heart, I don't want Mark left unguarded. I'll be right back."

With Karen now in the foyer, and Eric back home, I set to making some oatmeal for our breakfast, which Claire ate with renewed gusto.

"All we ever eat are wild greens, corn meal, and venison. I'm so tired of meat!" she said after cleaning her bowl.

"Not the best of diets, but at least you're eating," Mark said.

"Have you had any medical exams since your pregnancy started?"

"There isn't anybody and Art won't let us go into town," she said.

"Is this your first baby?" Another nod from her. I could tell the gentle, easy conversation seemed to be casual interest, but Mark was mentally taking her history.

"Why don't the three of us go into the exam room and listen to the baby's heart?" he suggested.

* * *

Claire lay back on my massage table—now exam table. Mark took his stethoscope down from the shelf, and listened to her protruding belly. I could see the look of concern on his face, although he masked it well.

"Allex, you should listen to this," his eyes held mine for a moment, which told me to check my reaction. I listened…to nothing. I lifted my eyes to his and gave him the slightest of nods.

"Can I listen?" Claire asked, smiling.

"The angle is poor, Claire. Sorry, you're too big," I lied to her.

Mark felt around her belly and asked her a few more questions and then we helped her back to the chair beside her husband.

Mark closed the door to the office behind us.

"The baby is dead, isn't it?" I asked.

"Either that or there is no baby," he paced the room. "Her belly is incredibly hard. I think it's a tumor; a fast growing one. We need to convince her to let me do a digital scan to be sure."

* * *

"No baby?" Art gasped at the news. Claire was beside him in tears.

"When I couldn't get a heartbeat, I did a scan," Mark informed him. "It's one large, dense mass. It's obviously a very fast growing tumor of some sort for it to have reached this size in less than five months. If it isn't removed, it will keep growing and it *will* kill her."

"We've been married for fifteen years and never gave up hope for a baby," Art rambled. "If this growth will kill her, then you *must* remove it. I couldn't stand to lose Claire." He squeezed his wife's hand.

We set up the exam room for the surgery, including a large bucket to hold whatever it was that was growing inside Claire, and Mark began.

Two and a half hours later he finished the final stitches across Claire's now deflated stomach. There was understandable swelling, and that would dissipate with time. The heartache of not having the baby she so desired would last much longer.

"That was incredible to watch, Mark. I can understand why Dr. Streiner wanted you to stay in town. You have impressive talent," I said, still in awe of what I had witnessed.

"Actually, I used some of the techniques she showed me. It's a shame that the tumor was inside the uterus. There will be no natural born children for the Collins'," he said.

He gave his patient a light sedative. We removed our surgical garments, and moved Claire out to her waiting bed on the makeshift stretcher.

"How is she, Doctor?" Collins asked. He had refused his next pain pill to be awake during his wife's surgery.

"The surgery was a success. We removed the tumor completely. It was encapsulated within the uterus, so the chance of any leakage is virtually non-existent. However, there is no way to know what may have been transferred via the blood during the past months. I don't even know if this growth was benign or cancerous," Mark stated with a sigh. "In better days, she would have had an early prenatal exam and the doctor would have quickly caught the growth and removed it. Physically, she will be fine. The incision will heal and within a few weeks she can resume normal activities. It's the psychological injury that will take longer. By removing the uterus all possibility of having a child is gone. You understand that don't you?"

Collins nodded. "What's important is that she's alive. Thank you, Doctor. I've been a jerk. I owe you for her life, and for mine." He looked down at his splints. "Even if those breaks healed on their own I probably wouldn't walk normal." He winced in pain. "Can I have that pain pill now?"

* * *

Eric showed up right before noon. I thought he was there to relieve Ken, who had relieved Karen last night, but he had a surprise for all of us.

"I heard you talking about a papier-mâché cast for Mr. Collins' leg so Jason and I have been working on something. Amanda knew the recipe for the papier-mâché, with flour, salt and water so we mixed it up, and used a piece of gutter for a mold. After digging around in the barn I found a bag of old massage sheets that I figured would be okay to cut up and would be stronger than newspapers." What he showed us was ingenious. They had made a half-round cast that tied on, complete with a foot to support the entire leg. It was removable for bathing or changing clothes.

"Oh, and I brought my crutches for Mr. Collins to use, too."

Collins looked at the cast and crutches, and then at Eric. "You did that for *me*? Why?"

"You need them," he said simply, looking bewildered at the question.

"I-I don't know what to s-say," Collins stammered.

"How about *thank you*?" Claire said from the other bed.

"When you're completely healed, I think the crutches should come back as property of the hospital," Mark said.

"I certainly have misjudged your group, Allexa," Collins confessed. "Please forgive me. In a day or two I'd like to have you as my guests for dinner. As many of you as want to attend will be welcomed. And I'd like to discuss a trade agreement at that time."

"Thank you, Art. We accept," I replied. Sometimes all it takes is an unselfish act in the midst of a crisis to forge a bond.

"I can't help wondering where your men are though. I suggested to Pete to come at noon yesterday," Mark said, puzzled.

"Oh, I told my brother Adam to wait until today. I knew Art might need the extra day here. Little did I know I would need it too," Claire responded.

Mark had finished fixing the cast to Collins' broken leg when Lenny and Adam arrived. The guys helped him stand and he practiced with the crutches.

When Claire told Adam about the tumor, he gave her a long, brotherly hug.

"I'm so sorry, Claire. I know how much you wanted a baby," Adam said. "I'm sure Alise would welcome your help when our baby arrives."

"That brings up a thought," Collins said, sitting down in a chair. "What kind of office hours do you plan on keeping? We have three other women that are expecting babies, and I think it wise for have you look at them."

I could see Mark was having a hard time suppressing a grin.

"I was thinking along the lines of Mondays from noon until four o'clock at the clinic next door," he answered. "Of course if there are any emergencies, all you need do is come and get me."

* * *

"Oh, that hot shower felt wonderful," I sighed as I towel dried my hair. It was the first thing I did when we got back home. Tomorrow would be plenty of time for Amanda and I to go back to the hospital and clean up. Right now, Mark and I needed some rest.

"I can't wait to sleep in our own bed!" Mark stated emphatically.

Outside, the thunder boomed and more rain fell.

"I'm really glad we harvested the garden when we did. All this rain would have made it impossible to get in there now and we might have lost much of the crop," I said.

"Which brings to mind, Allex, what do you intend on trading with Collins? Our food won't last much longer if we barter it away."

"I know. I intend on keeping the trade goods limited to what we can replace or don't need. Maybe a hen and a rooster, so they can start their own flock. Or a keg of beer, though that will be Eric's decision. I'd like to start with a couple of pounds of rice. They seemed to really like that."

"A couple of pounds won't go far with twenty people."

"True, but I don't want them thinking we have an unlimited supply, even though we still have hundreds of pounds sealed in buckets. So just a small amount to start with, then maybe some dried beans or a box of pasta. We need to earn each other's trust first. Besides, we don't know yet what they have to offer in return."

"I thought it was for hunting and fishing rights?"

"For now, maybe, though eventually the deer will come back to this area, and I think in the spring we should release these fish we have in the greenhouse, that's the reason we collected them." I stopped myself from saying more. It was John who helped collect the fish, not Mark. My love for both is blurring my memory.

CHAPTER TWENTY-THREE

With expectations and trepidation, Mark opened the clinic at noon. Our new hours would last until four o'clock.

"Do you think anyone will show?" he asked me nervously.

"You mean the pregnant women from Mathers Lake?" I chided him. "Mark, sweetheart, they will or they won't. I didn't feel any deceit from Collins, but all we can do is wait. Since you did promise these four hours every week, we will be here." I busied myself with wiping a thin film of dust off of everything.

At 1:30, there was a car pulling into the drive. Pete got out from the driver's side, followed by three young women, one who looked barely in her teens. I picked up a clipboard and greeted them.

"Pete, it's nice to see you again. How is the arm doing?" I asked.

"Much better, thanks. I was wondering if the doc could look at it and maybe take the stitches out. They itch."

"Sure, Pete, come on in," Mark said, coming out of his office. "These ladies will need a few minutes to fill out some basic information anyway." The two men disappeared into the exam room.

"I'm sorry, we only have one clipboard, so you'll have to take turns," I said. "It won't take long, I promise. This is only basic stuff the doctor should have, like you name, age, how far along you think you are. He'll fill the rest in, so he can monitor your pregnancies." They all looked scared. "By the way, I'm Allexa, Dr. Mark's wife and nurse. I'll be with you the entire time, so please don't be nervous, all he wants to do is help."

They seemed a little more at ease as they wrote on the forms I had created on the computer with Mark's guidance.

It only took ten minutes for Mark to remove Pete's stitches, and probably not that long. I'm sure my husband was asking plenty of questions.

"Tess, we'll see you first," I said, and the youngest stood. Her chart said she was only fourteen. This was a new world; girls became women overnight.

Mark took her blood pressure and listened to the baby's heart.

"Would you like to hear?" he asked her.

"Really? Oh, yeah!" Tess grinned. I fitted the second stethoscope into her ears, and Mark moved it around as he did his. Tess giggled with delight.

"Do you have any questions, Tess?" Mark asked, giving her his full attention when he finished writing on the new chart.

"I...I know I'm kinda young, Doctor, and my Mom says I'm not really fully grown yet. Do you think I'll have any problems delivering?" she asked, suddenly looking scared and even younger.

"I don't know, Tess. Much will depend on genetics. This baby is both you and its father. If he's a big man, maybe, but we will monitor you carefully as the time draws near," Mark said, trying to reassure her.

The next two exams, with Alise and Chloe, were equally quick and well received. Chloe was nearing term and very relieved to have a doctor near. When everyone stood to leave, Pete approached us.

"Mr. Collins wants to know if this Friday would be a good day for all of you to come to dinner at his house at two o'clock."

"Tell Mr. Collins we would be delighted to come. And inform him there will be nine or ten of us," I replied.

* * *

"Why did you say there would be nine *or* ten of us?" Mark asked.

"I want him to know that not all of us are coming. Strategy, my dear, strategy."

CHAPTER TWENTY-FOUR

"Thank goodness this land line still works!" I said to Jason.

"Yeah. Eric tests it every day, calling Rayn." He poked his brother in the ribs. Eric shrugged. "What can I say? I really like her."

"Jason, stop teasing your brother!" I had to smile. I dialed the private number Colonel Andrews had given me.

"What a pleasant surprise, Allexa. What can I do for you?"

"We've been invited out to Mathers Lake for dinner tomorrow and I was wondering if you and a few of your men would like to go with us? Oh, and Rayn, too," I added when I got a panicked look from Eric.

"I think we can use the break. This storm is still sitting on top of us and creating all kinds of havoc."

"I'm still hearing distant thunder and seeing flashes of lightning, though I thought it would have moved off by now. What kind of problems?"

"Fires mainly, and isolated flooding. The rain isn't hitting us directly, or it might help put out the fires. Seems it's raining inland, but moving downriver right at us." Jim sighed on the other end of the line. "What few firefighters that are left are being hampered by flooded streets, so whenever the lightning starts a new blaze, they can't get to it. They've managed to contain most of it, though that's about it. What time is dinner and how many men do you want me to bring?"

"Dinner is at two o'clock, and I think six personnel will be sufficient, but," I hesitated, "can you bring some new faces? Besides Rayn, of course."

"Ah, you want to keep Collins thinking there are more of you than there are, right?"

"I can't fool you," I laughed and hung up.

* * *

"Fires? From the lightning? Wow, I guess we really lucked out that this storm passed us with no real damage," Jason said.

We all sat around their kitchen table discussing tomorrow's events.

"Well, the colonel did say they had them mostly contained, so maybe it isn't all that bad," I said.

"Fire can get out of hand in a heartbeat," Mark commented. "And then no matter how many people are fighting it, the fire will win."

"Let's get back to our situation, okay? Besides the colonel, there will be five new faces, plus Rayn. Jason, do you and Amanda want to come with us this time? And what about the kids?"

"Yes, I'd like to go," Amanda was quick to say. "It would be nice to meet someone new."

"I think we should leave the kids here. I don't like the idea of possibly putting them into danger or maybe in the midst of a hostage situation," Eric said. "Once we feel these people out in a social setting, maybe next time."

We all agreed the children would stay home, with Ken, Karen, Joshua, and one of Jim's soldiers.

* * *

"I'm glad you could make it, Allexa, Doctor," Art Collins greeted us, balancing on the crutches Eric had loaned him, his casted arm resting in a sling attached to the crutch.

"Thank you for the invitation, Mr. Collins," I said looking around at his spacious house. "Nice place you have here."

"Thank you, I designed it myself ten years ago."

"Ten years ago? You mean this is *your* house?" Mark asked.

Collins ignored the implied accusation. I think we all assumed he was a squatter and had taken over the nicest house.

"Please, have a seat and allow me to explain our situation here," he said, being a polite host.

"Before we do," Mark interrupted, "would you mind if I checked over Claire's incision? Somewhere private of course." I helped Claire stand and she led us to one of the guest rooms.

"That's starting to heal quite nicely, Claire," Mark observed, when she lifted her baggy shirt. "The swelling is already much less. Come to the clinic in another week and I'll take the stitches out."

"Thank you again, Dr. Robbins. I actually feel better. I didn't realize I was feeling bad, sick-like, until I started to feel better. Could the tumor have been poisoning me or something?"

"Anything's possible, Claire. I am quite pleased that your health is improving." Mark flashed her a sincere smile.

When we rejoined the group, Collins was passing out mugs of warmed cider.

"I should probably start from the beginning," he began.

We all sat on the comfortable furniture. The overstuffed couch was a pleasant plaid pattern of greens, blues, and beige, with the side chairs in a matching deep hunter green. The end tables were a sturdy heavy dark oak. It was all nicely appealing.

"I know you think I just showed up and took over here, grabbing the nicest house on the block," he smiled ruefully. "My grandfather was Anthony Mathers, hence Mathers Lake. He purchased this land a hundred years ago. He was young, but he had great vision. There is a cabin on the other side of the lake that is the original homestead. When my mother Lilly married Abe Collins, Gramps gave her this side of the lake and half of the land, three hundred and twenty acres. When he died, she inherited the rest."

"Your grandfather bought a whole section of land? Wow," Jason remarked.

"She and my father sold much of it to the Resort at a good profit, and kept the lake and a hundred acres around it. I grew up here, roaming the woods as a child." He smiled as some pleasant memories seemed to intrude on his dissertation. He took a sip of his cider before going on. "When Claire and I married fifteen years ago, they gave it to me, and retired to Florida. I was fresh out of graduate school with a degree in architecture. What better way to practice my new profession than to build our own home?"

Just then we were interrupted by a young man whispering something to Collins.

"Ah, dinner is ready. I will continue as we eat." He stood, leading us into a formal dining room. "With so many of you attending I'm afraid most of my extended family will be dining in the kitchen. There isn't enough room at this table, big as it is. My mother loved to entertain and often had this table filled with friends every weekend. I'm not as gracious of a host as she was. I never have been—I like my privacy. But I love this table so I brought it here after she passed. It reminds me of her."

The table was set with a simple setting, and did include cloth napkins. Although it was a lovely touch, there were few paper products available, and many of us had fallen back on the old ways out of necessity. There was a platter filled with sliced turkey, and another with what I found out was smoked goose. A basket of corn muffins sat on either end of the table. We have bread, they have cornbread, and I found it to be a treat. There was a bowl full of corn on the cob, cut into thirds to stretch the servings, and a bowl of steaming stewed apples.

"I certainly hope the rest of your family is eating this well, Mr. Collins. It looks and smells wonderful," Mark commented, spearing a slice of goose.

"No one here goes hungry, though we certainly don't eat this elaborately every day," he answered. "I understand you have children, Allexa. May I ask why you didn't bring them? We have four here under the age of fourteen; they were looking forward to some new playmates."

I heard a few snickers around the table, and Mark coughed, trying to suppress his laugh.

"Oh, I did bring them, Mr. Collins," I said with a straight face. "The two young men sitting to your left are my sons. However, we did leave the two grandchildren at home, well protected. They're ten and twelve and we didn't know if they would have anything to do here during our visit. Perhaps another time they can come too." I smiled and made eye contact, letting him know there were more adults back in our community, and that our children's safety was of high priority.

"You wear your age well," he said. He munched on some cornbread and then set it aside. "I won't bore you with all the details of our lives over the past five years, but this is an intentional community. Over the years I kept building small homes here as a retreat of sorts, and carefully selecting those I felt would fit in. My group is of the beans and bullets mentality, though I should have listened more to my wife and stored more beans, not to mention rice. That was a real treat, by the way.

"This spring we did plant an extensive garden. We realized we were really short on certain supplies, so we raided the Resort and took every bit of food we could find. I think raid is a harsh term—there wasn't anyone there, and hasn't been since the first quake.

"My friends are all of the survivalist mindset, though I prefer to call ourselves isolationists. We only want to be left alone, although we are well prepared to defend what we have."

"Well, I can understand that. We want to be left alone too, but we also understand there are times when that isn't practical, like when someone gets injured," I replied.

"That has been made abundantly clear," Collins laughed. "And I now agree, which is why I invited all of you here today. I would like to make amends for my rude treatment before, and see what we can do about setting up some kind of trade."

"I'd like that," I said, smiling warmly, as the same young man came by and quickly removed our empty plates.

"Doctor, have you thought more about your 'terms' for medical treatment?" Collins asked.

"I've been working on it. I think one of the terms for an overnight stay at the hospital of more than one night is food. It needs to be either replaced or furnished," Mark stated.

"That's more than reasonable. If you like, I can make up a box to replace what Claire and I ate," Collins offered.

"Not necessary. I would say this meal more than took care of what we provided. And personally speaking, the smoked goose was excellent," Mark complimented. "I think too, that I'm going to limit my services to mainly injuries or other physical issues, like maternity care. If someone gets a cold or comes down with the measles, there's nothing I can do to help anyway, so that person would need to be cared for at home, also to limit exposure to others."

"Another reasonable term. What about payment?" Collins got right to the point.

"I was thinking of service for service. What you might have to offer, I don't know, so we can let it coast for now," Mark answered.

"Mr. Collins, if you don't mind, I'd like to know how you rode out the ash fall. Did you even know about it?" I asked.

"Oh, yes, we knew. One of the members here, Nathan, is a Ham operator. His set up is quite impressive and because we considered all possibilities, his equipment has its own solar array for power. From the first rumblings, he monitored several channels collecting information. We grouped all of our members into three housing units to ride out the ash. I feel incredibly fortunate that we were spared. Barely, but spared," Collins paused. "I understand Moose Creek didn't fare as well."

"I think I've thought of a service that you could provide for us that will pay your debt to me," Mark smiled. "We have a Ham radio and tower set up at one of the houses in our compound, and no one knows how to use it. Will this Nathan be willing to teach one of us?"

"I can guarantee he would do that! I think I'm going to like this barter system," Collins laughed. "Now, what can I trade you for some of that rice?"

* * *

"I must admit that all went better than I expected," Jim Andrews commented over a finger of iced vodka once we arrived back home.

We didn't stay much longer at Mathers Lake once we arranged a time for Nathan to come here, with Lenny, to begin teaching Joshua how to use the Ham radio.

"Yes, it did. I was fairly certain that all we needed to do was to appeal to fairness in trade, and he would come around. Art Collins is not stupid and he does have the best interest of his people in mind. Now we need to work out what we can barter and what we won't."

"Well, thank you again for including me in this, Allexa, Mark. Now it's time for me to collect my people and get back to Marquette. I can hear the thunder still going on from here, and it has me concerned." Jim sighed, downing the remnants of his drink.

CHAPTER TWENTY-FIVE

"Mark, will you come outside with me for a few minutes?" I called into the house. I had finished closing up the chickens for the night when I noticed something very odd.

"What is it, Allex?" he asked joining me out on the lawn as he slipped a jacket on.

I took him by the hand and led him out on to the quiet street, walking north away from the houses. We turned, looking south.

"Look at the sky," I said, pointing.

"It looks…reddish," he said, perplexed. "The setting sun?"

"Red, yes, but it's over the area where Marquette is, and that's southeast, not west. I wonder if that's from the fires Jim was talking about." There was another flash of lightning in the crimson colored sky and a rumble of thunder followed less than a minute later. Suddenly there was a rapid succession of lightning bolts and flashes and the rumbles seemed to be non-stop.

"Wow, I wonder if that's what we looked like when the storm hit us that hard," I commented. "I don't want to call it impressive, but it sure is a sight to behold!"

* * *

The four hours of clinic time were uneventful, but we stayed the entire time since Mark had promised. Around one o'clock, Lenny and Nathan stopped by when they saw our car in the parking area.

"There was no way to let you know we'd be by today. Mr. Collins thought it best if we got your radio up and running as soon as possible so we could have a means of communication," Nathan said. He was a plain man, perhaps forty years old, sandy hair and brown eyes, the kind that blended into a crowd.

"I'm sure Joshua will be delighted to get started on the lessons," I said, and then turned to Lenny. "He's one house down from mine, in David's house. I'm sure you can find it."

When Mark and I returned home just after four, the truck was still parked at Joshua's, so we decided to walk down and see how things were progressing.

I was extra surprised to see Emilee sitting at the console, with the radio muffs snug around her tiny ears, twisting a dial, deep in concentration.

"She's quite the apt student," Nathan said. "She caught on to every nuance quite quickly. I'm impressed."

"She's doing better than me," Joshua laughed. "Since Emi was already here playing with Matilda and wanted to learn, we agreed that it would be better to have two of us get lessons right from the get-go."

Nathan straightened up and stretched his back. "I think three hours are enough for the first day. I'll be back tomorrow, same time, and we'll do the next phase. If that's alright," he had turned to us for that last confirmation.

"Sounds good to me, as long as these two are up for it," I agreed.

"Nahna! This is so much fun!" Emi shrieked, sliding the muffs off her head.

"Don't forget your homework, Emilee. You have to learn all these codes before you can talk to anyone," Nathan reminded her, handing her a few sheets of paper.

* * *

Nathan showed up by himself to continue the lessons on how to operate the radio. Initially I was a bit alarmed, though we *are* trying to foster trust between the two communities so I didn't say anything.

At noon I walked down to Joshua's to talk with Nathan.

"Can you take a message to Mr. Collins for me?" I asked him.

"I've got him on the radio now, Ms. Allexa. You can deliver the message yourself, if you like. Just hold down this button when you talk and release it when you're finished. Emi, please let your grandmother sit there and use the ear phones." Emilee was quick to respond, which told me Nathan was a good teacher and she respected him.

"Mr. Collins, this is Allexa, are you there?" I asked after sitting.

"Yes, I'm here," he replied.

"Would it be alright for us to discuss a trade agreement tomorrow? We'll come to you; Mark doesn't think you should travel yet."

"How about two o'clock? Would that fit your schedule?"

"Yes, that would be perfect. See you then. Out." I handed the muffs back to Emi and stood.

"May I speak to you privately, Ms. Allexa?" Nathan asked, and we stepped outside.

"What is it Nathan?" I hoped he wasn't going to defect and ask for asylum!

"I wanted you to know that most everyone at the compound thought we were getting too isolated and we're all quite pleased your group came along," Nathan said. "And even though he might not admit it, I think Art is happy to have new company."

CHAPTER TWENTY-SIX

I carefully measured five pounds of rice and scooped it into a new cloth bag. Since our favorite is the basmati, with the second being long grain, I had selected the short grain rice to use for barter. I know I was being selfish, but why give up our favorites?

"Five pounds isn't very much is it?" Mark eyed the bag.

"No, it isn't though it will give them a meal or two, and tantalize them into wanting more. I want to see what Art is going to offer in return," I told my charming husband.

I tied the bag closed with a piece of string, then put the rice bag in one of my cloth carryalls, along with a loaf of fresh bread.

"Bread too?"

I smiled at him. "What I hope this instigates is baking lessons. I think it's important for us to share skills as well as extra supplies."

* * *

We arrived at two o'clock as agreed. Mark parked the car facing out, a habit we all have developed.

"And who is this?" Art Collins said, hobbling out onto the wooden porch. "Can it possibly be the little chatterbox from the radio?"

Emilee bounded up the steps to greet him and held out her hand.

"Hello, Mr. Collins, it's nice to meet you," she said very adult-like.

Art looked past Emilee at us and grinned.

"Thank you for this most delightful surprise!" he said. "Please come in." He took Emi by the hand and let us follow. She has a way of winning over the most stoic of adversaries.

A swinging door bumped open behind Collins and a golden retriever nosed his way out. When he spotted Emilee, his tail went into full wag-mode. She reached down to pet him, and he licked her face which got her giggling.

"This dog looks like Chivas, only bigger," she said, giving the dog a hug. "What's his name?"

"This is Captain Morgan; Morgan for short. Who is Chivas?" Art asked.

"She's my dog, a golden retriever too, but she's still a puppy. Karen found her last spring and gave her to Uncle Jason for his birthday but he let us keep her when he and Aunt Amanda moved back home," Emi stopped to take a breath. "Dad's been training her and she's a good dog to have around. She got shot a couple of months ago, but Dr. Mark saved her. He said it was the first dog he ever did surgery on."

Art smiled at Emi's monologue. "Maybe someday when she's older you can bring Chivas to meet Morgan." He looked up at us, and it was obvious he was thinking of breeding the two dogs.

"We don't intend on staying long, Art, but we thought you might want to meet another member of our group," I said. "Actually, she *insisted* on coming along, and she can be very persuasive."

"Are there any kids here, Mr. Collins?" Emi asked, getting right to the point.

"Yes, we have a few. Would you like to meet them?" He asked and she nodded her head vigorously. "Claire can take you where they are having their lessons, if it's okay."

"I think that would be fine, as long as they don't go off anywhere. As I said, we don't plan on staying," I answered.

Once Emi and Claire left, with Morgan right behind them, we got down to business.

"Claire is obviously getting around well," Mark said, his eyes had followed the duo out the door.

"Yes, she seems better and better every day. I still don't like her doing much, though walking appears to be good for her. Thank you again, Doctor."

"You're welcome. Now, I'd like to take a look at your arm, see how the wound is healing." Mark removed the bandages from Art's arm, touched and poked it a bit, then reached for his black bag. He spread some antibiotic cream over the stitches and re-wrapped it with fresh gauze.

"It's doing well, I say we can take the stitches out in a week, but the bones will need at least another six weeks to knit. We'll need to do a scan at that time to be sure," Mark finished, snapping the black bag closed.

"Let's get down to business," Art seemed uncomfortable with the attention.

"Of course," I replied, and I picked up my carryall. "We brought five pounds of rice for a start. I know it isn't a lot, but we both know that rationing of irreplaceable supplies is necessary. And as an extra incentive for our trading, here is a loaf of fresh bread."

"Real bread made with wheat flour and not corn? This is more priceless to me than the rice!" Art confided. "We had very little flour stored when the quakes hit. We thought we had time, you know, more time, more *warning* to pull in those extra supplies."

"That's one of the things that many failed at, preppers and survivalists alike. Everyone thinks they will have warning, because they *want* to believe that. In reality, the worst situations come without any warning at all!" I shrugged my shoulders. "I didn't have all I would have liked, but I had all I really needed."

"So what do you want for the rice and the bread?"

"The bread is yours, this loaf anyway," I smiled. "I think we could arrange one loaf every week. It will be up to you how to share it. I had initially thought of offering baking lessons, and I still could do that, but without flour to bake, lessons would be wasted. As for what you would want to give us in return for weekly bread, I will leave it up to you to make an offer. Likewise with the rice, you figure it out what it's worth to you."

Mark and I stood to leave. Collins struggled to stand.

"You don't have to see us out, Art. I'd rather you stay off that leg," Mark said.

"What direction did Emi go? We can find her."

We got to the building Collins had described, only to be met with silence instead of the sound of children playing that I was expecting. Claire was just coming out the door and met us on the steps.

"Where is Emilee? It's time for us to leave," I said.

"Oh, they decided to go for a walk and show Emi the lake," Claire smiled.

"We clearly said she was not to go anywhere else! Show me where they went," I said angrily.

Claire lost her smile. "This path leads to the lake. The kids left only a few minutes ago."

Mark and I hurried along the pine needle trail, catching up with the group when the shimmering lake came into view.

"Nahna, isn't this lake beautiful? Jeremy says they were swimming in it all summer! Can I go swimming?" Emilee said, clearly not realizing how distraught I was.

"Perhaps another time, Emilee, right now it's time to go home," Mark gentled his voice, a signal to me to calm down. I met his eyes, and took a deep breath, letting it out slowly.

* * *

In the car, I turned to Emilee who was buckled in the back seat.

"Emilee Rush, you clearly disobeyed me and I am not happy about that!" I said sternly.

"It was just a walk, Nahna," she replied in a small voice. "We didn't go far."

"That's not the point! You were told to not go anywhere else. We don't know these people well yet and you had us worried!"

"I'm sorry," she said to her chest, her chin tucked low. I could see the tears dripping onto her hands. I turned in my seat to look forward, or I would start crying too.

* * *

"What are you doing here?" Mark demanded, when Art Collins hobbled up our steps with the help of Adam. "You can't keep walking around like that and expect your bones to heal straight!"

"I understand that, Doc, however, I felt my personal attention was necessary in this case," he replied, settling into a kitchen chair.

"Can I get you a cup of coffee?" I asked, wondering what was so urgent that he would venture out of the security of his compound.

He looked at me skeptically. "You have coffee? Thank you, I would appreciate that. As fond as I've gotten of tea, I've missed coffee." I set the cup in front of him, along with the creamer and sugar. He sighed with contentment after two spoons of sugar and a healthy dose of Joshua's rich cream.

Mark and I sat side by side, waiting for Collins to tell us why he had come here.

He got right to the point. "I feel a personal apology is owed to you for the misconduct of my wife and the children during your visit. Claire told me how upset you were when you left yesterday and you had every right to be. Your request that your precious granddaughter not leave the designated area was completely reasonable, and for them to disregard that and go wandering off to the lake was unforgiveable." He paused for another sip of coffee. "I did explain to them that we were trying to build trust between our two groups and their actions have hurt us. I hope not irreparably."

"We had a similar discussion with Emilee," I said. "As a rule she is good at doing what she is told. I believe she was so excited about being with other children that she lost her common sense. She was as much to blame as anyone. I appreciate that you have come to us about this matter. It says to me that you have the same concerns about the safety of your children as we do."

"I would never have forgiven myself, or the others, if anything had happened to Emilee at the lake. Sometimes the children forget that not everyone can swim like they can," Art swallowed hard.

"That wasn't my concern, Art. Emi can swim just fine. I *was* concerned about her getting lost, or injured or even...abducted," I stated, leaving the veiled accusation hang in the air.

Collins was silent for a long moment.

"I would never let anyone harm a child, Allexa, not one of mine and not a guest in my home. Will you accept my deepest apologies?"

It was my turn to be silent in contemplation. Mark is my husband, but these children are of my flesh.

"Apology accepted. It tells me a great deal about your character coming here," I smiled. "More coffee?" The tension in the air dissolved.

"Would you ask Adam to bring in my bag?" Collins requested. After setting it down in front of him, Adam stepped outside again. They definitely had a pecking order.

"As a further apology, please accept this smoked goose, the one you liked so much, Doctor," Art said with a smile.

Mark looked at the package.

"I'm sorry, Art, we cannot accept this as a gift. Your verbal apology was sufficient," Mark stated. Collins looked affronted, until Mark continued. "However, we will accept it as payment for the rice we brought over the day."

Collins smiled. "I like your style, Doc."

So do I.

CHAPTER TWENTY-SEVEN

The temperatures had been holding at a moderate fifty-five to sixty degrees, and even though the sky was a smudgy gray with ash clouds, the day felt wonderful, even normal.

Mark was on the back deck reading so I decided to spend the morning in the greenhouse. The air was wonderfully humid and the fishpond gurgled. I tossed some breadcrumbs to the fish and smiled as they flickered back and forth grabbing each tiny piece.

Everything was growing remarkably well and the abundance of green plants made my heart happy. While I weeded and cultivated around the plants, I discovered some mature beans hiding among the leaves! Fresh vegetables were hard to come by even in here. The greenhouse was only so big and had only so much room. I looked up at the tomatoes in the hanging baskets to see a few of the green fruit starting to get a blush. The cornstalks in the pots by the pond were healthy, however there weren't any ears developing.

The biggest surprise for me was how well the kale plant was doing. A month ago when we harvested all the root crops, I had pulled the kale plant up by the roots and set it in a bucket of water. It had continued to grow and flourish and to give us crunchy leaves once a week. Kale had so many nutrients and it was obviously hardy. I would definitely have to grow more next year.

* * *

"What do you want for your birthday dinner, Eric?" I asked. I felt a bit of nostalgia looking at my oldest child. Where had the years gone?

"Would lasagna be too much trouble? I've got a real taste for it," he said, then looked around to see if we were being overheard. "Amanda is a good cook, but I'm getting tired of her casseroles almost every night."

"That won't be a problem," I said to him, also thinking of the new batch of green beans ready to harvest, maybe even a salad of kale greens.

* * *

We had just sat down for our morning coffee when I saw two vehicles pull in the driveway. Rayn got out of the military Hummer, and Tom White got out of the other one, a dark blue sedan.

"Sorry to barge in on you like this, Allex, but we've got a major problem," Tom said, getting right to the point.

"What's wrong, Tom?"

"Marquette is burning out of control from all the lightning. We're evacuating the city." He accepted the full coffee cup I set in front of him. "There are less than two thousand people left so we've decided to split them up into three groups: one will go to Escanaba, one to the Soo, and one group...to Moose Creek."

"What?! Why here? And why Sault Ste. Marie? " I asked, alarmed.

"Location, Allex. You have an established town that is virtually empty. The housing is in place, the schools, everything. It only needs to be populated and supplied." Tom paused, looking for words. "I know this is going to sound outrageous, but Canada is attempting to invade us, so we're placing mostly current or former military in the Soo to stop them."

"You gotta be kidding. Why would Canada want to invade the U.P.?" I was astounded.

"Though Lake Superior was almost untouched by the ash cloud, the other Great Lakes are now heavily polluted. It's the largest freshwater source in the world, and Canada wants total control of it."

I let out a big sigh and sank down in my chair.

"What is it you want us to do?" Mark asked.

"Jim figures we have less than twenty-four hours to take what we can and get everyone out safely. Marquette is now under martial law and nobody is objecting. People are massing at the sports dome.

"We've commandeered semi-trucks and all the package delivery trucks, and we're filling them with everything that might be needed. A crew worked a few hours at the university, hauling out books until it got too hot. The library was already burning when they thought of it.

"There is a mostly full semi that just arrived at the food warehouse and is being divided between two others that were sitting there. Jim has a volunteer group emptying the warehouse of everything into the three trucks equally, one for each evac location. They're positioned for easy escape should the fires spread even more. We aren't descending on any place empty handed.

"There are also three more big trucks parked at Walstroms and three delivery vans. That's where you come in, Doc. We want to fill the vans with medical supplies from the pharmacy, however, we only have two field medics and they don't know what medicines do what. Right now they're working on boxing up all the over the counter stuff — aspirin, cough syrups, those kinds of items — but they don't want to touch the heavy pharmaceuticals until you get there."

Mark stood. "Of course I'll help."

"Not yet, Doc," Tom said. "Before Rayn takes you in, I'd like us to take a few minutes and pump Allexa's prepper brain. Allexa, what else might be still in that store that a new location could use? The space in the semis is limited and so is our time. However, we don't want to overlook something that might be vital later. Right now they are concentrating on sporting goods, tools, lanterns, candles, and things like blankets and sleeping bags. We've got the manpower to spread out, what else should we be looking for?"

I took a sip of coffee; my thoughts whirling. "In the pharmacy department are also hygiene items. Have them get as many packs of bar soap as possible. It can be used as shampoo and clothes soap too, so take all of it," I stated. "Also toward the back of the store is the fabric department. Take all the bolts of everything. One aisle over is the sewing materials; it should take only three boxes to collect all of the threads, pins, needles, and scissors equally."

Tom stared at me for a moment and started writing.

"And yarn. That can go in large trash bags. Plus knitting needles, crochet hooks, and anything that even remotely looks useful, like patterns," I continued. "If you have two people doing only that, they should be able to empty that entire aisle equally into three or six bags in less than ten minutes."

He was still writing.

"May I make a suggestion, Tom?" I paused, and he nodded. "Write these down on separate sheets of paper. That way you can give the sheet to a two man team and they can go. It'll save minutes of instructions."

Tom grinned. "And now you see why I want her as my assistant!" he said to Mark, ripping the pages off and starting over.

"Canning supplies, if there are any left: jars, seals, canners. Plus spices and matches. Baby things—cloth diapers, bottles, a few soft toys maybe, though many things can be made from the fabric and yarn. Shoes! It will take a while to learn how to make them."

"Speaking of babies, Tom, you should add condoms to that pharmacy list!" Mark said.

"Someone needs to check the gardening area," I said. "I know its October and there likely isn't anything there, but even flower seeds should be kept."

"I think we should check out the hospital, too," Mark said. "I'm sure there are lots of useful supplies there."

"Sorry, Doc. The hospital was hit with a major lightning strike two days ago and it's nothing but smoldering rubble now." Tom glanced at his watch. "This is a good list. Okay, we need to move; time is running out." He handed the stack of papers to Rayn, who had been standing quietly by the door.

Mark stood, slipping on his jacket. He reached out for me and I slid into his arms.

"You bring him back to me safe and sound!" I said to Tom.

"I'm staying here, Allex. Sargent Jones will take care of him," he said. I looked at him with many questions on my mind, and before I could ask them, he continued. "You and I need to ready the town for a lot of new residents!"

They drove away in the Hummer, Rayn at the wheel. I felt a knot form in the pit of my stomach and wondered when or if I would see Mark again.

"What now?" I asked Tom.

"We need to come up with a plan for housing distribution. You know the town, I don't. Any ideas?"

"I think we should get the others involved in this," I said. "Besides, Moose Creek belongs to all of us now and I value their input."

* * *

We all sat around the large kitchen table: Ken and Karen, Eric, Jason and Amanda, Joshua, and the kids.

"Five hundred people coming in the next two days? Can we do this in time?" Jason asked.

"I think if we take it by groups it might work better," Amanda said. "Personally, from past experience, I think the people with kids should be closest to the school, and be dealt with first. There's nothing more distracting or disruptive than a room full of cranky kids! Maybe the couples without children could go to the motels."

"Great idea, Amanda." I smiled at her. "Tell you what. Why don't you and Jason go house to house across from the school and write down the addresses and how many bedrooms are in each house. That way we can assign the appropriate space."

"I like that idea," Tom said. "We can use that method for the other houses too. Ken, Karen, can you take around Lake Meade? Just addresses or fire numbers and any info you think might come in handy. We have to work quickly; the first wave will be here in a few hours."

There was a collective *"What?!"*

"It's a small group of women with children. Jim thought it best to get them out of harm's way. Besides, the less he has to worry about, the quicker things will fall into place," Tom said.

"Joshua, do you mind if both Emi and Jacob stay with you for the day?" I asked. "It would help us out not worrying about them."

* * *

"So what are you not telling me, Tom?" I asked as he drove with me in the front seat and Eric in the back.

He glanced toward the back.

"No secrets, Tom," I stated flatly.

"It's a mess in town, Allex. Jim hasn't slept more than an hour or two in three days. Not many *are* sleeping, not with the constant thunder. It's eerie. There's no rain, just all thunder and heavy lightning. Huge bolts, big jagged slashes across the sky, almost non-stop. The last meteorologist in town said he thought it was a system that is now caught in this valley and can't get out. Every now and then we get hit with hail but that doesn't help the fires.

"The fires started small, in isolated places that were quickly contained. Then one of the taller buildings was hit, and the bolt must have followed the pipes. An underground heating fuel tank blew and it took out more than a city block. That fire spread to the gas stations and those started to blow. Fortunately, right after the first explosion someone suggested we pump as much of the gas back out of the underground storage tanks and move any tankers away from town. That's how we came to have so many and already filled."

"Does that meteorologist say what is causing all this?" Eric asked from the back seat.

"He guessed it was the weather pattern disruption from the continuing volcanic eruptions in Yellowstone. We won't know now. He got hit during a big strike; died instantly, his body charred...right on TV during an in the field broadcast. People are scared now, Allex, terrified. I think that's why everyone is cooperating so well. They want to get out, and I don't blame them."

"When was the last time *you* got some sleep, Tom?" I asked quietly.

"I got a couple of hours last night. I'm okay, really, exhausted, stressed out beyond the max, but okay."

"So what is really bothering you, Tom? I've known you for a long time and you're holding something back," I said.

He glanced at Eric again. "We haven't been able to...to filter who is going where. There are some, ah, undesirables in each group."

"Swell," Eric said. "I guess we'll have to deal with them as we find out who they are, won't we?"

* * *

Tom pulled into the township office parking lot, followed by Jason with Amanda and Ken and Karen in the police car. I unlocked the doors and hit the light switch by habit, but nothing happened.

"Hold on, Mom, I threw the breakers last time to prevent a surge," Jason said. He headed toward the maintenance room, guided by the faint light streaming through the dirty windows. Soon, the building was flooded with artificial light.

In the vault where we've always kept office supplies I found several steno pads that still had several sheets each and handed them out to everyone, along with a couple of pens.

"Remember, work as quickly as you can—addresses, number of bedrooms, and anything that might be critical, like a wood stove, fenced yard, keep it short and simple. Amanda, Jason we need you back here within an hour."

* * *

"Just so you know, I believe there are a few evacuees coming here that are from Moose Creek. Chances are they will want their homes back," Tom said, looking out the window.

"I don't have a problem with that," I replied.

"And we did try to balance out the personnel. We asked for at least one electrician, plumber, carpenter, and teacher in each group, especially the Moose Creek group. Those going to Esky will be blending with a community already set up, Moose Creek is starting over."

"Are there any medical people?" I asked, thinking of the workload on Mark.

"The two medics I mentioned are going to Sault Ste. Marie with their units. I do believe that there is one coming here. Gray. Wasn't he one of your paramedics?" Tom asked.

"Gray is coming back? That's good to hear." I smiled, even though the vision that danced across my memory was of Gray sitting in the school gym with bodies piled around him.

While everyone was out surveying the houses for possible occupation, I found a street map of the town of Moose Creek. Using the copy machine I enlarged the map, a section at a time, and taped it together. In foresight, I made two copies. One was now tacked to the wall in the meeting room, where we also set up a couple dozen chairs and a desk. The other went on the wall in my old office, which made me wonder if Anna was coming back.

I took a red marker and put an "X" through several of the houses.

"What are the red Xs for?" Tom asked after he woke up from a short nap.

"This house is Pete's," I tapped with a pencil, "and this one is Lenny's. They are at Mathers Lake right now, but will want to come home at some point. This one is…was, my friend Kathy's house, and the one next door was Pastor Carolyn's. They are off limits." Tom didn't question why. I couldn't bear seeing them used right now. "There are a few more that aren't in Moose Creek proper, however we'll deal it with later.

"Tom, I have to ask: aren't we out here in danger of the fires spreading? We're not that far from Marquette and we're surrounded by forest."

"We've taken that into consideration," Tom said. "I saw a map of the county behind the zoning desk. Let me show you something." Standing in front of the map, he pointed with a pencil. "Here's Antler's Basin, and here is the dam that forms it."

"Natural waterways," I thought out loud.

"Not only there, also here at Three Shoes Corner, the Little Guppy, the Big Guppy, and Snake River." He pointed at all the rivers that cross county road 695, the main road to Moose Creek. "Natural *fire* breaks. Plus, Jim is sending a munitions crew to the dam. Once everyone is out of Marquette, they're blowing the dam to create a wider river right next to town."

"You do remember what happened the last time the dam was breeched, don't you, Tom? We had six inches of rain in two days during spring meltdown," I said. "The dam couldn't hold the water and it burst. The resulting flood took out three bridges, including the two that are Moose Creek's access to Marquette. We were completely cut off."

"Yes, I remember. We're hoping with a controlled detonation the bridges won't be compromised," he responded. "I hope it works."

"What about our electricity? Is that going to fail as the fires spread?"

"Anything is possible, Allex however the lines that feed Moose Creek that come from Wisconsin run here, on this side of the Antler Basin River." He pointed to an area outside of Marquette. "How long the power lasts is anybody's guess at this point. One tree down almost anywhere, and it's gone. We lost power in Marquette days ago. Jim had his men bring a couple of generators from Sawyer. You should see those things, they're huge. One is keeping Walstroms lit up so they can work in there; the other is keeping the arena cooled off and powered. With all the people in that confined space, it gets very warm, and with the heat from the fires, well, that generator is getting a workout. Jim says it's capable of running the entire airport, so he's not afraid of overloading it."

"Can you show me where the fires are concentrated?" I handed Tom a red marker. "Tom…" I pointed to a grouping of red dots near the shoreline just outside of town.

"Yes, we know, Allex. That's why the evacuation was called, the deciding factor so to speak. The fires have already hit the edges of the coal yard that feeds the power plant. Once it really takes hold, it will burn for years. Marquette is lost."

CHAPTER TWENTY-EIGHT

While I stood there contemplating the map and all those red dots, Jason and Amanda pulled into the parking lot.

"There are forty-five houses within Moose Creek proper, Mom, I'm sure you know that," Jason said, looking at my taped together map on the wall in the meeting room. "All of them are within walking distance to the school."

"I think the ten houses that actually face the school should be held for the families with the youngest children," Amanda stated. "Most of them are three bedrooms, and that bi-level house right across from the school has four bedrooms. On the next street, the houses that back up to these are all two bedrooms or have a third in a loft." She looked closer at my map. "What are the red Xs for?"

"Those are the ones that are off limits for one reason or another." I took the pad from her with all their notes. "You two did great. Jason, will you and Eric do the same thing for all the motels? I don't think I've ever paid attention to how many units each one has, and that's something we need to know." I tore the sheets from the pad and gave it back to Jason. "Amanda, can you stay and help us here when the first group arrives?"

"Of course! What do you want me to do?"

"I'm not sure. Tom, do you have any idea how many will be showing up today?" I asked.

"I can't be certain, maybe as many as a hundred women and their children," he responded.

I suddenly felt very overwhelmed! How were we going to process that many?

Amanda must have recognized the panicked look. "Mom, what if we issue numbers, like they do at the deli? We can take them one at a time."

I nodded. "There are packs of 3x5 index cards in the vault. Will you number a stack one through fifty? I'm going to put this list of addresses on the computer along with your information and print it out. After we get everyone assigned, we can add names to the list. Tom, we need to talk."

Once in the privacy of the office, I confided in him my growing concern.

568

"I'm worried about entitlement attitudes, Tom. We're giving these people free housing, free schooling, and for a time, free food. I don't want anyone thinking they are going to get a total free ride. We need to set down rules."

"I've been thinking about that myself, though your concern might be premature. I've seen these people, met them, and talked with them. Most of them are so thankful to have someone giving directions they'll do anything to be taken care of," he replied.

"That's what I mean, Tom, they want to be *taken care of*." I paced while I thought. "I still think we should lay some ground rules and go from there. You should be the one who addresses it though. I'll back you up."

The first busload arrived a half hour later, along with the semi-truck from the food warehouse. The truck parked at Fram's and the bus emptied into the township parking lot. Amanda passed out thirty-two numbers as they filed quietly in. The adults sat in the chairs and the children sat on the floor or wandered around.

While everyone was getting settled, I had a brief chat with Amanda, and she went across the street to the truck and secured a couple of large cans of soup, plastic spoons, and Styrofoam cups.

"I've met some of you already. For those I haven't, I'm Tom White, the Emergency Manager for Marquette County. This is Allexa Smeth, the Emergency Manager for Moose Creek. For the time being, we are in charge. If you have any questions or concerns, you bring them to us.

"The guidelines for your stay here are simple: Until everyone is here, the housing you are assigned is temporary. There may be some adjusting necessary. Plus, there are some who are coming *back* to Moose Creek, and it's only reasonable that they would want their own house back. We don't know who they may be yet.

"On the back of the card you were given, please print your full name, your husband or significant other's name if they will be joining you later, and your children's names and ages. Also, yours and your husband's occupation or any other skills you have. If you have hobbies like sewing, knitting, or gardening, write it down.

"Next: Everyone here has children, and all children from age four to sixteen *will* attend school once things settle down. Your housing is in the center of town and the closest to the school so the kids can walk.

"For the next week or so, meals will be furnished at the Inn. That's the big red and gray building across from the school. It has a commercial kitchen and restaurant seating. Remember, this whole situation is new to us too, so we need time to figure out how to handle things. So please be patient."

Just then one of the older boys pushed a smaller boy, who fell against another who pushed him back, and a little girl started screaming. A mother glanced over at the instigator, said something to him, and turned back to us. The boy pushed again and she ignored him.

I stood up. "The next thing we are going to address is your children's behavior! You," I pointed at the dyed redhead, "Get that boy under control or you will be both on the next bus back to Marquette." She looked ready to protest and then thought better of it. She took the boy by the arm and stepped outside.

"We are not your babysitters. Understand that and things will work much smoother. I know everyone is in a state of shock. Believe me, at this point, so am I. I found out three hours ago I was going to have five hundred people on my hands. I'll be blunt," I said, "I'm not happy about it. All I ask is you respect each other. We all need to work together. You or your kids act up, you're out of here." I sat back down and the room got very quiet.

"Who is number one?" Tom asked, barely suppressing a chuckle.

The first woman came to the desk and presented her 3x5 card. Tom checked her name on the back, how many children she had, their ages, and if she was expecting a husband to join them later. He then passed the card to me, and I did my best to match a house for them. I wrote an address on another 3x5 card and handed it to the subdued woman, who sat back down.

"Once you've been processed, you're welcome to get a cup of hot soup over at the kitchen here. Please take care of the containers yourself. Remember, *nothing* is disposable anymore. Even the Styrofoam cups will be washed and reused."

Tom called the next one up, a young woman with a very young and very pregnant daughter.

"I saw the sign across the road," she said. "You have a hospital here?"

"Yes…Judi," I said, glancing at the card Tom had handed me. "My husband is a doctor. And this is Marci?" I gave them a warm smile. Mark will be delighted to have another maternity case.

"Oh, thank God!" Judi leaned in to whisper, "Marci is only thirteen. She's only a child herself and I'm so worried about her delivery."

"Once everyone gets here and settles in, you can set up an appointment with him," I reassured her.

Tom called the next one and we processed all of the families in less than an hour. Once everyone had a cup of soup they were more cordial, even chatting and laughing amongst themselves.

I stood to address the room. "A few more things we need to cover. The clinic and hospital across the street are for trauma care. It's a field hospital with only four beds, and we have only one doctor. If you break your arm or get injured somehow, he can take care of it. If your kids come down with a cold or the measles, he *can't* fix it. Keep the child or yourself at home to prevent spreading whatever it is you have. This is *not* a clinic to run to with every sniffle or bruise.

"After you settle into your new house, please feel free to wander around town. There's a playground and tennis courts behind the school. There is also a picnic park and a ball field near the old post office. We hope to have the food service operating within the next couple of hours. That will also be where notices will be posted."

* * *

The women and children were loaded back onto the waiting bus. Tom decided to stay behind and work on the computerized list, while Amanda and I joined our new residents for the short ride to their new homes.

As we turned up Superior Lane, I pointed out the Inn on one side and the school on the other. Another twenty yards and I asked the driver to stop. After checking my handwritten list, I called out the first three names and they got off the bus, along with what luggage they had. They matched up the house number on their card and let themselves in.

We repeated this sequence every half block until the bus was empty.

Back at the township hall, I gave the bus driver a big bowl of soup. When he finished, he went back to Marquette and the sports arena to wait for the next load of refugees.

As rocky as this first processing was, I hoped they would all be this smooth.

* * *

"Mom, here's the list for the motels," Eric said, handing me his spiral pad. "I'm surprised so many of them have kitchenettes."

"That could be handy," I thought out loud. "What we really need at the moment, though, is some workable system of feeding everyone. Tom, did you see anything on those cards about cooks?"

"The only one that was remotely close was someone who said they loved to cook," he told me as he flipped through the cards. "Here it is: Piper Weston." He jotted down the address she had been assigned.

"Amanda, would you go talk to her and see if she could help? Once we get the women together again, we should recruit kitchen help. These people will have to learn right from the start to do things for themselves," I said. "Jason, can you drive that semi over to the service entrance of the Inn? The driver went back with the bus. Then you and Eric unload what looks useful, like cans of soup or stews, easy to fix items. Use your best judgment. It will give them a start, but keep the rest of it locked up."

"I can help with the cooking, Mom," Jason offered.

"If you want, but I need Eric back here before the next busload arrives," I reminded them.

Ken and Karen arrived back at the offices around one o'clock, looking a bit peaked. Ken handed me their list while Karen went into the bathroom and threw up.

"What's going on, Ken?" I asked, looking over at the bathroom door that was only partially closed.

Ken wiped his hand over his face and took a deep breath. "Everything was going really well and we were getting a lot done. Keith and Carron Kaye are still in their home by the way, and said to say hi. Anyway, we were almost finished when we ran into a problem on the east end of the lake. We knocked first like we had been doing, and someone answered, said to come in," he visibly shuddered. "It was Harvey Ward. He was sitting in a recliner, buck-naked, holding a shotgun, and he… wasn't alone. There were ten corpses in the living room, Allexa! He had them sitting in chairs, on the couch watching movies. There were even four sitting at the table like they were playing pinochle!"

"Harvey's House of Horrors," Karen said, joining us. She looked unusually pale. "That sick bastard had shot every one of them and posed them like they were company. Men, women, even a couple of teenage girls…I think they were girls." Karen ran back to the bathroom.

Ken looked in the direction his wife went for a long moment before continuing. "Harvey was giggling like a madman and talking to us about joining the party. Then he focused on Karen and stood up." He turned his back to me for a brief moment. "He was… aroused. Karen pulled her gun out and shot him in the face and then in the crotch." Ken let out a nervous chuckle.

"We need to mark that place completely off limits," I whispered.

"I ran a roll of police tape around the house. Anyone getting close should get the message," Ken said.

"Do you want to take Karen home?" I asked him gently.

"Actually, I think she'd rather keep working here, if that's okay."

* * *

It was mid-afternoon when the next busload arrived with perhaps a dozen personal cars following. We used the same procedure of issuing numbers. Though this group was all childless older couples, we still passed out fifty numbers. By assigning these couples to the various motels, it went quickly. There were a few exceptions.

"Is there any chance we can get a house with a yard?" one woman pleaded. "I'd really like to put in a garden. I do understand about using the housing space wisely, and if my daughter and her husband move in with us, it would save space and I'd have some help."

"I agree. Let's look at this other list," I said, shuffling some papers. I found the list Ken and Karen had dropped off before they started patrolling the parking areas. I assigned the family a house down on Lake Meade.

Four others came to Tom and asked about joint housing. Seems they had been close friends for many years and wanted to stay together. I really thought that if we made as many feel welcomed and as comfortable as possible, the fewer problems we would have. I assigned them a house next to the other family.

I gave the same speech about getting along, the hospital, and the food.

"Perhaps I can help," a middle aged woman said, approaching me. "I come from a really large family. I'm used to cooking a lot at a time, and I'd like to help somehow. I'm Marsha by the way."

"You just got yourself a job!" I said enthusiastically. "In fact, let me have your card back, I'm changing your housing to live right at the Inn. It has a dozen rooms on the upper floors. Let's take a walk and you can choose whichever room you want. That might be your only perk. The rest is going to be a lot of work."

I left Eric and Tom to escort the other couples to the various motels. As a tourist town, Moose Creek had several seasonal motels that had quickly become a benefit to us as instant housing.

I introduced Marsha and her husband to Jason and Amanda, and returned to the offices in time to see the three long commercial tankers backing into the lot at Fram's.

"What are those, Tom?" I asked.

"Propane, gas, and diesel. Each of the three locations gets the same thing. I thought it only fair." He leaned against the doorway. "It will still have to be rationed. When this is gone, it's gone."

What a daunting thought.

"That's it for today, Allexa," Tom yawned. "I don't know about you, but that was exhausting. I still need to get back to Marquette." He paused for a long time, not moving to leave.

"What, Tom?"

He looked at me, then away. "You know, this is what we trained for, and we did well today. But all of this has such a…a final feeling to it."

"Are you coming back?" I asked in a small voice.

He smiled at my obvious emotional pain. "Yes, Allex, I'm coming back. Jim and I discussed it and I volunteered to move here to Moose Creek and give you a hand in running it. We couldn't just dump five hundred people on your doorstep without some help."

"Is Jim coming too?" I asked. I'd grown quite fond of the colonel.

"No, he feels he will be of better use in the Soo fighting the Canadians." He laughed. "Who ever thought we would be at war with Canada?" That left me speechless and sad. "Let me give you and Eric a lift home, Allex. We're done for now and tomorrow is going to be a very long day."

* * *

Rayn's Hummer and a step-van were sitting in the driveway. Rayn was sitting on top of the picnic table with a glass of water, deep in thought. Mark was nowhere in sight.

"Rayn, where's Mark?" I asked, alarmed.

"He's in the house, having a drink. He's really upset and I think he's mad at me," she stated.

"Over what?" I asked.

She frowned. "Maybe you should ask him."

Just then Mark came out the back door. "She almost *killed* me!" he snapped, pointing at the young lady sitting quietly.

"I did *not*, Doctor Mark!" Rayn protested.

"What in the world happened?" I asked, wrapping my arms around Mark, so glad to see him home. "No, don't say anything yet. I think I need a drink for this. Tom, you want anything?"

"No, though I'd like to know what the fuss is all about." He grinned.

Mark followed me inside, and I saw Eric sit down next to Rayn and hug her. They were going to make a good couple.

"One of you start from the beginning," I pleaded, taking a sip of my spiced rum. It went down smoothly, just like it should on a rough day.

Mark and Rayn glared at each other.

"Mark, how did it go at the pharmacy?" I asked, hoping to get something started.

"Actually, it went quite well," Mark said. "We finished everything in less than two hours. The sorting, packaging, even marking all the boxes. There wasn't a great deal left. I did manage to get some vital things for the hospital."

"Since the pharmaceuticals were at the top of Colonel Andrews' priority list, those were loaded first and left with a guard, even though there isn't anyone left in town who's out to steal," Rayn chimed in. "After that all of us circulated with shopping carts. It was actually kind of fun. Three semis are now loaded with an amazing variety of things. One of them should arrive in Moose Creek in a few hours. The soldier driving it will sleep in the cab tonight to protect it. Oh, and he's staying with us so he will need quarters."

"Us?" Eric gasped. "Does that mean *you're* staying?"

"Of course I'm staying," she laughed. "I asked for this assignment as soon as it came up."

"Rayn, I'm delighted you will be here, but let's get on with what happened, please!"

"I volunteered to drive the pharmaceutical truck," Mark stated. "That's it over there." He pointed to the oversized step van. "I wanted to stop at the Medical Center before we came home since there is no going back." He looked at me; his eyes had a touch of fear. "Oh, Allex, it's bad there, really bad, there are fires everywhere."

"He told me that if I didn't stop with him, he would go alone." Rayn glared at him again. "I couldn't let that happen, so I went."

"The parking lot was empty. I pulled up as close to the doors by the rehab center as I could, and Rayn was right behind me. I went to the equipment supply room first and found what I wanted: a wheelchair. I went back for another one while Rayn stood guard. I also found several pairs of adjustable crutches and some limb stabilizers that I piled on top of the second wheelchair. When I was headed back to leave, some guy stepped out from one of the therapy rooms and pointed a gun at me." He swallowed hard. "I'm not afraid to admit that I was really scared, Allex."

"The guy didn't see me at first," Rayn stated calmly. "When he saw me and turned my direction, his whole body turned, including his gun hand. As soon as the weapon cleared the doctor's range, I fired."

"The Arc," Eric said, and Rayn nodded. "Once the perp began the Arc, that curve of space where the gun isn't pointed at anything, the doctor was no longer in danger of being shot by a reflex firing," Eric explained. "The Arc lasts only a fraction of a second."

"She could have hit *me*!" Mark yelled starting to pace.

"Mark, where did the bullet actually hit?" I asked.

"In the middle of his forehead."

"From what I understand, Rayn is an excellent shot, and that was a very short range. So it was exactly where she aimed. You were never in any danger from her hitting you. It sounds like she saved you." I hugged him tightly. "I'm really glad she did!"

"It was really loud," he said, his voice quieting. "My ears are still ringing."

"So did you bring the wheelchairs with you?" Tom asked.

"After all of that I was not about to leave them behind. Allex, I want to take one to Collins. He's having a rough time getting around on crutches with a broken arm."

When Tom was getting ready to leave, a moving van pulled into the driveway. It was getting busy here.

Staff Sargent Frank Sanders, one of the Colonel's private detail, stepped down from the driver's seat. Rayn and Eric both stood and Rayn gave him a quick nod, acknowledging his superior rank. He returned her gesture, also nodding to Eric, who outranked him. Even though Eric was no longer active military, it was all a sign of respect.

"Ma'am," Sargent Sanders said, "this is a special delivery from Col. Andrews. I'm to give only you or the doctor the keys. One key is for the truck, the other is for the padlock on the back doors."

"What's in there, Sargent?" I asked.

"I don't know, ma'am."

Mark took the keys and opened the padlock, looked inside, and then locked it again. He stood by my side, grinning.

"Do you need a ride back to Marquette?" Tom asked the young soldier.

"Yes, sir, I do, although I will be coming back tomorrow to stay."

* * *

After the two left for Marquette, I pulled Mark aside. "So what's in the van?" I asked.

"Christmas," he said, smiling even broader. "It looks like Jim emptied a liquor store."

Rayn coughed subtly.

"Ma'am," she looked really nervous, "would it be alright with you if I went home with Eric?"

"I'd be disappointed if you didn't," I replied, reaching out to give this new member of our family a hug.

CHAPTER TWENTY-NINE

With what we were to face today haunting my thoughts, I slept poorly, finally falling asleep at four o'clock in the morning. The alarm went off at six.

Freshly showered and fortified with coffee and toast with jam, we headed back to the township offices to organize the next wave. As prearranged the night before, we all drove our own vehicles, not knowing when someone might have to leave. Before we arrived at the township office, I noticed another large semi-truck in Fram's parking lot. It must be our Walstroms truck, filled with supplies.

Rayn and Eric came in casual fatigues with Eric proudly sporting his maroon beret. They also had rifles and side arms, and would be stationed inside by the check-in desk, in full view. Ken and Karen were to control the parking lot, while Jason and Amanda worked in the office kitchen preparing an easy meal. This next group could be the most disorderly of all.

A long line of personal vehicles began filling Fram's parking lot and a full school bus pulled into the township offices at ten o'clock. Men and women spilled out, dragging suitcases and plastic bags. The ones that caught my attention immediately were the two women with six children. I singled them out and ushered them into the meeting room.

"You should have been on yesterday's bus," I said.

"I'm sorry, but we were still rounding up the kids," the youngest one replied, clearly exhausted.

"I'm Holly Crawford, and this is my sister Ivy. Please, no jokes," the other one pleaded. "We are, or *were*, middle school teachers. All these children are orphans we've been caring for. If at all possible, could we stay together? The children have been traumatized enough."

"I have the perfect house for you two," I said, thinking of the big house with four bedrooms across the street from the school. "Here, fill out these cards, and I'll have Amanda take you to your new house."

Teachers! Another problem solved on its own.

Out of the corner of my eye I caught a familiar face. "Gray!" I called out to the town's only paramedic. He turned my way and smiled. "It's so good to see you. I heard you might be coming back."

"It is home, ya know? When everyone left or died, I felt I was more useful in Marquette. Now…" Gray looked around, "I think I can help again. Has my house been assigned to anyone?"

"No, it hasn't. I marked it off-limits. You can go home anytime you want. Have some lunch first."

"Ramen noodles again?" he asked with a grin.

"Nope, I think it's vegetable soup today," I said, remembering the two cases of noodles I gave him during the flu outbreak last winter.

I found Tom out in the parking lot organizing the restless bunch.

"Everyone whose wife or parents might already be here will be next. File into the meeting room and we'll find where your family is," Tom said. He had a very loud and commanding voice when he wanted to.

It took close to an hour to process the forty men that came forward; most were husbands, some were fathers and brothers. Only two didn't match up to anyone.

"I'm sorry, I don't have those names listed," I shrugged. "Are you sure they were to come here and not Escanaba?"

They both assured me their families were on the bus yesterday. All I could do was take their names and keep searching our records.

Tom had a small group of the remaining horde enter the office and take numbers. One young man swaggered up to my desk.

"What a pretty cougar," he leered at me, leaning across my paperwork where I got a good look at the tattoo on the side of his neck that disappeared down into his shirt. "I really get off on powerful women."

I was speechless.

Eric immediately stepped in between us. "Back off, sonny."

He smirked. "Oh, is she yours, soldier boy?"

"This 'cougar' is my *mother*," Eric replied, his voice turning to ice.

"And *my wife*," Mark said, stepping forward protectively.

The young man straightened up, looking guilty.

"I suggest you have a seat and wait for your number to be called," I said politely. "I'm not likely to forget that face."

Four women approached my desk.

"We need to be housed together," one of them stated simply.

"Your names?" I asked, a bit taken back by the abruptness.

"I'm Sister Agnes, this is Sister Margaret, Sister Doris, and Sister Lynn," she replied.

"Nuns?" I was astonished. They were dressed in jeans and sweaters, not even the casual short skirt habits I'd seen before.

"Yes, and I suppose our attire is misleading. However, we felt these garments were more practical and more suitable for the…occasion. We do have our habits packed in our suitcases," Sister Agnes gave me a smile that lit her makeup-less face.

"Somewhere around here is Father Constantine. He's always wandering off talking to someone," Sister Margaret commented.

"A priest," I stated, stunned. "Excuse me a moment. I'll be right back." I needed some privacy. I went out the maintenance service door that led to the grassy courtyard behind the offices. I felt the tears burning behind my eyes as I lifted my face to the morning sun.

"Oh, Carolyn, I don't know if you would approve or not, but I do know you would understand, and if you don't approve, forgive me anyway." I wiped my eyes with my cloth hanky and went back inside and sat down at my desk.

"Sisters, I know just the place for you. It's a large house, right next door to the church, and it even has a separate apartment over the garage for Father Constantine. I hope he's able to negotiate the stairs."

They all smiled at me, Sister Lynn giggled. At that moment a young blond man of about thirty, maybe thirty-five, joined the group. Although he too was dressed in jeans and a sweater, he also wore a clerical collar. If this was the priest, he certainly wouldn't be having an issue with the stairs. He looked very fit, possibly a runner.

"Sorry, Sisters, I got distracted," Father Constantine said, giving me a beatific smile that reminded me much of Pastor Carolyn. "I overheard you say the house was next door to a church. Is it the Catholic church?"

"Yes, it is, Father, although I have no idea what kind of congregation you may be having, if any."

"It matters not. God's word is God's word. In fact, I've always wanted to try non-denominational services, and it might even be wise considering our circumstances." He radiated kindness, and I knew I was making the right decision in housing them in Pastor Carolyn's former residence.

"If you don't mind waiting, I'll find someone to take you there. Meanwhile, help yourself to some coffee or tea. Soup will be available at the Inn after noon. They'll be feeding the children first."

* * *

It felt like we had barely put a dent in the parking lot numbers after three hours. Tom asked for a short conference.

"We still have maybe a hundred to go and I doubt we will finish today. All of you know this town better than I do—any suggestions?"

"We could drop off six or eight to each empty house and hope for the best," Ken said.

"What about Camp Tamarack?" Jason suggested.

"What's that?" Tom asked.

"It's a summer camp for underprivileged children," Jason said. "There are maybe twenty cabins that sleep four to eight each. The cabins are only used for six to eight weeks in the summer, so might be a bit rough. The men could stay there until more permanent houses are assigned."

"There are less than twenty women left. They shouldn't be difficult to relocate," I said, thinking out loud again. "Tom, you need housing too," I told my friend. "I think you should have Bob and Kathy's house. It's central and you could walk here."

"Are you sure?" he asked, knowing it was one of the places I had set aside.

"Absolutely sure, because *you* are going to run this town, not me, and you need to be available to the people. I'll help, but this group needs a man at the helm. You are by far more qualified for the job than I am. Why don't you come home with us for dinner tonight and we'll talk about it."

"Thanks, I might even take you up on that drink. Do you have enough?"

"You have no idea," I laughed, thinking of the van in our driveway.

* * *

I took the package of thawed venison out of the refrigerator and browned the meat in a large pot along with a chopped onion. After I snipped off the piece of nylon that contained the onion, I stuffed it into the top of the hanging pantyhose. Some day we will make a washable toy with those scraps.

I added a minced clove of garlic to the pot, then a jar of canned peas and a few dried herbs. While all of that simmered I made a paste of flour and water to thicken the juices into gravy. Mom always served this over mashed potatoes, with us making a "volcano" with the gravy ladle. Potatoes were too few right now, so I made a small batch of pasta and a larger batch of rice so the guys could have a choice.

Mark and Tom went out to the Christmas van and brought in a case of mixed liquor and a case of red wine.

"I propose we toast to Colonel James Andrews, for being thoughtful and generous in leaving this gift for us," Mark said. We were all in a good mood and a bit distracted, so when the vehicle with a very large trailer pulled in the drive, it startled us.

A much-disheveled colonel stepped down from the Hummer and we all rushed outside.

"Jim! I thought you were going to the Soo?" Tom greeted his friend. "Have things been delayed?"

"No, everyone is on their way," Jim sighed. "Can we open some of that Grey Goose?"

"With or without ice?" I asked, smiling as we went back indoors. It was really good to see him.

"With, please. We haven't had ice in a week," he replied.

I poured him two inches in an Old Fashioned glass, and added a couple of cubes to chill his drink.

"Not that we're complaining, Jim, but why are you here?" Mark asked.

The colonel sipped his drink and closed his eyes for a moment. "Would you mind if I washed up first? It's been a long and harrowing drive."

We waited patiently while Jim washed soot off of his hands and face. Meanwhile, I set another place and put the steaming food on the table.

Once everyone had food on their plate and a slice of buttered bread, Jim told his story.

"All of the semi-trucks, tankers, and vans had taken up positions on the west side of town where the fires were the least. They each had their instructions and directions and were only waiting for the school buses and other vehicles to show up so they could leave. While they were waiting, they had to move the tankers even further out when it started getting really hot," he paused for another forkful of rice and meat.

"I went back to the sports arena to hustle the buses and military transports. It was even hotter there—the air temperature was getting close to 110 degrees. Everyone was finally on the road that skirts town to the north, Fleet Street, and I knew they would meet up with their convoys within the half hour.

"It took me about ten more minutes to do one final sweep of the arena to make sure no one was left behind. I shut the big gennie down and attached it to the Hummer to take it to the new base at the Soo. That's when I heard the explosion. The power plant on the corner of Fleet and Alabaster blew. I was completely cut off from our escape route with fires burning all around me. There wasn't any way I could get through on Fleet. Even the pavement was burning, but there was a small break on 695. I had thought of trying to find another route south or east, then I remembered the munitions going off at the dam. I had less than five minutes to make it over the bridge before the water hit, maybe less. I had to make a choice, so I came here." He paused to take a drink. "It was less. When I crossed the bridge, the water was rising, and fast. I don't know if the bridge is still there—I never looked back."

The three of us stopped eating.

"Are you alright though, Jim? Did you get burned or anything?" Mark asked, concerned.

"No, I'm not hurt, though I think my tires are shot. Rubber doesn't stand up well to burning asphalt. I think some fresh air will help clear the smoke I inhaled."

"I don't know what to say, Jim," I said. "Your command and counsel to your men will be greatly missed by them, but at the same time, their loss is our gain. I'm so pleased to have you join us."

"Well, thank you, Allexa. If I had to be stranded, I couldn't have picked a better group to spend my life with." We all raised a glass. "The group going to Sault St. Marie has some good leaders; they will be fine." He helped himself to another slice of bread.

The four of us took a walk down to the end of my road as dusk settled fully in. In the distance we could see the crimson sky over Marquette. The darker the night became, the redder the sky. It was a very sobering reminder of our new and complete isolation.

"I think you should take this case of Grey Goose with you, Jim," Mark suggested when Jim and Tom got ready to leave.

"Thanks, I think I will," Jim replied. "I'll stay the night at Tom's new barracks, and find something else tomorrow. It's been a long day and I'm exhausted. Thank you again for the dinner, Allex, it was great."

CHAPTER THIRTY

When we arrived at the township office at nine o'clock, the place was in chaos.

"What's the matter with you people?" Jim Andrews bellowed, barely heard above the roar of the crowd.

Mark parked the car across the road at the clinic and we waited. With all the yelling going on, I couldn't hear what this group was so upset about.

"We need to get over there, Mark!" I said, and started to leave. Mark grabbed my arm to stop me.

"Let's wait a minute or two. I don't want you getting hurt."

While we waited a safe distance away, I could see Eric, Rayn, and Frank at the front door, rifles at the ready. How did this happen? Yesterday all was quiet.

I saw the group of five making their way toward the front of the crowd. The priest and his nuns!

"Come on, Mark, I think *someone* is about to get hurt," I said and bolted across the road. Eric saw us coming and fired a shot well over the heads of the crowd. That gave us enough time to make it through the mass of angry people and reach the doors.

A moment later that arrogant young man that had called me a cougar went nose to nose with the priest.

"You pussy, get out of my way!" he sneered at Father Constantine, who calmly smiled back at him.

"You're a very troubled young man," the priest said. "These good people are only trying to help us. What is your complaint this morning?"

"There's no food and we're all hungry!" he shouted. "We were supposed to be fed last night and we weren't! Nobody brought us anything over at that rat trap they're making us stay in!" Which got several affirmative yells from the crowd.

"You were supposed to go to the Inn on your own for dinner. It's only a short walk," I remarked.

"Shut up, bitch!" he screamed at me.

Father Constantine stepped up to the young man and told him to apologize to me.

"You gonna make me, pussy?"

Father Constantine smiled. "If need be, yes."

"Well, well, maybe you got some balls after all, padre. Let's go a round, see how you feel with a few loose teeth!"

The crowd backed up, creating a circle.

I could hear the nuns behind me, whispering to each other. "Oh, I don't think he wants to do that," Sister Agnes was saying.

"Can you stop him?" I asked Sister Agnes. "I don't want to see the Father hurt."

Sister Lynn started giggling again. "Don't worry about Father Constantine; you need to pray for that poor boy!"

"What do you mean?"

"Father Constantine not only was a champion boxer in college, he grew up on the south side of Chicago, and is very street smart," Sister Doris said matter-of-factly. "That young man picked the wrong guy to challenge and is about to get his butt kicked."

Someone standing close to us heard the conversation. "I'll still lay odds on Marlow. He learned to fight on the inside."

"Who?" I asked, alarmed.

"Kenny Marlow," the guy repeated. "His uncle was some big shot general until he was railroaded or something."

I know I paled.

Father Constantine walked over to the nuns and handed Sister Agnes his collar. "Will you hold this for me please?" He turned in time to duck a sucker punch from Marlow, and the fight was on.

It was impressive to watch this young priest fight. He avoided all of Kenny's punches, making the punk angrier as he landed hit after hit. He finally ended it with a well-placed uppercut, sending Marlow to the pavement.

Father Constantine reached down and grabbed a fist full of shirt, hauling Kenny to his feet.

"Now, apologize to the nice lady."

* * *

The crowd settled down after that, and we were finally able to understand the problem. It seemed that Kenny Marlow had been the instigator all along, insisting that *someone* was supposed to bring them meals, even though everyone had been told otherwise. The group left as one and walked down to the Inn for breakfast, with instructions to return for housing assignments.

I singled the colonel out once the meal problem was solved. "Jim, we have a problem."

DEBORAH D. MOORE

"I can see that. I think they understand now they aren't going to be spoon fed," he replied.

"No, not that. That kid, the one that was fighting the priest, his name is Kenny Marlow, and he's Hank Marlow's nephew!"

Colonel Andrews closed his eyes, trying to control his anger. "I'll take care of this, Allex. You needn't worry about that family anymore." I saw him talking to Eric, Rayn, and Frank, and then the four of them left in the direction of the Inn.

* * *

Two hours later, we were once again filling out cards and assigning houses to the eighty men who returned after lunch.

"Excuse me, ma'am, my name is Jeremy Smith," one of the younger men said as he approached the desk. "I'd like to apologize for our behavior earlier. I remembered what you said about going to the Inn, but that guy kept telling us we heard you wrong and that we should wait for someone to show up with our meals on wheels. When we realized no one was coming, it was too late and the Inn was closed. He's really good at getting people riled up."

"I appreciate your apology. Please let the others know we really are doing the best we can and we will try to get things running smoothly as soon as possible. We're going to need help and cooperation though," I replied. "We simply cannot do it by ourselves, especially not if half the people here are fighting us. If anyone has any suggestions that would help, I really do want to hear them. Anyone can talk to me or to Tom White, at any time."

* * *

Hours later we were done. I was exhausted and wanted to go home. After all the anxiety I wanted a relaxing hot shower and something to eat. Just as Mark and I were getting ready to leave, Jim showed up.

"Did that Kenny Marlow come back here?" he asked.

"No, he didn't."

"We can't find him anywhere, and that worries me," Jim growled, obviously frustrated.

584

CHAPTER THIRTY-ONE

JOURNAL ENTRY: October 29

It has been a grueling couple of days. I'm secretly wanting for us to go back to the days when we were left alone, but I know those days are long gone. I envy Art Collins in his isolation now, and I think Mark and I should take the news of the town's new citizens to him personally.

* * *

"Sorry to barge in on you, Art, but we have news we want to deliver firsthand," I said after Collins hobbled onto the deck when we pulled in.

"First, though, I have something for you." Mark beamed as he pulled one of the wheelchairs from the back hatch. "Again, it's on loan, but keep it as long as you need it."

Art gaped at the gift.

"Oh, and these might be better suited for you." Mark produced one set of adjustable crutches. "You're a bit taller than Eric, and those wooden ones were made custom for him."

"I...I don't know what to say," Art mumbled. "Please come in and tell me where you found these."

We sat at the smaller table in the kitchen, Art in his new wheelchair. Mark had him stand with my assistance, and he adjusted the crutches.

"Use the crutches as little as possible for now. I don't want you putting unnecessary pressure on that arm," Mark instructed. "In a few more weeks, you should need to exercise your good leg, and then we'll set up some physical therapy that Claire can help you with."

"This is wonderful! How do I thank you?"

"There really isn't any need to thank us. You never know though, someday we may need a favor," I interjected. "Now, for the main reason we came here..."

I think I scowled, because Art looked concerned. "Marquette is burning out of control, and the remaining population has been evacuated, some of them to Moose Creek."

"I see."

"I don't think you do. We didn't have a say in it, Art. We had a three hour warning that there would be up to five hundred people showing up needing places to live." I stood so I could pace. "For the most part, I think these are good people, scared and lost, however, there are a few..." I pursed my lips. "There are a few that are dangerous, and we wanted to warn you. You should keep the main gates locked again; maybe even post a guard until we can find one in particular. Once he's captured, I think the danger will have passed."

"Who is this person?" Art asked quietly.

"His name is Kenny Marlow, an ex con. His father was one of the gang that hit Moose Creek last spring and killed my brother," I replied.

"And his uncle, Hank Marlow, appointed himself general over the Marquette National Guard. His rule was nothing short of tyrannical. He also blamed Allex for the death of his brother and set out to kill her," Mark added.

"Until he was uncovered. He killed my best friend and her husband," I said through gritted teeth. "But he *was* found out by Colonel Andrews and was executed. Now this kid is in town, we don't know where he is and we don't know what he's up to."

I could see thoughts running through Art's mind. "What do you want us to do, Allexa?" he asked.

"Just be aware that he might show up here. I think he knows the colonel is looking for him, so he may be looking for someplace to hide out. He's mean and he's dangerous, Art, and I don't want anything to happen to any of your people, especially the children." I sat back down, fidgeting.

"What does this guy look like, Doc?" Art asked Mark, clearly avoiding my distress.

"He's dark haired, maybe five foot ten, lean, wiry, brown eyes. Allex, is there anything else about him you can remember?"

"The tattoo. He has some kind of tattoo on the right side of his neck that extends from below the ear down into his shirt."

"Okay, we'll keep an eye out for him. What do you want us to do if he does show up here?" Art asked.

"I suppose tie him up and let the colonel deal with him," I answered, though I really didn't feel that way.

"Anything else we should know about the new citizens of Moose Creek?"

I smiled. "There is good news in all of this. When they arrived, it wasn't empty handed."

"That's how I got the wheelchairs and crutches," Mark said. "There is also a nice stock of medical supplies for the hospital now. Knowing the city was burning out of control and everything there would eventually be lost, the place was stripped."

"What do you need, Art? What do you want? Once we get everything sorted out and inventoried, we can get you flour so the women can bake bread; books for the children; there are a couple of semi-trucks full of...of stuff! If you want, we'll bring it to you so you don't have to expose yourself."

Art's eyes dilated and he grinned. "Can I get back to you on that?"

* * *

I sat down across from Tom at the big oak desk, like I did with Anna so many times in the past. "Although it's only been a couple of days, I think we should start an inventory of the supplies in the trucks and put them somewhere."

"Interesting that you bring that up, Allexa," Tom said, leaning back in the oversized leather chair. "Marsha was just here and asked about getting more things out of the food truck. She wants to set up some staples in the lobby so people can take some food home with them. She mentioned keeping most in the back, under a strict inventory. That's one smart lady there. She was quick to bring up that the food won't last forever and it will have to be rationed, and that people need to start making some of their own decisions."

"That's great, Tom. I'm glad to see someone taking the initiative. That's going to be critical to the town surviving and thriving, not just maintaining," I agreed. "I've been thinking about the Walstroms truck and where to put all of those supplies. There is the Out Riggers gift shop. It's mostly empty, now, but could be a good place to sort things out. We need someone really organized for that job."

"Hmmmm," Tom thought out loud. "Those nuns were here earlier looking for something to do. Say, did you know all four of them are teachers? And from what I have seen, most teachers *have* to be organized. Do you want to talk to them?"

* * *

The day was unusually warm for late October, so I left my car at the township and walked across the street to talk with Mark.

"How is the stocking progressing?" I asked. He had driven the medical van today, and was emptying the over the counter medicines onto shelves.

"Slow but steady," Mark answered. "I'm amazed at how much was boxed up. There are more cough and cold treatments here than I have room for and I don't want to put everything out. That's not an efficient use of limited space." He moved a box to the floor and put another on top of his desk.

"I have a feeling we're going to run into the same problem with the other truckload of things."

"How are you going to handle it?"

"Well," I said, "if we put out just enough so we can see what we have, and leave the rest in the truck, we could use the truck as a warehouse. When items run low, we bring more in. Of course the truck will be parked right next to the building and kept locked."

"I like that idea, although with the vital pharmaceuticals in the same truck, I can't leave it parked here," Marked admitted. "With the lower gas mileage of this van, I also can't drive it back and forth all the time."

"Agreed. And with so many people here now, the gas will have to be rationed even more than before. What if you drive it only when you know you need to restock, and carry some of the drugs with you, leaving everything else in the van at home locked in the barn?" I suggested.

"That could work." He smiled at me. "What are you up to this afternoon?"

"I'm going to talk with the nuns about organizing a group to inventory the big semi-truck and putting things in the Out Riggers. It's such a nice day I think I'll walk down," I said. "I'll be back in an hour or two." I gave my husband a quick kiss. It felt like we'd been married a lot longer than the three months it has been.

* * *

"Oh, thank you, Allexa! This is exactly the kind of project we were looking for," Sister Agnes said, clapping her hands.

"Wonderful, that will really help us out a lot, Sister. I'll have someone move the semi-trailer over into the parking lot next door. I think we should check over the building first though, see how much work needs to be done to get it ready." This was going to work out better than I had hoped. "I'm rather anxious myself to see what's in the truck."

"You don't know?" Sister Margaret inquired.

"Sister, I didn't even know any of you were coming here until three days ago! That truck was mostly packed by then. It's as much of a mystery to me as anyone," I told them, as all of us walked over to the gift shop.

The gift shop definitely needed a good cleaning, and some of the display cases were cracked. All in all though, it would hold a great deal with little effort.

"I think this room on the main floor should be a children's play area," Sister Lynn suggested. "Hopefully there are some toys in there."

"What a wonderful idea, Sister. The mothers should have someplace they can safely leave their children while they 'shop.' If there aren't any toys in the truck we can get some from the pre-school room at the school for you."

"Although it might be premature, Allexa, how do you want us to handle who gets what and how much?" Sister Agnes asked.

"I'm not sure. All of what was brought with the new people is *for* the people. I do understand what you're getting at though; we can't have a free for all, with some getting a lot while others get little. That wouldn't be fair. It will take several days to get things cleaned and organized, so we have some time to think about it. I want to hear any suggestions you have."

* * *

That night over dinner, I told Mark about the new store.

"Sounds like you have a good crew to work with Allex. I had an interesting visitor today after you left," he said, barely able to contain himself. "A young man stopped by, James Geneva, a third year med student! I think I have a new assistant and protégé."

"So you don't need me anymore?" I had mixed feelings suddenly. Being Mark's aide had given me a satisfying purpose.

"I will *always* need you, Allex," Mark said, pulling me into his arms for a reassuring hug. "Although I think it will be good to have someone to help out with the routine stuff and someone who can take over for me when I get sick or too old. I will need *you* with me when I see a female patient; that's common practice. Besides," he tightened his hug, "with this many people, I don't want to spend all of my time at the clinic or hospital. I want for you and me to still have a life."

CHAPTER THIRTY-TWO

JOURNAL ENTRY: October 30

It's been an unbelievably busy three days in Moose Creek. The town has come alive again. People are milling around at the park; children are playing, and I hear laughter wherever I go.

Marsha selected another husband and wife team to help inventory and stock the food supplies. She was one hundred percent right that people need to make some of their own choices, and that begins with food. Now that they can pick up a few staples and cook at home, the Inn is less crowded at mealtime, and with less wait, everyone seems to be in a better mood. The variety of food prepared has expanded too, now that Marsha can see everything that was brought, although much of is still locked in the trailer.

The Sisters recruited help and had the Out Riggers cleaned and rearranged in only one day. The transformation has been a miracle.

* * *

"I had the ladies bring in a dozen boxes and open them," Sister Margaret laughed. "It was like Christmas. When they saw what was in a box they put it in a designated room. There is a room for sewing and knitting; another for outdoor activities; another for games, toys, and puzzles and one for toiletries. Now that one is a big hit! Just knowing there is soap and shampoo available has everyone giggling like Sister Lynn."

"Once there were a couple of boxes in one room, we stopped bringing them in, and started putting things on shelves or on tables," continued Sister Doris. "When the boxes were emptied, we went back for more. That way nothing got too cluttered."

"Sister Doris hates clutter," Sister Lynn giggled.

THE JOURNAL: CRIMSON SKIES

"Have you thought about how to keep track of everything?" I asked Sister Agnes, who seemed to be the alpha of the group.

"We're going to try a card system, sort of like what you had when we were all checking in," she said. "The first time in, a person will fill out a card, and when they leave we mark down what they took and when, like a ledger system. If it doesn't work, we'll try something else." She shrugged a thin shoulder.

* * *

The strange, mild weather was holding and no one was complaining. I took the opportunity to walk around the town and observe the changes. There were toys in the yards, clothes on lines and hanging over fences. Moose Creek had a lived in look again. As I passed the deserted community garden, Bradley's Backyard, a few green things caught my attention. Upon looking closer, I could see the leafy greens were tops from beets planted months ago! And dying vines foretold of hidden potatoes. I would have to let Marsha know there were fresh vegetables to be had.

"Well, if it isn't the pretty cougar out for a stroll," Kenny Marlow said, leaning casually against a tree, half hidden by an old twisted lilac bush.

My heart stumbled and I looked around, only to realize that although I could hear children playing at the school, there was no one in sight. I tucked my elbows into my body to feel the reassuring bulge of my Kel-Tec.

"Well, if it isn't the little troublemaker out from hiding under a rock," I retorted.

He laughed and straightened up, taking a few steps toward me. "I do know who you are, bitch. You killed my daddy and then you killed my uncle." He stepped closer. I backed up.

"Your father killed my brother and his wife, he deserved whoever's bullet ended his wretched life." I backed up two steps more. "As far as your uncle goes, he was executed by the military; I had nothing to do with it. However, I would gladly have pulled the trigger myself to end his pathetic existence after what he ordered done to my friends." I could feel the rage building inside of me as the memories swamped my heart with all my loss at the hands of this family.

He glowered at me. I could almost feel the hatred rolling off this young man, and it was all aimed, unjustifiably, at me.

A vehicle came around the corner and honked, demanding my attention. I glanced then I quickly looked back and Kenny Marlow was gone.

"Allex, glad I found you," Jim Andrews said, emerging from the Hummer. "Are you alright? You look pale."

"Did you see him?" I asked.

"Who?"

"Kenny Marlow was just here. He surprised me when I was checking this old garden spot," I said shakily, trying to get my breathing back under control.

"Marlow was here? Where did he go?" Jim pulled his service revolver while scanning the area.

"When you honked, he slipped away, back into the woods, I guess," I surmised.

"Did he hurt you or threaten you at all, Allex?" he asked, obviously concerned.

"In so many words, yeah you could call it a threat. He knows who I am, feels it's my fault his father and uncle are dead." I let loose an involuntary shiver. "I don't think he's going to be happy until I'm dead too."

"We are not going to let that happen, Allex. I'm assigning you and your family a bodyguard."

I laughed nervously. "You don't think Eric and Rayn are enough?"

"Are they here right now?" Jim stated more than asked. "No, they're not. Allex, please, until we catch this guy, you're not to ever be by yourself, is that clear?"

"I don't have a death wish, Colonel, but you can't give me orders." I folded my arms over my chest. Why was I being so belligerent? Maybe it was the adrenaline talking.

Jim sighed. "Let me at least give you a lift back to the office. Please."

"Sure, but I need to do something first." I grabbed the claw fork that was still hanging on the fence. After sweeping away some leaves and the dying vine, I pressed the fork into the soil and dragged it, pulling up a large tuber. I repeated the procedure until I was sure I had all the potatoes from that hill. I pulled out the hem of my shirt and piled the spuds in the makeshift apron.

"Fresh potatoes?" Jim said in awe. "Can I have one? Make that two, one for Tom."

"Help yourself," I said.

I was happy that Jim and Tom had decided to share Bob and Kathy's former home. The house was large and the two levels were individually fully functional with two bedrooms and a full bath each, perfect for two bachelors.

"The rest I want to take over to Marsha. I think these will make a nice addition to the stew I hear she's fixing for dinner tonight."

* * *

Jim pulled into the clinic parking lot next to Mark's gray compact car. When we didn't find Mark at the clinic, we walked over to the hospital.

"See, I told you she would come looking for you," Kenny Marlow sneered, holding a gun to Mark's temple. "Now that she's here, I'm going to take from her what she took from me: the person that means the most to her. You."

When I heard that, my blood ran cold.

"Lose the gun, Colonel," Kenny insisted when Jim pulled his weapon.

"Not gonna happen, Kenny," Jim said his voice calm. "Drop!"

Within a second, Mark was on the floor, giving Jim a clear shot. The Beretta discharged and the concussion rang out, echoing in the room. Kenny slumped to the floor, a large red blossom in the center of his chest.

I ran to Mark, afraid he'd been shot too. He stood up, brushing non-existent dirt from his slacks with shaky hands.

"How did you know to fall like that?" I asked in amazement.

"Well, after that situation with Rayn at the Rehab Center, she and Eric sat me down for a bit of a chat, and drummed it into me that if or when someone with a gun tells me to 'drop' I am to go limp and fall to the floor immediately. That when someone tells me that, there's good reason and I'm to get out of the way. So I did."

I hugged him tight in relief.

"If you're up to it, Doc, can you confirm death? Then I'll get this piece of garbage out of here," Jim said, all military now.

* * *

"I've been thinking, Allex," Mark said as we sat on the back deck having a pre-dinner cocktail. "Considering that I've had a gun pointed at me twice in the last week, maybe it's time I learned how to shoot one."

I grinned, even though I was shocked by this. "I'm sure Eric would be willing to teach you what you need to know. He's already taught Emi, so I know he's patient." I leaned over and gave him a kiss. "I think this is a wise decision you're making."

CHAPTER THIRTY-THREE

We haven't heard back from Collins concerning what he may want or need, so I thought I would take it upon myself to collect a few things. Mark and I should go see him anyway, and tell him the Marlow threat is no more.

* * *

"I'm spending the day giving the children school health exams, Allex. I should have told you that, I'm sorry," Mark said over breakfast. "It really can't wait; everyone is anxious to get the kids back in classes."

"I understand. Do you need me or is this something you can do on your own?"

"Doctor James is going to help out. I think it's important for the townspeople to get familiar with him," Mark said. "I don't like you going alone though."

"I won't go alone. Even though Kenny Marlow is dead, I've still promised Jim I won't venture anywhere by myself. That goes for *you* too," I said seriously. "I'll get Rayn or Amanda to go with me."

* * *

I stopped at the school first to pick out a couple of textbooks. The library was a hub of activity.

"What's going on, Sister Margaret?" I asked.

"This morning a couple of nice young men brought us boxes full of books from the university library. We're going through some now and putting them away. I'm setting aside any technical medical stuff that I think Dr. Mark would like to keep," she answered. "Is there something I can help you with, Allexa?"

"Yes, I need a half dozen textbooks, grades five, six, and seven. Maybe some fun reading too."

Sister Margaret nodded and walked off. She came back a moment later with a partially filled box and handed it to me.

"When the children have finished reading these young adult mysteries, bring them back and we'll exchange them for fresh material." She gave me a knowing smile.

What a great addition to the community the Sisters are. I may have to attend a Sunday service to see how Father Constantine is fitting in.

The next stop for Amanda and I was the new food pantry.

"Marsha, I need some flour and rice," I requested.

"How much?" she asked, without questioning me why.

"A twenty-five pound bag of flour would be good, and a big bag of rice. Is there any yeast? And can you spare some oil?"

Marsha had her husband put the supplies in the back of my car beside the box of books, and Amanda and I went to the Out Riggers.

"I know all this is going to Mathers Lake, Mom, but isn't it taking food from *these* people?" Amanda asked.

"Don't worry, Collins is going to pay for it. He just doesn't know it yet, and the people won't be disappointed." I had a plan.

"Good morning, Allexa, what can I do for you?" Sister Doris greeted us.

"If it's okay, I'd like a few things from the toiletry room: some soap, a bottle of shampoo, not much," I replied.

"Here's a shopping basket, take whatever you need."

"Where did you find these?" I asked, looking at the plastic basket that many stores once used.

"It was a Godsend, really. In the truck, there were several big shopping carts filled with these hand-carry baskets! I would like to hug whoever thought of adding them. We're giving the baskets to each household so they can pick up things to take home. They're even using them now at the food pantry. It's so convenient, and it's giving everyone a sense of ownership to be able to keep it."

"Do you want me to fill out a card?" I asked the Sister.

"Oh, no, Mr. White and the colonel both said your family is to have whatever you want. It's our way of thanking you for our...invasion," Sister Doris replied.

I added a bottle of shampoo and six bars of soap to the stash in the car.

* * *

The gate at the entrance to the Mathers Lake compound was closed and locked; a pickup truck parked just inside. A young man I didn't recognize came from the back of the truck, shotgun in hand.

I got out of my car and approached the heavy metal gate. "Hello, I'm Allexa Smeth. I've come to see Mr. Collins." He silently backed away, pulled out a walkie-talkie, and said something I couldn't hear, then came back to the gate and opened the padlock. He swung the gate open and stepped aside for me to drive through. In my rearview mirror I could see him relocking the gate.

* * *

"This is a pleasant surprise, Allexa," Art said after greeting us. "And it's Amanda, right? It's nice to see you again. What brings you here?" He brought his attention back to me.

"I've brought some supplies. I know you didn't request anything yet, but I selected what I thought you might appreciate." I said. It took Amanda and me two trips to bring everything into Art's kitchen.

"Twenty-five pounds of flour will make a lot of bread. Here's yeast, salt, a gallon of oil, twenty pounds of rice, and," I smiled as I opened the box, "I don't know if you need it, but we brought bar soap and shampoo. Oh, and books for the kids."

"This is very generous, Allexa," he said, his jaw twitching. "What do I owe you for it?"

"You don't owe me anything, Art, however, you do owe the town," I stated. "I think a couple of deer would be a good payment; they need meat. Unless you don't want this, then I can take it back."

He looked at the array of items on the table, then back at me. "I think we can spare a couple of deer." He smiled in relief.

* * *

"What ever became of the young man you warned me about?" Art asked later over tea.

"When he threatened to kill Mark, the colonel shot him." I shuddered with the memory of the close call. "He was a violent, hate-filled person, and I can't say I'm sorry he's dead."

Morgan nosed his way past a closed door and immediately started wagging his tail. He sniffed Amanda and gave her a dog-kiss that got her laughing. Then he butted my hand, demanding an ear scratch, while I gladly complied.

"Thank you for the tea, Art. If the women need any baking lessons, you know how to reach me," I said, standing. "When you've harvested the deer, you can either call us on the ham and we'll come for them, or you can have one of your men deliver them to the Inn. There are so many new faces in town your guys won't be noticed as not belonging." I turned to leave. "Oh, and I see this made you uncomfortable, and I apologize. We won't bring any other supplies until you request them."

* * *

After giving Collins the one-pound block of yeast, I thought it wise to check my own supply, only to realize I was getting low. I know I'd been baking a great deal, however, it still surprised me. This might be a good time to fall back on some old practices. The yeast that was available now won't last forever.

I got out a large glass canister and began working on a sourdough starter. Sourdough can be touchy, and I learned the hard way to *not* use any metal when working with it. So now it's only glass bowls and wooden spoons.

A cup and a half of warm water, a tablespoon of sugar in place of the honey I don't have, a tablespoon of dry yeast, and two cups of flour. I stirred it well, draped a towel over it and set it near the cook stove to stay warm. Tomorrow I will stir down the bubbling mixture and set it in the refrigerator for two days to cure and sour. Then I will take half out. Into the starter canister, I'll add another cup of water and a cup of flour and put it back in the refrigerator to ripen. With what I took out I think I'll make biscuits by adding equal amounts of water and flour, enough for a total of two cups. This time, I'll let the "sponge" sit out to ripen overnight. In the morning, the mixture gets some sugar, salt, oil, baking powder, and enough flour to work it.

Initially, it's a lot of work and time, but I remember back many years ago when I made sourdough regularly I had a starter sponge ready every morning, and it was much easier. Maybe next time I'll do pancakes.

Sourdough used to be the only way breads were made generations ago. There's a good reason to fall back on the old ways.

* * *

"Something feels different, Allex," Mark commented while we took our nightly walk. "I can't quite put my finger on it. Maybe something in the air."

"I feel it too," I answered, cocking my head. "I know what it is! It's quiet...I don't hear any thunder coming from Marquette. I wonder if that means the storms have moved out."

"Even if it has, two weeks of relentless pounding and non-stop lightning has done enough damage to last a lifetime."

CHAPTER THIRTY-FOUR

"It's been two weeks since the town has been infused with its new residents. I think it's time for a town meeting," I said to Tom from across his desk.

"Only two weeks? It feels much longer than that," he replied, leaning back in the big leather chair.

"Would you believe in two days it marks one year since the first earthquake hit the New Madrid Fault?" I got up and walked to the windows. One year. My thoughts flooded with memories of all the good and all the bad that's happened. John came to me and completed my life; the struggles with food shortages, and then the Wheelers' rampage which ended in my brother's death; Eric and Emilee making their way here, making our family whole again. We made it through that harsh winter, sometimes I wonder how.

"Demons?" Tom asked quietly from behind me in response to my silence.

"We all have them," I said, remembering that Tom had lost his wife and son in one of the flu sweeps. That's what we've been calling them, when a killer flu virus sweeps through the population, often infecting eighty percent and killing fifty percent.

"When should we have this town meeting?" Tom asked.

"I think on the anniversary would be significant. It was the day things began to fall apart, and now we're rebuilding. Besides, we need to let everyone know, *and* you and I need to plan the agenda."

* * *

Everyone congregated in the school gymnasium at three o'clock in the afternoon as school let out for the day. As pre-arranged, the older children would be watching the younger ones on the playground. A light snack had been provided for the kids before class was dismissed to keep them from getting cranky. The Inn kitchen was closed down so Marsha and her new staff could attend the meeting.

I didn't like the idea of a table and chairs being set up on the stage for us, however it did make sense and we would be heard easier that way too. Tom White, Mark, the colonel, and I took our places. Soon the crowd quieted. Tom stood and faced the group.

"On this day, the one year anniversary of the first earthquake that changed all of our lives forever, I ask you to please rise for the Pledge of Allegiance." A stunned crowd rose to face the flag.

"I pledge Allegiance, to the Flag, of the United States of America," Tom started, and we all joined in, hands over our hearts.

"And to the Republic for which it stands," the voices from the audience grew louder and stronger.

"One nation under God, indivisible, with liberty and justice for all."

The people all but shouted the final words.

Tom understood that a group of strangers needed a rallying point, something that they all believed in to make them united. What better way than to remind each other that no matter what disasters befell us, no matter what hardships we faced, we were still Americans, and indivisible.

"Welcome everyone. Welcome to your new home," Tom said loudly. The applause was thunderous. "I hope to keep this meeting, and future meetings, as short as possible, while still accomplishing what needs to be done.

"If you're not familiar with who we are," he paused to look back at us in recognition, "I'll introduce you. I'm Tom White, the former Emergency Manager of the *former* county of Marquette. Allexa Smeth is my reluctant assistant," which elicited a round of snickers. "Her husband, Dr. Mark Robbins, and Colonel James Andrews. Most everyone knows the colonel for organizing our flight here. He is now in charge of the security of the town. I will let him address those issues in a few minutes.

"Our agenda today will be to see how everyone is doing. Do you have any problems or questions that we might be able to help with? Think about that and we'll have a question and answer segment toward the end. For now, I will let the doctor give his report."

Mark stood and faced the group. "Several days ago I gave school physicals to forty-five students, with the help of Dr. James Geneva. Although Dr. James is only a third year med student, he's the closest thing you've got to a doctor next to me. Remember that. He's smart, he's good, and he's learning fast. Aside from Dr. James, my wife Allexa is my nurse and right arm. She will be my assistant during all prenatal exams, of which we have two expectant mothers in the town.

"As has been discussed before, the clinic and the hospital are limited. If you're injured somehow, we can take care of you. If you're pregnant, we can take care of you. If you have a cold, I'll give you a bottle of cough syrup and send you home, because we *can't* take care of you. The clinic is walk-in, no appointment necessary. The hours will be Mondays, noon until four, and Thursdays, noon until four. The hours will be adjusted as needed, and should an emergency arise, contact the colonel and he will come for me. Any questions?" When there were none, Mark sat back down.

Jim stood next. Even without his casual fatigues and brush haircut, he had a commanding presence. "Good afternoon," his voice boomed. "I will start by introducing those under my command. Staff Sargent Frank Sanders, Sargent Rayn Jones, Specialist Tony Ramirez, Corporal Ansell Perkins, Sargent First Class Eric Rush, and Officers Ken and Karen Gifford. They are my eyes and ears, my voice and my hands. I trust each of them with my life and so should you.

"So far we have had only one altercation and I'd like to keep it that way. Some of you met Kenny Marlow when we all first arrived here. Mr. Marlow had some unsubstantiated issues with Ms. Smeth and threatened her. Shortly after, he then threatened to kill Dr. Robbins. That is unacceptable, and I removed Mr. Marlow from our society.

"We are the only law here, people, and I mean to keep the peace. This panel of four, plus Father Constantine, will be your council of peers, your jury, and your judges if need be. Any questions?" There were none. Jim sat down.

This was news to me. I had lots of questions for Jim though I would ask them later. I stood next.

"Hi. I'm going to bring you up to date on some of the projects that are going on in town. At some point, most everyone has met Marsha, the new cook at the Inn. Marsha Maki and her husband Arnie are running the kitchen, along with help from Rick and Lisa Riley. These two couples have rooms right at the Inn to better serve you, literally.

"There is no way this town could have fed all of you without that semi-truck full of food, and with," I glanced down at my notes, "four hundred and fifty-seven of you, even all that food won't last long. Until we can plant gardens next spring, there *must* be deep rationing. The Inn will provide only one meal per day per person. With over four hundred, that will be split into two shifts, either an eleven o'clock lunch or a four o'clock dinner. Rick and Lisa are printing up meal cards, which will be punched each time you come in to eat. Sounds harsh, but it's necessary to make the food last through winter.

"They will also oversee the limited pantry items. If you want to fix meals at home, talk to them. They are here to work with you.

"The nuns that arrived with the last busload have organized both the school and the supply shop. They are gracious and I'm sure will help however they can.

"Father Constantine will be conducting non-denominational services at the Methodist Church on Sundays at ten o'clock. He will also be making all announcements we feel the need to get out to you, so going to church will be a good source of news for you. Any questions?"

One woman raised her hand. "The house I'm in doesn't have a washer or dryer. Is there any way to use that Laundromat?"

I jotted that down on my notepad. "I'm glad you brought that up. I've already been looking into it. Although the details haven't been completed yet, so far what

I can tell you is that within the next few days the Laundromat will be open. My daughter-in-law, Amanda, will be running the facilities during school hours, although it's still undecided which days it will be open. Once that is confirmed, it will be posted at the Inn." I sat down.

Tom stood once again. "The weather has been unseasonably mild, and I've lived here for over twenty years and I know it won't last. All of you know how brutal our winter weather can be. We don't know how long the electricity will stay on. It could last until next June or next week, which could mean a heating problem. If there are any engineers with us, I ask that you put on your thinking caps and come up with some kind of simple stove you can manufacture here, with what we have, that will keep the houses without wood stoves warm for the winter. And I suggest that everyone start collecting firewood."

Keith Kay stood up near the back. "I can help with that. I just need gas for the splitter and the truck to deliver the wood, plus a spot to pile it."

"Thank you, Keith, that would solve a huge problem," I said from my seat, aware that Tom didn't know who this was. "We'll get back to you on a central location." I made more notes on my pad.

"Are there any other questions?" Tom asked.

"I don't have a question," a small but confident voice came from the back of the room, "but I do have a suggestion."

"Anna?!" I stood, smiling in disbelief. "Ladies and gentlemen, I would like to introduce Anna Meyers, the elected supervisor of Moose Creek. Anna, would you like to join us up here?"

"No, Allexa, I wouldn't. None of these people elected me, so I no longer consider myself the supervisor," she said, stepping into the aisle. "However, I've been quietly watching the transition and rebuilding of this town and I'm more than impressed by what has been accomplished in such a short time. So I'm going to make a motion to these new residents that they elect Tom White as mayor of Moose Creek for a term of one year. At the end of that one year, hold elections based on what has transpired during that time." Anna sat down, coughing. She sipped on a bottle of water, and coughed again.

"I second that," Keith Kay called out.

"All in favor?" I asked, smiling at a bewildered Tom. The vote was unanimous. We have a mayor.

* * *

As everyone filed out, I caught up to Anna.

"Why didn't you let me know you were back in town, Anna? It's really good to see you," I said, giving her a brief hug.

"I wanted to watch for a while. I didn't need housing, I just moved back into my own place. You and Tom have done good work, Allexa. I see he finally got you to be his assistant," she laughed.

"It was a really good idea to elect Tom as the mayor, Anna."

"I was going to nominate *you*, but I knew you would refuse," she admitted. She hadn't forgotten my dislike for attention.

"Is George here too?" I asked, looking around.

"No. George, my sister, and her husband all died during the last outbreak of flu a few weeks ago, before the storms," she said, her voice laced with sadness. "I got sick too, but recovered. I guess that bout last winter gave me some antibodies to fight it with." She coughed again.

"Are you okay?"

"Sure. I'm not used to talking so much and it's made my throat dry," Anna said.

"Stop by the clinic and Mark can give you something for that cough," I suggested.

"I might do that, but first I want to tell you about Marquette. It was bad, Allexa, really bad. Now of course it's moot, but in the last two or three weeks before the evacuation it was deplorable. Everyone was afraid to go out, even during the day. Gangs would roam the streets all the time, day or night, and were good at hiding from the military. Then the flu hit again. It hit pockets, neighborhoods, anywhere there was a cluster of people. The best way to stay healthy was to isolate, but no one could do that, we needed to group for protection. I know the colonel's people were doing their best, though they couldn't be everywhere and they were getting sick too.

"Then the storms hit. I've never seen such lightning in my entire life! Once the fires got going, it was hard to breathe. The air was always thick with smoke. Sometimes the smoke was oily and we knew it was a gas station on fire nearby. Sometimes it was wood smoke from a house burning. And as much as I like the scent of wood burning, it was too thick and would be mixed with other smells like burning plastic from the house siding...and worse. It was that 'worse' that made me finally decide to leave. I would smell the burning 'meat' and my stomach actually rumbled from hunger. I had to get out.

"Once I was strong enough from my last go around with the virus, and everyone else in the house was gone, I gathered everything I could and filled the car. I went through the houses on either side of me and managed to get a few more cans of food. It took me three days, going out only a few minutes at a time, and I was finally ready. And I came home." Anna wiped the tears from her pale cheeks with the back of her hand, coughed, and took a sip of her water bottle. "I think the cough is from all the smoke I breathed."

"How long have you been here, Anna?"

"I left a few days before everyone else. I wanted to be alone for a while, Allexa, please understand. I needed to breathe some clean air and sleep in my own bed," she looked past me, haunted by something. Then she smiled. "You can't imagine how delighted I was to have electricity, a hot shower, and clean clothes!"

* * *

"It was good to see Anna again," I said to Mark after I cleared away our dinner dishes.

"Yes, it was."

"What's the matter, Mark? You sound distracted."

"I am. I've been neglecting you," he said softly.

"You've been busy."

"I've been neglecting you," he repeated, stepping closer, his voice husky with desire.

"*I've* been busy."

"I've been neglecting you," he repeated once more, brushing his lips across my temple and trailing his kisses across the thin scar on my chin.

"What are we going to do about that?" I asked, but it was getting hard to breathe.

He took my hand. We spent the rest of the evening in bed making up for hours lost.

CHAPTER THIRTY-FIVE

"Mom, I've having a problem with one of the women at the Laundromat," Amanda confided to me as we shared a cup of coffee.

"What kind of a problem?" I asked.

"She won't give back the quarters and I'm starting to run low."

"Who is it?" This was something I hadn't expected.

"Do you remember that girl with the funny red hair, the one with the son that was bullying the other kids that first day?"

"Oh, definitely. Tell me what happened."

"Her name is Tonya Germaine. She came in with a load of laundry and asked for her four quarters to run the machine. Then, like she's supposed to do, she used them for the dryer. When she was done, I asked for the quarters back, and she said she's coming back tomorrow so she'll use them tomorrow too, and she just pushed past me and out the door. When she came back, she said she forgot them and asked for more quarters." Amanda was clearly frustrated.

"How many times has this happened?"

"Six times now, almost every day. I know it's not a lot of money, and like I said, I'm running low. I don't have enough if all the machines are in use."

"Is she the only one doing this?"

"Yes. What can I do?"

"I'll take care of it," I answered. This young woman may need to be made an example of. It's time to talk to the colonel.

* * *

"I know it's a minor problem, Jim, but if we let her get away with breaking the rules, others will think they can get away with things too, and then we will have a real mess on our hands," I explained to the colonel when I tracked him down in Tom's office at the township.

"I completely agree," Jim said.

"What are you planning on doing, Jim?" Tom asked.

"Oh, I think a little humiliation will work wonders in this case," he snickered. "Let's find a couple of my boys and pay Ms. Germaine a visit."

* * *

I knocked on the door of the house we had assigned to her.

"Ms. Germaine, we need to have a talk," I said when she answered the door.

"Yeah? About what?" she replied, eying the colonel and his two men.

"About your behavior at the Laundromat and the theft of township property."

"Theft? I didn't steal anything!" Tonya protested in alarm.

"We have it on good authority you have in your possession twenty-four silver tokens that do not belong to you," Jim said, forcing his way in.

"Hey, you can't barge in here like that, I have my rights!"

"Oh, but I can and I did," Jim said. He leaned in close to her, forcing her to back up. "And that's because you *don't have any rights*, Ms. Germaine. You are here on the grace of the Moose Creek authorities, and you stole from them. You're under arrest."

I swear she was going to cry!

"Arrest?" she said, bewildered, as Sgt. Sanders and Cpl. Perkins moved to either side of her.

"You are banished from the Laundromat for a period of no less than one month and your punishment is two weeks in jail," Jim said reading from a blank sheet of paper, "which will be reduced to one week when you return the tokens." She hurried from the room and came back with a bowl of quarters, handing them to me with shaking hands.

"I can't spend a week in jail...what about my son?" she asked, her voice cracking.

"When he's not in school, he will stay in the jail cell with you."

She looked aghast. "But he didn't do anything wrong," she protested.

"The sins of the father," Jim stated simply. "Or in this case, the mother, and you were told when you first arrived here, no one is your babysitter. Sargent, take Ms. Germaine to the jail." He turned back to her. "You will be escorted to the school before it lets out, and both of you will be taken back to the jail to serve your time."

Tonya Germaine walked out the door weeping.

"Wow, Jim, don't you think that was excessive?" I asked when we were walking back to the offices alone.

"Yes," he chuckled, "and that's the point. Those here have to know we're serious. And before you ask the wisdom of including the boy, he's a bully. I've had reports that hasn't changed. A bit of humiliation should turn him around too."

"A week though?"

"Oh, I think we'll be able to reduce her sentence to three days for good behavior," Jim laughed.

* * *

Before going home, I stopped at the Inn to see Marsha, wondering how things were going.

"I'm glad you came by, Allexa, I wanted to tell you what showed up this morning," Marsha said, all flushed with excitement.

"Something good I hope. I can use some good news."

"Oh, yes! Two nice young men came by and brought us three whole deer! I didn't recognize them, but there are so many here that I don't know."

"That is great news, Marsha. I'm sure the fresh meat will be well received," I smiled. Art Collins had paid his debt, in spades.

CHAPTER THIRTY-SIX

JOURNAL ENTRY: November 14

The weather has taken a definite turn for the worse. I think our mild days are gone now, although it sure was nice while it lasted. The digital outdoor thermometer read only thirty-four degrees when I checked it this morning. I sipped a cup of tea while I started a fire in the wood stove that hopefully will take the chill out of the air.

* * *

I heard a vehicle pull in the driveway and saw a pickup truck I didn't recognize, then Lenny started pounding on the glass door.

"Is Dr. Mark here, Allexa? Chloe has gone into labor," Lenny reported. "She's waiting at the hospital."

Mark and I quickly got dressed. I poured the coffee I brewed for Mark into a thermos, and took what remained of the loaf of bread, setting it into a tote box. While Mark selected what drugs he thought might be needed, I grabbed a couple of jars of soup from the pantry.

We were ready to leave in five minutes.

* * *

Nathan jumped out of his SUV as soon as we pulled into the parking lot.

"Oh, thank God you're here," he said anxiously. "Chloe started having contractions during the night, and said they weren't bad. Her water broke about an hour ago so I got her ready to come here. She's in a lot of pain, Doc!"

"Calm down Nathan, she's going to be fine," Mark said. "This is your first baby isn't it?"

"Yeah, does it show?" Nathan let loose a nervous laugh, wringing his hands.

"Let's get her inside."

Mark and Nathan helped Chloe out of the Explorer and into the wheelchair I had brought out from the lobby. We got Chloe settled into one of the beds so Mark could examine her. I was surprised to see Dr. James coming down the stairs from our loft apartment.

"Just in time, James. You get to assist with our first delivery," Mark beamed. Just then a contraction hit, and Chloe screamed.

"Take a deep breath, Chloe, and blow it out through your mouth," I said gently. She laid back and breathed a few times.

"Thanks, Allexa, that helps." She closed her eyes to rest.

"She's almost fully dilated. Allex, can you prep the other bed for delivery?" Mark said to me, and I got to work.

We had discussed earlier what would be best to do for sanitation. Blankets and sheets could be washed, not so the mattresses. I stripped down the bed next to the one Chloe was in, one that Jason had fitted with rolling casters, and covered the bedding with a sheet of plastic, tucking it in. Next went an old blanket, folded so it became a pad, followed by a fitted sheet, topped with a flat sheet that would be used for modesty.

"Nathan, would you help me put Chloe into a delivery gown?" I asked the nervous new father. I pulled the shower curtain closed around us. Once we had removed her bulky clothes, I slipped a pink flowered cotton gown over her arms and used the Velcro to close it at the neck. I pushed the curtains back and let the three men move her while I held the bed steady.

I had put a blanket in the dryer before I started and it was now soothingly warm Chloe sighed in contentment when I tucked it around her shoulders. I went back to the kitchen and put another blanket and a towel in the dryer.

The next contraction hit, and she let out muffled moan. I wiped her forehead with a cool washcloth and Nathan held her hand. The two doctors were in quiet discussion. Contractions were now coming seconds apart.

"You're doing great, Chloe, the baby's head is crowning," Mark said with controlled glee. "Next contraction, push!" She did. Mark's head snapped up. "The umbilical cord is around the neck, do *not* push until I say, no matter how strong the urge is."

"Chloe, look at me," I said, moving into her view. "I need to you to control your breathing, can you do that?" She nodded, the sweat dampening her brown curls. "Good, now, take a deep breath, and let it out slow, now short breaths, like a dog panting. Great, keep it up." I looked down at Mark, but he was deep in concentration. Chloe groaned when another contraction hit. "Breathe, Chloe, do not push, breathe! Now pant again, in and out in short breaths. Again! Pant, don't push!"

Mark looked up, relieved, and said, "You're doing great, Chloe. Next contraction you can push!"

I could see a little fist waving in the air as the baby let out a cry. I grabbed the warmed large towel I had set nearby between two more heated ones, and held it out for James to wrap the baby. Mark took the baby and set him in the new mother's arms.

"Congratulations, you have a beautiful baby boy."

* * *

"I have to ask, Allex, how did you know what to do about the breathing? I will admit I have never delivered a baby under those conditions before. Of course, I haven't delivered very many babies at all. It was unnerving! Was that a Lamaze method?" Mark asked.

"Yes, it was Lamaze. Eric was born the same way. The umbilical was wrapped around his neck twice. I literally had to stop breathing so my son could live to take his first breath. A mother doesn't forget moments like that," I said, remembering that morning like it was last week.

"How is James doing?" I asked. "Was this his first delivery?"

Mark laughed. "Yes, this was his first and he's feeling a bit green at the moment. He'll be fine. I sent him back to the loft with a couple of books on obstetrics. We have four more pregnancies to get through and likely lots more after that."

"I didn't know he was staying here," I commented. I'm not sure how I feel about this arrangement, but it was Mark's call to make, not mine.

"I'm sorry, I forgot to tell you," he replied. "It seemed logical that someone should be here most if not all the time, and there certainly is enough room. If we need to stay, too, Allex, we have my place next door over the clinic."

* * *

"Mother and baby are doing quite well," Mark informed me. "I think they should go home this morning."

"That's good news. It will give me enough time to pick up a couple of things for them," I replied. "Like cloth diapers, some baby clothes, and a baby bottle. I saw some at the gift shop."

"Chloe is already breastfeeding the baby," Mark let me know.

"I know, but you can't breastfeed water and apple juice," I laughed. "After I pick those up I have a meeting with Jim and Tom across the street in case you need me."

* * *

"What is on the table for discussion today?" I asked, sitting down at the large conference table with Tom White and Colonel Jim.

"You look in a good mood," Tom observed, shuffling some papers. I think that's a nervous habit he has.

"Babies do that," I said. "We had our first delivery yesterday: A healthy little boy to one of the Mathers Lake women."

"We'll have to come up with a suitable gift," Jim said. "For now, though, we need to make some decisions about the rest of our supplies."

"Which supplies? I thought all the trucks were already being inventoried and made available?"

"Those supplies, yes, but I'm talking about the fuel," Jim answered. "We have tankers of diesel, gas, and propane. It's the propane I'd like to discuss first. Where would it be best utilized?"

I thought for a moment. "The township should have a refill of the thousand gallon tank out back. It's the heat for here and it powers an automatic generator in case the power goes out."

"Good start and I agree. Where else? You know this town better than either of us," Tom said.

"The Inn has the same situation: heat and a generator, plus the kitchen. It's become a focal point in the community. I've seen people there just hanging out, chatting or playing chess and checkers in the lobby. If we lose power before someone comes up with a simple wood burner design, those that need to can stay warm there," I explained.

"Does the hospital use propane?" Tom asked.

"Yes, however there's no generator there that I know of. Same for the school: propane heat but no generator." I leaned back in my padded chair, thinking. "I also think that the house you two share should be on the list for topping off the fuel tank. You're both highly important to the community now."

"I've seen lots of the blue tanks around, mostly on the edges of town, none in Moose Creek proper, other than the Inn," Tom observed. "How can we justify getting fuel when others don't?"

"That's why we're here today, to prioritize the distribution where it does the most good for the most people," Jim reminded us.

"Then we should add the house next door to you. There are five people there, and the priest and nuns have become a vital part of the town's functioning," I said. "As for your house, there's a gas fireplace in the basement that doesn't need power. It kept Bob and Kathy comfortable all last winter. In using that as heat you won't be using any wood that someone else might need. It's a tradeoff, guys."

"She has a point," Tom said, and kept writing as we bantered about more ideas.

"How much propane is there?" I asked.

"There is a five thousand gallon delivery truck and a fifty thousand gallon tanker, both full," Jim answered.

"Wow, that's a lot of fuel. I didn't realize those delivery trucks held so much. What about the other tankers? The diesel and gas? I know Keith needs diesel to cut and split the wood supply for everyone. Fortunately he won't need as much since he isn't going far to deliver. Have you seen the piles he's making at the ball field? It's impressive. I say we let him have as much as he asks for."

Tom and Jim agreed.

"There are also a couple of vehicles that run on diesel, like the Passat that Ken and Karen drive."

"I think after that we should save the balance of the diesel for the big generator," Jim said quietly. "Just in case."

"What generator?" I asked, confused.

"That massive trailer I towed out of Marquette is a city-sized power plant, and it takes diesel fuel."

I had forgotten about that. "Where is it, Jim?"

"I parked it behind the offices here, on the other side of the bay doors, completely out of sight."

"That reminds me of something else. The township water. The pumps are powered by the grid of course, and there is a big generator that runs them when the grid is down. I have no idea where it is or what kind of fuel it takes. Pete knows though. I'll ask him the next time I go up to Mathers Lake."

* * *

After our brainstorming session, which I found highly productive, I wandered over to the Inn to see how things were going for Marsha and was surprised to see Anna sitting at a table next to the curtained windows, a bowl of half-finished soup in front of her.

"Hi, Anna, how are you feeling today? Is the cough any better?" I sat down across from her. Her eyes were closed and her head was tilted, resting against the wall, sleeping, her gray curls stiffly framing her peaceful face.

"Anna?" I repeated and reached out to waken her. She wasn't sleeping. Anna wasn't breathing.

I found Marsha, and asked her to be sure no one disturbed Anna, and I ran back to the clinic.

"Mark!" I gasped. "Anna is at the Inn. I think she's...dead."

When we arrived back at the Inn, Mark confirmed Anna was gone.

"How long has she been sitting here?" Mark asked Marsha.

"She came in with the early lunch crowd, maybe 11:30, so about two hours," Marsha replied. "She was coughing something fierce, so I asked her to sit away from everyone else. Is she okay?"

"I have no idea why at this point, but Anna is dead," Mark answered. He looked at me, "I'd like to do an autopsy."

* * *

We had Anna on the surgical table. Mark, James, and I were fully gowned, masked and gloved. With all the coughing she'd been doing, Mark felt examination of her lungs was crucial.

"I know this may seem silly to the two of you, but Anna was my friend," I said, a catch in my voice as I placed a bleached white towel over her still, slack face. Mark made the common Y incision down her chest and I cringed.

Mark and James peeled skin and tissue back, held in place with the metal surgical clamps. When the rib bones were exposed, it was obvious there was a massive amount of hemorrhaging.

"Saw," Mark said, and I handed him a small device with a three-inch diameter circular blade. He turned it on and cut through the bone and cartilage on one side of Anna's chest cavity. "We only need one side exposed to see the lungs," he said, mostly to James.

"My God, are those her lungs?" James asked once the ribs were removed, "There's nothing left of them."

"No wonder she was always coughing," Mark said quietly. "I've seen enough. Dr. James, will you close?" Mark stepped back and moved to the large stainless steel sink where he washed his still gloved hands twice. He removed his mask, then his gloves, and washed a third time. I removed the clamps holding the skin aside, rinsed them off in the sink and dropped them into a metal bowl for sterilizing. Then I followed Mark's example of washing even though I didn't have any blood on me.

* * *

"What are your thoughts, Dr. Mark?" James asked politely. We had adjourned to the kitchen area, leaving Anna in the surgery for now.

"My guess, without having the benefit of a microscope for a biopsy, is a very aggressive virus." He turned to me. "Anna said she had been sick and had recovered, right?"

"That's what she told me. Everyone in her household had been sick and died, except she got better," I recalled.

"I'm guessing that the virus backed off into her lungs. She only *thought* she had recovered, when she was actually carrying around a time bomb." Mark looked at both of us. "She has now exposed everyone who was at lunch."

"And at the town meeting; she was coughing then too! Oh, Anna, what have you brought down on us?" I said to no one.

* * *

The first one to come down sick was Tonya Germaine. As part of a work release program the colonel had come up with, Tonya was let out of jail to help out in the kitchen during meals. She had escorted Anna to a private table and brought her soup. The contact was close enough to infect her with Anna's newly raging virus. Tonya gave the virus to her son that same day, who took it to school. The newly mutated virus moved fast and they both died three days later.

"After what you told me, Allexa, as soon as the first child got sick I thought it best to cancel school until we understood what was going on," Sister Agnes explained. "I hope I haven't overstepped."

"Oh no, Sister, I think you made the prudent choice. I hope it was in time," I reassured the nun. "However, it seems to be spreading anyway."

"How many now?" the nun asked quietly.

"The last count put the numbers over thirty," I said. One became two, which became six, which turned into two dozen. Two dozen becomes unstoppable in a small town like Moose Creek.

"I have an idea that may or may not help," Sister Margaret said. "What if we move all the sick people to Camp Tamarack? At least they won't be infecting anyone new."

"That's a really good idea, Margaret," Sister Agnes replied. "I know that you already buried Anna out there, Allexa, as well as Tonya and her son. There's bound to be many more causalities and to be practical, they might as well be close to the burial site. I do have to ask why you picked out there and not in the cemetery here or one of the open fields?"

I sighed. "The cemetery is full, Sister. Flu hit us last winter with high losses. When the ash cloud showed up, we turned the baseball field into a mass grave. Camp Tamarack is the only place left and the most accessible, plus there is equipment already there for digging." What an odd conversation this was. How had we gotten so casual about death and dying?

"We'll take care of the details, Allexa. It's what we do. I don't know if you've been told our history, but the four of us met working in South Africa during the last Ebola outbreak. We've been through this type of medical emergency before," Sister Agnes said. She turned to Sisters Margaret and Lynn. "Close down and lock up the school and the supply shop, and meet me back at the house. I need to check on Doris and Father Constantine."

"Are they okay?" I asked hesitantly.

"Father Constantine is sick," Agnes frowned. "Doris is tending him."

* * *

"Mark, I know that little can be done to fight a virus, but can anything be done to help Father Constantine?" I pleaded with my husband.

"I can't cure the virus, but the subsequent vulnerability often turns into pneumonia, which is bacterial, and that I *can* fight. Let me grab a few things and we'll go see them."

* * *

We let ourselves into the house that was once Carolyn's and called out, letting Sister Doris know we were here.

"Oh, thank you for coming by, Doctor. I don't think there's anything to be done though." She bit back a sob. "He's really sick."

"Help me sit him up more, Allex," Mark said from behind his mask. "Sister, can you put some extra pillows or anything behind his back to help keep him up? Lying flat will only cause his lungs to fill faster. A forty-five degree angle is best." Mark listened to Father Constantine's chest, looked in his eyes, throat, and felt his neck.

"Let's get a bowl of water and a towel. Keeping his face cool will make him more comfortable," I suggested, trying to keep the Sister occupied while Mark worked.

"I don't know what I would do if I lost Connie," Sister Doris whimpered as we left the room.

"How long have you known him?" I asked, thinking the attachment she had for a priest unusual.

"My entire life." She looked at me with tear filled eyes. "Connie is my brother, my *real* brother. There were only the two of us kids and our parents were so proud when we both dedicated our lives to the church."

"I gave the Father a shot of antibiotics," Mark said when we returned. "Has he taken any fluids?"

"I can get him to sip some water on threat of telling Mom if he didn't," Sister Doris chuckled, and then frowned. "Even though Mom has been gone for five years...he doesn't remember that. At first he would take some broth, though none today, only the water."

"Has he had anything like an aspirin?"

She shook her head.

"Then it's doubtful to I could get antibiotic pills down him. I'll be back later, and twice a day to give him a shot," Mark stated. "Keep pushing the fluids down, he's dehydrating."

"He will protest getting special treatment, Doctor; that's just a warning. He can be really stubborn," Doris said.

"I can be just as stubborn, Sister Doris." Mark winked at her. "Father Constantine is this town's spiritual leader now, and we need him. If he protests, remind him he still needs to baptize the new babies."

I left the Sister two extra masks and more surgical gloves. She'd need them.

* * *

Outside, a confused Mark asked, "What was that about telling Mom?"

"It seems that Father Constantine is Sister Doris' biological brother. She is totally devoted to his wellbeing, so I don't think we need to worry about the care he's getting."

Mark was reaching for the door to the hospital when James opened it. "I'm glad you're back. There are five new cases and three more deaths," he stated. "I don't know what to do."

"James, there isn't anything *to* do. If anyone shows up here, send them to the camp," a very weary Mark told him. "It's late and I'm exhausted. We're going home. I'll see you in the morning. Send someone if you need me."

* * *

The Sisters moved quickly getting the empty Camp Tamarack open and functioning as a field hospital, a triage center, and a morgue.

"Do you have enough supplies, Sister? What about help?" I asked Sister Agnes. I handed her a box each of masks and gloves that we retrieved from the medical supply van.

"So far the only supplies we need are these," she said, holding up the boxes I'd delivered. "Marsha gave us a number of large jars of bouillon. Most everyone here is too sick to eat, though they do manage to get down a cup of broth. As for help, well, few want to willingly expose themselves to a deadly virus, and we're making do with assistance from Gray."

We walked out into the cool afternoon air. The sun was straining to be seen through the ever-present muddy clouds. The fake cobblestone walkways were cluttered with road gravel and stray leaves. The air was strangely quiet, except for an occasional hacking cough from behind closed cabin doors.

"Even though there are enough buildings to separate people, we're keeping them together for ease of care," she explained as we passed a dark building. "The men are here, while we put the women next door. They may be sick, even dying, but their modesty is deeply ingrained. The ones that are the saddest are the children. At least one parent is staying when a sick child arrives, unfortunately that parent is usually sick too, and dies before the child."

This tour was making my heart hurt.

"Over here is the morgue," Agnes told me when we came to the last building. We rounded the corner and were blasted by an icy chill coming off Lake Superior. The building's roof hung low and the dirty windows were shuttered closed. "We've been open for twenty-four hours and have had that many die. A new mass grave was dug this morning, so Sisters Margaret and Lynn have been busy preparing the bodies." She stopped and turned to me. "Are you up for this? It's shocking even if you know what's coming."

We stepped inside. Table after table was filled with mounds of lifeless forms covered with unmoving sheets. I lifted a corner and quickly dropped it. Another vision filled my mind, one of lifeless bodies stacked on a mattress in the school gym. I shuddered.

"Why are they all nude?"

"We have been made fully aware by the colonel and Mr. White that we cannot afford to waste anything. That goes double for clothing, Allexa." Her voice was soft and gentle, and it held an edge of reality that comes from having seen some very bad things. "When someone is brought in, their information is recorded. Any jewelry or watches are put in an envelope with their name and held for the next of kin, if there is one. We remove all their clothing and set it aside for laundering; same for shoes. Eventually it will all be available for the taking at the gift and supply shop." She smiled at me. "You're shocked, aren't you?"

"Yes, I...I guess I am. The more I think about it though it's the logical thing to do. There's no good reason the survivors should be deprived of something they could use."

"Exactly, and those here don't care. They are with God now, their souls are at peace. Even though these bodies are just empty vessels now, they are treated and handled with the utmost care and respect, Allexa, be assured of that."

"I quite honestly don't think I have it in me help you here, with the living or the dead, but is there anything that I *can* do?" I asked, still mesmerized by the horrific sight in front of me.

"As a matter of fact, yes, there is something we very much need done and can't spare anyone to do it. Will you take this clothing to the Laundromat? Your son's wife is running it now, isn't she? Perhaps she can wash and fold for us," Sister Agnes suggested, with a faraway look in her eyes. I wondered how she compartmentalizes so well.

* * *

"Joshua," I called out. "Are you here?" I walked down to his house and didn't see him outside like he usually was.

"Oh yes, Miss Allexa, I'm on the radio talking to one of my new friends," he answered, a gleeful tone to his voice that I hadn't heard in way too long.

"I hate to interrupt you, but could you raise Mathers Lake? I need to talk with Mr. Collins and I don't want to drive all the way out there."

I heard him sign off and start with a calling out jargon that he apparently was taught.

"Here you are, Miss Allexa, they're getting Mr. Collins for you now," Joshua said, relinquishing his seat to me and handing me the headphones.

"And to what do I owe this pleasure, Allexa?" Art said a few minutes later.

"It's twofold, Art. First I wanted to make sure you were aware of the flu that has hit Moose Creek so you can keep your people away from here and safe."

"Yes, I heard. How bad is it?"

"Bad. We've had three dozen deaths so far and dozens more sick. So please, keep yourself isolated. If there are any medical emergencies, you can reach Mark through Joshua, or you can come straight to the clinic or here," I offered.

"I understand. And the other thing?"

"Peter used to be the township handyman. We need to see him about the town's water pumps. He's the only one who knows where the well pumps are and where the generator is located. Those in charge, Colonel Andrews and Tom White, have been careful about being masked and gloved whenever they are in contact with anyone, so they have escaped getting sick. I'll make sure Pete gets protective gear before talking to them, so he'll be safe. We really do need him for an hour or two though. Please."

"Your family has been more than kind and generous to us, Allexa, even after our rough start. I will make sure he comes to see you tomorrow," Art assured me. "Anything else?"

I thought for a moment. "How are the kids doing with the mystery novels?"

Art laughed. "They have blasted through them twice. It's refreshing to see them interested in reading again. They would love to have more if you can arrange it."

"Of course. Have Pete bring those back and I will give him another batch to take back. And one more thing, Art," I said quickly before he hung up. "I'm curious about something. What did you do with the hides from the deer you sent to the kitchen?"

"Over the past year one of my men has gotten exceptionally good at tanning. We don't waste anything," he replied.

"That's good to know, Art, and I'm glad the hides are being put to good use. What are the finished hides being turned into?"

"A variety of things, and right now shoes are high on our list, since the kids seem to grow out of everything so quickly. Next time you come up I'll take you on a tour of our tanning factory."

* * *

"Are you going into town soon?" I asked Mark. He looked tired even after a full night's sleep.

"Yes I am. I need to give Father Constantine his antibiotics and relieve James for a while. Will you come with me?"

I smiled, knowing he enjoyed my company even when we had unpleasant tasks to perform.

"Yep, and I need to stop at the school for some more books for the Mathers Lake kids. Art says they love the young adult mysteries. Pete should be coming in tomorrow, so I need to let Jim and Tom know. I hope you don't mind that I don't want to go out to Camp Tamarack again. It's just too depressing."

* * *

We drove Mark's fuel efficient little gray compact to Carolyn's old house. I'd like to find another way to refer to it, and I don't know what to call it yet. The Nunnery doesn't sound right and it isn't a chapel.

We let ourselves in as usual, and called out, but no one answered. Father Constantine was still in bed, still propped up to keep his lungs clear. Although he was sleeping, I could see his color was better.

"Father Constantine?" Mark said, placing his hand on the Father's shoulder. His eyes fluttered open and he smiled.

"Good morning, Doctor. It is morning, isn't it?" He coughed, and I was happy to hear that the rumblings in his chest were not as deep as before. Perhaps he was beating this flu!

"Close enough," Mark said, grinning. He must have noticed the improvement too. "Time for me to listen to you breathe again." He pulled out his stethoscope.

I wandered about looking for Sister Doris. She wasn't in the luxurious kitchen that Carolyn had loved so much, which had endless amounts of oak cupboards and granite counter space. I finally found her in the back room that overlooked Lake Meade. She was sitting in an overstuffed purple chair facing the picture window, enjoying the picturesque view. Blood dribbled from the corner of her mouth when she coughed. She had hidden her sickness from us very well. Sister Doris opened her bloodshot eyes.

"How's Connie doing?" she asked, and coughed again, spitting up more blood.

"He's doing much better, thanks to you, Doris." My voice cracked and I could feel the tears starting. "Why didn't you tell us you were sick? Maybe we could have helped."

"Taking care of my brother was always first and something I had to do on my own. He's such a good man, Allexa, and he must live. I owe that to him, and I promised our parents I wouldn't leave him, and now I must. I'm dying," she stated simply in a subdued voice. "I need to talk with him."

* * *

"Mark," I said, after leading him away from his patient, "Doris is in the other room, very sick, and feels she's dying. She wants to see Father Constantine. Is he strong enough to go there? I don't think she could make it in here."

We helped the priest walk with us on either side. He was still very weak and we sat him down in a soft chair across from Doris.

"Hey, little sister," Father said softly. "Did you catch my cold?"

Her eyes fluttered open and she smiled. "Father, forgive me, for I have sinned." She paused to cough, bringing up more blood. "Oh, Connie, I need your blessing and the Last Rites." Her voice was barely audible.

His face fell, and the tears gathered in his deep brown eyes. He placed his hand on her head and began the Latin incantation, "*Per istam sanctan unctionem et suam piissimam misericordiam, indulgeat tibi Dominus quidquid per visum, audtiotum, odorátum, gustum et locutiónem, tactum, gressum deliquisti.*"

We backed out of the room to give them privacy.

I leaned into Mark and sobbed.

* * *

Gray and Eric arrived in the township ambulance and quietly brought the gurney inside. We waited until Father Constantine made his way down the hall a half hour later, using the walls to hold himself up.

"She's yours now, Doctor," he said emotionlessly, and he sat down in the nearest chair, staring at the floor through his hands folded in prayer.

Mark checked Doris' vitals and pronounced her dead. I felt like I had been kicked in the chest. I moved back down the hall to wave the gurney forward. A few minutes later they reappeared with the still form of Sister Doris covered in a pink sheet. I barely had the strength to open the door for them.

I knelt down in front of the priest, his head still bowed in prayer. "Father Constantine, do you want to go with Doris, or ride with us when we take her to the other Sisters?"

He finally looked up at me, bewildered. "Yes, of course," he struggled to stand. "I'll go with her."

* * *

The ambulance followed us on the long winding road inside the Camp Tamarack gate. We stopped at the last building on the right, the morgue Sister Agnes had taken me to. She and Sister Margaret came out on the short front porch. As I got out of our car, I could see the confusion in their eyes; we had not used the ambulance for body delivery before.

When Father Constantine slowly got out of the back, they both ran to him, relieved...until the gurney was pulled out. Sister Agnes straightened her back, walked over to the shrouded body, and lifted the colorful sheet. When she saw whose body it was, she crumpled to her knees and gave out the most mournful wail I've ever heard.

Sister Lynn had been tending patients in another building when we arrived and started running toward us as Sister Agnes went down. The three Sisters and the priest gathered around the body of their beloved family member, holding hands, praying, and crying.

"I know this is asking for a special favor, Allexa," Sister Margaret said tearfully, "but...we can't bury her in this mass grave. We just can't." Tears spilled down her cheeks again.

"We will find room in the Catholic cemetery for her," I promised, my own heart breaking for their loss.

* * *

We laid Sister Doris to rest the next morning, dressed in her full habit, in the front of the sanctified ground. Jason had spent all night working on an appropriate grave marker, etched with flowers and smiling children.

CHAPTER THIRTY-SEVEN

Mark left early to visit patients at Camp Tamarack, which gave me the time and the privacy for what I needed to do. This was really something I didn't want company or help in doing.

Although the temperatures had been dropping it still had stayed above freezing and no snow had fallen yet. The cold ground was workable. I got a basket and a shovel from the greenhouse and knelt beside the four by four raised bed that held my spring bulbs. I dug up bulbs of blue and white crocus and fragrant yellow daffodils, striped tulips, and a hyacinth. Then I moved over to the flower garden that held all of my mother's flowers, and carefully lifted out some of the blue flags and the pale pink bleeding hearts. I put the shovel in the car and took it and my basket to the cemetery.

Kneeling in the freshly turned soil at Doris' grave, my hands shook and I let the tears fall again. I didn't know Doris all that well, and I would have liked to have had the chance to know her better. Now I never would.

I planted the bleeding heart close to the grave marker, knowing it wouldn't grow tall, at least not enough to obscure the writing Jason had done. The blue flags, those delicate miniature irises, went on either side. The other bulbs were planted in a random pattern down the center and would add an eye pleasing variety of color next spring. They would spread and create a blanket of color in the years to come.

* * *

"Has Pete been by yet?" I asked Tom. I was leaning against the doorjamb, momentarily swaying with a déjà vu of another time I did the same thing, but with Anna.

"Yes, and we've got it all squared away. Thanks for arranging that, Allex," Tom answered. "Are you all right?" Concern crept into his voice.

"Yeah, it's...been devastating to lose one of the nuns." My lip quivered and I caught it with my teeth to stop the trembling. "It's hard to lose so many in such a short time, Tom! *Again.* When will this end?"

"I don't know if it ever will, Allex," he replied softly. "What I do know is we have to keep doing what we can to help those left, until there aren't any left or we die."

Die? "How's your heart?" I asked, remembering he'd just had several stents put in.

He chuckled. "I'm fine. It's you I'm worried about. When was the last time you did something fun?"

"You gotta be kidding. There isn't any time for *fun*," I sneered. "It's all work, barely sleep, and then start over again." I dropped down into the nearest chair.

"I couldn't help but overhear your conversation," Jim Andrews said as he took my spot holding up the doorframe. "How would you like to take a short road trip with me tomorrow, Allex?"

"Where to?" I asked, straightening up in my seat. I could really use the diversion.

"It's been over a month and I'd like to check on the fires in Marquette. It might be good to get away from here for a few hours. I thought I'd ask Rayn and Eric to come along. We don't know what we might run into and four guns are better than two. You game?"

* * *

On my way home, I saw Amanda's car at the Laundromat and decided it was a good time to talk to her.

"Oh, hi Mom," she said when I entered. "I thought you might be one of the women coming in. I miss the chitchat with them."

"I'm surprised you're not busy," I said.

"I'm staying busy with all the laundry from the nuns," she said, folding yet another t-shirt and adding it to a growing pile. "The women think what I'm doing is too gruesome to be around. I sure hope this ends soon. It's depressing me too."

"I can fully understand that, and I know how much the Sisters appreciate what you're doing for them. What do you do with the clothes when you're done?"

"I take them to Pastor Carolyn's and leave the laundry bag in the breezeway. If there's one there, I take it with me. We don't see each other, which I think is good. They're with sick people all day, I don't know how they do it or how come they're not getting sick too," she said.

I instantly thought of Father Constantine and Sister Doris.

"Some of them *have* gotten sick." I looked out the grimy windows so she wouldn't see my anguish. I looked around at the Laundromat. "You've cleaned the place up, it looks nice. You spend so much time here, why don't you decorate? You know, make it cheery! I think that would help everyone's attitude."

"I can do that? You wouldn't mind?" Amanda looked hopeful.

"Dear, you can do anything you want here. I don't think there's any paint, though you could do new curtains or put things up on the walls. Use your imagination!"

There had been so much sadness and grief here, I felt that whatever we could do to cheer ourselves up, we should, and if Amada was happy, Jason was happy.

* * *

"You're going *where*?" Mark shouted. "I don't think it's a good idea!" He stood with his hands planted firmly on his narrow hips.

"And why not?" I glared right back at him. "We'll only be gone a few hours. It's been a month, Mark, we need updated information."

"Why you?"

"Why *not* me?" I shot back. "Besides, Eric and Rayn are coming too. We'll be in an armor-plated Hummer. What kind of danger could we possibly be in?"

Mark definitely did not like us going off to a hot zone, but we needed to find out how bad the fires had gotten, if the Antlers Basin Bridge was still intact and maybe, just maybe, there would be other survivors. We also needed to see if some of the outer stores were still standing. We would never have enough supplies and there wasn't enough time to check all of them.

"When are you leaving?" he asked sullenly.

"In about a half hour," I answered. "I need to pack some water and a few snacks." I wrapped my arms around his waist and looked up into his deep blue eyes. "We'll be fine, honest."

"Now I know how you felt when I left with Dr. Streiner," Mark admitted.

"That was a bit different. She had designs on you, remember?" He arched an eyebrow at me and was about to say something more when Jim pulled in. Instead, he leaned down and gave me a long, soulful kiss.

"You better be back before dinner."

* * *

"I stopped at the Inn first and had Marsha pack a cooler I found," Jim said. "Have you ever been up in that garage where I am? There is *everything* up there, and all neatly organized and labeled!"

"Yes, I have," I laughed, which felt good to do. "Kathy was the most organized person I've ever known. She also liked themes. There are bins filled with pirate outfits, Caribbean and Hawaiian garb, even pink flamingoes. She could lay her hands on just about anything in less than five minutes. Next Halloween we can outfit most of the town," I said, "if there's anyone left that is," I mumbled under my breath. The numbers were rising of those lost to this latest flu.

"So what did Marsha pack?" Mark asked.

"A half dozen sandwiches, some muffins, a thermos of coffee, and a gallon jug of water," Jim replied.

"All that for a few hours?" Mark sounded alarmed. "I thought this was to be a short excursion?"

"It is, dear," I said, laying my hand on his arm. "I'm sure Marsha was just being extra cautious. Besides, if we run into anyone, we should have food to share." I turned back to Jim. "What else do we need?"

Just then Eric and Rayn arrived from across the street.

"I managed to find a crowbar and bolt cutters," Jim said, "though I couldn't find a chainsaw."

"Mom's got one," Eric said, heading to the barn, with Rayn close behind. They returned with the chainsaw, a bottle of chain oil, and a canister of pre-mixed gas. "I also grabbed a longer crowbar. It could come in handy."

"What do you need all that for?" Mark asked. "It sounds like you plan on doing some breaking and entering."

"It might be necessary," Jim stated flatly. "I'm hoping we find some places that aren't burned to a crisp. This is a scouting trip, yes; it's also a preliminary scavenging expedition. We will never have enough supplies, Doc, I want to make sure we have all that we can. It's a matter of survival."

Mark looked perplexed. "I can understand that, but why the chainsaw?"

"It's thirty-five miles from here to the city limits, and it hasn't been traveled for a month. There could be trees down on the road from the last storms," Eric said.

"Are we ready?" Jim asked.

"I only need to grab my pack," I said. "Mark, can I see you in the house for a minute?"

Once inside, I turned to my husband, taking his big hands in my small ones.

"I'm going to need a basic first aid kit. Will you put one together for me? I believe in being over prepared, you know that, so it should include some pain killers and antibiotics – in case we run into someone who needs them."

While he was selecting a few things, I took my backpack that was always ready, and added an extra box of 9mm ammo, two more magazines for my Kel-Tec, and a box of .223 for my rifle. The pack was getting heavy.

Mark added the first aid kit to my pack, and then hugged me, whispering, "Please be careful and stay out of trouble."

* * *

The ride into town was relatively uneventful. There was zero traffic, as expected, and the road was surprisingly free of debris. We stopped at the Basin Bridge and all of us got out.

"Sargent Jones, will you accompany me across the bridge please?" Jim said.

"Excuse me?" I said. "Why are we being left behind?"

"Allex, you're not being left behind. Two should stay with the vehicle and cover our back. Rayn will cover us moving forward while I inspect the structure for damage," he said. When I raised an eyebrow, he laughed. "This is still a military operation, ma'am."

He turned without further word and started across. Halfway across he paused and leaned over the side. Rayn stopped and kept focused forward. Jim went to the other side and looked over the edge.

"Colonel," I called out, "on the other end of the bridge there is half of the old bridge that was kept for fishing. It will allow you a better view of underneath."

He nodded and they continued over. After searching the underside of the bridge for recent defects, the two of them came back to the Hummer.

"It would appear that the controlled detonation of the dam worked to prevent structural damage. The water is high, as to be expected, though not so high to matter...except that the old bridge is now six inches underwater." He shook a wet boot. "Let's go."

We went to the coal yards for the electric plant first, as close as we could get anyway. The fire was burning hot and the asphalt pavement leading into plant was liquid. The air was heavy with heat and the nauseating odor of petroleum tar. It was going to be burning for a very long time.

"Suggestions?" Jim said to all of us. "Allex, what would be the best route to get back to the shore line?"

Access to the shoreline road was blocked with melted asphalt and broken pavement. Every street we tried was buckled or blocked with fallen buildings. The streets leading through or around the university gave us a clear view of the devastation of that once proud school. It was now leveled to the ground, steel girders watching over it like silent behemoths. We made it to the next major artery only to be stopped again by pavement that was ripped up like it was a toy track.

"What caused the streets to do that, ma'am?" Rayn asked from the back seat.

"The worst road damage seems to be near gas stations, so I would guess the explosion of the underground tanks did this," I answered her as best I could. "Jim, let's get back to Fleet Street. There aren't any gas stations along that stretch. It will take us around to the west side of town and we can approach the shoreline from the south. Perhaps there's a way to get through."

Fleet was littered with massive potholes, and what wasn't was rippled from the heat that had passed over it a month ago. The damage was minimal compared to the other roads, and the military multi-wheeled drive vehicle took the challenge easily, though slowly. We ventured down a few of the main streets that intersected with Fleet, only to be turned back by blockage too great to go around. After the third such try, we stayed on Fleet until we came to Highway 41.

"As we feared, Walstroms has suffered major casualties," Jim said with a frown. We stared at the huge store and the caved in roof. "If it's any consolation, this makes me feel better about all the stuff that was commandeered."

We turned east and followed the highway to the lake.

"I tried to visualize what this might look like, Jim, but even my worst thoughts are no match for this," I remarked. The shells of burned out buildings stood like hulking monsters lying in wait. Others were just piles of rubble, some of which were still smoldering. Without the familiar landmarks I was quickly getting disoriented. The Big Lake, Lake Superior, looming in front of us was the only constant, and led us to Shoreline Drive and the harbor.

The scene was surreal. It was like viewing a disaster movie set after the money shot. The few buildings that dotted the marina were nothing but piles of charred rubbish while the playground equipment was untouched. A single swing moved listlessly in the pre-winter wind coming from the lake, squeaking with every push it got from that invisible hand. In the back of my mind it reminded me of a movie, and I couldn't or didn't want to remember which one.

In the harbor itself, skeletons of burned out watercraft bobbed aimlessly in the shallows, while other, bigger boats, untouched by the flames, were smashed against the ancient pylons of the long ago closed ore docks that were part of Marquette's boom and history. The water itself had a surprising clarity to it.

"I've seen enough," Jim stated, disturbing the absolute quiet of the car as we all took in the horrendous residue.

"Me, too. Let's go back west and see if there is anything beyond Walstroms," I suggested. "I'm not interested in seeing downtown. From what you saw before the evacuation, there isn't anything left anyway."

Passing back through the carnage was no better than the first time and in some ways even worse. With the wind now blowing at us we were enveloped in the smells.

"Ew, what is that?" Eric asked, wrinkling his nose as he rolled up his window.

Jim took a whiff, then rolled his window up too and turned on the air conditioner, even though the outside temperature hovered around forty-five degrees.

"Wood, plastics, fuels and...meat, that's what you smell," he stated simply. That he can say that so easily makes me wonder what he's seen during his long career.

"Meat?" Eric questioned. When he realized it was human flesh he smelled all he could say was, "Oh."

My stomach lurched at the cloying stench and I closed my eyes to battle the urge to vomit. I took a sip of water from my bottle to settle my stomach, but it didn't help much, only distance would do that.

It felt odd to stop in the middle of the road, even though it was completely vacant and had been for over a month. I must still be so conditioned by laws no longer enforceable that it made me edgy to sit here.

"There's another store about a half mile west of here: Shopmore. It's like a smaller version of Walstroms without the fresh food," I informed Jim when he started the Hummer moving again. He made a right turn where I indicated and we were headed north again. It was a surprise to see trees still standing, though they were leafless, and the road was smooth. Around the bend, the store came into view. It was unscathed by the fires!

"Before we start exploring, I think we should have some water, maybe one of these sandwiches," I suggested. "Believe it or not, we've been driving around for almost five hours."

We sat on the parched grassy island in the center of the Shopmore parking lot and opened the cooler, like a family having a picnic.

"What do you think we're going to find, Colonel?" Eric asked, taking a bite of a peanut butter and jelly sandwich, casually offering the other half to Rayn.

"Hopefully it's what and not who," he answered, chomping into tuna fish. "If it's occupied by scavengers, it could get dicey. I want us to stay close and keep weapons drawn when we go in."

I had difficulty swallowing the bit of muffin I had in my mouth when he issued those orders. So much for staying out of trouble.

Rayn moved the Hummer up close to the front doors while Jim and Eric circled the building, checking for forced entry. The main doors were closed and locked with no visible signs of damage.

"This could be our lucky day," Jim smiled, hefting one of the crowbars ready to smash the glass.

"Wait!" Rayn cried, and Jim stopped in mid-swing. The center doors were meant to slide open when activated by motion, reliant on electricity that was no longer available. The two doors on either side were designed to open with a push. She went to the nearest one and placed her hand on the glass, giving it a nudge. It swung open soundlessly. She turned around and grinned.

Rayn frowned. "Looks dark in here."

I pulled a mini mag-light from my pocket and looped the lanyard around my wrist. I noticed everyone did the same with various sizes of flashlights. The bright LED lights cast shadows over the displays.

"Recon only, everyone," the colonel ordered, pulling his Beretta from its holster. We all did likewise and headed up the center aisle. The lights barely cut through the gloom that permeated the building. It was enough, though, to see depleted racks of clothing still hanging silently waiting for a customer. Another aisle produced boxes of dry cereal and crackers that had been ravaged by rodents. What few cans of food were left had labels partially chewed off, but were otherwise untouched.

I headed up one more aisle toward the health care area, Eric on my heels.

"Looking for anything in particular, Mom?"

"Vitamins, supplements, that sort of thing," I replied as I spotted what I wanted.

"This was to be recon only, Allexa," the colonel said from behind me.

"For you maybe, but I may not have another chance." I started filling my pockets with bottles of garlic capsules, oil of oregano, and D-3.

626

"Why those?" he asked.

"The garlic and oregano are natural antibiotics and antivirals. The D-3 helps with the lack of sun depression that will eventually hit," I said. "With the flu on a rampage right now, this could be important."

"Here," the colonel said after having left for a few moments. He shook open a large plastic garbage bag, one for each of us. We all scooped bottles of everything into the sacks. I'd sort them out later.

"Back to the front," Jim barked once we had cleared out those shelves. We all stepped outside into the now fading light. "I think we've scored a jackpot!" he grinned.

Just then I felt a rumble under my feet, and saw the others sway. The rumble grew to a shaking and it was hard to stand upright. I grabbed onto the handle of the Hummer to keep from stumbling and saw the others do the same. Then it was over.

"What the hell was that?" Jim cried out.

"It felt like an earthquake," Rayn said. "I was born and raised in California, sir, and was stationed there for two years. Earthquakes were quite common. This one felt really strong, or really close, or both."

Feeling nervous, I said, "I think we should head back, at least get on the other side of the Basin Bridge." We tossed our booty into the back of the Hummer and climbed in. We were heading out the service road when the next tremor hit. The Humvee skittered sideways and Jim fought to keep control.

Once the shaking stopped, Jim floored it and we were soon speeding down Highway 41 and then Fleet Street, our discovery now secondary. He did a good job of dodging the biggest potholes, though still managed to hit a few that bounced us around and rattled our fillings.

"Jim, we'll be in world of hurt if you blow a tire on this thing!" I yelled at him over the whine of the engine. He immediately slowed, though not by much. Our turn was coming up quickly and I could see the pavement buckling. Fortunately, he saw it too and jumped the curb, cutting across the burnt lawn of whatever business had been there.

He swerved to miss a wall that tumbled across the road, and kept going. On 695 again with the bridge in sight, we all let out a collective sigh...then the next jolt hit. I could see the sides of the bridge start to crumble and gasped. I know Jim saw it too, but he didn't stop, didn't slow down.

We made it across with the bridge collapsing behind us.

"My God, that was close!" I gasped as we cleared the last of the bridge. "You two okay back there?"

Eric let out a long breath. "We're okay, Mom, but I sure don't want to try that again!"

Jim sped up and put a couple of miles between us and the bridge before anyone said anything else. As we approached Ravens Perch, he slowed the vehicle and stopped. He wiped his hands over his face and got out.

The three of us looked at each other and got out too.

"I'm getting too old for this shit," Jim said. He put his hands on his knees and took a couple of deep breaths.

"For being 'too old,' sir, you drive like an ace! That was some pretty fancy maneuvering!" Eric said, laughing to ease the tension we were all feeling.

Jim looked up from his bent over position to look at my son. "That's the most fun I've had in ages, though I'm not anxious to repeat it any time soon," he grinned. "Let's go home."

* * *

"I've been so worried about you, Allex!" Mark said, crushing me to his chest. "You were gone so long I was sure something had happened when the tremors hit. Did you feel them?"

"Oh, yes."

We were all gathered around the kitchen table, enjoying the heat from the wood stove. Eric pulled a bottle of rum from the cabinet and got down five glasses from the shelf. He looked at the colonel and Mark, and retrieved the bottle of Grey Goose and the Scotch.

"How bad were the quakes here?" I asked.

"Not super bad, though we did feel them. Where do you think was the epicenter?" Mark took a sip of his scotch.

"My guess is the main quake was to the east, since what we felt while in Marquette was a lot stronger than what you had," Rayn replied without thinking.

Mark looked alarmed and downed his drink. "Okay, so fess up. What happened?" he asked Jim, knowing I would downplay it.

"We felt three distinct tremors. We headed out of town right after the first one, Allexa insisted. Personally, I'm glad she did, because the next two got stronger. The last one hit as we were crossing the Basin Bridge," Jim replied in that deadpan, calm manner he had. "The bridge is now gone."

Mark turned pale.

"It's not as if we would have been stranded, though," I said quickly. "There *is* another way back—up country road 150. It's a gravel road and since we haven't had any snow, it's still open." I hoped I sounded more confident than I felt.

"I didn't know this, Allexa," Jim said with a scowl.

"It does mean, though, that we can go back!" Rayn piped in enthusiastically.

CHAPTER THIRTY-EIGHT

With the probability of being able to get back into Marquette and to the Shopmore store, Jim and Tom spent the morning planning and organizing while I took notes for them.

"Tell me what you know about this county road 150, Allexa," Jim requested. "What are we likely to find, things to watch out for, that kind of thing."

"It's eighty percent gravel with patches that were paved to protect the substructure from erosion. I used to live ten miles south and just off that road," I replied, thinking of my woods house, hidden away deep in the forest. "The county used to keep it plowed in the winter but I don't think it's been maintained at all for the past year. I would recommend taking at least two chainsaws to clear any fallen trees. Even during good times trees dropping were quite common."

"That makes sense. Anything else to watch for?"

"Some of the men that are going with you might know the area better than I do. I rarely ventured south of my own road. I do know that with it being plowed in the winter, the road would narrow to one vehicle in certain places, especially by the Hairpin."

"The Hairpin is a very tight loop in the road with rock shears on either side," Tom explained. "Even the loggers would use chains on their tires in that area. It could get real treacherous, so it's a good thing we haven't had any snow yet." Tom paused while he thought. "Come to think of it, I don't remember any turnouts in that area, do you Allex?"

"No, I don't. What I do remember is backing up a long way once, and it was the last time I traveled that road in the winter. I backed into an old logging trail on the west side of the road to turn around." I looked at Jim before going on. "A standard sized vehicle could make a five-point turn when the roadsides weren't reduced by snow banks."

"That's good info," Jim said. "I can see we might need to recon the road before sending a caravan in."

* * *

"Mark, don't be such a worrywart. I already told you I'm *not* going back into Marquette with the next crew." I stopped my pacing to face him.

"I'm glad to hear that. It's too dangerous for you," Mark said, looking up briefly from the medical charts he was working on at his desk.

"Have you taken any of the supplements I brought back yesterday?" I asked him quietly.

"No, I don't believe they will do any good. Besides, as long as we're careful, wear our masks and gloves, and wash our hands frequently, we'll be fine."

"Well, I'm taking them and I'm pushing the kids to take them too. Even if they don't help they certainly won't hurt." Upset with Mark's attitude, I walked back across the street to talk with Tom.

"Take these," I stated, and set a bottle of garlic capsules on his desk. "We can't afford for you to come down sick." I slumped in the chair. "When did Jim leave?"

Tom glowered, though it wasn't meant for me.

"They left a half hour ago to scout the road." Tom tossed his pen aside. "Jim refused to let me go with them! Said it was too dangerous for me. Can you believe that?"

"Yeah, Mark was adamant about me not going either." We looked at each other and started laughing. "Tom, when did we get to be so important?"

* * *

The colonel returned two hours later, dusty and disheveled.

"We had cut our way through two areas of downed trees, only to be stopped. There's a rockslide at a tight curve that I'm assuming is what you were calling the Hairpin. We tried moving some of it, but there are boulders that will require earth-moving equipment that we don't have," Jim informed us, clearly frustrated. "It's obvious that's a much higher elevation than here since there's snow on the ground. Not much, but enough. I think we're stuck until spring."

"Yes, it's part of a small mountain range and it's almost two thousand feet higher than right here on the lake," I said. "Can you get around the rubble on an ATV?"

"Doubtful, but we can try."

"Can you walk around it?" I was suddenly interested in finding a solution to this latest problem. It was unacceptable that all those supplies were sitting there for the taking and we couldn't get to them!

"Sure, we could walk around or over, though that doesn't do much good unless..." he sat up straighter, "...unless we had something on the other side! If we can get to town somehow, and commandeer a large vehicle, we could bring supplies to the other side. Then it would only be a matter of hauling everything from one side of the blockage to the other!"

"What about a motorcycle?" I asked, remembering one of our original town members was a Harley enthusiast.

The three of us headed out to Eagle Beach in Jim's dusty brown Hummer. I hadn't had any reason to be here in months, except for once. At the crossroads I motioned for him to turn right. Turning left would have taken us to the house where I met John. I shut the memory down.

We passed several nice and elegant houses, intermixed with much smaller and well-kept camps along the half-mile road until I spotted the place I recalled.

"Still got those bolt cutters?" I asked Jim with a sly grin as I hefted the padlock on the large gray and white metal pole-barn. Jim snapped the lock off easily, and slid the doors open to reveal not one, but six pristine Harley Davidson motorcycles of various models, some covered with heavy tarps. The keys were all hanging neatly on a pegboard, labeled with the year and model.

"Thank you, Dan," I whispered to myself, watching Jim run his hand over a black beauty of a roadster.

"An Electra Glide; 1200cc engine, looks to be maybe a 1970 with a Shovelhead engine and an electric start." Jim found the keys on the board and started it up. "Purrs like a happy kitten! Your friend sure took good care of his bikes," he said, straddling the quiet machine. He pushed with his feet and backed out of the barn.

I found a piece of chain to hold the doors closed, and slipped the now broken lock back in place.

* * *

"It's too late in the day to try again," Jim said, after he parked the bike in the safety of the big garage at his new home. "I would like to head out early in the morning though. You think Eric would mind if I took Rayn with me?"

I was puzzled. "I don't think he has any say in it, Jim. You're still her commanding officer, but why Rayn?"

"She's a small person and will ride easily on the back of the bike. Once we get to town and pick up a van or something large, I know she'll be fine driving it. She can drive anything," Jim grinned. "And there's no way I'm leaving my new ride behind! After that, we can take several of the guys."

"So ultimately you plan on driving up to the landslide, walking around it, and then taking the new vehicle back into town?" Tom asked.

"Yep, might even pick up a second car, so we can double our capacity, making as few trips as possible."

"That makes sense," I said.

CHAPTER THIRTY-NINE

"Nahna," Emi whined as she sat down at my table, "I'm bored. With school closed and most of you adults off into town being busy, there's nothing for me to do. I feel useless. Is there *anything* I can do to help?"

Oh my, she sounded so grown up. This new life of ours was making our children mature so fast. I admired that she wanted to do something helpful and productive.

"You and Jacob have been spending a lot of time with Joshua and the animals, that's being helpful."

"Sure, but there are only so many eggs to collect and Joshua says I'm too small to milk Bossy," she pouted.

Too small? She was almost as tall as I am!

"I think I have a solution to two problems, Emilee, yours and mine. I've been so busy in town with helping the new people settle in and working with Mark when needed, that I haven't had enough time to bake. If you could take over the baking duties, I would really appreciate it."

Her eyes lit up and she sat straighter in the chair.

"It won't be easy, though. To satisfy our family, I've been baking two loaves every day. Do you think you can do that?"

"Oh, yes!" Emi exclaimed. "Do I have to bake only bread? Can I try other things?"

I could sense her excitement and decided to capitalize on it.

"Sure. I have lots of cookbooks that can give you ideas. Any thoughts on what you want to try?"

She looked at me with a grin. "Cookies!" I laughed.

"Okay, here's one book on cookies and another on breads," I said, handing her two books from the bookshelves. There were so many books there she would be kept really busy. "The deal for today is two loaves of bread and a list of what kind of cookies you want to try. Remember, Emi, we might not have all the ingredients you need, so pick several recipes, okay? And tomorrow you and I will go over what you've selected and gather supplies.

"The other thing though, is you and Jacob still have to stay with Joshua when no one is here, is that understood? Joshua has a good working stove and oven, so you can do all your baking there."

"That's fine with me, Nahna, I like Joshua. He's fun and he lets me talk on the ham radio, and Jacob is happy almost anywhere as long as he has his letters, books to read, and can watch cartoons at least once during the day."

"Great! I'll get enough baking supplies together for you to make two loaves of bread every day for a week, while you get the wagon out of the barn. When you see Joshua, ask him to check his propane level. You'll be using more of his supply with the baking and I don't want him to run short."

"The propane truck came by when you were in town with Colonel Jim and filled all of our tanks. Didn't you know?" Emi looked surprised.

No, I didn't know. More stuff going on behind my back. This time though, I couldn't argue.

* * *

I was going to have a talk with Tom about filling our tanks while not wanting his own tank refilled, however, by the time I got into town it was snowing and it was coming down really hard.

"I think winter has finally caught up with us," I said, announcing my presence when I walked into Tom's office. "Oh, I didn't know you had someone here. Do you need privacy?"

"Not at all, Allexa, please join us. This is Earl Tyler, a really interesting man," Tom stated. "We were just going over the designs he's come up with for a workable, easy to build wood burner. Earl, please continue."

"I was explaining to the mayor that with the welding equipment across the street, and a few extra hands, I can mass produce a simple wood stove that can also be cooked on," Earl said. This young man, possibly in his middle thirties, blond and brown-eyed, was very animated as he talked.

I looked at the designs on Tom's desk. "May I ask your background, Earl?"

"Basically, I'm an auto mechanic, but I...*fix* things, and build things. Half the time at my shop in Ishpeming I had to manufacture a part for what I was working on. I've been welding for almost twenty years, Tig, Stick, Mig welding, as well as soldering, brazing. Give me a torch and I'll make you anything," he grinned.

"I'm impressed! Sounds like you're a good addition to the town," Tom said.

"There is something else I do, as a hobby more than anything, so I think I can shed some light on what's been happening," he said.

Colonel Jim was now beside me, listening with interest.

"I thought you were going to try getting into town," I said when I noticed him, changing the subject.

"Not in this snow!" he said, sounding disappointed.

"Now that we are all here, let's take this to the conference table where we have more room," Tom said. "I'm very interested in what Earl has to say."

"First of all, I'm not a Paleomagnetist, although I've studied under one," Earl began.

"A *what*?" I asked.

"A Paleomagnetist is one who studies the records of the Earth's magnetic field in rock and other archeological findings," he explained. "It's really quite fascinating. The different layers of rock show how and when the magnetic poles have shifted."

"I thought you said you were an auto mechanic. This seems to be a strange hobby for that profession."

"I started out wanting to be a geologist, but turning wrenches pays better," he confessed with a forlorn smile. "I've kept up with it though, taking classes at the U whenever possible."

"Please go on," Tom said, giving me a look that said to shut up.

"Anyway, the last study group I was in revealed that we are, or were, getting close to the next magnetic pole reversal, which happens every ten thousand years or so. The magnetic north has been drifting for years, mainly further into Russia, and I think it's into the shift now."

"What makes you think so?" Jim asked, "And what would that mean to us?"

"The Earth is held together by its magnetic forces, like this," he started drawing on the chalkboard behind him. "When the pole shifts this direction, it pulls on the tectonic plates," he drew more lines, "and that causes the plates to move and create earthquakes, mainly along the Ring of Fire. The last theory is the shift is moving the opposite direction and will now pull on the northern and eastern plates; like this." He tossed some finish nails on the table and produced a large magnet, moving it in different directions while the nails realigned.

"From the study group's previous findings, it might also explain the storms. It's really hard to determine if the pole shift triggered the tectonic plate shift that erupted Yellowstone, or if Yellowstone sling-slotted the shift. We may never know. Either way, both circumstances would create magnetic storms, and those would produce the kind of weather we've been seeing for the past several months, especially massive amounts of lightning. It would also produce some awesome Northern Lights, though we can't see them because of the ash clouds. I also believe we will continue to see some very erratic weather for months to come."

"Why didn't you bring this information forward before?" I asked.

"I tried to," Earl shrugged, "but I'm just a grease monkey..."

"Is there more?" Jim asked.

"Only that the tremors we felt recently seem to support the theory. My guess, and it's just that—a guess—is it isn't over. There could be another larger quake or even two, as the pole continues and finishes its shift. When it's over, we could be much closer to the magnetic equator than we were before."

"Earl, I have to ask why we are even feeling these tremors. I didn't think there were any fault lines under the U.P.," I said, looking back at his crude drawing on the board.

He chuckled. "Ma'am, there are tectonic plates literally everywhere on the planet and where there are plates, there are faults."

"So are you saying we could become the next tropical paradise?" Tom asked.

"Oh, no, sir. A magnetic pole shift is different than a geographic pole shift, although some of the side effects are similar, like the earthquakes and the weather changes, and there is speculation that at times they *have* occurred together. Magnetic poles change every ten thousand years or so, however geographic pole flips are millions of years apart. And let's all pray a geographic movement is *not* what's underway."

"What would happen?" Tom queried.

"Ever hear of an ELE? That's an Extinction Level Event," Earl said solemnly.

* * *

"So you're putting off your trip into town?" I asked Jim after Earl left and Tom went back to his office.

"The traveling will be done mostly by motorcycle, and that's not gonna happen in all this snow," he answered, gazing out the window as the wind picked up and turned the parking lot into a mini tornado of powdery snowflakes.

"Well, I think Eric will be relieved. He wasn't happy about Rayn going." I smiled. "Ah, young love."

"Young love? Mark doesn't like it when you go off on one of these excursions either," Jim reminded me.

"He has a difficult time remembering how independent I am. He *is* making progress in that direction though." I glanced out the window. "I'm trying to be understanding in return, considering I don't like the way he exposes himself to all the sickness going around."

"How many have we lost so far?" he asked quietly.

"Out of the 457 people who arrived here back on October 24th, there are now 243 left." I shut my eyes momentarily. "That's 214 lost. Fifteen of those were children."

"Are there any still sick and at Camp Tamarack?" he asked.

"About a dozen, however the Sisters think those may recover. The percentages are scary, Jim. Two-thirds of everyone here caught the virus, and eighty percent of those died. Are you and Tom taking those supplements I dropped off?"

"Yes, although I think staying away from sick people does the most good; can't catch it if I'm not exposed," Jim tried to reassure me.

"I wish I could convince my husband of that!"

CHAPTER FORTY

The heavy snow from yesterday melted quickly in the fifty degree sunlight, though there isn't much light to the sun these days.

* * *

"Jim, I've been meaning to ask you something," I said when I found him at the Inn. "Did any of the evacuees bring any guns with them?"

"No, I didn't think it wise. I'm doubting my wisdom now," he answered.

"How are they going to hunt?" I asked.

"That's why I doubt the wisdom of that decision. I'd like to know how someone took down the deer that we've been eating!"

"Oh, those came from Art Collins, as payment for some supplies."

"Ah, that makes sense," he looked up from his bowl of soup. "I was more concerned with violence than I was with hunting; my error. I should have remembered that the mind is the only true weapon, everything else is just a tool, and we need tools."

"My group members all have guns and rifles. I'm sure they would be happy to do the hunting. I haven't seen any deer moving though. They seem to be content to stay up at the Resort," I said.

"My team is well armed, too. Plus," he looked guilty, "I did control an armory." He laughed. "Even though I can safely say we have plenty of munitions, it won't last forever."

"True, but the best shots only need one bullet."

* * *

I did not want to go to Camp Tamarack. I did need to find one of the Sisters though, so it was my lucky day that I saw Sister Margaret coming out of the school.

"I've wanted to ask about the clothes Amanda's been washing," I stopped her on the sidewalk. "How is that working out?"

"It has been a Godsend having her help us that way, though we're done now," Sister said.

"Done? What do you mean?"

"There are only eight people left at the camp now and all well on the way to recovery. They should be going home tomorrow. "We haven't had any new patients in days. I truly feel we are over this flu. Thank God!" She crossed herself.

"How is Father Constantine doing?" I asked carefully.

"He has recovered fully from the flu. Recovering from losing Doris will take much longer," Sister Margaret said solemnly. "And on behalf of the other Sisters, I want to thank you and Dr. Mark for all you've done. As much as Doris was willing to do, without the doctor, Father Constantine would have died, we know this." She took a deep breath before continuing. "We won't forget, and neither will God, how thoughtful you were with Sister Doris. One of our greatest desires is to have Last Rites at our passing. That she was granted this means everything to us."

CHAPTER FORTY-ONE

I was getting a fire going in the stove when Mark came down the hall.

"Did we drink a lot of wine last night or something equally stupid? I feel like crap." He plopped down in the kitchen chair.

"We did have wine with dinner, only one glass each though," I brushed a wayward lock of curly hair off his forehead. "Mark, you're hot."

"Thank you sweetheart, you're hot too." He sniffled.

"No, I mean fever hot." I put my hand fully across his dry forehead. He was burning up. I retrieved his little black bag and pulled out the thermometer. I poured a small amount of rubbing alcohol in a glass and swished the thermometer in it, and then shook it a few times. After seeing it was down, I stuck it in Mark's mouth.

After a couple of minutes, I took it back and read it.

"Mark, you have a fever of 103. You're sick." My voice trembled and my hands started shaking.

He looked at me with such disbelief, I handed the glass tube to him so he could read it, just as he sneezed.

"No wonder you've been so tired lately, you've been fighting coming down with…this," I said, not wanting to say the word flu. "You need some antibiotics and back to bed!"

"I was to relieve James today. He's been working around the clock and needs a break," Mark said, putting his head down on his arms.

I retrieved a vial from the refrigerator that I knew was an antibiotic, and pulled a syringe from the box beside it. I filled it and stabbed Mark in the arm. He didn't seem to notice. Then I poured a half glass of water.

"Mark, you have to sit up for me and drink some water." I coaxed him upright in the chair and held the glass while he drank. "Now, let's get you back to bed."

It was difficult getting him down the narrow hall. I felt like I was supporting all of his weight and dragging him. If this was the flu everyone else had, it hit Mark hard and fast.

I managed to get him back into our bed, though he fought me when I tried to prop him up.

"I just want to lie down and sleep, Allex."

"All this time I've been listening to you tell every one of your patients that you can't lay completely down, you *have* to stay at a forty-five degree angle. Now do it!" He was finally compliant and I pushed both pillows behind his back, but the angle wasn't enough. He coughed. The phlegm was pink.

* * *

"Is there anyone listening?" I said into the FRS radio.

"I'm here, Mom," Eric said. "What's up?"

"I need some help." I hesitated to get him involved but I didn't have much choice. "Come with an N-99 mask and double gloved, Mark is sick."

"I'll be right there," he said after a momentary silence.

* * *

Eric was still affixing his mask standing at the door. I waited until he was done, then I opened it. He had a very worried and scared look in his eyes.

"I need to get Mark sitting up more in bed. I think one of the couch cushions should do it, but I can't move that and him too." I looked at my son. "I don't want you touching him; just put the cushion in place. I'm already exposed; I don't want you to be!"

It didn't take long. I grabbed Mark's wrists and pulled; he offered no resistance. Eric angled the cushion then backed away. I pulled the blankets up around Mark's chest and walked out with Eric.

"Mom...how are you feeling?" he asked, his voice trembling.

"Tired and worried," I answered. "I so want to give you a hug, but I can't! I know I'm sick too, maybe a day or two behind." I let the tears flow. Eric reached for me and I backed away. "No! Don't touch me! I gave Mark some antibiotics. I just hope it isn't too late," I choked on those words.

"Have *you* had any yet?" Eric asked quietly.

"No, not yet. Let me show you which vial and how to do it...just in case."

Just in case I'm too sick to do it for myself. Just in case this sickness spreads to your family. Just in case. I said it all in my head, but not out loud, never out loud.

"And *don't touch anything!*"

I gave myself a shot in the thigh while Eric watched, nodding that he understood what to do. I put the vial back in the refrigerator, away from the rest, and set the syringe in the jar of alcohol. Although they were designed for one time use, we didn't have that luxury.

"This is *my* syringe. I will keep Mark's in the other room. Now, go home, throw away these gloves and mask, and take a shower, wash your clothes. You don't want to be accidently carrying this back with you."

"Mom…I love you," my son broke down and cried.

"I love you too. I love all of you! I will use the FRS to call tonight around six o'clock. Now go. I'm going to fix some soup."

While I still can.

* * *

I heard the pounding, but felt it was more in my brain than on the door. I raised my aching head from my arms where I had been resting on the table. Everything hurt. I saw a shadow at the door, raising a fist to start pounding again. I lifted the mask that dangled around my neck and settled it over my nose and mouth before I opened the door.

"Oh, thank God you're here! I need the doctor right away!"

"Judi, right? What's the problem?" I coughed lightly.

"It's Marci, my daughter; she's gone into labor and something is wrong!" she cried. I remembered the case: Marci, a sweet, petite blond, had just turned thirteen and was walking home from school in Marquette when she was attacked and gang raped. Now she was pregnant and about to deliver.

"I'm sorry, the doctor is sick. He can't help you."

"I don't care, she needs him! I think the baby is stuck!" she wailed.

"You don't understand. The doctor is sick, very sick, with this flu. When he's awake he's delirious and can't function. Go see Dr. James." I really did feel sorry for her.

"No one can find him," she sobbed angrily.

"Maybe Gray can help."

She looked at me with sad brown eyes. "Gray died two days ago. If I can't find her help, Marci will die too."

"Just do the best you can," I answered her and as I went into a fit of coughing I closed and locked the door.

* * *

Mark's breathing was so strained, and I felt so helpless that I kicked the cushion out from behind him and wedged myself in place. I sat with Mark's head and shoulders in my lap, trying to ease his labored breathing, his dark, sweat drenched hair resting against my chest, and I held him until his breathing slowed then stopped. I lay down beside him and curled my feverish body around his cooling one and cried until I had nothing left, and then I cried some more.

I fell into a deep sleep while my body burned, and woke drenched in sweat. My fever had broken and I felt somewhat better until I turned and saw the still body of my husband on the other side of the bed. I let the tears flow one more time for my loss. We had only four months together, and it wasn't nearly enough.

* * *

I struggled to sit up, knowing I must. I stood on shaky legs and wrapped my robe around my shoulders, making my way to the kitchen.

After starting a fire in the wood stove, I set coffee to brew. Everything I did felt mechanical, and it felt all wrong. I was empty inside.

A chill was creeping into my bones from the sweat damp pajamas, so I retrieved fresh clothes from the back room, averting my eyes from the bed as I passed. In the shower, I set it on hot to ease the aches in my muscles, though it would not ease the ache in my heart. As I washed the greasy, sick sweat from my body and hair I knew that others still needed me and I must pull myself together. There were things that needed doing. Mark still needed me too, one last time.

After one glance in the mirror, I avoided looking at my haunted reflection. My eyes were bloodshot and swollen from my tears, my face splotchy and thin from the lack of food.

Dressed in flannel pants and a long sleeved t-shirt, I poured some coffee and headed to the table.

The coughing from the other room startled me and sent my full coffee cup crashing to the floor.

In the bedroom it was a shock to see Mark leaning over the side of the bed, coughing. I reached him in time to keep him from tumbling to the floor. He spat out a glob of dark brown phlegm onto the towel I had covering his chest.

"Oh, that hurt," he murmured. I held him, speechless. "Can you help me sit up?"

I stuffed some pillows behind him and pulled the covers tightly around him, still not having spoken a word.

"You look better," Mark said. "How long was I asleep?"

"Mark," I couldn't find the words I needed.

"What's wrong, Allex?"

"I thought…I thought you were dead," I whimpered. He stared at me, disbelieving. "You stopped breathing and I couldn't find a pulse. That was almost twelve hours ago."

"I see. Well, that might explain the strange dreams. I found myself here, yet not here. You were crying, weren't you?" he stroked my cheek as I nodded. "I didn't hear you and I couldn't really see you, but I…felt your anguish. Allex, I think I was in a coma."

"Do your vitals slow that much while in a coma?"

"For some, it's possible," Mark closed his eyes for a few moments. When he opened them again, the cloudy confusion was gone and the deep blueness had returned. "I wasn't ready to leave you."

I helped him to the bathroom and turned on the water for the shower he asked for. While he was bathing I retrieved his gray and burgundy flannel pants from a drawer, along with a gray t-shirt. I smiled when I remembered him wearing these the first night he came to stay here.

"Oh, that feels so much better," he said toweling his hair. He sat in the chair across from me and I poured him some coffee. "I'm so sorry you had to go through this, Allex, it must have been frightening."

"It was, Mark. I have never felt so hollow in my life." I reached across the table and took his cool hand in mine. He yawned.

"Even though I slept for over twelve hours, I'm exhausted. I think I'll go lay back down for a while. I love you, Allex, I always will, until death do us part."

"I love you too, Mark, until death do us part," I answered with our personal affirmation. I watched as he made his way down the hall and disappeared around the corner.

* * *

I raised my head off of my arms. I had a crick in my neck and my forearms were numb from sleeping like that for so long. I sat up, feeling a bit dizzy. The room was cold; the fire in the stove must have gone out. I looked around, and our coffee cups were gone. I must have cleared the table without thinking about it.

The sun was starting to set. I must have been sleeping for hours! I should wake Mark and fix us something to eat.

In our bedroom, Mark was lying there…just as he had been this morning; he was even still in his pajamas, not his flannels. I brushed my fingers across his cheek. He was icy cold. I felt my knees give out and I clutched the edge of the bed. Kneeling beside him, I laid my head on his still chest and cried.

I had wanted so much to tell him one last time that I loved him so much that I had hallucinated his recovery.

Mark was dead. Death had parted us.

I slipped my father's wedding band from his cold hand and put it back in the glass box. Then I took off my mother's ring and put it away too.

* * *

It was only five o'clock, still, I had to call my sons.

"Hey, Mom, how are you feeling?" Eric asked quietly.

"I'm doing better. My fever broke last night," I replied, trying to keep my voice even.

"How is Dr. Mark?"

I sniffled and swallowed the lump in my throat. "He's…he's gone. I need you and Jason to come over please." I heard the radio go quiet and moments later I saw them both running across the yards.

* * *

I handed them both gloves and a mask, saying, "I don't know how long the contamination lasts. We can't be too careful." I led them into the bedroom where Mark lay in his forever sleep. I heard Jason take a sobbing breath.

"Not now, Jason, please. There will be time for it later. You start crying now and *I* might never stop, so please, be strong for me."

I pulled the top sheet completely off and let it fall to the floor. I handed Eric one of my old massage sheets and together we spread it out on the floor beside the bed. Ever so gently the two of them lifted the stiffening body and lowered it onto the sheet. Once it was folded over they each lifted an end and we walked the body into the living room, where Mark would wait on the futon until we had a grave ready to receive him.

"I'm sure he will be fine there until tomorrow," I said in a monotone. "I want him buried here, not in the mass pit, not in the cemetery, here in the front lawn. I don't know how hard the digging will be, but I think the three of us can get that done." I paused, thinking. "I suppose Dr. James should come and pronounce him, though there isn't any doubt."

"I'll take care of that," Eric said, and after giving his brother a silent message, he left.

* * *

"Do you want coffee or tea, Mom?" Jason asked politely. He was busy rebuilding the fire in the stove.

"Neither. I'm going to have a glass of rum." I dropped two ice cubes in a short glass and filled it halfway with my spiced rum. I tipped it up and felt it burn all the way down, and then I poured another one, which sat on the table while the ice melted.

* * *

James knelt down beside Mark's corpse and searched for a heartbeat with his stethoscope.

"I'm very sorry for your loss, Allexa. The doctor will be missed by all," he said. I could only nod. His condolences said it all.

"Yesterday, or the day before, I don't remember, the woman with the pregnant daughter came here looking for Mark. She said no one could find you. Where were you?" I asked.

"Lenny came for me. One of the women at Mathers Lake had fallen and went into labor," James said. "I was there all night. It was a rough delivery; the baby is fine though. He's a bit small, only five pounds, and healthy. Mother and son are resting comfortably."

"What about Judi's daughter, Marci? I told her to find Gray since Mark was so sick. She said Gray died two days ago." My days were getting confused.

James looked down at his hands and shook his head.

"Without anyone who knew how to turn a breach baby, Judi tried pulling the baby out. Both Marci and the baby died," he said. "The loss of her daughter was too much for her to deal with. No one knows where Judi is now."

"And Gray?"

"He'd been helping the Sisters at the camp. The virus mutated and those who caught it were overwhelmed quickly." I could hear the sadness in his voice.

"How sad. We gain one new life and lose three." That empty feeling was creeping in again.

"Eric told me that Dr. Mark will be buried here tomorrow once a grave can be dug. I'm going to give you a single sleeping pill for tonight. You're going to need your rest to face the day." He handed Jason the pill and left.

Jason set a bowl of hot soup in front of me. I tried to tell him I wasn't hungry.

"Eat! Damn it! Do you want to have a relapse? We can't lose you, too!" he said, smacking his hand on the table, causing the soup to slosh, and then he stormed out.

I forced myself to eat the soup, all of it. Jason's outburst made me feel guilty. I took the pill with a gulp of rum. Tufts came out and pawed at my leg, wanting in my lap. I hugged and cuddled him until I became drowsy.

* * *

Even with the sleeping pill Dr. James had left for me, I slept fitfully. When I did manage to doze off, my dreams were dark and foreboding.

Eric was there early to make sure the stove was lit and coffee was brewing and that I was up and moving with no relapse of the flu that took Mark from me.

"We started digging an hour ago, Mom. There's lots of rock so it's slow progress, but we will be done by early afternoon," he said, sitting down across from me after handing me a cup of coffee. He searched my face and my lip quivered. "We set the burial for three o'clock. I hope it's okay we made that decision." I nodded. I really didn't care.

They finished digging at two o'clock and went home to shower. Amanda came across a few minutes later.

"Hi, Mom," she said quietly, and then burst into tears. "I'm sorry; I told myself I wasn't going to do that." She wiped her eyes with a hanky. Her hands were trembling. "I'm supposed to make sure you take a shower and get dressed. People will be starting to show up in a half hour or so."

"What people?" I asked.

"Half the town wanted to come and the colonel said no. Father Constantine will be here with the Sisters, and Mr. White, Dr. James and the colonel. I don't know who else." She led me to the bathroom and turned the water on for my shower. "I'm going to get you some clothes."

The hot water felt good on my skin. I let it cascade across my face, washing the tears away that kept escaping.

I dressed in dark brown pants and a brown turtle neck shirt. Amanda insisted on a black sweater she found in my closet.

"It's cool outside, plus it has pockets, Mom, for your hanky and sunglasses," she turned away, stifling a sob.

There was no sun out, though I know they were meant to hide my red and swollen eyes.

* * *

I went outside, escorted by my sons. I was surprised to see so many in attendance. There was Father Constantine and the Sisters, Tom, Jim, James, Art and Claire Collins, Nathan and Chloe with Lenny and Pete, Marsha and her husband, Ken and Karen, Joshua, Rayn, Amanda, Emilee and Jacob...and Chivas.

At 3:15, we all stood around this ugly gaping hole in the ground, and Eric, Jason, Ken, and Joshua brought Mark's body out.

I know the Father was talking, saying nice things about Mark, but I only heard half of what he said, my brain was in shutdown. Then there was a prayer and the four of them lowered Mark's body gently into the grave, and I tossed the first shovel of dirt in, and promptly collapsed.

* * *

I woke staring at the ceiling, and the concerned faces of my two sons and Dr. James, who was waving some old fashioned smelling salts under my nose.

"Okay, okay, stop! That stuff stinks." I wrinkled my nose and sat up.

"Are you alright, Mom?" Jason asked as Eric looked on.

"I think she'll be fine now," Dr. James answered for me. "I'm going to take a wild guess that you haven't had anything to eat today, right?"

I sighed. "And not much yesterday."

"Then we're getting you across the street," Eric said, helping me up. "There's a wake going on, and lots of food. You *have* to eat, Mom."

"A wake?"

"Yes, a celebration of life. Mark was a good man and we all want to remember him that way. You knew him best and you need to be there," Jason pleaded. "Amanda felt it was better to have the wake at our house instead of here, that it would be easier on you."

"I don't know... I don't think I'm up to it." I frowned, while memories washed over me.

"Your friends and family are there, waiting for you, Allexa. Mark would want you to do this for him," Dr. James said.

* * *

On the front porch of the house that was once my brother's, I paused in the growing darkness to listen to the chatter and laughter from within. I knew that once I entered, all that would change.

"Allexa! Are you better now? I was really worried when you fainted," a concerned Sister Agnes said.

"Yes, Sister, I forgot to eat today, so it must have been low blood sugar."

"No need to make excuses to us, dear, you've been through an incredible shock," she replied, leading me to the food table.

The array of food was impressive. There was a platter of thinly sliced meat that could only be venison, and another I knew to be smoked goose. A sob caught in my throat knowing that was a favorite of Mark's. I let my eyes wander over the rest of the table and found potato salad, macaroni salad, a dish of mostaccioli pasta in tomato sauce, deviled eggs, smoked fish, bread, and cookies.

Tom White was at my side, shoving a plate in my hands. "Eat, Allex, please," he pleaded. The pain in his eyes was all it took for me to start crying again.

I wiped my eyes with my sleeve, took a deep breath, and put on a brave face. I took the plate from him and took a spoonful of everything, except the goose.

"Are you going to try one of my angel wings?" Sister Lynn asked. I searched the table for what I knew as Chruscik, a Polish pastry.

"Did you make these?" I asked impressed, taking one.

"Oh, yes, one of the few things I make well is sweets," she grinned. I took a bite and the powdered sugar coating clung to my lips.

"It's heavenly," I said with a smile and she laughed.

Tom led me over to the colonel, who stood as I approached. He took my plate, handed it to Tom, and then hugged me gently. He gazed down at me briefly, then lowered me on to the couch and put the plate back in my hands.

I nibbled at the food, and drank from the glass of rum the colonel gave me.

"I hope you don't mind that we raided the liquor truck. It feels like a good use of it," he said.

"When Mark first opened it and saw what was inside he called it the Christmas truck," I said with a smile. The smile felt good; maybe I would get through this after all.

I set my plate on the sink with the other dirty dishes. When I turned, Art Collins was standing behind me, leaning on his crutches.

"I'm so sorry, Allexa," his voice quivered.

"Thank you, Art, and thank you for coming today." What else could I say?

"Any time you need to get away, please feel free to come and visit. In fact, with this strange warm weather we've been having the fish are still biting. Why don't you come out and wet a line with us?"

"That's very tempting. I haven't been fishing in a long time. Let me get back to you, okay?" I replied. Maybe I do need to get away.

That's when the tremors started and a moment later the lights went out.

"Got it!" I heard Jason's voice in the dark, and a flashlight came on. "If everyone will stand still for a minute, I'll get some light in here."

Another flashlight came on, this one in Eric's hands. Both made their way to the hutch where the oil lamps stood like sentinels across the top. Fortunately Nancy had insisted on a decorative but functional rail around the edge, so the lamps were intact. One by one, Eric and Jason lit the lamps and pushed the darkness back.

Another, stronger quake hit, lasting perhaps a minute.

"Let's hope that's the last one," Tom White said.

"Why would the lights go out?" Sister Margaret asked. Her soft voice drifted across the room since everyone had gone quiet.

"The lines must have come down. They've been vulnerable since this started, and the power may be gone for good now," I replied to her. "Rayn, you have the most experience with earthquakes, how strong would you say those were?"

"That depends on how far away they were," she answered. "If it was twenty miles away, I'd say a 6.0 or 7.0 on the Richter Scale. If it was fifty miles it would be stronger…a lot stronger for us to have felt it that much."

I took the flashlight with me and Eric walked me back home. I immediately smelled kerosene when I opened the door and found one of my oil lamps smashed on the floor.

"I need to clean this up right away. Not only is there glass all over the floor, the smell turns my stomach," I said. "Will you light the two hanging lanterns while I get the broom and some rags?" While Eric did that, I piled some rags on the oil to keep it from spreading. This would have to be cleaned and mopped before lighting the cook stove.

I hated losing one of my lamps, though there wasn't anything I could do about it. I scooped it all into the dustpan. When I was going to dump it into the trash, I stopped and removed the metal cap that held the wick. The glass might be shattered, though the metal and the wick could still be used. No matter how I felt, no matter how deep my sorrow, nothing could be wasted anymore.

CHAPTER FORTY-TWO

"Excuse me, Miss Allexa, may I come in?" Joshua stood at the entrance to the greenhouse where I was tending the plants. I found working with growing things that were green and thriving helped ease my sorrow.

"Of course, Joshua, it's good to see you. What's on your mind?" I stood, brushing the dirt from my hands.

"Without grid power, there are a lot of things we can't do like we used to, and I've been careful about using the generator," he said.

"That's wise. Do you need more gas?"

"Not yet, but thank you, ma'am." He looked down at his feet. Even after all this time, Joshua was still shy around me. "When Emilee and Jacob come over, I make sure we do all the power stuff at the same time. Jacob watches cartoons or a movie, Emilee talks on the Ham and I do laundry, wash dishes, and water the animals."

"That's a good use of the generator time." It was also a reminder to me I needed to do laundry, too.

"Emilee has some radio friends down in Owosso, near Lansing, that said they've been trying to reach her for days, wondering if she was okay. I guess I should have let her on the radio sooner," he said.

"Why is that, Joshua?" I said, wishing he would get to the point.

"The quake we felt the other night? It's all over the news down there." Joshua's eyes lit up. "It was right here, and it was really bad. I think you should come over and talk to these folks."

* * *

"My grandmother just came in, Felicia. Can you get your dad? Thanks," I heard Emilee speak into the radio mike. She stood so I could sit down.

"This is Allexa Smeth in Moose Creek. Who am I speaking with, please?" I said into the mike.

"My name is Glen Grant, Ms. Smeth. I work at the capital in the Department of Natural Resources. May I ask what your position is, other than Emi's grandma," he said, and I could hear the smile in his voice.

"I'm the township Emergency Manager, Mr. Grant, what there is left of the town. I understand you have some important news for us?" I was trying hard to be patient, something I wasn't good at lately.

"Yes, Emi said you felt the earthquakes that hit three days ago, is that correct?"

"Yes," I responded, trying hard not to remember where we all were at the time. "Though all of our power is gone now, as well as any satellite feeds, so we're completely cut off from information. What can you tell me about the quake?"

"I do hope you're sitting down, ma'am," he said, making me nervous. "The first quake that hit in the late afternoon on December 3rd registered a 7.5 and was centered in Au Train on the northern shore of the Upper Peninsula. Are you familiar with the area?"

"I know it well. It's rather rural there, was there any damage?"

"Because it's so sparsely populated the casualties were minimal. However, the quake that followed was a 10.9." He paused, I'm sure for that to sink in.

"Is that even possible? I don't think I've ever heard of one rated that high."

"Oh, it's possible alright. In fact it's possible it was even higher. Since earthquakes don't happen in Michigan there wasn't any seismic equipment in place, so we don't know."

"What was the damage, Mr. Grant?" I asked quietly.

"The 10.9 quake ran along the Whitefish River from Au Train to Gladstone and divided the U.P. into two sections."

"What?!"

"There is a chasm that appears to be almost a half mile wide. Gladstone was completely destroyed from what the aerial shots show, and Escanaba is mostly flooded." Another lengthy pause made me wonder if we'd lost our connection. "Lake Superior is draining into Lake Michigan, Ms. Smeth, and flooding areas in the upper half of Lower Michigan. The Mackinaw Bridge is gone, so is Mackinaw city, Traverse City too. In fact, everything from Cheboygan to Manistee is being evacuated."

I was stunned into silence. Everyone who lived on the Lake Superior shoreline had moved into town. I doubt if anyone had even noticed if the water level was going down.

"Are you still there, ma'am?" Grant asked.

"Yes, I'm here, just speechless. No one in our surviving community lives on the shore, so there have been no reports of the lake levels changing."

"Well, that's not all that has happened," he went on. "The quake also destroyed the Soo Locks. We don't have much information on that area yet though."

"Will you relay that to me when it comes in?" I requested.

"Certainly. I have a question for you," he said. "From our aerial photos we're reading extreme hot spots in the vicinity of Marquette. Can you shed any light on that?"

"In a nutshell, sir, Marquette is burning and will be for a long time. Massive lightning strikes set nearly everything on fire, including the coal yards for the power plant. Marquette was evacuated at the end of October. Three groups were formed and went to Sault Ste. Marie, Escanaba, and here."

"I'm thinking your group was the fortunate one," he commented ominously. He didn't know the horrors and the misery we were hiding.

"I need to get this information to our mayor. Thank you so much, Mr. Grant, and please let us know anything further. I'm allocating supplies that will keep this ham radio on the air from noon until six in the evening every day, unless and until you give us a more convenient time slot," and I signed off.

* * *

Tom, Colonel Andrews, and I stood on the narrow boardwalk that had been constructed years ago for tourists to enjoy the panoramic view from Lookout Point.

"You relayed to us all that Glen Grant told you, though it still didn't sink in. Not until now," Tom said, gazing out over the receding muddy shore of Lake Superior. Lake Meade shimmered in the foreground, held in place by a small dam.

"What do you think is the distance, a quarter of a mile?" I asked, referring to the new line where water began just past the mouth of the bay.

"Closer to a half mile, is my guess," Jim said. "Wish we had a range finder."

"It's devastating. I also find it fascinating. Look over at the bay. See that pond? That was a popular hole for Lake Perch. I wonder if any are trapped there," I thought out loud, remembering Art's offer to go fishing at Mathers Lake. "The bay is a port of refuge; maximum depth is less than fifty feet, mostly where that hole is."

"The bottom looks pretty rocky," Tom observed. "We might be able to make our way there without sinking. Say, Jim, think any of the new residents could build a dock out that far?"

"Might depend on how hungry they get for Lake Perch," he chuckled.

"The lake bottom for the most part is sandy and should drain quickly, at least here it is. Further out where the new shore is, I have no idea," I said. "I wonder how much more it will go down. At some point it will have to level out."

"Any idea how deep the lake is?" Jim asked.

"It has an average depth of 483 feet," Tom answered. "And one spot near Munising is over 1,300 feet deep."

"The surface is nearly 32,000 square miles, Jim. For it to have a new shore a half-mile out is one hell of a lot of water to lose. No wonder Lower Michigan is flooding!" I commented. "Think of all the shipwrecks that might now be exposed!"

Tom looked from me to Jim and back to me and started to laugh.

"This is one of the strangest conversations I've had in a very long time! We have been faced with multiple disasters of apocalyptic proportions and we're discussing finding old shipwrecks and building long docks to go fishing. Come on you two, let's go have a drink. I'm buying."

* * *

We sat at the bar in the lower level of the house that was once my best friend Kathy's and was now occupied by my two new best friends.

I picked up my glass of rum that was filled with ice cubes.

"I sure miss club soda," I lamented.

The two men were so quiet I looked up.

"Allexa, about Mark..." Jim said quietly.

I held up my hand. "No, don't. It's still too raw," I choked out. "This is the first day I have felt somewhat normal, please, let's just talk shop, you know, natural disasters and strategic planning, okay?" My laugh came out a half sob.

"Okay. So what are we going to do?" Jim asked.

"It's approaching winter, even though the weather says otherwise. There is little else *to* do until spring, except survive," Tom answered him.

"I forgot to mention, Tom, I've allocated Joshua more gas for his generator to have the ham radio on for six hours a day until we get a regular communication time," I slipped in.

"Sure, whatever, just keep me posted. Say, Jim, did you see the new prototypes of the heating stove Earl is working on?"

I leaned back and smiled behind my glass of ice and amber rum. Things might return to a kind of normal. Without Mark, though, nothing will be normal for me ever again.

CHAPTER FORTY-THREE

"Are you sure you want to do that, Mom?" Eric asked. They had been checking on me daily, often twice a day.

"It's only for two days, just overnight," I replied. "Art made the offer for Christmas, but I would rather be here with you two for that. I really need the diversion, boys, I'm feeling a bit...stressed, ya know? The weather is mild enough that I don't need to worry about heat. I just need someone to come over and feed Tufts. I'll be back tomorrow."

"Since you're going anyway, and since you brought up Christmas, would you invite Art and Claire for us? We'd like to have a party in the late afternoon on Christmas, no gifts, just dinner. We all think it would be a good idea to do something fun," Jason said.

* * *

"I'm so glad you decided to take me up on my offer, Allexa," Art said, balancing on his crutches.

"I see the cast is gone now, Art. How is your leg feeling?" I asked, stepping into the warm house.

"Dr. James removed it yesterday and said I could start exercising it a few minutes every day. Even though it's only been two months, it feels much longer," he replied, following me in. "I still need the crutches if I'm walking any distance, so I don't stress the bones."

"What a lovely Christmas tree!" I said entering the large living room. "It's so festive."

"Thank you. We love Christmas, and since we got power back on, I thought we might as well have all lights too," he said.

Power back on? My power wasn't on. I wonder if Jim got the big generator going. If he managed somehow to feed that power into the town grid, it *would* extend out here. I would have to ask him about that.

"I must say I'm looking forward to the fishing, Art. It's been so long since I've even thought about wetting a line." I smiled.

"I will admit that they haven't been biting very well since the quake. That won't stop us from trying though," he said.

Claire came into the room with a tray.

"I thought you might like some tea and scones, Allexa," Claire said, setting the tray down on the long low table in front of the chairs. "It's been wonderful to have regular flour, thank you so much for the supplies!"

"Speaking of supplies, I've brought you a gift." I set a half gallon bottle of Captain Morgan's rum on the table. "I noticed you drinking this brand, and since you named your dog after it, I'm assuming it's what you like."

Art's eyes lit up. "Oh, yes! It was a real treat to have some..." Then he stopped and I knew it was because he didn't want to mention Mark's funeral or wake.

"It's been two weeks, Art, I really am doing better. I will miss Mark forever, and I will admit there are times I can't even say his name aloud without falling apart, but I've been getting so much support from my family and friends that I know I'll be okay." I picked up the cup with trembling hands and sipped the minty tea. "Oh, and the boys are having a party on Christmas afternoon, and would like you and Claire to join us. It's a potluck dinner and they've asked for there to be no gifts. That's why I wanted to bring the rum today."

"It's greatly appreciated, Allexa, thank you. We know how hard these past few months have been on you, not only the last few weeks, which I've no doubt have been the worse anyone could bear. We want you to know, Allexa, that our home is open to you anytime you need a refuge," Art said, sympathy deep in his voice.

* * *

"I thought you might like to see our tanning factory since you had some interest in what we did with the hides," Art said as we followed a long, wide path. "We put this building away from the rest of the compound because of the potential odors. During the curing process it can get a bit smelly," he laughed. "And since it's an ongoing thing, it's always odorous."

We stepped inside the long, low building where there were two people sitting at large wooden tables cutting and sewing leather.

"This is the craft room, and through those doors is the curing room. We harvested two more deer and a bear, so those hides are being scraped, if you would care to see," he offered, and opened the door to the next section.

"Yep, it smells!" I said, and entered, fascinated by the steps needed to produce a workable hide. The three hides were draped over logs that had had the bark removed to provide a smooth surface. The skins were held in place by straps and someone was using a wide, dull knife to scrape all the tissue off the underside.

"What do you use for the curing agent?" I asked.

"Brains," Art grinned. "Every animal has enough brains to cure its hide, except for the human." At which point he laughed. "Over here are the stretching racks. If the hides aren't held in one shape while they dry, they start to curl." He turned and led me back to the craft room.

I looked around more closely this time. There were various pelts hanging from the ceiling: rabbit, marten, mink, and wolf. That made me think of the wolf pelts we had wasted back in July.

"What are you making?" I asked one of the workers.

"A muff," she explained. "These are easy. All I do is lace the ends together, trim it and turn it inside out. With the fur on the inside, the hands stay warm." I pictured old-fashioned Christmas scenes with women having their hands tucked inside a muff in front of them. It swept me with a warm, nostalgic feeling.

"Mittens are next. The children are forever wearing them out," Art continued.

"We are also experimenting with shoes, or moccasins to be more precise. We're not sure how long the leather on moccasins will hold up," the worker continued.

"You know, Art, you have quite a valuable barter commodity in this leather crafting," I said as we made our way down to the lake.

"Perhaps someday. Right now we're barely keeping up with our own needs."

* * *

Dinner that night was bear burgers, potato salad, and blackberry wine. I ate way too much and slept well for the first time in many days.

* * *

"I'm sorry you didn't catch any fish yesterday, Allexa," Art lamented.

"It's called fishing, not catching," I laughed, and that felt really good. "I do think it's time for me to head home. Art, Claire, this has been a wonderful, relaxing break for me. Thank you so much." I reached out and gave each a brief hug.

"Before you go, we have a gift for you," Claire said, presenting me with what looked like a pile of leather.

Upon closer inspection, I realized it was a large purse or satchel, with a long, wide strap. The exterior flap that closed and held the contents inside was held shut with a piece of antler pushed through a loop of matching leather. The flap was etched with designs of pine needles and pinecones. I was awestruck.

"This is beautiful," I whispered, admiring the well-oiled leather. "Thank you."

CHAPTER FOURTY-FOUR

I slipped inside the church and found a seat in the back, like I had done before with Pastor Carolyn. The place was packed, many looking for salvation or forgiveness or both; still others just seeking the company of others. I can't say I blamed them for any of it.

Father Constantine looked healthy, if not somewhat subdued, and gave a good, non-denominational sermon on what Christmas means to Christians. He's going to make an excellent spiritual leader for the community.

"Allexa," Father Constantine said as he greeted me in the throng of the parishioners in the narthex of the church. "It's really good to see you here for our Christmas Eve service. How are you doing?" His deep brown eyes searched my face compassionately.

"I'm doing as well as can be expected, Father. Will I be seeing you tomorrow afternoon at my son's party?"

He smiled instantly. "Absolutely, and we're looking forward to it." He then let go of my hand as the crowd pushed me onward and out the door.

* * *

I had no lights, no tree, and few presents to give my family tomorrow. I kept telling everyone I was doing fine, but I wasn't.

"Oh, Mark, I miss you so much!" I sobbed, and cried myself to sleep.

* * *

With the sun coming up later in the morning and with it usually shrouded with murky cloud cover, I didn't notice the dusting of snow at first. The snow gave a fresh look to the yard and the trees, especially the evergreens. The temperatures must have dropped during the night.

I lit the stove to take the chill off, just as Rayn came over.

"Good morning, Allexa! Isn't the snow beautiful?" She glowed with happiness.

"Yes, it is. Are you getting ready for the party this afternoon?"

"I've never been more excited about an event in my life! I was wondering if you had a dress I could borrow? Dress up was not part of my duffle bag."

I laughed along with her. "Certainly, let's take a look."

At my closet we stood and stared, until I found what I was looking for. It was a long, slim, peach colored dress with a scooped neck. I pulled it out, and held it up to her. The peach emphasized and complimented her exotic coloring.

"Here, try this on," I said, leaving her in the bedroom alone. Moments later she came out.

"The dress is lovely on you, Rayn, but the boots have to go!" I laughed. She looked down at her feet and laughed too. Then frowned.

"I suppose I could go barefoot," she grinned.

"No need. I have just the thing." I disappeared back to the closet and found her some beige slippers while she changed back into her own clothes.

"Thank you so much! These will be perfect. I'll see you around three o'clock!" and she slipped out the door, running home.

* * *

I made a batch of tortillas first, so they could rest before grilling. They should be cooled for what I had in mind as my potluck contribution.

I opened and drained two jars of canned fish, mashing the chunks in a medium bowl. Next was a glop of mayonnaise I had made a few days ago, a dash of Worcestershire sauce, and several dashes of liquid smoke. I stirred it until blended, and added one onion, finely chopped. I felt a twinge of sorrow, remembering I usually left out the onion because Kathy disliked it so.

I divided the mixture into six portions, and spread it evenly on the six tortillas, rolling each one tightly. I sliced the rolls an inch thick, forming pinwheels, and placed them on a Christmas platter. Covered with a clean sackcloth towel, they would keep in the cold pantry until I was ready to leave.

With the generator running for my shower, I also did the few dishes and ran a load of laundry. I drew off two gallons of water to put through the filter and set them aside for later.

Showered and dressed, I gazed at my reflection in the bathroom mirror. When had I gotten so thin and sad looking? This wouldn't do. The party my sons were having was to be a fun and festive occasion. I rooted around in the cupboard and found my makeup bag. It had been over a year that I'd even thought about using it. A touch of eyeliner, a swipe of mascara and a light dust of blush made all the difference in the world. I was ready to face my family and my friends.

* * *

"Hi, Mom!" Eric greeted me at the door. He was glowing with excitement. "Let me take that dish from you." He set it on the table while I took my coat off and added it to the growing pile in the anteroom off the kitchen.

It was good to see how many were already here. Jason thrust a glass in my hand and I made my way to the group on the other side of the room.

"You look lovely tonight, Allexa," Colonel Jim said, kissing my cheek.

"Thank you. Once Rayn borrowed a dress from me, I figured it was an occasion to spruce up a bit," I laughed, and noticed everyone was dressed up a bit. I'm not sure Joshua owned anything other than jeans, though the ones he had on were clean and looked like they had been pressed, as well as his button down shirt.

There were colored lights strung around the ceiling and over every doorway. Those two boys of mine must have done a great deal of searching the house and barn to have found Nancy's artificial tree and ornaments. The place sparkled with festivity.

Shortly after Sargent Sanders and Corporal Perkins arrived, Father Constantine and the three Sisters came in. I looked around at the crowded room. It seemed that everyone we knew was there. What a wonderful way to spend the holiday.

Father Constantine cleared his throat. "May I have everyone's attention please? Not only is this Christmas day, and we are celebrating the birth of Christ, but we are also celebrating another event."

Eric and Rayn were suddenly in front of me, holding hands.

"Mom, remember what you said when you announced that you and Dr. Mark were getting married? That you wanted to hold onto all the happiness you could find? Well that's what I want, too, with Rayn. I'm going to grab onto this happiness I've found with her, so I'm asking for your blessing on our marriage."

"Oh, Eric...." I barely got the words out. "Of course you have my blessing!" I turned to Rayn and said, "You are both very lucky! When is the wedding?"

Eric grinned. "Right now."

* * *

"What a joyous occasion this is," Father Constantine started, as Eric and Rayn took their places in front of him. "And I'm personally pleased to be part of it. When we first arrived here in Moose Creek two months ago, we were all strangers. Now, I feel we are all family, and that makes my heart sing. All the disasters that have befallen us and brought us such sorrow have also bonded us, and now Eric and Rayn have asked to be bonded in marriage."

Father Constantine talked on and my mind drifted.

It was a simple and lovely ceremony.

CHAPTER FORTY-FIVE

JOURNAL ENTRY: March 15

It's been an incredibly mild winter with very little snow. Rather than having the harsh winter and cold summer that everyone was expecting with the ash cloud still circling the Earth, it seems as if our seasons have been balanced to a more neutral zone, which may mean an early summer.

I pulled out all the vegetable seeds I had in storage and piled them by types: tomatoes, root crops, squash. With the greenhouse it is never too early to start some seedlings.

The greenhouse has produced well over the winter, and I was able to share green and wax beans, tomatoes and kale with my family and friends.

* * *

I pushed more of the fresh vegetables at Rayn, now that she was expecting a baby. Their news was what I needed to pull me out of the grief induced funk I was in. The prospect of them giving me another grandchild filled me with joy and hope for the future.

I was about done drawing out this year's garden when I spotted a familiar car pull in the driveway. Jim had arrived for our weekly game of cribbage.

"The weather sure has been good, Allexa," he said with a mischievous grin. "And with no snow, I bet we could make it around that other route we found and get to the city. Want to take a road trip?"

ACKNOWLEDGEMENTS

The Journal didn't start out as a novel. It was an exercise for teaching preparedness by storytelling — a what-if situation on a day-to-day basis. As I got further into it, it morphed and took on a life of its own. The blog entries were such a huge hit that I made the decision to publish. By the time I heard back on my submission to Permuted Press, book two was done and I was thinking about book three.

This brings me to thanking Michael L. Wilson, the publisher willing to take a risk on this unknown, unpublished author, who had never been rejected because I had never submitted anything. I hope your trust has been justified. And to Felicia Sullivan, my editor, and now my good friend, who takes my ramblings and makes sense of them.

My friend 'Boyne Suzie' deserves a spot for presenting me with the replica of a Civil War Diary, which gave me the idea of doing a journal.

Thank you to my son Eric, who has kept me straight and honest with everything military. Your twenty-plus years of dedication to Uncle Sam make me so very proud.

Another big thank you to my other son, Jason, who has helped with all my construction concerns and for putting up with my flights of fantasy on what and how something could be built with very little.

I could never forget to thank my sister Pam and my brother Tom for their support and suggestions and for Beta reading for me.

And last, but not least, thank you to my readers. Without your continued support, I wouldn't have written yet another glimpse into the life of Allexa Smeth. Yes, book four, *Raging Tide*, awaits you.

ABOUT THE AUTHOR

Deborah D. Moore lives in a remote region of the Upper Peninsula of Michigan with her cat Tufts, on ten acres of deeply wooded property.

A very private person, she has a hard time talking about herself and what she has done with her life. She had a rather normal childhood growing up in Detroit with a brother, three sisters and a stay at home mother. Her father, a career police officer, often worked two jobs to make ends meet. She started writing short stories when she was thirteen and wrote her first full length novel thirty years later.

After raising two wonderful sons, she has gone on to reinvent her life several times with artistic endeavors, travel, education and different successful careers, which now includes being a published author.

Deborah was a prepper long before the term had any meaning. Living in the woods and cooking on a wood cookstove during the long snowy winters reinforced her need to always be prepared and has given her first-hand experiences that she passes on to her characters.

A PREPPER'S COOKBOOK

20 Years of Cooking in the Woods

by Deborah D. Moore

In the event of a disaster, it isn't enough to have food. You also have to know what to do with it.

Deborah D. Moore, author of *The Journal* series and a passionate Prepper for over twenty years, gives you step-by-step instructions on making delicious meals from the emergency pantry.

PERMUTED
PRESS